Harry Potter
AND THE ORDER OF THE PHOENIX

J.K. ROWLING

5

英汉对照版

Harry Potter

哈利·波特与凤凰社 [下]

〔英〕J.K. 罗琳 / 著

马爱农　马爱新 / 译

人民文学出版社
PEOPLE'S LITERATURE PUBLISHING HOUSE

CHAPTER TWENTY

Hagrid's Tale

Harry sprinted up to the boys' dormitories to fetch the Invisibility Cloak and the Marauder's Map from his trunk; he was so quick that he and Ron were ready to leave at least five minutes before Hermione hurried back down from the girls' dormitories, wearing scarf, gloves and one of her own knobbly elf hats.

'Well, it's cold out there!' she said defensively, as Ron clicked his tongue impatiently.

They crept through the portrait hole and covered themselves hastily in the Cloak – Ron had grown so much he now needed to crouch to prevent his feet showing – then, moving slowly and cautiously, they proceeded down the many staircases, pausing at intervals to check on the map for signs of Filch or Mrs Norris. They were lucky; they saw nobody but Nearly Headless Nick, who was gliding along absent-mindedly humming something that sounded horribly like 'Weasley is our King'. They crept across the Entrance Hall and out into the silent, snowy grounds. With a great leap of his heart, Harry saw little golden squares of light ahead and smoke coiling up from Hagrid's chimney. He set off at a quick march, the other two jostling and bumping along behind him. They crunched excitedly through the thickening snow until at last they reached the wooden front door. When Harry raised his fist and knocked three times, a dog started barking frantically inside.

'Hagrid, it's us!' Harry called through the keyhole.

'Shoulda known!' said a gruff voice.

They beamed at each other under the Cloak; they could tell by Hagrid's voice that he was pleased. 'Bin home three seconds ... out the way, Fang ... *out the way*, yeh dozy dog ...'

The bolt was drawn back, the door creaked open and Hagrid's head appeared in the gap.

Hermione screamed.

第20章

海格的故事

哈利冲到男生宿舍,从箱子里拿出隐形衣和活点地图,他的动作那么快,结果他和罗恩起码等了五分钟,赫敏才急急忙忙从女生宿舍下来,戴着围巾、手套和她自己织的一顶织花小精灵帽。

"外面很冷!"看到罗恩不耐烦地咂嘴,她辩解说。

他们爬出肖像洞口,匆匆钻进隐形衣——罗恩个头长了不少,必须弯着腰才能把脚藏在里面。然后三人小心翼翼地走下许多级楼梯,时而停下来在地图上查看一下费尔奇和洛丽丝夫人的踪影。他们很幸运,路上只碰到了差点没头的尼克,他飘飘荡荡,无心地哼着歌曲,听上去与"韦斯莱是我们的王"惊人地相似。他们蹑手蹑脚地穿过门厅,来到静悄悄的雪地上。看到前面那一小方金色的灯光和海格烟囱上袅袅的青烟,哈利的心剧烈地跳了起来。他加快了步伐,另外两人跌跌撞撞地跟在后面。他们激动地踏着变厚的积雪走到木门前,哈利举手敲了三下,一条狗在里面狂吠起来。

"海格,是我们!"哈利对着钥匙孔叫道。

"应该想到的!"一个粗哑的声音说。

他们在隐形衣下相视而笑,听得出海格的声音很高兴:"刚回来三秒钟……让开,牙牙……让开,你这条瞌睡虫……"

拔门闩的声音,门吱吱嘎嘎地开了,门缝中露出海格的脑袋。

赫敏尖叫起来。

CHAPTER TWENTY Hagrid's Tale

'Merlin's beard, keep it down!' said Hagrid hastily, staring wildly over their heads. 'Under that Cloak, are yeh? Well, get in, get in!'

'I'm sorry!' Hermione gasped, as the three of them squeezed past Hagrid into the house and pulled the Cloak off themselves so he could see them. 'I just – oh, *Hagrid*!'

'It's nuthin', it's nuthin'!' said Hagrid hastily, shutting the door behind them and hurrying to close all the curtains, but Hermione continued to gaze up at him in horror.

Hagrid's hair was matted with congealed blood and his left eye had been reduced to a puffy slit amid a mass of purple and black bruising. There were many cuts on his face and hands, some of them still bleeding, and he was moving gingerly, which made Harry suspect broken ribs. It was obvious that he had only just got home; a thick black travelling cloak lay over the back of a chair and a haversack large enough to carry several small children leaned against the wall inside the door. Hagrid himself, twice the size of a normal man, was now limping over to the fire and placing a copper kettle over it.

'What happened to you?' Harry demanded, while Fang danced around them all, trying to lick their faces.

'Told yeh, *nuthin'*,' said Hagrid firmly. 'Want a cuppa?'

'Come off it,' said Ron, 'you're in a right state!'

'I'm tellin' yeh, I'm fine,' said Hagrid, straightening up and turning to beam at them all, but wincing. 'Blimey, it's good ter see yeh three again – had good summers, did yeh?'

'Hagrid, you've been attacked!' said Ron.

'Fer the las' time, it's nuthin'!' said Hagrid firmly.

'Would you say it was nothing if one of us turned up with a pound of mince instead of a face?' Ron demanded.

'You ought to go and see Madam Pomfrey, Hagrid,' said Hermione anxiously, 'some of those cuts look nasty.'

'I'm dealin' with it, all righ'?' said Hagrid repressively.

He walked across to the enormous wooden table that stood in the middle of his cabin and twitched aside a tea towel that had been lying on it. Underneath was a raw, bloody, green-tinged steak slightly larger than the average car tyre.

'You're not going to eat that, are you, Hagrid?' said Ron, leaning in for a closer look. 'It looks poisonous.'

第20章 海格的故事

"梅林的胡子啊,小声点!"海格急忙说,他越过他们的头顶使劲张望,"在隐形衣里呢,是不是?进来,进来!"

"对不起!"赫敏低声说,三人从海格身边挤进屋里,扯下隐形衣,让他能看到他们,"我只是——哦,海格!"

"没事儿,没事儿!"海格忙说,他关上门,又赶紧拉上所有的窗帘,但赫敏依然惊恐地望着他。

海格的头发乱糟糟的,上面结着血块,他的左眼肿成了一条缝,又青又紫,脸上和手上伤痕累累,有的还在流血,他动作很小心,哈利怀疑可能他的肋骨断了。他显然刚刚到家,一件厚厚的黑色旅行斗篷搭在椅背上,一个装得下几个小孩的大背包靠在墙边。海格有正常人的两倍高、三倍宽,他一瘸一拐地走向火炉,往火上搁了一个铜水壶。

"你遇到什么了?"哈利问,牙牙围着他们又蹦又跳,想要舔他们的脸蛋。

"我说了,没事儿。"海格固执地说,"喝杯茶吗?"

"算了吧,"罗恩说,"看你那副样子!"

"跟你们说了我很好。"海格说着直起腰,转身对他们微笑,但疼得皱了皱眉,"啊,看到你们真高兴——暑假过得不错,是不是?"

"海格,你遭到袭击了!"罗恩说。

"我说最后一遍,没事儿!"海格一口咬定。

"如果我们哪个的脸变成了一团肉酱,你会说没事吗?"罗恩说。

"你应该去让庞弗雷女士看看,海格,"赫敏焦急地说,"有些伤口看上去很严重。"

"我会处理的,行了吧?"海格威严地说。

他走到小屋中间那张巨大的木桌前,揭去桌上的一块茶巾,下面是一块带血的生肉,绿莹莹的,比普通的汽车轮胎稍大一点。

"你不会吃那个吧,海格?"罗恩凑过去看了看,"好像有毒啊。"

CHAPTER TWENTY   Hagrid's Tale

'It's s'posed ter look like that, it's dragon meat,' Hagrid said. 'An' I didn' get it ter eat.'

He picked up the steak and slapped it over the left side of his face. Greenish blood trickled down into his beard as he gave a soft moan of satisfaction.

'Tha's better. It helps with the stingin', yeh know.'

'So, are you going to tell us what's happened to you?' Harry asked.

'Can't, Harry. Top secret. More'n me job's worth ter tell yeh that.'

'Did the giants beat you up, Hagrid?' asked Hermione quietly.

Hagrid's fingers slipped on the dragon steak and it slid squelchily on to his chest.

'Giants?' said Hagrid, catching the steak before it reached his belt and slapping it back over his face, 'who said anythin' abou' giants? Who yeh bin talkin' to? Who's told yeh what I've – who's said I've bin – eh?'

'We guessed,' said Hermione apologetically.

'Oh, yeh did, did yeh?' said Hagrid, fixing her sternly with the eye that was not hidden by the steak.

'It was kind of … obvious,' said Ron. Harry nodded.

Hagrid glared at them, then snorted, threw the steak back on to the table and strode over to the kettle, which was now whistling.

'Never known kids like you three fer knowin' more'n yeh oughta,' he muttered, splashing boiling water into three of his bucket-shaped mugs. 'An' I'm not complimentin' yeh, neither. Nosy, some'd call it. Interferin'.'

But his beard twitched.

'So you have been to look for giants?' said Harry, grinning as he sat down at the table.

Hagrid set tea in front of each of them, sat down, picked up his steak again and slapped it back over his face.

'Yeah, all righ',' he grunted, 'I have.'

'And you found them?' said Hermione in a hushed voice.

'Well, they're not that difficult ter find, ter be honest,' said Hagrid. 'Pretty big, see.'

'Where are they?' said Ron.

'Mountains,' said Hagrid unhelpfully.

第20章 海格的故事

"它就是这个样子,是火龙肉,"海格说,"我没准备吃它。"

他拎起火龙肉,敷在自己的左脸上,绿色的血滴到胡子上,他满意地哼哼了一声。

"好些了,它有镇痛作用,你知道的。"

"你能告诉我们你遇到了什么吗?"哈利问。

"不行,哈利,这是绝对机密,不能告诉你们,拿我的工作都抵不了这责任。"

"是巨人打你的吗,海格?"赫敏轻声问。

海格的手一松,龙肉咕叽滑到了他的胸口。

"巨人?"海格在火龙肉滑到他的皮带上之前把它抓住,重新敷在脸上,"谁说巨人了?你们跟谁聊过?谁告诉你们——谁说我——啊?"

"我们猜的。"赫敏抱歉地说。

"哦,你们猜的,是吗?"海格用没被火龙肉遮住的那只眼睛严厉地盯着她。

"挺……明显的嘛。"罗恩说,哈利点点头。

海格瞪着他们,然后哼了一声,把火龙肉扔回桌上,走到呜呜响的水壶跟前。

"没见过像你们这么大的小孩知道这么多不该知道的事儿,"他嘟哝着,把滚开的水泼泼洒洒地倒进三个水桶形状的杯子里,"我不是夸你们。有人管这叫——包打听。多管闲事。"

但他的胡子在抖动。

"你去找巨人了?"哈利在桌边坐下笑着问。

海格把茶杯放在每个人面前,坐下来,又拎起火龙肉敷在脸上。

"嗯,去了。"他嘟哝道。

"找到他们了?"赫敏屏着气问。

"老实说,他们并不那么难找,"海格说,"个头大嘛。"

"他们在哪儿?"罗恩问。

"山里。"海格含糊地回答。

719

CHAPTER TWENTY Hagrid's Tale

'So why don't Muggles —?'

'They do,' said Hagrid darkly. 'On'y their deaths are always put down ter mountaineerin' accidents, aren' they?'

He adjusted the steak a little so that it covered the worst of the bruising.

'Come on, Hagrid, tell us what you've been up to!' said Ron. 'Tell us about being attacked by the giants and Harry can tell you about being attacked by the Dementors —'

Hagrid choked in his mug and dropped his steak at the same time; a large quantity of spit, tea and dragon blood was sprayed over the table as Hagrid coughed and spluttered and the steak slid, with a soft *splat*, on to the floor.

'Whadda yeh mean, attacked by Dementors?' growled Hagrid.

'Didn't you know?' Hermione asked him, wide-eyed.

'I don' know anythin' that's bin happenin' since I left. I was on a secret mission, wasn' I, didn' wan' owls followin' me all over the place — ruddy Dementors! Yeh're not serious?'

'Yeah, I am, they turned up in Little Whinging and attacked my cousin and me, and then the Ministry of Magic expelled me —'

'WHAT?'

'— and I had to go to a hearing and everything, but tell us about the giants first.'

'You were *expelled*?'

'Tell us about your summer and I'll tell you about mine.'

Hagrid glared at him through his one open eye. Harry looked right back, an expression of innocent determination on his face.

'Oh, all righ',' Hagrid said in a resigned voice.

He bent down and tugged the dragon steak out of Fang's mouth.

'Oh, Hagrid, don't, it's not hygien—' Hermione began, but Hagrid had already slapped the meat back over his swollen eye.

He took another fortifying gulp of tea, then said, 'Well, we set off righ' after term ended —'

'Madame Maxime went with you, then?' Hermione interjected.

'Yeah, tha's righ',' said Hagrid, and a softened expression appeared on the few inches of face that were not obscured by beard or green steak. 'Yeah, it was jus' the pair of us. An' I'll tell yeh this, she's not afraid of roughin' it, Olympe. Yeh know, she's a fine, well-dressed woman, an' knowin' where

第20章 海格的故事

"那为什么麻瓜没有——"

"不是没有，"海格低沉地说，"只是麻瓜的死因总被说成是登山事故，对不对？"

他把火龙肉移了移，盖住最严重的伤痕。

"海格，跟我们说说你干了什么吧！"罗恩说，"说说被巨人袭击的事，哈利可以说说被摄魂怪袭击的事——"

正在喝茶的海格呛了一下，火龙肉也掉了。他连连咳嗽，大量的唾液、茶水和火龙血溅到桌上，火龙肉啪嗒一声滑到地上。

"你说什么，被摄魂怪袭击了？"海格大声说。

"你不知道吗？"赫敏瞪大眼睛问。

"我走后发生的事我都不知道。我有秘密使命，不希望猫头鹰到处跟着我——讨厌的摄魂怪！不会是真的吧？"

"是真的，它们出现在小惠金区，袭击了我和我表哥，然后魔法部把我开除了——"

"什么？"

"——我只好去受审，好多的事情，可是，你还是先跟我们说说巨人的事吧。"

"你被开除了？"

"先说说你的暑假，然后我再说我的。"

海格用他能睁开的那只眼睛瞪着哈利。哈利与他对视着，脸上是直率而坚决的表情。

"唉，好吧。"海格无可奈何地说。

他弯下腰把火龙肉从牙牙的嘴里拽了出来。

"不要，海格，这不卫生——"赫敏说，但海格已经把火龙肉重新敷到他肿起来的眼睛上了。他又喝了一口茶提神，然后说道："我们学期一结束就出发了——"

"马克西姆女士跟你一起吗？"赫敏插嘴问。

"对，"海格说，他脸上没被胡子和绿色的火龙肉遮住的一点地方显出了温柔的表情，"只有我们两个。告诉你们吧，奥利姆她不怕吃苦。

we was goin' I wondered 'ow she'd feel abou' clamberin' over boulders an' sleepin' in caves an' tha', bu' she never complained once.'

'You knew where you were going?' Harry asked. 'You knew where the giants were?'

'Well, Dumbledore knew, an' he told us,' said Hagrid.

'Are they hidden?' asked Ron. 'Is it a secret, where they are?'

'Not really,' said Hagrid, shaking his shaggy head. 'It's jus' that mos' wizards aren' bothered where they are, 's'long as it's a good long way away. But where they are's very difficult ter get ter, fer humans anyway, so we needed Dumbledore's instructions. Took us abou' a month ter get there –'

'A *month*?' said Ron, as though he had never heard of a journey lasting such a ridiculously long time. 'But – why couldn't you just grab a Portkey or something?'

There was an odd expression in Hagrid's unobscured eye as he squinted at Ron; it was almost pitying.

'We're bein' watched, Ron,' he said gruffly.

'What d'you mean?'

'Yeh don' understand,' said Hagrid. 'The Ministry's keepin' an eye on Dumbledore an' anyone they reckon's in league with 'im, an' –'

'We know about that,' said Harry quickly, keen to hear the rest of Hagrid's story, 'we know about the Ministry watching Dumbledore –'

'So you couldn't use magic to get there?' asked Ron, looking thunderstruck, 'you had to act like Muggles *all the way*?'

'Well, not exactly all the way,' said Hagrid cagily. 'We jus' had ter be careful, 'cause Olympe an' me, we stick out a bit –'

Ron made a stifled noise somewhere between a snort and a sniff and hastily took a gulp of tea.

'– so we're not hard ter follow. We was pretendin' we was goin' on holiday together, so we got inter France an' we made like we was headin' fer where Olympe's school is, 'cause we knew we was bein' tailed by someone from the Ministry. We had to go slow, 'cause I'm not really s'posed ter use magic an' we knew the Ministry'd be lookin' fer a reason ter run us in. But we managed ter give the berk tailin' us the slip round abou' Dee-John –'

'Ooooh, Dijon?' said Hermione excitedly. 'I've been there on holiday, did you see –?'

第20章 海格的故事

你们知道，她是一位优雅的、穿得很考究的女士。我知道我们要去哪里，怕她受不了爬石头、睡岩洞什么的，可她一次都没抱怨过。"

"你知道你们要去哪里？"哈利问，"你知道巨人在哪儿？"

"邓布利多知道，他告诉了我们。"海格说。

"巨人是不是藏起来了？"罗恩问，"他们的藏身处是秘密的吗？"

"并不是，"海格摇着乱蓬蓬的脑袋说，"只是许多巫师都不操心巨人在哪儿，只要他们离得很远就行。但巨人住的地方很难进去，至少对人类是这样的。所以我们需要邓布利多的指引。我们花了一个月才到地方——"

"一个月？"罗恩说，好像他从没听说过长得这么离谱的旅行，"可是——你们为什么不拿门钥匙呢？"

海格看着罗恩，那只露在外面的眼睛里有一种近乎怜悯的奇怪表情。

"我们受到监视，罗恩。"他粗哑地说。

"什么意思？"

"你不明白，"海格说，"魔法部监视着邓布利多和他们认为跟邓布利多一道的人——"

"我们知道，"哈利忙说，急于听海格的故事，"我们知道魔法部在监视邓布利多——"

"所以你们不能用魔法过去？"罗恩震惊地问，"你们一路只能像麻瓜一样？"

"也不是一路，"海格狡黠地说，"我们只是必须多加小心，因为我和奥利姆，块头大了点——"

罗恩发出强忍着的噗嗤一声，赶紧喝了一大口茶。

"——很容易被跟踪。我们装作一起去度假，因为知道有魔法部的人在盯梢，所以我们去了法国，假装要去奥利姆的学校。我们只能慢慢走，因为我不能用魔法，而且知道魔法部在找借口拘留我们。但在地-龙附近我们终于甩掉了那个尾巴——"

"哦，是第戎吧？"赫敏兴奋地说，"我去那儿度过假，你有没有看见——"

CHAPTER TWENTY   Hagrid's Tale

She fell silent at the look on Ron's face.

'We chanced a bit o' magic after that an' it wasn' a bad journey. Ran inter a couple o' mad trolls on the Polish border an' I had a sligh' disagreement with a vampire in a pub in Minsk, bu' apart from tha' couldn't'a bin smoother.

'An' then we reached the place, an' we started trekkin' up through the mountains, lookin' fer signs of 'em …

'We had ter lay off the magic once we got near 'em. Partly 'cause they don' like wizards an' we didn' want ter put their backs up too soon, an' partly 'cause Dumbledore had warned us You-Know-Who was bound ter be after the giants an' all. Said it was odds on he'd sent a messenger off ter them already. Told us ter be very careful of drawin' attention ter ourselves as we got nearer in case there was Death Eaters around.'

Hagrid paused for a long draught of tea.

'Go on!' said Harry urgently.

'Found 'em,' said Hagrid baldly. 'Went over a ridge one nigh' an' there they was, spread ou' underneath us. Little fires burnin' below an' huge shadows … it was like watchin' bits o' the mountain movin'.'

'How big are they?' asked Ron in a hushed voice.

''Bout twenty feet,' said Hagrid casually. 'Some o' the bigger ones mighta bin twenty-five.'

'And how many were there?' asked Harry.

'I reckon abou' seventy or eighty,' said Hagrid.

'Is that all?' said Hermione.

'Yep,' said Hagrid sadly, 'eighty left, an' there was loads once, musta bin a hundred diff'rent tribes from all over the world. Bu' they've bin dyin' out fer ages. Wizards killed a few, o' course, bu' mostly they killed each other, an' now they're dyin' out faster than ever. They're not made ter live bunched up together like tha'. Dumbledore says it's our fault, it was the wizards who forced 'em to go an' made 'em live a good long way from us an' they had no choice bu' ter stick together fer their own protection.'

'So,' said Harry, 'you saw them and then what?'

'Well, we waited till morning, didn' want ter go sneakin' up on 'em in the dark, fer our own safety,' said Hagrid. ''Bout three in the mornin' they fell asleep jus' where they was sittin'. We didn' dare sleep. Fer one thing, we wanted ter make sure none of 'em woke up an' came up where we were, an' fer another, the snorin' was unbelievable. Caused an avalanche near mornin'.

第20章 海格的故事

看到罗恩的脸色,她不作声了。

"然后我们找机会用了一点魔法,旅行还不赖。在波兰边境遇到几个疯巨怪,我在明斯克的酒吧里跟一个吸血鬼闹了点小别扭,但刨去这些,就再顺利不过了。

"我们到了那个地方,开始在山里跋涉,寻找他们的踪影……

"接近他们后,我们又不得不收起魔法。一是因为巨人不喜欢巫师,我们不想太早惹火他们;另外邓布利多警告我们说,神秘人肯定也在寻找巨人,可能已经派出了使者。他嘱咐我们在那一带要非常小心,千万不能引人注意,提防附近有食死徒。"

海格停下来喝了一大口茶。

"说呀!"哈利性急地催促道。

"后来找到了。"海格直率地说,"一天晚上翻过山脊,他们就在下面,小小的篝火,巨大的影子……就像山在移动。"

"有多大?"罗恩屏着气问。

"大概二十英尺吧,"海格漫不经心地说,"大的可能有二十五英尺。"

"有多少人?"哈利问。

"我想有七八十个吧。"海格回答。

"全在那儿了吗?"赫敏问。

"嗯,"海格悲哀地说,"只剩八十个了,以前有好多,全世界起码有一百个部落,但是渐渐消亡了。当然,巫师杀了一些,但大部分死于自相残杀。现在他们死得更快了,因为不适合那样挤在一起生活。邓布利多说是我们的错,是巫师把他们赶到了老远的地方,他们没有办法,为了生存只能待在一起。"

"那么,"哈利说,"你们看到了巨人,后来呢?"

"我们一直等到早上,为了安全起见,不想在夜里悄悄走过去。"海格说,"凌晨三点左右他们在原地睡着了。我们不敢睡,一是怕哪个巨人醒了爬上来,二是呼噜声响得吓人。快天亮时引起了一场雪崩。

CHAPTER TWENTY Hagrid's Tale

'Anyway, once it was light we wen' down ter see 'em.'

'Just like that?' said Ron, looking awestruck. 'You just walked right into a giant camp?'

'Well, Dumbledore'd told us how ter do it,' said Hagrid. 'Give the Gurg gifts, show some respect, yeh know.'

'Give the *what* gifts?' asked Harry.

'Oh, the Gurg – means the chief.'

'How could you tell which one was the Gurg?' asked Ron.

Hagrid grunted in amusement.

'No problem,' he said. 'He was the biggest, the ugliest an' the laziest. Sittin' there waitin' ter be brought food by the others. Dead goats an' such like. Name o' Karkus. I'd put him at twenty-two, twenty-three feet an' the weight o' a couple o' bull elephants. Skin like rhino hide an' all.'

'And you just walked up to him?' said Hermione breathlessly.

'Well ... *down* ter him, where he was lyin' in the valley. They was in this dip between four pretty high mountains, see, beside a mountain lake, an' Karkus was lyin' by the lake roarin' at the others ter feed him an' his wife. Olympe an' I went down the mountainside –'

'But didn't they try and kill you when they saw you?' asked Ron incredulously.

'It was def'nitely on some o' their minds,' said Hagrid, shrugging, 'but we did what Dumbledore told us ter do, which was ter hold our gift up high an' keep our eyes on the Gurg an' ignore the others. So tha's what we did. An' the rest of 'em went quiet an' watched us pass an' we got right up ter Karkus's feet an' we bowed an' put our present down in front o' him.'

'What do you give a giant?' asked Ron eagerly. 'Food?'

'Nah, he can get food all righ' fer himself,' said Hagrid. 'We took him magic. Giants like magic, jus' don' like us usin' it against 'em. Anyway, that firs' day we gave 'im a branch o' Gubraithian fire.'

Hermione said, 'Wow!' softly, but Harry and Ron both frowned in puzzlement.

'A branch of –?'

'Everlasting fire,' said Hermione irritably, 'you ought to know that by now. Professor Flitwick's mentioned it at least twice in class!'

'Well, anyway,' said Hagrid quickly, intervening before Ron could answer

第20章 海格的故事

"天亮之后我们就下去了。"

"就那样?"罗恩敬畏地问,"你们直接走进了巨人的营地?"

"邓布利多告诉了我们该怎么做,"海格说,"给古戈礼物,表示敬意。"

"给谁礼物?"哈利问。

"哦,古戈——就是首领。"

"你怎么知道哪个是古戈?"罗恩问。

海格乐了。

"错不了,他最大,最丑,最懒,坐在那儿等别人拿东西给他吃,死羊什么的。他叫卡库斯。我估计他有二十二三英尺高,有两头公象那么重,皮肤像犀牛皮。"

"你们就直接走了过去?"赫敏提心吊胆地问。

"嗯……走了下去,他躺在山谷里。他们待在四座高山之间的洼地里,靠近一个高山湖泊。卡库斯躺在湖边,咆哮着让人喂他和他老婆。我跟奥利姆走下山坡——"

"可是他们看见你们的时候没有想杀你们吗?"罗恩难以置信地问。

"肯定有人这么想,"海格耸耸肩膀,"但我们按邓布利多说的那样,把礼物举得高高的,眼睛盯着古戈,没有理会其他人。就这样,其他人安静下来,看着我们走了过去,我们一直走到卡库斯的脚边,鞠了个躬,把礼物放在他面前。"

"送给巨人什么礼物?"罗恩感兴趣地问,"是吃的吗?"

"不是,他自己能搞到吃的。"海格说,"我们送他魔法。巨人喜欢魔法,只是不喜欢我们用魔法对付他们。总之,第一天我们给了他一支古卜莱仙火。"

赫敏轻轻地哇了一声,但哈利和罗恩都不解地皱起了眉头。

"一支——?"

"永恒的火,"赫敏不耐烦地说,"你们该知道的,弗立维教授在课上提了至少两次!"

"总之,"海格忙说,不等罗恩回嘴,"邓布利多用魔法使这支火

CHAPTER TWENTY   Hagrid's Tale

back, 'Dumbledore'd bewitched this branch to burn fer evermore, which isn' somethin' any wizard could do, an' so I lies it down in the snow by Karkus's feet and says, "A gift to the Gurg of the giants from Albus Dumbledore, who sends his respectful greetings."'

'And what did Karkus say?' asked Harry eagerly.

'Nothin',' said Hagrid. 'Didn' speak English.'

'You're kidding!'

'Didn' matter,' said Hagrid imperturbably, 'Dumbledore had warned us tha' migh' happen. Karkus knew enough to yell fer a couple o' giants who knew our lingo an' they translated fer us.'

'And did he like the present?' asked Ron.

'Oh yeah, it went down a storm once they understood what it was,' said Hagrid, turning his dragon steak over to press the cooler side to his swollen eye. 'Very pleased. So then I said, "Albus Dumbledore asks the Gurg to speak with his messenger when he returns tomorrow with another gift."'

'Why couldn't you speak to them that day?' asked Hermione.

'Dumbledore wanted us ter take it very slow,' said Hagrid. 'Let 'em see we kept our promises. *We'll come back tomorrow with another present,* an' then we do come back with another present – gives a good impression, see? An' gives them time ter test out the firs' present an' find out it's a good one, an' get 'em eager fer more. In any case, giants like Karkus – overload 'em with information an' they'll kill yeh jus' to simplify things. So we bowed outta the way an' went off an' found ourselves a nice little cave ter spend that night in an' the followin' mornin' we went back an' this time we found Karkus sittin' up waitin' fer us lookin' all eager.'

'And you talked to him?'

'Oh yeah. Firs' we presented him with a nice battle helmet – goblin-made an' indestructible, yeh know – an' then we sat down an' we talked.'

'What did he say?'

'Not much,' said Hagrid. 'Listened mostly. Bu' there were good signs. He'd heard o' Dumbledore, heard he'd argued against the killin' o' the last giants in Britain. Karkus seemed ter be quite int'rested in what Dumbledore had ter say. An' a few o' the others, 'specially the ones who had some English, they gathered round an' listened too. We were hopeful when we left that day. Promised ter come back next mornin' with another present.

第20章 海格的故事

把能永远燃烧，这不是一般巫师能做到的。我把它放在卡库斯脚边的雪地上，说：'阿不思·邓布利多给巨人古戈的礼物，向他表示敬意。'"

"卡库斯说什么？"哈利急切地问。

"什么也没说，"海格说，"他不会说我们的话。"

"你开玩笑吧？"

"这没关系，"海格平静地说，"邓布利多提醒过可能发生这种情况。还好，卡库斯叫来两个懂我们话的巨人，给我们做翻译。"

"他喜欢这礼物吗？"罗恩问。

"哦，是的，他们一明白是什么礼物，营地上就起了一片骚动。"海格把火龙肉翻过来，把凉的一面贴在他的肿眼上，"他们非常高兴。这时我说：'阿不思·邓布利多捎话，使者明天再带礼物来时，请古戈与他交谈。'"

"你为什么不当天跟他们谈？"赫敏问。

"邓布利多要我们慢慢来，"海格说，"让巨人看到我们守信用。明天再带礼物来，如果真的带了，会给他们一个好印象。而且让他们有时间检验一下第一份礼物，发现它是好东西，想要更多。总之，面对卡库斯这样的巨人——一下子说很多，他们会杀死你，免得多事。所以我们鞠躬退了回去，找了个舒服的小岩洞过夜；第二天早上再去时，看到卡库斯正在眼巴巴地等我们呢。"

"你们跟他谈了？"

"是啊，我们先送给他一顶漂亮的头盔——妖精做的，坚不可摧，然后就坐下来谈话。"

"他说什么？"

"没怎么说，主要是听。但苗头不错，他听说过邓布利多，知道他反对杀死英国最后一批巨人。卡库斯好像对邓布利多的话很感兴趣。还有几个人也围过来听，尤其是懂一点英语的。我们走的时候充满希望，答应第二天再带一个礼物来。

CHAPTER TWENTY   Hagrid's Tale

'Bu' that night it all wen' wrong.'

'What d'you mean?' said Ron quickly.

'Well, like I say, they're not meant ter live together, giants,' said Hagrid sadly. 'Not in big groups like that. They can' help themselves, they half kill each other every few weeks. The men fight each other an' the women fight each other; the remnants of the old tribes fight each other, an' that's even without squabbles over food an' the best fires an' sleepin' spots. Yeh'd think, seein' as how their whole race is abou' finished, they'd lay off each other, bu' ...'

Hagrid sighed deeply.

'That night a fight broke out, we saw it from the mouth of our cave, lookin' down on the valley. Went on fer hours, yeh wouldn' believe the noise. An' when the sun came up the snow was scarlet an' his head was lyin' at the bottom o' the lake.'

'Whose head?' gasped Hermione.

'Karkus's,' said Hagrid heavily. 'There was a new Gurg, Golgomath.' He sighed deeply. 'Well, we hadn' bargained on a new Gurg two days after we'd made friendly contact with the firs' one, an' we had a funny feelin' Golgomath wouldn' be so keen ter listen to us, bu' we had ter try.'

'You went to speak to him?' asked Ron incredulously. 'After you'd watched him rip off another giant's head?'

'Course we did,' said Hagrid, 'we hadn' gone all that way ter give up after two days! We wen' down with the next present we'd meant ter give ter Karkus.

'I knew it was no go before I'd opened me mouth. He was sitting there wearin' Karkus's helmet, leerin' at us as we got nearer. He's massive, one o' the biggest ones there. Black hair an' matchin' teeth an' a necklace o' bones. Human-lookin' bones, some of 'em. Well, I gave it a go – held out a great roll o' dragon skin – an' said, "A gift fer the Gurg of the giants –" Nex' thing I knew, I was hangin' upside-down in the air by me feet, two of his mates had grabbed me.'

Hermione clapped her hands to her mouth.

'How did you get out of *that*?' asked Harry.

'Wouldn'ta done if Olympe hadn' bin there,' said Hagrid. 'She pulled out her wand an' did some o' the fastes' spellwork I've ever seen. Ruddy marvellous. Hit the two holdin' me right in the eyes with Conjunctivitus

第20章 海格的故事

"可是那天晚上坏事了。"

"什么意思?"罗恩忙问。

"我说过,巨人们不适合住在一起,"海格悲哀地说,"不适合组成那么大的一群。他们不能控制自己,每隔几个星期就要互相打个半死。男的跟男的打,女的跟女的打。那些老部落的残余打来打去,还不算为了食物、火和睡觉地方的争斗。眼看他们整个种族都快灭绝了,你以为他们会停止自相残杀?但……"

海格深深地叹了口气。

"那天晚上发生了一场恶斗,我们在洞口看到的,在下面的山谷里。打了几小时,声音大得你都不敢相信。太阳出来时,雪都是红的,他的头沉入了湖底。"

"谁的头?"赫敏惊问。

"卡库斯的。"海格沉重地说,"换了个新古戈,叫高高马。"他长叹一声。"没想到,我们和古戈交朋友才两天就换了人。我们感到高高马可能不好说话,但也只能去试一试。"

"你们去找他说话?"罗恩不敢相信地问,"在看到他砍掉其他巨人的脑袋之后?"

"我们当然去了。"海格说,"这么大老远过去的,怎么能两天就放弃呢?我们带着本打算送给卡库斯的礼物走了下去。

"我还没开口就知道不行了。他坐在那儿,戴着卡库斯的头盔,斜眼看着我们走近。他非常魁梧,是那里最高大的之一,黑头发,大黑牙,戴着骨头项链,有的看着像人骨。我努力了一下——举起一大卷火龙皮说:'给巨人古戈的礼物——'话还没说完,就头朝下被吊了起来。他的两个手下抓住了我。"

赫敏用手捂住了嘴巴。

"你是怎么从那里脱身的?"哈利问。

"要不是奥利姆在,我就出不来了。"海格说,"她抽出魔杖,施了几个我这辈子见过的最快的魔法,真了不起。眼疾咒正中那两个家伙

CHAPTER TWENTY Hagrid's Tale

Curses an' they dropped me straightaway – bu' we were in trouble then, 'cause we'd used magic against 'em, an' that's what giants hate abou' wizards. We had ter leg it an' we knew there was no way we was going ter be able ter march inter the camp again.'

'Blimey, Hagrid,' said Ron quietly.

'So, how come it's taken you so long to get home if you were only there for three days?' asked Hermione.

'We didn' leave after three days!' said Hagrid, looking outraged. 'Dumbledore was relyin' on us!'

'But you've just said there was no way you could go back!'

'Not by daylight we couldn', no. We just had ter rethink a bit. Spent a couple o' days lyin' low up in the cave an' watchin'. An' wha' we saw wasn' good.'

'Did he rip off more heads?' asked Hermione, sounding squeamish.

'No,' said Hagrid, 'I wish he had.'

'What d'you mean?'

'I mean we soon found out he didn' object ter all wizards – just us.'

'Death Eaters?' said Harry quickly.

'Yep,' said Hagrid darkly. 'Couple of 'em were visitin' him ev'ry day, bringin' gifts ter the Gurg, an' he wasn' dangling them upside-down.'

'How d'you know they were Death Eaters?' said Ron.

'Because I recognised one of 'em,' Hagrid growled. 'Macnair, remember him? Bloke they sent ter kill Buckbeak? Maniac, he is. Likes killin' as much as Golgomath; no wonder they were gettin' on so well.'

'So Macnair's persuaded the giants to join You-Know-Who?' said Hermione desperately.

'Hold yer Hippogriffs, I haven' finished me story yet!' said Hagrid indignantly, who, considering he had not wanted to tell them anything in the first place, now seemed to be rather enjoying himself. 'Me an' Olympe talked it over an' we agreed, jus' 'cause the Gurg looked like favourin' You-Know-Who didn' mean all of 'em would. We had ter try an' persuade some o' the others, the ones who hadn' wanted Golgomath as Gurg.'

'How could you tell which ones they were?' asked Ron.

'Well, they were the ones bein' beaten to a pulp, weren' they?' said Hagrid patiently. 'The ones with any sense were keepin' outta Golgomath's way,

的眼睛,他们马上把我丢下了——但这下麻烦了,因为我们对巨人用了魔法,那正是巨人仇恨巫师的原因。我们只好逃走,知道不能再走进营地了。"

"哎呀,海格。"罗恩轻声说。

"你在那儿只待了三天,怎么这么晚才回来?"赫敏问。

"我们没有只待三天就走!"海格好像受了侮辱,"邓布利多还指望着我们呢!"

"可是你说你们不能再回去了!"

"白天是不能,我们必须重新考虑。趴在岩洞里观察了几天。情况不妙。"

"他又砍人脑袋了?"赫敏有点作呕。

"不是,"海格说,"那还好些。"

"什么意思?"

"我是说,我们很快发现他并不排斥所有的巫师——只排斥我们。"

"食死徒?"哈利马上问。

"对,"海格阴沉地说,"每天都有两个带着礼物来见他,他没有把他们吊起来。"

"你怎么知道是食死徒?"罗恩问。

"因为我认出了一个,"海格粗声说,"麦克尼尔,记得吗?他们派来杀巴克比克的那家伙。他是个疯子,像高高马一样喜欢杀人,难怪他们那么投缘。"

"麦克尼尔说服巨人跟神秘人联合了?"赫敏绝望地说。

"别着急呀,我还没讲完呢!"海格愤愤地叫道,他一开始什么也不肯说,现在倒好像说上瘾了,"我和奥利姆商量了一下,虽然古戈好像偏向神秘人,但并不意味着巨人都是这样,我们要想法说服其他巨人——那些不愿意高高马当古戈的人。"

"你怎么看得出哪些是呢?"罗恩问。

"他们是被打惨了的,对不对?"海格耐心地解释,"有点头脑的

CHAPTER TWENTY Hagrid's Tale

hidin' out in caves roun' the gully jus' like we were. So we decided we'd go pokin' round the caves by night an' see if we couldn' persuade a few o' them.'

'You went poking around dark caves looking for giants?' said Ron, with awed respect in his voice.

'Well, it wasn' the giants who worried us most,' said Hagrid. 'We were more concerned abou' the Death Eaters. Dumbledore had told us before we wen' not ter tangle with 'em if we could avoid it, an' the trouble was they knew we was around – 'spect Golgomath told 'em abou' us. At night, when the giants were sleepin' an' we wanted ter be creepin' inter the caves, Macnair an' the other one were sneakin' round the mountains lookin' fer us. I was hard put to stop Olympe jumpin' out at 'em,' said Hagrid, the corners of his mouth lifting his wild beard, 'she was rarin' ter attack 'em ... she's somethin' when she's roused, Olympe ... fiery, yeh know ... 'spect it's the French in her ...'

Hagrid gazed misty-eyed into the fire. Harry allowed him thirty seconds of reminiscence before clearing his throat loudly.

'So, what happened? Did you ever get near any of the other giants?'

'What? Oh ... oh, yeah, we did. Yeah, on the third night after Karkus was killed we crept outta the cave we'd bin hidin' in an' headed back down inter the gully, keepin' our eyes skinned fer the Death Eaters. Got inside a few o' the caves, no go – then, in abou' the sixth one, we found three giants hidin'.'

'Cave must've been cramped,' said Ron.

'Wasn' room ter swing a Kneazle,' said Hagrid.

'Didn't they attack you when they saw you?' asked Hermione.

'Probably woulda done if they'd bin in any condition,' said Hagrid, 'but they was badly hurt, all three o' them; Golgomath's lot had beaten 'em unconscious; they'd woken up an' crawled inter the nearest shelter they could find. Anyway, one o' them had a bit of english an' 'e translated fer the others, an' what we had ter say didn' seem ter go down too badly. So we kep' goin' back, visitin' the wounded ... I reckon we had abou' six or seven o' them convinced at one poin'.'

'Six or seven?' said Ron eagerly. 'Well that's not bad – are they going to come over here and start fighting You-Know-Who with us?'

But Hermione said, 'What do you mean "at one point", Hagrid?'

Hagrid looked at her sadly.

'Golgomath's lot raided the caves. The ones tha' survived didn' wan' no more ter to do with us after that.'

第20章 海格的故事

都会躲着高高马,像我们一样藏在周围的岩洞里。所以我们决定晚上到各个岩洞走走,看能不能说服几个人。"

"你们到漆黑的岩洞里去找巨人?"罗恩说,声音里满是敬畏。

"巨人倒不是我们最担心的,"海格说,"我们更怕食死徒。邓布利多嘱咐过尽量不要跟他们纠缠。问题是那帮人知道我们在那儿——大概是高高马说的。夜里我们想趁巨人睡觉时溜进岩洞,麦克尼尔那帮人却在山里找我们。我很难拦住奥利姆,"海格的嘴角牵动着大胡子,"她一心想教训教训他们……她被激怒时可真不得了,奥利姆……像团烈火……大概是因为她的法国血统吧……"

海格眼眶湿润地看着炉火,哈利给了他三十秒回忆时间,然后大声清了清嗓子。

"怎么样?你们接近其他巨人了吗?"

"什么?哦……哦,接近了。在卡库斯被杀后的第三个夜里,我们钻出岩洞,悄悄摸下山去,睁大眼睛提防着食死徒。我们进了几个岩洞,没有——然后,大约到第六个洞时,发现里面藏着三个巨人。"

"一定够挤的。"罗恩说。

"连悬挂猫狸子的地方都没有。"海格说。

"他们看到你们的时候没有打你们吗?"赫敏问。

"如果他们身体好一点的话,可能会的。"海格说,"但他们三个都伤得很重。高高马那一伙把他们打晕了,他们苏醒后,爬进了最近的藏身之处。总之,其中一个懂一点英语,给那两个当翻译,我们的话好像效果还不坏。后来我们就经常过去,探视被打伤的巨人……我想我们一度说服了六七个。"

"六七个?"罗恩兴奋地说,"那不错呀——他们会过来和我们一起对抗神秘人吗?"

但赫敏说:"'一度'是什么意思,海格?"

海格悲哀地看着她。

"高高马的人袭击了岩洞,活下来的再也不想跟我们打交道了。"

CHAPTER TWENTY   Hagrid's Tale

'So ... so there aren't any giants coming?' said Ron, looking disappointed.

'Nope,' said Hagrid, heaving a deep sigh as he turned over his steak and applied the cooler side to his face, 'but we did wha' we meant ter do, we gave 'em Dumbledore's message an' some o' them heard it an' I 'spect some o' them'll remember it. Jus' maybe, them that don' want ter stay around Golgomath'll move outta the mountains, an' there's gotta be a chance they'll remember Dumbledore's friendly to 'em ... could be they'll come.'

Snow was filling up the window now. Harry became aware that the knees of his robes were soaked through: Fang was drooling with his head in Harry's lap.

'Hagrid?' said Hermione quietly after a while.

'Mmm?'

'Did you ... was there any sign of ... did you hear anything about your ... your ... mother while you were there?'

Hagrid's unobscured eye rested upon her and Hermione looked rather scared.

'I'm sorry ... I ... forget it –'

'Dead,' Hagrid grunted. 'Died years ago. They told me.'

'Oh ... I'm ... I'm really sorry,' said Hermione in a very small voice. Hagrid shrugged his massive shoulders.

'No need,' he said shortly. 'Can't remember her much. Wasn' a great mother.'

They were silent again. Hermione glanced nervously at Harry and Ron, plainly wanting them to speak.

'But you still haven't explained how you got in this state, Hagrid,' Ron said, gesturing towards Hagrid's bloodstained face.

'Or why you're back so late,' said Harry. 'Sirius says Madame Maxime got back ages ago –'

'Who attacked you?' said Ron.

'I haven' bin attacked!' said Hagrid emphatically. 'I –'

But the rest of his words were drowned in a sudden outbreak of rapping on the door. Hermione gasped; her mug slipped through her fingers and smashed on the floor; Fang yelped. All four of them stared at the window beside the doorway. The shadow of somebody small and squat rippled across the thin curtain.

'*It's her!*' Ron whispered.

第20章 海格的故事

"那……那不会有巨人来了?"罗恩失望地问。

"是啊,"海格深深地叹了口气,又翻动火龙肉,把凉的一面贴在脸上,"但我们做了该做的事,传达了邓布利多的口信,有人听到了,我想会有人记得。假使那些不愿服从高高马的巨人住到山外,他们也许会想起邓布利多是友好的……说不定会过来……"

雪正在积满窗棂。哈利感到膝头都湿透了,牙牙把脑袋搁在他的腿上,流着口水。

"海格?"过了一会儿赫敏轻声问道。

"嗯?"

"你有没有……你在那儿的时候……有没有听到你……你……妈妈的消息?"

海格露在外面的眼睛看着她,赫敏似乎很害怕。

"对不起……我……我忘了——"

"死了,"海格嘟哝道,"好些年前就死了。他们告诉我的。"

"哦……我……真对不起。"赫敏声音小小地说。海格耸了耸宽大的肩膀。

"没必要,"他干脆地说,"不大记得她。不是个好母亲。"

又沉默了,赫敏不安地瞟着哈利和罗恩,显然希望他们开口说话。

"可你还没解释你怎么会变成这样的,海格。"罗恩指了指海格那血污的面孔。

"还有你为什么回来得这么晚。"哈利说,"小天狼星说马克西姆女士早就回去了——"

"谁袭击了你?"罗恩问。

"我没受到袭击!"海格强调道,"我——"

但他的话被一阵骤然的敲门声淹没。赫敏倒吸了一口凉气,手里的杯子掉到地上摔碎了。牙牙叫了起来。四个人瞪着门旁的窗户,一个矮胖的身影在薄窗帘上晃动。

"是她!"罗恩低声说。

CHAPTER TWENTY Hagrid's Tale

'Get under here!' Harry said quickly; seizing the Invisibility Cloak, he whirled it over himself and Hermione while Ron tore around the table and dived under the Cloak as well. Huddled together, they backed away into a corner. Fang was barking madly at the door. Hagrid looked thoroughly confused.

'Hagrid, hide our mugs!'

Hagrid seized Harry and Ron's mugs and shoved them under the cushion in Fang's basket. Fang was now leaping up at the door; Hagrid pushed him out of the way with his foot and pulled it open.

Professor Umbridge was standing in the doorway wearing her green tweed cloak and a matching hat with earflaps. Lips pursed, she leaned back so as to see Hagrid's face; she barely reached his navel.

'*So*,' she said slowly and loudly, as though speaking to somebody deaf. 'You're Hagrid, are you?'

Without waiting for an answer she strolled into the room, her bulging eyes rolling in every direction.

'Get away,' she snapped, waving her handbag at Fang, who had bounded up to her and was attempting to lick her face.

'Er – I don' want ter be rude,' said Hagrid, staring at her, 'but who the ruddy hell are you?'

'My name is Dolores Umbridge.'

Her eyes were sweeping the cabin. Twice they stared directly into the corner where Harry stood, sandwiched between Ron and Hermione.

'Dolores Umbridge?' Hagrid said, sounding thoroughly confused. 'I thought you were one o' them Ministry – don' you work with Fudge?'

'I was Senior Undersecretary to the Minister, yes,' said Umbridge, now pacing around the cabin, taking in every tiny detail within, from the haversack against the wall to the abandoned travelling cloak. 'I am now the Defence Against the Dark Arts teacher –'

'Tha's brave of yeh,' said Hagrid, 'there's not many'd take tha' job any more.'

'– and Hogwarts High Inquisitor,' said Umbridge, giving no sign that she had heard him.

'Wha's that?' said Hagrid, frowning.

'Precisely what I was going to ask,' said Umbridge, pointing at the broken

第20章 海格的故事

"钻进来！"哈利急忙说，抓起隐形衣披在自己和赫敏身上，罗恩也奔过去钻进了隐形衣。三人挨挨挤挤地退到一个角落里。牙牙对着门口狂吠。海格似乎完全不知所措了。

"海格，把我们的杯子藏起来！"

海格抓起哈利和罗恩的茶杯，塞到牙牙的篮筐垫子底下。牙牙在跳着抓门。海格用脚把它推开到一边，拉开了门。

乌姆里奇教授站在门口，穿着她的绿花呢斗篷，戴着一顶同样颜色的带耳罩的帽子。她噘着嘴，身体后仰，好看到海格的脸，她的个头还不到海格的肚脐眼呢。

"这么说，"她说得又慢又响，好像对聋子讲话似的，"你就是海格，是吗？"

没等海格回答，她就走进屋来，凸出的眼睛骨碌碌乱转。

"走开。"她挥着皮包对牙牙喝道，因为牙牙跳到她跟前，想舔她的脸。

"呃——我不想没礼貌，"海格瞪着她说，"可你到底是谁啊？"

"我的名字叫多洛雷斯·乌姆里奇。"

她扫视着小屋，两次直瞪着哈利站的角落，哈利像三明治一样夹在罗恩和赫敏中间。

"多洛雷斯·乌姆里奇？"海格好像彻底被搞糊涂了，"我以为你是魔法部的——你不是跟福吉在一起吗？"

"对，我之前是对部长负责的高级副部长。"乌姆里奇说。她开始在屋里踱步，留意每个细节，从墙边的背包到搭在那儿的黑色旅行斗篷。"我现在是黑魔法防御术课的教师——"

"你很勇敢，"海格说，"现在没多少人肯教这个了——"

"——兼霍格沃茨高级调查官。"乌姆里奇好像没听见海格的话一样。

"那是什么？"海格皱眉问。

"正是我要问的问题。"乌姆里奇指着地上的碎瓷片，那是赫敏摔

CHAPTER TWENTY Hagrid's Tale

shards of china on the floor that had been Hermione's mug.

'Oh,' said Hagrid, with a most unhelpful glance towards the corner where Harry, Ron and Hermione stood hidden, 'oh, tha' was ... was Fang. He broke a mug. So I had ter use this one instead.'

Hagrid pointed to the mug from which he had been drinking, one hand still clamped over the dragon steak pressed to his eye. Umbridge stood facing him now, taking in every detail of his appearance instead of the cabin's.

'I heard voices,' she said quietly.

'I was talkin' ter Fang,' said Hagrid stoutly.

'And was he talking back to you?'

'Well ... in a manner o' speakin',' said Hagrid, looking uncomfortable. 'I sometimes say Fang's near enough human –'

'There are three sets of footprints in the snow leading from the castle doors to your cabin,' said Umbridge sleekly.

Hermione gasped; Harry clapped a hand over her mouth. Luckily, Fang was sniffing loudly around the hem of Professor Umbridge's robes and she did not appear to have heard.

'Well, I on'y jus' got back,' said Hagrid, waving an enormous hand at the haversack. 'Maybe someone came ter call earlier an' I missed 'em.'

'There are no footsteps leading away from your cabin door.'

'Well, I ... I don' know why that'd be ...' said Hagrid, tugging nervously at his beard and again glancing towards the corner where Harry, Ron and Hermione stood, as though asking for help. 'Erm ...'

Umbridge wheeled round and strode the length of the cabin, looking around carefully. She bent and peered under the bed. She opened Hagrid's cupboards. She passed within two inches of where Harry, Ron and Hermione stood pressed against the wall; Harry actually pulled in his stomach as she walked by. After looking carefully inside the enormous cauldron Hagrid used for cooking, she wheeled round again and said, 'What has happened to you? How did you sustain those injuries?'

Hagrid hastily removed the dragon steak from his face, which in Harry's opinion was a mistake, because the black and purple bruising all around his eye was now clearly visible, not to mention the large amount of fresh and congealed blood on his face. 'Oh, I ... had a bit of an accident,' he said lamely.

'What sort of accident?'

碎的茶杯。"

"哦，真要命，"海格欲盖弥彰地朝哈利、罗恩和赫敏站的地方瞥了一眼，"哦，那是……是牙牙，它打碎了茶杯，所以我只好用这一只。"

海格指指他的茶杯，一只手还按着敷在眼上的火龙肉。乌姆里奇站在他面前，注意着他脸上的每个细节。

"我刚才听到了说话声。"她低声说。

"我在跟牙牙说话。"海格坚定地回答。

"它也跟你说话吗？"

"啊……以某种方式，"海格说，显得不大自在，"我有时说牙牙很像人——"

"雪地上有三对脚印，从城堡门口通到你的小屋。"乌姆里奇圆滑地说。

赫敏倒吸了一口气，哈利赶紧捂住她的嘴巴。幸好，牙牙大声地嗅着乌姆里奇教授的袍摆，她似乎没有听见。

"哦，我刚回来。"海格说，一只大手朝背包挥了挥，"也许有人来过，我没见着。"

"你的小屋门口没有离开的脚印。"

"这……我不知道……"海格紧张地揪着胡须，又求助似的朝哈利三人站的角落瞟去，"呃……"

乌姆里奇转身从屋子这头走向那头，仔细巡视。她弯腰看看床下；她打开海格的碗柜；她从哈利他们跟前不到两英寸处走过，三人贴墙而立，哈利使劲收着肚子。在仔细检查过海格煮饭用的大锅之后，她转身问道："你怎么了？这些伤是怎么回事？"

海格赶紧把火龙肉从脸上拿了下来，哈利认为这是个错误，他眼睛周围黑紫的瘀肿都露出来了，更别提脸上那么多的鲜血和血块。"哦，我……出了点事故。"海格无力地说。

"什么样的事故？"

741

CHAPTER TWENTY Hagrid's Tale

'I – I tripped.'

'You tripped,' she repeated coolly.

'Yeah, tha's right. Over ... over a friend's broomstick. I don' fly, meself. Well, look at the size o' me, I don' reckon there's a broomstick that'd hold me. Friend o' mine breeds Abraxan horses, I dunno if you've ever seen 'em, big beasts, winged, yeh know, I've had a bit of a ride on one o' them an' it was –'

'Where have you been?' asked Umbridge, cutting coolly through Hagrid's babbling.

'Where've I –?'

'Been, yes,' she said. 'Term started two months ago. Another teacher has had to cover your classes. None of your colleagues has been able to give me any information as to your whereabouts. You left no address. Where have you been?'

There was a pause in which Hagrid stared at her with his newly uncovered eye. Harry could almost hear his brain working furiously.

'I – I've been away for me health,' he said.

'For your health,' said Professor Umbridge. Her eyes travelled over Hagrid's discoloured and swollen face; dragon blood dripped gently and silently on to his waistcoat. 'I see.'

'Yeah,' said Hagrid, 'bit o' – o' fresh air, yeh know –'

'Yes, as gamekeeper fresh air must be so difficult to come by,' said Umbridge sweetly. The small patch of Hagrid's face that was not black or purple, flushed.

'Well – change o' scene, yeh know –'

'Mountain scenery?' said Umbridge swiftly.

She knows, Harry thought desperately.

'Mountains?' Hagrid repeated, clearly thinking fast. 'Nope, South o' France fer me. Bit o' sun an' ... an' sea.'

'Really?' said Umbridge. 'You don't have much of a tan.'

'Yeah ... well ... sensitive skin,' said Hagrid, attempting an ingratiating smile. Harry noticed that two of his teeth had been knocked out. Umbridge looked at him coldly; his smile faltered. Then she hoisted her handbag a little higher into the crook of her arm and said, 'I shall, of course, be informing the Minister of your late return.'

'Righ',' said Hagrid, nodding.

第20章 海格的故事

"我——我摔了一跤。"

"摔了一跤。"她冷冷地重复道。

"是的。被……被朋友的飞天扫帚绊的。我自己不会飞。看我这块头,我想没有一把扫帚载得了我。我朋友养神符马,不知你见过没有,大牲口,长着翅膀,我骑过一回——"

"你去哪儿了?"乌姆里奇冷冷地打断了海格的胡扯。

"我去……?"

"哪儿了?对,开学两个多月了,你的课由别的老师代着,同事都不知道你的去向,你没留下地址,你到底去哪儿了?"

一阵沉默,海格用他新露出的眼睛瞪着乌姆里奇,哈利几乎能听到他的大脑在疯狂地转动。

"我——我去疗养了。"他说。

"疗养。"乌姆里奇教授说。她打量着海格那没有血色的青肿的脸,静默中,火龙血缓缓地滴到他的皮马甲上。"看得出来。"

"是啊,"海格说,"享受点——新鲜空气,你知道——"

"是啊,猎场看守一定很难呼吸到新鲜空气。"乌姆里奇亲切地说。海格脸上没有瘀青的那一小块皮肤变红了。

"嗯——换换风景,你知道——"

"高山风景?"乌姆里奇马上说。

她知道了,哈利绝望地想。

"高山?"海格重复道,显然在使劲动脑子,"不,是法国南部,阳光和……和大海。"

"是吗?"乌姆里奇说,"你没怎么晒黑啊。"

"啊……是……皮肤敏感。"海格想做出一个讨好的笑容,哈利注意到他掉了两颗牙齿。乌姆里奇冷冷地看着海格,他的笑容挂不住了。然后乌姆里奇把皮包往臂弯里拉了拉说:"我自然会向部长报告你这么晚回来的。"

"是。"海格点头说。

CHAPTER TWENTY Hagrid's Tale

'You ought to know, too, that as High Inquisitor it is my unfortunate but necessary duty to inspect my fellow teachers. So I daresay we shall meet again soon enough.'

She turned sharply and marched back to the door.

'You're inspectin' us?' Hagrid echoed blankly, looking after her.

'Oh, yes,' said Umbridge softly, looking back at him with her hand on the door handle. 'The Ministry is determined to weed out unsatisfactory teachers, Hagrid. Goodnight.'

She left, closing the door behind her with a snap. Harry made to pull off the Invisibility Cloak but Hermione seized his wrist.

'Not yet,' she breathed in his ear. 'She might not be gone yet.'

Hagrid seemed to be thinking the same way; he stumped across the room and pulled back the curtain an inch or so.

'She's goin' back ter the castle,' he said in a low voice. 'Blimey ... inspectin' people, is she?'

'Yeah,' said Harry, pulling off the Cloak. 'Trelawney's on probation already ...'

'Um ... what sort of thing are you planning to do with us in class, Hagrid?' asked Hermione.

'Oh, don' you worry abou' that, I've got a great load o' lessons planned,' said Hagrid enthusiastically, scooping up his dragon steak from the table and slapping it over his eye again. 'I've bin keepin' a couple o' creatures saved fer yer O.W.L. year; you wait, they're somethin' really special.'

'Erm ... special in what way?' asked Hermione tentatively.

'I'm not sayin',' said Hagrid happily. 'I don' want ter spoil the surprise.'

'Look, Hagrid,' said Hermione urgently, dropping all pretence, 'Professor Umbridge won't be at all happy if you bring anything to class that's too dangerous.'

'Dangerous?' said Hagrid, looking genially bemused. 'Don' be silly, I wouldn' give yeh anythin' dangerous! I mean, all righ', they can look after themselves –'

'Hagrid, you've got to pass Umbridge's inspection, and to do that it would really be better if she saw you teaching us how to look after Porlocks, how to tell the difference between Knarls and hedgehogs, stuff like that!' said Hermione earnestly.

'But tha's not very interestin', Hermione,' said Hagrid. 'The stuff I've got's much more impressive. I've bin bringin' 'em on fer years, I reckon I've got the on'y domestic herd in Britain.'

第20章 海格的故事

"你还应该知道,作为高级调查官,我有一个不幸但必要的任务,就是调查其他教师的教学。所以我敢说我们很快又会见面的。"

她猛然转身朝门口走去。

"你要调查我们?"海格望着她的后背茫然地问。

"对,"乌姆里奇手放在门把上,回头看着他,轻声说,"魔法部决心清除不合格的教师,海格。晚安。"

她出去了,啪地把门带上。哈利想掀开隐形衣,但赫敏抓住了他的手腕。

"等等,"她耳语道,"她可能还没走。"

海格似乎也这么想,他大步走到窗前,把窗帘拉开一条缝。

"她回城堡去了。"他低声说,"邪门……她还要调查别人?"

"是啊,"哈利扯掉隐形衣说,"特里劳妮已经留用察看了……"

"嗯……海格,你打算在课上让我们干什么?"赫敏问。

"哦,别担心,我准备了一堆内容,"海格兴致勃勃地说,又从桌上拿起火龙肉敷在眼睛上,"我为你们的 O.W.L. 学年专门留了一些动物。等着吧,它们非常特别。"

"嗯……特别在哪里?"赫敏试探性地问。

"不能说,"海格快活地答道,"我想给你们一个惊喜。"

"哎呀,海格,"赫敏一着急,顾不得掩饰了,"乌姆里奇教授会挑毛病的,要是你课上用太危险的——"

"危险?"海格似乎觉得好笑,"别说傻话了,我不会给你们危险东西的!我是说,它们能照看好自己——"

"海格,你必须通过乌姆里奇的检查,所以,如果让她看到你教我们怎样寻找庞洛克,怎样区分刺佬儿和刺猬等等,真的会好得多!"赫敏急切地说。

"可那不大有趣,赫敏,"海格说,"我准备的东西要神奇得多,我养了好些年了,我想全英国只有我这一批驯养的——"

CHAPTER TWENTY Hagrid's Tale

'Hagrid ... please ...' said Hermione, a note of real desperation in her voice. 'Umbridge is looking for any excuse to get rid of teachers she thinks are too close to Dumbledore. Please, Hagrid, teach us something dull that's bound to come up in our O.W.L.'

But Hagrid merely yawned widely and cast a one-eyed look of longing towards the vast bed in the corner.

'Lis'en, it's bin a long day an' it's late,' he said, patting Hermione gently on the shoulder, so that her knees gave way and hit the floor with a thud. 'Oh – sorry –' He pulled her back up by the neck of her robes. 'Look, don' you go worryin' abou' me, I promise yeh I've got really good stuff planned fer yer lessons now I'm back ... now you lot had better get back up to the castle, an' don' forget ter wipe yer footprints out behind yeh!'

'I dunno if you got through to him,' said Ron a short while later when, having checked that the coast was clear, they walked back up to the castle through the thickening snow, leaving no trace behind them due to the Obliteration Charm Hermione was performing as they went.

'Then I'll go back again tomorrow,' said Hermione determinedly. 'I'll plan his lessons for him if I have to. I don't care if she throws out Trelawney but she's not getting rid of Hagrid!'

第20章 海格的故事

"海格……求求你……"赫敏的声音真有点绝望了,"乌姆里奇在找借口除掉她认为跟邓布利多关系太密切的教师,求求你,教点平常的、O.W.L.考试中肯定会有的东西……"

但海格只是打了个大大的哈欠,独眼朝屋角的大床投去渴望的一瞥。

"好了,今天够累的,天也晚了。"他轻轻拍了拍赫敏的肩膀,赫敏膝盖一软,扑通跪到地上。"哦——对不起——"他揪着袍领把赫敏拉了起来,"不要为我担心,现在我回来了,我发誓我给你们的保护神奇动物课准备了很好的东西……现在你们最好回城堡去,别忘了擦掉脚印!"

"我不知道他有没有听懂你的话。"罗恩后来在路上说。看看四下安全,他们便踏着渐渐加厚的积雪走回城堡,一路没有留下痕迹,因为赫敏用了擦除咒。

"那我明天再来,"赫敏坚决地说,"必要的话我会帮他备课,解雇特里劳尼我不在乎,但是她不能赶走海格!"

CHAPTER TWENTY-ONE

The Eye of the Snake

Hermione ploughed her way back to Hagrid's cabin through two feet of snow on Sunday morning. Harry and Ron wanted to go with her, but their mountain of homework had reached an alarming height again, so they remained grudgingly in the common room, trying to ignore the gleeful shouts drifting up from the grounds outside, where students were enjoying themselves skating on the frozen lake, tobogganing and, worst of all, bewitching snowballs to zoom up to Gryffindor Tower and rap hard on the windows.

'Oi!' bellowed Ron, finally losing patience and sticking his head out of the window, 'I am a prefect and if one more snowball hits this window – OUCH!'

He withdrew his head sharply, his face covered in snow.

'It's Fred and George,' he said bitterly, slamming the window behind him. 'Gits ...'

Hermione returned from Hagrid's just before lunch, shivering slightly, her robes damp to the knees.

'So?' said Ron, looking up when she entered. 'Got all his lessons planned for him?'

'Well, I tried,' she said dully, sinking into a chair beside Harry. She pulled out her wand and gave it a complicated little wave so that hot air streamed out of the tip; she then pointed this at her robes, which began to steam as they dried out. 'He wasn't even there when I arrived, I was knocking for at least half an hour. And then he came stumping out of the Forest –'

Harry groaned. The Forbidden Forest was teeming with the kind of creatures most likely to get Hagrid the sack. 'What's he keeping in there? Did he say?' he asked.

'No,' said Hermione miserably. 'He says he wants them to be a surprise. I tried to explain about Umbridge, but he just doesn't get it. He kept saying nobody in their right mind would rather study Knarls than Chimaeras – oh, I don't think he's *got* a Chimaera,' she added at the appalled look on Harry

第21章

蛇 眼

星期天早上,赫敏踏着两英尺深的积雪走向海格的小屋。哈利和罗恩想陪她去,但他们的"家庭作业山"又增到了骇人的高度,只好不情愿地留在了公共休息室里,努力不去理睬楼下传来的欢叫声。同学们在湖上溜冰、滑雪橇,更糟糕的是,他们还用魔法使雪球飞上格兰芬多塔楼,重重地砸在窗户上。

"喂!"罗恩终于失去了耐心,把头伸出窗外吼道,"我是级长,再有一个雪球砸到这扇窗户——哎哟!"

他猛地缩回头,脸上全是雪。

"是弗雷德和乔治,"他砰地关上窗户,恨恨地说,"臭小子们……"

午饭前赫敏才从海格那儿回来,微微哆嗦着,袍子膝部以下都湿了。

"怎么样?"她进来时罗恩抬起头来问,"帮他备好课了?"

"我努力了。"赫敏没精打采地说,坐进哈利旁边的椅子,抽出魔杖,花样复杂地舞了一下,杖尖冒出热气。赫敏用它指着自己的袍子,水汽从袍子上蒸发了出去。"我去的时候他不在,我在外面敲门敲了至少半小时,他才从林子里走出来——"

哈利呻吟了一声,禁林里多的是容易让海格被解雇的生物。"他在那儿养了什么?他说了吗?"哈利问。

"没有,"赫敏苦恼地说,"他说他要给我们一个惊喜。我想说明乌姆里奇的情况,可他就是听不进去。他一个劲儿地说脑子正常的人都不会愿意研究刺佬儿而放弃客迈拉兽——哦,我想他没有客迈拉兽。"

CHAPTER TWENTY-ONE — The Eye of the Snake

and Ron's faces, 'but that's not for lack of trying, from what he said about how hard it is to get eggs. I don't know how many times I told him he'd be better off following Grubbly-Plank's plan, I honestly don't think he listened to half of what I said. He's in a bit of a funny mood, you know. He still won't say how he got all those injuries.'

Hagrid's reappearance at the staff table at breakfast next day was not greeted by enthusiasm from all students. Some, like Fred, George and Lee, roared with delight and sprinted up the aisle between the Gryffindor and Hufflepuff tables to wring Hagrid's enormous hand; others, like Parvati and Lavender, exchanged gloomy looks and shook their heads. Harry knew that many of them preferred Professor Grubbly-Plank's lessons, and the worst of it was that a very small, unbiased part of him knew that they had good reason: Grubbly-Plank's idea of an interesting class was not one where there was a risk that somebody might have their head ripped off.

It was with a certain amount of apprehension that Harry, Ron and Hermione headed down to Hagrid's on Tuesday, heavily muffled against the cold. Harry was worried, not only about what Hagrid might have decided to teach them, but also about how the rest of the class, particularly Malfoy and his cronies, would behave if Umbridge was watching them.

However, the High Inquisitor was nowhere to be seen as they struggled through the snow towards Hagrid, who stood waiting for them on the edge of the forest. He did not present a reassuring sight; the bruises that had been purple on Saturday night were now tinged with green and yellow and some of his cuts still seemed to be bleeding. Harry could not understand this: had Hagrid perhaps been attacked by some creature whose venom prevented the wounds it inflicted from healing? As though to complete the ominous picture, Hagrid was carrying what looked like half a dead cow over his shoulder.

'We're workin' in here today!' Hagrid called happily to the approaching students, jerking his head back at the dark trees behind him. 'Bit more sheltered! Anyway, they prefer the dark.'

'What prefers the dark?' Harry heard Malfoy say sharply to Crabbe and Goyle, a trace of panic in his voice. 'What did he say prefers the dark – did you hear?'

Harry remembered the only other occasion on which Malfoy had entered the forest before now; he had not been very brave then, either. He smiled to himself; after the Quidditch match anything that caused Malfoy discomfort was all right with him.

第21章 蛇眼

看到哈利和罗恩惊恐的表情,她赶紧加了一句,"但他不是没试过,他说那是因为客迈拉的蛋不容易弄到……我不知多少次对他讲,用格拉普兰的教法更有利。可我真觉得他连一半都没听进去。你们知道,他有些怪怪的,还是不肯说他是怎么受的伤……"

海格第二天早饭时重新出现在教工桌子旁,并不是所有学生都反应热烈。弗雷德、乔治和李·乔丹等人热烈欢呼,冲到格兰芬多与赫奇帕奇桌子之间的过道上,拉着海格巨大的手握了又握。另一些人,像帕瓦蒂和拉文德等则郁闷地交换着眼色,摇着头。哈利知道他们许多人更喜欢格拉普兰教授的课。最糟糕的是,他心里一小块公正的地方知道他们是有理由的:格拉普兰概念中有趣的课,决不是可能有人被揪掉脑袋的那种。

星期二,哈利、罗恩和赫敏穿得严严实实地去上海格的课,心里有些害怕。哈利不仅担心海格可能会教的东西,还担心其他同学,尤其是马尔福及其心腹,在乌姆里奇听课时的表现。

然而,当他们在雪地上深一脚浅一脚地朝等在树林边的海格走去时,却没有看到高级调查官的影子。海格的样子不让人宽心,星期六夜里紫色的伤痕现在显出了黄绿色,有些伤口好像还在流血。哈利不明白:难道海格受了什么怪兽的袭击,它的毒液能阻止伤口愈合?仿佛是为了让这幅不祥的画面更加完整,海格肩上似乎还扛着半头死牛。

"我们今天在这儿上课!"海格愉快地对正在走近的学生们说,把头朝身后黑乎乎的林子一摆,"林子里密了点儿!不过,它们喜欢黑暗……"

"什么东西喜欢黑暗?"哈利听到马尔福尖声问克拉布和高尔,声音中带着一丝恐惧,"他说什么喜欢黑暗——你们听见了吗?"

哈利想起马尔福以前唯一一次进这个林子的情形,那时他自己也不是很勇敢。哈利笑了,魁地奇比赛后凡是能让马尔福不自在的事情他都赞成。

CHAPTER TWENTY-ONE   The Eye of the Snake

'Ready?' said Hagrid cheerfully, looking around at the class. 'Right, well, I've bin savin' a trip inter the forest fer yer fifth year. Thought we'd go an' see these creatures in their natural habitat. Now, what we're studyin' today is pretty rare, I reckon I'm probably the on'y person in Britain who's managed ter train 'em.'

'And you're sure they're trained, are you?' said Malfoy, the panic in his voice even more pronounced. 'Only it wouldn't be the first time you'd brought wild stuff to class, would it?'

The Slytherins murmured agreement and a few Gryffindors looked as though they thought Malfoy had a fair point, too.

'Course they're trained,' said Hagrid, scowling and hoisting the dead cow a little higher on his shoulder.

'So what happened to your face, then?' demanded Malfoy.

'Mind yer own business!' said Hagrid, angrily. 'Now, if yeh've finished askin' stupid questions, follow me!'

He turned and strode straight into the forest. Nobody seemed much disposed to follow. Harry glanced at Ron and Hermione, who sighed but nodded, and the three of them set off after Hagrid, leading the rest of the class.

They walked for about ten minutes until they reached a place where the trees stood so closely together that it was as dark as twilight and there was no snow at all on the ground. With a grunt, Hagrid deposited his half a cow on the ground, stepped back and turned to face his class, most of whom were creeping from tree to tree towards him, peering around nervously as though expecting to be set upon at any moment.

'Gather roun', gather roun',' Hagrid encouraged. 'Now, they'll be attracted by the smell o' the meat but I'm goin' ter give 'em a call anyway, 'cause they'll like ter know it's me.'

He turned, shook his shaggy head to get the hair out of his face and gave an odd, shrieking cry that echoed through the dark trees like the call of some monstrous bird. Nobody laughed: most of them looked too scared to make a sound.

Hagrid gave the shrieking cry again. A minute passed in which the class continued to peer nervously over their shoulders and around trees for a first glimpse of whatever it was that was coming. And then, as Hagrid shook his hair back for a third time and expanded his enormous chest, Harry nudged Ron and pointed into the black space between two gnarled yew trees.

第21章 蛇眼

"准备好了吗？"海格快活地扫视着同学们说，"好。我为你们五年级留了一堂林中考察课，想让你们看看这些动物在自然环境中的生活。我们今天要学习的动物非常稀有，我想我可能是全英国唯一一个驯服了它们的人——"

"你肯定它们被驯服了吗？"马尔福问，声音中的恐惧更明显了，"反正这不会是你第一次把野兽带到课堂上，对吧？"

斯莱特林的学生小声附和，几个格兰芬多的学生好像也觉得马尔福说的不无道理。

"当然被驯服了。"海格皱起眉头，把肩上的死牛朝上提了提。

"那你的脸是怎么回事？"马尔福问。

"不关你的事！"海格火了，"好了，如果你们问完了愚蠢的问题，就跟我走！"

他转身大步走进森林。大家似乎都不大愿意跟进去。哈利望望罗恩与赫敏，他们叹了口气，点点头。于是三人带头跟在海格后面。

走了大约十分钟，来到一处林木茂密、暗如黄昏的地方，地上一点积雪也没有。海格吭哧一声把那半头牛撂到地上，退后两步，转身面对着全体同学。许多人都用树干做掩护，紧张地东张西望，小心翼翼地向他靠近，似乎在防备随时受到袭击。

"靠拢，靠拢。"海格鼓励地说，"现在，它们会被肉味引来，但我还是叫它们一声，因为它们愿意听到是我……"

他转过身，摇摇脑袋甩开挡在脸上的头发，发出一种古怪的、尖厉的叫声。声音在幽暗的林子里回响，像是巨鸟的鸣叫。没有人笑，大部分人似乎都吓得不敢出声了。

海格又叫了一声。一分钟过去了，学生们一直在紧张地越过肩膀和树木窥视四周，想看一眼正在靠近的不知什么东西。当海格第三次甩开头发，扩张他那宽大的胸脯时，哈利推推罗恩，指了指两棵多节的紫杉之间的暗处。

CHAPTER TWENTY-ONE   The Eye of the Snake

A pair of blank, white, shining eyes were growing larger through the gloom and a moment later the dragonish face, neck and then skeletal body of a great, black, winged horse emerged from the darkness. It looked around at the class for a few seconds, swishing its long black tail, then bowed its head and began to tear flesh from the dead cow with its pointed fangs.

A great wave of relief broke over Harry. Here at last was proof that he had not imagined these creatures, that they were real: Hagrid knew about them too. He looked eagerly at Ron, but Ron was still staring around into the trees and after a few seconds he whispered, 'Why doesn't Hagrid call again?'

Most of the rest of the class were wearing expressions as confused and nervously expectant as Ron's and were still gazing everywhere but at the horse standing feet from them. There were only two other people who seemed to be able to see them: a stringy Slytherin boy standing just behind Goyle was watching the horse eating with an expression of great distaste on his face; and Neville, whose eyes were following the swishing progress of the long black tail.

'Oh, an' here comes another one!' said Hagrid proudly, as a second black horse appeared out of the dark trees, folded its leathery wings closer to its body and dipped its head to gorge on the meat. 'Now ... put yer hands up, who can see 'em?'

Immensely pleased to feel that he was at last going to understand the mystery of these horses, Harry raised his hand. Hagrid nodded at him.

'Yeah ... yeah, I knew you'd be able ter, Harry,' he said seriously. 'An' you too, Neville, eh? An' –'

'Excuse me,' said Malfoy in a sneering voice, 'but what exactly are we supposed to be seeing?'

For an answer, Hagrid pointed at the cow carcass on the ground. The whole class stared at it for a few seconds, then several people gasped and Parvati squealed. Harry understood why: bits of flesh stripping themselves away from the bones and vanishing into thin air had to look very odd indeed.

'What's doing it?' Parvati demanded in a terrified voice, retreating behind the nearest tree. 'What's eating it?'

'Thestrals,' said Hagrid proudly and Hermione gave a soft '*Oh!*' of comprehension at Harry's shoulder. 'Hogwarts has got a whole herd of 'em in here. Now, who knows –?'

'But they're really, really unlucky!' interrupted Parvati, looking alarmed.

第21章 蛇眼

一对发亮空洞的白眼睛在昏暗中渐渐变大，随后是火龙一样的脸、颈部和骨骼毕露的身体，一匹巨大的、长着翅膀的黑马从黑暗中显现出来。它朝学生们看了几秒钟，甩了甩长长的黑尾巴，然后低下头开始用尖牙撕咬死牛。

哈利感到如释重负。现在终于证明这些动物不是他的幻想，而是真的：海格也知道。他急切地望着罗恩，但罗恩还在朝林间张望，过了片刻他小声地问："海格为什么不叫了？"

大部分同学也带着像罗恩一样困惑、紧张而又期待的表情东张西望，但就是看不到站在几英尺外的黑马。只有另外两人好像看到了：高尔身后一个瘦瘦的斯莱特林男生正在看黑马吃肉，脸上露出非常厌恶的表情；纳威的目光盯着那条不停甩动的长长黑尾。

"哦，又来了一位！"海格自豪地说，第二匹黑马从林中出现了，收起皮革一样的翅膀，低头贪婪地吃起了生肉，"现在……有谁看见了，举个手。"

哈利举起手，非常高兴终于有机会了解这些怪马的秘密了。海格朝他点了点头。

"嗯……我知道你会的，哈利。"他严肃地说，"还有你，纳威？还有——"

"对不起，"马尔福用讥讽的口气说，"我们到底应该看到什么？"

海格指了指地上的死牛作为回答。同学们盯着它看了几秒钟，有几个人倒吸了一口冷气，帕瓦蒂尖叫起来。哈利知道为什么。一块块肉自动从骨头上剥离，消失在空气中，看上去一定非常诡异。

"什么东西？"帕瓦蒂退到离她最近的一棵树后，恐惧地问，"什么东西在吃它？"

"夜骐，"海格自豪地说，赫敏在哈利旁边领悟地"哦！"了一声，"霍格沃茨这里有一大群呢。现在，有谁知道——？"

"可它们非常非常不吉利！"帕瓦蒂插嘴说，看上去很惊恐，"会给

CHAPTER TWENTY-ONE   The Eye of the Snake

'They're supposed to bring all sorts of horrible misfortune on people who see them. Professor Trelawney told me once –'

'No, no, no,' said Hagrid, chuckling, 'tha's jus' superstition, that is, they aren' unlucky, they're dead clever an' useful! Course, this lot don' get a lot o' work, it's mainly jus' pullin' the school carriages unless Dumbledore's takin' a long journey an' don' want ter Apparate – an' here's another couple, look –'

Two more horses came quietly out of the trees, one of them passing very close to Parvati, who shivered and pressed herself closer to the tree, saying, 'I think I felt something, I think it's near me!'

'Don' worry, it won' hurt yeh,' said Hagrid patiently. 'Righ', now, who can tell me why some o' yeh can see 'em an' some can't?'

Hermione raised her hand.

'Go on then,' said Hagrid, beaming at her.

'The only people who can see Thestrals,' she said, 'are people who have seen death.'

'Tha's exactly right,' said Hagrid solemnly, 'ten points ter Gryffindor. Now, Thestrals –'

'*Hem, hem.*'

Professor Umbridge had arrived. She was standing a few feet away from Harry, wearing her green hat and cloak again, her clipboard at the ready. Hagrid, who had never heard Umbridge's fake cough before, was gazing in some concern at the closest Thestral, evidently under the impression that it had made the sound.

'*Hem, hem.*'

'Oh, hello!' Hagrid said, smiling, having located the source of the noise.

'You received the note I sent to your cabin this morning?' said Umbridge, in the same loud, slow voice she had used with him earlier, as though she were addressing somebody both foreign and very slow. 'Telling you that I would be inspecting your lesson?'

'Oh, yeah,' said Hagrid brightly. 'Glad yeh found the place all righ'! Well, as you can see – or, I dunno – can you? We're doin' Thestrals today –'

'I'm sorry?' said Professor Umbridge loudly, cupping her hand around her ear and frowning. 'What did you say?'

Hagrid looked a little confused.

'Er – *Thestrals*!' he said loudly. 'Big – er – winged horses, yeh know!'

第21章 蛇 眼

看到它们的人带来各种可怕的灾祸，特里劳尼教授有一次跟我说过——"

"不不不，"海格笑道，"那只是迷信，没什么不吉利的，它们很聪明也很有用。当然，这一群没多少事可干，主要也就拉拉学校的马车，除非邓布利多要出远门又不想用幻影移形——又来了一对，瞧——"

又有两匹马悄然显现了，其中一匹从帕瓦蒂身旁擦过。她浑身发抖，紧紧抱着树干说："我觉得有什么东西，它好像在我旁边！"

"别害怕，它不会伤害你的。"海格耐心地说，"现在，谁能告诉我为什么有人看得见，有人看不见？"

赫敏举起手。

"你说。"海格对她一笑说。

"只有见过死亡的人才能看见夜骐。"赫敏说。

"对了，"海格严肃地说，"格兰芬多加十分。夜骐——"

"咳，咳。"

乌姆里奇教授来了。她站在离哈利几英尺远的地方，仍是绿帽子、绿斗篷，手拿写字板。没听过乌姆里奇假咳的海格有点担心地望着旁边的一匹夜骐，显然以为是它发出的声音。

"咳，咳。"

"哦，你好！"海格微笑道，发现了怪声的来源。

"你有没有收到我早上送到你小屋的字条？"乌姆里奇还是像她前一次对海格说话时那样，说得又慢又响，似乎对方是个外国人，而且智力迟钝，"我说要来听你的课。"

"哦，收到了，"海格爽朗地说，"很高兴你找到了地方！你看——我不知道——你能看到吗？我们今天讲夜骐——"

"对不起，"乌姆里奇教授把手放在耳朵边握成杯子形状，皱着眉头大声说，"你说什么？"

海格显得有点疑惑。

"呃——夜骐！"他响亮地说，"大马——呃——长着翅膀的，你知道！"

CHAPTER TWENTY-ONE The Eye of the Snake

He flapped his gigantic arms hopefully. Professor Umbridge raised her eyebrows at him and muttered as she made a note on her clipboard: '*Has ... to ... resort ... to ... crude ... sign ... language.*'

'Well ... anyway ...' said Hagrid, turning back to the class and looking slightly flustered, 'erm ... what was I sayin'?'

'*Appears ... to ... have ... poor ... short ... term ... memory,*' muttered Umbridge, loudly enough for everyone to hear her. Draco Malfoy looked as though Christmas had come a month early; Hermione, on the other hand, had turned scarlet with suppressed rage.

'Oh, yeah,' said Hagrid, throwing an uneasy glance at Umbridge's clipboard, but ploughing on valiantly. 'Yeah, I was gonna tell yeh how come we got a herd. Yeah, so, we started off with a male an' five females. This one,' he patted the first horse to have appeared, 'name o' Tenebrus, he's my special favourite, firs' one born here in the Forest –'

'Are you aware,' Umbridge said loudly, interrupting him, 'that the Ministry of Magic has classified Thestrals as "dangerous"?'

Harry's heart sank like a stone, but Hagrid merely chuckled.

'Thestrals aren' dangerous! All righ', they might take a bite outta yeh if yeh really annoy them –'

'*Shows ... signs ... of ... pleasure ... at ... idea ... of ... violence,*' muttered Umbridge, scribbling on her clipboard again.

'No – come on!' said Hagrid, looking a little anxious now. 'I mean, a dog'll bite if yeh bait it, won' it – but Thestrals have jus' got a bad reputation because o' the death thing – people used ter think they were bad omens, didn' they? Jus' didn' understand, did they?'

Umbridge did not answer; she finished writing her last note, then looked up at Hagrid and said, again very loudly and slowly, 'Please continue teaching as usual. I am going to walk,' she mimed walking (Malfoy and Pansy Parkinson were having silent fits of laughter) 'among the students' (she pointed around at individual members of the class) 'and ask them questions.' She pointed at her mouth to indicate talking.

Hagrid stared at her, clearly at a complete loss to understand why she was acting as though he did not understand normal English. Hermione had tears of fury in her eyes now.

'You hag, you evil hag!' she whispered, as Umbridge walked towards Pansy Parkinson. 'I know what you're doing, you awful, twisted, vicious –'

第21章 蛇眼

他把粗胳膊扑扇了两下,希望她明白。乌姆里奇教授朝他挑起眉毛,在写字板上边念边写,"要靠……笨拙的……手势……"

"好……"海格说,转身面向学生,看上去有点慌乱,"呃……我说到哪儿了?"

"似乎……记性……很差……"乌姆里奇说,声音响得大家都能听见。德拉科·马尔福的样子好像圣诞节提前一个月到了,赫敏则气得涨红了脸。

"哦,"海格不安地瞟了瞟乌姆里奇的写字板,但还是勇敢地讲了下去。"对,我正要告诉你们这群夜骐是怎么来的。开始只有一匹公马和五匹母马。这匹叫乌乌,"他拍拍最先出现的那匹,"是我最喜欢的,这个林子里出生的第一匹——"

"你知不知道,"乌姆里奇高声打断他,"魔法部已把夜骐列为'危险动物'?"

哈利的心陡地一沉,但海格只是笑笑。

"夜骐不危险!当然,要真给惹急了,它们可能会咬你——"

"对……残暴……表现出……快意……"乌姆里奇又边说边在笔记本上写道。

"不——不是!"海格说,看上去有点着急了,"我是说,狗急了还会咬人呢,对吧——夜骐只是因为死人的关系名声不好——人们过去以为它不吉利,对吧?只是无知,对吧?"

乌姆里奇没有回答。她记完最后一笔,抬头看着海格,依旧又慢又响地说:"请像往常一样继续讲课,我要在学生中——"她指着一个个学生,"——走一走,"她做出走路的样子,马尔福和潘西·帕金森在偷笑,"提点问题。"她又指指自己的嘴巴,表示说话。

海格瞪着她,显然完全不明白她为什么装成他听不懂正常英语的样子。赫敏眼中含着愤怒的泪花。

"女妖,邪恶的女妖!"她小声说,看着乌姆里奇走向潘西·帕金森,"我知道你要干什么,你这丑陋的、变态的、恶毒的——"

CHAPTER TWENTY-ONE   The Eye of the Snake

'Erm ... anyway,' said Hagrid, clearly struggling to regain the flow of his lesson, 'so – Thestrals. Yeah. Well, there's loads o' good stuff abou' them ...'

'Do you find,' said Professor Umbridge in a ringing voice to Pansy Parkinson, 'that you are able to understand Professor Hagrid when he talks?'

Just like Hermione, Pansy had tears in her eyes, but these were tears of laughter; indeed, her answer was almost incoherent because she was trying to suppress her giggles.

'No ... because ... well ... it sounds ... like grunting a lot of the time ...'

Umbridge scribbled on her clipboard. The few unbruised bits of Hagrid's face flushed, but he tried to act as though he had not heard Pansy's answer.

'Er ... yeah ... good stuff abou' Thestrals. Well, once they're tamed, like this lot, yeh'll never be lost again. 'Mazin' sense o' direction, jus' tell 'em where yeh want ter go –'

'Assuming they can understand you, of course,' said Malfoy loudly, and Pansy Parkinson collapsed in a fit of renewed giggles. Professor Umbridge smiled indulgently at them and then turned to Neville.

'You can see the Thestrals, Longbottom, can you?' she said.

Neville nodded.

'Who did you see die?' she asked, her tone indifferent.

'My ... my grandad,' said Neville.

'And what do you think of them?' she said, waving her stubby hand at the horses, who by now had stripped a great deal of the carcass down to bone.

'Erm,' said Neville nervously, with a glance at Hagrid. 'Well, they're ... er ... OK ...'

'*Students ... are ... too ... intimidated ... to ... admit ... they ... are ... frightened,*' muttered Umbridge, making another note on her clipboard.

'No!' said Neville, looking upset. 'No, I'm not scared of them!'

'It's quite all right,' said Umbridge, patting Neville on the shoulder with what she evidently intended to be an understanding smile, though it looked more like a leer to Harry. 'Well, Hagrid,' she turned to look up at him again, speaking once more in that loud, slow voice, 'I think I've got enough to be getting along with. You will receive' (she mimed taking something from the air in front of her) 'the results of your inspection' (she pointed at the clipboard) 'in ten days' time.' She held up ten stubby little fingers, then,

第21章 蛇 眼

"哦……总之,"海格试图继续讲下去,"这个——夜骐,对,它们浑身都是宝……"

"你觉得,"乌姆里奇教授清脆地问潘西·帕金森,"你能听懂海格教授讲话吗?"

像赫敏一样,潘西也含着眼泪,但这些眼泪是笑出来的。她使劲忍着笑,回答得断断续续。

"不能……因为……听起来……很多时候……像呜噜呜噜……"

乌姆里奇在写字板上唰唰地写着。海格脸上几小块没有瘀青的皮肤一下红了,但他努力装作没听见潘西的回答。

"呃……这个……夜骐的好东西。对了,当它们被驯服之后,像这群一样,你就不会迷路了。方向感好得惊人,只要告诉它们你想去哪儿——"

"当然啦,得假定他们能听懂你的话。"马尔福大声说,潘西·帕金森又咯咯地笑了起来。乌姆里奇教授纵容地朝他们笑笑,然后转向纳威。

"你能看到夜骐,是吗,隆巴顿?"她问。

纳威点点头。

"你看到谁死了?"她语气冷漠地问。

"我……我爷爷。"纳威说。

"你觉得它们怎么样?"她说,粗短的手指朝黑色的飞马挥了挥,它们已经把很大一部分牛身撕得只剩骨头了。

"嗯,"纳威瞟了一眼海格,紧张地说,"嗯,它们……呃……挺好的……"

"学生……不敢……承认……害怕。"乌姆里奇念道,又在写字板上记了几笔。

"不!"纳威不安地说,"我不害怕它们——!"

"没关系。"乌姆里奇拍拍纳威的肩膀,她显然想露出一副理解的笑容,但在哈利看来却更像狞笑。"好了,海格,"她转身仰视着他,再

CHAPTER TWENTY-ONE   The Eye of the Snake

her smile wider and more toadlike than ever before beneath her green hat, she bustled from their midst, leaving Malfoy and Pansy Parkinson in fits of laughter, Hermione actually shaking with fury and Neville looking confused and upset.

'That foul, lying, twisting old gargoyle!' stormed Hermione half an hour later, as they made their way back up to the castle through the channels they had made earlier in the snow. 'You see what she's up to? It's her thing about half-breeds all over again – she's trying to make out Hagrid's some kind of dimwitted troll, just because he had a giantess for a mother – and oh, it's not fair, that really wasn't a bad lesson at all – I mean, all right, if it had been Blast-Ended Skrewts again, but Thestrals are fine – in fact, for Hagrid, they're really good!'

'Umbridge said they're dangerous,' said Ron.

'Well, it's like Hagrid said, they can look after themselves,' said Hermione impatiently, 'and I suppose a teacher like Grubbly-Plank wouldn't usually show them to us before N.E.W.T. level, but, well, they *are* very interesting, aren't they? The way some people can see them and some can't! I wish I could.'

'Do you?' Harry asked her quietly.

She looked suddenly horrorstruck.

'Oh, Harry – I'm sorry – no, of course I don't – that was a really stupid thing to say.'

'It's OK,' he said quickly, 'don't worry.'

'I'm surprised so many people *could* see them,' said Ron. 'Three in a class –'

'Yeah, Weasley, we were just wondering,' said a malicious voice. Unheard by any of them in the muffling snow, Malfoy, Crabbe and Goyle were walking along right behind them. 'D'you reckon if you saw someone snuff it you'd be able to see the Quaffle better?'

He, Crabbe and Goyle roared with laughter as they pushed past on their way to the castle, then broke into a chorus of 'Weasley is our King'. Ron's ears turned scarlet.

'Ignore them, just ignore them,' intoned Hermione, pulling out her wand and performing the charm to produce hot air again, so that she could melt them an easier path through the untouched snow between them and the greenhouses.

第21章 蛇 眼

一次用又慢又响的声音说,"我想我已经掌握了足够的情况……你会在十天之内——"她伸出短粗的十指,"收到——"(她做出从空中取东西状)"你的调查结果。"她指了指写字板。然后,她更加得意地微笑着,从学生中匆匆走了出去,在绿帽子下比以前更像一只癞蛤蟆。马尔福和潘西·帕金森笑个不停,赫敏气得浑身发抖,纳威看上去迷惑而懊恼。

"那个邪恶、虚伪、变态的滴水嘴石兽!"半小时后赫敏愤怒地说,他们沿着来时在雪地上踩出的小道走回城堡,"你们看出她想干什么吗?又是她那套歧视半人半兽的把戏——她想把海格说成是智力低下的巨怪,就因为海格的妈妈是个巨人——哦,这不公平,其实课上得不赖——我是说,如果又是炸尾螺也就罢了,但是夜骐挺好的——老实讲,对海格来说,它们真是很不错了!"

"乌姆里奇说它们有危险。"罗恩说。

"咳,就像海格说的,它们能照看好自己。"赫敏不耐烦地说,"我想格拉普兰那样的老师一般是不会在提高班之前教这个的,但是,它们确实很有趣,是不是? 有人看见,有人看不见! 我希望我能看见。"

"是吗?"哈利平静地问。

她一下子显得很惊恐。

"哦,哈利——对不起——我当然不希望——那真是句蠢话——"

"没关系,"哈利赶忙说,"别担心。"

"我奇怪竟有这么多人看得见,"罗恩说,"班上有三个——"

"对啊,韦斯莱,我们也在纳闷呢。"一个阴阳怪气的声音说。因为雪太深,他们都没听见马尔福、克拉布和高尔就走在身后。"你以为如果你见过人咽气,就能把鬼飞球看得更清楚些吗?"

他和克拉布、高尔放声大笑,从旁边挤过,朝城堡走去,又高唱起"韦斯莱是我们的王"。罗恩耳朵通红。

"别理他们,千万别理他们。"赫敏急忙劝道。她抽出魔杖,又用咒语产生热气,在没人踏过的雪地上融化出一条通向温室的路。

763

CHAPTER TWENTY-ONE

The Eye of the Snake

December arrived, bringing with it more snow and a positive avalanche of homework for the fifth-years. Ron and Hermione's prefect duties also became more and more onerous as Christmas approached. They were called upon to supervise the decoration of the castle ('You try putting up tinsel when Peeves has got the other end and is trying to strangle you with it,' said Ron), to watch over first- and second-years spending their break-times inside because of the bitter cold ('And they're cheeky little snot-rags, you know, we definitely weren't that rude when we were in first year,' said Ron) and to patrol the corridors in shifts with Argus Filch, who suspected that the holiday spirit might show itself in an outbreak of wizard duels ('He's got dung for brains, that one,' said Ron furiously). They were so busy that Hermione had even stopped knitting elf hats and was fretting that she was down to her last three.

'All those poor elves I haven't set free yet, having to stay here over Christmas because there aren't enough hats!'

Harry, who had not had the heart to tell her that Dobby was taking everything she made, bent lower over his History of Magic essay. In any case, he did not want to think about Christmas. For the first time in his school career, he very much wanted to spend the holidays away from Hogwarts. Between his Quidditch ban and worry about whether or not Hagrid was going to be put on probation, he felt highly resentful towards the place at the moment. The only thing he really looked forward to were the DA meetings, and they would have to stop over the holidays, as nearly everybody in the DA would be spending the time with their families. Hermione was going skiing with her parents, something that greatly amused Ron, who had never heard of Muggles strapping narrow strips of wood on to their feet to slide down mountains. Ron was going home to The Burrow. Harry endured several days of envy before Ron said, in response to Harry asking him how he was going to get home for Christmas: 'But you're coming too! Didn't I say? Mum wrote and told me to invite you weeks ago!'

Hermione rolled her eyes, but Harry's spirits soared: the thought of Christmas at The Burrow was truly wonderful, though slightly marred by Harry's guilty feeling that he would not be able to spend the holiday with Sirius. He wondered whether he could possibly persuade Mrs Weasley to invite his godfather for the festivities. Even though he doubted whether Dumbledore would permit Sirius to leave Grimmauld Place anyway, he could not help but think Mrs Weasley might not want him; they were so often at loggerheads. Sirius had not contacted Harry at all since his last appearance in the fire, and although Harry knew that with Umbridge on constant watch it would be unwise to attempt to contact him, he did not like to think of Sirius alone in his mother's old house, perhaps pulling a lonely cracker with Kreacher.

第21章 蛇 眼

十二月带来了更多的雪，也给五年级学生带来了雪崩般的家庭作业。随着圣诞节的临近，罗恩、赫敏的级长工作越来越繁重。他们要负责监督装饰城堡（"你去挂彩带，皮皮鬼却抓着另一头要把你勒死。"罗恩说），要看着课间因为天冷而待在室内的一二年级学生（"他们脸皮真厚，我们一年级时绝对没那么放肆。"罗恩说），还要轮班和阿格斯·费尔奇在走廊里巡视，因为费尔奇怀疑节日气氛会使巫师决斗增多（"那家伙脑子里有大粪。"罗恩气愤地说）。赫敏忙得没工夫织小精灵帽，心里很着急，她只剩三顶了。

"那些我还没有解放的可怜的小精灵，圣诞节只好待在这里，因为帽子不够！"

哈利不忍心讲多比把她织的帽子全拿走了，便埋下头写魔法史课的论文。反正他不愿去想圣诞节。上学以来，他这是第一次很想在假期离开霍格沃茨。不能打球，又担心海格会被留用察看，他现在恨透了这个地方。他唯一盼望的就是D.A.的活动，可是假期中只能暂停，因为几乎所有成员都要和家人一起过节。赫敏要跟父母去滑雪，罗恩觉得非常有趣，他从没听说过麻瓜把木条绑在脚上从山上滑下去。罗恩自己要回陋居。哈利妒忌了好几天，后来他问罗恩打算怎么回家过节，罗恩说："你也去呀！我没说过吗？妈妈几星期前就写信叫我邀请你了！"

赫敏翻了个白眼，但哈利的心飞了起来。在陋居过圣诞节真是太棒了，只是哈利有点内疚不能和小天狼星一起过节。他也想过能不能说服韦斯莱夫人邀请他的教父，但他不仅怀疑邓布利多不会让小天狼星离开格里莫广场，而且深感韦斯莱夫人可能也不欢迎他去，她跟小天狼星总是不和。小天狼星自从上次在火中消失后还没跟哈利联系过，哈利知道，在乌姆里奇严密的监视下试图联系是不明智的，但他不愿想到小天狼星独自待在他母亲的老房子里，也许只能寂寞地和克利切拉开一个彩包爆竹。

CHAPTER TWENTY-ONE The Eye of the Snake

Harry arrived early in the Room of Requirement for the last DA meeting before the holidays and was very glad he had, because when the torches burst into flame he saw that Dobby had taken it upon himself to decorate the place for Christmas. He could tell the elf had done it, because nobody else would have strung a hundred golden baubles from the ceiling, each showing a picture of Harry's face and bearing the legend: *HAVE A VERY HARRY CHRISTMAS!*

Harry had only just managed to get the last of them down before the door creaked open and Luna Lovegood entered, looking as dreamy as usual.

'Hello,' she said vaguely, looking around at what remained of the decorations. 'These are nice, did you put them up?'

'No,' said Harry, 'it was Dobby the house-elf.'

'Mistletoe,' said Luna dreamily, pointing at a large clump of white berries placed almost over Harry's head. He jumped out from under it.

'Good thinking,' said Luna very seriously. 'It's often infested with Nargles.'

Harry was saved the necessity of asking what Nargles were by the arrival of Angelina, Katie and Alicia. All three of them were breathless and looked very cold.

'Well,' said Angelina dully, pulling off her cloak and throwing it into a corner, 'we've finally replaced you.'

'Replaced me?' said Harry blankly.

'You and Fred and George,' she said impatiently. 'We've got another Seeker!'

'Who?' said Harry quickly.

'Ginny Weasley,' said Katie.

Harry gaped at her.

'Yeah, I know,' said Angelina, pulling out her wand and flexing her arm, 'but she's pretty good, actually. Nothing on you, of course,' she said, throwing him a very dirty look, 'but as we can't have you ...'

Harry bit back the retort he was longing to utter: did she imagine for a second that he did not regret his expulsion from the team a hundred times more than she did?

'And what about the Beaters?' he asked, trying to keep his voice even.

'Andrew Kirke,' said Alicia without enthusiasm, 'and Jack Sloper. Neither of them are brilliant, but compared to the rest of the idiots who turned up ...'

第21章 蛇眼

哈利早早来到有求必应屋，参加节前的最后一次 D.A. 活动。他很高兴自己来得早，因为所有的火把亮起时，他看出多比为了过节已经把这里装饰过了。一看就知道是小精灵干的，因为没有别人会在天花板上吊一百个金色的小球，每个球上都有哈利的大头照，还刻着一行字：**圣诞哈利路亚！**

哈利刚把最后一个小金球摘下来，门吱呀一声开了，卢娜·洛夫古德像往常一样做梦似的走了进来。

"你好，"她含糊地说，打量着其他的装饰，"很漂亮，是你搞的吗？"

"不，"哈利说，"是家养小精灵多比。"

"槲寄生。"卢娜做梦似的说，指着几乎罩在哈利头顶上的一大丛白浆果。哈利赶快从它下面跳了出来。"这就对了，"卢娜严肃地说，"它里面经常会长蛹钩。"

正在这时，安吉利娜、凯蒂和艾丽娅进来了，哈利也就用不着追问蛹钩是什么了。三个女生都气喘吁吁，看上去冻得够呛。

"咳，"安吉利娜没精打采地说，扯下斗篷扔到角落里，"我们终于找到你的替补了。"

"替补我？"哈利傻乎乎地问。

"你、弗雷德和乔治，"安吉利娜不耐烦地说，"我们有新的找球手了！"

"谁？"哈利忙问。

"金妮·韦斯莱。"凯蒂说。

哈利愣愣地望着她。

"没错，我知道。"安吉利娜说着抽出魔杖，活动着胳膊，"可她很不错，真的。当然不如你，"她狠狠地白了哈利一眼说，"可是既然你不能参加……"

哈利咽回了已到嘴边的反驳：她难道没有想过，他被迫离队，不比她遗憾一百倍吗？

"击球手呢？"他问，努力使语气保持平静。

"安德鲁·柯克，"艾丽娅毫无热情地说，"杰克·斯劳珀，都不是很灵，但跟别的木头比起来……"

CHAPTER TWENTY-ONE   The Eye of the Snake

The arrival of Ron, Hermione and Neville brought this depressing discussion to an end, and within five minutes the room was full enough to prevent Harry seeing Angelina's burning, reproachful looks.

'OK,' he said, calling them all to order. 'I thought this evening we should just go over the things we've done so far, because it's the last meeting before the holidays and there's no point starting anything new right before a three-week break –'

'We're not doing anything new?' said Zacharias Smith, in a disgruntled whisper loud enough to carry through the room. 'If I'd known that, I wouldn't have come.'

'We're all really sorry Harry didn't tell you, then,' said Fred loudly.

Several people sniggered. Harry saw Cho laughing and felt the familiar swooping sensation in his stomach, as though he had missed a step going downstairs.

'– we can practise in pairs,' said Harry. 'We'll start with the Impediment Jinx, for ten minutes, then we can get out the cushions and try Stunning again.'

They all divided up obediently; Harry partnered Neville as usual. The room was soon full of intermittent cries of '*Impedimenta!*' People froze for a minute or so, during which their partner would stare aimlessly around the room watching other pairs at work, then would unfreeze and take their turn at the jinx.

Neville had improved beyond all recognition. After a while, when Harry had unfrozen three times in a row, he had Neville join Ron and Hermione again so that he could walk around the room and watch the others. When he passed Cho she beamed at him; he resisted the temptation to walk past her several more times.

After ten minutes on the Impediment Jinx, they laid out cushions all over the floor and started practising Stunning again. Space was really too confined to allow them all to work this spell at once; half the group observed the others for a while, then swapped over. Harry felt himself positively swelling with pride as he watched them all. True, Neville did Stun Padma Patil rather than Dean, at whom he had been aiming, but it was a much closer miss than usual, and everybody else had made enormous progress.

At the end of an hour, Harry called a halt.

'You're getting really good,' he said, beaming around at them. 'When we get back from the holidays we can start doing some of the big stuff – maybe even Patronuses.'

There was a murmur of excitement. The room began to clear in the usual

第21章 蛇 眼

罗恩、赫敏和纳威的到来结束了这场压抑的谈话,不到五分钟,屋子里已经满得看不到安吉利娜灼人的责备目光了。

"好,"哈利叫大家安静,"我想今晚我们就复习一下以前练过的内容,因为这是节前最后一次集会,在三星期的假期之前学新东西没有意义——"

"不学新东西?"扎卡赖斯·史密斯不满地嘟哝道,声音传遍了全屋,"早知道就不来了……"

"那我们都很遗憾哈利没有早点告诉你。"弗雷德大声说。

几个人偷偷地笑。哈利看到秋也在笑,心里又是一跳,好像下楼时一脚踩空了似的。

"——我们两两练习,"哈利说,"从障碍咒开始,练十分钟,然后把垫子拿出来,再练昏迷咒。"

众人顺从地分组,哈利照例和纳威一组。屋里很快便充斥了"障碍重重"之声,被点中的人会僵住一分钟左右,对手无所事事地看着他人练习,然后他们活动起来,跟对手交换角色。

纳威进步得像换了个人。过了一会儿,当哈利连着僵住三次之后,他又让纳威去跟罗恩、赫敏练,自己在屋里转转,看看别人。走过秋的身旁时,秋朝他嫣然一笑。哈利努力抵制老想往那边走的诱惑。

练了十分钟障碍咒之后,他们摆开垫子,又练起了昏迷咒。地方太小,不够他们一起练,一半人先在旁边看着,然后交换。哈利看着大家,心里充满了自豪。诚然,纳威击昏了帕德玛·佩蒂尔,而不是他所瞄准的迪安,但比起以前,他的准头已经好多了,其他人也都有很大的进步。

一小时后,哈利叫大家停了下来。

"练得很好了,"他笑望着大家说,"假期结束回来后我们可以开始一些难度大的——甚至可以包括守护神咒。"

一片兴奋的议论声。人们像往常一样三三两两地走出房间,许多

CHAPTER TWENTY-ONE   The Eye of the Snake

twos and threes; most people wished Harry a 'Happy Christmas' as they went. Feeling cheerful, he collected up the cushions with Ron and Hermione and stacked them neatly away. Ron and Hermione left before he did; he hung back a little, because Cho was still there and he was hoping to receive a 'Merry Christmas' from her.

'No, you go on,' he heard her say to her friend Marietta and his heart gave a jolt that seemed to take it into the region of his Adam's apple.

He pretended to be straightening the cushion pile. He was quite sure they were alone now and waited for her to speak. Instead, he heard a hearty sniff.

He turned and saw Cho standing in the middle of the room, tears pouring down her face.

'Wha–?'

He didn't know what to do. She was simply standing there, crying silently.

'What's up?' he said, feebly.

She shook her head and wiped her eyes on her sleeve.

'I'm – sorry,' she said thickly. 'I suppose … it's just … learning all this stuff … it just makes me … wonder whether … if *he'd* known it all … he'd still be alive.'

Harry's heart sank right back past its usual spot and settled somewhere around his navel. He ought to have known. She wanted to talk about Cedric.

'He did know this stuff,' Harry said heavily. 'He was really good at it, or he could never have got to the middle of that maze. But if Voldemort really wants to kill you, you don't stand a chance.'

She hiccoughed at the sound of Voldemort's name, but stared at Harry without flinching.

'*You* survived when you were just a baby,' she said quietly.

'Yeah, well,' said Harry wearily, moving towards the door, 'I dunno why, nor does anyone else, so it's nothing to be proud of.'

'Oh, don't go!' said Cho, sounding tearful again. 'I'm really sorry to get all upset like this … I didn't mean to …'

She hiccoughed again. She was very pretty even when her eyes were red and puffy. Harry felt thoroughly miserable. He'd have been so pleased with just a 'Merry Christmas'.

'I know it must be horrible for you,' she said, mopping her eyes on her sleeve again. 'Me mentioning Cedric, when you saw him die … I suppose you just want to forget about it?'

第21章 蛇眼

人祝哈利"圣诞快乐"。哈利心情很好,跟罗恩、赫敏一起收起垫子,堆放整齐。罗恩与赫敏先走了,他多待了一会儿,因为秋还在,他希望听到她说"圣诞快乐"。

"你先走吧。"他听到秋对她的朋友玛丽埃塔说,他的心一下蹦到了嗓子眼儿。

哈利假装把垫子摞齐,知道屋里没有别人了,他等着秋开口,可是听到的却是一声抽泣。

他转过身,看到秋站在屋子中间,脸上流着泪。

"怎么——?"

哈利不知道怎么办,她只是站在那儿,默默地哭泣。

"怎么啦?"他无力地问。

她摇摇头,用衣袖拭了拭眼泪。

"对不起,"她含混地说,"我想……只是因为……学这些东西……让我……我想起……要是他会这些……他现在就会还活着……"

哈利的心一下子掉过原来的位置,沉到了肚脐眼附近。他该知道的,她想谈塞德里克。

"他会这些。"哈利沉重地说,"他使用得很好,要不也走不到迷宫中央。可如果伏地魔真想杀你,你没有机会。"

听到伏地魔的名字,秋哽噎了一下,但无畏地望着哈利。

"你当时还是婴儿却活了下来。"她轻声说。

"哦,是的。"哈利疲惫地说,一边朝门口走去,"我不知道为什么,谁也不知道,所以没什么可骄傲的。"

"哦,别走!"秋又带着哭腔说,"真对不起,我这个样子……我本来不想……"

她又哽噎了。即使眼眶红肿,她还是很好看。哈利难过极了,本来只要一句"圣诞快乐",他就会非常高兴……

"我提到塞德里克,"秋又用袖子拭了拭眼泪,"我知道你一定很难过,你看到了他的死……我想你只是希望忘掉……"

CHAPTER TWENTY-ONE   The Eye of the Snake

Harry did not say anything to this; it was quite true, but he felt heartless saying it.

'You're a r-really good teacher, you know,' said Cho, with a watery smile. 'I've never been able to Stun anything before.'

'Thanks,' said Harry awkwardly.

They looked at each other for a long moment. Harry felt a burning desire to run from the room and, at the same time, a complete inability to move his feet.

'Mistletoe,' said Cho quietly, pointing at the ceiling over his head.

'Yeah,' said Harry. His mouth was very dry. 'It's probably full of Nargles, though.'

'What are Nargles?'

'No idea,' said Harry. She had moved closer. His brain seemed to have been Stunned. 'You'd have to ask Loony. Luna, I mean.'

Cho made a funny noise halfway between a sob and a laugh. She was even nearer to him now. He could have counted the freckles on her nose.

'I really like you, Harry.'

He could not think. A tingling sensation was spreading through him, paralysing his arms, legs and brain.

She was much too close. He could see every tear clinging to her eyelashes …

He returned to the common room half an hour later to find Hermione and Ron in the best seats by the fire; nearly everybody else had gone to bed. Hermione was writing a very long letter; she had already filled half a roll of parchment, which was dangling from the edge of the table. Ron was lying on the hearthrug, trying to finish his Transfiguration homework.

'What kept you?' he asked, as Harry sank into the armchair next to Hermione's.

Harry didn't answer. He was in a state of shock. Half of him wanted to tell Ron and Hermione what had just happened, but the other half wanted to take the secret with him to the grave.

'Are you all right, Harry?' Hermione asked, peering at him over the tip of her quill.

Harry gave a half-hearted shrug. In truth, he didn't know whether he was all right or not.

'What's up?' said Ron, hoisting himself up on his elbow to get a clearer view of Harry. 'What's happened?'

第21章 蛇 眼

哈利什么也没说。这是事实,但他觉得说出来太残忍了。

"你真——真是个好老师,"秋含泪微笑道,"我以前从来没有击昏过什么东西。"

"谢谢。"哈利笨拙地说。

他们对视了很久,哈利有从屋里逃出去的强烈冲动,可脚根本挪不动。

"槲寄生。"秋指指他头顶的天花板说。

"没错,"哈利说,感到唇干舌燥,"但里面可能长满了蛴钩。"

"蛴钩是什么?"

"不知道。"哈利说。秋靠近了些,哈利的脑子好像被击昏了。"你得问疯姑娘,我是说卢娜。"

秋发出一种半哭半笑的滑稽声音。她离他更近了,他几乎数得清她鼻子上的雀斑。

"我真的喜欢你,哈利。"

他无法思考。一种震颤的感觉传遍他的全身,麻痹了他的手臂、双腿和大脑。

她太近了。他能看见她睫毛上的每颗泪珠……

半小时后他回到公共休息室,发现罗恩与赫敏坐在壁炉前最好的位置上,几乎所有的人都回去睡觉了。赫敏在写一封很长很长的信,半卷羊皮纸已经写满了,从桌边垂下来。罗恩趴在炉前的地毯上,试图完成变形课作业。

"什么把你绊住了?"罗恩问。哈利倒在了赫敏旁边的扶手椅上。

哈利没有回答。他沉浸在震惊中,既想告诉罗恩和赫敏刚才发生了什么,又想把这秘密带进坟墓。

"你还好吧,哈利?"赫敏问,从笔尖上抬起目光看着他。

哈利心不在焉地耸了耸肩。其实他也不知道自己是好还是不好。

"怎么啦?"罗恩用胳膊肘支起身子,好看清哈利,"发生了什么事?"

CHAPTER TWENTY-ONE   The Eye of the Snake

Harry didn't quite know how to set about telling them, and still wasn't sure whether he wanted to. Just as he had decided not to say anything, Hermione took matters out of his hands.

'Is it Cho?' she asked in a businesslike way. 'Did she corner you after the meeting?'

Numbly surprised, Harry nodded. Ron sniggered, breaking off when Hermione caught his eye.

'So – er – what did she want?' he asked in a mock casual voice.

'She –' Harry began, rather hoarsely; he cleared his throat and tried again. 'She – er –'

'Did you kiss?' asked Hermione briskly.

Ron sat up so fast he sent his ink bottle flying all over the rug. Disregarding this completely, he stared avidly at Harry.

'Well?' he demanded.

Harry looked from Ron's expression of mingled curiosity and hilarity to Hermione's slight frown, and nodded.

'HA!'

Ron made a triumphant gesture with his fist and went into a raucous peal of laughter that made several timid-looking second-years over beside the window jump. A reluctant grin spread over Harry's face as he watched Ron rolling around on the hearthrug. Hermione gave Ron a look of deep disgust and returned to her letter.

'Well?' Ron said finally, looking up at Harry. 'How was it?'

Harry considered for a moment.

'Wet,' he said truthfully.

Ron made a noise that might have indicated jubilation or disgust, it was hard to tell.

'Because she was crying,' Harry continued heavily.

'Oh,' said Ron, his smile fading slightly. 'Are you that bad at kissing?'

'Dunno,' said Harry, who hadn't considered this, and immediately felt rather worried. 'Maybe I am.'

'Of course you're not,' said Hermione absently, still scribbling away at her letter.

'How do you know?' said Ron very sharply.

'Because Cho spends half her time crying these days,' said Hermione vaguely. 'She does it at mealtimes, in the loos, all over the place.'

第21章 蛇 眼

哈利不知道该怎么对他们开口,也拿不准要不要说。就在他决定不说的时候,赫敏把问题接了过去。

"是秋吗?"她淡淡地问,"她在会后堵住了你吧?"

哈利微微有些吃惊,点了点头。罗恩哧哧地笑,看到赫敏的目光,赶忙止住了。

"那——呃——她想干吗?"他装出随便的口气问。

"她——"哈利的声音有点儿哑,他清了清嗓子,又说,"她——呃——"

"你们接吻了吗?"赫敏干脆地问。

罗恩腾地坐了起来,把墨水瓶碰得骨碌碌地滚在地毯上。他全然不管,只顾眼巴巴地盯着哈利。

"接了吗?"他问。

哈利从罗恩好奇而兴奋的面孔望向赫敏微蹙的双眉,点了点头。

"哈!"

罗恩得意地一挥拳头,嘎嘎大笑,把窗前几个怯怯的二年级学生惊得跳了起来。看到罗恩在地毯上打滚,哈利脸上勉强浮现出一丝笑容。赫敏厌恶地看了罗恩一眼,继续写她的信。

"哎,"罗恩最后抬头看着哈利说,"怎么样?"

哈利想了一会儿。

"湿的。"他诚实地说。

罗恩发出一声怪叫,很难说是表示祝贺还是恶心。

"因为她在哭。"哈利沉重地说。

"哦,"罗恩说,脸上的笑容减退了一些,"你接吻水平那么差吗?"

"不知道,"哈利说,他没有想过这一点,顿时担心起来,"可能是吧。"

"当然不是。"赫敏随口说道,还在忙着写她的信。

"你怎么知道?"罗恩尖刻地问。

"因为秋最近一半时间都在哭,"赫敏含糊地说,"吃饭时哭,上盥洗室也哭,到哪儿都哭。"

CHAPTER TWENTY-ONE The Eye of the Snake

'You'd think a bit of kissing would cheer her up,' said Ron, grinning.

'Ron,' said Hermione in a dignified voice, dipping the point of her quill into her inkpot, 'you are the most insensitive wart I have ever had the misfortune to meet.'

'What's that supposed to mean?' said Ron indignantly. 'What sort of person cries while someone's kissing them?'

'Yeah,' said Harry, slightly desperately, 'who does?'

Hermione looked at the pair of them with an almost pitying expression on her face.

'Don't you understand how Cho's feeling at the moment?' she asked.

'No,' said Harry and Ron together.

Hermione sighed and laid down her quill.

'Well, obviously, she's feeling very sad, because of Cedric dying. Then I expect she's feeling confused because she liked Cedric and now she likes Harry, and she can't work out who she likes best. Then she'll be feeling guilty, thinking it's an insult to Cedric's memory to be kissing Harry at all, and she'll be worrying about what everyone else might say about her if she starts going out with Harry. And she probably can't work out what her feelings towards Harry are, anyway, because he was the one who was with Cedric when Cedric died, so that's all very mixed up and painful. Oh, and she's afraid she's going to be thrown off the Ravenclaw Quidditch team because she's been flying so badly.'

A slightly stunned silence greeted the end of this speech, then Ron said, 'One person can't feel all that at once, they'd explode.'

'Just because you've got the emotional range of a teaspoon doesn't mean we all have,' said Hermione nastily, picking up her quill again.

'She was the one who started it,' said Harry. 'I wouldn't've – she just sort of came at me – and next thing she's crying all over me – I didn't know what to do –'

'Don't blame you, mate,' said Ron, looking alarmed at the very thought.

'You just had to be nice to her,' said Hermione, looking up anxiously. 'You were, weren't you?'

'Well,' said Harry, an unpleasant heat creeping up his face, 'I sort of – patted her on the back a bit.'

Hermione looked as though she was restraining herself from rolling her eyes with extreme difficulty.

第21章 蛇 眼

"我还以为一点接吻能让她开心起来呢。"罗恩咧嘴笑道。

"罗恩,"赫敏板着脸说,把羽毛笔伸到墨水瓶里,"你是我不幸遇到的最迟钝的笨蛋。"

"这是什么意思?"罗恩不平地问,"什么人会在别人亲她的时候哭鼻子?"

"是啊,"哈利有点绝望地说,"谁会呢?"

赫敏带着几乎是怜悯的表情看着他们这一对。

"你们不明白秋现在的心情吗?"她问。

"不明白。"哈利和罗恩一齐说。

赫敏叹了口气,搁下羽毛笔。

"显而易见,她心里很悲伤,因为塞德里克的死。同时我想她有些困惑,因为她以前喜欢塞德里克,现在又喜欢哈利,她搞不清到底最喜欢谁。同时她还感到内疚,觉得和哈利接吻是对心中的塞德里克的亵渎。她还担心,要是她跟哈利好的话,别人会怎么说。而且,她可能还搞不清对哈利的感情,因为塞德里克死时哈利在场。所以这一切非常矛盾和痛苦。哦,她还怕被踢出拉文克劳魁地奇球队,因为她近来飞得那么差。"

她的话把两人说愣了。然后罗恩说:"一个人不能同时有那么多感情,会爆炸的。"

"你自己只有一茶匙的感情,并不代表人人都是这样。"赫敏挖苦道,又拿起了她的笔。

"是她主动的,"哈利说,"我本来不想——她靠过来——然后就趴在我身上哭——我不知道怎么办——"

"怨不得你,伙计。"罗恩说,似乎被吓着了。

"你只需要对她温柔点儿。"赫敏担心地抬起眼睛说,"你有没有啊?"

"嗯,"哈利脸上热得难受,"我好像——拍了拍她的背。"

赫敏似乎用了很大努力才忍住没有翻白眼。

CHAPTER TWENTY-ONE   The Eye of the Snake

'Well, I suppose it could have been worse,' she said. 'Are you going to see her again?'

'I'll have to, won't I?' said Harry. 'We've got DA meetings, haven't we?'

'You know what I mean,' said Hermione impatiently.

Harry said nothing. Hermione's words opened up a whole new vista of frightening possibilities. He tried to imagine going somewhere with Cho – Hogsmeade, perhaps – and being alone with her for hours at a time. Of course, she would have been expecting him to ask her out after what had just happened ... the thought made his stomach clench painfully.

'Oh well,' said Hermione distantly, buried in her letter once more, 'you'll have plenty of opportunities to ask her.'

'What if he doesn't want to ask her?' said Ron, who had been watching Harry with an unusually shrewd expression on his face.

'Don't be silly,' said Hermione vaguely, 'Harry's liked her for ages, haven't you, Harry?'

He did not answer. Yes, he had liked Cho for ages, but whenever he had imagined a scene involving the two of them it had always featured a Cho who was enjoying herself, as opposed to a Cho who was sobbing uncontrollably into his shoulder.

'Who're you writing the novel to, anyway?' Ron asked Hermione, trying to read the bit of parchment now trailing on the floor. Hermione hitched it up out of sight.

'Viktor.'

'*Krum?*'

'How many other Viktors do we know?'

Ron said nothing, but looked disgruntled. They sat in silence for another twenty minutes, Ron finishing his Transfiguration essay with many snorts of impatience and crossings-out, Hermione writing steadily to the very end of the parchment, rolling it up carefully and sealing it, and Harry staring into the fire, wishing more than anything that Sirius's head would appear there and give him some advice about girls. But the fire merely crackled lower and lower, until the red-hot embers crumbled into ash and, looking around, Harry saw that they were, yet again, the last ones in the common room.

'Well, night,' said Hermione, yawning widely as she set off up the girls' staircase.

'What does she see in Krum?' Ron demanded, as he and Harry climbed the boys' stairs.

第21章 蛇眼

"我想这还不算最糟糕。"她说,"你还打算见她吗?"

"我非见不可,是不是?"哈利说,"有 D.A. 集会呀。"

"你知道我指的是什么。"赫敏不耐烦地说。

哈利沉默了。赫敏的话展现了一幕幕吓人的前景。他试着想象跟秋一起出去——或许去霍格莫德村——跟她单独相处几小时。在发生了刚才那件事之后,秋当然会期望他约她出去的……这念头使得他的胃痛苦地紧缩起来。

"反正,"赫敏漠然地说,又埋在她的信里了,"你会有很多机会约她的……"

"要是他不想约她呢?"罗恩一直盯着哈利,脸上现出一种不常见的精明。

"别犯傻,"赫敏含糊地说,"哈利早就喜欢她了,是不是,哈利?"

哈利没有回答。不错,他是早就喜欢秋了,但他想象的两人相处的画面中,秋总是快乐的,而不是趴在他肩上哭得不可收拾。

"你在给谁写小说呢?"罗恩问赫敏,伸头去读已经垂到地上的羊皮纸。赫敏把它拖了上去。

"威克多尔。"

"克鲁姆?"

"我们还知道几个威克多尔呀?"

罗恩没说话,但看上去怏怏的。他们又沉默地坐了二十分钟,罗恩在不耐烦的哼哼和涂涂擦擦中完成了他的变形课论文;赫敏沉着地写到羊皮纸的最后,把它仔细地卷起封好;哈利盯着炉火,特别希望小天狼星的脑袋出现,给他一些关于女孩子的忠告。但炉火只是噼噼啪啪地越烧越低,直到红热的余炭化成了灰烬。哈利环顾四周,发现屋里又只剩他们三个了。

"好了,晚安。"赫敏说,打着大哈欠朝女生宿舍的楼梯走去。

"她看上克鲁姆什么啦?"罗恩和哈利一起上楼时问道。

CHAPTER TWENTY-ONE

The Eye of the Snake

'Well,' said Harry, considering the matter, 'I s'pose he's older, isn't he ... and he's an international Quidditch player ...'

'Yeah, but apart from that,' said Ron, sounding aggravated. 'I mean, he's a grouchy git, isn't he?'

'Bit grouchy, yeah,' said Harry, whose thoughts were still on Cho.

They pulled off their robes and put on pyjamas in silence; Dean, Seamus and Neville were already asleep. Harry put his glasses on his bedside table and got into bed but did not pull the hangings closed around his four-poster; instead, he stared at the patch of starry sky visible through the window next to Neville's bed. If he had known, this time last night, that in twenty-four hours' time he would have kissed Cho Chang ...

'Night,' grunted Ron, from somewhere to his right.

'Night,' said Harry.

Maybe next time ... if there was a next time ... she'd be a bit happier. He ought to have asked her out; she had probably been expecting it and was now really angry with him ... or was she lying in bed, still crying about Cedric? He did not know what to think. Hermione's explanation had made it all seem more complicated rather than easier to understand.

That's what they should teach us here, he thought, turning over on to his side, *how girls' brains work ... it'd be more useful than Divination, anyway ...*

Neville snuffled in his sleep. An owl hooted somewhere out in the night.

Harry dreamed he was back in the DA room. Cho was accusing him of luring her there under false pretences; she said he had promised her a hundred and fifty Chocolate Frog Cards if she showed up. Harry protested ... Cho shouted, '*Cedric gave me loads of Chocolate Frog Cards, look!*' And she pulled out fistfuls of Cards from inside her robes and threw them into the air. Then she turned into Hermione, who said, '*You did promise her, you know, Harry ... I think you'd better give her something else instead ... how about your Firebolt?*' And Harry was protesting that he could not give Cho his Firebolt, because Umbridge had it, and anyway the whole thing was ridiculous, he'd only come to the DA room to put up some Christmas baubles shaped like Dobby's head ...

The dream changed ...

His body felt smooth, powerful and flexible. He was gliding between shining metal bars, across dark, cold stone ... he was flat against the floor, sliding along on his belly ... it was dark, yet he could see objects around him

第21章 蛇眼

"嗯,"哈利思考着说,"我想他岁数大些,是不是……又是国际球星……"

"可是除了这个之外,"罗恩似乎很恼火,"我说,他不就是个暴躁的饭桶吗?"

"确实有点暴躁。"哈利说,他还在想着秋。

他们默默地脱掉袍子,换上睡衣。迪安、西莫和纳威都已睡着了。哈利把眼镜放在床头桌上,钻进被里,但没有拉上帷帐,而是盯着纳威床边窗户外的那一片星空。要是他昨晚这个时候知道,二十四小时之内他会亲吻秋·张……

"晚安。"罗恩在他右边咕哝着说。

"晚安。"哈利说。

也许下次……如果有下次的话……她会快乐一些。他应该约她出去的,她当时可能在期待他开口,现在正生着他的气……或者她正躺在床上,为塞德里克哭泣?他不知道该怎么想。赫敏的解释似乎使这一切变得更复杂,而不是更好懂了。

学校应该教这个,他翻了个身想道,女孩子的心思……这至少比占卜课有用得多。

纳威在睡梦中抽了抽鼻子,远处传来一只猫头鹰的叫声。

哈利梦见他回到了D.A.集会的房间,秋埋怨他把她骗来了,说他答应只要她来了就给她一百五十张巧克力蛙画片。哈利辩白着……秋叫了起来:"塞德里克给了我好多好多巧克力蛙画片,看!"她从袍子里掏出一把把的画片撒到空中,然后她又变成了赫敏。赫敏说:"你答应过她的,哈利……我想你最好给她点别的……你的火弩箭怎么样?"哈利争辩说他不能把火弩箭送给秋,因为它被乌姆里奇拿走了,而且这一切是荒唐的,他只是到D.A.房间里来挂一些多比脑袋形状的圣诞彩球……

梦境幻化了……

他的身体柔软、有力而又灵活,在闪亮的金属栅栏间,在阴暗、冰冷的石头上滑过……他身体贴着地面,用腹部滑行……光线很暗,

CHAPTER TWENTY-ONE — The Eye of the Snake

shimmering in strange, vibrant colours ... he was turning his head ... at first glance the corridor was empty ... but no ... a man was sitting on the floor ahead, his chin drooping on to his chest, his outline gleaming in the dark ...

Harry put out his tongue ... he tasted the man's scent on the air ... he was alive but drowsy ... sitting in front of a door at the end of the corridor ...

Harry longed to bite the man ... but he must master the impulse ... he had more important work to do ...

But the man was stirring ... a silver Cloak fell from his legs as he jumped to his feet; and Harry saw his vibrant, blurred outline towering above him, saw a wand withdrawn from a belt ... he had no choice ... he reared high from the floor and struck once, twice, three times, plunging his fangs deeply into the man's flesh, feeling his ribs splinter beneath his jaws, feeling the warm gush of blood ...

The man was yelling in pain ... then he fell silent ... he slumped backwards against the wall ... blood was splattering on to the floor ...

His forehead hurt terribly ... it was aching fit to burst ...

'Harry! HARRY!'

He opened his eyes. Every inch of his body was covered in icy sweat; his bed covers were twisted all around him like a straitjacket; he felt as though a white-hot poker were being applied to his forehead.

'*Harry!*'

Ron was standing over him looking extremely frightened. There were more figures at the foot of Harry's bed. He clutched his head in his hands; the pain was blinding him ... he rolled right over and vomited over the edge of the mattress.

'He's really ill,' said a scared voice. 'Should we call someone?'

'Harry! *Harry!*'

He had to tell Ron, it was very important that he tell him ... taking great gulps of air, Harry pushed himself up in bed, willing himself not to throw up again, the pain half blinding him.

'Your dad,' he panted, his chest heaving. 'Your dad's ... been attacked ...'

'What?' said Ron uncomprehendingly.

'Your dad! He's been bitten, it's serious, there was blood everywhere ...'

'I'm going for help,' said the same scared voice, and Harry heard footsteps running out of the dormitory.

第21章 蛇 眼

但他能看到周围物体的光亮，一些奇异的、鲜明的色彩……他转动脑袋……一眼看去，走廊是空的……不对……有个人坐在地上，头垂在胸前，他的轮廓在昏暗中闪烁。

哈利伸出舌头……他尝了尝那人的气味……他活着，但在打瞌睡……坐在走廊尽头那扇门的前面……

哈利渴望咬那个人……但他必须克制住这种冲动……有更重要的事要做……

那人惊醒了……跳了起来，一件银斗篷从他腿上滑落下来，哈利看到他明亮、模糊的轮廓屹立在面前，一根魔杖从皮带上抽出……他别无选择……他从地板上竖起身子，袭击了一下、两下、三下，把他的尖牙深深地扎进那人的身体，感到肋骨在他的牙齿间碎裂，热乎乎的鲜血涌出……

那人痛得大叫……然后没声音了……瘫倒在墙脚……鲜血溅到地上……

他的前额疼得要命……好像要炸开了……

"哈利！哈利！"

他睁开眼睛，浑身浸满冷汗，床单全裹在身上，像紧身衣。他觉得额头上好像插了一把滚烫的火钳。

"哈利！"

罗恩站在床前，好像吓坏了，床脚还有几个人影。哈利抱紧脑袋，痛得眼前发黑……他滚到床边吐了起来。

"他真的病了，"一个惊恐的声音说，"要喊人吗？"

"哈利！哈利！"

他要告诉罗恩，这至关重要……哈利大口吸着气，从床上撑起身子，下决心不再呕吐，他痛得视线模糊。

"你爸爸，"他气喘吁吁地说，胸口起伏着，"你爸爸……出事了……"

"什么？"罗恩没听懂。

"你爸爸！他被咬了，很严重，到处都是血……"

"我去叫人。"那个惊恐的声音说，哈利听见脚步声跑出了宿舍。

CHAPTER TWENTY-ONE — The Eye of the Snake

'Harry, mate,' said Ron uncertainly, 'you ... you were just dreaming ...'

'No!' said Harry furiously; it was crucial that Ron understand. 'It wasn't a dream ... not an ordinary dream ... I was there, I saw it ... I *did* it ...'

He could hear Seamus and Dean muttering but did not care. The pain in his forehead was subsiding slightly, though he was still sweating and shivering feverishly. He retched again and Ron leapt backwards out of the way.

'Harry, you're not well,' he said shakily. 'Neville's gone for help.'

'I'm fine!' Harry choked, wiping his mouth on his pyjamas and shaking uncontrollably. 'There's nothing wrong with me, it's your dad you've got to worry about – we need to find out where he is – he's bleeding like mad – I was – it was a huge snake.'

He tried to get out of bed but Ron pushed him back into it; Dean and Seamus were still whispering somewhere nearby. Whether one minute passed or ten, Harry did not know; he simply sat there shaking, feeling the pain recede very slowly from his scar ... then there were hurried footsteps coming up the stairs and he heard Neville's voice again.

'Over here, Professor.'

Professor McGonagall came hurrying into the dormitory in her tartan dressing gown, her glasses perched lopsidedly on the bridge of her bony nose.

'What is it, Potter? Where does it hurt?'

He had never been so pleased to see her; it was a member of the Order of the Phoenix he needed now, not someone fussing over him and prescribing useless potions.

'It's Ron's dad,' he said, sitting up again. 'He's been attacked by a snake and it's serious, I saw it happen.'

'What do you mean, you saw it happen?' said Professor McGonagall, her dark eyebrows contracting.

'I don't know ... I was asleep and then I was there ...'

'You mean you dreamed this?'

'No!' said Harry angrily; would none of them understand? 'I was having a dream at first about something completely different, something stupid ... and then this interrupted it. It was real, I didn't imagine it. Mr Weasley was asleep on the floor and he was attacked by a gigantic snake, there was a load of blood, he collapsed, someone's got to find out where he is ...'

第21章 蛇眼

"哈利，哥们儿，"罗恩将信将疑，"你……你只是在做梦……"

"不是！"哈利愤怒地说，一定要让罗恩明白，"不是梦……不是一般的梦……我在那儿，我看到了……我干的……"

他听到西莫和迪安在嘀嘀咕咕，但他顾不了这么多了。额头上的剧痛稍稍减轻了些，但他还在出汗，发高烧一样浑身哆嗦着。他又呕吐起来，罗恩朝后一跳闪开了。

"哈利，你病了，"他不安地说，"纳威去找人了……"

"我没事！"哈利呛了一下，用睡衣擦擦嘴巴，控制不住地哆嗦着，"我没生病，该担心的是你爸爸——我们要找到他在哪儿——他流血不止——我是——那是一条大蛇。"

他想下床，但罗恩把他按了回去。迪安和西莫还在旁边小声嘀咕。过了一分钟还是十分钟，哈利不知道，他只是坐在那儿瑟瑟发抖，感到伤疤的剧痛在缓慢消退……楼梯上传来急促的脚步声，他又听到了纳威的声音。

"这边，教授。"

麦格教授穿着格子呢的晨衣匆匆走进宿舍，眼镜歪架在瘦削的鼻梁上。

"怎么了，波特？哪儿疼？"

哈利从没像现在这样高兴见到她，他现在正需要凤凰社的成员，而不是紧张兮兮给他开些没用的汤药的人。

"是罗恩的爸爸，"他说着又坐了起来，"他被蛇咬了，非常严重，我看到的。"

"什么意思，你看到的？"麦格教授的黑眉毛拧了起来。

"我也说不清……我在睡觉，后来就到了那儿……"

"你是说你梦见的？"

"不是！"哈利烦躁地说。没人听得懂吗？"我先做了一个完全不同的梦，一些傻事……后来这个插了进来，是真的，不是我的幻想，韦斯莱先生在地上睡觉，被一条大蛇咬了，好多的血，他倒了下去，必须找到他在哪儿……"

CHAPTER TWENTY-ONE   The Eye of the Snake

Professor McGonagall was gazing at him through her lopsided spectacles as though horrified at what she was seeing.

'I'm not lying and I'm not mad!' Harry told her, his voice rising to a shout. 'I tell you, I saw it happen!'

'I believe you, Potter,' said Professor McGonagall curtly. 'Put on your dressing gown – we're going to see the Headmaster.'

第21章 蛇眼

麦格教授透过歪斜的眼镜盯着他,好像被看到的东西吓坏了。

"我没说谎,我也没有发疯!"哈利喊了起来,"跟你说,我是亲眼看到的!"

"我相信你,波特,"麦格教授干脆地说,"穿上你的晨衣——我们去见校长。"

CHAPTER TWENTY-TWO

St Mungo's Hospital for Magical Maladies and Injuries

Harry was so relieved she was taking him seriously that he did not hesitate, but jumped out of bed at once, pulled on his dressing gown and pushed his glasses back on to his nose.

'Weasley, you ought to come too,' said Professor McGonagall.

They followed Professor McGonagall past the silent figures of Neville, Dean and Seamus, out of the dormitory, down the spiral stairs into the common room, through the portrait hole and off along the Fat Lady's moonlit corridor. Harry felt as though the panic inside him might spill over at any moment; he wanted to run, to yell for Dumbledore; Mr Weasley was bleeding as they walked along so sedately, and what if those fangs (Harry tried hard not to think 'my fangs') had been poisonous? They passed Mrs Norris, who turned her lamplike eyes upon them and hissed faintly, but Professor McGonagall said, 'Shoo!' Mrs Norris slunk away into the shadows, and in a few minutes they had reached the stone gargoyle guarding the entrance to Dumbledore's office.

'Fizzing Whizzbee,' said Professor McGonagall.

The gargoyle sprang to life and leapt aside; the wall behind it split in two to reveal a stone staircase that was moving continually upwards like a spiral escalator. The three of them stepped on to the moving stairs; the wall closed behind them with a thud and they were moving upwards in tight circles until they reached the highly polished oak door with the brass knocker shaped like a griffin.

Though it was now well past midnight there were voices coming from inside the room, a positive babble of them. It sounded as though Dumbledore was entertaining at least a dozen people.

Professor McGonagall rapped three times with the griffin knocker and the voices ceased abruptly as though someone had switched them all off. The door opened of its own accord and Professor McGonagall led Harry and Ron inside.

第22章

圣芒戈魔法伤病医院

她认真对待他的话了,哈利大感欣慰。他没有迟疑,一下子就从床上蹦起来,套上晨衣,把眼镜推到鼻梁上。

"韦斯莱,你也应该一起来。"麦格教授说。

他们跟着麦格教授走过默立一旁的纳威、迪安和西莫,出了宿舍,从螺旋形楼梯下到公共休息室,钻出肖像洞口,沿着胖夫人那道洒满月光的走廊往前走。哈利觉得他内心的恐惧随时都可能决堤。他想跑,想大声叫邓布利多。他们这样慢腾腾地走着,而韦斯莱先生正在流血。要是那些尖牙(哈利努力不去想"我的尖牙")有毒呢?路上遇到洛丽丝夫人,它把灯泡般的眼睛转向他们,发出微弱的嘶嘶声,麦格教授说了一声"嘘!"洛丽丝夫人溜进了阴影中。几分钟后,他们来到了邓布利多办公室入口处的滴水嘴石兽跟前。

"滋滋蜜蜂糖。"麦格教授说。

石兽活过来跳到一边,后面的墙壁裂成两半,露出一段不断上升的石梯,好像一架螺旋形的自动扶梯。三人踏上楼梯,墙壁在他们身后咔嚓合拢。他们转着小圈上升,来到那一扇闪闪发亮的橡木门前,门上有狮身鹰首兽形状的铜门环。

虽然早已过了午夜,屋里却传出说话声,乱哄哄的,好像邓布利多在招待至少十二个人。

麦格教授把兽形门环叩了三下,说话声突然停止,好像被关掉了似的。门自动打开,麦格教授领着哈利和罗恩走了进去。

CHAPTER TWENTY-TWO

St Mungo's Hospital for Magical Maladies and Injuries

The room was in half-darkness; the strange silver instruments standing on tables were silent and still rather than whirring and emitting puffs of smoke as they usually did; the portraits of old headmasters and headmistresses covering the walls were all snoozing in their frames. Behind the door, a magnificent red and gold bird the size of a swan dozed on its perch with its head under its wing.

'Oh, it's you, Professor McGonagall ... and ... *ah.*'

Dumbledore was sitting in a high-backed chair behind his desk; he leaned forward into the pool of candlelight illuminating the papers laid out before him. He was wearing a magnificently embroidered purple and gold dressing gown over a snowy white nightshirt, but seemed wide-awake, his penetrating light blue eyes fixed intently upon Professor McGonagall.

'Professor Dumbledore, Potter has had a ... well, a nightmare,' said Professor McGonagall. 'He says ...'

'It wasn't a nightmare,' said Harry quickly.

Professor McGonagall looked round at Harry, frowning slightly.

'Very well, then, Potter, you tell the Headmaster about it.'

'I ... well, I *was* asleep ...' said Harry and, even in his terror and his desperation to make Dumbledore understand, he felt slightly irritated that the Headmaster was not looking at him, but examining his own interlocked fingers. 'But it wasn't an ordinary dream ... it was real ... I saw it happen ...' He took a deep breath, 'Ron's dad – Mr Weasley – has been attacked by a giant snake.'

The words seemed to reverberate in the air after he had said them, sounding slightly ridiculous, even comic. There was a pause in which Dumbledore leaned back and stared meditatively at the ceiling. Ron looked from Harry to Dumbledore, white-faced and shocked.

'How did you see this?' Dumbledore asked quietly, still not looking at Harry.

'Well ... I don't know,' said Harry, rather angrily – what did it matter? 'Inside my head, I suppose –'

'You misunderstand me,' said Dumbledore, still in the same calm tone. 'I mean ... can you remember – er – where you were positioned as you watched this attack happen? Were you perhaps standing beside the victim, or else looking down on the scene from above?'

This was such a curious question that Harry gaped at Dumbledore; it was almost as though he knew ...

第22章 圣芒戈魔法伤病医院

屋里半明半暗,桌上那些古怪的银质仪器静静地待着,而不是像往常那样嗡嗡转动,吐出阵阵烟雾。墙上历届校长的肖像都在相框里打瞌睡。门后面,一只个头像天鹅、羽毛金红相间、美丽非凡的大鸟在栖木上打瞌睡,头藏在翅膀下面。

"哦,是你,麦格教授……还有……啊。"

邓布利多坐在他书桌后的高背椅上,凑在蜡烛光前看文件。他穿着雪白的睡衣,外罩一件刺绣华丽、紫金相间的便袍,但看上去精神抖擞,锐利的蓝眼睛紧盯着麦格教授。

"邓布利多教授,波特刚才做了一个……一个噩梦。"麦格教授说,"他说……"

"不是噩梦。"哈利马上说。

麦格教授回头看看哈利,微微皱起眉头。

"好吧,波特,你自己跟校长说吧。"

"我……嗯,我确实在睡觉……"哈利说,虽然他又害怕又着急让邓布利多明白,但仍然有点气恼校长没有看他,而是望着自己交叉的十指,"可这不是一般的梦……它是真的……我看到它发生了……"他深深吸了口气,"罗恩的爸爸——韦斯莱先生——被一条大蛇咬了。"

他说完后,这些话似乎在空气中回响,有点荒唐,甚至可笑。短暂的沉默中,邓布利多向后一靠,凝视着天花板。罗恩望望哈利,又望望邓布利多,面孔苍白而震惊。

"你是怎么看到的?"邓布利多轻声问,依然没有看哈利。

"嗯……我不知道,"哈利有点恼火地说——这有什么关系?"在我脑子里吧——"

"你误会了,"邓布利多依然是平静的语气,"我是说……你记不记得——嗯——你看到袭击时是在什么位置?你是站在受害者旁边,还是从上面俯瞰着这一幕?"

这个问题很怪,哈利呆呆地望着邓布利多,他好像知道似的……

'I was the snake,' he said. 'I saw it all from the snake's point of view.'

Nobody else spoke for a moment, then Dumbledore, now looking at Ron, who was still whey-faced, asked in a new and sharper voice, 'Is Arthur seriously injured?'

'*Yes*,' said Harry emphatically – why were they all so slow on the uptake, did they not realise how much a person bled when fangs that long pierced their side? And why could Dumbledore not do him the courtesy of looking at him?

But Dumbledore stood up, so quickly it made Harry jump, and addressed one of the old portraits hanging very near the ceiling. 'Everard?' he said sharply. 'And you too, Dilys!'

A sallow-faced wizard with a short black fringe and an elderly witch with long silver ringlets in the frame beside him, both of whom seemed to have been in the deepest of sleeps, opened their eyes immediately.

'You were listening?' said Dumbledore.

The wizard nodded; the witch said, 'Naturally.'

'The man has red hair and glasses,' said Dumbledore. 'Everard, you will need to raise the alarm, make sure he is found by the right people –'

Both nodded and moved sideways out of their frames, but instead of emerging in neighbouring pictures (as usually happened at Hogwarts) neither reappeared. One frame now contained nothing but a backdrop of dark curtain, the other a handsome leather armchair. Harry noticed that many of the other headmasters and mistresses on the walls, though snoring and drooling most convincingly, kept sneaking peeks at him from under their eyelids, and he suddenly understood who had been talking when they had knocked.

'Everard and Dilys were two of Hogwarts's most celebrated Heads,' Dumbledore said, now sweeping around Harry, Ron and Professor McGonagall to approach the magnificent sleeping bird on his perch beside the door. 'Their renown is such that both have portraits hanging in other important wizarding institutions. As they are free to move between their own portraits, they can tell us what may be happening elsewhere ...'

'But Mr Weasley could be anywhere!' said Harry.

'Please sit down, all three of you,' said Dumbledore, as though Harry had not spoken, 'Everard and Dilys may not be back for several minutes. Professor McGonagall, if you could draw up extra chairs.'

Professor McGonagall pulled her wand from the pocket of her dressing

"我就是那条蛇，"哈利说，"我都是从蛇的角度看到的……"

一时没人吭声，然后邓布利多看着脸色仍然煞白的罗恩，换了一种比较强烈的语气说："亚瑟伤得严重吗？"

"很严重。"哈利强调地说——他们为什么领会得这么慢呢？难道不知道一个人被那么长的尖牙刺穿之后会流多少血吗？邓布利多为什么不能看他一眼呢？

邓布利多猛地站起来，把哈利吓了一跳。他对离天花板很近的一幅旧肖像说："埃弗拉？"他厉声说，"还有你，戴丽丝！"

一个额前留着短黑头发的黄脸男巫和旁边相框中一个垂着长长银发卷的老女巫立刻睁开了眼睛，两人刚才好像都睡得很酣。

"你们听见了吗？"邓布利多问。

男巫点点头，女巫说："当然。"

"那男子红头发，戴眼镜。"邓布利多说，"埃弗拉，你需要发警报，以确保他被自己人发现——"

两位巫师点点头，从侧面出了相框，但并没有出现在旁边的相框里（像在霍格沃茨经常发生的那样），而是消失不见了。一个相框里只剩下了深色的帘子，另一个剩下了一把漂亮的皮椅。哈利注意到墙上其他许多老校长虽然逼真地打着呼噜，流着口水，却从眼皮底下偷偷地看他，他突然明白了刚才敲门时是谁在说话。

"埃弗拉和戴丽丝是霍格沃茨鼎鼎有名的两位校长，"邓布利多快步从哈利、罗恩和麦格教授身旁走到门边睡觉的美丽大鸟跟前，"其他重要的巫师机构也挂有他们的肖像。他们能在自己的肖像之间随意来去，所以能告诉我们别处发生的事情……"

"但韦斯莱先生可能在任何地方！"哈利说。

"三位请坐一会儿，"邓布利多说，好像哈利没说话一样，"埃弗拉和戴丽丝可能要几分钟之后才能回来……麦格教授，你能不能再拉几把椅子过来。"

麦格教授从睡袍兜里抽出魔杖，挥了一下，凭空变出三把椅子，

gown and waved it; three chairs appeared out of thin air, straight-backed and wooden, quite unlike the comfortable chintz armchairs that Dumbledore had conjured up at Harry's hearing. Harry sat down, watching Dumbledore over his shoulder. Dumbledore was now stroking Fawkes's plumed golden head with one finger. The phoenix awoke immediately. He stretched his beautiful head high and observed Dumbledore through bright, dark eyes.

'We will need,' Dumbledore said very quietly to the bird, 'a warning.'

There was a flash of fire and the phoenix had gone.

Dumbledore now swooped down upon one of the fragile silver instruments whose function Harry had never known, carried it over to his desk, sat down facing them again and tapped it gently with the tip of his wand.

The instrument tinkled into life at once with rhythmic clinking noises. Tiny puffs of pale green smoke issued from the minuscule silver tube at the top. Dumbledore watched the smoke closely, his brow furrowed. After a few seconds, the tiny puffs became a steady stream of smoke that thickened and coiled in the air ... a serpent's head grew out of the end of it, opening its mouth wide. Harry wondered whether the instrument was confirming his story: he looked eagerly at Dumbledore for a sign that he was right, but Dumbledore did not look up.

'Naturally, naturally,' murmured Dumbledore apparently to himself, still observing the stream of smoke without the slightest sign of surprise. 'But in essence divided?'

Harry could make neither head nor tail of this question. The smoke serpent, however, split itself instantly into two snakes, both coiling and undulating in the dark air. With a look of grim satisfaction, Dumbledore gave the instrument another gentle tap with his wand: the clinking noise slowed and died and the smoke serpents grew faint, became a formless haze and vanished.

Dumbledore replaced the instrument on its spindly little table. Harry saw many of the old headmasters in the portraits follow him with their eyes, then, realising that Harry was watching them, hastily pretend to be sleeping again. Harry wanted to ask what the strange silver instrument was for, but before he could do so, there was a shout from the top of the wall to their right; the wizard called Everard had reappeared in his portrait, panting slightly.

'Dumbledore!'

'What news?' said Dumbledore at once.

第22章 圣芒戈魔法伤病医院

是直背的木椅,与哈利受审时邓布利多变出的软椅不同。哈利坐下来,回头看着邓布利多,邓布利多用一根手指抚摸着福克斯头上的金色羽毛,凤凰立刻醒了过来,仰起美丽的头颈,用明亮的黑眼睛望着他。

"我们需要一点警报。"邓布利多轻轻对它说。

一道火光,凤凰不见了。

邓布利多现在快步走到一台精巧的银质仪器前,哈利一直不知道这些银仪器的用途。邓布利多把那台仪器搬到书桌上,重新面对他们坐下,用魔杖尖轻轻敲打着仪器。

仪器立刻运转起来,发出有节奏的叮当声,顶部的小银管喷出一缕缕淡绿色的轻烟,在空气中汇聚缭绕。邓布利多专注地望着轻烟,眉头紧锁。几秒钟后,几缕轻烟变成一股稳定的烟雾,越来越浓,在空气中盘旋……顶端化成了一个蛇头,蛇嘴大张着。哈利想知道仪器是否在证实他的描述,他急切地看着邓布利多,急于得到肯定的表示,但校长没有抬头。

"自然,自然,"他自言自语地说,依然注视着烟气,一点也没有惊讶,"但实质上是分开的吧?"

哈利对这个问题完全摸不着头脑,但烟蛇马上分成了两条,在昏暗的空气中盘旋、扭动。邓布利多带着严峻而满意的神情,又用魔杖轻轻敲了敲仪器。叮当声减慢停止了,烟蛇渐渐淡去,化成无形的烟雾消失了。

邓布利多把仪器放回细长的小桌上。哈利看到肖像中许多老校长在窥视,他们发现哈利在看着他们,又赶忙假装睡着了。哈利正想问那奇怪的银仪器是干什么的,右边墙壁上方一声喊叫,那个叫埃弗拉的男巫已经回到相框中,有点气喘吁吁。

"邓布利多!"

"什么消息?"邓布利多马上问。

CHAPTER TWENTY-TWO St Mungo's Hospital for Magical Maladies and Injuries

'I yelled until someone came running,' said the wizard, who was mopping his brow on the curtain behind him, 'said I'd heard something moving downstairs – they weren't sure whether to believe me but went down to check – you know there are no portraits down there to watch from. Anyway, they carried him up a few minutes later. He doesn't look good, he's covered in blood, I ran along to Elfrida Cragg's portrait to get a good view as they left –'

'Good,' said Dumbledore as Ron made a convulsive movement. 'I take it Dilys will have seen him arrive, then –'

And moments later, the silver-ringleted witch had reappeared in her picture, too; she sank, coughing, into her armchair and said, 'Yes, they've taken him to St Mungo's, Dumbledore ... they carried him past my portrait ... he looks bad ...'

'Thank you,' said Dumbledore. He looked round at Professor McGonagall.

'Minerva, I need you to go and wake the other Weasley children.'

'Of course ...'

Professor McGonagall got up and moved swiftly to the door. Harry cast a sideways glance at Ron, who was looking terrified.

'And Dumbledore – what about Molly?' said Professor McGonagall, pausing at the door.

'That will be a job for Fawkes when he has finished keeping a lookout for anybody approaching,' said Dumbledore. 'But she may already know ... that excellent clock of hers ...'

Harry knew Dumbledore was referring to the clock that told, not the time, but the whereabouts and conditions of the various Weasley family members, and with a pang he thought that Mr Weasley's hand must, even now, be pointing at *mortal peril*. But it was very late. Mrs Weasley was probably asleep, not watching the clock. Harry felt cold as he remembered Mrs Weasley's Boggart turning into Mr Weasley's lifeless body, his glasses askew, blood running down his face ... but Mr Weasley wasn't going to die ... he couldn't ...

Dumbledore was now rummaging in a cupboard behind Harry and Ron. He emerged from it carrying a blackened old kettle, which he placed carefully on his desk. He raised his wand and murmured, '*Portus!* ' for a moment the kettle trembled, glowing with an odd blue light; then it quivered to rest, as solidly black as ever.

Dumbledore marched over to another portrait, this time of a clever-

第22章 圣芒戈魔法伤病医院

"我一直喊到有人跑来,"男巫用帘子擦着额头说,"说我听到楼下有东西在动——他们半信半疑,但还是下去看了——你知道下面没有肖像可以供我瞭望。总之,几分钟后他们把他抬了上来。他看上去不妙,浑身是血,他们离开时我跑到艾芙丽达·克拉格的肖像中去好好看了一眼——"

"很好,"邓布利多说,罗恩抽搐了一下,"我想戴丽丝会看到他进去,然后——"

过了一会儿,拖着银发卷的女巫也回到了相框中,她咳嗽着坐到皮椅上说:"对,他们把他送进了圣芒戈,邓布利多……他们从我的肖像下面走过……他看上去状况很不好……"

"谢谢你。"邓布利多说,转身望着麦格教授。

"米勒娃,我需要你去叫醒韦斯莱家的其他孩子。"

"当然……"

麦格教授站起来快步走向门口。哈利瞥了瞥罗恩,他现在看上去很害怕。

"邓布利多——还有莫丽呢?"麦格教授在门口说。

"让福克斯放完哨之后去吧,"邓布利多说,"但她可能已经知道了……她那奇妙的挂钟……"

哈利知道邓布利多指的是那个不显示时间,只显示韦斯莱家各人位置和情况的挂钟。他揪心地想到韦斯莱先生的指针此时此刻一定指着生命危险。可是天太晚了……韦斯莱夫人也许在睡觉,没有看钟……他心里发寒,想起韦斯莱夫人的博格特变成她丈夫的尸体,眼镜歪斜,脸上流着血……但韦斯莱先生不会死……他不能死……

邓布利多在哈利和罗恩身后的一个柜子里摸索着,找出了一个熏黑的旧茶壶,小心地放到桌上。他举起魔杖,念了一声"门托斯!"茶壶颤动了一会儿,发出奇异的蓝光,然后渐渐静止,又变得乌黑。

邓布利多走到另一幅肖像前,这是一个留着山羊胡、一副聪明相

looking wizard with a pointed beard, who had been painted wearing the Slytherin colours of green and silver and was apparently sleeping so deeply that he could not hear Dumbledore's voice when he attempted to rouse him.

'Phineas. *Phineas.*'

The subjects of the portraits lining the room were no longer pretending to be asleep; they were shifting around in their frames, the better to watch what was happening. When the clever-looking wizard continued to feign sleep, some of them shouted his name, too.

'Phineas! *Phineas!* PHINEAS!'

He could not pretend any longer; he gave a theatrical jerk and opened his eyes wide.

'Did someone call?'

'I need you to visit your other portrait again, Phineas,' said Dumbledore. 'I've got another message.'

'Visit my other portrait?' said Phineas in a reedy voice, giving a long, fake yawn (his eyes travelling around the room and focusing on Harry). 'Oh, no, Dumbledore, I am too tired tonight.'

Something about Phineas's voice was familiar to Harry, where had he heard it before? But before he could think, the portraits on the surrounding walls broke into a storm of protest.

'Insubordination, sir!' roared a corpulent, red-nosed wizard, brandishing his fists. 'Dereliction of duty!'

'We are honour-bound to give service to the present Headmaster of Hogwarts!' cried a frail-looking old wizard whom Harry recognised as Dumbledore's predecessor, Armando Dippet. 'Shame on you, Phineas!'

'Shall I persuade him, Dumbledore?' called a gimlet-eyed witch, raising an unusually thick wand that looked not unlike a birch rod.

'Oh, very *well*,' said the wizard called Phineas, eyeing the wand with mild apprehension, 'though he may well have destroyed my picture by now, he's done away with most of the family –'

'Sirius knows not to destroy your portrait,' said Dumbledore, and Harry realised immediately where he had heard Phineas's voice before: issuing from the apparently empty frame in his bedroom in Grimmauld Place. 'You are to give him the message that Arthur Weasley has been gravely injured and that his wife, children and Harry Potter will be arriving at his house shortly. Do you understand?'

的男巫。画中的他身着银绿相间的斯莱特林服装，似乎睡得很香，没听见邓布利多在叫他。

"菲尼亚斯，菲尼亚斯！"

现在墙上肖像中的人都不再装睡了，他们在相框中走来走去，想看得更清楚些。聪明相的男巫继续装睡时，他们有些人也开始叫他。

"菲尼亚斯！菲尼亚斯！**菲尼亚斯**！"

他装不下去了，夸张地动了一下，睁大眼睛。

"有人叫我吗？"

"我需要你再到你的另外一幅肖像中跑一趟，菲尼亚斯，"邓布利多说，"我又得到了一个消息。"

"到我的那幅肖像中跑一趟？"菲尼亚斯尖声说，假装打了一个长长的哈欠（他的目光在屋里扫了一圈，落到哈利身上），"哦，不行，邓布利多，我今晚太累了……"

哈利觉得菲尼亚斯的声音有点耳熟。在哪儿听到过呢？没等他细想，周围的肖像突然爆发出一片抗议。

"不听命令，先生！"一个红鼻子的大胖男巫挥着拳头吼道，"不守职责！"

"我们有义务为现任的霍格沃茨校长效力！"一个看上去体质虚弱的老男巫喊道，哈利认出是邓布利多的前任，阿芒多·迪佩特，"不害臊，菲尼亚斯！"

"要我来说服他吗，邓布利多？"一个目光精明的女巫举起一根极粗的魔杖，看上去有点像桦树条。

"哦，好吧，"菲尼亚斯有点害怕地瞟着这根魔杖说，"不过他这会儿可能早把我的肖像毁了，他已经毁了家里大部分——"

"小天狼星不会打坏你的肖像。"邓布利多说。哈利一下想起他在哪儿听到过菲尼亚斯的声音了：是从格里莫广场12号他卧室里那看似空空的相框里传出的。"你要告诉他，亚瑟·韦斯莱受了重伤，其夫人、儿女和哈利·波特很快会去他家。明白吗？"

CHAPTER TWENTY-TWO   St Mungo's Hospital for Magical Maladies and Injuries

'Arthur Weasley, injured, wife and children and Harry Potter coming to stay,' recited Phineas in a bored voice. 'Yes, yes ... very well ...'

He sloped away into the frame of the portrait and disappeared from view at the very moment the study door opened again. Fred, George and Ginny were ushered inside by Professor McGonagall, all three of them looking dishevelled and shocked, still in their night things.

'Harry – what's going on?' asked Ginny, who looked frightened. 'Professor McGonagall says you saw Dad get hurt –'

'Your father has been injured in the course of his work for the Order of the Phoenix,' said Dumbledore, before Harry could speak. 'He has been taken to St Mungo's Hospital for Magical Maladies and Injuries. I am sending you back to Sirius's house, which is much more convenient for the hospital than The Burrow. You will meet your mother there.'

'How're we going?' asked Fred, looking shaken. 'Floo powder?'

'No,' said Dumbledore, 'Floo powder is not safe at the moment, the Network is being watched. You will be taking a Portkey.' He indicated the old kettle lying innocently on his desk. 'We are just waiting for Phineas Nigellus to report back ... I want to be sure that the coast is clear before sending you –'

There was a flash of flame in the very middle of the office, leaving behind a single golden feather that floated gently to the floor.

'It is Fawkes's warning,' said Dumbledore, catching the feather as it fell. 'Professor Umbridge must know you're out of your beds ... Minerva, go and head her off – tell her any story –'

Professor McGonagall was gone in a swish of tartan.

'He says he'll be delighted,' said a bored voice behind Dumbledore; the wizard called Phineas had reappeared in front of his Slytherin banner. 'My great-great-grandson has always had an odd taste in house-guests.'

'Come here, then,' Dumbledore said to Harry and the Weasleys. 'And quickly, before anyone else joins us.'

Harry and the others gathered around Dumbledore's desk.

'You have all used a Portkey before?' asked Dumbledore, and they nodded, each reaching out to touch some part of the blackened kettle. 'Good. On the count of three, then ... one ... two ...'

It happened in a fraction of a second: in the infinitesimal pause before Dumbledore said 'three', Harry looked up at him – they were very close together –

第22章 圣芒戈魔法伤病医院

"亚瑟·韦斯莱受伤,老婆孩子和哈利·波特要来。"菲尼亚斯懒洋洋地说,"行,行……好吧……"

他从相框中溜了出去,消失了,这时书房的门又开了,弗雷德、乔治和金妮由麦格教授领了进来,三人都还穿着睡衣,头发凌乱,神色惊恐。

"哈利——怎么回事?"金妮问,看起来吓坏了,"麦格教授说你看到爸爸受伤了——"

"你父亲在为凤凰社工作时受了伤,"邓布利多不等哈利开口就说,"他已被送往圣芒戈魔法伤病医院。我要把你们送回小天狼星的住处,那里比陋居更方便去医院,你们在那里会见到你们的母亲。"

"我们怎么去?"弗雷德忧心忡忡地问,"用飞路粉吗?"

"不,"邓布利多说,"这个时候用飞路粉不安全,网络被监视了。你们要用门钥匙。"他指了指桌上那把看上去很平常的旧茶壶,"现在只等菲尼亚斯·奈杰勒斯回来……我想确保没有危险再把你们送去——"

屋子中央火光一现,留下一根金羽毛,轻盈地飘向地面。

"是福克斯的警报。"邓布利多接住羽毛说,"乌姆里奇教授一定知道你们都不在床上……米勒娃,去把她支开——不管用什么借口——"

在格子呢的沙沙声中,麦格教授走了。

"他说欢迎,"邓布利多身后一个懒洋洋的声音说,那个叫菲尼亚斯的男巫重新出现在斯莱特林的旗帜前,"我的玄孙有留人住宿的怪癖……"

"来吧,"邓布利多对哈利和韦斯莱他们说,"快,趁现在还没有人来……"

哈利等人围在邓布利多桌前。

"你们都用过门钥匙吧?"邓布利多问,大家点点头,每人都把手放到黑茶壶上,"好。我数到三,一……二……"

只是一瞬间的工夫:在邓布利多数到"三"之前那短暂的停顿中,哈利抬头看了他一眼——他们离得很近,邓布利多清澈的目光从门钥

and Dumbledore's clear blue gaze moved from the Portkey to Harry's face.

At once, Harry's scar burned white-hot, as though the old wound had burst open again – and unbidden, unwanted, but terrifyingly strong, there rose within Harry a hatred so powerful he felt, for that instant, he would like nothing better than to strike – to bite – to sink his fangs into the man before him –

'... *three.*'

Harry felt a powerful jerk behind his navel, the ground vanished from beneath his feet, his hand was glued to the kettle; he was banging into the others as they all sped forwards in a swirl of colours and a rush of wind, the kettle pulling them onwards ... until his feet hit the ground so hard his knees buckled, the kettle clattered to the ground, and somewhere close at hand a voice said:

'Back again, the blood-traitor brats. Is it true their father's dying?'

'OUT!' roared a second voice.

Harry scrambled to his feet and looked around; they had arrived in the gloomy basement kitchen of number twelve, Grimmauld Place. The only sources of light were the fire and one guttering candle, which illuminated the remains of a solitary supper. Kreacher was disappearing through the door to the hall, looking back at them malevolently as he hitched up his loincloth; Sirius was hurrying towards them all, looking anxious. He was unshaven and still in his day clothes; there was also a slightly Mundungus-like whiff of stale drink about him.

'What's going on?' he said, stretching out a hand to help Ginny up. 'Phineas Nigellus said Arthur's been badly injured –'

'Ask Harry,' said Fred.

'Yeah, I want to hear this for myself,' said George.

The twins and Ginny were staring at him. Kreacher's footsteps had stopped on the stairs outside.

'It was –' Harry began; this was even worse than telling McGonagall and Dumbledore. 'I had a – a kind of – vision ...'

And he told them all that he had seen, though he altered the story so that it sounded as though he had watched from the sidelines as the snake attacked, rather than from behind the snake's own eyes. Ron, who was still very white, gave him a fleeting look, but did not speak. When Harry had finished, Fred, George and Ginny continued to stare at him for a moment. Harry did not know whether he was imagining it or not, but he fancied there was something accusatory in their looks. Well, if they were going to blame

匙移到哈利的脸上。

顿时，哈利的伤疤火烧火燎地痛起来，像伤口重新裂开了一样——哈利心中升起一股强烈的憎恨，毫无来由，但强烈得可怕，他那一刻只想袭击——想咬——想把他的尖牙插进面前这个人的身体——

"……三。"

他感到肚脐眼后被猛地一扯，地面从他脚下消失了，他的手粘在茶壶上，跟其他人碰撞着，在旋转的色彩和呼呼的风声中飞速前进。茶壶一直牵引着他们……直到他的脚突然撞到地面，震得他膝盖一弯。茶壶哗啦落地。近旁一个声音说话了。

"又回来了，这些败类渣滓，他们的爸爸是要死了吗？"

"**出去！**"另一个声音咆哮道。

哈利爬起来环顾四周，他们来到了格里莫广场12号阴暗的地下厨房里。唯一的光源是炉火和一根摇曳的蜡烛，照出残留的清冷的晚饭。克利切走向前厅门口，拉着缠腰布，回头恶意地看了看他们，消失了。小天狼星疾步向他们走来，显得很焦急。他没刮胡子，还穿着白天的衣服，身上还带着一股类似蒙顿格斯身上的陈酒味儿。

"怎么啦？"他伸手把金妮拉了起来，"菲尼亚斯·奈杰勒斯说亚瑟受了重伤——"

"问哈利吧。"弗雷德说。

"对，我也想听听。"乔治说。

双胞胎和金妮都盯着哈利，克利切的脚步声在外面楼梯上停住了。

"是——"哈利开口道，这比告诉麦格教授和邓布利多还要难，"我好像——做了个梦……"

他讲了他看到的一切，但稍有改动，好像他是在旁边看到了大蛇袭击，而不是直接通过蛇的眼睛……脸色依然煞白的罗恩快速地看了他一眼，但没有说话。哈利讲完之后，弗雷德、乔治和金妮又盯了他好一会儿。哈利觉得他们的目光中有责备的成分，他不知道这是不是自己的想象。如果他们光是这样就要责备他，他真庆幸没有说出自己

him just for seeing the attack, he was glad he had not told them that he had been inside the snake at the time.

'Is Mum here?' said Fred, turning to Sirius.

'She probably doesn't even know what's happened yet,' said Sirius. 'The important thing was to get you away before Umbridge could interfere. I expect Dumbledore's letting Molly know now.'

'We've got to go to St Mungo's,' said Ginny urgently. She looked around at her brothers; they were of course still in their pyjamas. 'Sirius, can you lend us cloaks or anything?'

'Hang on, you can't go tearing off to St Mungo's!' said Sirius.

'Course we can go to St Mungo's if we want,' said Fred, with a mulish expression. 'He's our dad!'

'And how are you going to explain how you knew Arthur was attacked before the hospital even let his wife know?'

'What does that matter?' said George hotly.

'It matters because we don't want to draw attention to the fact that Harry is having visions of things that are happening hundreds of miles away!' said Sirius angrily. 'Have you any idea what the Ministry would make of that information?'

Fred and George looked as though they could not care less what the Ministry made of anything. Ron was still ashen-faced and silent.

Ginny said, 'Somebody else could have told us ... we could have heard it somewhere other than Harry.'

'Like who?' said Sirius impatiently. 'Listen, your dad's been hurt while on duty for the Order and the circumstances are fishy enough without his children knowing about it seconds after it happened, you could seriously damage the Order's –'

'We don't care about the dumb Order!' shouted Fred.

'It's our dad dying we're talking about!' yelled George.

'Your father knew what he was getting into and he won't thank you for messing things up for the Order!' said Sirius, equally angry. 'This is how it is – this is why you're not in the Order – you don't understand – there are things worth dying for!'

'Easy for you to say, stuck here!' bellowed Fred. 'I don't see you risking your neck!'

第22章 圣芒戈魔法伤病医院

当时就附在蛇的身上……

"妈妈来了吗？"弗雷德转向小天狼星问。

"她可能还不知道。"小天狼星说，"重要的是在乌姆里奇干涉之前你们就得离开。我想邓布利多正在通知莫丽吧。"

"我们要去圣芒戈医院，"金妮着急地说，看了看她的哥哥们，他们当然还穿着睡衣，"小天狼星，你能借我们几件斗篷什么的吗——？"

"等等，你们不能冲到圣芒戈去！"小天狼星说。

"我们要去的话当然能去。"弗雷德犟头犟脑地说，"他是我们的爸爸！"

"你们怎么解释，在医院通知家属之前你们就知道亚瑟受伤了呢？"

"那有什么关系？"乔治激烈地说。

"有关系，因为我们不想声张哈利能看见千里之外的事！"小天狼星恼怒地说，"你知道魔法部会就此做什么文章吗？"

弗雷德和乔治的神情表示他们才不管魔法部会做什么呢。罗恩依旧脸色苍白，一言不发。

金妮说："可以说是别人告诉我们的……我们是从别处听说的，不提哈利……"

"听谁说的？"小天狼星不耐烦地说，"听着，你爸爸是在为凤凰社工作时受伤的，这事本身已经够可疑了，再添上他的子女几秒钟后就知道了情况，你们会严重损害凤凰社的——"

"我们不关心什么愚蠢的凤凰社！"弗雷德叫了起来。

"我们的爸爸生命垂危！"乔治嚷道。

"你们的父亲知道他在干什么，他不会感谢你们搅乱凤凰社的大事！"小天狼星也火了，"就是这样——这就是你们不是凤凰社成员的原因——你们不懂——有些东西是值得为之去死的！"

"你说得轻松，缩在这儿！"弗雷德吼道，"我没看到你有生命危险！"

CHAPTER TWENTY-TWO — St Mungo's Hospital for Magical Maladies and Injuries

The little colour remaining in Sirius's face drained from it. He looked for a moment as though he would quite like to hit Fred, but when he spoke, it was in a voice of determined calm.

'I know it's hard, but we've all got to act as though we don't know anything yet. We've got to stay put, at least until we hear from your mother, all right?'

Fred and George still looked mutinous. Ginny, however, took a few steps over to the nearest chair and sank into it. Harry looked at Ron, who made a funny movement somewhere between a nod and a shrug, and they sat down too. The twins glared at Sirius for another minute, then took seats either side of Ginny.

'That's right,' said Sirius encouragingly, 'come on, let's all ... let's all have a drink while we're waiting. *Accio Butterbeer!*'

He raised his wand as he spoke and half a dozen bottles came flying towards them out of the pantry, skidded along the table, scattering the debris of Sirius's meal, and stopped neatly in front of the six of them. They all drank, and for a while the only sounds were those of the crackling of the kitchen fire and the soft thud of their bottles on the table.

Harry was only drinking to have something to do with his hands. His stomach was full of horrible hot, bubbling guilt. They would not be here if it were not for him; they would all still be asleep in bed. And it was no good telling himself that by raising the alarm he had ensured that Mr Weasley was found, because there was also the inescapable business of it being he who had attacked Mr Weasley in the first place.

Don't be stupid, you haven't got fangs, he told himself, trying to keep calm, though the hand on his Butterbeer bottle was shaking, *you were lying in bed, you weren't attacking anyone ...*

But then, what just happened in Dumbledore's office? He asked himself. *I felt like I wanted to attack Dumbledore, too ...*

He put the bottle down a little harder than he meant to, and it slopped over on to the table. No one took any notice. Then a burst of fire in midair illuminated the dirty plates in front of them and, as they gave cries of shock, a scroll of parchment fell with a thud on to the table, accompanied by a single golden phoenix tail feather.

'Fawkes!' said Sirius at once, snatching up the parchment. 'That's not Dumbledore's writing – it must be a message from your mother – here –'

He thrust the letter into George's hand, who ripped it open and read aloud: '*Dad is still alive. I am setting out for St Mungo's now. Stay where you are. I will*

第22章 圣芒戈魔法伤病医院

小天狼星脸上仅有的一点血色一下子消失了,有一会儿他看上去似乎想揍弗雷德,但开口时却是坚定而平静。

"我知道这很难,但我们大家要装作还不知道,不要急躁,至少等听到你母亲的消息再说,好吗?"

弗雷德和乔治还不服气,但金妮走到最近的椅子前坐了下来。哈利看看罗恩,罗恩做了个介于点头和耸肩之间的古怪动作,两人也坐下了。双胞胎兄弟又瞪了小天狼星一分钟,才坐到了金妮的两边。

"这就对了,"小天狼星鼓励地说,"来,我们……一边喝一边等。黄油啤酒飞来!"

他举起魔杖,六个酒瓶从食品间朝他们飞来,滑过桌面,冲散了小天狼星的剩饭剩菜,刚巧停在六人的面前。他们喝了起来,一时间只听见厨房炉火的噼啪声和酒瓶轻碰桌面的声音。

哈利喝酒只是为了手上有点事做,他的胃里充满了可怕的、烧灼般的负疚感。要不是他,他们就不会在这里,而是好端端地在床上睡觉。虽然他可以对自己说是他的警报保证了韦斯莱先生被及时发现,但这也没有什么用,因为有一个无法逃避的事实:是他袭击了韦斯莱先生……

别瞎想,你没有尖牙,他对自己说,竭力保持镇静,但握着啤酒瓶的手在颤抖。你当时躺在床上,没有袭击任何人……

可是,在邓布利多办公室又是怎么回事呢?他问自己。我觉得我想袭击邓布利多……

他把酒瓶放到桌上,不料动作重了些,酒洒了出来,但没人注意。突然间,一道火光照亮了他们面前的脏盘子,他们惊叫起来,一卷羊皮纸啪地落到桌上,伴着一根金色的凤凰尾羽。

"福克斯!"小天狼星马上说,抓起了羊皮纸,"不是邓布利多的笔迹——一定是你妈妈的信,给——"

他把信塞到乔治手里。乔治撕开信读道:"爸爸还活着。我现在去

CHAPTER TWENTY-TWO · St Mungo's Hospital for Magical Maladies and Injuries

send news as soon as I can. Mum.'

George looked around the table.

'Still alive ...' he said slowly. 'But that makes it sound ...'

He did not need to finish the sentence. It sounded to Harry, too, as though Mr Weasley was hovering somewhere between life and death. Still exceptionally pale, Ron stared at the back of his mother's letter as though it might speak words of comfort to him. Fred pulled the parchment out of George's hands and read it for himself, then looked up at Harry, who felt his hand shaking on his Butterbeer bottle again and clenched it more tightly to stop the trembling.

If Harry had ever sat through a longer night than this one, he could not remember it. Sirius suggested once, without any real conviction, that they all go to bed, but the Weasleys' looks of disgust were answer enough. They mostly sat in silence around the table, watching the candle wick sinking lower and lower into liquid wax, occasionally raising a bottle to their lips, speaking only to check the time, to wonder aloud what was happening, and to reassure each other that if there was bad news, they would know straightaway, for Mrs Weasley must long since have arrived at St Mungo's.

Fred fell into a doze, his head lolling sideways on to his shoulder. Ginny was curled like a cat on her chair, but her eyes were open; Harry could see them reflecting the firelight. Ron was sitting with his head in his hands, whether awake or asleep it was impossible to tell. Harry and Sirius looked at each other every so often, intruders upon the family grief, waiting ... waiting ...

At ten past five in the morning by Ron's watch, the door swung open and Mrs Weasley entered the kitchen. She was extremely pale, but when they all turned to look at her, Fred, Ron and Harry half rising from their chairs, she gave a wan smile.

'He's going to be all right,' she said, her voice weak with tiredness. 'He's sleeping. We can all go and see him later. Bill's sitting with him now; he's going to take the morning off work.'

Fred fell back into his chair with his hands over his face. George and Ginny got up, walked swiftly over to their mother and hugged her. Ron gave a very shaky laugh and downed the rest of his Butterbeer in one.

'Breakfast!' said Sirius loudly and joyfully, jumping to his feet. 'Where's that accursed house-elf? Kreacher! KREACHER!'

But Kreacher did not answer the summons.

'Oh, forget it, then,' muttered Sirius, counting the people in front of him.

第22章 圣芒戈魔法伤病医院

圣芒戈。待在那儿,我会尽快通报消息。妈妈。"

乔治看看大家。

"还活着……"他慢慢地说,"可这听上去……"

他不必说完,哈利也觉得听上去韦斯莱先生像是在生死之间徘徊。罗恩还是脸色异常苍白,盯着他母亲的信的背面,好像它能对他说些安慰的话似的。弗雷德从乔治手中抽过信纸,自己念了一遍,抬头看着哈利。哈利觉得他握着酒瓶的手又颤抖起来,赶忙紧紧攥住瓶子。

哈利不记得他几时熬过比这更漫长的夜晚。小天狼星提过一次叫大家去睡觉,但语气不是很有力,韦斯莱兄弟反感的表情就足以回答了。他们大部分时间都默默地围坐在桌边,看着烛芯在液体蜡中越燃越低,时而把酒瓶举到唇边,说话也只是问问时间,猜测发生了什么,或相互安慰几句,说如果有坏消息会立刻知道的,因为韦斯莱夫人一定早就到了圣芒戈医院。

弗雷德打起盹来,脑袋歪垂到肩上。金妮像小猫一样蜷缩在椅子上,但眼睛还睁着,哈利看到她的眸子里映着炉火的光。罗恩托着脑袋坐在那里,看不出是醒着还是睡了。哈利和小天狼星偶尔看一看对方,他们两个是侵入这场家庭悲剧的外人。等啊……等啊……

罗恩的表走到五点十分时,厨房门开了,韦斯莱夫人走了进来。她脸色非常苍白,但当他们都转过头看着她,弗雷德、罗恩和哈利站起身来时,她无力地笑了一下。

"他脱离危险了。"她说,声音虚弱而疲惫,"他在睡觉。我们待会儿可以一起去看他。比尔在陪他呢,他上午请假了。"

弗雷德一屁股坐回椅子上,双手捂着脸。乔治和金妮站起来,快步走过去和母亲拥抱。罗恩虚弱地笑了一声,把剩下的黄油啤酒一饮而尽。

"早饭!"小天狼星跳了起来,愉快地大声说,"那个可恶的家养小精灵呢?克利切!**克利切!**"

但克利切没有回应。

"哦,算了吧,"小天狼星嘟哝道,一边点着人数,"我来看看——

CHAPTER TWENTY-TWO   St Mungo's Hospital for Magical Maladies and Injuries

'So, it's breakfast for – let's see – seven ... bacon and eggs, I think, and some tea, and toast –'

Harry hurried over to the stove to help. He did not want to intrude on the Weasleys' happiness and he dreaded the moment when Mrs Weasley would ask him to recount his vision. However, he had barely taken plates from the dresser when Mrs Weasley lifted them out of his hands and pulled him into a hug.

'I don't know what would have happened if it hadn't been for you, Harry,' she said in a muffled voice. 'They might not have found Arthur for hours, and then it would have been too late, but thanks to you he's alive and Dumbledore's been able to think up a good cover story for Arthur being where he was, you've no idea what trouble he would have been in otherwise, look at poor Sturgis ...'

Harry could hardly bear her gratitude, but fortunately she soon released him to turn to Sirius and thank him for looking after her children through the night. Sirius said he was very pleased to have been able to help, and hoped they would all stay with him as long as Mr Weasley was in hospital.

'Oh, Sirius, I'm so grateful ... they think he'll be there a little while and it would be wonderful to be nearer ... of course, that might mean we're here for Christmas.'

'The more the merrier!' said Sirius with such obvious sincerity that Mrs Weasley beamed at him, threw on an apron and began to help with breakfast.

'Sirius,' Harry muttered, unable to stand it a moment longer. 'Can I have a quick word? Er – *now?*'

He walked into the dark pantry and Sirius followed. Without preamble, Harry told his godfather every detail of the vision he had had, including the fact that he himself had been the snake who had attacked Mr Weasley.

When he paused for breath, Sirius said, 'Did you tell Dumbledore this?'

'Yes,' said Harry impatiently, 'but he didn't tell me what it meant. Well, he doesn't tell me anything any more.'

'I'm sure he would have told you if it was anything to worry about,' said Sirius steadily.

'But that's not all,' said Harry, in a voice only a little above a whisper. 'Sirius, I ... I think I'm going mad. Back in Dumbledore's office, just before we took the Portkey ... for a couple of seconds there I thought I was a snake, I *felt* like one – my scar really hurt when I was looking at Dumbledore – Sirius, I wanted to attack him!'

He could only see a sliver of Sirius's face; the rest was in darkness.

第22章 圣芒戈魔法伤病医院

七个人……咸肉加鸡蛋,再来点茶,还有烤面包——"

哈利忙跑到炉边帮忙。他不想打搅韦斯莱一家的喜悦,而且害怕韦斯莱夫人让他讲那个梦。然而,他刚把盘子从碗柜中拿出来,韦斯莱夫人就接了过去,并且拥抱了他一下。

"要不是你,真不知道会怎么样,哈利。"她低声说,"亚瑟可能再过几小时都不会被发现,那样就晚了。多亏你,救了他一命,而且邓布利多想出了一个好的说法解释亚瑟为什么会在那儿,不然的话,真不知道他会遇到多大的麻烦,看看可怜的斯多吉吧……"

哈利无法承受她的感激,幸好她很快放开了他,去感谢小天狼星通宵照看她的孩子们。小天狼星说他很高兴能帮忙,并希望他们在韦斯莱先生住院期间留在他家。

"哦,小天狼星,我真感激……医院说他要住一阵子,能离得近就太好了……当然,这就是说我们可能得在这儿过圣诞节了……"

"那更好!"小天狼星说得如此真诚,韦斯莱夫人对他笑了一下,系上围裙,开始帮着做早饭。

"小天狼星,"哈利小声说,他再也忍不住了,"我能跟你说句话吗?嗯——现在?"

他走进昏暗的食品间,小天狼星跟了进来。哈利开门见山地对他教父讲了梦里的每个细节,讲了他自己就是袭击韦斯莱先生的那条蛇。

他停下来喘息时,小天狼星说:"你跟邓布利多说了吗?"

"说了,"哈利烦躁地说,"可他没给我解释,他现在什么也不跟我讲了……"

"如果是严重的事,我相信,他会跟你讲的。"小天狼星镇定地说。

"可不止这些,"哈利的声音低得像耳语,"小天狼星,我……我觉得我要疯了……在邓布利多的办公室里,在我们触摸门钥匙之前……有一两秒钟我觉得自己是一条蛇,我感觉像蛇——当我看着邓布利多的时候,我的伤疤特别痛——小天狼星,我想咬他——"

他只能看到小天狼星的一小条脸,其余都在暗处。

CHAPTER TWENTY-TWO St Mungo's Hospital for Magical Maladies and Injuries

'It must have been the aftermath of the vision, that's all,' said Sirius. 'You were still thinking of the dream or whatever it was and –'

'It wasn't that,' said Harry, shaking his head, 'it was like something rose up inside me, like there's a *snake* inside me.'

'You need to sleep,' said Sirius firmly. 'You're going to have breakfast, then go upstairs to bed, and after lunch you can go and see Arthur with the others. You're in shock, Harry; you're blaming yourself for something you only witnessed, and it's lucky you *did* witness it or Arthur might have died. Just stop worrying.'

He clapped Harry on the shoulder and left the pantry, leaving Harry standing alone in the dark.

Everyone but Harry spent the rest of the morning sleeping. He went up to the bedroom he and Ron had shared over the last few weeks of summer, but while Ron crawled into bed and was asleep within minutes, Harry sat fully clothed, hunched against the cold metal bars of the bedstead, keeping himself deliberately uncomfortable, determined not to fall into a doze, terrified that he might become the serpent again in his sleep and wake to find that he had attacked Ron, or else slithered through the house after one of the others ...

When Ron woke up, Harry pretended to have enjoyed a refreshing nap too. Their trunks arrived from Hogwarts while they were eating lunch, so they could dress as Muggles for the trip to St Mungo's. Everybody except Harry was riotously happy and talkative as they changed out of their robes into jeans and sweatshirts. When Tonks and Mad-Eye turned up to escort them across London, they greeted them gleefully, laughing at the bowler hat Mad-Eye was wearing at an angle to conceal his magical eye and assuring him, truthfully, that Tonks, whose hair was short and bright pink again, would attract far less attention on the Underground.

Tonks was very interested in Harry's vision of the attack on Mr Weasley, something Harry was not remotely interested in discussing.

'There isn't any *Seer* blood in your family, is there?' she enquired curiously, as they sat side by side on a train rattling towards the heart of the city.

'No,' said Harry, thinking of Professor Trelawney and feeling insulted.

'No,' said Tonks musingly, 'no, I suppose it's not really prophecy you're

第22章 圣芒戈魔法伤病医院

"准是幻觉的残留影响，你还在想那个梦——管它是什么呢——"小天狼星说。

"不是，"哈利摇头说，"就像我心里有东西冒出来，就像我身体里面有一条蛇——"

"你需要睡觉。"小天狼星坚决地说，"吃点早饭，上楼休息去，午饭后可以跟他们一起去看亚瑟。你受了刺激，哈利，你在自责，其实你只是目击了这件事，幸好你看到了，不然亚瑟可能就完了。别胡思乱想……"

他拍拍哈利的肩膀，离开了食品间，剩下哈利一个人站在黑暗中。

大家都睡了一上午，除了哈利。他上楼进了他和罗恩暑假最后几个星期住过的卧室。罗恩爬到床上，几分钟就睡着了，哈利却和衣而坐，蜷曲着靠在冰冷的金属床栏上，故意让自己不舒服，决心不打瞌睡，唯恐睡着后再变成蛇，醒来发现他袭击了罗恩，或者游到其他房间袭击了别人……

罗恩醒来后，哈利假装自己也睡了个好觉。午饭时，他们的行李从霍格沃茨运来了，这样他们可以穿着麻瓜的衣服去圣芒戈。除了哈利之外，所有的人都兴高采烈，有说有笑，脱下袍子，换上了牛仔裤和运动衫。他们高兴地招呼来陪他们横穿伦敦城的唐克斯和疯眼汉，大家开心地取笑疯眼汉歪戴在头上挡住魔眼的圆礼帽，对他说，这会让头发又变得短而亮粉的唐克斯在地铁里不再那么惹人注意。这倒是实话。

唐克斯对哈利梦见韦斯莱先生遭蛇咬一事很感兴趣，而哈利一点也不想谈这个话题。

"你家里不会有先知的血统吧？"唐克斯好奇地问，他们并排坐在车厢里，哐啷哐啷地朝市中心驶去。

"没有。"哈利说，想到特里劳尼教授，他觉得受到了侮辱。

"不是，"唐克斯自己琢磨道，"我想你做的不是真正的预言，对

813

doing, is it? I mean, you're not seeing the future, you're seeing the present ... it's odd, isn't it? Useful, though ...'

Harry didn't answer; fortunately, they got out at the next stop, a station in the very heart of London, and in the bustle of leaving the train he was able to allow Fred and George to get between himself and Tonks, who was leading the way. They all followed her up the escalator, Moody clunking along at the back of the group, his bowler tilted low and one gnarled hand stuck in between the buttons of his coat, clutching his wand. Harry thought he sensed the concealed eye staring hard at him. Trying to avoid any more questions about his dream, he asked Mad-Eye where St Mungo's was hidden.

'Not far from here,' grunted Moody as they stepped out into the wintry air on a broad store-lined street packed with Christmas shoppers. He pushed Harry a little ahead of him and stumped along just behind; Harry knew the eye was rolling in all directions under the tilted hat. 'Wasn't easy to find a good location for a hospital. Nowhere in Diagon Alley was big enough and we couldn't have it underground like the Ministry – wouldn't be healthy. In the end they managed to get hold of a building up here. Theory was, sick wizards could come and go and just blend in with the crowd.'

He seized Harry's shoulder to prevent them being separated by a gaggle of shoppers plainly intent on nothing but making it into a nearby shop full of electrical gadgets.

'Here we go,' said Moody a moment later.

They had arrived outside a large, old-fashioned, red-brick department store called Purge & Dowse Ltd. The place had a shabby, miserable air; the window displays consisted of a few chipped dummies with their wigs askew, standing at random and modelling fashions at least ten years out of date. Large signs on all the dusty doors read: *Closed for Refurbishment.* Harry distinctly heard a large woman laden with plastic shopping bags say to her friend as they passed, 'It's *never* open, that place ...'

'Right,' said Tonks, beckoning them towards a window displaying nothing but a particularly ugly female dummy. Its false eyelashes were hanging off and it was modelling a green nylon pinafore dress. 'Everybody ready?'

They nodded, clustering around her. Moody gave Harry another shove between the shoulder blades to urge him forward and Tonks leaned close to the glass, looking up at the very ugly dummy, her breath steaming up the glass. 'Wotcher,' she said, 'we're here to see Arthur Weasley.'

第22章 圣芒戈魔法伤病医院

吧？你没有看到未来，你看到的是现在……真奇怪，是不是？但挺有用的……"

哈利没有回答，幸好他们到站了，在伦敦的市中心。挤着下车时，他让弗雷德和乔治插到了领路的唐克斯和自己中间。他们都跟着她登上自动扶梯，穆迪噔噔噔地走在最后，圆礼帽拉得低低的，一只粗糙的大手插在上衣纽扣之间握着魔杖。哈利感到那只遮住的眼睛紧紧盯着他，他怕别人又提起那个梦，就问疯眼汉圣芒戈藏在哪儿。

"离这儿不远。"穆迪嘟哝道。他们走到寒冷的街上，这是一条宽阔的街道，两旁的商店里挤满了圣诞节的顾客。穆迪把哈利推到前面，自己压后。哈利知道他帽檐下的眼睛在四下转动。"不容易找到一个好地址建医院，对角巷地皮不够，又不能像魔法部一样建在地下——不利于健康。最后他们在这儿搞到了一栋楼，理由是病号可以混在人群中来来往往……"

他抓住哈利的肩膀，免得他们被一群显然只想挤进旁边那家电器店的购物者冲散。

"到了。"过了一会儿穆迪说。

面前是一座老式的红砖百货商店，叫淘淘有限公司，看上去衰败冷清，橱窗里只有几个破裂的假人，歪戴着假发，姿态各异，穿的是至少十年以前的服装。积满灰尘的门上挂着停业装修的大牌子。哈利分明听到一个拎着大包小包的高个子女人对同伴说："这个地方从来没有开张过……"

"这儿，"唐克斯招手把他们领到一个橱窗前，里面只有一个特别丑的女假人，假睫毛都要掉了，穿着绿色尼龙背心裙，"都准备好了吗？"

大家点点头，向她靠拢过去。穆迪又在哈利后背上推了一把，让他往前去。唐克斯凑近橱窗，抬头望着那个丑陋的假人，呼出的气模糊了玻璃，"你好哇，我们来看亚瑟·韦斯莱。"

CHAPTER TWENTY-TWO   St Mungo's Hospital for Magical Maladies and Injuries

Harry thought how absurd it was for Tonks to expect the dummy to hear her talking so quietly through a sheet of glass, with buses rumbling along behind her and all the racket of a street full of shoppers. Then he reminded himself that dummies couldn't hear anyway. Next second, his mouth opened in shock as the dummy gave a tiny nod and beckoned with its jointed finger, and Tonks had seized Ginny and Mrs Weasley by the elbows, stepped right through the glass and vanished.

Fred, George and Ron stepped after them. Harry glanced around at the jostling crowd; not one of them seemed to have a glance to spare for window displays as ugly as those of Purge & Dowse Ltd; nor did any of them seem to have noticed that six people had just melted into thin air in front of them.

'C'mon,' growled Moody, giving Harry yet another poke in the back, and together they stepped forward through what felt like a sheet of cool water, emerging quite warm and dry on the other side.

There was no sign of the ugly dummy or the space where she had stood. They were in what seemed to be a crowded reception area where rows of witches and wizards sat upon rickety wooden chairs, some looking perfectly normal and perusing out-of-date copies of *Witch Weekly*, others sporting gruesome disfigurements such as elephant trunks or extra hands sticking out of their chests. The room was scarcely less quiet than the street outside, for many of the patients were making very peculiar noises: a sweaty-faced witch in the centre of the front row, who was fanning herself vigorously with a copy of the *Daily Prophet*, kept letting off a high-pitched whistle as steam came pouring out of her mouth; a grubby-looking warlock in the corner clanged like a bell every time he moved and, with each clang, his head vibrated horribly so that he had to seize himself by the ears to hold it steady.

Witches and wizards in lime-green robes were walking up and down the rows, asking questions and making notes on clipboards like Umbridge's. Harry noticed the emblem embroidered on their chests: a wand and bone, crossed.

'Are they doctors?' he asked Ron quietly.

'Doctors?' said Ron, looking startled. 'Those Muggle nutters that cut people up? Nah, they're Healers.'

'Over here!' called Mrs Weasley, above the renewed clanging of the warlock in the corner, and they followed her to the queue in front of a plump blonde witch seated at a desk marked *Enquiries*. The wall behind her was covered in notices and posters saying things like: A CLEAN CAULDRON KEEPS

第22章 圣芒戈魔法伤病医院

一刹那间，哈利觉得唐克斯很滑稽，隔着玻璃用这么小的声音说话，街上人来人往，汽车声那么响，假人怎么能听得见呢。然后他想起假人本来就听不见。但他随即吃惊地张大了嘴巴，只见假人微微点一下头，招了招连在一起的手指。唐克斯抓住金妮和韦斯莱夫人的胳膊，径直穿过玻璃消失了。

弗雷德、乔治和罗恩也走了进去。哈利看看熙熙攘攘的人群，似乎谁也没工夫瞥一眼淘淘公司这样难看的橱窗，也没人注意到六个人刚刚在他面前融入了空气中。

"走吧。"穆迪粗声说着，又捅了哈利的后背一下。他们俩一起走上前，好像穿过了一层凉水，却不冷也不湿地从对面出来了。

丑陋的假人和她站的地方都消失了。他们好像来到了一个拥挤的候诊室，一排排男女巫师坐在摇摇晃晃的木椅上，有些看上去很正常，在读过期的《女巫周刊》，另一些则有可怕的畸形，如长着象鼻子或胸口多生出了一只手等。室内比街上安静不到哪儿去，因为有许多病人发出非常奇怪的声音。前排中间一个满头大汗的女巫使劲扇着一份《预言家日报》，不断发出尖锐的汽笛声，口吐蒸汽。角落里一个邋遢的男巫一动就像钟那样当当响，每响一声他的脑袋就可怕地摆动起来，他只好抓住耳朵把它稳住。

穿着绿袍的男女巫师在候诊者中走来走去，询问情况，在乌姆里奇那样的写字板上作记录。哈利注意到他们胸口绣的徽章：一根魔杖与骨头组成的十字。

"他们是医生吗？"他小声问罗恩。

"医生？"罗恩好像很吃惊，"那些把人切开的麻瓜疯子？不是，他们是治疗师。"

"这边！"在角落里的男巫刚发出的一阵当当声中，韦斯莱夫人喊道。他们跟她排到队伍里，一个胖胖的金发女巫坐在标有问讯处字样的桌子前，她身后的墙上贴满通知和招贴，如**干净坩埚防止魔药变毒药**，

CHAPTER TWENTY-TWO   St Mungo's Hospital for Magical Maladies and Injuries

POTIONS FROM BECOMING POISONS and ANTIDOTES ARE ANTI-DON'TS UNLESS APPROVED BY A QUALIFIED HEALER. There was also a large portrait of a witch with long silver ringlets which was labelled:

DILYS DERWENT
St Mungo's Healer 1722–1741
Headmistress of Hogwarts School
of Witchcraft and Wizardry
1741–1768

Dilys was eyeing the Weasley party as though counting them; when Harry caught her eye she gave a tiny wink, walked sideways out of her portrait and vanished.

Meanwhile, at the front of the queue, a young wizard was performing an odd on-the-spot jig and trying, in between yelps of pain, to explain his predicament to the witch behind the desk.

'It's these – ouch – shoes my brother gave me – ow – they're eating my – OUCH – feet – look at them, there must be some kind of – AARGH – jinx on them and I can't – AAAAARGH – get them off.' He hopped from one foot to the other as though dancing on hot coals.

'The shoes don't prevent you reading, do they?' said the blonde witch, irritably pointing at a large sign to the left of her desk. 'You want Spell Damage, fourth floor. Just like it says on the floor guide. Next!'

As the wizard hobbled and pranced sideways out of the way, the Weasley party moved forward a few steps and Harry read the floor guide:

ARTEFACT ACCIDENTS   GROUND FLOOR
CAULDRON EXPLOSION, WAND BACKFIRING,
BROOM CRASHES, ETC.
CREATURE-INDUCED INJURIES   FIRST FLOOR
BITES, STINGS, BURNS, EMBEDDED SPINES, ETC.
MAGICAL BUGS   SECOND FLOOR
CONTAGIOUS MALADIES, E.G. DRAGON POX,
VANISHING SICKNESS, SCROFUNGULUS, ETC.

第22章 圣芒戈魔法伤病医院

解药不可乱用，需经合格治疗师认可。还有一幅垂着长长银发卷的女巫的大肖像，上面注明：

戴丽丝·德文特

圣芒戈治疗师（1722—1741）

霍格沃茨魔法学校

校长（1741—1768）

戴丽丝在仔细打量韦斯莱的亲友团，好像在点人数。遇到哈利的目光时，她微微眨了眨眼，从侧面走出相框消失了。

队伍前头有一个年轻男巫正在跳一种奇异的快步舞，一边喊痛一边试图向桌后的女巫解释他的困境。

"是——嗷——我哥哥给我的鞋子——哎哟——它在咬我的——嗷——脚——看看，上面一定有——啊——恶咒，我——啊——脱不下来——"他轮流跳着两只脚，好像在热炭上跳舞。

"鞋子没妨碍你阅读吧？"金发女巫不耐烦地指着桌子左边的大牌子说，"你得去五楼的咒语伤害科，指示牌上写着呢。下一个！"

那男巫一跳一拐地让到一边，韦斯莱亲友团等人往前挪了几步。哈利读着指示牌：

器物事故科……………………………………一楼

（坩埚爆炸、魔杖走火、扫帚碰撞等）

生物伤害科……………………………………二楼

（蜇咬、灼伤、嵌刺等）

奇异病菌感染科………………………………三楼

（龙痘疮、消失症、淋巴真菌炎等传染病）

CHAPTER TWENTY-TWO — St Mungo's Hospital for Magical Maladies and Injuries

POTION AND PLANT POISONING   THIRD FLOOR
RASHES, REGURGITATION, UNCONTROLLABLE GIGGLING, ETC.

SPELL DAMAGE   FOURTH FLOOR
UNLIFTABLE JINXES, HEXES, INCORRECTLY APPLIED CHARMS, ETC.

VISITORS' TEAROOM/HOSPITAL SHOP FIFTH FLOOR

IF YOU ARE UNSURE WHERE TO GO, INCAPABLE OF NORMAL SPEECH OR UNABLE TO REMEMBER WHY YOU ARE HERE, OUR WELCOMEWITCH WILL BE PLEASED TO HELP.

A very old, stooped wizard with a hearing trumpet had shuffled to the front of the queue now. 'I'm here to see Broderick Bode!' he wheezed.

'Ward forty-nine, but I'm afraid you're wasting your time,' said the witch dismissively. 'He's completely addled, you know – still thinks he's a teapot. Next!'

A harassed-looking wizard was holding his small daughter tightly by the ankle while she flapped around his head using the immensely large, feathery wings that had sprouted right out through the back of her romper suit.

'Fourth floor,' said the witch, in a bored voice, without asking, and the man disappeared through the double doors beside the desk, holding his daughter like an oddly shaped balloon. 'Next!'

Mrs Weasley moved forward to the desk.

'Hello,' she said, 'my husband, Arthur Weasley, was supposed to be moved to a different ward this morning, could you tell us –?'

'Arthur Weasley?' said the witch, running her finger down a long list in front of her. 'Yes, first floor, second door on the right, Dai Llewellyn Ward.'

'Thank you,' said Mrs Weasley. 'Come on, you lot.'

They followed her through the double doors and along the narrow corridor beyond, which was lined with more portraits of famous Healers and lit by crystal bubbles full of candles that floated up on the ceiling, looking like giant soapsuds. More witches and wizards in lime-green robes walked in and out of the doors they passed; a foul-smelling yellow gas wafted into the passageway as they passed one door, and every now and then they heard distant wailing. They climbed a flight of stairs and entered the Creature-

药剂和植物中毒科……………………………四楼

（皮疹、反胃、大笑不止等）

咒语伤害科………………………………………五楼

（去不掉的魔咒、恶咒、错误使用的魔咒等）

茶室和商店………………………………………六楼

如果不知去哪一科，不能正常说话，或不记得为何事而来，我们的接待员愿意帮忙。

一个老态龙钟、戴着喇叭形助听器的男巫慢慢蹭到前面："我来看望布罗德里克·博德！"他带着哮喘声说。

"四十九号病房，但恐怕你是在浪费时间，"女巫随口答道，"他完全糊涂了，还当自己是茶壶呢。下一个！"

一个脸色疲惫的男巫紧紧抓着小女儿的脚脖子，她的连裤衫背部长出来一对大羽毛翅膀，在他脑袋旁边拍打着。

"五楼。"女巫问都没问就厌倦地说，那男子举着女儿从旁边的双扇门走了出去，像举着一个奇特的气球。"下一个！"

韦斯莱夫人走到桌前。

"你好，"她说，"我丈夫亚瑟·韦斯莱今天早上换的病房，请问——？"

"亚瑟·韦斯莱？"女巫用手指顺着一张长长的单子往下找，"哦，二楼，右边第二个门，戴伊·卢埃林病房。"

"谢谢。"韦斯莱夫人说，"跟我来。"

他们随她穿过双扇门，走过一条狭窄的走廊，两边是著名治疗师的肖像，装有蜡烛的水晶泡泡飘在天花板上，看上去像巨大的肥皂泡。他们路过的门口都有穿着绿袍的巫师进进出出，有一扇门里飘出一股黄色的臭气，不时听到隐隐的哀号声。他们登上楼梯，进了生物伤害科，右边第二个门上写着"危险的"戴伊·卢埃林病房：重度咬伤。底下

Induced Injuries corridor, where the second door on the right bore the words: *'Dangerous' Dai Llewellyn Ward: Serious Bites.* Underneath this was a card in a brass holder on which had been handwritten: *Healer-in-Charge: Hippocrates Smethwyck. Trainee Healer: Augustus Pye.*

'We'll wait outside, Molly,' Tonks said. 'Arthur won't want too many visitors at once ... it ought to be just the family first.'

Mad-Eye growled his approval of this idea and set himself with his back against the corridor wall, his magical eye spinning in all directions. Harry drew back, too, but Mrs Weasley reached out a hand and pushed him through the door, saying, 'Don't be silly, Harry, Arthur wants to thank you.'

The ward was small and rather dingy, as the only window was narrow and set high in the wall facing the door. Most of the light came from more shining crystal bubbles clustered in the middle of the ceiling. The walls were of panelled oak and there was a portrait of a rather vicious-looking wizard on the wall, captioned:

URQUHART RACKHARROW
1612–1697
Inventor of the
Entrail-expelling Curse

There were only three patients. Mr Weasley was occupying the bed at the far end of the ward beside the tiny window. Harry was pleased and relieved to see that he was propped up on several pillows and reading the *Daily Prophet* by the solitary ray of sunlight falling on to his bed. He looked up as they walked towards him and, seeing who it was, beamed.

'Hello!' he called, throwing the *Prophet* aside. 'Bill just left, Molly, had to get back to work, but he says he'll drop in on you later.'

'How are you, Arthur?' asked Mrs Weasley, bending down to kiss his cheek and looking anxiously into his face. 'You're still looking a bit peaky.'

'I feel absolutely fine,' said Mr Weasley brightly, holding out his good arm to give Ginny a hug. 'If they could only take the bandages off, I'd be fit to go home.'

'Why can't they take them off, Dad?' asked Fred.

'Well, I start bleeding like mad every time they try,' said Mr Weasley cheerfully, reaching across for his wand, which lay on his bedside cabinet, and waving it so that six extra chairs appeared at his bedside to seat them all.

第22章 圣芒戈魔法伤病医院

一张铜框镶嵌的卡片上有手写的字样：主治疗师：希伯克拉特·斯梅绥克；实习治疗师：奥古斯都·派伊。

"我们在外面等吧，莫丽，"唐克斯说，"亚瑟一次不能见太多的人……应该让家里人先进。"

疯眼汉赞同地咕噜了一声，背靠在墙上，魔眼骨碌碌地转动着。哈利也往后缩，但韦斯莱夫人伸手把他推进了门，说："别傻了，哈利，亚瑟想谢谢你……"

病房很小，暗暗的，只有门对面的墙上高处开了一个窄窄的窗户。光线主要由聚在天花板中央的水晶泡泡提供。橡木镶板的墙上挂着一个邪里邪气的男巫的肖像，上面写着：

厄克特·拉哈罗
（1612—1697），
掏肠咒发明者。

病房里只有三个病人。韦斯莱先生的病床在房间的最里头，小窗户旁边。哈利欣慰地看到他靠在几个枕头上，就着那正好落到他床上的唯一一道阳光看《预言家日报》。他们走过去时他抬起头，看到是谁之后，高兴地笑了起来。

"你们好！"他把《预言家日报》扔到一边，叫道，"莫丽，比尔刚走，上班去了，但他说会去看你。"

"你怎么样，亚瑟？"韦斯莱夫人俯身吻了吻他的面颊，担心地看着他的脸问，"看上去还有点憔悴。"

"我感觉很好，"韦斯莱先生愉快地说，伸出那只没受伤的胳膊抱了抱金妮，"要是他们能把绷带拆掉的话，我都可以回家了。"

"为什么不能拆，爸爸？"弗雷德问。

"因为每次拆的时候我都流血不止，"韦斯莱先生轻松地说，伸手拿过搁在床头柜上的魔杖，轻轻一挥，床边多了六把椅子，"好像那条

'It seems there was some rather unusual kind of poison in that snake's fangs that keeps wounds open. They're sure they'll find an antidote, though; they say they've had much worse cases than mine, and in the meantime I just have to keep taking a Blood-Replenishing Potion every hour. But that fellow over there,' he said, dropping his voice and nodding towards the bed opposite in which a man lay looking green and sickly and staring at the ceiling. 'Bitten by a *werewolf*, poor chap. No cure at all.'

'A werewolf?' whispered Mrs Weasley, looking alarmed. 'Is he safe in a public ward? Shouldn't he be in a private room?'

'It's two weeks till full moon,' Mr Weasley reminded her quietly. 'They've been talking to him this morning, the Healers, you know, trying to persuade him he'll be able to lead an almost normal life. I said to him – didn't mention names, of course – but I said I knew a werewolf personally, very nice man, who finds the condition quite easy to manage.'

'What did he say?' asked George.

'Said he'd give me another bite if I didn't shut up,' said Mr Weasley sadly. 'And that woman over *there*,' he indicated the only other occupied bed, which was right beside the door, 'won't tell the Healers what bit her, which makes us all think it must have been something she was handling illegally. Whatever it was took a real chunk out of her leg, *very* nasty smell when they take off the dressings.'

'So, you going to tell us what happened, Dad?' asked Fred, pulling his chair closer to the bed.

'Well, you already know, don't you?' said Mr Weasley, with a significant smile at Harry. 'It's very simple – I'd had a very long day, dozed off, got sneaked up on and bitten.'

'Is it in the *Prophet*, you being attacked?' asked Fred, indicating the newspaper Mr Weasley had cast aside.

'No, of course not,' said Mr Weasley, with a slightly bitter smile, 'the Ministry wouldn't want everyone to know a dirty great serpent got –'

'Arthur!' Mrs Weasley warned him.

'– got – er – me,' Mr Weasley said hastily, though Harry was quite sure that was not what he had meant to say.

'So where were you when it happened, Dad?' asked George.

'That's my business,' said Mr Weasley, though with a small smile. He

第22章 圣芒戈魔法伤病医院

蛇的毒牙里有一种特殊的毒液，能阻止伤口愈合……但他们相信能找到解药，他们说见过比我严重得多的情况，我现在只是要每小时服用一种补血药。可那一位，"他压低嗓门，把头朝对面床上一点，一个脸色发绿的男子躺在那儿，眼睛盯着天花板，"被狼人咬了，可怜的人，治不好了。"

"狼人？"韦斯莱夫人惊恐地小声说，"他在公共病房安全吗？不用单独隔离吗？"

"离满月还有两星期呢，"韦斯莱先生平静地提醒她，"治疗师今天早上跟他谈话了，想让他相信他可以过几乎正常的生活。我跟他说我认识一个狼人——当然没提名字。我说他人很好，状态也不难控制。"

"他说什么？"乔治问。

"他说我要是不闭嘴，他就让我再挨一下咬。"韦斯莱先生悲哀地说，"那边那个女的，"他指指门边的那一张有人的病床，"不肯告诉治疗师她是被什么东西咬的，我们猜一定是她非法搞来的东西。那东西把她腿上的肉咬下了一大块，换绷带的时候那个难闻哪。"

"跟我们说说你是怎么受伤的吧，爸爸？"弗雷德把椅子朝床边拖了拖，问道。

"你们都知道了，是不是？"韦斯莱先生说，意味深长地朝哈利笑了一下，"很简单——我这天过得很辛苦，打了个瞌睡，就被咬了。"

"《预言家日报》里说你受伤了吗？"弗雷德指着他爸爸丢在一边的报纸问。

"没有，当然没有，"韦斯莱先生略带苦涩地一笑，"魔法部不会希望人人都知道有一条肮脏的大蛇——"

"亚瑟！"韦斯莱夫人警告道。

"——啊——偷袭了我。"韦斯莱先生忙说，但哈利觉得这不是他本来要说的话。

"当时你在哪儿，爸爸？"乔治问。

"这事跟你无关。"韦斯莱先生说，但嘴角还带着笑。他抓起《预

CHAPTER TWENTY-TWO   St Mungo's Hospital for Magical Maladies and Injuries

snatched up the *Daily Prophet*, shook it open again and said, 'I was just reading about Willy Widdershins's arrest when you arrived. You know Willy turned out to be behind those regurgitating toilets back in the summer? One of his jinxes backfired, the toilet exploded and they found him lying unconscious in the wreckage covered from head to foot in –'

'When you say you were "on duty",' Fred interrupted in a low voice, 'what were you doing?'

'You heard your father,' whispered Mrs Weasley, 'we are not discussing this here! Go on about Willy Widdershins, Arthur.'

'Well, don't ask me how, but he actually got off the toilet charge,' said Mr Weasley grimly. 'I can only suppose gold changed hands –'

'You were guarding it, weren't you?' said George quietly. 'The weapon? The thing You-Know-Who's after?'

'George, be quiet!' snapped Mrs Weasley.

'Anyway,' said Mr Weasley, in a raised voice, 'this time Willy's been caught selling biting doorknobs to Muggles and I don't think he'll be able to worm his way out of it because, according to this article, two Muggles have lost fingers and are now in St Mungo's for emergency bone regrowth and memory modification. Just think of it, Muggles in St Mungo's! I wonder which ward they're in?'

And he looked eagerly around as though hoping to see a signpost.

'Didn't you say You-Know-Who's got a snake, Harry?' asked Fred, looking at his father for a reaction. 'A massive one? You saw it the night he returned, didn't you?'

'That's enough,' said Mrs Weasley crossly. 'Mad-Eye and Tonks are outside, Arthur, they want to come and see you. And you lot can wait outside,' she added to her children and Harry. 'You can come and say goodbye afterwards. Go on.'

They trooped back into the corridor. Mad-Eye and Tonks went in and closed the door of the ward behind them. Fred raised his eyebrows.

'Fine,' he said coolly, rummaging in his pockets, 'be like that. Don't tell us anything.'

'Looking for these?' said George, holding out what looked like a tangle of flesh-coloured string.

'You read my mind,' said Fred, grinning. 'Let's see if St Mungo's puts

言家日报》，抖开来说："我刚刚正在看威利·威德辛被捕的报道。你们知道夏天的时候厕所污水回涌是威利干的吗？他的一个咒语出了问题，厕所爆炸了，他们发现他昏迷不醒地躺在一片废墟中，从头到脚淹在——"

"你说你当时在'值班'，"弗雷德低声打断他问，"你究竟做什么呢？"

"你爸爸说了，"韦斯莱夫人小声说，"在这里不谈这个！继续说威利·威德辛吧，亚瑟——"

"别问我为什么，厕所爆炸一事居然没定他的罪，"韦斯莱先生严肃地说，"我只能猜测有金钱交易——"

"你在看守它，是不是？"乔治低声问，"那件武器，神秘人要找的东西？"

"乔治，安静！"他母亲训斥道。

"反正，"韦斯莱先生提高了嗓门，"这一回威利是在向麻瓜出售咬人的门把手时被抓获的。我想他逃不掉了，因为文章里说，两个麻瓜被咬掉了手指，正在圣芒戈接受骨骼再生和记忆修改的急救。想想吧，麻瓜进了圣芒戈！不知道他们在哪个病房？"

他环顾四周，好像希望看到指示牌。

"哈利，你不是说神秘人有条蛇吗？"弗雷德问，一边看着他爸爸的反应，"好大的一条？你在他恢复肉身的那天晚上看到的，对不对？"

"够了。"韦斯莱夫人生气地说，"疯眼汉和唐克斯在外面呢，亚瑟，他们想进来看你。你们可以出去等，"她又对她的孩子和哈利说，"待会儿再进来说再见。去吧……"

他们退到走廊上。疯眼汉和唐克斯走进去关上了房门。弗雷德扬起了眉毛。

"好啊，"他冷冷地说，手在口袋里摸索着，"就那样吧，什么也别告诉我们。"

"找这个吗？"乔治说，递过一团肉色细绳状的东西。

"你真是我肚里的蛔虫啊。"弗雷德咧嘴一笑，"看看圣芒戈是不是

CHAPTER TWENTY-TWO   St Mungo's Hospital for Magical Maladies and Injuries

Imperturbable Charms on its ward doors, shall we?'

He and George disentangled the string and separated five extendable ears from each other. Fred and George handed them around. Harry hesitated to take one.

'Go on, Harry, take it! You saved Dad's life. If anyone's got the right to eavesdrop on him, it's you.'

Grinning in spite of himself, Harry took the end of the string and inserted it into his ear as the twins had done.

'OK, go!' Fred whispered.

The flesh-coloured strings wriggled like long skinny worms and snaked under the door. At first, Harry could hear nothing, then he jumped as he heard Tonks whispering as clearly as though she were standing right beside him.

'... they searched the whole area but couldn't find the snake anywhere. It just seems to have vanished after it attacked you, Arthur ... but You-Know-Who can't have expected a snake to get in, can he?'

'I reckon he sent it as a lookout,' growled Moody, ''cause he's not had any luck so far, has he? No, I reckon he's trying to get a clearer picture of what he's facing and if Arthur hadn't been there the beast would've had a lot more time to look around. So, Potter says he saw it all happen?'

'Yes,' said Mrs Weasley. She sounded rather uneasy. 'You know, Dumbledore seems almost to have been waiting for Harry to see something like this.'

'Yeah, well,' said Moody, 'there's something funny about the Potter kid, we all know that.'

'Dumbledore seemed worried about Harry when I spoke to him this morning,' whispered Mrs Weasley.

'Course he's worried,' growled Moody. 'The boy's seeing things from inside You-Know-Who's snake. Obviously, Potter doesn't realise what that means, but if You-Know-Who's possessing him –'

Harry pulled the extendable ear out of his own, his heart hammering very fast and heat rushing up his face. He looked around at the others. They were all staring at him, the strings still trailing from their ears, looking suddenly fearful.

第22章 圣芒戈魔法伤病医院

在病房门上加了抗扰咒,好吗?"

他和乔治打开线团,分开五个伸缩耳分给大家,哈利犹豫着要不要拿。

"拿着吧,哈利!你救了爸爸的命,如果谁有权利偷听他讲话,那就是你了……"

哈利禁不住笑了,拿起线头,像兄弟俩那样把它塞到耳朵里。

"好,走吧!"弗雷德小声说。

肉色的细绳像长虫般蠕动着,一扭一扭地从门底下钻了进去。一开始哈利什么也听不见,然后他听到唐克斯在小声说话,清晰得就像在他身边一样,把他吓了一跳。

"……他们把那里搜遍了,就是找不到那条蛇,它好像咬了你之后就消失了……可是神秘人不可能指望一条蛇进去吧?"

"我想他是放蛇出来侦察的,"穆迪的粗嗓门说,"因为他至今没什么进展,对吧?我估计他是想探探情况,如果亚瑟不在那儿,那畜生就会有时间多看看。波特说他看到了全过程?"

"对,"韦斯莱夫人的声音有点不安,"你知道,邓布利多似乎一直在等着哈利看到这种事……"

"啊,"穆迪说,"波特那孩子是有点怪,我们都知道。"

"今天早上邓布利多跟我说话的时候,好像有些担心哈利。"韦斯莱夫人小声说。

"他当然担心了,"穆迪粗声说,"那孩子通过神秘人的蛇的眼睛看东西。波特显然不知道这意味着什么,但如果神秘人附在他身上——"

哈利把伸缩耳摘了下来,心怦怦乱跳,脸上火辣辣的。他看看其他人,他们都望着他,线还挂在耳朵上,脸上带着突如其来的惊恐。

CHAPTER TWENTY-THREE

Christmas on the Closed Ward

Was this why Dumbledore would no longer meet Harry's eyes? Did he expect to see Voldemort staring out of them, afraid, perhaps, that their vivid green might turn suddenly to scarlet, with catlike slits for pupils? Harry remembered how the snakelike face of Voldemort had once forced itself out of the back of Professor Quirrell's head and ran his hand over the back of his own, wondering what it would feel like if Voldemort burst out of his skull.

He felt dirty, contaminated, as though he were carrying some deadly germ, unworthy to sit on the Underground train back from the hospital with innocent, clean people whose minds and bodies were free of the taint of Voldemort ... he had not merely seen the snake, he had *been* the snake, he knew it now ...

A truly terrible thought then occurred to him, a memory bobbing to the surface of his mind, one that made his insides writhe and squirm like serpents.

What's he after, apart from followers?

Stuff he can only get by stealth ... like a weapon. Something he didn't have last time.

I'm the weapon, Harry thought, and it was as though poison were pumping through his veins, chilling him, bringing him out in a sweat as he swayed with the train through the dark tunnel. I'm the one Voldemort's trying to use, that's why they've got guards around me everywhere I go, it's not for my protection, it's for other people's, only it's not working, they can't have someone on me all the time at Hogwarts ... I *did* attack Mr Weasley last night, it was me. Voldemort made me do it and he could be inside me, listening to my thoughts right now –

'Are you all right, Harry, dear?' whispered Mrs Weasley, leaning across Ginny to speak to him as the train rattled along through its dark tunnel. 'You don't look very well. Are you feeling sick?'

第23章

封闭病房中的圣诞节

这就是邓布利多不再正视哈利目光的原因吗？他是不是担心会在里面看到伏地魔，怕那翠绿的眼睛会突然变得血红，瞳孔像猫眼那样只有一条缝？哈利想起伏地魔那张蛇脸从奇洛教授的后脑勺上露出来的情形，他用手摸摸自己的后脑勺，想象着伏地魔从自己脑壳里钻出来会是什么感觉。

他感到自己很脏，受了污染，好像带着某种致命的病菌，不配与干净、清白、身体和心灵没有被伏地魔玷污的人们一起坐地铁从医院回去……他不只是看到了那条蛇，他就是那条蛇。他现在知道了……

然后他生出一个真正可怕的念头，一个记忆跳出脑海，使他的五脏六腑像毒蛇一样翻腾起来……

"除了追随者以外，他还想得到什么呢？"

"某种只有偷偷摸摸才能得到的东西……比如一件武器。他以前所没有的东西。"

我就是那件武器，哈利想，好像毒液正在他的血管里奔突，使他浑身冰凉，出了一身冷汗。他在漆黑的隧道中随着地铁车厢摇摇晃晃。我就是伏地魔想利用的东西，所以他们到处都让人守着我，不是为了保护我，是为了保护别人，只是不管用，在霍格沃茨不可能一直有人看着我……昨晚我还是袭击了韦斯莱先生，是我，伏地魔让我干的，他现在可能就在我的肚子里，听见我在想什么……

"你没事吧，哈利，亲爱的？"韦斯莱夫人隔着金妮凑过来问他，地铁列车在隧道里哐当哐当地行驶，"你脸色不大好，不舒服吗？"

CHAPTER TWENTY-THREE — Christmas on the Closed Ward

They were all watching him. He shook his head violently and stared up at an advertisement for home insurance.

'Harry, dear, are you *sure* you're all right?' said Mrs Weasley in a worried voice, as they walked around the unkempt patch of grass in the middle of Grimmauld Place. 'You look ever so pale ... are you sure you slept this morning? You go upstairs to bed right now and you can have a couple of hours of sleep before dinner, all right?'

He nodded; here was a ready-made excuse not to talk to any of the others, which was precisely what he wanted, so when she opened the front door he hurried straight past the troll's-leg umbrella stand, up the stairs and into his and Ron's bedroom.

Here, he began to pace up and down, past the two beds and Phineas Nigellus's empty picture frame, his brain teeming and seething with questions and ever more dreadful ideas.

How had he become a snake? Perhaps he was an Animagus ... no, he couldn't be, he would know ... perhaps *Voldemort* was an Animagus ... yes, thought Harry, that would fit, he *would* turn into a snake of course ... and when he's possessing me, then we both transform ... that still doesn't explain how I got to London and back to my bed in the space of about five minutes ... but then Voldemort's about the most powerful wizard in the world, apart from Dumbledore, it's probably no problem at all to him to transport people like that.

And then, with a terrible stab of panic, he thought, *but this is insane — if Voldemort's possessing me, I'm giving him a clear view into the Headquarters of the Order of the Phoenix right now! He'll know who's in the Order and where Sirius is ... and I've heard loads of stuff I shouldn't have, everything Sirius told me the first night I was here ...*

There was only one thing for it: he would have to leave Grimmauld Place straightaway. He would spend Christmas at Hogwarts without the others, which would keep them safe over the holidays at least ... but no, that wouldn't do, there were still plenty of people at Hogwarts to maim and injure. What if it was Seamus, Dean or Neville next time? He stopped his pacing and stood staring at Phineas Nigellus's empty frame. A leaden sensation was settling in the pit of his stomach. He had no alternative: he was going to have to return to Privet Drive, cut himself off from other wizards entirely.

Well, if he had to do it, he thought, there was no point hanging around. Trying with all his might not to think how the Dursleys were going to react when they found him on their doorstep six months earlier than they had

第23章 封闭病房中的圣诞节

大家都看着他,他使劲摇摇头,抬头盯着一幅家庭保险广告。

"哈利,亲爱的,你真的没事吗?"走过格里莫广场中央那片杂乱的草坪时,韦斯莱夫人担心地问,"你脸色这么苍白……上午真的睡着了吗?你马上回楼上躺着,晚饭前还能睡两小时,好吗?"

哈利点点头,正好有借口不用跟别人说话,他求之不得。所以韦斯莱夫人一打开前门,他就径直走过巨怪腿做的伞架,上楼逃进了他和罗恩的卧室。

他在屋里踱来踱去,走过两张床和菲尼亚斯·奈杰勒斯的空相框,脑子里翻涌着一个个问题和可怕的念头……

他是怎么变成蛇的?也许他是阿尼马格斯……不,不可能,他会知道的……也许伏地魔是阿尼马格斯……对,哈利想,这就说得通了,他当然能变成一条蛇……当他附在我身上时,我们都变成了蛇……可这还不能解释我怎么会在五分钟之内去了伦敦又回到床上……但除了邓布利多之外,伏地魔几乎是世界上最厉害的巫师,把人运来运去对他来说可能不成问题……

然后他心中猛地一惊,想道:这太可怕了——如果伏地魔附在我身上,我现在就让他清楚地看到了凤凰社的总部!他会知道哪些人是凤凰社的,小天狼星在哪儿……我还听了很多不该听的东西,我在这儿的第一个晚上小天狼星对我说的那些话……

只有一个办法:他必须马上离开格里莫广场。他要在霍格沃茨一个人过圣诞节,这样至少可以在节日期间保证他们的安全……不行,还是没有用,霍格沃茨也有许多人可以伤害,如果下一个是西莫、迪安或纳威呢?他停止了踱步,望着菲尼亚斯·奈杰勒斯的空相框,肚子里像灌了铅。他别无选择,只有回女贞路,同其他巫师彻底隔离……

好吧,他想,如果必须走,再耽搁已经没有意义。他竭力不去想象德思礼一家看见他提前六个月回来了会有什么反应,而是大步走到他的箱子前,关上盖子,锁好,然后习惯性地回头找海德薇,这才想

CHAPTER TWENTY-THREE   Christmas on the Closed Ward

expected, he strode over to his trunk, slammed the lid shut and locked it, then glanced around automatically for Hedwig before remembering that she was still at Hogwarts – well, her cage would be one less thing to carry – he seized one end of his trunk and had dragged it halfway towards the door when a snide voice said, 'Running away, are we?'

He looked around. Phineas Nigellus had appeared on the canvas of his portrait and was leaning against the frame, watching Harry with an amused expression on his face.

'Not running away, no,' said Harry shortly, dragging his trunk a few more feet across the room.

'I thought,' said Phineas Nigellus, stroking his pointed beard, 'that to belong in Gryffindor house you were supposed to be *brave*? It looks to me as though you would have been better off in my own house. We Slytherins are brave, yes, but not stupid. For instance, given the choice, we will always choose to save our own necks.'

'It's not my own neck I'm saving,' said Harry tersely, tugging the trunk over a patch of particularly uneven, moth-eaten carpet right in front of the door.

'Oh, I *see*,' said Phineas Nigellus, still stroking his beard, 'this is no cowardly flight – you are being *noble*.'

Harry ignored him. His hand was on the doorknob when Phineas Nigellus said lazily, 'I have a message for you from Albus Dumbledore.'

Harry spun round.

'What is it?'

'"Stay where you are."'

'I haven't moved!' said Harry, his hand still upon the doorknob. 'So what's the message?'

'I have just given it to you, dolt,' said Phineas Nigellus smoothly. 'Dumbledore says, "*Stay where you are.*"'

'Why?' said Harry eagerly, dropping the end of his trunk. 'Why does he want me to stay? What else did he say?'

'Nothing whatsoever,' said Phineas Nigellus, raising a thin black eyebrow as though he found Harry impertinent.

Harry's temper rose to the surface like a snake rearing from long grass. He was exhausted, he was confused beyond measure, he had experienced terror, relief, then terror again in the last twelve hours, and still Dumbledore did not want to talk to him!

第 23 章 封闭病房中的圣诞节

起它还在霍格沃茨——也好,少拎一个笼子。他提起箱子的一头,把它向门口拖去,忽听一个讽刺的声音说道:"想逃,是不是?"

哈利扭头一看,菲尼亚斯·奈杰勒斯又回到了画布上,正倚在相框上看着他,脸上带着揶揄的表情。

"不是逃,不是。"哈利简单地说,拖着箱子又走了几步。

"我想,"菲尼亚斯·奈杰勒斯抚摸着山羊胡须说,"做格兰芬多的学生需要很勇敢,是不是?依我看你来我们学院可能更合适。斯莱特林人勇敢,但是不傻。比方说,如果有机会,我们总是选择保命。"

"我不是为了保自己的命。"哈利干脆地说,把箱子拖过门口一块虫蛀的、特别毛糙的地毯。

"哦,我知道了,"菲尼亚斯·奈杰勒斯依然抚摸着胡须,"这不是胆怯的逃跑——你这是高尚行为!"

哈利没理他。可当他抓住门把手时,菲尼亚斯·奈杰勒斯懒洋洋地说:"我有阿不思·邓布利多的口信。"

哈利急忙转身。

"什么口信?"

"待在这儿。"

"我没动呀!"哈利的手还放在门把手上,"什么口信?"

"我已经告诉你了,傻瓜,"菲尼亚斯·奈杰勒斯平和地说,"邓布利多说:'待在这儿。'"

"为什么?"哈利丢下箱子,急切地问,"他为什么要我待在这儿?他还说了什么?"

"什么也没说。"菲尼亚斯·奈杰勒斯挑起一根细细的黑眉毛,好像觉得哈利很无礼。

哈利的火气腾地蹿了上来,像一条蛇从高草中猛地竖起。他已精疲力竭,困惑到极点,他在这十二个小时内经历了恐惧、宽慰,然后又是恐惧,可邓布利多还是不肯跟他谈!

CHAPTER TWENTY-THREE   Christmas on the Closed Ward

'So that's it, is it?' he said loudly. '"*Stay where you are*"? That's all anyone could tell me after I got attacked by those Dementors, too! Just stay put while the grown-ups sort it out, Harry! We won't bother telling you anything, though, because your tiny little brain might not be able to cope with it!'

'You know,' said Phineas Nigellus, even more loudly than Harry, 'this is precisely why I *loathed* being a teacher! Young people are so infernally convinced that they are absolutely right about everything. Has it not occurred to you, my poor puffed-up popinjay, that there might be an excellent reason why the Headmaster of Hogwarts is not confiding every tiny detail of his plans to you? Have you never paused, while feeling hard-done-by, to note that following Dumbledore's orders has never yet led you into harm? No. No, like all young people, you are quite sure that you alone feel and think, you alone recognise danger, you alone are the only one clever enough to realise what the Dark Lord may be planning –'

'He *is* planning something to do with me, then?' said Harry swiftly.

'Did I say that?' said Phineas Nigellus, idly examining his silk gloves. 'Now, if you will excuse me, I have better things to do than listen to adolescent agonising … good-day to you.'

And he strolled to the edge of his frame and out of sight.

'Fine, go then!' Harry bellowed at the empty frame. 'And tell Dumbledore thanks for nothing!'

The empty canvas remained silent. fuming, Harry dragged his trunk back to the foot of his bed, then threw himself face down on the moth-eaten covers, his eyes shut, his body heavy and aching.

He felt as though he had journeyed for miles and miles … it seemed impossible that less than twenty-four hours ago Cho Chang had been approaching him under the mistletoe … he was so tired … he was scared to sleep … yet he did not know how long he could fight it … Dumbledore had told him to stay … that must mean he was allowed to sleep … but he was scared … what if it happened again?

He was sinking into shadows …

It was as though a film in his head had been waiting to start. He was walking down a deserted corridor towards a plain black door, past rough stone walls, torches, and an open doorway on to a flight of stone steps leading downstairs on the left …

第23章 封闭病房中的圣诞节

"就这样，是不是？"他大声说，"待在这儿？我被摄魂怪袭击之后，也是人人都对我这么说！哈利，待着别动，等大人去查清楚！但我们什么也不会告诉你，因为你的小脑瓜搞不懂！"

"你知道，"菲尼亚斯·奈杰勒斯的声音比哈利的还大，"这就是我讨厌当老师的原因！年轻人总以为他们什么事都绝对正确，真让人讨厌。可怜的自负的小家伙，你有没有想过，霍格沃茨的校长可能有很好的理由不把他计划的每个细节都告诉你？你在感觉委屈的时候，就没有想一想，服从邓布利多的命令曾经害了你吗？没有，没有！你像所有的年轻人一样，以为就你有感情，有思想，就你看到了危险，就你能看出黑魔头的阴谋……"

"那他是在制订跟我有关的计划了？"哈利马上问。

"我说了吗？"菲尼亚斯·奈杰勒斯懒懒地看着他的丝绸手套，"现在，对不起，我有比听少年的烦恼更重要的事要做……日安……"

他走出相框不见了。

"好，走吧！"哈利朝空相框吼道，"对邓布利多说，我感激涕零！"

空相框不再出声。哈利气呼呼地把箱子拖回床脚，然后扑到虫蛀的床罩上，闭着眼睛，身子沉重而酸痛……

他觉得像走了好远好远的路……真不能相信不到二十四小时之前秋·张还在槲寄生下向他靠近……他太累了……他害怕睡着……但他不知道自己能坚持多久……邓布利多叫他留下来……那一定表示他可以睡觉……但他还是害怕……要是再……？

他渐渐沉入了阴影中……

好像他脑子里有一段胶片在等着放映。他在空荡荡的走廊上朝一扇黑门走去，经过粗糙的石墙、火把，左边一个门洞连着通到楼下的石阶。

CHAPTER TWENTY-THREE   Christmas on the Closed Ward

He reached the black door but could not open it ... he stood gazing at it, desperate for entry ... something he wanted with all his heart lay beyond ... a prize beyond his dreams ... if only his scar would stop prickling ... then he would be able to think more clearly ...

'Harry,' said Ron's voice, from far, far away, 'Mum says dinner's ready, but she'll save you something if you want to stay in bed.'

Harry opened his eyes, but Ron had already left the room.

He doesn't want to be on his own with me, Harry thought. *Not after what he heard Moody say.*

He supposed none of them would want him there any more, now that they knew what was inside him.

He would not go down to dinner; he would not inflict his company on them. He turned over on to his other side and, after a while, dropped back off to sleep. He woke much later, in the early hours of the morning, his insides aching with hunger and Ron snoring in the next bed. Squinting around the room, he saw the dark outline of Phineas Nigellus standing again in his portrait and it occurred to Harry that Dumbledore had probably sent Phineas Nigellus to watch over him, in case he attacked somebody else.

The feeling of being unclean intensified. He half wished he had not obeyed Dumbledore ... if this was how life was going to be for him in Grimmauld Place from now on, maybe he would be better off in Privet Drive after all.

Everybody else spent the following morning putting up Christmas decorations. Harry could not remember Sirius ever being in such a good mood; he was actually singing carols, apparently delighted that he was to have company over Christmas. Harry could hear his voice echoing up through the floor in the cold drawing room where he was sitting alone, watching the sky growing whiter outside the windows, threatening snow, all the time feeling a savage pleasure that he was giving the others the opportunity to keep talking about him, as they were bound to be doing. When he heard Mrs Weasley calling his name softly up the stairs around lunchtime, he retreated further upstairs and ignored her.

Around six o'clock in the evening the doorbell rang and Mrs Black started screaming again. Assuming that Mundungus or some other Order member had come to call, Harry merely settled himself more comfortably against the wall of Buckbeak's room where he was hiding, trying to ignore how hungry he felt as he fed dead rats to the Hippogriff. It came as a slight shock when somebody hammered hard on the door a few minutes later.

第23章 封闭病房中的圣诞节

他摸到了黑门，可是打不开……他站在那儿看着门，渴望能进去……那后面有他一心想要的东西……他梦想不到的宝贝……只希望他的伤疤不那么刺痛……他可以想清楚些……

"哈利，"罗恩的声音从遥远的地方传来，"妈妈说晚饭好了，但如果你不想起来，她可以给你留一点儿……"

哈利睁开眼睛，但罗恩已经离开了。

他不想单独跟我待在一起，哈利想，在听了穆迪的话之后……

他想，知道了他身上有什么，他们谁也不会要他了……

他不想下去吃饭，不想去讨人嫌。他翻了一下身，过一会儿又迷糊过去，醒来时已是凌晨，肚子饿得发痛，罗恩在旁边床上打着呼噜。哈利眯眼环顾四周，看见菲尼亚斯·奈杰勒斯又站在肖像中了，哈利想到邓布利多可能是派菲尼亚斯·奈杰勒斯来监视他的，怕他再伤人。

不洁的感觉增强了，他几乎希望自己没有听邓布利多的话留下来……如果以后在格里莫广场的生活就是这样，也许他还不如在女贞路呢。

上午其他人都忙着布置圣诞节的装饰。哈利不记得小天狼星什么时候有过这好的兴致，他居然唱起了圣诞颂歌，显然很高兴有人陪他过节。哈利听到小天狼星的声音穿过地板传来，而他一个人坐在这间冷冰冰的客厅里，看着窗外的天空越来越白，要下雪了。与此同时，想到别人有机会不停地议论他，他有一种残酷的快感。他们肯定会这么做的。午饭时听见韦斯莱夫人在楼梯上轻轻喊他的名字，他又往楼上躲了躲，没有答应。

晚上六点左右门铃响了，布莱克夫人又尖叫起来。哈利以为是蒙顿格斯或其他凤凰社成员来访，于是他躲在巴克比克的房间，在墙上靠得更舒服些，一边喂死老鼠给巴克比克，一边努力忘记自己有多饿。几分钟后有人咚咚敲门，他微微吃了一惊。

CHAPTER TWENTY-THREE   Christmas on the Closed Ward

'I know you're in there,' said Hermione's voice. 'Will you please come out? I want to talk to you.'

'What are *you* doing here?' Harry asked her, pulling open the door as Buckbeak resumed his scratching at the straw-strewn floor for any fragments of rat he may have dropped. 'I thought you were skiing with your mum and dad?'

'Well, to tell the truth, skiing's not *really* my thing,' said Hermione. 'So, I've come here for Christmas.' There was snow in her hair and her face was pink with cold. 'But don't tell Ron. I told him skiing's really good because he kept laughing so much. Mum and Dad are a bit disappointed, but I've told them that everyone who is serious about the exams is staying at Hogwarts to study. They want me to do well, they'll understand. Anyway,' she said briskly, 'let's go to your bedroom, Ron's mum has lit a fire in there and she's sent up sandwiches.'

Harry followed her back to the second floor. When he entered the bedroom, he was rather surprised to see both Ron and Ginny waiting for them, sitting on Ron's bed.

'I came on the Knight Bus,' said Hermione airily, pulling off her jacket before Harry had time to speak. 'Dumbledore told me what had happened yesterday morning, but I had to wait for term to end officially before setting off. Umbridge is already livid that you lot disappeared right under her nose, even though Dumbledore told her Mr Weasley was in St Mungo's and he'd given you all permission to visit. So ...'

She sat down next to Ginny, and the two girls and Ron all looked up at Harry.

'How're you feeling?' asked Hermione.

'Fine,' said Harry stiffly.

'Oh, don't lie, Harry,' she said impatiently. 'Ron and Ginny say you've been hiding from everyone since you got back from St Mungo's.'

'They do, do they?' said Harry, glaring at Ron and Ginny. Ron looked down at his feet but Ginny seemed quite unabashed.

'Well, you have!' she said. 'And you won't look at any of us!'

'It's you lot who won't look at me!' said Harry angrily.

'Maybe you're taking it in turns to look, and keep missing each other,' suggested Hermione, the corners of her mouth twitching.

'Very funny,' snapped Harry, turning away.

'Oh, stop feeling all misunderstood,' said Hermione sharply. 'Look, the others have told me what you overheard last night on the Extendable Ears –'

第23章 封闭病房中的圣诞节

"我知道你在这儿,"赫敏的声音说,"你出来好吗？我想跟你谈谈。"

"你到这儿来干什么？"哈利拉开门问,巴克比克又开始在铺着稻草的地上扒找它可能漏掉的老鼠肉,"我还以为你跟你爸妈去滑雪了呢。"

"唉,说实话,滑雪真不适合我,所以我是来过圣诞节的。"她头上沾着雪花,脸冻得红扑扑的,"可是别告诉罗恩,我对他说滑雪很棒,因为他老是笑我。总之,爸妈有点失望,但我说认真准备考试的人都留在霍格沃茨学习。他们希望我考好,所以会理解的。好了,"她轻松地说,"到你的卧室去吧,罗恩的妈妈在那儿生了火,还送了三明治上去。"

哈利跟她回到三楼,进屋时惊讶地看到罗恩和金妮正坐在罗恩的床上等着他们。

"我是坐骑士公共汽车来的。"哈利还没来得及开口,赫敏就活泼地说,一边脱掉外衣,"邓布利多昨天早上就告诉我了。可我必须等到学期正式结束才能走。你们在乌姆里奇眼皮底下消失,把她鼻子都气歪了,尽管邓布利多对她说韦斯莱先生在圣芒戈医院,是他批准你们去探视的。所以……"

她在金妮身边坐了下来,两个女孩和罗恩一起看着哈利。

"你感觉怎么样？"赫敏问。

"很好。"哈利生硬地答道。

"别撒谎了,哈利,"她不耐烦地说,"罗恩和金妮说你从圣芒戈回来后就一直躲着大家。"

"他们这么说的？"哈利瞪着罗恩和金妮。罗恩低头看着脚,金妮好像并没有什么不好意思。

"就是嘛！"她说,"你都不看我们！"

"是你们不看我！"哈利气愤地说。

"也许你们轮流看来看去,就是对不上。"赫敏说,嘴角轻轻颤动。

"很有趣吧。"哈利抢白了一句,背过脸去。

"喂,别老觉得别人误解你。"赫敏尖刻地说,"他们都告诉我了,你昨天用伸缩耳听到了什么——"

CHAPTER TWENTY-THREE   Christmas on the Closed Ward

'Yeah?' growled Harry, his hands deep in his pockets as he watched the snow now falling thickly outside. 'All been talking about me, have you? Well, I'm getting used to it.'

'We wanted to talk *to you*, Harry,' said Ginny, 'but as you've been hiding ever since we got back –'

'I didn't want anyone to talk to me,' said Harry, who was feeling more and more nettled.

'Well, that was a bit stupid of you,' said Ginny angrily, 'seeing as you don't know anyone but me who's been possessed by You-Know-Who, and I can tell you how it feels.'

Harry remained quite still as the impact of these words hit him. Then he turned on the spot to face her.

'I forgot,' he said.

'Lucky you,' said Ginny coolly.

'I'm sorry,' Harry said, and he meant it. 'So ... so, do you think I'm being possessed, then?'

'Well, can you remember everything you've been doing?' Ginny asked. 'Are there big blank periods where you don't know what you've been up to?'

Harry racked his brains.

'No,' he said.

'Then You-Know-Who hasn't ever possessed you,' said Ginny simply. 'When he did it to me, I couldn't remember what I'd been doing for hours at a time. I'd find myself somewhere and not know how I got there.'

Harry hardly dared believe her, yet his heart was lightening almost in spite of himself.

'That dream I had about your dad and the snake, though –'

'Harry, you've had these dreams before,' Hermione said. 'You had flashes of what Voldemort was up to last year.'

'This was different,' said Harry, shaking his head. 'I was *inside* that snake. It was like I *was* the snake ... what if Voldemort somehow transported me to London –?'

'One day,' said Hermione, sounding thoroughly exasperated, 'you'll read *Hogwarts: A History*, and perhaps it will remind you that you can't Apparate or Disapparate inside Hogwarts. Even Voldemort couldn't just make you fly out of your dormitory, Harry.'

第23章 封闭病房中的圣诞节

"是吗?"哈利吼道,他手插在兜里,看着外面纷纷扬扬的雪花,"都在说我,是不是?好啊,我都快习惯了……"

"我们希望跟你说话,哈利,"金妮说,"可你回来之后就一直躲着——"

"我不需要别人跟我说话。"哈利越来越火了。

"那你可有点傻,"金妮生气地说,"你认识的人里,只有我被神秘人附身过,我可以告诉你那是什么感觉。"

哈利呆立了一会儿,被这些话震住了,然后回过味来,转身看着金妮。

"我忘了。"

"你真走运。"金妮冷冷地说。

"对不起,"哈利真心地说,"那……你认为我是被附身了吗?"

"你能记得你做过的所有事吗?"金妮问,"有没有大段的空白,你不知道自己干了什么?"

哈利努力回想。

"没有。"他说。

"那神秘人就没有附在你身上。"金妮干脆地说,"他附到我身上的时候,我有几个小时都不知道干了些什么。我发现自己在一个地方,但不知道是怎么去的。"

哈利不大敢相信她,但他的心几乎不由自主地轻松起来。

"可我梦见你爸爸和蛇——"

"哈利,你以前也做过这种噩梦,"赫敏说,"去年你就看到过伏地魔在干什么。"

"这次不一样,"哈利摇头道,"我在蛇的身体里,好像我就是那条蛇……要是伏地魔用法力把我运到了伦敦——?"

"你哪天能看看《霍格沃茨:一段校史》就好了,"赫敏似乎大为气恼,"也许那会提醒你,在霍格沃茨不可能用幻影显形和移形,就连伏地魔也无法让你飞出宿舍,哈利。"

CHAPTER TWENTY-THREE   Christmas on the Closed Ward

'You didn't leave your bed, mate,' said Ron. 'I saw you thrashing around in your sleep for at least a minute before we could wake you up.'

Harry started pacing up and down the room again, thinking. What they were all saying was not only comforting, it made sense ... without really thinking, he took a sandwich from the plate on the bed and crammed it hungrily into his mouth.

I'm not the weapon after all, thought Harry. His heart swelled with happiness and relief, and he felt like joining in as they heard Sirius tramping past their door towards Buckbeak's room, singing 'God Rest Ye, Merry Hippogriffs' at the top of his voice.

How could he have dreamed of returning to Privet Drive for Christmas? Sirius's delight at having the house full again, and especially at having Harry back, was infectious. He was no longer their sullen host of the summer; now he seemed determined that everyone should enjoy themselves as much, if not more than they would have done at Hogwarts, and he worked tirelessly in the run-up to Christmas Day, cleaning and decorating with their help, so that by the time they all went to bed on Christmas Eve the house was barely recognisable. The tarnished chandeliers were no longer hung with cobwebs but with garlands of holly and gold and silver streamers; magical snow glittered in heaps over the threadbare carpets; a great Christmas tree, obtained by Mundungus and decorated with live fairies, blocked Sirius's family tree from view, and even the stuffed elf-heads on the hall wall wore Father Christmas hats and beards.

Harry awoke on Christmas morning to find a stack of presents at the foot of his bed and Ron already halfway through opening his own, rather larger, pile.

'Good haul this year,' he informed Harry through a cloud of paper. 'Thanks for the Broom Compass, it's excellent; beats Hermione's – she got me a *homework planner* –'

Harry sorted through his presents and found one with Hermione's handwriting on it. She had given him, too, a book that resembled a diary except that every time he opened a page it said aloud things like: '*Do it today or later you'll pay!*'

Sirius and Lupin had given Harry a set of excellent books entitled *Practical Defensive Magic and its Use Against the Dark Arts*, which had superb, moving colour

第23章 封闭病房中的圣诞节

"你没离开过你的床,哥们儿,"罗恩说,"在叫醒你至少一分钟前我还看到你在那儿翻来滚去……"

哈利又开始踱步,思考。他们的话不只是一种安慰,而且很有道理……他几乎想也没想就从床上的盘子里抓起一块三明治,贪婪地塞进了嘴里。

我不是那件武器,哈利想,他的心里涨满了快乐和解脱的感觉,听到小天狼星在门外高唱着"上帝保佑你,快乐的鹰头马身有翼兽"朝巴克比克的房间走去,他都想跟着唱。

他怎么会想回女贞路过圣诞节呢?小天狼星的快乐是有传染性的。小天狼星因为家里又住满了人而高兴,哈利的回来尤其让他高兴。他不再是夏天那个阴沉的主人了,现在他似乎决心要让每个人都像在霍格沃茨一样开心,如果不是更开心的话。他不知疲倦地为过节做准备,在大家的帮助下打扫和装饰房间。圣诞节前夜他们上床睡觉时,家里简直都认不出来了。生锈的吊灯上挂的不再是蜘蛛网,而是冬青花环和金银彩带,魔法变出的雪花亮晶晶地堆在破地毯上,蒙顿格斯搞来的一棵大圣诞树挡住了小天狼星的家谱,上面装饰着活的小仙子,就连门厅墙上摆放的那些小精灵脑袋也戴上了圣诞老人的帽子和胡子。

圣诞节早上哈利醒来后发现床脚有一堆礼物,罗恩的那堆更大一些,他已经拆了一半。

"今年大丰收,"罗恩在一堆包装纸中对哈利说,"谢谢你的扫帚指南针,太棒了,比赫敏的礼物好,她送了一个家庭作业计划簿——"

哈利翻到了一个有赫敏笔迹的礼包,她也送了他一个小本子,看上去跟日记本差不多,只是每翻开一页,它就会说"今日事,今日毕!"之类的话。

小天狼星和卢平送了哈利一套精美的图书:《实用防御魔法及其对抗黑魔法的应用》,里面的咒语和逆转咒都有彩色动画图解。哈利急切

CHAPTER TWENTY-THREE   Christmas on the Closed Ward

illustrations of all the counter-jinxes and hexes it described. Harry flicked through the first volume eagerly; he could see it was going to be highly useful in his plans for the DA. Hagrid had sent a furry brown wallet that had fangs, which were presumably supposed to be an anti-theft device, but unfortunately prevented Harry putting any money in without getting his fingers ripped off. Tonks's present was a small, working model of a Firebolt, which Harry watched fly around the room, wishing he still had his full-size version; Ron had given him an enormous box of Every-Flavour Beans, Mr and Mrs Weasley the usual hand-knitted jumper and some mince pies, and Dobby a truly dreadful painting that Harry suspected had been done by the elf himself. He had just turned it upside-down to see whether it looked better that way when, with a loud *crack*, Fred and George Apparated at the foot of his bed.

'Merry Christmas,' said George. 'Don't go downstairs for a bit.'

'Why not?' said Ron.

'Mum's crying again,' said Fred heavily. 'Percy sent back his Christmas jumper.'

'Without a note,' added George. 'Hasn't asked how Dad is or visited him or anything.'

'We tried to comfort her,' said Fred, moving around the bed to look at Harry's portrait. 'Told her Percy's nothing more than a humungous pile of rat droppings.'

'Didn't work,' said George, helping himself to a Chocolate Frog. 'So Lupin took over. Best let him cheer her up before we go down for breakfast, I reckon.'

'What's that supposed to be, anyway?' asked Fred, squinting at Dobby's painting. 'Looks like a gibbon with two black eyes.'

'It's Harry!' said George, pointing at the back of the picture, 'says so on the back!'

'Good likeness,' said Fred, grinning. Harry threw his new homework diary at him; it hit the wall opposite and fell to the floor where it said happily: '*If you've dotted the "i"s and crossed the "t"s then you may do whatever you please!*'

They got up and dressed. They could hear the various inhabitants of the house calling 'Merry Christmas' to one another. On their way downstairs they met Hermione.

'Thanks for the book, Harry,' she said happily. 'I've been wanting that *New Theory of Numerology* for ages! And that perfume's really unusual, Ron.'

第23章 封闭病房中的圣诞节

地翻了翻第一册，看出这书对他准备 D.A. 的活动很有用。海格送了他一个带尖牙的毛皮钱包，尖牙大概是防盗装置，可惜哈利往里面放钱时有被咬掉手指的可能。唐克斯的礼物是一个小小的火弩箭模型，哈利看着它在屋子里飞，希望那把真的扫帚还在他手里。罗恩给了他一大盒比比多味豆，韦斯莱夫妇的礼物还是手织的套头衫以及肉馅饼。多比送了一张很难看的图画，哈利怀疑是这小精灵自己画的。他刚要把图画倒过来看会不会好一点儿，只听响亮的啪的一声，弗雷德和乔治在床脚幻影显形了。

"圣诞快乐，"乔治说，"暂时别下楼。"

"为什么？"罗恩问。

"妈妈又哭了，"弗雷德沉重地说，"珀西把圣诞套头衫寄回来了。"

"连个字条都没有，"乔治说，"没问爸爸怎么样，也不去看他……"

"我们想安慰妈妈，"弗雷德一边说一边绕过床来看哈利手里的画，"对她说珀西不过是一堆老鼠屎——"

"——没用，"乔治说着拿了一块巧克力蛙吃，"所以卢平接了过去，最好等他把妈妈劝好了，我们再下去吃早饭。"

"这是什么？"弗雷德打量着多比的画问，"像一只长臂猿，长了两个黑眼睛。"

"是哈利！"乔治指着画的背面说，"后头写了。"

"很像。"弗雷德嘻嘻笑道。哈利把新的作业计划簿朝他扔过去，本子撞墙落地后开心地说："只要你在 i 上加了点，t 上加了横，什么事情都能干得成！"

他们起床穿衣，听见住在家里的人互道"圣诞快乐！"下楼时，他们碰到了赫敏。

"谢谢你的书，哈利！"她高兴地说，"我一直想要一本《数字占卜学新原理》！那瓶香水非常特别，罗恩。"

CHAPTER TWENTY-THREE Christmas on the Closed Ward

'No problem,' said Ron. 'Who's that for, anyway?' he added, nodding at the neatly wrapped present she was carrying.

'Kreacher,' said Hermione brightly.

'It had better not be clothes!' Ron warned her. 'You know what Sirius said: Kreacher knows too much, we can't set him free!'

'It isn't clothes,' said Hermione, 'although if I had my way I'd certainly give him something to wear other than that filthy old rag. No, it's a patchwork quilt, I thought it would brighten up his bedroom.'

'What bedroom?' said Harry, dropping his voice to a whisper as they were passing the portrait of Sirius's mother.

'Well, Sirius says it's not so much a bedroom, more a kind of – *den*,' said Hermione. 'Apparently he sleeps under the boiler in that cupboard off the kitchen.'

Mrs Weasley was the only person in the basement when they arrived there. She was standing at the stove and sounded as though she had a bad head cold as she wished them 'Merry Christmas', and they all averted their eyes.

'So, is this Kreacher's bedroom?' said Ron, strolling over to a dingy door in the corner opposite the pantry. Harry had never seen it open.

'Yes,' said Hermione, now sounding a little nervous. 'Er ... I think we'd better knock.'

Ron rapped on the door with his knuckles but there was no reply.

'He must be sneaking around upstairs,' he said, and without further ado pulled open the door. '*Urgh!*'

Harry peered inside. Most of the cupboard was taken up with a very large and old-fashioned boiler, but in the foot of space underneath the pipes Kreacher had made himself something that looked like a nest. A jumble of assorted rags and smelly old blankets were piled on the floor and the small dent in the middle of it showed where Kreacher curled up to sleep every night. Here and there among the material were stale bread crusts and mouldy old bits of cheese. In a far corner glinted small objects and coins that Harry guessed Kreacher had saved, magpie-like, from Sirius's purge of the house, and he had also managed to retrieve the silver-framed family photographs that Sirius had thrown away over the summer. Their glass might be shattered, but still the little black-and-white people inside them peered up at him haughtily, including – he felt a little jolt in his stomach – the dark, heavy-lidded woman whose trial he had witnessed in Dumbledore's

第23章 封闭病房中的圣诞节

"别客气,"罗恩说,"那是给谁的?"他看着她手里那个漂亮的礼包问。

"克利切。"赫敏愉快地说。

"最好别是衣服!"罗恩警告道,"你知道小天狼星说的,克利切知道得太多,我们不能把他放走!"

"不是衣服,"赫敏说,"虽然要按我的意思,准会让他换下那块臭烘烘的破布。这只是一条花被子,我想可以让他的卧室亮堂一点儿。"

"什么卧室?"哈利压低了嗓门,因为他们正从小天狼星母亲的肖像旁走过。

"哦,小天狼星说算不上卧室,不过是个——窝。"赫敏说,"克利切似乎睡在厨房锅炉间里的锅炉下面。"

韦斯莱夫人独自待在地下室,她站在炉边祝他们圣诞快乐的时候,听上去像得了重感冒。他们都移开了目光。

"这就是克利切的房间?"罗恩说,走到食品间对面角落里一扇黑乎乎的门前,哈利从没看到这扇门打开过。

"是,"赫敏现在听起来有点紧张,"嗯……我想我们最好敲敲门……"

罗恩用指节敲了敲门,里面没声音。

"他一定溜上楼了。"他说,不管三七二十一拉开了房门,"啊!"

哈利朝里面看去,空间大部分都被一个老式的大锅炉占了,但在管子下面一尺来宽的地方,克利切给自己弄了一个窝,地上堆着各种各样的破布和气味难闻的旧毯子,中间一小块凹陷处便是克利切每天晚上蜷着身子睡觉的地方。到处散落着变质的面包屑和发了霉的奶酪。紧里头的角落里有一些闪闪发光的小玩意儿和硬币,哈利估计是克利切一点一滴从小天狼星的手里抢救下来的。连小天狼星夏天扔掉的那些银相框的家庭照片也在。玻璃虽然碎了,但里面黑白照片上的人还高傲地望着他,包括他在邓布利多的冥想盆里看到的那个黑头发、肿眼皮的女人:贝拉特里克斯·莱斯特兰奇——哈利觉得胃里抽搐了一下。

CHAPTER TWENTY-THREE   Christmas on the Closed Ward

Pensieve: Bellatrix Lestrange. By the looks of it, hers was Kreacher's favourite photograph; he had placed it to the fore of all the others and had mended the glass clumsily with Spellotape.

'I think I'll just leave his present here,' said Hermione, laying the package neatly in the middle of the depression in the rags and blankets and closing the door quietly. 'He'll find it later, that'll be fine.'

'Come to think of it,' said Sirius, emerging from the pantry carrying a large turkey as they closed the cupboard door, 'has anyone actually seen Kreacher lately?'

'I haven't seen him since the night we came back here,' said Harry. 'You were ordering him out of the kitchen.'

'Yeah ...' said Sirius, frowning. 'You know, I think that's the last time I saw him, too ... he must be hiding upstairs somewhere.'

'He couldn't have left, could he?' said Harry. 'I mean, when you said *"out"*, maybe he thought you meant get out of the house?'

'No, no, house-elves can't leave unless they're given clothes. They're tied to their family's house,' said Sirius.

'They can leave the house if they really want to,' Harry contradicted him. 'Dobby did, he left the Malfoys' to give me warnings three years ago. He had to punish himself afterwards, but he still managed it.'

Sirius looked slightly disconcerted for a moment, then said, 'I'll look for him later, I expect I'll find him upstairs crying his eyes out over my mother's old bloomers or something. Of course, he might have crawled into the airing cupboard and died ... but I mustn't get my hopes up.'

Fred, George and Ron laughed; Hermione, however, looked reproachful.

Once they had eaten their Christmas lunch, the Weasleys, Harry and Hermione were planning to pay Mr Weasley another visit, escorted by Mad-Eye and Lupin. Mundungus turned up in time for Christmas pudding and trifle, having managed to 'borrow' a car for the occasion, as the Underground did not run on Christmas Day. The car, which Harry doubted very much had been taken with the consent of its owner, had been enlarged with a spell like the Weasleys' old Ford Anglia had once been. Although normally proportioned outside, ten people with Mundungus driving were able to fit into it quite comfortably. Mrs Weasley hesitated before getting inside – Harry knew her disapproval of Mundungus was battling with her dislike of

第23章 封闭病房中的圣诞节

看来她是克利切最喜欢的照片，他把她放在最前面，而且用魔术胶带笨拙地把玻璃粘了起来。

"我就把给他的礼物留在这儿吧，"赫敏利落地把礼包放在破布和毯子中间的凹处，轻轻带上房门，"他会发现的，没关系……"

"想想看，"他们关上锅炉间的门时，小天狼星刚好从食品间端了一只大火鸡出来，"最近谁见到克利切了？"

"我从来的那天晚上之后就没见过他。"哈利说，"你把他从厨房里轰了出去。"

"对了……"小天狼星皱着眉说，"我想那也是我最后一次见他……他准是藏在楼上……"

"他不会走了吧？"哈利说，"你说'出去'，他可能会以为你叫他离开这所房子？"

"不会，家养小精灵没有衣服不能离开，他们被束缚在主人家里。"小天狼星说。

"他们要真想离开的话是可以走的。"哈利提出了异议，"多比就是，三年前他就离开了马尔福家来给我报信。他后来不得不惩罚自己，但他还是出来了。"

小天狼星似乎有点不安，然后说："我过会儿去找他，我想我会发现他正在楼上对着我妈妈的旧布鲁姆女裤痛哭流涕呢……当然，他也可能爬到晾衣柜里一命呜呼……但我不能抱太大的希望……"

弗雷德、乔治和罗恩笑了起来，但赫敏用责备的眼光看着他们。

吃了圣诞午餐之后，韦斯莱一家、哈利和赫敏打算再去看看韦斯莱先生，由疯眼汉和卢平护送。蒙顿格斯赶上了吃圣诞布丁和果冻蛋糕，因为圣诞节地铁不开，他"借"了一辆车子，但哈利很怀疑他是否征得了主人同意。这部车子也像韦斯莱家的老福特安格里亚一样加了扩大咒，外面大小正常，但十个人坐进去再加上开车的蒙顿格斯都不挤。韦斯莱夫人犹豫了一阵子，哈利知道，她对蒙顿格斯不满，但又不愿用非魔法的方式旅行，因而内心十分纠结。最后车外的严寒和子女们

CHAPTER TWENTY-THREE   Christmas on the Closed Ward

travelling without magic – but, finally, the cold outside and her children's pleading triumphed, and she settled herself into the back seat between Fred and Bill with good grace.

The journey to St Mungo's was quite quick as there was very little traffic on the roads. A small trickle of witches and wizards was creeping furtively up the otherwise deserted street to visit the hospital. Harry and the others got out of the car, and Mundungus drove off around the corner to wait for them. They strolled casually towards the window where the dummy in green nylon stood, then, one by one, stepped through the glass.

The reception area looked pleasantly festive: the crystal orbs that illuminated St Mungo's had been coloured red and gold to become gigantic, glowing Christmas baubles; holly hung around every doorway; and shining white Christmas trees covered in magical snow and icicles glittered in every corner, each one topped with a gleaming gold star. It was less crowded than the last time they had been there, although halfway across the room Harry found himself shunted aside by a witch with a satsuma jammed up her left nostril.

'Family argument, eh?' smirked the blonde witch behind the desk. 'You're the third I've seen today ... Spell Damage, fourth floor.'

They found Mr Weasley propped up in bed with the remains of his turkey dinner on a tray on his lap and a rather sheepish expression on his face.

'Everything all right, Arthur?' asked Mrs Weasley, after they had all greeted Mr Weasley and handed over their presents.

'Fine, fine,' said Mr Weasley, a little too heartily. 'You – er – haven't seen Healer Smethwyck, have you?'

'No,' said Mrs Weasley suspiciously, 'why?'

'Nothing, nothing,' said Mr Weasley airily, starting to unwrap his pile of gifts. 'Well, everyone had a good day? What did you all get for Christmas? Oh, *Harry* – this is absolutely *wonderful*!' For he had just opened Harry's gift of fuse-wire and screwdrivers.

Mrs Weasley did not seem entirely satisfied with Mr Weasley's answer. As her husband leaned over to shake Harry's hand, she peered at the bandaging under his nightshirt.

'Arthur,' she said, with a snap in her voice like a mousetrap, 'you've had your bandages changed. Why have you had your bandages changed a day early, Arthur? They told me they wouldn't need doing until tomorrow.'

第23章 封闭病房中的圣诞节

的恳求取得了胜利，韦斯莱夫人高高兴兴地坐到了后排弗雷德和乔治的中间。

他们很快就到了圣芒戈，一路上车辆稀少，只有一些去医院的巫师悄悄走在寂静无人的街上。哈利等人下了车，蒙顿格斯把车开过街角去等他们。他们溜达到穿绿尼龙裙的假人站的橱窗跟前，然后一个一个穿过了玻璃。

候诊室里一派节日的气氛：明亮的水晶泡泡变成了红色和金色，像巨大的圣诞彩球不断闪烁。每个门口都挂着冬青，用魔法加盖了白雪和冰凌的圣诞树在每个屋角闪闪发亮，树尖顶着一颗闪烁的金星。人没有上次那么多，但在屋子中间哈利还是被一个左鼻孔塞了个小蜜橘的女巫挤到了一边。

"家庭纠纷，嗯？"问讯台后面那个金发女巫幸灾乐祸地说，"你是我今天看到的第三位……咒语伤害科，五楼……"

他们发现韦斯莱先生倚在床上，腿上的托盘里放着吃剩的火鸡套餐，脸上带着绵羊般温顺的表情。

"情况怎么样，亚瑟？"大家向他问过好，送了礼物之后，韦斯莱夫人问。

"很好，很好。"韦斯莱先生的语气有点过分热情，"你——呃——没见到斯梅绥克治疗师吧？"

"没有啊，"韦斯莱夫人起了疑心，"怎么啦？"

"没什么，没什么。"韦斯莱先生轻松地说，开始拆那堆礼物，"今天都过得开心吗？得了什么礼物？哦，哈利——这个太棒了——"他打开了哈利送的保险丝和螺丝刀。

韦斯莱夫人似乎对他的回答不大满意。当韦斯莱先生侧过来和哈利握手时，她看了看他睡衣里的绷带。

"亚瑟，"她说，嗓音像捕鼠夹发出的声音一样尖脆，"你换了绷带。为什么早换了一天，亚瑟？他们说要明天才换呢。"

CHAPTER TWENTY-THREE   Christmas on the Closed Ward

'What?' said Mr Weasley, looking rather frightened and pulling the bed covers higher up his chest. 'No, no – it's nothing – it's – I –'

He seemed to deflate under Mrs Weasley's piercing gaze.

'Well – now don't get upset, Molly, but Augustus Pye had an idea ... he's the Trainee Healer, you know, lovely young chap and very interested in ... um ... complementary medicine ... I mean, some of these old Muggle remedies ... well, they're called *stitches*, Molly, and they work very well on – on Muggle wounds –'

Mrs Weasley let out an ominous noise somewhere between a shriek and a snarl. Lupin strolled away from the bed and over to the werewolf, who had no visitors and was looking rather wistfully at the crowd around Mr Weasley; Bill muttered something about getting himself a cup of tea and Fred and George leapt up to accompany him, grinning.

'Do you mean to tell me,' said Mrs Weasley, her voice growing louder with every word and apparently unaware that her fellow visitors were scurrying for cover, 'that you have been messing about with Muggle remedies?'

'Not messing about, Molly, dear,' said Mr Weasley imploringly, 'it was just – just something Pye and I thought we'd try – only, most unfortunately – well, with these particular kinds of wounds – it doesn't seem to work as well as we'd hoped –'

'*Meaning?*'

'Well ... well, I don't know whether you know what – what stitches are?'

'It sounds as though you've been trying to sew your skin back together,' said Mrs Weasley with a snort of mirthless laughter, 'but even you, Arthur, wouldn't be *that* stupid –'

'I fancy a cup of tea, too,' said Harry, jumping to his feet.

Hermione, Ron and Ginny almost sprinted to the door with him. As it swung closed behind them, they heard Mrs Weasley shriek, 'WHAT DO YOU MEAN, THAT'S THE GENERAL IDEA?'

'Typical Dad,' said Ginny, shaking her head as they set off up the corridor. 'Stitches ... I ask you ...'

'Well, you know, they do work well on non-magical wounds,' said Hermione fairly. 'I suppose something in that snake's venom dissolves them or something. I wonder where the tearoom is?'

'Fifth floor,' said Harry, remembering the sign over the welcome-witch's desk.

第23章 封闭病房中的圣诞节

"啊?"韦斯莱先生好像很害怕,把被单拉到了胸口以上,"没有——没什么——这是——我——"

他似乎在韦斯莱夫人锐利的目光下泄了气。

"唉——别生气,莫丽,奥古斯都·派伊出了个主意……你知道,他是实习治疗师,一个可爱的年轻人,爱研究……这个……辅助性治疗……我是说一些麻瓜的老疗法……叫作缝线,莫丽,它对——对麻瓜的伤口很有效——"

韦斯莱夫人发出一声介于尖叫和咆哮之间的可怕声音。卢平走到狼人床前——他没人探视,正愁闷地望着韦斯莱先生身边的这群人。比尔嘀咕说要去拿杯茶,弗雷德和乔治跳起来要跟他一起去,一边咧着嘴笑。

"你想告诉我,"韦斯莱夫人一个字比一个字说得响,似乎没发觉其他人都在惊慌逃窜,"你在瞎用麻瓜的疗法?"

"不是瞎用,莫丽,亲爱的,"韦斯莱先生恳求地说,"只是——只是派伊和我想试试——只可惜——对这种特殊的伤口——它没有我们预期的那么有效——"

"什么意思?"

"呃……这个,我不知道你懂不懂——缝线是怎么回事?"

"听上去好像你想把你的皮肤缝起来,"韦斯莱夫人冷笑一声说,"可是,亚瑟,你也不至于那么愚蠢——"

"我也想要一杯茶。"哈利跳起来说。

赫敏、罗恩和金妮几乎是和他一起冲到门口的。关门时他们听到了韦斯莱夫人的尖叫:"**你说什么?原理就是这样?**"

"这就是爸爸。"金妮摇头说,他们沿着过道走去,"缝线……我问你……"

"哦,它对非魔法伤口挺有效的,"赫敏公正地说,"我想蛇毒里准是有什么东西把它化掉了……茶室在哪儿呀?"

"六楼。"哈利想起了问讯处的牌子。

855

CHAPTER TWENTY-THREE   Christmas on the Closed Ward

They walked along the corridor, through a set of double doors and found a rickety staircase lined with more portraits of brutal-looking Healers. As they climbed it, the various Healers called out to them, diagnosing odd complaints and suggesting horrible remedies. Ron was seriously affronted when a medieval wizard called out that he clearly had a bad case of spattergroit.

'And what's that supposed to be?' he asked angrily, as the Healer pursued him through six more portraits, shoving the occupants out of the way.

'''Tis a most grievous affliction of the skin, young master, that will leave you pockmarked and more gruesome even than you are now –'

'Watch who you're calling gruesome!' said Ron, his ears turning red.

'– the only remedy is to take the liver of a toad, bind it tight about your throat, stand naked at the full moon in a barrel of eels' eyes –'

'I have not got spattergroit!'

'But the unsightly blemishes upon your visage, young master –'

'They're freckles!' said Ron furiously. 'Now get back in your own picture and leave me alone!'

He rounded on the others, who were all keeping determinedly straight faces. 'What floor's this?'

'I think it's the fifth,' said Hermione.

'Nah, it's the fourth,' said Harry, 'one more –'

But as he stepped on to the landing he came to an abrupt halt, staring at the small window set into the double doors that marked the start of a corridor signposted SPELL DAMAGE. A man was peering out at them all with his nose pressed against the glass. He had wavy blond hair, bright blue eyes and a broad vacant smile that revealed dazzlingly white teeth.

'Blimey!' said Ron, also staring at the man.

'Oh, my goodness,' said Hermione suddenly, sounding breathless. 'Professor Lockhart!'

Their ex-Defence Against the Dark Arts teacher pushed open the doors and moved towards them, wearing a long lilac dressing gown.

'Well, hello there!' he said. 'I expect you'd like my autograph, would you?'

'Hasn't changed much, has he?' Harry muttered to Ginny, who grinned.

'Er – how are you, Professor?' said Ron, sounding slightly guilty. It had been Ron's malfunctioning wand that had damaged Professor Lockhart's memory so badly that he had landed in St Mungo's in the first place, though

第23章 封闭病房中的圣诞节

他们沿着走廊走过一道道双扇门,看到了一架摇摇晃晃的楼梯,墙上挂着面目狰狞的治疗师的肖像。爬楼梯的时候,那些治疗师冲他们嚷嚷,诊断出稀奇古怪的病症,想出种种可怕的疗法。罗恩气得够呛,有个中世纪的巫师叫喊说他显然有严重的散花痘。

"那是什么东西?"他气愤地问,那治疗师把画中人推到一边,追了罗恩六个相框。

"此乃皮肤沉疴,少爷,会留有疤痕,令您比目前还不中看——"

"你说谁不中看?"罗恩的耳根红了。

"唯有取蟾蜍之肝贴于喉部,于望日月光朗朗之时赤身裸体立于一桶鳗鱼目中——"

"我没有散花痘!"

"可您面现触目瑕疵,少爷——"

"这是雀斑!"罗恩大怒,"回你自己的相框里去,别缠着我!"

他转向竭力绷着脸的其他几个人。

"这是几楼?"

"我想是六楼。"赫敏说。

"不,是五楼,"哈利说,"还有一层——"

可是走上平台时,他突然停住了脚步,瞪着标有**咒语伤害科**的双扇门上的小窗。一个男子鼻子压在玻璃上,在盯着他们看:金色的鬈发,明亮的蓝眼睛,一副茫然的笑容,露出白得耀眼的牙齿。

"哎呀!"罗恩也瞪着那男子。

"天哪,"赫敏突然惊叫道,听起来像喘不过气一样,"洛哈特教授!"

前黑魔法防御术课教师推门走了出来,穿着一件丁香紫色的长袍。

"你们好!"他说,"我想你们是要我签名,是不是?"

"没变多少。"哈利小声地对金妮说,金妮笑了。

"呃——您好吗,教授?"罗恩的语气有点内疚,是他的魔杖出了故障,破坏了洛哈特教授的记忆,才使他住进了圣芒戈。当时洛哈特是想永远抹去哈利和罗恩的记忆,所以哈利此时对洛哈特的同

CHAPTER TWENTY-THREE Christmas on the Closed Ward

as Lockhart had been attempting to permanently wipe Harry and Ron's memories at the time, Harry's sympathy was limited.

'I'm very well indeed, thank you!' said Lockhart exuberantly, pulling a rather battered peacock-feather quill from his pocket. 'Now, how many autographs would you like? I can do joined-up writing now, you know!'

'Er – we don't want any at the moment, thanks,' said Ron, raising his eyebrows at Harry, who asked, 'Professor, should you be wandering around the corridors? Shouldn't you be in a ward?'

The smile faded slowly from Lockhart's face. For a few moments he gazed intently at Harry, then he said, 'Haven't we met?'

'Er ... yeah, we have,' said Harry. 'You used to teach us at Hogwarts, remember?'

'Teach?' repeated Lockhart, looking faintly unsettled. 'Me? Did I?'

And then the smile reappeared upon his face so suddenly it was rather alarming.

'Taught you everything you know, I expect, did I? Well, how about those autographs, then? Shall we say a round dozen, you can give them to all your little friends then and nobody will be left out!'

But just then a head poked out of a door at the far end of the corridor and a voice called, 'Gilderoy, you naughty boy, where have you wandered off to?'

A motherly-looking Healer wearing a tinsel wreath in her hair came bustling up the corridor, smiling warmly at Harry and the others.

'Oh, Gilderoy, you've got visitors! How *lovely*, and on Christmas Day, too! Do you know, he *never* gets visitors, poor lamb, and I can't think why, he's such a sweetie, aren't you?'

'We're doing autographs!' Gilderoy told the Healer with another glittering smile. 'They want loads of them, won't take no for an answer! I just hope we've got enough photographs!'

'Listen to him,' said the Healer, taking Lockhart's arm and beaming fondly at him as though he were a precocious two-year-old. 'He was rather well known a few years ago; we very much hope that this liking for giving autographs is a sign that his memory might be starting to come back. Will you step this way? He's in a closed ward, you know, he must have slipped out while I was bringing in the Christmas presents, the door's usually kept locked ... not that he's dangerous! But,' she lowered her voice to a whisper, 'he's a bit of a danger to himself, bless him ... doesn't know who he is, you see, wanders off and can't remember how to get back ... it *is* nice of you to have come to see him.'

情有限。

"我很好,谢谢!"洛哈特热情洋溢地说,从兜里掏出一支磨破的孔雀羽毛笔,"你们想要多少签名?你们知道,我能写连笔字了!"

"哦……我们现在不需要,谢谢。"罗恩说着对哈利扬起了眉毛,于是哈利问:"教授,您怎么在走廊里闲逛?您不应该在病房里吗?"

洛哈特脸上的笑容渐渐消失了,他盯着哈利看了一会儿,然后说:"我们以前见过吗?"

"哦……见过。"哈利说,"您在霍格沃茨教过我们,记得吗?"

"教过?"洛哈特说,显得有点疑惑,"我吗?"

然后笑容又回到他的脸上,突然得令人害怕。

"教了你们所有的知识,是吧?好,你要多少签名?整整一打怎么样,你可以送给所有的小朋友,一个也不漏!"

但这时一个脑袋从走廊另一头的门后探出来叫道:"吉德罗,淘气的孩子,你跑到哪儿去了?"

一个头上戴着金银丝花环的如母亲般的治疗师匆匆跑来,热情地对哈利等人微笑着。

"哦,吉德罗,有人来看你!太好了,而且是圣诞节!你们知道吗,从来没有人探视过他,可怜的小羊羔,我想不出为什么,他这么可爱,对不对?"

"我们在签名!"吉德罗又对治疗师灿烂地一笑,"他们要好多,不给不答应!但愿我有那么多照片!"

"听听,"治疗师拉起洛哈特的手臂,宠爱地看着他,仿佛他是个早熟的两岁儿童,"他几年前很有名,我们希望这种给人签名的爱好意味着他的记忆有所恢复。请这边走好吗?他住的是封闭式病房,一定是趁我拿礼物进去的时候溜出来的,那扇门通常都锁着……他不危险!只是,"她压低了声音,"对他自己有点危险,上帝保佑他……不知道自己是谁,走出去了就不记得怎么回来……你们来看他真是太好了——"

CHAPTER TWENTY-THREE — Christmas on the Closed Ward

'Er,' said Ron, gesturing uselessly at the floor above, 'actually, we were just – er –'

But the Healer was smiling expectantly at them, and Ron's feeble mutter of 'going to have a cup of tea' trailed away into nothingness. They looked at each other helplessly, then followed Lockhart and his Healer along the corridor.

'Let's not stay long,' Ron said quietly.

The Healer pointed her wand at the door of the Janus Thickey Ward and muttered, '*Alohomora.*' The door swung open and she led the way inside, keeping a firm grasp on Gilderoy's arm until she had settled him into an armchair beside his bed.

'This is our long-term residents' ward,' she informed Harry, Ron, Hermione and Ginny in a low voice. 'For permanent spell damage, you know. Of course, with intensive remedial potions and charms and a bit of luck, we can produce some improvement. Gilderoy does seem to be getting back some sense of himself; and we've seen a real improvement in Mr Bode, he seems to be regaining the power of speech very well, though he isn't speaking any language we recognise yet. Well, I must finish giving out the Christmas presents, I'll leave you all to chat.'

Harry looked around. The ward bore unmistakeable signs of being a permanent home to its residents. They had many more personal effects around their beds than in Mr Weasley's ward; the wall around Gilderoy's headboard, for instance, was papered with pictures of himself, all beaming toothily and waving at the new arrivals. He had autographed many of them to himself in disjointed, childish writing. The moment he had been deposited in his chair by the Healer, Gilderoy pulled a fresh stack of photographs towards him, seized a quill and started signing them all feverishly.

'You can put them in envelopes,' he said to Ginny, throwing the signed pictures into her lap one by one as he finished them. 'I am not forgotten, you know, no, I still receive a very great deal of fan mail ... Gladys Gudgeon writes *weekly* ... I just wish I knew *why* ...' He paused, looking faintly puzzled, then beamed again and returned to his signing with renewed vigour. 'I suspect it is simply my good looks ...'

A sallow-skinned, mournful-looking wizard lay in the bed opposite staring at the ceiling; he was mumbling to himself and seemed quite unaware of anything around him. Two beds along was a woman whose entire head was covered in fur; Harry remembered something similar happening to Hermione during their second year, although fortunately the damage, in her case, had not been permanent. At the far end of the ward flowery curtains had been drawn around two beds to give the occupants and their visitors some privacy.

第23章 封闭病房中的圣诞节

"啊,"罗恩徒然地指着楼上,"其实,我们只是——哦——"

可是治疗师期待地冲着他们微笑,罗恩"想去喝杯茶"的嗫嚅低得听不见了。他们无可奈何地对视了一下,跟着洛哈特和治疗师走去。

"别待太久。"罗恩小声说。

治疗师用魔杖指着杰纳斯·西奇病房的门,念了声"阿拉霍洞开",门应声而开。她领头走了进去,一只手紧紧抓着吉德罗的胳膊,让他坐在了床边的扶手椅上。

"这是我们的长住病房,"她低声对哈利、罗恩、赫敏和金妮说,"永久性咒语伤害。当然,依靠药物和咒语强化治疗再加上一点运气,可以使病情有所好转……吉德罗确实好像恢复了一些意识。博德先生进步很大,他的说话能力恢复得不错,尽管他还没说过我们能听懂的话……好了,我得发完圣诞礼物,你们聊一会儿……"

哈利打量着这间病房,它显然是病人长住的家。病床周围的私人物品比韦斯莱先生那边的多得多。吉德罗的床头板周围的墙上贴着他自己的照片,都在向新来者露齿微笑,挥手致意。许多照片是他签给自己的,笔画幼稚零乱。他刚被治疗师按到椅子上,就拉过一沓照片,抓起羽毛笔,疯狂地签起名来。

"你可以把它们放在信封里,"他对金妮说,把签好的照片一张张扔到她膝上,"我没被遗忘,没有,我仍然收到许多崇拜者的来信……格拉迪丝·古吉翁每周都写……我真搞不懂为什么……"他停了下来,似乎有点困惑,随即又露出笑容,起劲地签起名来,"我想只是因为我相貌英俊……"

一个面色灰黄、愁眉苦脸的男巫躺在对面的床上,盯着天花板自言自语,仿佛对周围事物不知不觉。隔了两张床是一个满脸长毛的女人,哈利想起二年级时赫敏也有过类似的经历,幸好她的损容不是永久性的。病房另一头的两张床有花帘子围着,给病人和探视者一些隐私。

CHAPTER TWENTY-THREE   Christmas on the Closed Ward

'Here you are, Agnes,' said the Healer brightly to the furry-faced woman, handing her a small pile of Christmas presents. 'See, not forgotten, are you? And your son's sent an owl to say he's visiting tonight, so that's nice, isn't it?'

Agnes gave several loud barks.

'And look, Broderick, you've been sent a pot plant and a lovely calendar with a different fancy Hippogriff for each month; they'll brighten things up, won't they?' said the Healer, bustling along to the mumbling man, setting a rather ugly plant with long, swaying tentacles on the bedside cabinet and fixing the calendar to the wall with her wand. 'And – oh, Mrs Longbottom, are you leaving already?'

Harry's head spun round. The curtains had been drawn back from the two beds at the end of the ward and two visitors were walking back down the aisle between the beds: a formidable-looking old witch wearing a long green dress, a moth-eaten fox fur and a pointed hat decorated with what was unmistakeably a stuffed vulture and, trailing behind her looking thoroughly depressed – *Neville*.

With a sudden rush of understanding, Harry realised who the people in the end beds must be. He cast around wildly for some means of distracting the others so that Neville could leave the ward unnoticed and unquestioned, but Ron had also looked up at the sound of the name 'Longbottom', and before Harry could stop him had called out, '*Neville!*'

Neville jumped and cowered as though a bullet had narrowly missed him.

'It's us, Neville!' said Ron brightly, getting to his feet. 'Have you seen –? Lockhart's here! Who've you been visiting?'

'Friends of yours, Neville, dear?' said Neville's grandmother graciously, bearing down upon them all.

Neville looked as though he would rather be anywhere in the world but here. A dull purple flush was creeping up his plump face and he was not making eye contact with any of them.

'Ah, yes,' said his grandmother, peering at Harry and sticking out a shrivelled, clawlike hand for him to shake. 'Yes, yes, I know who you are, of course. Neville speaks most highly of you.'

'Er – thanks,' said Harry, shaking hands. Neville did not look at him, but stared at his own feet, the colour deepening in his face all the while.

'And you two are clearly Weasleys,' Mrs Longbottom continued, proffering her hand regally to Ron and Ginny in turn. 'Yes, I know your parents – not well,

第23章 封闭病房中的圣诞节

"你的,阿格尼丝,"治疗师愉快地跟脸上长毛的女人打招呼,递给她一小堆圣诞礼物,"看,没有被忘记吧?你儿子派了猫头鹰来说他晚上来看你,真不错,是不是?"

阿格尼丝响亮地吠叫了几声。

"布罗德里克,你看,有人送给你一盆植物,还有一个漂亮的日历,每个月是不同的鹰头马身有翼兽,会带给你好心情的,是不是?"治疗师快步走到自言自语的男子跟前,把一盆怪难看的植物放在他的床头柜上,又用魔杖把日历挂到墙上,那植物上的长触手摆来摆去。"还有——哦,隆巴顿夫人,您这就走吗?"

哈利猛地转过头。病房那头的帘子已经拉开,有两人从床边走了出来:一个可怕的老女巫,穿着一件绿色的长袍,披着虫蛀的狐皮,尖帽子上装饰的无疑是一只秃鹫的标本,她后面跟着一个看上去闷闷不乐的——纳威。

哈利突然意识到那边两张床上的病人是谁了。他拼命想转移其他人的注意,让纳威悄悄走出病房,不被询问。但罗恩听到"隆巴顿"也抬起头来,哈利没来得及制止,他已经叫出了声:"纳威!"

纳威浑身一震,畏缩了一下,仿佛一颗子弹刚从他身旁擦过。

"是我们,纳威!"罗恩高兴地站了起来,"你看见了吗?洛哈特在这儿!你来看谁?"

"是你的朋友吗,纳威,小乖乖?"纳威的奶奶亲切地说着,向他们走来。

纳威似乎宁愿自己在世界上任何地方,就是不要在这里。他圆鼓鼓的脸上泛起紫红色,没有接触他们的目光。

"啊,对了,"他奶奶凝视着哈利,伸出一只枯干的、鹰爪般的手给他握,"对,对,我当然知道你是谁。纳威对你评价很高。"

"呃——谢谢。"哈利和她握了握手。纳威没有看哈利,只盯着自己的脚,脸上越来越紫。

"你们两个显然是韦斯莱家的,"隆巴顿夫人高贵地把手伸给了罗

CHAPTER TWENTY-THREE   Christmas on the Closed Ward

of course – but fine people, fine people ... and you must be Hermione Granger?'

Hermione looked rather startled that Mrs Longbottom knew her name, but shook hands all the same.

'Yes, Neville's told me all about you. Helped him out of a few sticky spots, haven't you? He's a good boy,' she said, casting a sternly appraising look down her rather bony nose at Neville, 'but he hasn't got his father's talent, I'm afraid to say.' And she jerked her head in the direction of the two beds at the end of the ward, so that the stuffed vulture on her hat trembled alarmingly.

'What?' said Ron, looking amazed. (Harry wanted to stamp on Ron's foot, but that sort of thing is much harder to bring off unnoticed when you're wearing jeans rather than robes.) 'Is that your *dad* down the end, Neville?'

'What's this?' said Mrs Longbottom sharply. 'Haven't you told your friends about your parents, Neville?'

Neville took a deep breath, looked up at the ceiling and shook his head. Harry could not remember ever feeling sorrier for anyone, but he could not think of any way of helping Neville out of the situation.

'Well, it's nothing to be ashamed of!' said Mrs Longbottom angrily. 'You should be *proud*, Neville, *proud*! They didn't give their health and their sanity so their only son would be ashamed of them, you know!'

'I'm not ashamed,' said Neville, very faintly, still looking anywhere but at Harry and the others. Ron was now standing on tiptoe to look over at the inhabitants of the two beds.

'Well, you've got a funny way of showing it!' said Mrs Longbottom. 'My son and his wife,' she said, turning haughtily to Harry, Ron, Hermione and Ginny, 'were tortured into insanity by You-Know-Who's followers.'

Hermione and Ginny both clapped their hands over their mouths. Ron stopped craning his neck to catch a glimpse of Neville's parents and looked mortified.

'They were Aurors, you know, and very well respected within the wizarding community,' Mrs Longbottom went on. 'Highly gifted, the pair of them. I – yes, Alice dear, what is it?'

Neville's mother had come edging down the ward in her nightdress. She no longer had the plump, happy-looking face Harry had seen in Moody's old photograph of the original Order of the Phoenix. Her face was thin and worn now, her eyes seemed overlarge and her hair, which had turned white, was wispy and dead-looking. She did not seem to want to speak, or perhaps

第23章 封闭病房中的圣诞节

恩和金妮,"对,我认识你们的父母——当然,不大熟——是好人,好人……你一定是赫敏·格兰杰吧?"

赫敏听隆巴顿夫人叫出自己的名字似乎吃了一惊,但也和她握了握手。

"对,纳威跟我说起过你。帮他渡过了一些难关,是不是?他是个好孩子,"她用严厉审视的眼光沿着尖鼻子向下瞅着纳威,"但没有他爸爸的才气,我不得不说。"她把头朝里边那两张床一点,帽子上的秃鹫吓人地抖动起来。

"怎么?"罗恩惊奇地问(哈利想踩他的脚,但穿着牛仔裤做这种动作比穿袍子要显眼得多),"那边是你爸爸吗,纳威?"

"什么?"隆巴顿夫人厉声问,"你没跟朋友说过你父母的事吗,纳威?"

纳威深深吸了口气,抬头看着天花板,摇了摇头。哈利不记得他为哪个人这么难受过,可是他想不出有什么办法可以帮纳威解围。

"哼,这不是什么羞耻的事!"隆巴顿夫人生气地说,"你应该感到自豪,纳威,自豪!他们牺牲了健康和理智,不是为了让唯一的儿子以他们为耻的!"

"我没觉得羞耻。"纳威无力地说,还是不看哈利等人。罗恩踮着脚往那两张床上看。

"你不羞耻的样子可有些奇怪!"隆巴顿夫人说,"我儿子和儿媳被神秘人的手下折磨疯了。"她高傲地转向哈利、罗恩、赫敏和金妮说。

赫敏和金妮都捂住了嘴巴。罗恩不再伸着脖子去看纳威的父母,显得十分羞愧。

"他们是傲罗,在魔法界很受尊敬。"隆巴顿夫人继续说,"天分很高,他们两个。我——哎,艾丽斯,什么事?"

纳威的母亲穿着睡衣缓缓走来。她已不再有穆迪那张凤凰社最早成员合影上的那样圆润快乐的脸庞。她的脸现在消瘦而憔悴,眼睛特别大,头发已经白了,零乱而枯干。她似乎不想说话,或是不能说,

CHAPTER TWENTY-THREE   Christmas on the Closed Ward

she was not able to, but she made timid motions towards Neville, holding something in her outstretched hand.

'Again?' said Mrs Longbottom, sounding slightly weary. 'Very well, Alice dear, very well – Neville, take it, whatever it is.'

But Neville had already stretched out his hand, into which his mother dropped an empty Drooble's Best Blowing Gum wrapper.

'Very nice, dear,' said Neville's grandmother in a falsely cheery voice, patting his mother on the shoulder.

But Neville said quietly, 'Thanks, Mum.'

His mother tottered away, back up the ward, humming to herself. Neville looked around at the others, his expression defiant, as though daring them to laugh, but Harry did not think he'd ever found anything less funny in his life.

'Well, we'd better get back,' sighed Mrs Longbottom, drawing on long green gloves. 'Very nice to have met you all. Neville, put that wrapper in the bin, she must have given you enough of them to paper your bedroom by now.'

But as they left, Harry was sure he saw Neville slip the sweet wrapper into his pocket.

The door closed behind them.

'I never knew,' said Hermione, who looked tearful.

'Nor did I,' said Ron rather hoarsely.

'Nor me,' whispered Ginny.

They all looked at Harry.

'I did,' he said glumly. 'Dumbledore told me but I promised I wouldn't tell anyone ... that's what Bellatrix Lestrange got sent to Azkaban for, using the Cruciatus Curse on Neville's parents until they lost their minds.'

'Bellatrix Lestrange did that?' whispered Hermione, horrified. 'That woman Kreacher's got a photo of in his den?'

There was a long silence, broken by Lockhart's angry voice.

'Look, I didn't learn joined-up writing for nothing, you know!'

第23章 封闭病房中的圣诞节

但她怯怯地朝纳威比画着,手里捏着什么东西。

"又一个?"隆巴顿夫人有点疲倦地说,"很好,艾丽斯,很好——纳威,拿着吧,管它是什么……"

纳威已经伸出手来,他母亲丢给他一张吹宝超级泡泡糖的包装纸。

"很好,亲爱的。"纳威的奶奶拍着她的肩膀,装出高兴的样子。

纳威轻声说:"谢谢,妈妈。"

他母亲蹒跚地走了回去,一边哼着歌曲。纳威挑战地看着大家,好像准备接受他们的嘲笑,但哈利觉得他从没遇到过比这更不好笑的事。

"好吧,我们该回去了。"隆巴顿夫人叹息着说,一边戴上长长的绿手套,"很高兴见到你们大家。纳威,把那张糖纸扔到垃圾箱里,她给你的都够贴满你的卧室了吧……"

但祖孙二人离开时,哈利相信他看到纳威把糖纸塞进了口袋里。

门关上了。

"我一直不知道。"赫敏眼泪汪汪地说。

"我也不知道。"罗恩声音嘶哑。

"我也是。"金妮小声说。

他们都看着哈利。

"我知道,"他难过地说,"邓布利多跟我讲过,但我保证过不说出去……贝拉特里克斯·莱斯特兰奇就是为这事进阿兹卡班的,她对纳威的父母用了钻心咒,害得他们发了疯。"

"贝拉特里克斯·莱斯特兰奇干的?"赫敏惊恐地说,"就是克利切窝里的照片上那个女人?"

长时间的沉默,然后是洛哈特气愤的声音。

"喂,我的连笔字可不是白练的,知道吧!"

CHAPTER TWENTY-FOUR

Occlumency

Kreacher, it transpired, had been lurking in the attic. Sirius said he had found him up there, covered in dust, no doubt looking for more relics of the Black family to hide in his cupboard. Though Sirius seemed satisfied with this story, it made Harry uneasy. Kreacher seemed to be in a better mood on his reappearance, his bitter muttering had subsided somewhat and he submitted to orders more docilely than usual, though once or twice Harry caught the house-elf staring at him avidly, but always looking quickly away whenever he saw that Harry had noticed.

Harry did not mention his vague suspicions to Sirius, whose cheerfulness was evaporating fast now that Christmas was over. As the date of their departure back to Hogwarts drew nearer, he became more and more prone to what Mrs Weasley called 'fits of the sullens', in which he would become taciturn and grumpy, often withdrawing to Buckbeak's room for hours at a time. His gloom seeped through the house, oozing under doorways like some noxious gas, so that all of them became infected by it.

Harry didn't want to leave Sirius again with only Kreacher for company; in fact, for the first time in his life, he was not looking forward to returning to Hogwarts. Going back to school would mean placing himself once again under the tyranny of Dolores Umbridge, who had no doubt managed to force through another dozen decrees in their absence; there was no Quidditch to look forward to now that he had been banned; there was every likelihood that their burden of homework would increase as the exams drew even nearer; and Dumbledore remained as remote as ever. In fact, if it hadn't been for the DA, Harry thought he might have begged Sirius to let him leave Hogwarts and remain in Grimmauld Place.

Then, on the very last day of the holidays, something happened that made Harry positively dread his return to school.

第 24 章

大脑封闭术

　　克利切原来躲在阁楼上。小天狼星说在那儿找到了他,他满身灰尘,无疑又在翻寻布莱克家的其他古董,想藏到他的锅炉间里。虽然小天狼星听了这个说法放下心来,哈利却有些不安。克利切出来后情绪似乎有所好转,他那怨恨的嘀咕减少了,也比平常听话了,但有一两次哈利发现这个小精灵在贪婪地盯着他,一见哈利发觉就赶忙移开目光。

　　哈利没有向小天狼星提起这些隐隐的怀疑。圣诞节过完了,小天狼星的快乐在迅速消散。随着众人返回霍格沃茨之日的临近,他越来越容易陷入韦斯莱夫人称之为"间歇性忧郁症"的状态:沉默寡言,脾气暴躁,经常躲到巴克比克的房间里一待就是几小时。他的忧郁在整所房子里蔓延,像毒气一样从门底下泄出来,所有的人都被感染了。

　　哈利不想留下小天狼星一个人跟克利切做伴。事实上,他生平第一次不再盼望返回霍格沃茨。返校意味着回到乌姆里奇的专制之下,她一定在他们离校期间又强行通过了十来条法令;再说他现在被禁飞了,也没有魁地奇球赛可盼。考试临近,作业量很可能又要增加。邓布利多还是那么遥远。说实话,要不是有 D.A.,哈利觉得他可能会去求小天狼星想办法让他离开霍格沃茨,留在格里莫广场。

　　假期最后一天发生了一件事,让哈利真正害怕返校了。

CHAPTER TWENTY-FOUR   Occlumency

'Harry, dear,' said Mrs Weasley, poking her head into his and Ron's bedroom, where the pair of them were playing wizard chess watched by Hermione, Ginny and Crookshanks, 'could you come down to the kitchen? Professor Snape would like a word with you.'

Harry did not immediately register what she had said; one of his castles was engaged in a violent tussle with a pawn of Ron's and he was egging it on enthusiastically.

'Squash him – *squash him*, he's only a pawn, you idiot. Sorry, Mrs Weasley, what did you say?'

'Professor Snape, dear. In the kitchen. He'd like a word.'

Harry's mouth fell open in horror. He looked around at Ron, Hermione and Ginny, all of whom were gaping back at him. Crookshanks, whom Hermione had been restraining with difficulty for the past quarter of an hour, leapt gleefully on to the board and set the pieces running for cover, squealing at the top of their voices.

'Snape?' said Harry blankly.

'*Professor* Snape, dear,' said Mrs Weasley reprovingly. 'Now come on, quickly, he says he can't stay long.'

'What's he want with you?' said Ron, looking unnerved as Mrs Weasley withdrew from the room. 'You haven't done anything, have you?'

'No!' said Harry indignantly, racking his brains to think what he could have done that would make Snape pursue him to Grimmauld Place. Had his last piece of homework perhaps earned a 'T'?

A minute or two later, he pushed open the kitchen door to find Sirius and Snape both seated at the long kitchen table, glaring in opposite directions. The silence between them was heavy with mutual dislike. A letter lay open on the table in front of Sirius.

'Er,' said Harry, to announce his presence.

Snape looked around at him, his face framed between curtains of greasy black hair.

'Sit down, Potter.'

'You know,' said Sirius loudly, leaning back on his rear chair legs and speaking to the ceiling, 'I think I'd prefer it if you didn't give orders here, Snape. It's my house, you see.'

An ugly flush suffused Snape's pallid face. Harry sat down in a chair beside Sirius, facing Snape across the table.

第24章 大脑封闭术

"哈利，亲爱的，"韦斯莱夫人把头伸进他和罗恩的卧室，他们俩在下巫师棋，赫敏、金妮和克鲁克山在旁边观看，"你到厨房来一下好吗？斯内普教授有话跟你说。"

哈利一时没反应过来，他的车在和罗恩的一个卒子激烈搏斗，他正兴奋地给它加油鼓劲呢。

"压扁它——压扁它，它不过是个小卒子，你这个笨蛋——对不起，韦斯莱夫人，你说什么？"

"斯内普教授在厨房里，他想和你谈谈。"

哈利惊恐地张大了嘴巴。他望望罗恩、赫敏和金妮，他们都目瞪口呆地看着他。赫敏好不容易才把克鲁克山管住了一刻钟，此时黄猫欢喜地跳到棋盘上，棋子尖叫着四散奔逃。

"斯内普？"哈利茫然地问。

"斯内普教授，亲爱的。"韦斯莱夫人责备地说，"快来吧，他说他待不了多久。"

"他找你干吗？"韦斯莱夫人走了，罗恩忐忑地问，"你没干什么吧？"

"没有！"哈利愤慨地说，一边拼命回想自己有什么过错会让斯内普追到格里莫广场来。莫非他上次作业得了一个"T"？

一两分钟后，他推开了厨房的门，看到小天狼星和斯内普坐在长桌前，气呼呼地瞪着相反的方向，沉默中充满了对彼此的厌恶。小天狼星面前有一封打开的信。

"呃。"哈利出声报告他的存在。

斯内普回过头来，一张脸镶在油油的黑发帘中。

"坐下，波特。"

"我说，"小天狼星往后一靠，翘起椅子，对着天花板大声说，"我希望你不要在这儿发号施令，斯内普，这是我的家。"

斯内普苍白的脸上涌起一阵难看的红潮，哈利在小天狼星身边坐了下来，望着桌子对面的斯内普。

CHAPTER TWENTY-FOUR   Occlumency

'I was supposed to see you alone, Potter,' said Snape, the familiar sneer curling his mouth, 'but Black —'

'I'm his godfather,' said Sirius, louder than ever.

'I am here on Dumbledore's orders,' said Snape, whose voice, by contrast, was becoming more and more quietly waspish, 'but by all means stay, Black, I know you like to feel ... involved.'

'What's that supposed to mean?' said Sirius, letting his chair fall back on to all four legs with a loud bang.

'Merely that I am sure you must feel — ah — frustrated by the fact that you can do nothing *useful*,' Snape laid a delicate stress on the word, 'for the Order.'

It was Sirius's turn to flush. Snape's lip curled in triumph as he turned to Harry.

'The Headmaster has sent me to tell you, Potter, that it is his wish for you to study Occlumency this term.'

'Study what?' said Harry blankly.

Snape's sneer became more pronounced.

'Occlumency, Potter. The magical defence of the mind against external penetration. An obscure branch of magic, but a highly useful one.'

Harry's heart began to pump very fast indeed. Defence against external penetration? But he was not being possessed, they had all agreed on that ...

'Why do I have to study Occlu— thing?' he blurted out.

'Because the Headmaster thinks it a good idea,' said Snape smoothly. 'You will receive private lessons once a week, but you will not tell anybody what you are doing, least of all Dolores Umbridge. You understand?'

'Yes,' said Harry. 'Who's going to be teaching me?'

Snape raised an eyebrow.

'I am,' he said.

Harry had the horrible sensation that his insides were melting. Extra lessons with Snape — what on earth had he done to deserve this? He looked quickly round at Sirius for support.

'Why can't Dumbledore teach Harry?' asked Sirius aggressively. 'Why you?'

'I suppose because it is a headmaster's privilege to delegate less enjoyable tasks,' said Snape silkily. 'I assure you I did not beg for the job.' He got to his feet. 'I will expect you at six o'clock on Monday evening, Potter. My office. If anybody asks, you are taking remedial Potions. Nobody who has seen you in my classes could deny you need them.'

第24章 大脑封闭术

"我本该和你一个人谈，波特，"斯内普嘴角浮现出惯常的冷笑，"但布莱克——"

"我是他的教父。"小天狼星嗓门更大了。

"我是奉邓布利多之命来的，"斯内普说，声音则越来越微弱而尖刻，"不过请留下，布莱克，我知道你喜欢有……参与感。"

"这话什么意思？"小天狼星问，重重地把椅腿落回了地面。

"意思是我想你一定挺——啊——挺心烦的，不能为凤凰社做任何有用的事。"斯内普故意强调"有用"一词。

这一下轮到小天狼星涨红了脸，斯内普嘴角带着胜利的笑容转向哈利。

"校长让我来通知你，波特，他希望你这学期学习大脑封闭术。"

"学习什么？"哈利愣愣地问。

斯内普的冷笑更明显了。

"大脑封闭术，波特。防止头脑受到外来入侵。是魔法中冷僻的一门，但非常有用。"

哈利的心脏剧烈地跳了起来。防止外来入侵？可他没有被附身啊，大家都这么说……

"为什么我要学大——这玩意儿？"他脱口而出。

"因为校长认为有必要，"斯内普和缓地说，"你一周接受一次单独辅导，但不能告诉任何人，尤其是多洛雷斯·乌姆里奇。明白吗？"

"明白。"哈利说，"谁来教我？"

斯内普扬了扬眉毛。

"本人。"他说。

哈利感到他的五脏六腑在融化，由斯内普单独辅导——他到底做了什么要受到这种惩罚？他急忙求助地看着小天狼星。

"为什么邓布利多不能教他？"小天狼星咄咄逼人地问，"为什么是你？"

"我想是因为校长有权把不愉快的差使下放吧，"斯内普圆滑地说，"我向你保证这不是我要来的。"他站起身来，"我星期一晚上六点在我办公室等你，波特。如果有人问，就说是魔药课补习，见过你在我课上表现的人都不会否认有这个必要。"

CHAPTER TWENTY-FOUR Occlumency

He turned to leave, his black travelling cloak billowing behind him.

'Wait a moment,' said Sirius, sitting up straighter in his chair.

Snape turned back to face them, sneering.

'I am in rather a hurry, Black. Unlike you, I do not have unlimited leisure time.'

'I'll get to the point, then,' said Sirius, standing up. He was rather taller than Snape who, Harry noticed, balled his fist in the pocket of his cloak over what Harry was sure was the handle of his wand. 'If I hear you're using these Occlumency lessons to give Harry a hard time, you'll have me to answer to.'

'How touching,' Snape sneered. 'But surely you have noticed that Potter is very like his father?'

'Yes, I have,' said Sirius proudly.

'Well then, you'll know he's so arrogant that criticism simply bounces off him,' Snape said sleekly.

Sirius pushed his chair roughly aside and strode around the table towards Snape, pulling out his wand as he went. Snape whipped out his own. They were squaring up to each other, Sirius looking livid, Snape calculating, his eyes darting from Sirius's wand-tip to his face.

'Sirius!' said Harry loudly, but Sirius appeared not to hear him.

'I've warned you, *Snivellus*,' said Sirius, his face barely a foot from Snape's, 'I don't care if Dumbledore thinks you've reformed, I know better –'

'Oh, but why don't you tell him so?' whispered Snape. 'Or are you afraid he might not take very seriously the advice of a man who has been hiding inside his mother's house for six months?'

'Tell me, how is Lucius Malfoy these days? I expect he's delighted his lapdog's working at Hogwarts, isn't he?'

'Speaking of dogs,' said Snape softly, 'did you know that Lucius Malfoy recognised you last time you risked a little jaunt outside? Clever idea, Black, getting yourself seen on a safe station platform ... gave you a cast-iron excuse not to leave your hidey-hole in future, didn't it?'

Sirius raised his wand.

'NO!' Harry yelled, vaulting over the table and trying to get in between them. 'Sirius, don't!'

'Are you calling me a coward?' roared Sirius, trying to push Harry out of the way, but Harry would not budge.

第24章 大脑封闭术

他转身离开,黑色的旅行斗篷旋起了一股风。

"等一等。"小天狼星说着坐直了身子。

斯内普回身看着他冷笑。

"我很忙,布莱克……不像你。我没有无限的空闲……"

"那我直话直说吧。"小天狼星站了起来。他比斯内普高得多,哈利注意到斯内普的手在斗篷口袋里攥紧了,猜想他一定是握住了魔杖柄。"如果我听到你借教哈利大脑封闭术来整他,我会找你算账的。"

"多么动人哪,"斯内普冷笑道,"但你一定发现波特很像他父亲吧?"

"不错。"小天狼星自豪地说。

"那你该知道他骄傲自大,批评对他就像耳旁风。"斯内普圆滑地说。

小天狼星一把推开椅子,绕过桌子大步朝斯内普走去,一边抽出了魔杖。斯内普也亮出了魔杖。两人摆开架式,小天狼星脸色铁青,斯内普在算计,目光在小天狼星的脸和杖尖之间扫来扫去。

"小天狼星!"哈利叫道,但他好像没听见。

"我警告过你,鼻涕精,"小天狼星的脸离斯内普的脸不到一尺,"邓布利多或许认为你改造好了,可我不这么想——"

"哦,那你为什么不对他说呢?"斯内普低声说,"是不是担心他不会把在老妈家躲六个月的人的话当回事?"

"告诉我,卢修斯·马尔福近来怎么样?我想他一定很高兴他的哈巴狗在霍格沃茨任教吧?"

"提到狗,"斯内普轻轻地说,"你知道吗,你上次冒险外出时,卢修斯·马尔福认出了你。很聪明啊,布莱克,在安全的站台上被人看到……让你有铁打的理由以后不用出洞了,是不是?"

小天狼星举起了魔杖。

"**不要!**"哈利叫了起来,从桌上翻过去挡在他们中间,"小天狼星,别——"

"你在说我是懦夫吗?"小天狼星咆哮道,想把哈利推开,但哈利坚决不动。

875

CHAPTER TWENTY-FOUR   Occlumency

'Why, yes, I suppose I am,' said Snape.

'Harry – get – out – of – it!' snarled Sirius, pushing him aside with his free hand.

The kitchen door opened and the entire Weasley family, plus Hermione, came inside, all looking very happy, with Mr Weasley walking proudly in their midst dressed in a pair of striped pyjamas covered by a mackintosh.

'Cured!' he announced brightly to the kitchen at large. 'Completely cured!'

He and all the other Weasleys froze on the threshold, gazing at the scene in front of them, which was also suspended in mid-action, both Sirius and Snape looking towards the door with their wands pointing into each other's faces and Harry immobile between them, a hand stretched out to each, trying to force them apart.

'Merlin's beard,' said Mr Weasley, the smile sliding off his face, 'what's going on here?'

Both Sirius and Snape lowered their wands. Harry looked from one to the other. Each wore an expression of utmost contempt, yet the unexpected entrance of so many witnesses seemed to have brought them to their senses. Snape pocketed his wand and swept back across the kitchen, passing the Weasleys without comment. At the door he looked back.

'Six o'clock, Monday evening, Potter.'

And he was gone. Sirius glared after him, his wand at his side.

'What's been going on?' asked Mr Weasley again.

'Nothing, Arthur,' said Sirius, who was breathing heavily as though he had just run a long distance. 'Just a friendly little chat between two old school friends.' With what looked like an enormous effort, he smiled. 'So … you're cured? That's great news, really great.'

'Yes, isn't it?' said Mrs Weasley, leading her husband forward to a chair. 'Healer Smethwyck worked his magic in the end, found an antidote to whatever that snake's got in its fangs, and Arthur's learned his lesson about dabbling in Muggle medicine, *haven't you, dear?*' she added, rather menacingly.

'Yes, Molly, dear,' said Mr Weasley meekly.

That night's meal should have been a cheerful one, with Mr Weasley back amongst them. Harry could tell Sirius was trying to make it so, yet when his godfather was not forcing himself to laugh loudly at Fred and George's jokes or offering everyone more food, his face fell back into a moody, brooding expression. Harry was separated from him by Mundungus and Mad-Eye,

第24章 大脑封闭术

"嗯，我想是吧。"斯内普说。

"哈利——让开——！"小天狼星大吼一声，没拿魔杖的手一掌把他推到旁边。

厨房门开了，韦斯莱全家和赫敏一拥而入，个个兴高采烈，韦斯莱先生骄傲地走在中间，穿着条纹布的睡衣，外罩一件防水雨衣。

"治好了！"他兴冲冲地向厨房里的人宣布，"完全好了！"

他们全都僵立在门口，瞪着眼前这定格的一幕：小天狼星和斯内普都扭头望着门口，魔杖直指对方的面门，哈利张着手臂站在两人中间，想把他们推开。

"梅林的胡子啊，"韦斯莱先生的笑容消失了，"这是怎么一回事？"

小天狼星和斯内普都垂下了魔杖。哈利左右看看，两人脸上都带着极度的轻蔑，但突然进来这么多的目击者似乎使他们恢复了理智。斯内普把魔杖插进口袋，大步走出厨房，没有理睬韦斯莱一家人。走到门口，他又回过头来。

"星期一晚上六点，波特。"

他扬长而去，小天狼星瞪着他的背影，魔杖垂在一旁。

"到底是怎么回事？"韦斯莱先生又问。

"没什么，亚瑟，"小天狼星喘着粗气，像刚跑完长跑，"只是两个老同学叙叙旧……"他好像用了极大努力似的微笑道，"……你治好了？好，真好……"

"可不是嘛！"韦斯莱夫人把丈夫领到一把椅子跟前，"斯梅绥克治疗师终于找到了那条蛇尖牙里毒素的解药，亚瑟也从捣鼓麻瓜医术中吸取了教训，是不是，亲爱的？"她带着威胁问。

"是的，莫丽，亲爱的。"韦斯莱先生温顺地说。

由于韦斯莱先生回到了他们中间，那天的晚餐本应是非常愉快的，哈利看得出小天狼星竭力想活跃气氛，他强迫自己听了弗雷德和乔治的笑话后高声大笑，殷勤地劝大家多吃，但除此之外，他的脸就会阴沉下去，显得心事重重。他和哈利之间隔着来向韦斯莱先生道贺的蒙

CHAPTER TWENTY-FOUR Occlumency

who had dropped in to offer Mr Weasley their congratulations. He wanted to talk to Sirius, to tell him he shouldn't listen to a word Snape said, that Snape was goading him deliberately and that the rest of them didn't think Sirius was a coward for doing as Dumbledore told him and remaining in Grimmauld Place. But he had no opportunity to do so, and, eyeing the ugly look on Sirius's face, Harry wondered occasionally whether he would have dared to mention it even if he had the chance. Instead, he told Ron and Hermione under his voice about having to take Occlumency lessons with Snape.

'Dumbledore wants to stop you having those dreams about Voldemort,' said Hermione at once. 'Well, you won't be sorry not to have them any more, will you?'

'Extra lessons with Snape?' said Ron, sounding aghast. 'I'd rather have the nightmares!'

They were to return to Hogwarts on the Knight Bus the following day, escorted once again by Tonks and Lupin, both of whom were eating breakfast in the kitchen when Harry, Ron and Hermione came down next morning. The adults seemed to have been mid-way through a whispered conversation as Harry opened the door; all of them looked round hastily and fell silent.

After a hurried breakfast, they all pulled on jackets and scarves against the chilly grey January morning. Harry had an unpleasant constricted sensation in his chest; he did not want to say goodbye to Sirius. He had a bad feeling about this parting; he didn't know when they would next see each other and he felt it was incumbent upon him to say something to Sirius to stop him doing anything stupid – Harry was worried that Snape's accusation of cowardice had stung Sirius so badly he might even now be planning some foolhardy trip beyond Grimmauld Place. Before he could think of what to say, however, Sirius had beckoned him to his side.

'I want you to take this,' he said quietly, thrusting a badly wrapped package roughly the size of a paperback book into Harry's hands.

'What is it?' Harry asked.

'A way of letting me know if Snape's giving you a hard time. No, don't open it in here!' said Sirius, with a wary look at Mrs Weasley, who was trying to persuade the twins to wear hand-knitted mittens. 'I doubt Molly would approve – but I want you to use it if you need me, all right?'

'OK,' said Harry, stowing the package away in the inside pocket of his jacket, but he knew he would never use whatever it was. It would not be he, Harry, who lured Sirius from his place of safety, no matter how foully Snape treated him in their forthcoming Occlumency classes.

第24章 大脑封闭术

顿格斯和疯眼汉。哈利想对小天狼星说别把斯内普的话放在心上,斯内普是故意激他的,他们都不认为小天狼星听邓布利多的话待在格里莫广场是贪生怕死,可是没有找到机会。看着小天狼星那可怕的表情,哈利怀疑即使有机会他也未必敢讲。他只是小声地对罗恩和赫敏说了要跟斯内普学大脑封闭术的事。

"邓布利多想让你不再做那些关于伏地魔的梦,"赫敏马上说,"你不会舍不得它们吧?"

"跟斯内普补课?"罗恩声音中充满了恐惧,"我宁可做噩梦。"

第二天,他们准备乘骑士公共汽车回霍格沃茨,仍由唐克斯和卢平护送。早上哈利、罗恩和赫敏进厨房时,他们俩正在吃早饭。大人们好像在小声交谈,但哈利一开门,他们马上回过头来不说了。

他们匆匆吃过早饭,穿上外套,戴好围巾,准备上路。一月的清晨天色灰白,寒意袭人。哈利的胸口堵得难受,他不想跟小天狼星说再见,他对这次分别有一种不祥之感,不知道何时才能再见。他觉得自己有责任提醒小天狼星别做傻事——他担心小天狼星受了斯内普说他是懦夫的刺激,可能现在就已盘算着贸然离开格里莫广场。但他还没想好怎么说,小天狼星就把他叫到了一边。

"你带上这个。"他悄悄地说,塞给哈利一个包得很不像样的、平装书大小的东西。

"这是什么?"哈利问。

"如果斯内普欺负你,你可以用它告诉我。别在这儿打开!"小天狼星提防地看了看韦斯莱夫人,她正在劝双胞胎戴上她自己织的手套,"我怀疑莫丽不赞成——但我希望你在需要我的时候用它,好吗?"

"好的。"哈利答应着,把小包塞到上衣内侧的口袋里,但他知道自己不会用的。他,哈利,决不会把小天狼星引出安全地带,无论斯内普在教他大脑封闭术时怎么虐待他。

CHAPTER TWENTY-FOUR   Occlumency

'Let's go, then,' said Sirius, clapping Harry on the shoulder and smiling grimly, and before Harry could say anything else, they were heading upstairs, stopping before the heavily chained and bolted front door, surrounded by Weasleys.

'Goodbye, Harry, take care,' said Mrs Weasley, hugging him.

'See you, Harry, and keep an eye out for snakes for me!' said Mr Weasley genially, shaking his hand.

'Right – yeah,' said Harry distractedly; it was his last chance to tell Sirius to be careful; he turned, looked into his godfather's face and opened his mouth to speak, but before he could do so Sirius was giving him a brief, one-armed hug, and saying gruffly, 'Look after yourself, Harry.' Next moment, Harry found himself being shunted out into the icy winter air, with Tonks (today heavily disguised as a tall, tweedy woman with iron-grey hair) chivvying him down the steps.

The door of number twelve slammed shut behind them. They followed Lupin down the front steps. As he reached the pavement, Harry looked round. Number twelve was shrinking rapidly as those on either side of it stretched sideways, squeezing it out of sight. One blink later, it had gone.

'Come on, the quicker we get on the bus the better,' said Tonks, and Harry thought there was nervousness in the glance she threw around the square. Lupin flung out his right arm.

BANG.

A violently purple, triple-decker bus had appeared out of thin air in front of them, narrowly avoiding the nearest lamppost, which jumped backwards out of its way.

A thin, pimply, jug-eared youth in a purple uniform leapt down on to the pavement and said, 'Welcome to the –'

'Yes, yes, we know, thank you,' said Tonks swiftly. 'On, on, get on –'

And she shoved Harry forwards towards the steps, past the conductor, who goggled at Harry as he passed.

''Ere – it's 'Arry –!'

'If you shout his name I will curse you into oblivion,' muttered Tonks menacingly, now shunting Ginny and Hermione forwards.

'I've always wanted to go on this thing,' said Ron happily, joining Harry on board and looking around.

It had been evening the last time Harry had travelled by Knight Bus and

第24章 大脑封闭术

"走吧。"小天狼星拍拍哈利的肩膀,强打笑容说。哈利还没来得及说话,他们已经上了楼,停在了带粗铁链和门闩的正门前,韦斯莱一家围在那里。

"再见,哈利,多保重。"韦斯莱夫人拥抱了他一下。

"再见,哈利,替我看着点蛇!"韦斯莱先生握着他的手亲切地说。

"好——好的。"哈利心不在焉地答道。这是他提醒小天狼星的最后一个机会,他转身望着教父的脸,张嘴刚要说话,但小天狼星用一只胳膊搂了他一下,粗声粗气地说:"照顾好自己,哈利。"然后哈利就被推进了凛冽的空气中,唐克斯追着他下了台阶(她今天扮成了一个身着粗花呢的高个女人,头发是铁灰色的)。

12号的门在身后关上了,他们跟着卢平下了台阶。走到人行道上时,哈利回头看了看,12号在迅速缩小,两边的房屋延伸过来挤着它,一眨眼的工夫它就不见了。

"快点儿,越早上车越好。"唐克斯扫了一眼广场说,哈利觉得她眼神中有一些紧张。卢平挥起右手。

砰!

一辆鲜艳的紫色三层公共汽车凭空出现在他们面前,差点撞到了路灯柱,灯柱朝后一跳躲开了。

一个穿着紫色制服、长着招风耳、满脸粉刺的瘦小伙跳下来说:"欢迎乘坐——"

"我们知道了,谢谢你,"唐克斯迅速说,"上车,上车——"

她把哈利推向汽车踏板,售票员瞪眼看着哈利走过去。

"哎——是哈——!"

"你要喊他的名字我就让你万劫不复。"唐克斯小声威胁道,一边把金妮和赫敏也推向前去。

"我一直想坐这个。"罗恩高兴地说,他也上了车,只顾东看西看。

哈利上次乘骑士公共汽车是晚上,三层车厢里排满了铜床架。现

its three decks had been full of brass bedsteads. Now, in the early morning, it was crammed with an assortment of mismatched chairs grouped haphazardly around windows. Some of these appeared to have fallen over when the bus stopped abruptly in Grimmauld Place; a few witches and wizards were still getting to their feet, grumbling, and somebody's shopping bag had slid the length of the bus: an unpleasant mixture of frogspawn, cockroaches and custard creams was scattered all over the floor.

'Looks like we'll have to split up,' said Tonks briskly, looking around for empty chairs. 'Fred, George and Ginny, if you just take those seats at the back ... Remus can stay with you.'

She, Harry, Ron and Hermione proceeded up to the very top deck, where there were two unoccupied chairs at the very front of the bus and two at the back. Stan Shunpike, the conductor, followed Harry and Ron eagerly to the back. Heads turned as Harry passed and, when he sat down, he saw all the faces flick back to the front again.

As Harry and Ron handed Stan eleven Sickles each, the bus set off again, swaying ominously. It rumbled around Grimmauld Place, weaving on and off the pavement, then, with another tremendous BANG, they were all flung backwards; Ron's chair toppled right over and Pigwidgeon, who had been on his lap, burst out of his cage and flew twittering wildly up to the front of the bus where he fluttered down on to Hermione's shoulder instead. Harry, who had narrowly avoided falling by seizing a candle bracket, looked out of the window: they were now speeding down what appeared to be a motorway.

'Just outside Birmingham,' said Stan happily, answering Harry's unasked question as Ron struggled up from the floor. 'You keepin' well, then, 'Arry? I seen your name in the paper loads over the summer, but it weren't never nuffink very nice. I said to Ern, I said, 'e didn't seem like a nutter when we met 'im, just goes to show, dunnit?'

He handed over their tickets and continued to gaze, enthralled, at Harry. Apparently, Stan did not care how nutty somebody was, if they were famous enough to be in the paper. The Knight Bus swayed alarmingly, overtaking a line of cars on the inside. Looking towards the front of the bus, Harry saw Hermione cover her eyes with her hands, Pigwidgeon swaying happily on her shoulder.

BANG.

Chairs slid backwards again as the Knight Bus jumped from the

第24章 大脑封闭术

在是清晨，车上摆满了各式各样的椅子，也不讲究搭配，胡乱地挤在窗边，有的似乎是在汽车突然停在格里莫广场时翻倒的，几个巫师正在嘟嘟囔囔地爬起来。不知是谁的购物袋滑到了车厢那头，青蛙卵、蟑螂和蛋奶饼干撒了一地。

"看来我们得分开了，"唐克斯果断地说，一边寻找空座位，"弗雷德、乔治和金妮，你们坐到后面去……卢平可以跟你们一起……"

她和哈利、罗恩和赫敏走到了顶上那一层，最前面和最后面各有两把空椅子，售票员斯坦·桑帕克热心地跟着哈利和罗恩走到了后面。哈利走过时许多人回头看他，他坐下后，看到那些脑袋都赶忙转了过去。

哈利和罗恩每人递给斯坦十一个西可，汽车又开了起来，危险地摇晃着，轰隆隆地绕过格里莫广场，车身扭来扭去的，时而还会驶上人行道。然后又是砰的一声巨响，他们都被往后甩去，罗恩的椅子翻了，他膝上的小猪从笼子里挣了出来，啾啾地飞到车厢前面，拍着翅膀落到赫敏的肩头。哈利抓住了蜡烛架才勉强没有摔倒，他朝窗外望去，他们好像正沿着一条高速公路疾驶。

"伯明翰城外。"斯坦愉快地回答了哈利心里的问题，罗恩努力从地上爬了起来，"你挺好的，哈利？我夏天老是在报上看到你的名字，可是没什么好话……我对厄恩说，我们见到他的时候他不像个疯子啊，慢慢显出来的，是不是？"

他把票递给他们，继续着迷地盯着哈利。斯坦显然不在乎一个人有多疯，只要他的名字能上报。骑士公共汽车吓人地倾斜着，超过了内侧的一溜小汽车。哈利望望前面，看见赫敏捂住了眼睛，小猪在她肩上快乐地摇摆着。

砰！

椅子又朝后滑去，骑士公共汽车从伯明翰公路跳到了一条幽静的乡间小道上，一路尽是险弯。车子忽左忽右压上路边时，一道道树篱跳着闪开了。他们又开上了一条闹市区的主干道、一座崇山峻岭

CHAPTER TWENTY-FOUR   Occlumency

Birmingham motorway to a quiet country lane full of hairpin bends. Hedgerows on either side of the road were leaping out of their way as they mounted the verges. From here they moved to a main street in the middle of a busy town, then to a viaduct surrounded by tall hills, then to a windswept road between high-rise flats, each time with a loud BANG.

'I've changed my mind,' muttered Ron, picking himself up from the floor for the sixth time, 'I never want to ride on this thing again.'

'Listen, it's 'Ogwarts stop after this,' said Stan brightly, swaying towards them. 'That bossy woman up front 'oo got on with you, she's given us a little tip to move you up the queue. We're just gonna let Madam Marsh off first, though –' there was a retching sound from downstairs, followed by a horrible spattering noise '– she's not feeling 'er best.'

A few minutes later, the Knight Bus screeched to a halt outside a small pub, which squeezed itself out of the way to avoid a collision. They could hear Stan ushering the unfortunate Madam Marsh out of the bus and the relieved murmurings of her fellow passengers on the second deck. The bus moved on again, gathering speed, until –

BANG.

They were rolling through a snowy Hogsmeade. Harry caught a glimpse of the Hog's Head down its side street, the severed boar's head sign creaking in the wintry wind. Flecks of snow hit the large window at the front of the bus. At last they rolled to a halt outside the gates to Hogwarts.

Lupin and Tonks helped them off the bus with their luggage, then got off to say goodbye. Harry glanced up at the three decks of the Knight Bus and saw all the passengers staring down at them, noses flat against the windows.

'You'll be safe once you're in the grounds,' said Tonks, casting a careful eye around at the deserted road. 'Have a good term, OK?'

'Look after yourselves,' said Lupin, shaking hands all round and reaching Harry last. 'And listen …' he lowered his voice while the rest of them exchanged last-minute goodbyes with Tonks, 'Harry, I know you don't like Snape, but he is a superb Occlumens and we all – Sirius included – want you to learn to protect yourself, so work hard, all right?'

'Yeah, all right,' said Harry heavily, looking up into Lupin's prematurely lined face. 'See you, then.'

The six of them struggled up the slippery drive towards the castle,

第24章 大脑封闭术

中的高架桥,然后是高楼间一条冷风飕飕的街道,每次都是**砰**的一声巨响。

"我改主意了,"罗恩第六次从地上爬起来时嘟哝道,"我再也不想坐这玩意儿了。"

"注意,下一站是霍格沃茨。"斯坦快活地说,摇摇晃晃地走过来,"前面那个跟你们一起上车的霸道女人给了点小费,要让你们先下。不过我们得先让马什女士下去。"下层传来呕吐声和可怕的哗啦声,"她不舒服。"

几分钟后骑士公共汽车在一个小酒吧外尖声刹住,小店闪身躲避,才没有被撞上。他们听见斯坦把可怜的马什女士扶下了车,二层乘客都嘀咕着舒了口气。汽车继续前行,加速,直到——

砰!

他们已经行驶在白雪覆盖的霍格莫德村,哈利瞥见了小巷里的猪头酒吧,砍下的猪头招牌在寒风中吱嘎作响。片片雪花打在车前的大窗子上。车子终于摇摇晃晃地停在了霍格沃茨大门外。

卢平和唐克斯帮他们把行李弄下车,然后下来说再见。哈利望了一眼三层的骑士公共汽车,见所有乘客都把鼻子贴在窗子上看着他们。

"进学校就安全了。"唐克斯警惕地扫了一眼僻静的街道,"过得愉快,啊?"

"保重。"卢平和每个人握手,最后轮到哈利时,"听着……"他低声说,其他人都在和唐克斯作最后的道别,"哈利,我知道你不喜欢斯内普,但他是高超的大脑封闭术师,我们——包括小天狼星都希望你学会保护自己,所以刻苦学习,好吗?"

"好。"哈利沉重地说,抬眼望着卢平那过早显出皱纹的脸,"再见了……"

六个人吃力地拖着箱子,沿着结冰的车道往城堡走去,赫敏说要在睡觉前织出几顶小精灵帽。来到橡木大门前,哈利回头看了一眼,

CHAPTER TWENTY-FOUR Occlumency

dragging their trunks. Hermione was already talking about knitting a few elf hats before bedtime. Harry glanced back when they reached the oaken front doors; the Knight Bus had already gone and he half wished, given what was coming the following evening, that he was still on board.

Harry spent most of the next day dreading the evening. His morning double-Potions lesson did nothing to dispel his trepidation, as Snape was as unpleasant as ever. His mood was further lowered by the DA members constantly approaching him in the corridors between classes, asking hopefully if there would be a meeting that night.

'I'll let you know in the usual way when the next one is,' Harry said over and over again, 'but I can't do it tonight, I've got to go to – er – remedial Potions.'

'You take *remedial Potions*?' asked Zacharias Smith superciliously, having cornered Harry in the Entrance Hall after lunch. 'Good Lord, you must be terrible. Snape doesn't usually give extra lessons, does he?'

As Smith strode away in an annoyingly buoyant fashion, Ron glared after him.

'Shall I jinx him? I can still get him from here,' he said, raising his wand and taking aim between Smith's shoulder blades.

'Forget it,' said Harry dismally. 'It's what everyone's going to think, isn't it? That I'm really stup–'

'Hi, Harry,' said a voice behind him. He turned round and found Cho standing there.

'Oh,' said Harry as his stomach leapt uncomfortably. 'Hi.'

'We'll be in the library, Harry,' said Hermione firmly as she seized Ron above the elbow and dragged him off towards the marble staircase.

'Had a good Christmas?' asked Cho.

'Yeah, not bad,' said Harry.

'Mine was pretty quiet,' said Cho. For some reason, she was looking rather embarrassed. 'Erm ... there's another Hogsmeade trip next month, did you see the notice?'

'What? Oh, no, I haven't checked the noticeboard since I got back.'

'Yes, it's on Valentine's Day ...'

'Right,' said Harry, wondering why she was telling him this. 'Well, I suppose you want to –?'

'Only if you do,' she said eagerly.

第24章 大脑封闭术

骑士公共汽车已经不见了。想到明天晚上的事情,他倒有点希望自己还在车上。

第二天,哈利大部分时间都在为晚上的到来而害怕。上午的魔药课丝毫没有消除他的恐惧,斯内普还是那么可恶。课间走廊上不断有 D.A. 的成员满怀希望地来问他晚上要不要聚会,他的情绪更加低落。

"我会像往常一样通知你们下一次的时间,"哈利一遍遍地说,"但今天晚上不行,我要——补魔药课……"

"你要补魔药课?"午饭后扎卡赖斯·史密斯把哈利堵在门厅里,傲慢地说,"老天,你一定糟透了,斯内普不经常给人补课的,是不是?"

史密斯趾高气扬地走开了,罗恩气愤地瞪着他。

"要我对他施恶咒吗?我现在还能击中他。"他举起魔杖对准了史密斯的后背。

"算了,"哈利沮丧地说,"谁都会这么想,是不是?觉得我笨——"

"嗨,哈利。"哈利身后一个声音叫道。他转过身,发现秋站在那儿。

"嗯,"哈利的胃揪紧了,"嗨。"

"我们去图书馆,哈利。"赫敏果断地说,抓着罗恩的胳膊把他朝大理石楼梯拽去。

"圣诞节过得好吗?"秋问。

"嗯,还不错。"哈利说。

"我过得挺安静。"不知为什么,秋似乎有些不好意思,"嗯……下个月又要去一次霍格莫德村,你看到通知了吗?"

"什么?哦,没有,我回来后还没看过布告栏呢。"

"是在情人节……"

"哦,"哈利不明白她为什么要跟他说这个,"你是不是想——?"

"要是你愿意。"她热切地说。

CHAPTER TWENTY-FOUR Occlumency

Harry stared. He had been about to say, 'I suppose you want to know when the next DA meeting is?' but her response did not seem to fit.

'I – er –' he said.

'Oh, it's OK if you don't,' she said, looking mortified. 'Don't worry. I – I'll see you around.'

She walked away. Harry stood staring after her, his brain working frantically. Then something clunked into place.

'Cho! Hey – CHO!'

He ran after her, catching her halfway up the marble staircase.

'Er – d'you want to come into Hogsmeade with me on Valentine's Day?'

'Oooh, yes!' she said, blushing crimson and beaming at him.

'Right ... well ... that's settled then,' said Harry, and feeling that the day was not going to be a complete loss after all, he virtually bounced off to the library to pick up Ron and Hermione before their afternoon lessons.

By six o'clock that evening, however, even the glow of having successfully asked out Cho Chang could not lighten the ominous feelings that intensified with every step Harry took towards Snape's office.

He paused outside the door when he reached it, wishing he were almost anywhere else, then, taking a deep breath, he knocked and entered.

The shadowy room was lined with shelves bearing hundreds of glass jars in which slimy bits of animals and plants were suspended in variously coloured potions. In one corner stood the cupboard full of ingredients that Snape had once accused Harry – not without reason – of robbing. Harry's attention was drawn towards the desk, however, where a shallow stone basin engraved with runes and symbols lay in a pool of candlelight. Harry recognised it at once – it was Dumbledore's Pensieve. Wondering what on earth it was doing there, he jumped when Snape's cold voice came out of the shadows.

'Shut the door behind you, Potter.'

Harry did as he was told, with the horrible feeling that he was imprisoning himself. When he turned back into the room, Snape had moved into the light and was pointing silently at the chair opposite his desk. Harry sat down and so did Snape, his cold black eyes fixed unblinkingly upon Harry, dislike etched in every line of his face.

第24章 大脑封闭术

哈利呆住了，他本想说："你是不是想问下次 D.A. 活动的时间？"但她的回答好像对不上。

"我——呃——"他说。

"噢，你不愿意就算了，"她说，似乎感到有些屈辱，"没关系，回头见。"

她讪讪离去，哈利瞪着她的背影，脑子在疯狂地转动，突然醒悟了过来。

"秋！嗨——秋！"

他跑过去，在大理石楼梯上追到了秋。

"呃——你想在情人节跟我去霍格莫德吗？"

"哦，是的！"秋羞红了脸，灿烂地一笑。

"好……那么……就说定了。"哈利感到这一天还不算完全失败，他在下午上课前到图书馆去找罗恩和赫敏时，脚步不知不觉也变轻快了。

但到了晚上六点钟，就连成功地约了秋·张也不足以减轻哈利的不祥之感，这感觉随着他朝斯内普办公室迈出的每一步而增强。

他在门外停了一会儿，希望自己是在别处。只要不是在这里，在哪儿都行。然后他深深吸了口气，敲门进去。

这是一间昏暗的屋子，架子上放着几百个玻璃瓶，黏糊糊的动植物标本浮在五颜六色的药剂中。角落上一个柜子里装满了斯内普曾经——不无根据地——指责哈利盗取的药材。但哈利的注意力被吸引到了书桌上，烛光里有一个刻着神秘字母和符号的浅浅的石盆。哈利一下认出来了——邓布利多的冥想盆——他正在纳闷把它摆在这儿干什么，斯内普冷冰冰的声音从阴影处传来，把他吓了一跳。

"把你身后的门关上，波特。"

哈利照办了，恐惧地感到他把自己关了起来。他转过身，斯内普已经走到亮处，无声地指指书桌对面的椅子。哈利过去坐了，斯内普也坐下来，冷酷的黑眼睛一眨不眨地盯着哈利，脸上的每一道纹路里都刻着厌恶。

CHAPTER TWENTY-FOUR   Occlumency

'Well, Potter, you know why you are here,' he said. 'The Headmaster has asked me to teach you Occlumency. I can only hope that you prove more adept at it than at Potions.'

'Right,' said Harry tersely.

'This may not be an ordinary class, Potter,' said Snape, his eyes narrowed malevolently, 'but I am still your teacher and you will therefore call me "sir" or "Professor" at all times.'

'Yes ... *sir*,' said Harry.

'Now, Occlumency. As I told you back in your dear godfather's kitchen, this branch of magic seals the mind against magical intrusion and influence.'

'And why does Professor Dumbledore think I need it, sir?' said Harry, looking directly into Snape's eyes and wondering whether Snape would answer.

Snape looked back at him for a moment and then said contemptuously, 'Surely even you could have worked that out by now, Potter? The Dark Lord is highly skilled at Legilimency –'

'What's that? *Sir*?'

'It is the ability to extract feelings and memories from another person's mind –'

'He can read minds?' said Harry quickly, his worst fears confirmed.

'You have no subtlety, Potter,' said Snape, his dark eyes glittering. 'You do not understand fine distinctions. It is one of the shortcomings that makes you such a lamentable potion-maker.'

Snape paused for a moment, apparently to savour the pleasure of insulting Harry, before continuing.

'Only Muggles talk of "mind-reading". The mind is not a book, to be opened at will and examined at leisure. Thoughts are not etched on the inside of skulls, to be perused by any invader. The mind is a complex and many-layered thing, Potter – or at least, most minds are.' He smirked. 'It is true, however, that those who have mastered Legilimency are able, under certain conditions, to delve into the minds of their victims and to interpret their findings correctly. The Dark Lord, for instance, almost always knows when somebody is lying to him. Only those skilled at Occlumency are able to shut down those feelings and memories that contradict the lie, and so can utter falsehoods in his presence without detection.'

Whatever Snape said, Legilimency sounded like mind-reading to Harry, and he didn't like the sound of it at all.

第24章 大脑封闭术

"好,波特,你知道来这儿干什么。"他说,"校长要我教你大脑封闭术,我只能希望你比在魔药课上聪明一点儿。"

"是。"哈利不敢多话地答道。

"这也许不是一般的课,波特,"斯内普的眼睛阴险地眯缝起来,"但我还是你的老师,你任何时候都要叫我'先生'或'教授'。"

"是……先生。"哈利说。

"言归正传,大脑封闭术。在你亲爱的教父的厨房里我告诉过你,这门魔法能够防止头脑受到魔法的入侵和影响。"

"为什么邓布利多教授认为我需要它,先生?"哈利直视着斯内普冷酷的黑眼睛,不知他会不会回答。

斯内普瞪了他一会儿,轻蔑地说:"就算是你,到现在也该想通了吧,波特?黑魔王极其擅长摄神取念——"

"那是什么意思,先生?"

"即从另一个人的头脑中提取感觉和记忆——"

"他能读人心吗?"哈利马上问,他最担心的事被证实了。

"你没用心,波特,"斯内普说,他的黑眼睛闪着冷光,"你不懂得微妙的区别,这是使你把药剂配得如此糟糕的缺陷之一。"

斯内普停顿了一会儿,显然在品味侮辱哈利的快感,然后继续说:

"只有麻瓜才讲'读人心'。人心不是一本书,不可以随意翻阅和研究。思想也不是刻在脑壳里的,不可以让人钻进去读。人心是一种复杂的、多层次的东西,波特——至少多数头脑是。"他得意地笑道,"然而,会摄神取念的人可以在某些情况下研究别人的头脑,并做出正确的解释。比如说,黑魔王几乎总能看出别人对他说谎。只有擅长大脑封闭术的人才能封住与谎话相矛盾的感觉和记忆,在他面前说谎而不被发现。"

不管斯内普怎么说,摄神取念在哈利听来还是像读人心,而他一点也不喜欢有人这样做。

CHAPTER TWENTY-FOUR Occlumency

'So he could know what we're thinking right now? Sir?'

'The Dark Lord is at a considerable distance and the walls and grounds of Hogwarts are guarded by many ancient spells and charms to ensure the bodily and mental safety of those who dwell within them,' said Snape. 'Time and space matter in magic, Potter. Eye contact is often essential to Legilimency.'

'Well then, why do I have to learn Occlumency?'

Snape eyed Harry, tracing his mouth with one long, thin finger as he did so.

'The usual rules do not seem to apply with you, Potter. The curse that failed to kill you seems to have forged some kind of connection between you and the Dark Lord. The evidence suggests that at times, when your mind is most relaxed and vulnerable – when you are asleep, for instance – you are sharing the Dark Lord's thoughts and emotions. The Headmaster thinks it inadvisable for this to continue. He wishes me to teach you how to close your mind to the Dark Lord.'

Harry's heart was pumping fast again. None of this added up.

'But why does Professor Dumbledore want to stop it?' he asked abruptly. 'I don't like it much, but it's been useful, hasn't it? I mean ... I saw that snake attack Mr Weasley and if I hadn't, Professor Dumbledore wouldn't have been able to save him, would he? Sir?'

Snape stared at Harry for a few moments, still tracing his mouth with his finger. When he spoke again, it was slowly and deliberately, as though he weighed every word.

'It appears that the Dark Lord has been unaware of the connection between you and himself until very recently. Up till now it seems that you have been experiencing his emotions, and sharing his thoughts, without his being any the wiser. However, the vision you had shortly before Christmas –'

'The one with the snake and Mr Weasley?'

'Do not interrupt me, Potter,' said Snape in a dangerous voice. 'As I was saying, the vision you had shortly before Christmas represented such a powerful incursion upon the Dark Lord's thoughts –'

'I saw inside the snake's head, not his!'

'I thought I just told you not to interrupt me, Potter?'

But Harry did not care if Snape was angry; at last he seemed to be getting to the bottom of this business; he had moved forwards in his chair so that, without realising it, he was perched on the very edge, tense as though poised for flight.

第24章 大脑封闭术

"那他能知道我们现在想什么吗，先生？"

"黑魔王离得很远，霍格沃茨的院墙和场地有许多古老的咒语守护着，保证了校内人员的身心安全。"斯内普说，"时间和空间对魔法是有影响的，波特。目光接触对摄神取念往往十分关键。"

"那我为什么还要学大脑封闭术？"

斯内普瞟着哈利，用一根细长的手指摸着嘴巴。

"常规似乎不适用于你，波特。那个没能杀死你的咒语似乎在你和黑魔王之间建立了某种联系。迹象表明，有些时候，当你的头脑最放松、最脆弱时——比如在睡梦中，你就能感知黑魔王的思想和情绪。校长认为不应该任其继续下去，他要我教你怎样对黑魔王封闭你的思想。"

哈利的心咚咚直跳。这解释不通啊。

"可邓布利多教授为什么要制止呢？"他突然问，"我不大喜欢这感觉，可是这感觉挺有用呀。我是说……我看到了大蛇袭击韦斯莱先生，不然邓布利多教授可能救不了他，是不是，先生？"

斯内普看了哈利一会儿，依然用手指摸着嘴巴，然后缓缓开口，仿佛在斟酌每个字眼。

"黑魔王似乎直到最近才发觉你和他之间的这种联系。在此之前似乎是你能感知他的情绪和思想，他却浑然不知。但是，你圣诞节前的那个梦——"

"韦斯莱先生和蛇？"

"别打断我，波特。"斯内普凶狠地说，"我说到，你圣诞节前的那个梦，如此严重地侵入了黑魔王的思想——"

"我是在蛇的脑子里，不是他的！"

"我似乎刚说过别打断我，波特！"

但哈利不在意斯内普发火，他终于抓到了问题的根本。他身子往前探了过去，不知不觉已经坐在椅子的边缘，身体绷得紧紧的，就像随时准备逃跑一样。

CHAPTER TWENTY-FOUR Occlumency

'How come I saw through the snake's eyes if it's Voldemort's thoughts I'm sharing?'

'*Do not say the Dark Lord's name!*' spat Snape.

There was a nasty silence. They glared at each other across the Pensieve.

'Professor Dumbledore says his name,' said Harry quietly.

'Dumbledore is an extremely powerful wizard,' Snape muttered. 'While *he* may feel secure enough to use the name … the rest of us …' He rubbed his left forearm, apparently unconsciously, on the spot where Harry knew the Dark Mark was burned into his skin.

'I just wanted to know,' Harry began again, forcing his voice back to politeness, 'why –'

'You seem to have visited the snake's mind because that was where the Dark Lord was at that particular moment,' snarled Snape. 'He was possessing the snake at the time and so you dreamed you were inside it, too.'

'And Vol– he – realised I was there?'

'It seems so,' said Snape coolly.

'How do you know?' said Harry urgently. 'Is this just Professor Dumbledore guessing, or –?'

'I told you,' said Snape, rigid in his chair, his eyes slits, 'to call me "sir".'

'Yes, sir,' said Harry impatiently, 'but how do you know –?'

'It is enough that we know,' said Snape repressively. 'The important point is that the Dark Lord is now aware that you are gaining access to his thoughts and feelings. He has also deduced that the process is likely to work in reverse; that is to say, he has realised that he might be able to access your thoughts and feelings in return –'

'And he might try and make me do things?' asked Harry. '*Sir?*' he added hurriedly.

'He might,' said Snape, sounding cold and unconcerned. 'Which brings us back to Occlumency.'

Snape pulled out his wand from an inside pocket of his robes and Harry tensed in his chair, but Snape merely raised the wand to his temple and placed its tip into the greasy roots of his hair. When he withdrew it, some silvery substance came away, stretching from temple to wand like a thick gossamer strand, which broke as he pulled the wand away from it and fell gracefully into the Pensieve, where it swirled silvery-white, neither gas nor liquid. Twice more, Snape raised the wand to his temple and deposited the

"我感知的是伏地魔的思想,怎么又用蛇眼看东西呢?"

"不要说黑魔王的名字!"斯内普喝道。

一阵难堪的沉默,他们隔着冥想盆怒目相对。

"邓布利多教授也说他的名字。"哈利小声说。

"邓布利多是本领高强的巫师,"斯内普咕哝道,"他可能不讳言这个名字……但我们其他人……"他似乎是不自觉地摸了摸左胳膊,哈利知道那是烙有黑魔标记的地方。

"我只是想知道,"哈利竭力使语气保持礼貌,"为什么——"

"看来是你进入了蛇的脑子,因为黑魔王当时正在那里,"斯内普咆哮道,"他正附在蛇的体内,所以你梦见你也在里面。"

"那伏——他——发现我了吗?"

"看来是的。"斯内普冷冷地说。

"你怎么知道的?"哈利忙问,"这只是邓布利多教授的猜测,还是——?"

"我说过,"斯内普硬板板地坐在椅子上,眼睛像两条缝,"叫我先生。"

"是,先生。"哈利不耐烦地说,"可是你怎么知道——?"

"我们知道就够了。"斯内普厉声道,"重要的是黑魔王现在已经察觉你能感知他的思想和感觉。他还推断出这种情况是可以反过来的,也就是说,他已想到他或许能感知你的思想和感觉——"

"他可能想操纵我?"哈利问,赶紧又补上一句,"先生?"

"可能。"斯内普冷淡、漠然地说,"这就又回到了大脑封闭术。"

斯内普从袍子里抽出魔杖,哈利绷紧了身体。但斯内普只是把杖尖举到太阳穴上,插到油腻的发根中。当他拿开魔杖时,杖尖上连着一缕银色的东西,像粗粗的蛛丝。他把魔杖拿开时,银丝断开了,轻柔地落到了冥想盆里,在盆中旋转成了银白色,既非气体又非液体。斯内普又两次把魔杖举到太阳穴上,把银色的物质加入石盆中。他没

CHAPTER TWENTY-FOUR   Occlumency

silvery substance into the stone basin, then, without offering any explanation of his behaviour, he picked up the Pensieve carefully, removed it to a shelf out of their way and returned to face Harry with his wand held at the ready.

'Stand up and take out your wand, Potter.'

Harry got to his feet, feeling nervous. They faced each other with the desk between them.

'You may use your wand to attempt to disarm me, or defend yourself in any other way you can think of,' said Snape.

'And what are you going to do?' Harry asked, eyeing Snape's wand apprehensively.

'I am about to attempt to break into your mind,' said Snape softly. 'We are going to see how well you resist. I have been told that you have already shown aptitude at resisting the Imperius Curse. You will find that similar powers are needed for this ... brace yourself, now. *Legilimens!*'

Snape had struck before Harry was ready, before he had even begun to summon any force of resistance. The office swam in front of his eyes and vanished; image after image was racing through his mind like a flickering film so vivid it blinded him to his surroundings.

He was five, watching Dudley riding a new red bicycle, and his heart was bursting with jealousy ... he was nine, and Ripper the bulldog was chasing him up a tree and the Dursleys were laughing below on the lawn ... he was sitting under the Sorting Hat, and it was telling him he would do well in Slytherin ... Hermione was lying in the hospital wing, her face covered with thick black hair ... a hundred Dementors were closing in on him beside the dark lake ... Cho Chang was drawing nearer to him under the mistletoe ...

No, said a voice inside Harry's head, as the memory of Cho drew nearer, *you're not watching that, you're not watching it, it's private –*

He felt a sharp pain in his knee. Snape's office had come back into view and he realised that he had fallen to the floor; one of his knees had collided painfully with the leg of Snape's desk. He looked up at Snape, who had lowered his wand and was rubbing his wrist. There was an angry weal there, like a scorch mark.

'Did you mean to produce a Stinging Hex?' asked Snape coolly.

'No,' said Harry bitterly, getting up from the floor.

'I thought not,' said Snape contemptuously. 'You let me get in too far. You lost control.'

'Did you see everything I saw?' Harry asked, unsure whether he wanted to hear the answer.

第24章 大脑封闭术

有解释，只是小心地把冥想盆捧到靠边的架子上，然后转过来手持魔杖对着哈利。

"站起来，拿出你的魔杖，波特。"

哈利紧张地站了起来，两人隔着桌子对峙着。

"你可以用魔杖解除我的武器，或者用你能想到的其他方式自卫。"斯内普说。

"你要做什么？"哈利害怕地看着斯内普的魔杖问。

"我要进入你的大脑，"斯内普轻声说，"我们要看看你的抵抗能力。我听说你已经显示出对夺魂咒的抵抗力……你会发现这里要用到类似的能力……现在，准备……摄神取念！"

斯内普突然出手，哈利还没来得及准备，没来得及做任何抵抗：办公室在他眼前晃动着消失了，一幅幅画面像放电影般生动地在他脑海中闪过，他已看不到周围的东西。

五岁时他看着达力骑在红色的新自行车上，他心中充满了嫉妒……九岁时他被斗牛犬利皮赶到树上，德思礼一家在草坪上哈哈大笑……他戴着分院帽，听见它说他可以去斯莱特林……赫敏躺在校医院，满脸黑毛……一百个摄魂怪在黑暗的湖边把他包围了……秋·张在槲寄生下向他靠近……

不，记忆中的秋靠近时，哈利脑子里有个声音叫道，你不能看这个，你不能看，这是隐私——

他感到膝盖一阵剧痛，斯内普的办公室回来了，他发现自己倒在地上，一只膝盖在桌腿上重重地磕了一下。他抬头望望斯内普，见他放下了魔杖，正揉着手腕，那儿有一道红肿的鞭痕，像一个烙印。

"你想施蜇人咒吗？"斯内普冷冷地问。

"没有。"哈利怨恨地说，一边从地上爬了起来。

"我想也是。"斯内普轻蔑地说，"你让我进得太深，你失去了控制。"

"你全看到了？"哈利不知自己想不想听到回答。

CHAPTER TWENTY-FOUR   Occlumency

'Flashes of it,' said Snape, his lip curling. 'To whom did the dog belong?'

'My Aunt Marge,' Harry muttered, hating Snape.

'Well, for a first attempt that was not as poor as it might have been,' said Snape, raising his wand once more. 'You managed to stop me eventually, though you wasted time and energy shouting. You must remain focused. Repel me with your brain and you will not need to resort to your wand.'

'I'm trying,' said Harry angrily, 'but you're not telling me how!'

'Manners, Potter,' said Snape dangerously. 'Now, I want you to close your eyes.'

Harry threw him a filthy look before doing as he was told. He did not like the idea of standing there with his eyes shut while Snape faced him, carrying a wand.

'Clear your mind, Potter,' said Snape's cold voice. 'Let go of all emotion ...'

But Harry's anger at Snape continued to pound through his veins like venom. Let go of his anger? He could as easily detach his legs ...

'You're not doing it, Potter ... you will need more discipline than this ... focus, now ...'

Harry tried to empty his mind, tried not to think, or remember, or feel ...

'Let's go again ... on the count of three ... one – two – three – *Legilimens!*'

A great black dragon was rearing in front of him ... his father and mother were waving at him out of an enchanted mirror ... Cedric Diggory was lying on the ground with blank eyes staring at him ...

'NOOOOOOO!'

Harry was on his knees again, his face buried in his hands, his brain aching as though someone had been trying to pull it from his skull.

'Get up!' said Snape sharply. 'Get up! You are not trying, you are making no effort. You are allowing me access to memories you fear, handing me weapons!'

Harry stood up again, his heart thumping wildly as though he had really just seen Cedric dead in the graveyard. Snape looked paler than usual, and angrier, though not nearly as angry as Harry was.

'I – am – making – an – effort,' he said through clenched teeth.

'I told you to empty yourself of emotion!'

'Yeah? Well, I'm finding that hard at the moment,' Harry snarled.

'Then you will find yourself easy prey for the Dark Lord!' said Snape savagely. 'Fools who wear their hearts proudly on their sleeves, who cannot

第24章 大脑封闭术

"一些片段。"斯内普说着撇了撇嘴,"那条狗是谁的?"

"玛姬姑妈的。"哈利小声说,心里恨透了斯内普。

"不过,作为第一次,还不算太差。"斯内普又举起魔杖,"你在最后阻止了我,尽管你浪费了时间和精力大喊大叫。你必须集中精神,用你的脑子抵抗我,不需要用魔杖。"

"我会努力的。"哈利愤怒地说,"但你没告诉我怎么做!"

"礼貌,波特。"斯内普凶狠地说,"现在,我要你闭上眼睛。"

哈利狠狠地瞪了他一眼才照办了。他不喜欢闭眼站在那儿,让斯内普拿着魔杖站在他面前。

"排除杂念,波特,"斯内普冷冷的声音说,"丢开所有的感情……"

但对斯内普的愤怒仍像毒液一样冲击着哈利的血管。丢开愤怒?还不如丢掉一条腿更容易些……

"你没有做到,波特……你需要约束自己……集中思想,开始……"

哈利努力清空头脑,不去思考,不去回忆,不去感觉……

"再来……我数到三……一——二——三——摄神取念!"

一条黑色的巨龙在他面前张牙舞爪……他的父母在魔镜中向他招手……塞德里克·迪戈里躺在地上,两眼无神地瞪着他……

"不——!"

他又跪在了地上,脸埋在手心里,脑子生疼,好像有人要把它从脑壳中抽出去一样。

"起来!"斯内普厉声说,"起来!你没有做,没有努力,你让我看到了你所害怕的记忆,等于在给我武器!"

哈利站了起来,心脏怦怦狂跳,好像真的刚看到塞德里克死在墓地里一样。斯内普看上去比平常更苍白,更愤怒,尽管远不如哈利愤怒。

"我——努——力——了。"他咬着牙说。

"我叫你丢开感情!"

"是吗?我现在觉得很难做到。"哈利吼道。

"那你就很容易被黑魔王利用!"斯内普残酷地说,"把心事写在

CHAPTER TWENTY-FOUR Occlumency

control their emotions, who wallow in sad memories and allow themselves to be provoked so easily – weak people, in other words – they stand no chance against his powers! He will penetrate your mind with absurd ease, Potter!'

'I am not weak,' said Harry in a low voice, fury now pumping through him so that he thought he might attack Snape in a moment.

'Then prove it! Master yourself!' spat Snape. 'Control your anger, discipline your mind! We shall try again! Get ready, now! *Legilimens!*'

He was watching Uncle Vernon hammering the letterbox shut ... a hundred Dementors were drifting across the lake in the grounds towards him ... he was running along a windowless passage with Mr Weasley ... they were drawing nearer to the plain black door at the end of the corridor ... Harry expected to go through it ... but Mr Weasley led him off to the left, down a flight of stone steps ...

'I KNOW! I KNOW!'

He was on all fours again on Snape's office floor, his scar was prickling unpleasantly, but the voice that had just issued from his mouth was triumphant. He pushed himself up again to find Snape staring at him, his wand raised. It looked as though, this time, Snape had lifted the spell before Harry had even tried to fight back.

'What happened then, Potter?' he asked, eyeing Harry intently.

'I saw – I remembered,' Harry panted. 'I've just realised ...'

'Realised what?' asked Snape sharply.

Harry did not answer at once; he was still savouring the moment of blinding realisation as he rubbed his forehead ...

He had been dreaming about a windowless corridor ending in a locked door for months, without once realising that it was a real place. Now, seeing the memory again, he knew that all along he had been dreaming about the corridor down which he had run with Mr Weasley on the twelfth of August as they hurried to the courtrooms in the Ministry; it was the corridor leading to the Department of Mysteries and Mr Weasley had been there the night that he had been attacked by Voldemort's snake.

He looked up at Snape.

'What's in the Department of Mysteries?'

'What did you say?' Snape asked quietly and Harry saw, with deep satisfaction, that Snape was unnerved.

'I said, what's in the Department of Mysteries, *sir*?' Harry said.

第24章 大脑封闭术

脸上的傻瓜们，不会控制自己的感情，沉溺在悲伤的回忆中，让自己那么容易受刺激——一句话，软弱的人，他们在他的力量面前不堪一击！他要侵入你的思想易如反掌，波特！"

"我不软弱。"哈利低声说，他怒火中烧，觉得自己马上就有可能揍斯内普了。

"那就证明一下！控制自己！"斯内普训斥道，"克制你的怒气，管好你的大脑！我们再来！准备！摄神取念！"

他看着弗农姨父把信箱钉死……一百个摄魂怪从湖上朝他飘来……他和韦斯莱先生在一条没有窗户的走廊上疾行……离走廊尽头的黑门越来越近……哈利以为要进去……但韦斯莱先生把他领向左边，走下石阶……

"我知道了！我知道了！"

他又扑倒在斯内普办公室的地上，伤疤针扎一般地痛，但从他嘴里发出的声音却是欢喜的。他撑起身子，看到斯内普手举魔杖瞪着他。这次斯内普好像没等哈利反抗就撤除了咒语。

"怎么回事，波特？"他盯着哈利问。

"我看见——我想起，"哈利喘着气说，"我刚刚意识到……"

"意识到什么？"斯内普厉声问。

哈利没有马上回答，他揉着额头，还在回味那一刻令人目眩的顿悟……

他几个月来经常梦见一条没有窗户的走廊，尽头有一扇上锁的门，但从未意识到它是个真实的地方。现在在回忆中看到，他发现那就是他和韦斯莱先生八月十二日赶往审判室时经过的那条走廊，它通向神秘事务司，韦斯莱先生就是在那儿被伏地魔的蛇咬伤的……

他抬头望着斯内普。

"神秘事务司里有什么？"

"你说什么？"斯内普轻声问，哈利快意地看到他有些慌张。

"我说，神秘事务司里有什么，先生？"哈利说。

CHAPTER TWENTY-FOUR Occlumency

'And why,' said Snape slowly, 'would you ask such a thing?'

'Because,' said Harry, watching Snape closely for a reaction, 'that corridor I've just seen – I've been dreaming about it for months – I've just recognised it – it leads to the Department of Mysteries ... and I think Voldemort wants something from –'

'*I have told you not to say the Dark Lord's name!*'

They glared at each other. Harry's scar seared again, but he did not care. Snape looked agitated; but when he spoke again he sounded as though he was trying to appear cool and unconcerned.

'There are many things in the Department of Mysteries, Potter, few of which you would understand and none of which concern you. Do I make myself plain?'

'Yes,' Harry said, still rubbing his prickling scar, which was becoming more painful.

'I want you back here same time on Wednesday. We will continue work then.'

'Fine,' said Harry. He was desperate to get out of Snape's office and find Ron and Hermione.

'You are to rid your mind of all emotion every night before sleep; empty it, make it blank and calm, you understand?'

'Yes,' said Harry, who was barely listening.

'And be warned, Potter ... I shall know if you have not practised ...'

'Right,' Harry mumbled. He picked up his schoolbag, swung it over his shoulder and hurried towards the office door. As he opened it, he glanced back at Snape, who had his back to Harry and was scooping his own thoughts out of the Pensieve with the tip of his wand and replacing them carefully inside his own head. Harry left without another word, closing the door carefully behind him, his scar still throbbing painfully.

Harry found Ron and Hermione in the library, where they were working on Umbridge's most recent ream of homework. Other students, nearly all of them fifth-years, sat at lamp-lit tables nearby, noses close to books, quills scratching feverishly, while the sky outside the mullioned windows grew steadily blacker. The only other sound was the slight squeaking of one of Madam Pince's shoes, as the librarian prowled the aisles menacingly, breathing down the necks of those touching her precious books.

Harry felt shivery; his scar was still aching, he felt almost feverish. When he sat down opposite Ron and Hermione, he caught sight of himself in the window opposite; he was very white and his scar seemed to be showing up

第24章 大脑封闭术

"你为什么问这个?"斯内普缓缓地问。

"因为,"哈利紧盯着斯内普,看他有什么反应,"我看到的那条走廊——我几个月来一直梦见它——我刚刚意识到——它通向神秘事务司……我想伏地魔渴望得到那——"

"我叫你别说黑魔王的名字!"

他们怒目相向,哈利的伤疤又灼痛起来,但他没管它。斯内普似乎有些紧张,说话时却努力装出冷淡和漠不关心的样子。

"神秘事务司里有许多东西,波特,没有几样是你搞得懂的,而且每一样都不关你的事。我说清楚了吗?"

"清楚了。"哈利说,还在揉着伤疤,它越来越疼了。

"我希望你星期三同一时间过来,我们继续练习。"

"好的。"哈利说。他迫不及待地想离开斯内普的办公室去找罗恩与赫敏。

"你每天晚上睡觉前要排除一切情感——使你的头脑变得空而静,明白吗?"

"明白。"哈利说,但他几乎没有听。

"小心,波特……我会知道你有没有练习……"

"是。"哈利小声说。他把书包甩到肩上,快步朝门口走去。开门时他回头看了看斯内普,他正背对着哈利,用魔杖把他的思想从冥想盆里挑出来,小心地放回脑子里。哈利没再说话就离开了,他轻轻带上门,伤疤还在突突地痛着。

他在图书馆里找到了罗恩与赫敏,两人正在赶乌姆里奇新布置的一堆作业。其他学生,几乎全是五年级的,也都坐在点着灯的桌前,鼻子凑近书本,羽毛笔在唰唰地狂写。竖框窗子外的天色越来越黑,唯一的声音就是平斯女士的鞋子发出的哒哒轻响。她在过道里威胁地来回巡视,把呼吸喷到碰她那些宝贝图书的人的脖子上。

哈利有点哆嗦,伤疤还在痛着,他觉得有点发烧。在罗恩、赫敏对面坐下时,他在窗户中照见了自己,脸色十分苍白,伤疤似乎比平

more clearly than usual.

'How did it go?' Hermione whispered, and then, looking concerned. 'Are you all right, Harry?'

'Yeah ... fine ... I dunno,' said Harry impatiently, wincing as pain shot through his scar again. 'Listen ... I've just realised something ...'

And he told them what he had just seen and deduced.

'So ... so are you saying ...' whispered Ron, as Madam Pince swept past, squeaking slightly, 'that the weapon – the thing You-Know-Who's after – is in the Ministry of Magic?'

'In the Department of Mysteries, it's got to be,' Harry whispered. 'I saw that door when your dad took me down to the courtrooms for my hearing and it's definitely the same one he was guarding when the snake bit him.'

Hermione let out a long, slow sigh.

'Of course,' she breathed.

'Of course what?' said Ron rather impatiently.

'Ron, think about it ... Sturgis Podmore was trying to get through a door at the Ministry of Magic ... it must have been that one, it's too much of a coincidence!'

'How come Sturgis was trying to break in when he's on our side?' said Ron.

'Well, I don't know,' Hermione admitted. 'That is a bit odd ...'

'So what's in the Department of Mysteries?' Harry asked Ron. 'Has your dad ever mentioned anything about it?'

'I know they call the people who work in there "Unspeakables",' said Ron, frowning. 'Because no one really seems to know what they do – weird place to have a weapon.'

'It's not weird at all, it makes perfect sense,' said Hermione. 'It will be something top secret that the Ministry has been developing, I expect ... Harry, are you sure you're all right?'

For Harry had just run both his hands hard over his forehead as though trying to iron it.

'Yeah ... fine ...' he said, lowering his hands, which were trembling. 'I just feel a bit ... I don't like Occlumency much.'

'I expect anyone would feel shaky if they'd had their mind attacked over and over again,' said Hermione sympathetically. 'Look, let's get back to the common room, we'll be a bit more comfortable there.'

But the common room was packed and full of shrieks of laughter and excitement;

第24章 大脑封闭术

常更显眼了。

"怎么样？"赫敏小声问，然后露出担心的表情，"你没事吧，哈利？"

"嗯……没事……我不知道。"哈利烦躁地说，痛得皱了皱眉，"告诉你们……我刚发现了一件事……"

他讲了刚才看到和推想的那件事。

"你……你是说……"罗恩小声说，平斯女士走了过去，带着哒哒的轻响，"那件武器——神秘人要找的东西——藏在魔法部？"

"应该是在神秘事务司。"哈利悄声道，"你爸爸带我去审判室受审时看到过那扇门，跟他被蛇咬时看守的门就是同一扇。"

赫敏长长地吁了一口气。

"当然啦。"她说。

"什么当然啦？"罗恩不耐烦地问。

"罗恩，想想吧……斯多吉·波德摩企图闯入魔法部的一扇门……一定就是那扇，这不像是巧合！"

"为什么斯多吉要闯进去呢，他不是我们这一边的吗？"

"嗯，我不知道，"赫敏承认道，"是有点奇怪……"

"神秘事务司里到底有什么呢？"哈利问罗恩，"你爸爸提过什么吗？"

"我知道他们管在那儿工作的人叫'缄默人'，"罗恩皱眉道，"因为好像没人知道他们在那儿干什么……那种地方会有武器？这可够怪的……"

"一点也不怪，合情合理，"赫敏说，"我想那是魔法部开发的什么绝密玩意儿……哈利，你真的没事吗？"

这时哈利正用两手搓着额头，像是要熨平它。

"嗯……没事……"他放下手，双手在颤抖，"只是有点……我不大喜欢大脑封闭术……"

"脑子一次次地受到袭击，我想谁都会发虚的。"赫敏同情地说，"我们回公共休息室去吧，那儿会舒服一点儿……"

但公共休息室里闹哄哄地挤满了人，弗雷德和乔治在演示笑话店

CHAPTER TWENTY-FOUR — Occlumency

Fred and George were demonstrating their latest bit of joke shop merchandise.

'Headless Hats!' shouted George, as Fred waved a pointed hat decorated with a fluffy pink feather at the watching students. 'Two Galleons each, watch Fred, now!'

Fred swept the hat on to his head, beaming. For a second he merely looked rather stupid; then both hat and head vanished.

Several girls screamed, but everyone else was roaring with laughter.

'And off again!' shouted George, and Fred's hand groped for a moment in what seemed to be thin air over his shoulder; then his head reappeared as he swept the pink-feathered hat from it.

'How do those hats work, then?' said Hermione, distracted from her homework and watching Fred and George. 'I mean, obviously it's some kind of Invisibility Spell, but it's rather clever to have extended the field of invisibility beyond the boundaries of the charmed object ... I'd imagine the charm wouldn't have a very long life though.'

Harry did not answer; he was feeling ill.

'I'm going to have to do this tomorrow,' he muttered, pushing the books he had just taken out of his bag back inside it.

'Well, write it in your homework planner then!' said Hermione encouragingly. 'So you don't forget!'

Harry and Ron exchanged looks as he reached into his bag, withdrew the planner and opened it tentatively.

'*Don't leave it till later, you big second-rater!*' chided the book as Harry scribbled down Umbridge's homework. Hermione beamed at it.

'I think I'll go to bed,' said Harry, stuffing the homework planner back into his bag and making a mental note to drop it in the fire the first opportunity he got.

He walked across the common room, dodging George, who tried to put a Headless Hat on him, and reached the peace and cool of the stone staircase to the boys' dormitories. He was feeling sick again, just as he had the night he had had the vision of the snake, but thought that if he could just lie down for a while he would be all right.

He opened the door of his dormitory and was one step inside it when he experienced pain so severe he thought that someone must have sliced into the top of his head. He did not know where he was, whether he was standing or lying down, he did not even know his own name.

Maniacal laughter was ringing in his ears ... he was happier than he had been in a very long time ... jubilant, ecstatic, triumphant ... a wonderful, wonderful

第 24 章 大脑封闭术

的最新产品。

"无头帽!"乔治吆喝道,弗雷德对观看的学生挥舞着一顶饰有粉红色羽毛的尖帽子,"两个加隆一顶……诸位请看弗雷德!"

弗雷德笑嘻嘻地把帽子套到头上,一刹那间他显得呆头呆脑,然后帽子和头一起消失了。

几个女生尖叫起来,其他人哄堂大笑。

"脱帽!"乔治喊道,弗雷德的手在肩膀上方的空间摸索了一阵子,他的头重新出现了,粉红色羽毛的帽子被摘了下来。

"那帽子是怎么做到的?"赫敏也从作业上分了神,仔细观察着弗雷德和乔治,"显然是一种隐形咒,但把隐形区域扩大到施了魔法的物体之外倒是蛮聪明的……不过我想这魔法不会持续太久……"

哈利没有回答,他还是不舒服。

"我明天再做吧。"他低声说,把刚从书包里拿出来的课本又塞了回去。

"记在你的家庭作业计划簿上!"赫敏建议道,"这样你就不会忘了!"

哈利和罗恩交换了一下眼色,他从书包里掏出计划簿,小心地打开了它。

"不要说以后做,你这个二流货!"本子叱责道,哈利草草记下乌姆里奇的作业,赫敏满意地笑了。

"我去睡觉了。"哈利把作业计划簿塞进了书包,心想一有机会就把它丢到火里去。

他穿过公共休息室,躲开想给他戴无头帽的乔治,走到通往男生宿舍的安静凉爽的石楼梯上。他感觉很难受,就像梦见蛇的那天夜里一样。但他想也许躺一会儿就好了。

他打开宿舍的门,刚往里走了一步,脑袋就像被切开似的疼了起来。他不知道身在何处,站着还是躺着,甚至不知道自己的名字。

疯狂的笑声在他耳中回响……他好久没有这么开心过了……兴高

CHAPTER TWENTY-FOUR Occlumency

thing had happened ...

'Harry? HARRY!'

Someone had hit him around the face. The insane laughter was punctuated with a cry of pain. The happiness was draining out of him, but the laughter continued ...

He opened his eyes and, as he did so, he became aware that the wild laughter was coming out of his own mouth. The moment he realised this, it died away; Harry lay panting on the floor, staring up at the ceiling, the scar on his forehead throbbing horribly. Ron was bending over him, looking very worried.

'What happened?' he said.

'I ... dunno ...' Harry gasped, sitting up again. 'He's really happy ... really happy ...'

'You-Know-Who is?'

'Something good's happened,' mumbled Harry. He was shaking as badly as he had done after seeing the snake attack Mr Weasley and felt very sick. 'Something he's been hoping for.'

The words came, just as they had back in the Gryffindor changing room, as though a stranger was speaking them through Harry's mouth, yet he knew they were true. He took deep breaths, willing himself not to vomit all over Ron. He was very glad that Dean and Seamus were not here to watch this time.

'Hermione told me to come and check on you,' said Ron in a low voice, helping Harry to his feet. 'She says your defences will be low at the moment, after Snape's been fiddling around with your mind ... still, I suppose it'll help in the long run, won't it?'

He looked doubtfully at Harry as he helped him towards his bed. Harry nodded without any conviction and slumped back on his pillows, aching all over from having fallen to the floor so often that evening, his scar still prickling painfully. He could not help feeling that his first foray into Occlumency had weakened his mind's resistance rather than strengthening it, and he wondered, with a feeling of great trepidation, what had happened to make Lord Voldemort the happiest he had been in fourteen years.

第24章 大脑封闭术

采烈，欣喜若狂，得意忘形……一件大大的好事发生了……

"哈利？**哈利！**"

有人打了他一记耳光。疯狂的笑声中插入一声疼痛的叫喊。快乐渐渐消失，但笑声还在持续……

他睁开眼睛，发现那疯狂的笑声是从他自己嘴里发出来的。他一意识到这点，笑声就消失了。哈利气喘吁吁地躺在地上，瞪着天花板，额头的伤疤可怕地跳动着。罗恩俯身看着他，看上去很担心。

"你怎么啦？"

"我……不知道……"哈利喘着气，坐了起来，"他很高兴……很高兴……"

"神秘人？"

"有一件好事发生了，"哈利嘟哝道，他像梦见韦斯莱先生被蛇咬之后那样浑身发抖，非常难受，"他一直盼望的事情。"

像在格兰芬多队更衣室那次一样，这些话仿佛是一个陌生人用哈利的嘴说出来的，但他知道这是实情。他深深地呼吸，不让自己吐在罗恩身上。他很庆幸迪安和西莫不在场。

"赫敏让我来看看你。"罗恩低声说，一边把哈利拉了起来，"她说你这会儿抵抗力很弱，斯内普刚折腾过你的脑子……但我想长远看会有用的，是吧？"

罗恩怀疑地看看哈利，把他扶到床边。哈利没信心地点点头，瘫靠在枕头上，因为晚上摔的那些跤而浑身疼痛，他的伤疤仍像针扎般地疼。他不禁怀疑第一次学习的大脑封闭术不仅没有加强他的抵抗力，反而将其削弱了。同时他怀着极大的恐惧揣测着，究竟是什么事让伏地魔感觉到了十四年来从没有过的开心。

CHAPTER TWENTY-FIVE

The Beetle at Bay

Harry's question was answered the very next morning. When Hermione's *Daily Prophet* arrived she smoothed it out, gazed for a moment at the front page and gave a yelp that caused everyone in the vicinity to stare at her.

'What?' said Harry and Ron together.

For answer she spread the newspaper on the table in front of them and pointed at ten black-and-white photographs that filled the whole of the front page, nine showing wizards' faces and the tenth, a witch's. Some of the people in the photographs were silently jeering; others were tapping their fingers on the frame of their pictures, looking insolent. Each picture was captioned with a name and the crime for which the person had been sent to Azkaban.

Antonin Dolohov, read the legend beneath a wizard with a long, pale, twisted face who was sneering up at Harry, *convicted of the brutal murders of Gideon and Fabian Prewett.*

Augustus Rookwood, said the caption beneath a pockmarked man with greasy hair who was leaning against the edge of his picture, looking bored, *convicted of leaking Ministry of Magic secrets to He Who Must Not Be Named.*

But Harry's eyes were drawn to the picture of the witch. Her face had leapt out at him the moment he had seen the page. She had long, dark hair that looked unkempt and straggly in the picture, though he had seen it sleek, thick and shining. She glared up at him through heavily lidded eyes, an arrogant, disdainful smile playing around her thin mouth. Like Sirius, she retained vestiges of great good looks, but something – perhaps Azkaban – had taken most of her beauty.

Bellatrix Lestrange, convicted of the torture and permanent incapacitation of Frank and Alice Longbottom.

第 25 章

无奈的甲虫

哈利的问题第二天一早就找到了答案。赫敏的《预言家日报》送来后,她打开报纸先看头版,突然大声尖叫,周围的人都朝她看了过来。

"怎么啦?"哈利和罗恩一齐问。

赫敏把报纸摊到他们面前的桌上,指着占满头版的十张黑白照片,九个男巫和一个女巫的面孔,有的在无声嗤笑,有的傲慢地用手指敲着他们照片的边。每张照片下注有姓名和被关进阿兹卡班的罪行。

安东宁·多洛霍夫,一个男巫苍白、扭曲的长脸正对着哈利冷笑,凶残地杀害了吉迪翁和费比安·普威特兄弟俩。

奥古斯特·卢克伍德,一个头发油光光的麻脸男子倚在照片的边上,一副厌倦的表情,向神秘人泄露魔法部机密。

但哈利的目光被那个女巫吸引住了。第一眼看报纸时她的面孔就跳入了他的视线,她黑色的长发在照片上显得乱蓬蓬的,但哈利见过它光滑乌亮的样子。她厚眼皮下的眼睛瞪着他,薄嘴唇浮现出一丝高傲的、轻蔑的微笑。像小天狼星一样,她还保留着一些俊美的痕迹,但某种东西——也许是阿兹卡班,已经夺走了她大部分的美丽。

贝拉特里克斯·莱斯特兰奇,酷刑折磨弗兰克和艾丽斯·隆巴顿夫妇,导致二人永久性残废。

CHAPTER TWENTY-FIVE   The Beetle at Bay

Hermione nudged Harry and pointed at the headline over the pictures, which Harry, concentrating on Bellatrix, had not yet read.

MASS BREAKOUT FROM AZKABAN
MINISTRY FEARS BLACK IS 'RALLYING POINT' FOR OLD DEATH EATERS

'Black?' said Harry loudly. 'Not –?'

'*Shhh!*' whispered Hermione desperately. 'Not so loud – just read it!'

The Ministry of Magic announced late last night that there has been a mass breakout from Azkaban.

Speaking to reporters in his private office, Cornelius Fudge, Minister for Magic, confirmed that ten high-security prisoners escaped in the early hours of yesterday evening and that he has already informed the Muggle Prime Minister of the dangerous nature of these individuals.

'We find ourselves, most unfortunately, in the same position we were two and a half years ago when the murderer Sirius Black escaped,' said Fudge last night. 'Nor do we think the two breakouts are unrelated. An escape of this magnitude suggests outside help, and we must remember that Black, as the first person ever to break out of Azkaban, would be ideally placed to help others follow in his foot-steps. We think it likely that these individuals, who include Black's cousin, Bellatrix Lestrange, have rallied around Black as their leader. We are, however, doing all we can to round up the criminals, and we beg the magical community to remain alert and cautious. On no account should any of these individuals be approached.'

'There you are, Harry,' said Ron, looking awestruck. 'That's why he was happy last night.'

'I don't believe this,' snarled Harry, 'Fudge is blaming the breakout on *Sirius*?'

'What other options does he have?' said Hermione bitterly. 'He can hardly say, "Sorry, everyone, Dumbledore warned me this might happen, the Azkaban guards have joined Lord Voldemort" – stop *whimpering*, Ron – "and

第25章 无奈的甲虫

赫敏推推哈利，指指照片上方的标题。哈利只顾看贝拉特里克斯，都没看标题。

阿兹卡班多人越狱
魔法部担心布莱克是食死徒的"号召人"

"布莱克？"哈利大声说，"不是——？"
"嘘！"赫敏急道，"小声点儿——往下看！"

魔法部昨天夜间宣布阿兹卡班发生大规模越狱事件。

部长康奈利·福吉在办公室接受采访时证实十名重犯于昨晚脱逃，他已向麻瓜首相通报了逃犯的危险性。

"非常遗憾，我们陷入了与两年半前杀人犯小天狼星布莱克脱逃时相同的处境，"福吉昨夜说，"而且我们认为两次越狱并非没有联系。如此大规模的越狱令人怀疑有外面的接应，要知道布莱克作为从阿兹卡班脱逃的第一人，最有条件帮助他人越狱。逃犯中还包括布莱克的堂姐贝拉特里克斯·莱斯特兰奇。我们认为这些逃犯可能把布莱克当作领袖。但魔法部正不遗余力地追缉逃犯，并请公众保持警惕，切勿接近这些要犯。"

"你看，哈利，"罗恩颇为震惊地说，"怪不得他昨天晚上那么高兴……"

"我不能相信，"哈利吼道，"福吉竟会把越狱怪到小天狼星的头上？"

"他还能怎么样？"赫敏挖苦地说，"他能说'对不起，邓布利多提醒过我，阿兹卡班的看守投靠了伏地魔'——别哼哼，罗恩——'现在伏地魔的得力助手也跑了'吗？他花了六个月对大家说你和邓布利

CHAPTER TWENTY-FIVE   The Beetle at Bay

now Voldemort's worst supporters have broken out, too." I mean, he's spent a good six months telling everyone you and Dumbledore are liars, hasn't he?'

Hermione ripped open the newspaper and began to read the report inside while Harry looked around the Great Hall. He could not understand why his fellow students were not looking scared or at least discussing the terrible piece of news on the front page, but very few of them took the newspaper every day like Hermione. There they all were, talking about homework and Quidditch and who knew what other rubbish, when outside these walls ten more Death Eaters had swollen Voldemort's ranks.

He glanced up at the staff table. It was a different story there: Dumbledore and Professor McGonagall were deep in conversation, both looking extremely grave. Professor Sprout had the *Prophet* propped against a bottle of ketchup and was reading the front page with such concentration that she was not noticing the gentle drip of egg yolk falling into her lap from her stationary spoon. Meanwhile, at the far end of the table, Professor Umbridge was tucking into a bowl of porridge. For once her pouchy toad's eyes were not sweeping the Great Hall looking for misbehaving students. She scowled as she gulped down her food and every now and then she shot a malevolent glance up the table to where Dumbledore and McGonagall were talking so intently.

'Oh my –' said Hermione wonderingly, still staring at the newspaper.

'What now?' said Harry quickly; he was feeling jumpy.

'It's ... *horrible*,' said Hermione, looking shaken. She folded back page ten of the newspaper and handed it to Harry and Ron.

TRAGIC DEMISE OF MINISTRY OF MAGIC WORKER

St Mungo's Hospital promised a full inquiry last night after Ministry of Magic worker Broderick Bode, 49, was discovered dead in his bed, strangled by a pot plant. Healers called to the scene were unable to revive Mr Bode, who had been injured in a workplace accident some weeks prior to his death.

Healer Miriam Strout, who was in charge of Mr Bode's ward at the time of the incident, has been suspended on full pay and was unavailable for comment yesterday, but a spokeswizard for the hospital said in a statement:

'St Mungo's deeply regrets the death of Mr Bode, whose

第25章 无奈的甲虫

多都是骗子，不是吗？"

赫敏翻开报纸，开始读里面的报道。哈利环顾礼堂，不明白其他学生为什么没有显得恐慌，或至少在议论这可怕的头版新闻，但很少有人像赫敏那样每天拿到报纸。他们还在聊着作业、魁地奇球和鬼知道是什么的废话，而墙外又有十个食死徒壮大了伏地魔的力量……

他朝教工桌子望去，那儿是另一番景象：邓布利多和麦格教授在密切交谈，两人面容都异常严峻。斯普劳特教授把《预言家日报》靠在番茄酱的瓶子上，专心致志地读着第一版，勺子举在空中，连勺里的蛋黄滴到了腿上都没发觉。桌子另一头的乌姆里奇教授正在大口地喝麦片粥，她眼皮松垂的眼睛第一次没有在礼堂里搜寻行为不当的学生。她皱着眉头吃饭，不时恶毒地朝邓布利多和麦格教授那边瞥上一眼，他们正在专心谈话。

"呃，天——"赫敏惊叫一声，还在看着报纸。

"又怎么了？"哈利忙问，感觉心惊肉跳。

"……太可怕了。"赫敏看上去非常震惊，把第十版折过来，递给了哈利和罗恩。

魔法部职员死于非命

圣芒戈医院昨晚保证对魔法部职员布罗德里克·博德之死做出全面调查。四十九岁的博德先生被一盆植物勒死在病床上，治疗师抢救无效。博德先生数周前在一次工作事故中受伤。

出事时分管博德先生病房的治疗师梅莲姆·斯特劳带薪停职，昨天未接受采访。但医院发言人称：

"圣芒戈对博德先生之死深表遗憾，惨剧发生前他正在日渐康复。

CHAPTER TWENTY-FIVE   The Beetle at Bay

health was improving steadily prior to this tragic accident.

'We have strict guidelines on the decorations permitted on our wards but it appears that Healer Strout, busy over the Christmas period, overlooked the dangers of the plant on Mr Bode's bedside table. As his speech and mobility improved, Healer Strout encouraged Mr Bode to look after the plant himself, unaware that it was not an innocent Flitterbloom, but a cutting of Devil's Snare which, when touched by the convalescent Mr Bode, throttled him instantly.

'St Mungo's is as yet unable to account for the presence of the plant on the ward and asks any witch or wizard with information to come forward.'

'Bode ...' said Ron. '*Bode*. It rings a bell ...'

'We saw him,' Hermione whispered. 'In St Mungo's, remember? He was in the bed opposite Lockhart's, just lying there, staring at the ceiling. And we saw the Devil's Snare arrive. She – the Healer – said it was a Christmas present.'

Harry looked back at the story. A feeling of horror was rising like bile in his throat.

'How come we didn't recognise Devil's Snare? We've seen it before ... we could've stopped this from happening.'

'Who expects Devil's Snare to turn up in a hospital disguised as a pot plant?' said Ron sharply. 'It's not our fault, whoever sent it to the bloke is to blame! They must be a real prat, why didn't they check what they were buying?'

'Oh, come on, Ron!' said Hermione shakily. 'I don't think anyone could put Devil's Snare in a pot and not realise it tries to kill whoever touches it? This – this was murder ... a clever murder, as well ... if the plant was sent anonymously, how's anyone ever going to find out who did it?'

Harry was not thinking about Devil's Snare. He was remembering taking the lift down to the ninth level of the Ministry on the day of his hearing and the sallow-faced man who had got in on the Atrium level.

'I met Bode,' he said slowly. 'I saw him at the Ministry with your dad.'

Ron's mouth fell open.

'I've heard Dad talk about him at home! He was an Unspeakable – he worked in the Department of Mysteries!'

第25章 无奈的甲虫

"我们对病房中的装饰物有严格规定,但斯特劳治疗师在圣诞节的忙碌中,忽视了博德先生床头植物的危险性。随着博德先生语言和行动能力的恢复,治疗师鼓励他亲自照料那盆植物,却没看出它不是无害的蟹爪兰,而是一枝魔鬼网。康复中的博德先生一碰到它,马上就被勒死了。

"圣芒戈医院还不能解释这盆植物怎么会出现在病房里,望知情者提供线索。"

"博德……"罗恩说,"博德,挺耳熟的……"

"我们见过他,"赫敏小声说,"在圣芒戈,记得吗?他住在洛哈特对面的床上,光躺在那儿瞪着天花板。我们还看到了魔鬼网,她——那个治疗师说它是圣诞礼物。"

哈利记起当时的情景,恐怖感涌上心头,像胆汁堵在他的喉咙里。

"我们怎么会没有认出魔鬼网呢……?以前见过的呀……我们本来可以阻止……"

"谁想得到魔鬼网会伪装成盆栽植物出现在医院里?"罗恩尖刻地说,"这不怪我们,要怪那个送礼的!准是个蠢货,为什么不看看买的是什么呢?"

"得了吧,罗恩!"赫敏不安地说,"我想,没人会把魔鬼网放在花盆里而看不出它想勒死碰它的人。这——这是谋杀……很聪明的谋杀……如果送植物的人没留下姓名,谁能查得出来?"

哈利没有考虑魔鬼网,他记起受审那天乘升降梯下到魔法部第九层时,从门厅进来的那个黄脸男子。

"我见过博德,"他缓缓地说,"跟你爸爸在魔法部……"

罗恩张大了嘴巴。

"我在家听爸爸提到过他!他是个缄默人——他在神秘事务司工作!"

CHAPTER TWENTY-FIVE The Beetle at Bay

They looked at each other for a moment, then Hermione pulled the newspaper back towards her, closed it, glared for a moment at the pictures of the ten escaped Death Eaters on the front, then leapt to her feet.

'Where are you going?' said Ron, startled.

'To send a letter,' said Hermione, swinging her bag on to her shoulder. 'It ... well, I don't know whether ... but it's worth trying ... and I'm the only one who can.'

'I *hate* it when she does that,' grumbled Ron, as he and Harry got up from the table and made their own, slower way out of the Great Hall. 'Would it kill her to tell us what she's up to for once? It'd take her about ten more seconds – hey, Hagrid!'

Hagrid was standing beside the doors into the Entrance Hall, waiting for a crowd of Ravenclaws to pass. He was still as heavily bruised as he had been on the day he had come back from his mission to the giants and there was a new cut right across the bridge of his nose.

'All righ', you two?' he said, trying to muster a smile but managing only a kind of pained grimace.

'Are you OK, Hagrid?' asked Harry, following him as he lumbered after the Ravenclaws.

'Fine, fine,' said Hagrid with a feeble assumption of airiness; he waved a hand and narrowly missed concussing a frightened-looking Professor Vector, who was passing. 'Jus' busy, yeh know, usual stuff – lessons ter prepare – couple o' salamanders got scale rot – an' I'm on probation,' he mumbled.

'*You're on probation?*' said Ron very loudly, so that many of the passing students looked around curiously. 'Sorry – I mean – you're on probation?' he whispered.

'Yeah,' said Hagrid. ''S'no more'n I expected, ter tell yeh the truth. Yeh migh' not've picked up on it, bu' that inspection didn' go too well, yeh know ... anyway,' he sighed deeply. 'Bes' go an' rub a bit more chilli powder on them salamanders or their tails'll be hangin' off 'em next. See yeh, Harry ... Ron ...'

He trudged away, out of the front doors and down the stone steps into the damp grounds. Harry watched him go, wondering how much more bad news he could stand.

The fact that Hagrid was now on probation became common knowledge within the school over the next few days, but to Harry's indignation, hardly anybody appeared to be upset about it; indeed, some people, Draco Malfoy prominent among them, seemed positively gleeful. As for the freakish death of an obscure Department of Mysteries employee in St Mungo's, Harry, Ron and Hermione seemed to be the only people who knew or cared. There was only one topic of conversation in the corridors now: the ten escaped

第25章 无奈的甲虫

三人面面相觑，赫敏把报纸抽过去，翻到头版，瞪着十名越狱的食死徒瞧了一会儿，然后跳了起来。

"你要干吗？"罗恩吃惊地问。

"发一封信，"赫敏说，把书包甩到肩上，"可能……嗯，我不知道……但值得试一试……只有我能够……"

"我讨厌她那样，"罗恩嘟哝道，他和哈利也站起来，慢慢走出礼堂，"她就告诉我们一次会死吗？只需要十秒钟——嘿，海格！"

海格站在门厅的入口让一群拉文克劳的学生过去。他还像寻找巨人刚回来时那样伤痕累累，而且鼻梁上又多了一个新的伤口。

"你们好啊？"他想笑，但只做出了一个痛苦的鬼脸。

"你没事吧，海格？"哈利跟着他问，海格沉重地走在拉文克劳的学生后面。

"很好，很好，"海格假装快活地说，还挥了挥手，差点打到了旁边惊恐的维克多教授，"就是忙，你知道，还是那些事儿——备课——两只火蜥蜴的鳞烂了——我被留用察看了。"他嘟哝道。

"你被留用察看了？"罗恩大声问，许多学生都好奇地回头看了看，"对不起——我是说——你留用察看了？"他压低了嗓门。

"是啊，"海格说，"说实话，这是意料中的。你可能不理解，但那次调查结果不好……算了。"他长叹一声，"得再去给火蜥蜴抹点辣椒粉，不然它们的尾巴也要掉了。再见，哈利……罗恩……"

他沉重地走开了，出了前门，下了台阶，走进潮湿的场地。哈利望着他，不知道自己还能承受多少坏消息。

海格留用察看的事几天就在学校里传开了，让哈利感到愤慨的是，几乎没有人看上去有什么难过，有些人，尤其是德拉科·马尔福，显得很高兴。至于不知名的魔法部职员在圣芒戈蹊跷身亡，似乎只有哈利、罗恩和赫敏才知道或关心。现在走廊上只有一个话题：十名在逃的食

CHAPTER TWENTY-FIVE   The Beetle at Bay

Death Eaters, whose story had finally filtered through the school from those few people who read the newspapers. Rumours were flying that some of the convicts had been spotted in Hogsmeade, that they were supposed to be hiding out in the Shrieking Shack and that they were going to break into Hogwarts, just as Sirius Black had once done.

Those who came from wizarding families had grown up hearing the names of these Death Eaters spoken with almost as much fear as Voldemort's; the crimes they had committed during the days of Voldemort's reign of terror were legendary. There were relatives of their victims among the Hogwarts students, who now found themselves the unwilling objects of a gruesome sort of reflected fame as they walked the corridors: Susan Bones, whose uncle, aunt and cousins had all died at the hands of one of the ten, said miserably during Herbology that she now had a good idea what it felt like to be Harry.

'And I don't know how you stand it – it's horrible,' she said bluntly, dumping far too much dragon manure on her tray of Screechsnap seedlings, causing them to wriggle and squeak in discomfort.

It was true that Harry was the subject of much renewed muttering and pointing in the corridors these days, yet he thought he detected a slight difference in the tone of the whisperers' voices. They sounded curious rather than hostile now, and once or twice he was sure he overheard snatches of conversation that suggested that the speakers were not satisfied with the *Prophet*'s version of how and why ten Death Eaters had managed to break out of the Azkaban fortress. In their confusion and fear, these doubters now seemed to be turning to the only other explanation available to them: the one that Harry and Dumbledore had been expounding since the previous year.

It was not only the students' mood that had changed. It was now quite common to come across two or three teachers conversing in low, urgent whispers in the corridors, breaking off their conversations the moment they saw students approaching.

'They obviously can't talk freely in the staff room any more,' said Hermione in a low voice, as she, Harry and Ron passed Professors McGonagall, Flitwick and Sprout huddled together outside the Charms classroom one day. 'Not with Umbridge there.'

'Reckon they know anything new?' said Ron, gazing back over his shoulder at the three teachers.

'If they do, we're not going to hear about it, are we?' said Harry angrily. 'Not after Decree ... what number are we on now?' For new notices had appeared on the house noticeboards the morning after news of the Azkaban breakout:

第25章 无奈的甲虫

死徒。这个消息终于通过少数读报的人渗透到了校园里。谣传说在霍格莫德有人认出了几名逃犯,还说逃犯藏在尖叫棚屋,可能会像小天狼星那样闯进霍格沃茨。

魔法家庭的孩子从小就听说过这些食死徒,他们的名字几乎和伏地魔一样令人觉得恐惧,他们在伏地魔的恐怖统治下所犯的罪行众所周知。霍格沃茨的学生中就有受害者的家属,这些学生发现自己不情愿地成了走廊里注意的焦点:苏珊·博恩斯的叔叔、婶婶和堂兄弟都死在一个逃犯手里,她在草药课上痛苦地说,现在深深体会到了哈利的感觉。

"我不知道你怎么受得了,真可怕。"她坦率地说,一边往叫咬藤幼苗上加了太多的火龙粪,使得它们难受地扭动尖叫起来。

哈利这些天在走廊里又成了小声议论和指指点点的对象,但他发现议论者的语气稍有变化。现在是好奇代替了敌意,有一两次他肯定听到有人对《预言家日报》关于十名食死徒为什么以及如何逃出阿兹卡班的说法表示不满。在困惑和恐惧中,这些怀疑者似乎转向了仅剩的一种解释,即哈利和邓布利多去年以来所讲的内容。

不仅学生的情绪变了,现在还经常能看到两三个教师在走廊里低声紧张地交谈,一见有学生走近就不说了。

"显然他们不能在教工休息室自由讲话了,"赫敏小声说,她和哈利、罗恩碰到麦格、弗立维和斯普劳特教授聚在魔咒课教室外,"有乌姆里奇在那儿呢。"

"你说他们有新的消息吗?"罗恩回头望着三位教师。

"就算有,我们也不能听,是不是?"哈利气愤地说,"在教育令……第多少号来着?在那之后我们就不能听了。"因为阿兹卡班越狱事件见报的第二天早上,学院的布告栏上又贴出了新的告示:

CHAPTER TWENTY-FIVE   The Beetle at Bay

BY ORDER OF THE HIGH INQUISITOR OF HOGWARTS

Teachers are hereby banned from giving students
any information that is not strictly related to the
subjects they are paid to teach.

The above is in accordance with
Educational Decree Number Twenty-six.

Signed:

*Dolores Jane Umbridge,
High Inquisitor*

This latest Decree had been the subject of a great number of jokes among the students. Lee Jordan had pointed out to Umbridge that by the terms of the new rule she was not allowed to tell Fred and George off for playing Exploding Snap in the back of the class.

'Exploding Snap's got nothing to do with Defence Against the Dark Arts, Professor! That's not information relating to your subject!'

When Harry next saw Lee, the back of his hand was bleeding rather badly. Harry recommended essence of Murtlap.

Harry had thought the breakout from Azkaban might have humbled Umbridge a little, that she might have been abashed at the catastrophe that had occurred right under the nose of her beloved Fudge. It seemed, however, to have only intensified her furious desire to bring every aspect of life at Hogwarts under her personal control. She seemed determined at the very least to achieve a sacking before long, and the only question was whether it would be Professor Trelawney or Hagrid who went first.

Every single Divination and Care of Magical Creatures lesson was now conducted in the presence of Umbridge and her clipboard. She lurked by the fire in the heavily perfumed tower room, interrupting Professor Trelawney's increasingly hysterical talks with difficult questions about ornithomancy and heptomology, insisting that she predict students' answers before they gave them and demanding that she demonstrate her skill at the crystal ball, the tea leaves and the rune stones in turn. Harry thought Professor Trelawney might soon crack under the strain. Several times he passed her in the corridors – in itself a very unusual occurrence as she generally remained in her tower room – muttering wildly to herself, wringing her hands and shooting terrified glances over her shoulder, and all the while giving off a powerful smell of

第 25 章 无奈的甲虫

霍格沃茨高级调查官令

兹禁止教师向学生提供任何与其任教科目无密切关联的信息。

以上条例符合《第二十六号教育令》。

签名：

高级调查官

多洛雷斯·简·乌姆里奇

M.O.M.

这条最新法令在学生中引出了许多玩笑。李·乔丹向乌姆里奇指出，依据新法令她不能责备弗雷德和乔治在教室后面玩噼啪爆炸牌。

"噼啪爆炸牌跟黑魔法防御术不相干，教授！那是跟您任教科目无关的信息！"

哈利再见到李时，李的手背鲜血淋漓，哈利建议用一点莫特拉鼠汁。

哈利以为阿兹卡班越狱事件会使乌姆里奇收敛一点儿，以为她会为她亲爱的福吉眼皮底下出的这个大纰漏而感到羞愧。然而，这件事似乎只是使她更疯狂地想把霍格沃茨的生活控制在掌心里。她好像正下定决心近期内至少要解雇一个人，只不过是特里劳尼和海格谁先走的问题。

现在每堂占卜课和保护神奇动物课都在乌姆里奇和她的写字板前面进行。在香气熏人的塔楼楼顶的房间里，乌姆里奇坐在火炉边，不时打断特里劳尼教授越来越歇斯底里的讲课，问她鸟相学和七字学之类刁钻古怪的问题，坚持要她预言学生的回答，并要求她展示用水晶球、茶叶和如尼文石占卜的能力。哈利觉得特里劳尼快要崩溃了，他有几次在走廊里碰到她（这本身就很反常，因为她一般只待在她的塔楼里），都见她在激动地自言自语，绞着双手，惊恐地回头张望，身

CHAPTER TWENTY-FIVE   The Beetle at Bay

cooking sherry. If he had not been so worried about Hagrid, he would have felt sorry for her – but if one of them was to be ousted from their job, there could be only one choice for Harry as to who should remain.

Unfortunately, Harry could not see that Hagrid was putting up a better show than Trelawney. Though he seemed to be following Hermione's advice and had shown them nothing more frightening than a Crup – a creature indistinguishable from a Jack Russell terrier except for its forked tail – since before Christmas, he too seemed to have lost his nerve. He was oddly distracted and jumpy during lessons, losing the thread of what he was saying to the class, answering questions wrongly, and all the time glancing anxiously at Umbridge. He was also more distant with Harry, Ron and Hermione than he had ever been before, and had expressly forbidden them to visit him after dark.

'If she catches yeh, it'll be all of our necks on the line,' he told them flatly, and with no desire to do anything that might jeopardise his job further they abstained from walking down to his hut in the evenings.

It seemed to Harry that Umbridge was steadily depriving him of everything that made his life at Hogwarts worth living: visits to Hagrid's house, letters from Sirius, his Firebolt and Quidditch. He took his revenge the only way he could – by redoubling his efforts for the DA.

Harry was pleased to see that all of them, even Zacharias Smith, had been spurred on to work harder than ever by the news that ten more Death Eaters were now on the loose, but in nobody was this improvement more pronounced than in Neville. The news of his parents' attackers' escape had wrought a strange and even slightly alarming change in him. He had not once mentioned his meeting with Harry, Ron and Hermione on the closed ward in St Mungo's and, taking their lead from him, they had kept quiet about it too. Nor had he said anything on the subject of Bellatrix and her fellow torturers' escape. In fact, Neville barely spoke during the DA meetings any more, but worked relentlessly on every new jinx and counter-curse Harry taught them, his plump face screwed up in concentration, apparently indifferent to injuries or accidents and working harder than anyone else in the room. He was improving so fast it was quite unnerving and when Harry taught them the Shield Charm – a means of deflecting minor jinxes so that they rebounded upon the attacker – only Hermione mastered the charm faster than Neville.

Harry would have given a great deal to be making as much progress at Occlumency as Neville was making during the DA meetings. Harry's sessions with Snape, which had started badly enough, were not improving. On the contrary, Harry felt he was getting worse with every lesson.

第 25 章 无奈的甲虫

上散发着一股强烈的烹调雪利酒的味道。若不是太为海格担心，他都要为她难过了——可是如果两人中必须有一个丢掉工作，哈利只有一个选择。

不幸的是，哈利看不出海格比特里劳尼好到哪儿去。虽然他好像听了赫敏的劝告，自从快到圣诞节之后就没在课上用过比燕尾狗（它除了尾巴分叉之外与杰克·罗素狸犬没什么区别）更吓人的东西，但他似乎也受了刺激。他在课堂上心烦意乱，魂不守舍，经常忘了讲课的思路，答错问题，还老紧张地去瞟乌姆里奇。他跟哈利三人也前所未有地疏远，特别叫他们不要在天黑后去看他。

"如果被她抓到了，我们都会完蛋的。"他直截了当地说。他们不想进一步连累他，晚上就不再去他的小屋了。

哈利觉得，乌姆里奇在一步步剥夺让他的霍格沃茨生活有意义的东西：访问海格的小屋、小天狼星的来信、他的火弩箭，还有魁地奇球。他只能用他唯一的方式进行报复：加倍投入 D.A. 的活动。

哈利高兴地看到，得知十名食死徒在逃后，大家（包括扎卡赖斯·史密斯）都训练得更刻苦了。然而谁的进步都没有纳威明显，残害他父母的凶手逃跑的消息使他发生了奇特的甚至有些吓人的变化。他一次都没有提过在圣芒戈的封闭病房里见过哈利等人的事，见他这样，他们也守口如瓶。纳威也从来不提贝拉特里克斯及其同伙的在逃，事实上，他在 D.A. 活动时几乎一句话都不说了，只是埋头苦练哈利教的每个咒语和破解咒，圆脸蛋绷得紧紧的，似乎不在乎受伤和事故，练得比屋里任何人都卖力。他的进步快得令人害怕，当哈利教一种能把小恶咒反弹到敌人身上的铁甲咒时，只有赫敏比纳威先学会。

其实哈利非常希望自己在学习大脑封闭术时也能有纳威那样大的进步。斯内普对哈利的第一次辅导很糟糕，以后也没有改善，相反，哈利觉得他的状态越来越差了。

CHAPTER TWENTY-FIVE   The Beetle at Bay

Before he had started studying Occlumency, his scar had prickled occasionally, usually during the night, or else following one of those strange flashes of Voldemort's thoughts or mood that he experienced every now and then. Nowadays, however, his scar hardly ever stopped prickling, and he often felt lurches of annoyance or cheerfulness that were unrelated to what was happening to him at the time, which were always accompanied by a particularly painful twinge from his scar. He had the horrible impression that he was slowly turning into a kind of aerial that was tuned in to tiny fluctuations in Voldemort's mood, and he was sure he could date this increased sensitivity firmly from his first Occlumency lesson with Snape. What was more, he was now dreaming about walking down the corridor towards the entrance to the Department of Mysteries almost every night, dreams which always culminated in him standing longingly in front of the plain black door.

'Maybe it's a bit like an illness,' said Hermione, looking concerned when Harry confided in her and Ron. 'A fever or something. It has to get worse before it gets better.'

'The lessons with Snape are making it worse,' said Harry flatly. 'I'm getting sick of my scar hurting and I'm getting bored with walking down that corridor every night.' He rubbed his forehead angrily. 'I just wish the door would open, I'm sick of standing staring at it –'

'That's not funny,' said Hermione sharply. 'Dumbledore doesn't want you to have dreams about that corridor at all, or he wouldn't have asked Snape to teach you Occlumency. You're just going to have to work a bit harder in your lessons.'

'I am working!' said Harry, nettled. 'You try it some time – Snape trying to get inside your head – it's not a bundle of laughs, you know!'

'Maybe ...' said Ron slowly.

'Maybe what?' said Hermione, rather snappishly.

'Maybe it's not Harry's fault he can't close his mind,' said Ron darkly.

'What do you mean?' said Hermione.

'Well, maybe Snape isn't really trying to help Harry ...'

Harry and Hermione stared at him. Ron looked darkly and meaningfully from one to the other.

'Maybe,' he said again, in a lower voice, 'he's actually trying to open Harry's mind a bit wider ... make it easier for You-Know–'

'Shut up, Ron,' said Hermione angrily. 'How many times have you suspected Snape, and when have you *ever* been right? Dumbledore trusts him,

第25章 无奈的甲虫

在学习大脑封闭术以前，他的伤疤偶尔也会痛，通常是在夜里，或是在他几次突然感应到伏地魔的思想和情绪之后。但现在伤疤几乎是不间断地刺痛，他经常感到一阵阵与他当时行为无关的烦恼或喜悦，总是伴随着伤疤的剧烈疼痛。他恐惧地觉得自己正在逐渐变成一种天线，能接收伏地魔情绪的微小波动。他能肯定这种灵敏度的提高是第一次跟斯内普学习大脑封闭术后开始的。而且，他现在几乎每天晚上都梦见自己在走廊上朝神秘事务司走去，最后总是充满渴望地站在那扇黑门前。

"也许有点儿像生病，"听了哈利的倾诉之后，赫敏关切地说，"像发烧那样，要先加重，之后再变好。"

"是斯内普的辅导使它加重的。"哈利断言，"伤疤疼得太难受了，而且我讨厌每天晚上走那条走廊。"他恼火地揉着额头，"我希望那扇门快点儿打开，盯着它都看厌了——"

"这可不是开玩笑，"赫敏厉声说，"邓布利多不想让你梦见那条走廊，要不他也不会让斯内普教你大脑封闭术。你还得努点力。"

"我努力了！"哈利火了起来，"你倒试试看，斯内普想进到你脑子里，这不是什么开心的事！"

"也许……"罗恩开口道。

"也许什么？"赫敏没好气地问。

"也许不能封闭大脑并不是哈利的错。"罗恩阴沉地说。

"你是什么意思？"赫敏问。

"嗯，也许斯内普不是真想帮助哈利……"

两人都瞪着罗恩，他意味深长地看着他们。

"也许，"他低声说，"斯内普实际上是想把哈利的头脑打开得更大一点儿……让神秘人——"

"别胡说，罗恩，"赫敏生气地打断他，"你怀疑过斯内普多少次了，哪次是对的？邓布利多信任他，他为凤凰社工作，这就够了。"

CHAPTER TWENTY-FIVE The Beetle at Bay

he works for the Order, that ought to be enough.'

'He used to be a Death Eater,' said Ron stubbornly. 'And we've never seen proof that he *really* swapped sides.'

'Dumbledore trusts him,' Hermione repeated. 'And if we can't trust Dumbledore, we can't trust anyone.'

With so much to worry about and so much to do – startling amounts of homework that frequently kept the fifth-years working until past mid-night, secret DA sessions and regular classes with Snape – January seemed to be passing alarmingly fast. Before Harry knew it, February had arrived, bringing with it wetter and warmer weather and the prospect of the second Hogsmeade visit of the year. Harry had had very little time to spare for conversations with Cho since they had agreed to visit the village together, but suddenly found himself facing a Valentine's Day spent entirely in her company.

On the morning of the fourteenth he dressed particularly carefully. He and Ron arrived at breakfast just in time for the arrival of the post owls. Hedwig was not there – not that Harry had expected her – but Hermione was tugging a letter from the beak of an unfamiliar brown owl as they sat down.

'And about time! If it hadn't come today …' she said, eagerly tearing open the envelope and pulling out a small piece of parchment. Her eyes sped from left to right as she read through the message and a grimly pleased expression spread across her face.

'Listen, Harry,' she said, looking up at him, 'this is really important. Do you think you could meet me in the Three Broomsticks around midday?'

'Well … I dunno,' said Harry uncertainly. 'Cho might be expecting me to spend the whole day with her. We never said what we were going to do.'

'Well, bring her along if you must,' said Hermione urgently. 'But will you come?'

'Well … all right, but why?'

'I haven't got time to tell you now, I've got to answer this quickly.'

And she hurried out of the Great Hall, the letter clutched in one hand and a piece of toast in the other.

'Are you coming?' Harry asked Ron, but he shook his head, looking glum.

'I can't come into Hogsmeade at all; Angelina wants a full day's training. Like it's going to help; we're the worst team I've ever seen. You should see Sloper and Kirke, they're pathetic, even worse than I am.' He heaved a great sigh. 'I dunno why Angelina won't just let me resign.'

第25章 无奈的甲虫

"他以前是食死徒,"罗恩固执地说,"我们从没见过他真正转变的证据……"

"邓布利多信任他,"赫敏坚持道,"要是我们不相信邓布利多,就没人可相信了。"

有那么多烦心的事和要做的事——使五年级学生经常熬夜的惊人作业量、秘密的D.A.集会、斯内普的定期辅导——一月份过起来快得可怕。在不知不觉中,二月已经来临,带来了较为温暖湿润的天气,以及本学年的第二次霍格莫德之行。哈利自上次约定之后一直没什么时间跟秋说话,现在突然发现要跟她度过整整一个情人节。

二月十四日早上哈利特意打扮了一下,他和罗恩来到礼堂吃早饭时正赶上猫头鹰送信,海德薇不在——他也没指望它来,但他们坐下时,赫敏从一只陌生的褐色猫头鹰嘴里抽出了一封信。

"还算及时!要是今天不来……"她急切地撕开信封,抽出一小张羊皮纸,读了起来,目光迅速地来回移动,脸上现出恶狠狠的快意。

"哈利,"她抬头看着他,"这很重要,你中午能到三把扫帚来找我吗?"

"嗯……我不知道,"哈利没把握地说,"秋可能希望我一直陪着她。我们还没说过今天要干什么呢。"

"那就带她一起来好了。"赫敏急切地说,"你会来吗?"

"嗯……好吧,可为什么呢?"

"我现在没时间告诉你,我得赶快回信——"

她匆匆走出礼堂,一手拿着信一手捏着片面包。

"你去吗?"哈利问罗恩。但罗恩沮丧地摇摇头。

"我去不了霍格莫德,安吉利娜要训练一整天,好像会有用似的——我们是我见过的最差的队。你没看见过斯劳珀和柯克,太臭了,比我还臭。"他重重地叹了口气,"不知道安吉利娜为什么不让我离队……"

CHAPTER TWENTY-FIVE   The Beetle at Bay

'It's because you're good when you're on form, that's why,' said Harry irritably.

He found it very hard to be sympathetic to Ron's plight, when he himself would have given almost anything to be playing in the forthcoming match against Hufflepuff. Ron seemed to have noticed Harry's tone, because he did not mention Quidditch again during breakfast, and there was a slight frostiness in the way they said goodbye to each other shortly afterwards. Ron departed for the Quidditch pitch and Harry, after attempting to flatten his hair while staring at his reflection in the back of a teaspoon, proceeded alone to the Entrance Hall to meet Cho, feeling very apprehensive and wondering what on earth they were going to talk about.

She was waiting for him a little to the side of the oak front doors, looking very pretty with her hair tied back in a long ponytail. Harry's feet seemed to be too big for his body as he walked towards her and he was suddenly horribly aware of his arms and how stupid they must look swinging at his sides.

'Hi,' said Cho slightly breathlessly.

'Hi,' said Harry.

They stared at each other for a moment, then Harry said, 'Well – er – shall we go, then?'

'Oh – yes …'

They joined the queue of people being signed out by Filch, occasionally catching each other's eye and grinning shiftily, but not talking to each other. Harry was relieved when they reached the fresh air, finding it easier to walk along in silence than just stand about looking awkward. It was a fresh, breezy sort of a day and as they passed the Quidditch stadium Harry glimpsed Ron and Ginny skimming along over the stands and felt a horrible pang that he was not up there with them.

'You really miss it, don't you?' said Cho.

He looked round and saw her watching him.

'Yeah,' sighed Harry. 'I do.'

'Remember the first time we played against each other?' she asked him.

'Yeah,' said Harry, grinning. 'You kept blocking me.'

'And Wood told you not to be a gentleman and knock me off my broom if you had to,' said Cho, smiling reminiscently. 'I heard he got taken on by Pride of Portree, is that right?'

'Nah, it was Puddlemere United; I saw him at the World Cup last year.'

'Oh, I saw you there, too, remember? We were on the same campsite. It

第25章 无奈的甲虫

"因为你状态好的时候挺不错的。"哈利烦躁地说。

他觉得很难同情罗恩的处境，因为他自己几乎愿意花一切代价参加这次对赫奇帕奇的比赛。罗恩似乎觉出了哈利的语气，吃早饭时没再提魁地奇球，说"再见"的时候两人态度也有一点儿冷淡。罗恩去了魁地奇球场，哈利用饭勺当镜子理了理头发，一个人去门厅找秋，心里惴惴不安，不知道和她说些什么。

她站在橡木门旁等他，梳着长长的马尾辫，非常美丽。哈利的脚好像太大了，变得与身体不协调起来。他向她走过去的时候，他突然感到他的手臂在身边摆动得那么蠢笨。

"嗨。"秋有点儿紧张地说。

"嗨。"哈利说。

两人对视了一会儿，哈利说："那——我们走吧？"

"噢——好的……"

他们排到等费尔奇签字出校的队伍中，偶尔接触到对方的目光，躲闪地笑笑，但没有说话。走到外面时哈利松了一口气，觉得默默走路要比尴尬地站在那儿自在一些。清风习习，路过魁地奇球场时，哈利瞥见罗恩和金妮在看台上空掠过，他心里一阵剧痛：他没法和他们一起。

"你很想打球，是吗？"秋说。

他回过头，见她正望着他。

"是，"哈利叹道，"很想。"

"还记得我们第一次比赛吗，三年级的时候？"她问他。

"记得，"哈利笑道，"你老是挡着我。"

"伍德叫你别讲绅士风度，该撞就把我撞下去。"秋怀念地微笑道，"我听说他被波特利队选走了，是吗？"

"不，是普德米尔联队，我去年在世界杯上见过他。"

"嗯，我在那儿看到过你，记得吗？我们在同一个营地上。真棒，

CHAPTER TWENTY-FIVE   The Beetle at Bay

was really good, wasn't it?'

The subject of the Quidditch World Cup carried them all the way down the drive and out through the gates. Harry could hardly believe how easy it was to talk to her – no more difficult, in fact, than talking to Ron and Hermione – and he was just starting to feel confident and cheerful when a large gang of Slytherin girls passed them, including Pansy Parkinson.

'Potter and Chang!' screeched Pansy, to a chorus of snide giggles. 'Urgh, Chang, I don't think much of your taste ... at least Diggory was good-looking!'

The girls sped up, talking and shrieking in a pointed fashion with many exaggerated glances back at Harry and Cho, leaving an embarrassed silence in their wake. Harry could think of nothing else to say about Quidditch, and Cho, slightly flushed, was watching her feet.

'So ... where d'you want to go?' Harry asked as they entered Hogsmeade. The High Street was full of students ambling up and down, peering into the shop windows and messing about together on the pavements.

'Oh ... I don't mind,' said Cho, shrugging. 'Um ... shall we just have a look in the shops or something?'

They wandered towards Dervish and Banges. A large poster had been stuck up in the window and a few Hogsmeaders were looking at it. They moved aside when Harry and Cho approached and Harry found himself staring once more at the pictures of the ten escaped Death Eaters. The poster, 'By Order of the Ministry of Magic', offered a thousand-Galleon reward to any witch or wizard with information leading to the recapture of any of the convicts pictured.

'It's funny, isn't it,' said Cho in a low voice, gazing up at the pictures of the Death Eaters, 'remember when that Sirius Black escaped, and there were Dementors all over Hogsmeade looking for him? And now ten Death Eaters are on the loose and there are no Dementors anywhere ...'

'Yeah,' said Harry, tearing his eyes away from Bellatrix Lestrange's face to glance up and down the High Street. 'Yeah, that is weird.'

He wasn't sorry that there were no Dementors nearby, but now he came to think of it, their absence was highly significant. They had not only let the Death Eaters escape, they weren't bothering to look for them ... it looked as though they really were outside Ministry control now.

The ten escaped Death Eaters were staring out of every shop window he and Cho passed. It started to rain as they passed Scrivenshaft's; cold, heavy drops of water kept hitting Harry's face and the back of his neck.

第25章 无奈的甲虫

是不是？"

魁地奇世界杯的话题伴着他们一直走出了校门。哈利简直不能相信跟她聊天这么轻松，并不比跟罗恩、赫敏说话困难。他正开始感到自信和愉快时，旁边走过一大帮斯莱特林女生，里面有潘西·帕金森。

"波特和张！"潘西尖叫道，女生们一片哄笑，"啊，张，你的眼光不怎么样嘛……迪戈里至少长得还不错！"

她们加快了步子，一边尖声议论，放肆地回头看哈利和秋，留下一阵难堪的沉默。哈利想不出除了魁地奇球还有什么可说的，秋有点儿脸红，看着自己的脚。

"嗯……你想去哪儿？"进霍格莫德村时哈利问道。大街上全是学生，在街上溜达，看商店的橱窗，聚在一起玩闹。

"哦……我无所谓，"秋耸了耸肩，"嗯……就逛逛商店怎么样？"

他们朝德维斯－班斯商店走去。橱窗里贴出了一张大告示，几个当地人正在围着看，哈利和秋走近时他们就走开了。哈利发现他再次面对着十个越狱的食死徒的照片，告示说，"根据魔法部命令"，如有人能提供缉拿逃犯的线索，奖赏一千个加隆。

"真有意思，"秋也望着食死徒的照片，低声说，"你记得吗？小天狼星布莱克逃走的那次，霍格莫德村到处都是派来抓他的摄魂怪。现在十个食死徒在外面，却看不到摄魂怪……"

"是啊，"哈利把目光从贝拉特里克斯·莱斯特兰奇的脸上移开，往大街上张望了一下，"是很奇怪。"

他并不为附近没有摄魂怪而遗憾，但想起来这个现象的确耐人寻味。它们不仅让食死徒逃掉了，而且还不积极搜捕他们……摄魂怪现在好像真的脱离了魔法部的控制。

他和秋走过的每个橱窗里都贴着十个食死徒的照片。走过文人居羽毛笔店时下起了雨，冰冷的雨滴打在哈利的脸上和脖颈里。

CHAPTER TWENTY-FIVE   The Beetle at Bay

'Um ... d'you want to get a coffee?' said Cho tentatively, as the rain began to fall more heavily.

'Yeah, all right,' said Harry, looking around. 'Where?'

'Oh, there's a really nice place just up here; haven't you ever been to Madam Puddifoot's?' she said brightly, leading him up a side road and into a small teashop that Harry had never noticed before. It was a cramped, steamy little place where everything seemed to have been decorated with frills or bows. Harry was reminded unpleasantly of Umbridge's office.

'Cute, isn't it?' said Cho happily.

'Er ... yeah,' said Harry untruthfully.

'Look, she's decorated it for Valentine's Day!' said Cho, indicating a number of golden cherubs that were hovering over each of the small, circular tables, occasionally throwing pink confetti over the occupants.

'Aaah ...'

They sat down at the last remaining table, which was over by the steamy window. Roger Davies, the Ravenclaw Quidditch Captain, was sitting about a foot and a half away with a pretty blonde girl. They were holding hands. The sight made Harry feel uncomfortable, particularly when, looking around the teashop, he saw that it was full of nothing but couples, all of them holding hands. Perhaps Cho would expect him to hold *her* hand.

'What can I get you, m'dears?' said Madam Puddifoot, a very stout woman with a shiny black bun, squeezing between their table and Roger Davies's with great difficulty.

'Two coffees, please,' said Cho.

In the time it took for their coffees to arrive, Roger Davies and his girlfriend had started kissing over their sugar bowl. Harry wished they wouldn't; he felt that Davies was setting a standard with which Cho would soon expect him to compete. He felt his face growing hot and tried staring out of the window, but it was so steamed up he couldn't see the street outside. To postpone the moment when he would have to look at Cho, he stared up at the ceiling as though examining the paintwork and received a handful of confetti in the face from their hovering cherub.

After a few more painful minutes, Cho mentioned Umbridge. Harry seized on the subject with relief and they passed a few happy moments abusing her, but the subject had already been so thoroughly canvassed during DA meetings it did not last very long. Silence fell again. Harry was very conscious of the slurping noises coming from the table next door and cast wildly around for something else to say.

第25章 无奈的甲虫

"嗯……你想喝杯咖啡吗?"雨下得大起来,秋试探地问。

"好啊,"哈利环顾四周,"哪儿有——?"

"对了,附近有个很好的地方,你去过帕笛芙吗?"秋高兴地说,带他拐到侧路上,走进了一家他从来没注意到的小茶馆。这地方很小,里面雾气腾腾,好像所有的东西都用褶边或蝴蝶结装饰着。哈利不快地想起了乌姆里奇的办公室。

"很可爱,是不是?"秋快乐地说。

"呃……是啊。"哈利言不由衷地答道。

"看,情人节的装饰!"秋说,每个小圆桌上方都飞翔着金色的小天使,时而向人们撒下粉红的纸屑。

"啊……"

两人在仅剩的一张圆桌旁坐下,挨着雾蒙蒙的窗户。旁边大约一英尺半以外坐着拉文克劳球队队长罗杰·戴维斯,跟一个漂亮的金发姑娘在一起,两人握着手。哈利有些不自在,尤其是他发现屋里净是一对一对的,全都手拉着手。也许秋也希望他握着她的手。

"两位要点什么?"帕笛芙夫人问,她身材肥胖,梳着光亮的黑发髻,艰难地从两张桌子间挤过来。

"请来两杯咖啡。"秋说。

在等咖啡的时候,罗杰·戴维斯和他的女友开始隔着糖罐接吻。哈利希望他们不要这样。他感到戴维斯在做出一个秋很快会希望他效仿的榜样。他脸上发热,望着窗户,但是水汽太多,看不到外面的街道。为了推迟面对秋的时刻,他抬眼看着天花板,好像在研究上面的油漆,脸上被小天使撒了一把彩纸屑。

又过了痛苦的几分钟,秋提起了乌姆里奇,哈利如释重负地抓住话头,两人愉快地骂了她一阵子,但这个话题在D.A.活动时已经谈过很多了,所以没能聊多久。又是一阵沉默。哈利听到邻桌传来的吧嗒声,急于要找点儿别的话说。

CHAPTER TWENTY-FIVE   The Beetle at Bay

'Er ... listen, d'you want to come with me to the Three Broomsticks at lunchtime? I'm meeting Hermione Granger there.'

Cho raised her eyebrows.

'You're meeting Hermione Granger? Today?'

'Yeah. Well, she asked me to, so I thought I would. D'you want to come with me? She said it wouldn't matter if you did.'

'Oh ... well ... that was nice of her.'

But Cho did not sound as though she thought it was nice at all. On the contrary, her tone was cold and all of a sudden she looked rather forbidding.

A few more minutes passed in total silence, Harry drinking his coffee so fast that he would soon need a fresh cup. Beside them, Roger Davies and his girlfriend seemed glued together at the lips.

Cho's hand was lying on the table beside her coffee and Harry was feeling a mounting pressure to take hold of it. *Just do it*, he told himself, as a fount of mingled panic and excitement surged up inside his chest, *just reach out and grab it*. Amazing, how much more difficult it was to extend his arm twelve inches and touch her hand than it was to snatch a speeding Snitch from midair ...

But just as he moved his hand forwards, Cho took hers off the table. She was now watching Roger Davies kissing his girlfriend with a mildly interested expression.

'He asked me out, you know,' she said in a quiet voice. 'A couple of weeks ago. Roger. I turned him down, though.'

Harry, who had grabbed the sugar bowl to excuse his sudden lunging movement across the table, could not think why she was telling him this. If she wished she were sitting at the next table being heartily kissed by Roger Davies, why had she agreed to come out with him?

He said nothing. Their cherub threw another handful of confetti over them; some of it landed in the last cold dregs of coffee Harry had been about to drink.

'I came in here with Cedric last year,' said Cho.

In the second or so it took for him to take in what she had said, Harry's insides had become glacial. He could not believe she wanted to talk about Cedric now, while kissing couples surrounded them and a cherub floated over their heads.

Cho's voice was rather higher when she spoke again.

'I've been meaning to ask you for ages ... did Cedric – did he – m – m – mention me at all before he died?'

This was the very last subject on earth Harry wanted to discuss, and least of all with Cho.

第25章 无奈的甲虫

"呃……你中午想跟我去三把扫帚酒馆吗？我要去见赫敏·格兰杰。"秋扬起了眉毛。

"你要见赫敏·格兰杰？今天？"

"对，她叫我去的，我觉得应该去。你想跟我一起去吗？她说没关系。"

"哼……她真好。"

但是从秋的语气听来，她一点儿也不觉得好，相反，她的声音冷冷的，一下子疏远起来。

又是几分钟的沉默，哈利大口喝着咖啡，很快就该换杯新的了。邻桌罗杰和他女友的嘴唇好像粘在了一起。

秋的手放在杯子旁边，哈利感到越来越大的压力要求他去握住它。豁出去吧，他对自己说，恐惧与兴奋交织的感觉涌上心头，伸手握住它……真奇怪，只要越过一尺远的距离去碰碰她的手，竟比在空中抓高速移动的飞贼还难得多……

正当他伸出手时，秋的手却从桌面上拿了下去。她有些感兴趣地看着罗杰和女友接吻。

"他约过我，"她轻声说，"罗杰，两个星期之前，但我拒绝了。"

哈利抓住糖罐，掩饰住刚才突然伸手的动作。他不明白秋为什么要说这个。如果她想坐在那儿被罗杰热烈地亲吻，又为什么要跟他出来呢？

他没有说话。小天使又撒下一把彩纸屑，有的飘到了哈利正要喝的最后一点儿冷咖啡里。

"我去年和塞德里克来过这里。"秋说。

在领会这句话的一两秒钟里，哈利的心结成了冰。周围都是接吻的情侣，小天使在他们的头顶上飞翔，他无法相信她现在想谈塞德里克。

秋的声音高了一些。

"我一直想问……塞德里克——他临死前提到了我吗？"

这是哈利最不想谈的话题，更不想和秋谈。

CHAPTER TWENTY-FIVE   The Beetle at Bay

'Well – no –' he said quietly. 'There – there wasn't time for him to say anything. Erm ... so ... d'you ... d'you get to see a lot of Quidditch in the holidays? You support the Tornados, right?'

His voice sounded falsely bright and cheery. To his horror, he saw that her eyes were swimming with tears again, just as they had been after the last DA meeting before Christmas.

'Look,' he said desperately, leaning in so that nobody else could overhear, 'let's not talk about Cedric right now ... let's talk about something else ...'

But this, apparently, was quite the wrong thing to say.

'I thought,' she said, tears spattering down on to the table, 'I thought *you'd* u – u – understand! I *need* to talk about it! Surely you n – need to talk about it t – too! I mean, you saw it happen, d – didn't you?'

Everything was going nightmarishly wrong; Roger Davies's girlfriend had even unglued herself to look round at Cho crying.

'Well – I have talked about it,' Harry said in a whisper, 'to Ron and Hermione, but –'

'Oh, you'll talk to Hermione Granger!' she said shrilly, her face now shining with tears. Several more kissing couples broke apart to stare. 'But you won't talk to me! P – perhaps it would be best if we just ... just p – paid and you went and met up with Hermione G – Granger, like you obviously want to!'

Harry stared at her, utterly bewildered, as she seized a frilly napkin and dabbed at her shining face with it.

'Cho?' he said weakly, wishing Roger would seize his girlfriend and start kissing her again to stop her goggling at him and Cho.

'Go on, leave!' she said, now crying into the napkin. 'I don't know why you asked me out in the first place if you're going to make arrangements to meet other girls right after me ... how many are you meeting after Hermione?'

'It's not like that!' said Harry, and he was so relieved at finally understanding what she was annoyed about that he laughed, which he realised a split second too late was also a mistake.

Cho sprang to her feet. The whole tearoom was quiet and everybody was watching them now.

'I'll see you around, Harry,' she said dramatically, and hiccoughing slightly she dashed to the door, wrenched it open and hurried off into the pouring rain.

'Cho!' Harry called after her, but the door had already swung shut behind her with a tuneful tinkle.

第 25 章 无奈的甲虫

"噢——没有——"他低声说,"当时——他没有时间说话。唔……你……你假期里看了很多魁地奇比赛吗?你支持龙卷风队,是不是?"

他装出轻松愉快的口气,却惊恐地发现秋又眼泪汪汪了,就像圣诞节前那次 D.A. 集会之后一样。

"哎呀,"他着了慌,凑近一些,怕给别人听见,"现在不谈塞德里克好吗……我们聊点别的……"

但这显然是句错话。

"我以为,"她说,眼泪扑簌簌地掉到桌上,"我以为你会—会懂!我需要谈这个!你当然也—也需—需要!你亲眼看到的,是—是不是?"

就像一场噩梦:罗杰的女友甚至让自己脱了胶,回头看着秋哭泣。

"嗯——我谈过,"哈利小声说,"跟罗恩和赫敏,但是——"

"呃,你跟赫敏·格兰杰谈!"她尖声说,满脸泪光,又有几对接吻的情侣分开来看着他们,"可是不愿跟我谈!也—也许我们最好……付—付账,你去见赫敏·格—格兰杰,你显然很想去!"

哈利瞪着她,完全给弄蒙了。秋抓起一块有花边的餐巾擦了擦脸。

"秋?"哈利无力地说,希望罗杰搂住他的女友继续吻她,免得她一直盯着他和秋。

"走啊!"秋用餐巾捂着脸哭泣,"我不知道你为什么要约我出来,既然你马上又要去见别的女孩……赫敏后面还有几个?"

"不是这样的!"哈利终于明白了她气恼的原因,轻松地笑了起来,他马上发现这又是个错误,但为时已晚。

秋跳了起来。整个茶馆都安静下来,每个人都在看着他们。

"再会,哈利。"秋引人注目地说,哽噎着跑到门口,甩开门冲进了瓢泼大雨中。

"秋!"哈利叫道,但门已经当啷一声关上了。

CHAPTER TWENTY-FIVE   The Beetle at Bay

There was total silence within the teashop. Every eye was on Harry. He threw a Galleon down on to the table, shook pink confetti out of his hair, and followed Cho out of the door.

It was raining hard now and she was nowhere to be seen. He simply did not understand what had happened; half an hour ago they had been getting along fine.

'Women!' he muttered angrily, sloshing down the rain-washed street with his hands in his pockets. 'What did she want to talk about Cedric for, anyway? Why does she always want to drag up a subject that makes her act like a human hosepipe?'

He turned right and broke into a splashy run, and within minutes he was turning into the doorway of the Three Broomsticks. He knew he was too early to meet Hermione, but he thought it likely there would be someone in here with whom he could spend the intervening time. He shook his wet hair out of his eyes and looked around. Hagrid was sitting alone in a corner, looking morose.

'Hi, Hagrid!' he said, when he had squeezed through the crammed tables and pulled up a chair beside him.

Hagrid jumped and looked down at Harry as though he barely recognised him. Harry saw that he had two fresh cuts on his face and several new bruises.

'Oh, it's yeh, Harry,' said Hagrid. 'Yeh all righ'?'

'Yeah, I'm fine,' lied Harry; but, next to this battered and mournful-looking Hagrid, he felt he didn't really have much to complain about. 'Er – are you OK?'

'Me?' said Hagrid. 'Oh yeah, I'm grand, Harry, grand.'

He gazed into the depths of his pewter tankard, which was the size of a large bucket, and sighed. Harry didn't know what to say to him. They sat side by side in silence for a moment. Then Hagrid said abruptly, 'In the same boat, yeh an' me, aren' we, 'Arry?'

'Er –' said Harry.

'Yeah ... I've said it before ... both outsiders, like,' said Hagrid, nodding wisely. 'An' both orphans. Yeah ... both orphans.'

He took a great swig from his tankard.

'Makes a diff'rence, havin' a decent family,' he said. 'Me dad was decent. An' your mum an' dad were decent. If they'd lived, life woulda bin diff'rent, eh?'

'Yeah ... I s'pose,' said Harry cautiously. Hagrid seemed to be in a very strange mood.

第25章 无奈的甲虫

茶馆里静悄悄的，所有的眼睛都盯着哈利。他丢下一个加隆，甩掉头发上的彩纸屑，追了出去。

雨哗哗地下着，哈利看不到秋的影子。他不明白是怎么回事，半小时前他们还很融洽呀。

"女人！"他恼火地咕哝道，手插在兜里，水花四溅地走在被雨水冲刷的街道上，"她为什么要谈塞德里克？为什么总要扯出一个让她变成自来水管的话题呢？"

他朝右一拐，啪嗒啪嗒地跑了起来，几分钟后就来到了三把扫帚的门口。他知道见赫敏还太早，但心想可能会碰到某个熟人打发这段时间。他甩掉挡在眼睛上的湿头发，环顾四周，看到海格一个人闷闷地坐在角落里。

"嘿，海格！"他从桌子间挤过去，拉把椅子坐了下来。

海格跳了起来，低头看着哈利，好像一下子没认出来。哈利看到他脸上又添了两道伤口和几处青紫。

"哦，是你啊，哈利，"海格说，"你好吗？"

"挺好的。"哈利撒了个谎，事实上，在伤痕累累、面容愁苦的海格面前，他觉得自己没什么可抱怨的，"呃——你好吗？"

"我？"海格说，"啊，我很好，哈利，很好……"

他盯着水桶那么大的白镴酒杯，叹了口气。哈利不知道说什么好。两人默默地坐了一会儿。海格突然说："我们差不多，是吧，哈利？"

"呃——"哈利说。

"嗯……我以前说过……都是外人，差不多是吧，"海格明白地点点头，"又都是孤儿。嗯……都是孤儿。"

他喝了一大口酒。

"有个好家庭大不一样，"他说，"我爸爸是好的，你爸妈也是好的，要是他们活着，生活就会不一样，是吧？"

"嗯……可能吧。"哈利谨慎地说，海格的心情似乎很奇怪。

CHAPTER TWENTY-FIVE The Beetle at Bay

'Family,' said Hagrid gloomily. 'Whatever yeh say, blood's important ...'

And he wiped a trickle of it out of his eye.

'Hagrid,' said Harry, unable to stop himself, 'where are you getting all these injuries?'

'Eh?' said Hagrid, looking startled. 'Wha' injuries?'

'All those!' said Harry, pointing at Hagrid's face.

'Oh ... tha's jus' normal bumps an' bruises, Harry,' said Hagrid dismissively, 'I got a rough job.'

He drained his tankard, set it back on the table and got to his feet.

'I'll be seein' yeh, Harry ... take care now.'

And he lumbered out of the pub looking wretched, and disappeared into the torrential rain. Harry watched him go, feeling miserable. Hagrid was unhappy and he was hiding something, but he seemed determined not to accept help. What was going on? But before Harry could think about it any further, he heard a voice calling his name.

'Harry! Harry, over here!'

Hermione was waving at him from the other side of the room. He got up and made his way towards her through the crowded pub. He was still a few tables away when he realised that Hermione was not alone. She was sitting at a table with the unlikeliest pair of drinking mates he could ever have imagined: Luna Lovegood and none other than Rita Skeeter, ex-journalist on the *Daily Prophet* and one of Hermione's least favourite people in the world.

'You're early!' said Hermione, moving along to give him room to sit down. 'I thought you were with Cho, I wasn't expecting you for another hour at least!'

'Cho?' said Rita at once, twisting round in her seat to stare avidly at Harry. 'A *girl*?'

She snatched up her crocodile-skin handbag and groped within it.

'It's none of *your* business if Harry's been with a hundred girls,' Hermione told Rita coolly. 'So you can put that away right now.'

Rita had been on the point of withdrawing an acid-green quill from her bag. Looking as though she had been forced to swallow Stinksap, she snapped her bag shut again.

'What are you up to?' Harry asked, sitting down and staring from Rita to Luna to Hermione.

第25章 无奈的甲虫

"家庭,"海格阴郁地说,"不管你怎么说,血缘是很重要的……"

他擦去了眼中流出的一滴血。

"海格,"哈利忍不住说,"你从哪儿受的这些伤?"

"呃?"海格似乎吓了一跳,"什么伤?"

"这么多!"哈利指着海格的脸说。

"哦……一般的磕磕碰碰,哈利,"海格轻描淡写地说,"我干的是粗活。"

他喝干了酒,把杯子放到桌上,站了起来。

"再见,哈利……多保重……"

他笨重地走出酒吧,一副潦倒的样子,消失在倾盆大雨中。哈利看着他离开,心里很难受。海格不开心,而且掩藏着什么,但他好像决心不接受帮助。这到底是怎么回事?可是哈利还没来得及往深处想,就听见有人叫他的名字。

"哈利!哈利,这边!"

赫敏在房间另一头向他招手。他站起来,穿过拥挤的酒吧朝她走去。还隔着几张桌子时,他发现赫敏不是一个人。她身边坐着两位最让他想象不到的同伴:卢娜·洛夫古德和丽塔·斯基特——《预言家日报》前记者,天底下赫敏最不喜欢的人之一。

"你来得真早!"赫敏说,往旁边挪了挪,让他坐下来,"我以为你跟秋在一起,起码还要过一个小时才能来呢!"

"秋?"丽塔马上问,扭过身子贪婪地盯着哈利,"女孩子?"

她抓起鳄鱼皮手提包,在包里摸索着。

"哈利跟一百个女孩约会也不关你的事,"赫敏冷冷地对丽塔说,"你可以把那东西放下。"

丽塔正要抽出一根绿色的羽毛笔,她的表情就像被迫喝了臭汁一样,她把皮包又关上了。

"你们在做什么?"哈利坐下来,看着丽塔、卢娜和赫敏。

CHAPTER TWENTY-FIVE The Beetle at Bay

'Little Miss Perfect was just about to tell me when you arrived,' said Rita, taking a large slurp of her drink. 'I suppose I'm allowed to *talk* to him, am I?' she shot at Hermione.

'Yes, I suppose you are,' said Hermione coldly.

Unemployment did not suit Rita. The hair that had once been set in elaborate curls now hung lank and unkempt around her face. The scarlet paint on her two-inch talons was chipped and there were a couple of false jewels missing from her winged glasses. She took another great gulp of her drink and said out of the corner of her mouth, 'Pretty girl, is she, Harry?'

'One more word about Harry's love life and the deal's off and that's a promise,' said Hermione irritably.

'What deal?' said Rita, wiping her mouth on the back of her hand. 'You haven't mentioned a deal yet, Miss Prissy, you just told me to turn up. Oh, one of these days ...' She took a deep shuddering breath.

'Yes, yes, one of these days you'll write more horrible stories about Harry and me,' said Hermione indifferently. 'Find someone who cares, why don't you?'

'They've run plenty of horrible stories about Harry this year without my help,' said Rita, shooting a sideways look at him over the top of her glass and adding in a rough whisper, 'How has that made you feel, Harry? Betrayed? Distraught? Misunderstood?'

'He feels angry, of course,' said Hermione in a hard, clear voice. 'Because he's told the Minister for Magic the truth and the Minister's too much of an idiot to believe him.'

'So you actually stick to it, do you, that He Who Must Not Be Named is back?' said Rita, lowering her glass and subjecting Harry to a piercing stare while her finger strayed longingly to the clasp of the crocodile bag. 'You stand by all this garbage Dumbledore's been telling everybody about You-Know-Who returning and you being the sole witness?'

'I wasn't the sole witness,' snarled Harry. 'There were a dozen-odd Death Eaters there as well. Want their names?'

'I'd love them,' breathed Rita, now fumbling in her bag once more and gazing at him as though he was the most beautiful thing she had ever seen. 'A great bold headline: "*Potter Accuses* ..." A sub-heading, "*Harry Potter Names Death Eaters Still Among Us*". And then, beneath a nice big photograph of you, "*Disturbed teenage survivor of You-Know-Who's attack, Harry Potter, 15, caused outrage yesterday by accusing respectable and prominent members of the wizarding community of being Death Eaters ...*"'

第25章 无奈的甲虫

"你进来的时候十全十美小姐正要告诉我——"丽塔啜了一大口饮料,"我可以跟他说话吧?"她尖刻地问赫敏。

"可以。"赫敏淡淡地说。

失业不适合丽塔。以前精心烫过的鬈发现已变直,乱糟糟地挂着。两寸长的尖指甲上的红指甲油已经剥落,眼镜上掉了两颗假珠宝。她又吸了一大口饮料,几乎不动嘴唇地说:"她很漂亮吧,哈利?"

"再提一句哈利的感情生活,交易就告吹。"赫敏恼火地说。

"什么交易?"丽塔用手背擦着嘴问,"你还没提过交易呢,一本正经小姐,你只是叫我过来。好了,总有一天……"她颤抖地吸了口气。

"对,总有一天你还会写文章攻击我和哈利,"赫敏无动于衷地说,"为什么不找个在乎的人呢?"

"他们今年已经写了很多攻击哈利的文章,没用我帮忙。"丽塔从杯子上方瞟了他一眼,沙哑地低声问,"你感觉如何,哈利?被出卖了?心烦意乱了?被误解了?"

"他感到愤怒,当然是这样,"赫敏斩钉截铁地说,"因为他把真相告诉过魔法部部长,可部长竟蠢得不相信他。"

"你真的坚持认为,那个连名字都不能提的人回来了?"丽塔把眼镜往下推了推,锐利地盯着哈利,手指渴望地摸着鳄鱼皮包的搭扣,"你还抱着邓布利多的那套鬼话:神秘人回来了,你是唯一的见证人——?"

"我不是唯一的见证人,"哈利吼道,"还有十几个食死徒在场。想知道他们的名字吗?"

"非常愿意,"丽塔轻声说,又在皮包里摸索,看她那眼神,好像哈利是她见过的最美丽的东西似的,"一个醒目的大标题:波特控告……副标题:哈利·波特指出我们中间的食死徒。然后,在你的一张大照片底下:不安的少年,神秘人袭击的幸存者——十五岁少年哈利·波特昨指控魔法界有名望人士是食死徒,舆论哗然……"

CHAPTER TWENTY-FIVE   The Beetle at Bay

The Quick-Quotes Quill was actually in her hand and halfway to her mouth when the rapturous expression on her face died.

'But of course,' she said, lowering the quill and looking daggers at Hermione, 'Little Miss Perfect wouldn't want that story out there, would she?'

'As a matter of fact,' said Hermione sweetly, 'that's exactly what Little Miss Perfect *does* want.'

Rita stared at her. So did Harry. Luna, on the other hand, sang 'Weasley is our King' dreamily under her breath and stirred her drink with a cocktail onion on a stick.

'You *want* me to report what he says about He Who Must Not Be Named?' Rita asked Hermione in a hushed voice.

'Yes, I do,' said Hermione. 'The true story. All the facts. Exactly as Harry reports them. He'll give you all the details, he'll tell you the names of the undiscovered Death Eaters he saw there, he'll tell you what Voldemort looks like now – oh, get a grip on yourself,' she added contemptuously, throwing a napkin across the table, for, at the sound of Voldemort's name, Rita had jumped so badly she had slopped half her glass of Firewhisky down herself.

Rita blotted the front of her grubby raincoat, still staring at Hermione. Then she said baldly, 'The *Prophet* wouldn't print it. In case you haven't noticed, nobody believes his cock-and-bull story. Everyone thinks he's delusional. Now, if you let me write the story from that angle –'

'We don't need another story about how Harry's lost his marbles!' said Hermione angrily. 'We've had plenty of those already, thank you! I want him given the opportunity to tell the truth!'

'There's no market for a story like that,' said Rita coldly.

'You mean the *Prophet* won't print it because Fudge won't let them,' said Hermione irritably.

Rita gave Hermione a long, hard look. Then, leaning forwards across the table towards her, she said in a businesslike tone, 'All right, Fudge is leaning on the *Prophet*, but it comes to the same thing. They won't print a story that shows Harry in a good light. Nobody wants to read it. It's against the public mood. This last Azkaban breakout has got people quite worried enough. People just don't want to believe You-Know-Who's back.'

'So the *Daily Prophet* exists to tell people what they want to hear, does it?' said Hermione scathingly.

第25章 无奈的甲虫

速记羽毛笔已经在她的手上，正要放进嘴巴里，但陶醉的表情突然从她脸上消失了。

"当然，"她放下羽毛笔，狠狠剜了赫敏一眼，"十全十美小姐不希望登这篇文章，是不是？"

"实际上，"赫敏甜甜地说，"十全十美小姐正希望登这篇文章。"

丽塔瞪着赫敏，哈利也愣了。卢娜做梦似的轻声哼起了"韦斯莱是我们的王"，用插在棍子上的鸡尾酒洋葱搅动着她的饮料。

"你希望我报道他说的关于那个连名字都不能提的人的情况？"丽塔小声问赫敏。

"对，"赫敏说，"真实报道。所有的事实。就像哈利讲的一样。他会提供全部细节，他会说出他在那儿看到的所有别人不知道的食死徒的名字，他会告诉你伏地魔现在是什么样子——哎，稳重一点儿。"她轻蔑地说，扔过去一张餐巾纸，因为听到伏地魔的名字，丽塔浑身一震，把半杯火焰威士忌都泼到了身上。

丽塔擦了擦她那脏兮兮的雨衣，仍然瞪着赫敏。然后她直率地说："《预言家日报》不会登的。我想你也知道，没人相信他那个荒唐的故事，大家都认为他是妄想。如果你让我从那个角度来写——"

"我们不需要再来一篇说哈利疯了的文章！"赫敏生气地说，"已经够多的了，谢谢你！我想让他有机会说出真相！"

"那种文章没有市场。"丽塔冷淡地说。

"你是说《预言家日报》不会登，因为福吉不让他们登。"赫敏愤然说道。

丽塔狠狠地瞪了赫敏一会儿，然后往前凑过去，不带感情地说："好吧，福吉靠着《预言家日报》，但结果都是一样的。他们不会刊登说哈利好话的文章，没人要看，它跟公众心理相抵触。这次阿兹卡班越狱已经搞得人心惶惶，人们不愿相信神秘人回来了。"

"这么说《预言家日报》存在的目的就是说人们愿意听的话，是吗？"赫敏尖刻地说。

Rita sat up straight again, her eyebrows raised, and drained her glass of Firewhisky.

'The *Prophet* exists to sell itself, you silly girl,' she said coldly.

'My dad thinks it's an awful paper,' said Luna, chipping into the conversation unexpectedly. Sucking on her cocktail onion, she gazed at Rita with her enormous, protuberant, slightly mad eyes. 'He publishes important stories he thinks the public needs to know. He doesn't care about making money.'

Rita looked disparagingly at Luna.

'I'm guessing your father runs some stupid little village newsletter?' she said. 'Probably, *Twenty-five Ways to Mingle With Muggles* and the dates of the next Bring and fly Sale?'

'No,' said Luna, dipping her onion back into her Gillywater, 'he's the editor of *The Quibbler*.'

Rita snorted so loudly that people at a nearby table looked round in alarm.

'"Important stories he thinks the public needs to know", eh?' she said witheringly. 'I could manure my garden with the contents of that rag.'

'Well, this is your chance to raise the tone of it a bit, isn't it?' said Hermione pleasantly. 'Luna says her father's quite happy to take Harry's interview. That's who'll be publishing it.'

Rita stared at them both for a moment, then let out a great whoop of laughter.

'*The Quibbler!*' she said, cackling. 'You think people will take him seriously if he's published in *The Quibbler*?'

'Some people won't,' said Hermione in a level voice. 'But the *Daily Prophet's* version of the Azkaban breakout had some gaping holes in it. I think a lot of people will be wondering whether there isn't a better explanation of what happened, and if there's an alternative story available, even if it is published in a –' she glanced sideways at Luna, 'in a – well, an *unusual* magazine – I think they might be rather keen to read it.'

Rita didn't say anything for a while, but eyed Hermione shrewdly, her head a little to one side.

'All right, let's say for a moment I'll do it,' she said abruptly. 'What kind of fee am I going to get?'

'I don't think Daddy exactly pays people to write for the magazine,' said Luna dreamily. 'They do it because it's an honour and, of course, to see their names in print.'

第25章 无奈的甲虫

丽塔坐直了身体，扬起眉毛，喝干了她的火焰威士忌。

"《预言家日报》存在的目的是把自己推销出去，小傻瓜。"她冷冷地说。

"我爸爸说那是一份糟糕的报纸。"卢娜突然插话说。她吮着鸡尾酒洋葱，用她那大大的、凸出的、有一点儿疯狂的眼睛盯着丽塔。"我爸爸总是登他认为人们需要知道的重要消息，他不在乎赚不赚钱。"

丽塔轻蔑地看着卢娜。

"我猜你爸爸办的是什么可笑的乡村小报吧？很可能是《与麻瓜交往二十五法》，还有下次飞蚤市场的日期？"

"不是，"卢娜把洋葱浸到她那杯鳃囊草水中，"他是《唱唱反调》的主编。"

丽塔冷笑一声，声音很响，惊得邻桌的人都回过头来。

"'他认为人们需要知道的重要消息'？"她挖苦道，"我可以用那破报纸上的货色给我的花园施肥。"

"你正好可以提高一下它的品位嘛，"赫敏愉快地说，"卢娜说她爸爸很愿意刊登采访哈利的文章。就在那儿发吧。"

丽塔瞪了她们两个一会儿，突然大笑起来。

"《唱唱反调》！"她嘎嘎地笑道，"登在《唱唱反调》上，你认为人家会把他的话当真吗？"

"有的人不会，"赫敏冷静地说，"但《预言家日报》对阿兹卡班越狱事件的报道有很大的漏洞，我想有很多人会想有没有更好的解释。如果有另外一个说法，即使是登在一份——"她瞟了瞟卢娜，"嗯——一份特别的刊物上，我想他们也会愿意读的。"

丽塔没有马上答腔，而是偏着头精明地打量着赫敏。

"好吧，假设我同意写，"她突然说，"给我多少稿酬？"

"我想爸爸不会花钱请人写文章，"卢娜做梦似的说，"他们写是因为觉得光荣，当然，也是为了看到自己的名字上报纸。"

CHAPTER TWENTY-FIVE   The Beetle at Bay

Rita Skeeter looked as though the taste of Stinksap was strong in her mouth again as she rounded on Hermione.

'I'm supposed to do this *for free*?'

'Well, yes,' said Hermione calmly, taking a sip of her drink. 'Otherwise, as you very well know, I will inform the authorities that you are an unregistered Animagus. Of course, the *Prophet* might give you rather a lot for an insider's account of life in Azkaban.'

Rita looked as though she would have liked nothing better than to seize the paper umbrella sticking out of Hermione's drink and thrust it up her nose.

'I don't suppose I've got any choice, have I?' said Rita, her voice shaking slightly. She opened her crocodile bag once more, withdrew a piece of parchment, and raised her Quick-Quotes Quill.

'Daddy will be pleased,' said Luna brightly. A muscle twitched in Rita's jaw.

'OK, Harry?' said Hermione, turning to him. 'Ready to tell the public the truth?'

'I suppose,' said Harry, watching Rita balancing the Quick-Quotes Quill at the ready on the parchment between them.

'Fire away, then, Rita,' said Hermione serenely, fishing a cherry out from the bottom of her glass.

第 25 章 无奈的甲虫

丽塔看起来就像又咽了一口臭汁，转身冲着赫敏："要我白写？"

"是的，"赫敏喝了一口饮料，平静地说，"否则，你心里有数，我会去报告你是没有登记过的阿尼马格斯。当然，《预言家日报》也许会出很多钱请你从内部写一写阿兹卡班的生活……"

丽塔似乎恨不得抓过赫敏杯子上的小纸伞塞到她的鼻子里。

"看来我没什么选择，是不是？"丽塔的声音有点儿颤抖。她重新打开鳄鱼皮包，抽出一张羊皮纸，举起了速记羽毛笔。

"爸爸会很高兴的。"卢娜开心地说。丽塔嘴部的肌肉抽搐了一下。

"好，哈利，"赫敏转向他说，"准备好把真相告诉公众了吗？"

"我想是吧。"哈利说，看着丽塔铺开羊皮纸，把速记羽毛笔竖在上面。

"问吧，丽塔。"赫敏平静地说，从杯底捞上来一颗樱桃。

CHAPTER TWENTY-SIX

Seen and Unforeseen

Luna said vaguely that she did not know how soon Rita's interview with Harry would appear in *The Quibbler*, that her father was expecting a lovely long article on recent sightings of Crumple-Horned Snorkacks, '– and of course, that'll be a very important story, so Harry's might have to wait for the following issue,' said Luna.

Harry had not found it an easy experience to talk about the night when Voldemort had returned. Rita had pressed him for every little detail and he had given her everything he could remember, knowing that this was his one big opportunity to tell the world the truth. He wondered how people would react to the story. He guessed that it would confirm a lot of people in the view that he was completely insane, not least because his story would be appearing alongside utter rubbish about Crumple-Horned Snorkacks. But the breakout of Bellatrix Lestrange and her fellow Death Eaters had given Harry a burning desire to do *something*, whether or not it worked ...

'Can't wait to see what Umbridge thinks of you going public,' said Dean, sounding awestruck at dinner on Monday night. Seamus was shovelling down large amounts of chicken and ham pie on Dean's other side, but Harry knew he was listening.

'It's the right thing to do, Harry,' said Neville, who was sitting opposite him. He was rather pale, but went on in a low voice, 'It must have been ... tough ... talking about it ... was it?'

'Yeah,' mumbled Harry, 'but people have got to know what Voldemort's capable of, haven't they?'

'That's right,' said Neville, nodding, 'and his Death Eaters, too ... people should know ...'

Neville left his sentence hanging and returned to his baked potato. Seamus looked up, but when he caught Harry's eye he looked quickly back at his plate again. After a while, Dean, Seamus and Neville departed for the common room, leaving Harry and Hermione at the table waiting for Ron, who had not yet had dinner because of Quidditch practice.

第26章

梦境内外

卢娜含糊地说她不知道丽塔的文章什么时候能登出来,她爸爸正等着发一篇关于最近发现了弯角鼾兽的精彩长文章。"当然,那是一篇非常重要的文章,所以哈利的可能要等下一期了。"

讲述伏地魔回来那天晚上的情景对哈利来说并不轻松。丽塔追问每个细节,哈利把能记得起来的都告诉了她,知道这是他把真相公之于众的重要机会。他不知道人们会有什么反应,猜想文章会使不少人确信他完全疯了,何况还要和弯角鼾兽之类的无稽之谈登在一起。但贝拉特里克斯·莱斯特兰奇等食死徒的越狱使哈利迫切希望做点儿什么,不管成不成功……

"真想看看乌姆里奇对你登报的反应。"星期一晚饭时,迪安钦佩地说。西莫在迪安旁边大口地吃着鸡肉和火腿馅饼,但哈利知道他在听。

"做得对,哈利。"坐在对面的纳威说。他脸色苍白,但接着低声说:"一定……挺难的吧……讲这些……?"

"嗯,"哈利嘟哝道,"但人们必须知道伏地魔会干什么,是不是?"

"是,"纳威点头道,"还有他的食死徒……人们应该知道……"

纳威没有说完,继续吃起他的烤土豆。西莫抬起头来,但看到哈利的眼睛,马上又垂眼看着盘子。过了一会儿,迪安、西莫和纳威去了公共休息室,哈利和赫敏留下来等罗恩,他训练还没回来。

CHAPTER TWENTY-SIX — Seen and Unforeseen

Cho Chang walked into the Hall with her friend Marietta. Harry's stomach gave an unpleasant lurch, but she did not look over at the Gryffindor table, and sat down with her back to him.

'Oh, I forgot to ask you,' said Hermione brightly, glancing over at the Ravenclaw table, 'what happened on your date with Cho? How come you were back so early?'

'Er ... well, it was ...' said Harry, pulling a dish of rhubarb crumble towards him and helping himself to seconds, 'a complete fiasco, now you mention it.'

And he told her what had happened in Madam Puddifoot's teashop.

'... so then,' he finished several minutes later, as the final bit of crumble disappeared, 'she jumps up, right, and says, "I'll see you around, Harry," and runs out of the place!' He put down his spoon and looked at Hermione. 'I mean, what was all that about? What was going on?'

Hermione glanced over at the back of Cho's head and sighed.

'Oh, Harry,' she said sadly. 'Well, I'm sorry, but you were a bit tactless.'

'*Me*, tactless?' said Harry, outraged. 'One minute we were getting on fine, next minute she was telling me that Roger Davies asked her out and how she used to go and snog Cedric in that stupid teashop — how was I supposed to feel about that?'

'Well, you see,' said Hermione, with the patient air of someone explaining that one plus one equals two to an over-emotional toddler, 'you shouldn't have told her that you wanted to meet me halfway through your date.'

'But, but,' spluttered Harry, 'but — you told me to meet you at twelve and to bring her along, how was I supposed to do that without telling her?'

'You should have told her differently,' said Hermione, still with that maddeningly patient air. 'You should have said it was really annoying, but I'd *made* you promise to come along to the Three Broomsticks, and you really didn't want to go, you'd much rather spend the whole day with her, but unfortunately you thought you really ought to meet me and would she please, please come along with you and hopefully you'd be able to get away more quickly. And it might have been a good idea to mention how ugly you think I am, too,' Hermione added as an afterthought.

'But I don't think you're ugly,' said Harry, bemused.

Hermione laughed.

'Harry, you're worse than Ron ... well, no, you're not,' she sighed, as Ron himself came stumping into the Hall splattered with mud and looking grumpy. 'Look — you upset Cho when you said you were going to meet me, so she tried to

第26章 梦境内外

秋·张跟她的朋友玛丽埃塔走进了礼堂,哈利的心一沉,但秋没有看格兰芬多的桌子,而是背对着他坐了下来。

"对了,我忘了问你,"赫敏望望拉文克劳的桌子,轻松地说,"你跟秋的约会怎么样?你怎么那么早就回来了?"

"咳……别提了……"哈利拉过一盘大黄馅的酥皮派吃起来,"一塌糊涂。"

他跟她讲了帕笛芙茶馆里的事。

"……就这样,"几分钟后他讲到了结尾,最后一点酥皮派也消失了,"她跳起来说'再会,哈利',就跑出去了!"他放下勺子看着赫敏,"这是为什么?到底怎么回事?"

赫敏望着秋的背影,叹了口气。

"噢,哈利,"她悲哀地说,"我很遗憾,但你真是缺点儿心眼。"

"我缺心眼?"哈利不平地说,"前一分钟还挺好的,下一分钟她却告诉我罗杰·戴维斯约过她,还说她在那个叫人腻味的茶馆里跟塞德里克亲嘴——我能有什么感觉?"

"哦,你看,"赫敏用对一个情绪冲动的小毛娃解释一加一等于二那么耐心的口气说,"你不应该在跟她约会的时候说你要见我。"

"可是,可是——"哈利急道,"是你叫我十二点去见你,把她也带去的,我要是不告诉她,怎么能过去?"

"你应该换一种方式说,"赫敏用的还是那种能把人气疯的耐心口气,"你应该说真烦人,我逼你答应去三把扫帚,你实在不想去,很想一天都陪着她,可惜没办法,请求她跟你一起去,希望这样能早点离开。还可以说说你觉得我长得多丑。"赫敏补充道。

"可我不觉得你丑啊。"哈利迷惑不解地说。

赫敏笑了。

"哈利,你比罗恩还差……噢,不,你要好些。"她叹了口气,此时罗恩正好拖着沉重的身子走进礼堂,满身泥点,好像心情很坏,"你看——你说要来见我,秋不高兴了,所以她想让你嫉妒,那是她试探

CHAPTER TWENTY-SIX   Seen and Unforeseen

make you jealous. It was her way of trying to find out how much you liked her.'

'Is that what she was doing?' said Harry, as Ron dropped on to the bench opposite them and pulled every dish within reach towards him. 'Well, wouldn't it have been easier if she'd just asked me whether I liked her better than you?'

'Girls don't often ask questions like that,' said Hermione.

'Well, they should!' said Harry forcefully. 'Then I could've just told her I fancy her, and she wouldn't have had to get herself all worked up again about Cedric dying!'

'I'm not saying what she did was sensible,' said Hermione, as Ginny joined them, just as muddy as Ron and looking equally disgruntled. 'I'm just trying to make you see how she was feeling at the time.'

'You should write a book,' Ron told Hermione as he cut up his potatoes, 'translating mad things girls do so boys can understand them.'

'Yeah,' said Harry fervently, looking over at the Ravenclaw table. Cho had just got up, and, still not looking at him, she left the Great Hall. Feeling rather depressed, he looked back at Ron and Ginny. 'So, how was Quidditch practice?'

'It was a nightmare,' said Ron in a surly voice.

'Oh come on,' said Hermione, looking at Ginny, 'I'm sure it wasn't that —'

'Yes, it was,' said Ginny. 'It was appalling. Angelina was nearly in tears by the end of it.'

Ron and Ginny went off for baths after dinner; Harry and Hermione returned to the busy Gryffindor common room and their usual pile of homework. Harry had been struggling with a new star-chart for Astronomy for half an hour when Fred and George turned up.

'Ron and Ginny not here?' asked Fred, looking around as he pulled up a chair, and when Harry shook his head, he said, 'Good. We were watching their practice. They're going to be slaughtered. They're complete rubbish without us.'

'Come on, Ginny's not bad,' said George fairly, sitting down next to Fred. 'Actually, I dunno how she got so good, seeing how we never let her play with us.'

'She's been breaking into your broom shed in the garden since the age of six and taking each of your brooms out in turn when you weren't looking,' said Hermione from behind her tottering pile of Ancient Rune books.

'Oh,' said George, looking mildly impressed. 'Well — that'd explain it.'

'Has Ron saved a goal yet?' asked Hermione, peering over the top of *Magical Hieroglyphs and Logograms*.

第26章 梦境内外

你有多喜欢她的方式。"

"是吗？"哈利问，罗恩一屁股坐在对面的凳子上，把所有够得到的盘子都拖到他面前，"她为什么不直接问我更喜欢谁，那不是简单得多吗？"

"女孩子一般不问那种问题。"赫敏说。

"咳，她们应该问的！"哈利恼火地说，"那样我就会告诉她我喜欢她，她也不用又为塞德里克的死那么伤心了！"

"我没说她的行为是理智的，"赫敏说，金妮走了过来，跟罗恩一样满身泥点，一脸的不高兴，"我只是想让你了解她当时的感觉。"

"你应该写本书，"罗恩一边切土豆一边说，"解释女孩子的奇怪行为，让男孩子能搞懂她们。"

"对。"哈利热烈地说，望了望拉文克劳的桌子。秋刚刚站起来，还是没看他一眼，就离开了礼堂。他感到很懊恼，回头看着罗恩和金妮问："训练怎么样？"

"一场噩梦。"罗恩粗声说。

"不会吧，"赫敏看着金妮，"我相信没那么——"

"是的，"金妮说，"糟透了，结束时安吉利娜都快哭了。"

晚饭后罗恩和金妮去洗澡了，哈利跟赫敏回到热闹的格兰芬多公共休息室做他们那做不完的作业。哈利正在琢磨天文课的一张新的星图时，弗雷德和乔治来了。

"罗恩和金妮不在？"弗雷德拖过一把椅子，四下看看，见哈利摇头，他说，"那就好。我们去看训练了，他们会输得落花流水，没有我们，他们整个就是一堆废物。"

"别么说，金妮还不错，"乔治公正地说，挨着弗雷德坐了下来，"说实话，我不知道她怎么会打得这么好，我们从来没带她玩……"

"她从六岁起就钻进花园的扫帚棚，轮流偷用你们的扫帚。"赫敏在她那堆摇摇欲倒的古代如尼文书后面说。

"噢，"乔治叹服道，"噢——那就明白了。"

"罗恩扑到球没有？"赫敏从《魔法图符集》上面望过来。

957

CHAPTER TWENTY-SIX Seen and Unforeseen

'Well, he can do it if he doesn't think anyone's watching him,' said Fred, rolling his eyes. 'So all we have to do is ask the crowd to turn their backs and talk among themselves every time the Quaffle goes up his end on Saturday.'

He got up again and moved restlessly to the window, staring out across the dark grounds.

'You know, Quidditch was about the only thing in this place worth staying for.'

Hermione cast him a stern look.

'You've got exams coming!'

'Told you already, we're not fussed about N.E.W.T.,' said Fred. 'The Snackboxes are ready to roll, we found out how to get rid of those boils, just a couple of drops of Murtlap essence sorts them, Lee put us on to it.'

George yawned widely and looked out disconsolately at the cloudy night sky.

'I dunno if I even want to watch this match. If Zacharias Smith beats us I might have to kill myself.'

'Kill him, more like,' said Fred firmly.

'That's the trouble with Quidditch,' said Hermione absent-mindedly, once again bent over her Runes translation, 'it creates all this bad feeling and tension between the houses.'

She looked up to find her copy of *Spellman's Syllabary*, and caught Fred, George and Harry all staring at her with expressions of mingled disgust and incredulity on their faces.

'Well, it does!' she said impatiently. 'It's only a game, isn't it?'

'Hermione,' said Harry, shaking his head, 'you're good on feelings and stuff, but you just don't understand about Quidditch.'

'Maybe not,' she said darkly, returning to her translation, 'but at least my happiness doesn't depend on Ron's goalkeeping ability.'

And though Harry would rather have jumped off the Astronomy Tower than admit it to her, by the time he had watched the game the following Saturday he would have given any number of Galleons not to care about Quidditch either.

The very best thing you could say about the match was that it was short; the Gryffindor spectators had to endure only twenty-two minutes of agony. It was hard to say what the worst thing was: Harry thought it was a close-run contest between Ron's fourteenth failed save, Sloper missing the Bludger but hitting Angelina in the mouth with his bat, and Kirke shrieking and falling backwards off his broom when Zacharias Smith zoomed at him

第26章 梦境内外

"如果他觉得没人看他的话,他是能扑到的,"弗雷德翻着白眼说,"所以星期六鬼飞球一飞到他那边,我们只能叫观众背过身去讲话。"

他站起来烦躁地走到窗前,望着黑漆漆的校园。

"你知道,魁地奇球是唯一值得让你待在这儿的东西。"

赫敏瞪了他一眼。

"你们要考试了!"

"告诉过你,我们不在乎 N.E.W.T. 考试。"弗雷德说,"速效逃课糖大功告成了,我们找到了去脓包的办法,几滴莫特拉鼠汁就能解决问题,是受了李的启发……"

乔治打了个大哈欠,郁闷地看着多云的夜空。

"我不知道要不要去看这场比赛,如果扎卡赖斯·史密斯打败了我们,我可能会自杀的。"

"杀了他更可能。"弗雷德坚决地说。

"这就是魁地奇球的问题,"赫敏心不在焉地说,又在埋头做古代如尼文翻译,"它把学院之间的关系搞得这么紧张。"

她抬头找她的《魔法字音表》,发现弗雷德、乔治和哈利都在瞪着她,脸上带着厌恶和难以置信的表情。

"就是嘛,"她不耐烦地说,"它不过是个游戏,对不对?"

"赫敏,"哈利摇头说,"你对感情方面很在行,但你一点儿也不懂魁地奇球。"

"也许吧,"她绷着脸说,继续翻译,"但我的快乐不用依赖于罗恩的守门能力。"

尽管哈利宁可从天文塔上跳下去也不愿对赫敏承认,但星期六看完比赛之后他真是觉得,要是能让他也不再关心魁地奇,花多少加隆他都愿意。

这场比赛唯一的好处就是时间短,格兰芬多的观众只需忍受二十二分钟的痛苦。很难说最糟糕的是哪一个,哈利认为难分上下:罗恩十四次扑漏了球;斯劳珀没打到游走球,一棍子抽到了安吉利娜的嘴

CHAPTER TWENTY-SIX   Seen and Unforeseen

carrying the Quaffle. The miracle was that Gryffindor only lost by ten points: Ginny managed to snatch the Snitch from right under Hufflepuff Seeker Summerby's nose, so that the final score was two hundred and forty versus two hundred and thirty.

'Good catch,' Harry told Ginny back in the common room, where the atmosphere resembled that of a particularly dismal funeral.

'I was lucky,' she shrugged. 'It wasn't a very fast Snitch and Summerby's got a cold, he sneezed and closed his eyes at exactly the wrong moment. Anyway, once you're back on the team –'

'Ginny, I've got a *lifelong* ban.'

'You're banned as long as Umbridge is in the school,' Ginny corrected him. 'There's a difference. Anyway, once you're back, I think I'll try out for Chaser. Angelina and Alicia are both leaving next year and I prefer goal-scoring to Seeking anyway.'

Harry looked over at Ron, who was hunched in a corner, staring at his knees, a bottle of Butterbeer clutched in his hand.

'Angelina still won't let him resign,' Ginny said, as though reading Harry's mind. 'She says she knows he's got it in him.'

Harry liked Angelina for the faith she was showing in Ron, but at the same time thought it would really be kinder to let him leave the team. Ron had left the pitch to another booming chorus of 'Weasley is our King' sung with great gusto by the Slytherins, who were now favourites to win the Quidditch Cup.

Fred and George wandered over.

'I haven't even got the heart to take the mickey out of him,' said Fred, looking over at Ron's crumpled figure. 'Mind you ... when he missed the fourteenth –'

He made wild motions with his arms as though doing an upright doggy-paddle.

'– well, I'll save it for parties, eh?'

Ron dragged himself up to bed shortly after this. Out of respect for his feelings, Harry waited a while before going up to the dormitory himself, so that Ron could pretend to be asleep if he wanted to. Sure enough, when Harry finally entered the room Ron was snoring a little too loudly to be entirely plausible.

Harry got into bed, thinking about the match. It had been immensely frustrating watching from the sidelines. He was quite impressed by Ginny's performance but he knew if he had been playing he could have caught the Snitch sooner ... there had been a moment when it had been fluttering near Kirke's ankle; if Ginny hadn't hesitated, she might have been able to scrape a

第26章 梦境内外

巴上；看到扎卡赖斯·史密斯带着鬼飞球冲过来，柯克尖叫一声，仰面摔下了扫帚。奇迹是格兰芬多队只输了十分：金妮在赫奇帕奇找球手夏比的鼻子底下抓住了飞贼，最后的比分是二百四十比二百三十。

"你抓得好。"哈利对金妮说，公共休息室里的气氛很像一场特别凄惨的葬礼。

"很幸运，"金妮耸了耸肩，"那飞贼不是很快，夏比感冒了，在关键时候打了个大喷嚏，闭上了眼睛。反正，等你归队后——"

"金妮，我终身禁赛。"

"是乌姆里奇在学校期间禁赛，"金妮纠正他，"这不一样。反正，等你归队后，我想我会争取当追球手。安吉利娜和艾丽娅明年都要走了，我更喜欢进球而不是找球。"

哈利看看罗恩，他缩在角落里，眼睛盯着膝盖，手里攥着一瓶黄油啤酒。

"安吉利娜还是不肯让他离队，"金妮好像看出哈利在想什么，"她说知道他有潜力。"

哈利喜欢安吉利娜对罗恩的信心，但同时又觉得让罗恩离队其实更仁慈些。罗恩离开球场时，斯莱特林人兴高采烈地高唱着"韦斯莱是我们的王"，他们可望夺得魁地奇杯了。

弗雷德和乔治走了过来。

"我都不忍心取笑他了，"弗雷德看着罗恩那委顿的样子说，"跟你们说吧……当他扑漏第十四个球的时候……"

他两只胳膊乱舞，好像在做狗爬式。

"算了，我把它留到联欢会上吧，好吗？"

罗恩此后不久便恹恹地上楼睡觉了。为了照顾他的情绪，哈利过了一会儿才回宿舍，这样罗恩可以假装睡着了。果然，当哈利终于回屋时，罗恩的鼾声响得有点不大真实。

哈利上了床，想着这场比赛。在场外观看真是急死人，他很欣赏金妮的表现，但是觉得如果他在场上可能会更早抓住飞贼……有一刻它

CHAPTER TWENTY-SIX Seen and Unforeseen

win for Gryffindor.

Umbridge had been sitting a few rows below Harry and Hermione. Once or twice she had turned squatly in her seat to look at him, her wide toad's mouth stretched in what he thought had been a gloating smile. The memory of it made him feel hot with anger as he lay there in the dark. After a few minutes, however, he remembered that he was supposed to be emptying his mind of all emotion before he slept, as Snape kept instructing him at the end of every Occlumency lesson.

He tried for a moment or two, but the thought of Snape on top of memories of Umbridge merely increased his sense of grumbling resentment and he found himself focusing instead on how much he loathed the pair of them. Slowly, Ron's snores died away, to be replaced by the sound of deep, slow breathing. It took Harry much longer to get to sleep; his body was tired, but it took his brain a long time to close down.

He dreamed that Neville and Professor Sprout were waltzing around the Room of Requirement while Professor McGonagall played the bagpipes. He watched them happily for a while, then decided to go and find the other members of the DA.

But when he left the room he found himself facing, not the tapestry of Barnabas the Barmy, but a torch burning in its bracket on a stone wall. He turned his head slowly to the left. There, at the far end of the windowless passage, was a plain, black door.

He walked towards it with a sense of mounting excitement. He had the strangest feeling that this time he was going to get lucky at last, and find the way to open it ... he was feet from it, and saw with a leap of excitement that there was a glowing strip of faint blue light down the right-hand side ... the door was ajar ... he stretched out his hand to push it wide and –

Ron gave a loud, rasping, genuine snore and Harry awoke abruptly with his right hand stretched in front of him in the darkness, to open a door that was hundreds of miles away. He let it fall with a feeling of mingled disappointment and guilt. He knew he should not have seen the door, but at the same time felt so consumed with curiosity about what was behind it that he could not help feeling annoyed with Ron ... if only he could have saved his snore for just another minute.

They entered the Great Hall for breakfast at exactly the same moment as the post owls on Monday morning. Hermione was not the only person eagerly awaiting her *Daily Prophet*: nearly everyone was eager for more news about

第 26 章 梦境内外

在柯克的脚边闪烁,要是金妮没有犹豫的话,格兰芬多也许能赢呢……

乌姆里奇坐在哈利和赫敏下面,比他们低几排。有一两次她转身望着哈利,大蛤蟆嘴咧开着,在他看来分明是幸灾乐祸的笑容。躺在黑暗中一想到这里哈利就气得热血上涌。但几分钟后他想起睡觉前应该驱除所有的感情,斯内普在每次教完他大脑封闭术时都这么说。

他试了一会儿,可是在乌姆里奇之后想到斯内普只是增加了他的怨恨,他发现自己想的全是多么厌恶他们两个。罗恩的鼾声渐渐消失,变成了低沉、缓慢的呼吸声。哈利过了很久才睡着。他的身体很疲劳,但脑子久久关不上。

他梦见纳威和斯普劳特教授在有求必应屋里跳华尔兹,麦格教授吹风笛。他愉快地看了一会儿,然后决定去找其他 D.A. 成员。

可是走出房间,他发现面前不是傻巴拿巴的挂毯,而是一支火把,插在一堵石墙上。他缓缓把头转向左边,那儿,在没有窗户的走廊尽头,有一扇黑门。

他朝它走去,心中越来越兴奋。他有一种非常奇怪的感觉:这一次他终于要交好运,能有办法打开它……还差几步时,他狂喜地看到右边有一道微弱的蓝光……门虚掩着……他伸手去推——

罗恩发出一声响亮的、刺耳的、真实的鼾声,哈利突然醒来,黑暗中他的右手举在面前,正要推开千里之外的一扇门。他让手垂落下去,有一种混杂了失望与负疚的感觉。他知道他不该看到那扇门,但同时他又那么想知道门里有什么,以至于不禁有些怨恨罗恩……要是他的呼噜晚打一分钟……

星期一早晨他们进礼堂时,正赶上猫头鹰送信来。赫敏不是唯一一个焦急等待《预言家日报》的人。几乎人人都急于知道那些在逃食死徒的新消息,尽管有许多人报告看到过他们,但至今一个都没抓到。赫敏给了送报的猫头鹰一个铜纳特,便迫不及待地打开报纸。哈利喝

CHAPTER TWENTY-SIX Seen and Unforeseen

the escaped Death Eaters, who, despite many reported sightings, had still not been caught. She gave the delivery owl a Knut and unfolded the newspaper eagerly while Harry helped himself to orange juice; as he had only received one note during the entire year, he was sure, when the first owl landed with a thud in front of him, that it had made a mistake.

'Who're you after?' he asked it, languidly removing his orange juice from underneath its beak and leaning forwards to see the recipient's name and address:

> HARRY POTTER
> GREAT HALL
> HOGWARTS SCHOOL

Frowning, he made to take the letter from the owl, but before he could do so, three, four, five more owls had fluttered down beside it and were jockeying for position, treading in the butter and knocking over the salt as each one attempted to give him their letter first.

'What's going on?' Ron asked in amazement, as the whole of Gryffindor table leaned forwards to watch and another seven owls landed amongst the first ones, screeching, hooting and flapping their wings.

'Harry!' said Hermione breathlessly, plunging her hands into the feathery mass and pulling out a screech owl bearing a long, cylindrical package. 'I think I know what this means – open this one first!'

Harry ripped off the brown packaging. Out rolled a tightly furled copy of the March edition of *The Quibbler*. He unrolled it to see his own face grinning sheepishly at him from the front cover. In large red letters across this picture were the words:

HARRY POTTER SPEAKS OUT AT LAST: THE TRUTH ABOUT HE WHO MUST NOT BE NAMED AND THE NIGHT I SAW HIM RETURN

'It's good, isn't it?' said Luna, who had drifted over to the Gryffindor table and now squeezed herself on to the bench between Fred and Ron. 'It came out yesterday, I asked Dad to send you a free copy. I expect all these,' she waved a hand at the assembled owls still scrabbling around on the table in front of Harry, 'are letters from readers.'

第26章 梦境内外

着橙汁,他这一年才收到过一封短信,所以当第一只猫头鹰砰地落到他面前时,他以为它准是搞错了。

"你要找谁?"他懒洋洋地把橙汁从鸟嘴下移开,凑过去看收信人的姓名地址:

霍格沃茨学校
礼堂
哈利·波特

他皱皱眉,伸手去取信,可是又有三只、四只、五只猫头鹰拍着翅膀落到他旁边,挤来挤去,踩着了黄油,碰翻了盐罐,都想第一个把信给他。

"怎么回事?"罗恩惊奇地问,又有七只猫头鹰落在第一批中间。它们尖叫着,拍着翅膀,整个格兰芬多桌子上的人都伸着头朝这里看。

"哈利!"赫敏激动地说,把手伸进羽毛堆里,抓出了一只带着个长筒形包裹的长耳猫头鹰,"我想我知道是怎么回事——先看这个!"

哈利撕开棕色的包皮,里面滚出一份卷得很紧的《唱唱反调》三月刊。他把它展开,看到他自己的面孔在封面上向他腼腆地微笑。照片上印着一行红色的大字:

哈利·波特终于说出真相:
那天晚上我看到神秘人复活

"挺棒的,是不是?"卢娜游荡到格兰芬多桌子旁,挤坐在弗雷德和罗恩中间,"昨天出来的,我叫爸爸送给你一份。我想这些都是读者来信。"她扬手指了指还在哈利面前挤挤撞撞的猫头鹰。

CHAPTER TWENTY-SIX Seen and Unforeseen

'That's what I thought,' said Hermione eagerly. 'Harry, d'you mind if we –?'

'Help yourself,' said Harry, feeling slightly bemused.

Ron and Hermione both started ripping open envelopes.

'This one's from a bloke who thinks you're off your rocker,' said Ron, glancing down his letter. 'Ah well ...'

'This woman recommends you try a good course of Shock Spells at St Mungo's,' said Hermione, looking disappointed and crumpling up a second.

'This one looks OK, though,' said Harry slowly, scanning a long letter from a witch in Paisley. 'Hey, she says she believes me!'

'This one's in two minds,' said Fred, who had joined in the letter-opening with enthusiasm. 'Says you don't come across as a mad person, but he really doesn't want to believe You-Know-Who's back so he doesn't know what to think now. Blimey, what a waste of parchment.'

'Here's another one you've convinced, Harry!' said Hermione excitedly. '*Having read your side of the story, I am forced to the conclusion that the* Daily Prophet *has treated you very unfairly ... little though I want to think that He Who Must Not Be Named has returned, I am forced to accept that you are telling the truth ...* Oh, this is wonderful!'

'Another one who thinks you're barking,' said Ron, throwing a crumpled letter over his shoulder '... but this one says you've got her converted and she now thinks you're a real hero – she's put in a photograph, too – wow!'

'What is going on here?' said a falsely sweet, girlish voice.

Harry looked up with his hands full of envelopes. Professor Umbridge was standing behind Fred and Luna, her bulging toad's eyes scanning the mess of owls and letters on the table in front of Harry. Behind her he saw many of the students watching them avidly.

'Why have you got all these letters, Mr Potter?' she asked slowly.

'Is that a crime now?' said Fred loudly. 'Getting mail?'

'Be careful, Mr Weasley, or I shall have to put you in detention,' said Umbridge. 'Well, Mr Potter?'

Harry hesitated, but he did not see how he could keep what he had done quiet; it was surely only a matter of time before a copy of *The Quibbler* came to Umbridge's attention.

第26章 梦境内外

"我也是这么想,"赫敏热切地说,"哈利,你不介意我们——?"

"随便。"哈利说,觉得有点儿晕乎。

罗恩和赫敏一起拆起信来。

"这家伙说你是神经病,"罗恩看着信说,"嘿……"

"有个女的建议你到圣芒戈接受一段时间的魔法休克治疗。"赫敏失望地说,把信揉成了一团。

"这个看着还行,"哈利慢吞吞地说,一边读着一个在佩斯利的女巫写来的长信,"嘿,她说她相信我!"

"这位有点儿矛盾,"弗雷德也兴致勃勃地参加了拆信,"说你不像是个疯子,但他实在不愿相信神秘人回来了,所以他现在不知道该怎么想。老天,真是浪费羊皮纸。"

"又有一个人被你说服了,哈利!"赫敏激动地叫道,"读了你这一边的陈述,我不得不认为《预言家日报》对你很不公正……虽然我不愿相信那个连名字都不能提的人回来了,但我必须承认你说的是真话……啊,太棒了!"

"又一个人说你是狂叫的疯狗。"罗恩说着把揉皱的信朝后一扔,"但这一位说你转变了她,她现在认为你是真正的英雄——还附了一张照片——哇——"

"这儿在干什么?"一个装出来的甜甜的、小姑娘般的声音说。

哈利抬起头来,手上抓满了信封。乌姆里奇教授站在弗雷德和卢娜的身后,癞蛤蟆眼扫视着哈利面前乱糟糟的猫头鹰和信。她身后有许多学生在关心地看着。

"你为什么有这么多信,波特先生?"她缓慢地问。

"现在收信也犯法吗?"弗雷德大声说。

"小心点儿,韦斯莱先生,不然我罚你关禁闭。"乌姆里奇说,"波特先生?"

哈利犹豫着,但他看不出这事怎么瞒得住,《唱唱反调》迟早会引起乌姆里奇注意的。

CHAPTER TWENTY-SIX   Seen and Unforeseen

'People have written to me because I gave an interview,' said Harry. 'About what happened to me last June.'

For some reason he glanced up at the staff table as he said this. Harry had the strangest feeling that Dumbledore had been watching him a second before, but when he looked towards the Headmaster he seemed to be absorbed in conversation with Professor Flitwick.

'An interview?' repeated Umbridge, her voice thinner and higher than ever. 'What do you mean?'

'I mean a reporter asked me questions and I answered them,' said Harry. 'Here –'

And he threw the copy of *The Quibbler* to her. She caught it and stared down at the cover. Her pale, doughy face turned an ugly, patchy violet.

'When did you do this?' she asked, her voice trembling slightly.

'Last Hogsmeade weekend,' said Harry.

She looked up at him, incandescent with rage, the magazine shaking in her stubby fingers.

'There will be no more Hogsmeade trips for you, Mr Potter,' she whispered. 'How you dare … how you could …' She took a deep breath. 'I have tried again and again to teach you not to tell lies. The message, apparently, has still not sunk in. Fifty points from Gryffindor and another week's worth of detentions.'

She stalked away, clutching *The Quibbler* to her chest, the eyes of many students following her.

By mid-morning enormous signs had been put up all over the school, not just on house noticeboards, but in the corridors and classrooms too.

BY ORDER OF THE HIGH INQUISITOR OF HOGWARTS
Any student found in possession of the magazine
The Quibbler will be expelled.

The above is in accordance with
Educational Decree Number Twenty-seven.

Signed:
Dolores Jane Umbridge,
High Inquisitor

第26章 梦境内外

"人们给我写信了,因为我接受了采访,讲了我去年六月遇到的事。"哈利说。

他鬼使神差地望了望教工桌子。哈利有一种十分奇怪的感觉,似乎邓布利多一秒钟前还在看他,可是当他望过去时,邓布利多好像在专注地和弗立维教授交谈。

"采访?"乌姆里奇的声音比平时更尖更高了,"你说什么?"

"有个记者向我提问,我做了回答。"哈利说,"在这里——"

他把《唱唱反调》朝乌姆里奇扔过去,她接住了,看见那封面,面团一样苍白的脸上泛起一块块难看的紫红色。

"你什么时候干的?"她问,声音有点儿颤抖。

"上次去霍格莫德的时候。"哈利说。

她抬头看着哈利,气急败坏,杂志在她粗短的手指间颤抖。

"你不许再去霍格莫德了,波特先生,"她轻声说,"你怎么敢……你怎么能……"她深深吸了口气,"我一次次地教育你不要撒谎,但你显然把它当作了耳旁风。格兰芬多扣五十分,再加一个星期的关禁闭。"

她噔噔地走开了,把《唱唱反调》紧攥在胸口,许多学生的目光跟随着她。

不到中午,巨大的告示就贴满了学校,不光贴在学院布告栏上,连走廊和教室里都是。

霍格沃茨高级调查官令

任何学生如被发现携有《唱唱反调》杂志,立即开除。

以上条例符合《第二十七号教育令》。

签名:

高级调查官

多洛雷斯·简·乌姆里奇

CHAPTER TWENTY-SIX — Seen and Unforeseen

For some reason, every time Hermione caught sight of one of these signs she beamed with pleasure.

'What exactly are you so happy about?' Harry asked her.

'Oh, Harry, don't you see?' Hermione breathed. 'If she could have done one thing to make absolutely sure that every single person in this school will read your interview, it was banning it!'

And it seemed that Hermione was quite right. By the end of the day, though Harry had not seen so much as a corner of *The Quibbler* anywhere in the school, the whole place seemed to be quoting the interview to each other. Harry heard them whispering about it as they queued up outside classes, discussing it over lunch and in the back of lessons, while Hermione even reported that every occupant of the cubicles in the girls' toilets had been talking about it when she nipped in there before Ancient Runes.

'Then they spotted me, and obviously they know I know you, so they bombarded me with questions,' Hermione told Harry, her eyes shining, 'and Harry, I think they believe you, I really do, I think you've finally got them convinced!'

Meanwhile, Professor Umbridge was stalking the school, stopping students at random and demanding that they turn out their books and pockets: Harry knew she was looking for copies of *The Quibbler*, but the students were several steps ahead of her. The pages carrying Harry's interview had been bewitched to resemble extracts from textbooks if anyone but themselves read it, or else wiped magically blank until they wanted to peruse it again. Soon it seemed that every single person in the school had read it.

The teachers were of course forbidden from mentioning the interview by Educational Decree Number Twenty-six, but they found ways to express their feelings about it all the same. Professor Sprout awarded Gryffindor twenty points when Harry passed her a watering can; a beaming Professor Flitwick pressed a box of squeaking sugar mice on him at the end of Charms, said, 'Shh!' and hurried away; and Professor Trelawney broke into hysterical sobs during Divination and announced to the startled class, and a very disapproving Umbridge, that Harry was not going to suffer an early death after all, but would live to a ripe old age, become Minister for Magic and have twelve children.

But what made Harry happiest was Cho catching up with him as he was hurrying along to Transfiguration the next day. Before he knew what had happened, her hand was in his and she was breathing in his ear, 'I'm really, really sorry. That interview was so brave ... it made me cry.'

第26章 梦境内外

不知为何，赫敏一看到这些告示就抿着嘴乐。

"你高兴什么？"哈利问她。

"哦，哈利，你看不出来吗？"赫敏小声说，"如果她能做一件事保证学校里每个人都去读采访你的文章，那就是下个禁令！"

看来赫敏说得很对。到那天结束时，虽然哈利在学校里连《唱唱反调》的一个角都没见着，但似乎全校都在引用那篇采访中的话。哈利听到学生们在教室外排队时小声地讲，吃午饭时也在讲，上课时则在教室后面议论。赫敏甚至报告说，她在古代如尼文课前急急忙忙去盥洗室时，听到每个小间里的人都在说它。

"然后她们看到了我，显然都知道我认识你，就连珠炮似的向我发问。"赫敏眼睛亮晶晶的对哈利说，"哈利，我觉得她们相信你，真的，我想你终于说服了她们！"

乌姆里奇教授在学校里到处拦学生，要求检查他们的书包和口袋。哈利知道她在找《唱唱反调》，但学生们比她高了几招，哈利的采访被施了魔法，在别人看时就跟课本上的文章一样，或是变成了空白，等他们想看时才显出字来。很快学校里每个人好像都读过那篇文章了。

当然，《第二十六号教育令》禁止教师们提起这篇采访，但他们还是以各种方式表达了自己的感情。当哈利递给斯普劳特教授一个喷壶时，她给格兰芬多加了二十分。弗立维教授在魔咒课结束时笑眯眯地塞给哈利一盒会尖叫的糖老鼠，说了一声"嘘！"就急忙走开了。特里劳妮教授在占卜课上歇斯底里地抽泣起来，对吃惊的学生们和大为不满的乌姆里奇宣布，哈利不会早死，而是注定要长寿，当魔法部部长，还会有十二个小孩。

最让哈利高兴的是，第二天他匆匆去上变形课时，秋追了上来。他还没弄清是怎么回事，秋的手已经在他手里了，她在他耳边轻声说："真是对不起。那篇采访真勇敢……我都哭了。"

CHAPTER TWENTY-SIX   Seen and Unforeseen

He was sorry to hear she had shed even more tears over it, but very glad they were on speaking terms again, and even more pleased when she gave him a swift kiss on the cheek and hurried off again. And unbelievably, no sooner had he arrived outside Transfiguration than something just as good happened: Seamus stepped out of the queue to face him.

'I just wanted to say,' he mumbled, squinting at Harry's left knee, 'I believe you. And I've sent a copy of that magazine to me mam.'

If anything more was needed to complete Harry's happiness, it was the reaction he got from Malfoy, Crabbe and Goyle. He saw them with their heads together later that afternoon in the library; they were with a weedy-looking boy Hermione whispered was called Theodore Nott. They looked round at Harry as he browsed the shelves for the book he needed on Partial Vanishment: Goyle cracked his knuckles threateningly and Malfoy whispered something undoubtedly malevolent to Crabbe. Harry knew perfectly well why they were acting like this: he had named all of their fathers as Death Eaters.

'And the best bit,' whispered Hermione gleefully, as they left the library, 'is they can't contradict you, because they can't admit they've read the article!'

To cap it all, Luna told him over dinner that no issue of *The Quibbler* had ever sold out faster.

'Dad's reprinting!' she told Harry, her eyes popping excitedly. 'He can't believe it, he says people seem even more interested in this than the Crumple-Horned Snorkacks!'

Harry was a hero in the Gryffindor common room that night. Daringly, Fred and George had put an Enlargement Charm on the front cover of *The Quibbler* and hung it on the wall, so that Harry's giant head gazed down upon the proceedings, occasionally saying things like 'THE MINISTRY ARE MORONS' and 'EAT DUNG, UMBRIDGE' in a booming voice. Hermione did not find this very amusing; she said it interfered with her concentration, and she ended up going to bed early out of irritation. Harry had to admit that the poster was not quite as funny after an hour or two, especially when the talking spell had started to wear off, so that it merely shouted disconnected words like 'DUNG' and 'UMBRIDGE' at more and more frequent intervals in a progressively higher voice. In fact, it started to make his head ache and his scar began prickling uncomfortably again. To disappointed moans from the many people who were sitting around him, asking him to relive his interview for the umpteenth time, he announced that he too needed an early night.

第26章 梦境内外

哈利遗憾地听到秋为它掉了更多的眼泪,但很高兴他们又言归于好,更让他高兴的是,秋飞快地亲了他的脸颊一下,急忙跑了。简直令人难以置信,他刚走到变形课教室门口,就又碰到一件同样高兴的事:西莫从队里走出来迎向他。

"我想说,"他望着哈利的左膝说,"我相信你。我寄了一份杂志给我妈妈。"

如果还需要什么使哈利的快乐变得更加完满,那就是马尔福、克拉布和高尔的反应。他那天下午在图书馆看到他们脑袋凑在一起,旁边还有一个瘦弱的男生,赫敏小声说那是西奥多·诺特。哈利在书架上找关于局部隐形的书时,他们回头看着他,高尔威胁地把指关节捏得嘎吱响,马尔福低声对克拉布说了些什么,显然是恶意的话。哈利很明白他们为什么会这样:三人的父亲都被他指控为食死徒。

"最妙的是,"离开图书馆时,赫敏开心地小声说,"他们不能反驳你,因为他们不能承认看过那篇文章!"

还有,卢娜晚饭时告诉他《唱唱反调》从来没有销得这么快过。

"爸爸在重印了!"她兴奋地瞪大了眼睛说,"他简直不敢相信,说人们对这个似乎比对弯角鼾兽还感兴趣!"

那天晚上哈利成了格兰芬多公共休息室里的英雄,弗雷德和乔治大胆地对《唱唱反调》的封面施了放大咒,把它挂到墙上,哈利的大头像俯视着全场,时而洪亮地喊出**魔法部是糊涂蛋**和**乌姆里奇去吃屎**之类的口号。赫敏不觉得这多么有趣,说是妨碍了她集中思想,最后被烦得早早回去睡觉了。一两个小时之后,哈利也不得不承认大头像没那么有趣了,尤其是当说话咒开始消失,它只会喊**屎**和**乌姆里奇**等不连贯的字眼时,间隔越来越短,音调越来越高。哈利被弄得头痛,伤疤又针扎般地疼起来。于是他宣布他也需要早点儿睡觉,令围坐在他身边无数次让他重温采访经过的人们发出失望的抱怨。

CHAPTER TWENTY-SIX   Seen and Unforeseen

The dormitory was empty when he reached it. He rested his forehead for a moment against the cool glass of the window beside his bed; it felt soothing against his scar. Then he undressed and got into bed, wishing his headache would go away. He also felt slightly sick. He rolled over on to his side, closed his eyes, and fell asleep almost at once ...

He was standing in a dark, curtained room lit by a single branch of candles. His hands were clenched on the back of a chair in front of him. They were long-fingered and white as though they had not seen sunlight for years and looked like large, pale spiders against the dark velvet of the chair.

Beyond the chair, in a pool of light cast upon the floor by the candles, knelt a man in black robes.

'I have been badly advised, it seems,' said Harry, in a high, cold voice that pulsed with anger.

'Master, I crave your pardon,' croaked the man kneeling on the floor. The back of his head glimmered in the candlelight. He seemed to be trembling.

'I do not blame you, Rookwood,' said Harry in that cold, cruel voice.

He relinquished his grip on the chair and walked around it, closer to the man cowering on the floor, until he stood directly over him in the darkness, looking down from a far greater height than usual.

'You are sure of your facts, Rookwood?' asked Harry.

'Yes, My Lord, yes ... I used to work in the Department after – after all ...'

'Avery told me Bode would be able to remove it.'

'Bode could never have taken it, Master ... Bode would have known he could not ... undoubtedly, that is why he fought so hard against Malfoy's Imperius Curse ...'

'Stand up, Rookwood,' whispered Harry.

The kneeling man almost fell over in his haste to obey. His face was pockmarked; the scars were thrown into relief by the candlelight. He remained a little stooped when standing, as though halfway through a bow, and he darted terrified looks up at Harry's face.

'You have done well to tell me this,' said Harry. 'Very well ... I have wasted months on fruitless schemes, it seems ... but no matter ... we begin again, from now. You have Lord Voldemort's gratitude, Rookwood ...'

'My Lord ... yes, My Lord,' gasped Rookwood, his voice hoarse with relief.

'I shall need your help. I shall need all the information you can give me.'

'Of course, My Lord, of course ... anything ...'

第26章 梦境内外

宿舍里没人。他把额头贴在床边冰凉的窗玻璃上，感觉伤疤舒服了一些。然后他脱了衣服躺到床上，希望头痛能够消失。他还感觉有点儿恶心。他侧过来躺着，闭上眼睛，几乎立刻就睡着了……

他站在一间挂着帘子、只有几支蜡烛照明的黑屋子里。他的手抓着椅背，手指长而苍白，仿佛多年没见阳光，抓在深色的天鹅绒椅背上，像苍白的大蜘蛛。

椅子前面，昏暗的蜡烛光中，跪着个穿黑袍的男子。

"看来我上当了。"哈利的声音尖厉而冷酷，怒气冲冲。

"主人，求您恕罪……"地上那人嘶哑地说。他的后脑勺在烛光中闪烁。他似乎在发抖。

"我不怪你，卢克伍德。"哈利用那冷酷的声音说。

他放开椅背，走近那个瑟缩发抖的男子，在黑暗中立在他跟前，从比平时高得多的角度俯视着他。

"你的情报可靠吗，卢克伍德？"哈利问。

"可靠，主人，可靠……我——我毕竟在部里工作过……"

"埃弗里对我说博德可能会把它弄走。"

"博德本来绝对不可能去拿的，主人……博德本来应该知道他不能拿……这无疑就是他竭力抵抗马尔福的夺魂咒的原因……"

"站起来，卢克伍德。"哈利轻声说。

跪着的男子急忙从命，差一点儿栽倒。他脸上满是伤疤；烛光一照，他的伤疤变得更加明显了。他站起来时背还是有点弯，好像鞠躬鞠到了一半。他恐惧地瞟着哈利的脸色。

"你的报告很好，"哈利说，"很好……看来我白花了几个月的时间……可是没关系……我们现在重新开始。伏地魔感谢你，卢克伍德……"

"主人……是，主人。"卢克伍德松了口气，嘶哑地说。

"我还需要你的帮助，我需要你能提供的所有信息。"

"当然，主人，当然……在所不辞……"

CHAPTER TWENTY-SIX   Seen and Unforeseen

'Very well ... you may go. Send Avery to me.'

Rookwood scurried backwards, bowing, and disappeared through a door.

Left alone in the dark room, Harry turned towards the wall. A cracked, age-spotted mirror hung on the wall in the shadows. Harry moved towards it. His reflection grew larger and clearer in the darkness ... a face whiter than a skull ... red eyes with slits for pupils ...

'NOOOOOOOOO!'

'What?' yelled a voice nearby.

Harry flailed around madly, became entangled in the hangings and fell out of his bed. For a few seconds he did not know where he was; he was convinced he was about to see the white, skull-like face looming at him out of the dark again, then very near to him Ron's voice spoke.

'Will you stop acting like a maniac so I can get you out of here!'

Ron wrenched the hangings apart and Harry stared up at him in the moonlight, flat on his back, his scar searing with pain. Ron looked as though he had just been getting ready for bed; one arm was out of his robes.

'Has someone been attacked again?' asked Ron, pulling Harry roughly to his feet. 'Is it Dad? Is it that snake?'

'No – everyone's fine –' gasped Harry, whose forehead felt as though it were on fire. 'Well ... Avery isn't ... he's in trouble ... he gave him the wrong information ... Voldemort's really angry ...'

Harry groaned and sank, shaking, on to his bed, rubbing his scar.

'But Rookwood's going to help him now ... he's on the right track again ...'

'What are you talking about?' said Ron, sounding scared. 'D'you mean ... did you just see You-Know-Who?'

'I *was* You-Know-Who,' said Harry, and he stretched out his hands in the darkness and held them up to his face, to check that they were no longer deathly white and long-fingered. 'He was with Rookwood, he's one of the Death Eaters who escaped from Azkaban, remember? Rookwood's just told him Bode couldn't have done it.'

'Done what?'

'Remove something ... he said Bode would have known he couldn't have done it ... Bode was under the Imperius Curse ... I think he said Malfoy's dad put it on him.'

'Bode was bewitched to remove something?' Ron said. 'But – Harry, that's got to be –'

第 26 章 梦境内外

"很好……你可以走了。叫埃弗里来。"

卢克伍德躬身快步倒退,从一个门退了出去。

独自留在黑屋子里,哈利转身对着墙壁,阴影中的墙面上挂着一面裂了缝的、污渍斑斑的镜子。哈利走过去,他的模样在黑暗中渐渐变大,清晰起来……一张比骷髅还白的脸……红眼睛里的瞳孔是两条缝……

"不——!"

"怎么啦?"旁边一个声音喊道。

哈利乱蹬乱踢,缠到了帷帐里,滚下了床,有几秒钟他甚至不知道自己在什么地方,他相信黑暗中还会出现那苍白的骷髅般的面孔,然而罗恩的声音在他身旁响起。

"你能不能不像疯子那样乱动?我好把你弄出来!"

罗恩扯开帷帐,哈利仰面躺在地上,在月光中瞪着罗恩,伤疤在灼痛。罗恩好像正准备睡觉,袍子已经脱下一只袖子。

"又有人出事了吗?"罗恩问,一边把哈利拉了起来,"是我爸爸吗?是那条蛇吗?"

"不——大家都没事——"哈利喘着气说,他的额头好像又着了火,"不……埃弗里有事……他倒霉了……他给了他错误的情报……他非常生气……"

哈利呻吟一声,哆嗦着坐到床上,揉着伤疤。

"但现在有卢克伍德帮他……他又走对路了……"

"你说什么呀?"罗恩惊恐地问,"你是说……你刚才看见神秘人了?"

"我就是神秘人。"哈利说,他在黑暗中伸出双手,举到眼前,看它们是不是还苍白而细长,"他和卢克伍德在一起,就是从阿兹卡班跑出去的食死徒之一,记得吗?卢克伍德对他说博德本不可能做到……"

"做到什么?"

"拿走什么东西……他说博德应该知道他不能……博德中了夺魂咒……我想是马尔福的爸爸施的……"

"博德中了魔法要去拿什么东西?"罗恩说,"可是——哈利,那一定是——"

CHAPTER TWENTY-SIX Seen and Unforeseen

'The weapon,' Harry finished the sentence for him. 'I know.'

The dormitory door opened; Dean and Seamus came in. Harry swung his legs back into bed. He did not want to look as though anything odd had just happened, seeing as Seamus had only just stopped thinking Harry was a nutter.

'Did you say,' murmured Ron, putting his head close to Harry's on the pretence of helping himself to water from the jug on his bedside table, 'that you *were* You-Know-Who?'

'Yeah,' said Harry quietly.

Ron took an unnecessarily large gulp of water; Harry saw it spill over his chin on to his chest.

'Harry,' he said, as Dean and Seamus clattered around noisily, pulling off their robes and talking, 'you've got to tell –'

'I haven't got to tell anyone,' said Harry shortly. 'I wouldn't have seen it at all if I could do Occlumency. I'm supposed to have learned to shut this stuff out. That's what they want.'

By 'they' he meant Dumbledore. He got back into bed and rolled over on to his side with his back to Ron and after a while he heard Ron's mattress creak as he, too, lay back down. Harry's scar began to burn; he bit hard on his pillow to stop himself making a noise. Somewhere, he knew, Avery was being punished.

Harry and Ron waited until break next morning to tell Hermione exactly what had happened; they wanted to be absolutely sure they could not be overheard. Standing in their usual corner of the cool and breezy courtyard, Harry told her every detail of the dream he could remember. When he had finished, she said nothing at all for a few moments, but stared with a kind of painful intensity at Fred and George, who were both headless and selling their magical hats from under their cloaks on the other side of the yard.

'So that's why they killed him,' she said quietly, withdrawing her gaze from Fred and George at last. 'When Bode tried to steal this weapon, something funny happened to him. I think there must be defensive spells on it, or around it, to stop people touching it. That's why he was in St Mungo's, his brain had gone all funny and he couldn't talk. But remember what the Healer told us? He was recovering. And they couldn't risk him getting better, could they? I mean, the shock of whatever happened when he touched that weapon probably made the Imperius Curse lift. Once he'd got his voice back, he'd explain what he'd been doing, wouldn't he? They would have known

第26章 梦境内外

"武器,"哈利替他把话说完,"我知道。"

宿舍的门开了,迪安和西莫走了进来。哈利把腿搁到床上,不想让他们看出有什么异常,因为西莫刚刚不再认为哈利是个疯子。

"你是说,"罗恩假装到床头柜上拿水,把头凑近哈利问道,"你就是神秘人?"

"对。"哈利小声说。

罗恩吞了一大口水,哈利看到水从他的下巴流到了胸口。

"哈利,"他说,迪安和西莫在屋里动静很大,脱衣服,说话,"你必须告诉——"

"我不能告诉任何人,"哈利马上说,"要是我会大脑封闭术的话,根本就不该看到这个。我应该学会不让这些东西进来,他们希望这样。"

他说的"他们"指的是邓布利多。他躺下来,翻身背对着罗恩,过了一会儿他听见罗恩的床吱扭一响,知道他也睡下了。伤疤火烧火燎地痛了起来,他咬住枕头,尽量不发出声音。他知道,在某个地方,埃弗里在受惩罚……

第二天上午,哈利和罗恩等到课间休息时才把这件事告诉了赫敏。他们希望确保没人听见。站在凉风拂面的院子里他们惯常待的角落,哈利对赫敏讲了他能记得的每个细节。听完之后,赫敏有一会儿没说话,只是带着极其专注的表情看着院子那头的弗雷德和乔治,他们两个的头不见了,正躲在斗篷底下,推销他们的魔法帽。

"所以他们杀死了他,"赫敏终于把目光从弗雷德和乔治身上转了回来,轻轻地说,"当博德去偷武器的时候,发生了一件古怪的事,我想武器上面或周围一定有防御咒,不让人碰它。所以他进了圣芒戈,他神经错乱了,不能说话。但你记得治疗师说的话吗?他在渐渐康复。他们不能让他好起来,是不是?我是说,他碰武器时中的魔法可能冲掉了夺魂咒,一旦他能讲话,就会说出他干的事情,对不对?人家就会知道他被派去偷武器。当然,卢修斯·马尔福对他施夺魂咒很容易,

CHAPTER TWENTY-SIX Seen and Unforeseen

he'd been sent to steal the weapon. Of course, it would have been easy for Lucius Malfoy to put the curse on him. Never out of the Ministry, is he?'

'He was even hanging around that day I had my hearing,' said Harry. 'In the – hang on ...' he said slowly. 'He was in the Department of Mysteries corridor that day! Your dad said he was probably trying to sneak down and find out what happened in my hearing, but what if –'

'Sturgis!' gasped Hermione, looking thunderstruck.

'Sorry?' said Ron, looking bewildered.

'Sturgis Podmore –' said Hermione breathlessly, 'arrested for trying to get through a door! Lucius Malfoy must have got him too! I bet he did it the day you saw him there, Harry. Sturgis had Moody's Invisibility Cloak, right? So, what if he was standing guard by the door, invisible, and Malfoy heard him move – or guessed someone was there – or just did the Imperius Curse on the off-chance there'd be a guard there? So, when Sturgis next had an opportunity – probably when it was his turn on guard duty again – he tried to get into the Department to steal the weapon for Voldemort – Ron, be quiet – but he got caught and sent to Azkaban ...'

She gazed at Harry.

'And now Rookwood's told Voldemort how to get the weapon?'

'I didn't hear all the conversation, but that's what it sounded like,' said Harry. 'Rookwood used to work there ... maybe Voldemort'll send Rookwood to do it?'

Hermione nodded, apparently still lost in thought. Then, quite abruptly, she said, 'But you shouldn't have seen this at all, Harry.'

'What?' he said, taken aback.

'You're supposed to be learning how to close your mind to this sort of thing,' said Hermione, suddenly stern.

'I know I am,' said Harry. 'But –'

'Well, I think we should just try and forget what you saw,' said Hermione firmly. 'And you ought to put in a bit more effort on your Occlumency from now on.'

The week did not improve as it progressed. Harry received two more 'D's in Potions; he was still on tenterhooks that Hagrid might get the sack; and he couldn't stop himself dwelling on the dream in which he had been Voldemort – though he didn't bring it up with Ron and Hermione again; he didn't want another telling-off from Hermione. He wished very much that he could have talked to Sirius about it, but that was out of the question, so he tried to push the matter to the back of his mind.

第26章 梦境内外

他和魔法部一直关系密切,是不是?"

"我受审的那天他还在呢,"哈利说,"在——等等……"他回忆着,"他那天在神秘事务司的走廊上!你爸爸说他可能想溜进去听我的审讯,但假设——"

"斯多吉。"赫敏恐惧地惊叫一声。

"什么?"罗恩问,一脸迷惑。

"斯多吉·波德摩,"赫敏透不过气地说,"因企图闯入魔法部的一扇门而被捕。卢修斯·马尔福也对他下了手。哈利,我打赌他就是在你看到他的那天干的。斯多吉有穆迪的隐形衣,对不对?说不定他就隐身守在那扇门口,马尔福听到动静,或猜到那儿有人,或只是为防止有守卫而施了夺魂咒?所以当斯多吉下次有机会时——可能是又轮到他值班的时候,就企图溜进神秘事务司去为伏地魔偷武器——罗恩,别吵——但是他被抓住了,进了阿兹卡班……"

她望着哈利。

"卢克伍德告诉伏地魔怎么能拿到武器了吗?"

"我没有听全,但好像是的,"哈利说,"卢克伍德在那儿工作过……也许伏地魔会派卢克伍德去?"

赫敏点点头,显然还在沉思。突然她说:"可是你不应该看到这些,哈利。"

"什么?"哈利大吃一惊。

"你应该学习不让这些东西进到你的脑子里。"赫敏突然严厉起来。

"我知道,"哈利说,"可是——"

"我想我们应该设法忘掉你看到的东西,"赫敏坚决地说,"从现在起你要多下功夫练大脑封闭术。"

这个星期也没见什么起色:哈利在魔药课上又得了两个"D",还在担心海格会被解雇,而且总是不由自主地想到那个梦。可是他没有对罗恩和赫敏提起,因为不想再听赫敏的训斥。他非常希望能跟小天狼星谈谈,但那是不可能的,他只好努力把这件事推到脑子后面。

CHAPTER TWENTY-SIX — Seen and Unforeseen

Unfortunately, the back of his mind was no longer the secure place it had once been.

'Get up, Potter.'

A couple of weeks after his dream of Rookwood, Harry was to be found, yet again, kneeling on the floor of Snape's office, trying to clear his head. He had just been forced, yet again, to relive a stream of very early memories he had not even realised he still had, most of them concerning humiliations Dudley and his gang had inflicted upon him in primary school.

'That last memory,' said Snape. 'What was it?'

'I don't know,' said Harry, getting wearily to his feet. He was finding it increasingly difficult to disentangle separate memories from the rush of images and sound that Snape kept calling forth. 'You mean the one where my cousin tried to make me stand in the toilet?'

'No,' said Snape softly. 'I mean the one with a man kneeling in the middle of a darkened room ...'

'It's ... nothing,' said Harry.

Snape's dark eyes bored into Harry's. Remembering what Snape had said about eye contact being crucial to Legilimency, Harry blinked and looked away.

'How do that man and that room come to be inside your head, Potter?' said Snape.

'It –' said Harry, looking everywhere but at Snape, 'it was – just a dream I had.'

'A dream?' repeated Snape.

There was a pause during which Harry stared fixedly at a large dead frog suspended in a jar of purple liquid.

'You do know why we are here, don't you, Potter?' said Snape, in a low, dangerous voice. 'You do know why I am giving up my evenings to this tedious job?'

'Yes,' said Harry stiffly.

'Remind me why we are here, Potter.'

'So I can learn Occlumency,' said Harry, now glaring at a dead eel.

'Correct, Potter. And dim though you may be –' Harry looked back at Snape, hating him '– I would have thought that after over two months of lessons you might have made some progress. How many other dreams about the Dark Lord have you had?'

'Just that one,' lied Harry.

'Perhaps,' said Snape, his dark, cold eyes narrowing slightly, 'perhaps you actually enjoy having these visions and dreams, Potter. Maybe they make you feel special – important?'

第26章 梦境内外

不幸的是,他的脑子后面不再像以前那么安全了。

"站起来,波特。"

在梦见卢克伍德的两个星期之后,哈利又跪在斯内普办公室的地上,努力清空他的大脑。他刚刚又被迫重温了一串他自己都不知道还储存着的幼年记忆,大部分是达力那伙人在小学里对他的羞辱。

"最后一个记忆是什么?"斯内普问。

"我不知道,"哈利说,他疲惫地站了起来,发觉越来越难以分清斯内普不断引出的画面和声音,"是我表哥想让我站在马桶里的那个吗?"

"不是,"斯内普轻声说,"是一个男人跪在黑暗的屋子中间……"

"那……没什么。"哈利说。

斯内普的黑眼睛像钻子一样看到了哈利的眼睛里。哈利想起目光接触对摄神取念很关键,他眨了眨眼,移开了目光。

"那个人和那间屋子怎么会进到你的脑子里,波特?"斯内普说。

"那——"哈利回避着他的目光,"那——只是我做的一个梦。"

"一个梦?"斯内普说。

一阵沉寂,哈利盯着一只泡在紫色液体里的死青蛙。

"你知道我们在这儿干什么吗,波特?"斯内普凶恶地低声问,"你知道我为什么放弃晚上的时间来做这份讨厌的工作吗?"

"知道。"哈利生硬地说。

"说说我们在这儿干什么,波特。"

"教我大脑封闭术。"哈利又盯着一条死鳗鱼说。

"对,波特。就算你很笨——"哈利回瞪着斯内普,憎恨着他,"——我以为两个多月的课下来,你总该有些进步了吧。你还做了多少关于黑魔王的梦?"

"就这一个。"哈利撒谎道。

"或许,"斯内普那冷酷的黑眼睛眯了起来,"或许你喜欢有这些幻觉和怪梦,波特。或许它们让你觉得自己很特殊——很重要?"

983

CHAPTER TWENTY-SIX   Seen and Unforeseen

'No, they don't,' said Harry, his jaw set and his fingers clenched tightly around the handle of his wand.

'That is just as well, Potter,' said Snape coldly, 'because you are neither special nor important, and it is not up to you to find out what the Dark Lord is saying to his Death Eaters.'

'No – that's your job, isn't it?' Harry shot at him.

He had not meant to say it; it had burst out of him in temper. For a long moment they stared at each other, Harry convinced he had gone too far. But there was a curious, almost satisfied expression on Snape's face when he answered.

'Yes, Potter,' he said, his eyes glinting. 'That is my job. Now, if you are ready, we will start again.'

He raised his wand: 'One – two – three – *Legilimens!*'

A hundred Dementors were swooping towards Harry across the lake in the grounds ... he screwed up his face in concentration ... they were coming closer ... he could see the dark holes beneath their hoods ... yet he could also see Snape standing in front of him, his eyes fixed on Harry's face, muttering under his breath ... and somehow, Snape was growing clearer, and the Dementors were growing fainter ...

Harry raised his own wand.

'*Protego!*'

Snape staggered – his wand flew upwards, away from Harry – and suddenly Harry's mind was teeming with memories that were not his: a hook-nosed man was shouting at a cowering woman, while a small dark-haired boy cried in a corner ... a greasy-haired teenager sat alone in a dark bedroom, pointing his wand at the ceiling, shooting down flies ... a girl was laughing as a scrawny boy tried to mount a bucking broomstick –

'ENOUGH!'

Harry felt as though he had been pushed hard in the chest; he staggered several steps backwards, hit some of the shelves covering Snape's walls and heard something crack. Snape was shaking slightly, and was very white in the face.

The back of Harry's robes was damp. One of the jars behind him had broken when he fell against it; the pickled slimy thing within was swirling in its draining potion.

'*Reparo,*' hissed Snape, and the jar sealed itself at once. 'Well, Potter ... that was certainly an improvement ...' Panting slightly, Snape straightened the Pensieve in which he had again stored some of his thoughts before

第26章 梦境内外

"没有。"哈利咬着牙,手指紧紧地攥着魔杖。

"那就好,波特,"斯内普冷冷地说,"因为你既不特殊也不重要,也不需要你去弄清楚黑魔王对他的食死徒说了什么。"

"对——那是你的工作,是不是?"哈利向他吼道。

他本来没想这么说,是气头上冲口而出的。很长一段时间里他们瞪着对方,哈利觉得他说得太过火了。但斯内普的脸上却现出一种奇怪的、几乎是满意的表情。

"对,波特,"他的眼里闪出亮光,"那是我的工作。现在,准备好了吗,我们再来……"

他举起魔杖:"一——二——三——摄神取念!"

一百个摄魂怪从湖上朝哈利扑来……他的脸紧张得扭曲起来……他们越来越近……他看到了兜帽下的黑洞……但他同时看到斯内普站在他面前,盯着他的面孔,口里念念有词……不知为什么,斯内普清晰起来,摄魂怪变淡了……

哈利举起魔杖。

"盔甲护身!"

斯内普跟跄了一下,他的魔杖向上飞起,远离了哈利——突然哈利觉得脑子里充满了陌生的记忆——一个鹰钩鼻的男人在朝一个畏缩的女人吼叫,一个黑头发的小男孩在角落里哭泣……一个头发油腻腻的少年独自坐在黑暗的卧室里,用魔杖指着天花板射苍蝇……一个瘦骨嶙峋的男孩想骑上一把乱跳的扫帚,旁边一个女孩在笑他——

"够了!"

哈利感到胸口被猛推了一把,他跟跟跄跄地倒退了几步,撞在墙边的几个架子上,什么东西咔嚓一声碎了。斯内普在微微颤抖,脸色煞白。

哈利袍子后面湿了,他刚才撞破了身后的一个瓶子,里面一个黏糊糊的东西在渐渐流干的魔药中旋转。

"恢复如初!"斯内普嘶声说,瓶子又自动修复,"啊,波特……这

CHAPTER TWENTY-SIX Seen and Unforeseen

starting the lesson, almost as though he was checking they were still there. 'I don't remember telling you to use a Shield Charm ... but there is no doubt that it was effective ...'

Harry did not speak; he felt that to say anything might be dangerous. He was sure he had just broken into Snape's memories, that he had just seen scenes from Snape's childhood. It was unnerving to think that the little boy who had been crying as he watched his parents shouting was actually standing in front of him with such loathing in his eyes.

'Let's try again, shall we?' said Snape.

Harry felt a thrill of dread; he was about to pay for what had just happened, he was sure of it. They moved back into position with the desk between them, Harry feeling he was going to find it much harder to empty his mind this time.

'On the count of three, then,' said Snape, raising his wand once more. 'One – two –'

Harry did not have time to gather himself together and attempt to clear his mind before Snape cried, '*Legilimens!*'

He was hurtling along the corridor towards the Department of Mysteries, past the blank stone walls, past the torches – the plain black door was growing ever larger; he was moving so fast he was going to collide with it, he was feet from it and again he could see that chink of faint blue light –

The door had flown open! He was through it at last, inside a black-walled, black-floored circular room lit with blue-flamed candles, and there were more doors all around him – he needed to go on – but which door ought he to take –?

'POTTER!'

Harry opened his eyes. He was flat on his back again with no memory of having got there; he was also panting as though he really had run the length of the Department of Mysteries corridor, really had sprinted through the black door and found the circular room.

'Explain yourself!' said Snape, who was standing over him, looking furious.

'I ... dunno what happened,' said Harry truthfully, standing up. There was a lump on the back of his head from where he had hit the ground and he felt feverish. 'I've never seen that before. I mean, I told you, I've dreamed about the door ... but it's never opened before ...'

'You are not working hard enough!'

第26章 梦境内外

倒是个进步……"斯内普微微喘着气,摆正了冥想盆,好像在检查他上课前存进去的那些思想还在不在,"我不记得说过叫你用铁甲咒……但它无疑是有效的……"

哈利没说话,他觉得说什么都有危险。他知道自己刚才闯进了斯内普的记忆,看到了斯内普小时候的情景。他心里很不舒服,想到那个看着父母吵架而哭泣的小男孩此刻正站在他面前,眼里带着如此强烈的憎恨……

"再来一次,怎么样?"斯内普说。

哈利感到一阵恐惧:他猜到他要为刚才的事付出代价。两人隔着桌子站好,哈利感到这次清空大脑要困难得多……

"数到三,"斯内普说着再次举起魔杖,"一——二——"

哈利还没有来得及集中精神清空大脑,斯内普就已经喊出:"摄神取念!"

他在走廊上朝神秘事务司飞奔,空白的石墙、火把在两旁掠过——那扇黑门越来越大,他跑得太快,几乎要一头撞上去了,还差几步,他又看到了那道微弱的蓝光——

门突然打开了!他终于进去了,一间黑墙壁、黑地板的圆屋子,燃着蓝火苗的蜡烛,周围还有好几扇门——他要继续前进——可是该走哪个门呢——?

"**波特!**"

哈利睁开眼睛,他又仰面躺在地上,但不记得是怎么摔倒的。他喘着粗气,好像真的跑了那么长的走廊,真的冲过了黑门,发现了那间圆屋子……

"自己解释!"斯内普站在他面前,怒不可遏。

"我……不知道是怎么回事,"哈利诚实地说,站了起来,后脑勺在地上磕了一个包,他感到有点发烧,"我以前从来没见过。我跟你说过,我梦见过那扇门……可它以前从来没打开过……"

"你不够努力!"

CHAPTER TWENTY-SIX — Seen and Unforeseen

For some reason, Snape seemed even angrier than he had done two minutes before, when Harry had seen into his teacher's memories.

'You are lazy and sloppy, Potter, it is small wonder that the Dark Lord –'

'Can you tell me something, *sir?*' said Harry, firing up again. 'Why do you call Voldemort the Dark Lord? I've only ever heard Death Eaters call him that.'

Snape opened his mouth in a snarl – and a woman screamed from somewhere outside the room.

Snape's head jerked upwards; he was gazing at the ceiling.

'What the –?' he muttered.

Harry could hear a muffled commotion coming from what he thought might be the Entrance Hall. Snape looked round at him, frowning.

'Did you see anything unusual on your way down here, Potter?'

Harry shook his head. Somewhere above them, the woman screamed again. Snape strode to his office door, his wand still held at the ready, and swept out of sight. Harry hesitated for a moment, then followed.

The screams were indeed coming from the Entrance Hall; they grew louder as Harry ran towards the stone steps leading up from the dungeons. When he reached the top he found the Entrance Hall packed; students had come flooding out of the Great Hall, where dinner was still in progress, to see what was going on; others had crammed themselves on to the marble staircase. Harry pushed forwards through a knot of tall Slytherins and saw that the onlookers had formed a great ring, some of them looking shocked, others even frightened. Professor McGonagall was directly opposite Harry on the other side of the Hall; she looked as though what she was watching made her feel faintly sick.

Professor Trelawney was standing in the middle of the Entrance Hall with her wand in one hand and an empty sherry bottle in the other, looking utterly mad. Her hair was sticking up on end, her glasses were lopsided so that one eye was magnified more than the other; her innumerable shawls and scarves were trailing haphazardly from her shoulders, giving the impression that she was falling apart at the seams. Two large trunks lay on the floor beside her, one of them upside-down; it looked very much as though it had been thrown down the stairs after her. Professor Trelawney was staring, apparently terrified, at something Harry could not see but which seemed to be standing at the foot of the stairs.

'No!' she shrieked. 'NO! This cannot be happening ... it cannot ... I refuse to accept it!'

第26章 梦境内外

不知为什么,斯内普好像比两分钟前哈利看到他本人的记忆时更生气了。

"你又懒惰又马虎,波特,难怪黑魔王——"

"您能不能解释一下,先生?"哈利又火了起来,"您为什么管伏地魔叫黑魔王?我只听过食死徒那样叫他——"

斯内普张开嘴巴咆哮——外面有个女人尖叫起来。

斯内普抬头望着天花板。

"什么——?"他嘟哝道。

哈利听到好像是从门厅那边传来了吵吵嚷嚷的声音。斯内普皱眉看着他。

"你下来的时候看到什么异常情况了吗,波特?"

哈利摇摇头。上面的女人又尖叫起来。斯内普手持魔杖走到门口,闪身出去了。哈利犹豫了一会儿,跟了出去。

叫声果然是从门厅传来的,哈利跑向通往地下教室的台阶时声音更响了。跑到顶上,他发现门厅里挤满了人。吃晚饭的学生从礼堂里拥出来看发生了什么事,还有很多人挤在大理石楼梯上。哈利从一群高大的斯莱特林学生中间挤过去,看见旁观者围成了一个大圈,有的人显得很震惊,有的甚至神色惶恐。麦格教授站在门厅的另一端,正好在哈利的对面,她似乎对眼前这一幕感到很难受。

特里劳尼教授站在门厅中间,一手拿着魔杖,一手握着个空酒瓶,看上去完全疯了。她的头发都耷着,眼镜也歪了,显得一只眼睛比另一只放大了许多,她那数不清的围巾和披肩凌乱地挂了下来,让人感觉她似乎要崩溃了。她旁边有两个大箱子,一个倒立着,好像是从楼梯上扔下来的。特里劳尼教授恐惧地盯着楼梯底下的什么东西,但哈利看不见。

"不!"她尖叫道,"**不**!这不可能发生……不可能……我拒绝接受!"

CHAPTER TWENTY-SIX   Seen and Unforeseen

'You didn't realise this was coming?' said a high girlish voice, sounding callously amused, and Harry, moving slightly to his right, saw that Trelawney's terrifying vision was nothing other than Professor Umbridge. 'Incapable though you are of predicting even tomorrow's weather, you must surely have realised that your pitiful performance during my inspections, and lack of any improvement, would make it inevitable that you would be sacked?'

'You c – can't!' howled Professor Trelawney, tears streaming down her face from behind her enormous lenses, 'you c – can't sack me! I've b – been here sixteen years! H – Hogwarts is m – my h – home!'

'It *was* your home,' said Professor Umbridge, and Harry was revolted to see the enjoyment stretching her toadlike face as she watched Professor Trelawney sink, sobbing uncontrollably, on to one of her trunks, 'until an hour ago, when the Minister for Magic countersigned your Order of Dismissal. Now kindly remove yourself from this Hall. You are embarrassing us.'

But she stood and watched, with an expression of gloating enjoyment, as Professor Trelawney shuddered and moaned, rocking backwards and forwards on her trunk in paroxysms of grief. Harry heard a muffled sob to his left and looked around. Lavender and Parvati were both crying quietly, their arms round each other. Then he heard footsteps. Professor McGonagall had broken away from the spectators, marched straight up to Professor Trelawney and was patting her firmly on the back while withdrawing a large handkerchief from within her robes.

'There, there, Sybill ... calm down ... blow your nose on this ... it's not as bad as you think, now ... you are not going to have to leave Hogwarts ...'

'Oh really, Professor McGonagall?' said Umbridge in a deadly voice, taking a few steps forward. 'And your authority for that statement is ... ?'

'That would be mine,' said a deep voice.

The oaken front doors had swung open. Students beside them scuttled out of the way as Dumbledore appeared in the entrance. What he had been doing out in the grounds Harry could not imagine, but there was something impressive about the sight of him framed in the doorway against an oddly misty night. Leaving the doors wide open behind him he strode forwards through the circle of onlookers towards Professor Trelawney, tear-stained and trembling, on her trunk, Professor McGonagall alongside her.

'Yours, Professor Dumbledore?' said Umbridge, with a singularly unpleasant little laugh. 'I'm afraid you do not understand the position. I have

第26章 梦境内外

"你没想到会这样？"一个尖尖的小姑娘般的声音冷酷地说，似乎感到很好笑。哈利朝右边挪了挪，看到特里劳尼眼里可怕的东西正是乌姆里奇教授。"虽然你连明天的天气都预测不了，但你总该意识到，你在我听课时的糟糕表现和此后的毫无改进，必然会导致你被解雇吧？"

"你——你不能！"特里劳尼教授号叫道，眼泪从大镜片后面涌出，"你—你不能解雇我！我在—在这儿待了十六年！霍—霍格沃茨是我—我的家！"

"曾经是你的家，"乌姆里奇教授说。看到特里劳尼教授跌坐在一个箱子上痛哭流涕，她的癞蛤蟆脸上露出得意的笑容，哈利感到一阵恶心，"直到一小时前，魔法部部长签了你的解雇令为止。现在请你离开大厅，你让我们感到难为情。"

但她站在那里，幸灾乐祸地看着特里劳尼教授发抖，呜咽，随着一阵阵的悲痛在箱子上前后摇晃。哈利听见左边一声抽噎，回头一看，拉文德和帕瓦蒂正抱在一起默默哭泣。然后他听到脚步声，麦格教授从人群中挤了出来，径直走到特里劳尼教授面前，有力地拍着她的后背，从袍子里抽出一块大手帕。

"好了，好了，西比尔……镇定些……擤擤鼻子……没有你想的那么糟……你不会离开霍格沃茨……"

"哦，是吗，麦格教授？"乌姆里奇朝前走了几步，恶毒地说，"这是谁批准的……？"

"我。"一个低沉的声音说。

橡木大门打开了，门边的学生赶忙闪开，邓布利多出现在门口。哈利想象不出他在外面做什么，但他站在门框中，衬着雾霭缭绕的夜色，有一种威严之感。他让大门敞开着，大步穿过人群走向特里劳尼教授。特里劳尼教授还坐在箱子上，满脸泪痕，浑身发抖，麦格教授陪着她。

"你，邓布利多教授？"乌姆里奇发出一声特别难听的尖笑，"恐

CHAPTER TWENTY-SIX   Seen and Unforeseen

here –' she pulled a parchment scroll from within her robes '– an Order of Dismissal signed by myself and the Minister for Magic. Under the terms of Educational Decree Number Twenty-three, the High Inquisitor of Hogwarts has the power to inspect, place upon probation and sack any teacher she – that is to say, I – feel is not performing to the standards required by the Ministry of Magic. I have decided that Professor Trelawney is not up to scratch. I have dismissed her.'

To Harry's very great surprise, Dumbledore continued to smile. He looked down at Professor Trelawney, who was still sobbing and choking on her trunk, and said, 'You are quite right, of course, Professor Umbridge. As High Inquisitor you have every right to dismiss my teachers. You do not, however, have the authority to send them away from the castle. I am afraid,' he went on, with a courteous little bow, 'that the power to do that still resides with the Headmaster, and it is my wish that Professor Trelawney continue to live at Hogwarts.'

At this, Professor Trelawney gave a wild little laugh in which a hiccough was barely hidden.

'No – no, I'll g – go, Dumbledore! I sh – shall – leave Hogwarts and s – seek my fortune elsewhere –'

'No,' said Dumbledore sharply. 'It is my wish that you remain, Sybill.'

He turned to Professor McGonagall.

'Might I ask you to escort Sybill back upstairs, Professor McGonagall?'

'Of course,' said McGonagall. 'Up you get, Sybill ...'

Professor Sprout came hurrying forwards out of the crowd and grabbed Professor Trelawney's other arm. Together, they guided her past Umbridge and up the marble stairs. Professor Flitwick went scurrying after them, his wand held out before him; he squeaked '*Locomotor trunks!*' and Professor Trelawney's luggage rose into the air and proceeded up the staircase after her, Professor Flitwick bringing up the rear.

Professor Umbridge was standing stock-still, staring at Dumbledore, who continued to smile benignly.

'And what,' she said, in a whisper that carried all around the Entrance Hall, 'are you going to do with her once I appoint a new Divination teacher who needs her lodgings?'

'Oh, that won't be a problem,' said Dumbledore pleasantly. 'You see, I have already found us a new Divination teacher, and he will prefer lodgings on the ground floor.'

'You've found –?' said Umbridge shrilly. '*You've* found? Might I remind

第26章 梦境内外

怕你还不知情吧。我这儿有——"她从袍子里抽出一卷羊皮纸"——我本人和魔法部部长签的解雇令。根据《第二十三号教育令》,霍格沃茨高级调查官有权检查、留用察看和解雇任何其——也就是我——认为不符合魔法部标准的教师。我认为特里劳尼教授不合格。我已经解雇了她。"

令哈利大为惊讶的是,邓布利多仍然面带微笑。他低头看着还在箱子上抽泣的特里劳尼教授,说道:"您说的当然对,乌姆里奇教授。作为最高调查官您完全有权解雇我的教师。但是,您恐怕无权将他们逐出城堡,这个权力恐怕——"他礼貌地欠了欠身说,"还属于校长,我希望特里劳尼教授继续住在霍格沃茨。"

特里劳尼激动地笑了一声,还夹着一点儿抽噎。

"不——不,我要走,邓布利多!我要离——离开霍格沃茨,去别处谋生——"

"不,"邓布利多坚决地说,"我希望你留下,西比尔。"

他转向麦格教授。

"请你带西比尔上楼好吗,麦格教授?"

"当然,"麦格说,"上楼吧,西比尔……"

斯普劳特教授赶忙从人群中挤出来搀住了特里劳尼教授的另一只胳膊。两人带她从乌姆里奇身边走过,上了大理石楼梯。弗立维教授举着魔杖追上去,尖声叫道:"箱子移动!"特里劳尼教授的箱子升到空中,跟着她上了楼,弗立维教授断后。

乌姆里奇教授呆立在那里,瞪着邓布利多,他依然在和蔼地微笑。

"等我任命了新的占卜课教师,需要用她的房间时,你打算拿她怎么办?"乌姆里奇小声说,但声音还是传遍了整个大厅。

"噢,那不成问题,"邓布利多愉快地说,"您看,我已经找到了一位占卜课教师,他愿意住在一层。"

"你已经找到了——?"乌姆里奇尖厉地说,"你已经找到了?我

CHAPTER TWENTY-SIX — Seen and Unforeseen

you, Dumbledore, that under Educational Decree Number Twenty-two –'

'The Ministry has the right to appoint a suitable candidate if – and only if – the Headmaster is unable to find one,' said Dumbledore. 'And I am happy to say that on this occasion I have succeeded. May I introduce you?'

He turned to face the open front doors, through which night mist was now drifting. Harry heard hooves. There was a shocked murmur around the Hall and those nearest the doors hastily moved even further backwards, some of them tripping over in their haste to clear a path for the newcomer.

Through the mist came a face Harry had seen once before on a dark, dangerous night in the Forbidden Forest: white-blond hair and astonishingly blue eyes; the head and torso of a man joined to the palomino body of a horse.

'This is Firenze,' said Dumbledore happily to a thunderstruck Umbridge. 'I think you'll find him suitable.'

第26章 梦境内外

提醒你,邓布利多,按照《第二十二号教育令》——"

"——当且只有当校长找不到合适人选时,魔法部有权任命教师。我很高兴宣布这一次我找到了。要我介绍一下吗?"

他把头转向门口,夜雾从门中飘入。哈利听到了马蹄声,大厅中响起惊恐的低语,为了给新来的教师让路,门边的人赶紧退得更远些,有的还绊倒了。

雾中出现了一张脸,哈利曾于一个黑暗、危险的夜晚在禁林中见过:白金色的头发,蓝得惊人的眼睛,人的头和躯干安在一匹银鬃马身上。

"这位是费伦泽,"邓布利多愉快地对目瞪口呆的乌姆里奇说,"我想你会发现他很合适吧。"

CHAPTER TWENTY-SEVEN

The Centaur and the Sneak

'I'll bet you wish you hadn't given up Divination now, don't you, Hermione?' asked Parvati, smirking.

It was breakfast time, two days after the sacking of Professor Trelawney, and Parvati was curling her eyelashes around her wand and examining the effect in the back of her spoon. They were to have their first lesson with Firenze that morning.

'Not really,' said Hermione indifferently, who was reading the *Daily Prophet*. 'I've never really liked horses.'

She turned a page of the newspaper and scanned its columns.

'He's not a horse, he's a centaur!' said Lavender, sounding shocked.

'A *gorgeous* centaur ...' sighed Parvati.

'Either way, he's still got four legs,' said Hermione coolly. 'Anyway, I thought you two were all upset that Trelawney had gone?'

'We are!' Lavender assured her. 'We went up to her office to see her; we took her some daffodils – not the honking ones that Sprout's got, nice ones.'

'How is she?' asked Harry.

'Not very good, poor thing,' said Lavender sympathetically. 'She was crying and saying she'd rather leave the castle for ever than stay here where Umbridge is, and I don't blame her, Umbridge was horrible to her, wasn't she?'

'I've got a feeling Umbridge has only just started being horrible,' said Hermione darkly.

'Impossible,' said Ron, who was tucking into a large plate of eggs and bacon. 'She can't get any worse than she's been already.'

第 27 章

马人和告密生

"**我**敢说,你现在一定觉得要是没放弃占卜课就好了,是不是,赫敏?"帕瓦蒂带着得意的笑容问道。

此时正是早饭时间,特里劳尼教授被解雇的事已经过去两天了,帕瓦蒂用魔杖卷起自己的眼睫毛,对着饭勺背面看效果。今天上午,费伦泽要给他们上第一堂课。

"那倒不见得,"赫敏一边阅读《预言家日报》一边淡淡地说,"我向来不喜欢马。"

她翻过一页报纸,浏览了一下几个专栏。

"他不是一匹马,他是个马人!"拉文德惊异地说。

"而且是个帅气的马人……"帕瓦蒂叹息着说。

"不管怎么说,反正他有四条腿。"赫敏冷冷地说,"对了,我想特里劳尼离职的事让你们两个很难过吧?"

"是很难过!"拉文德对她肯定地说,"我们去她的办公室看望过她,还送给了她几株黄水仙花——是漂亮的黄水仙花,不是斯普劳特那些会叫唤的。"

"她还好吗?"哈利问道。

"不太好,可怜的人。"拉文德同情地说,"她哭着说,有乌姆里奇在这里,她宁可离开城堡。这不能怪她,乌姆里奇对她也太霸道了,是不是?"

"我有种感觉,乌姆里奇的霸道劲儿不过刚刚开了个头。"赫敏黯然地说。

"不可能,"罗恩说,他正狼吞虎咽地吃一大盘鸡蛋和熏咸肉,"她已经坏得不能再坏了。"

CHAPTER TWENTY-SEVEN   The Centaur and the Sneak

'You mark my words, she's going to want revenge on Dumbledore for appointing a new teacher without consulting her,' said Hermione, closing the newspaper. 'Especially another part-human. You saw the look on her face when she saw Firenze.'

After breakfast Hermione departed for her Arithmancy class as Harry and Ron followed Parvati and Lavender into the Entrance Hall, heading for Divination.

'Aren't we going up to North Tower?' asked Ron, looking puzzled, as Parvati bypassed the marble staircase.

Parvati looked at him scornfully over her shoulder.

'How d'you expect Firenze to climb that ladder? We're in classroom eleven now, it was on the noticeboard yesterday.'

Classroom eleven was on the ground floor along the corridor leading off the Entrance Hall from the opposite side to the Great Hall. Harry knew it was one of those classrooms that were never used regularly, and therefore had the slightly neglected feeling of a cupboard or storeroom. When he entered it right behind Ron, and found himself in the middle of a forest clearing, he was therefore momentarily stunned.

'What the –?'

The classroom floor had become springily mossy and trees were growing out of it; their leafy branches fanned across the ceiling and windows, so that the room was full of slanting shafts of soft, dappled, green light. The students who had already arrived were sitting on the earthy floor with their backs resting against tree trunks or boulders, arms wrapped around their knees or folded tightly across their chests, and all looking rather nervous. In the middle of the clearing, where there were no trees, stood Firenze.

'Harry Potter,' he said, holding out a hand when Harry entered.

'Er – hi,' said Harry, shaking hands with the centaur, who surveyed him unblinkingly through those astonishingly blue eyes but did not smile. 'Er – good to see you.'

'And you,' said the centaur, inclining his white-blond head. 'It was foretold that we would meet again.'

Harry noticed there was the shadow of a hoof-shaped bruise on Firenze's chest. As he turned to join the rest of the class on the ground, he saw they were all looking at him in awe, apparently deeply impressed that he was on

第27章 马人和告密生

"你们记住我的话吧,邓布利多没征求她的意见就指定了新老师,她会报复的,"赫敏合上报纸说,"更何况又是一个半人类。乌姆里奇见到费伦泽时,她脸上那副表情你们也看到了。"

早饭后,赫敏动身去上算术占卜课,哈利和罗恩跟在帕瓦蒂与拉文德身后走进门厅,前去上占卜课。

"我们不是要上北塔楼吗?"帕瓦蒂从大理石楼梯旁绕过时,罗恩一脸迷惑地问道。

帕瓦蒂回头轻蔑地看着他。

"你认为费伦泽怎么爬上活梯啊?现在我们用十一号教室,昨天布告栏上通知了。"

在礼堂对面,有一条走廊从门厅通向一楼的十一号教室。哈利知道,那是平常从不使用的教室之一,感觉有点像无人照管的橱柜或储藏室。他紧跟罗恩走了进去,发现自己来到了一片林间空地之中,这让他一时有些目瞪口呆。

"这是怎——?"

教室的地板变成了满地有弹性的苔藓,树木就是从苔藓下面长出来的;枝条上长满繁茂的树叶,成扇形从天花板和窗户上横贯而过,于是一束束柔和、斑驳的绿色光线倾泻在整间屋子里。先到的学生们背靠树干或大石头坐在泥地上,有的用胳膊搂着膝盖,有的两臂紧紧交叉在胸前,都显得很紧张。费伦泽就站在没有树木的空地中央。

"哈利·波特。"哈利进来后,他伸出一只手说。

"呃——嘿,"哈利说着和马人握了握手,马人那对蓝得出奇的眼睛一眨不眨地打量着哈利,脸上却没有露出笑容,"呃——真高兴见到你。"

"我也是,"长着白金色头发的马人说着点了点脑袋,"我们命中注定将要重逢。"

哈利注意到,费伦泽胸前有一块黑色的马蹄形瘀伤。他转过身,想和同学们一起坐在地上,这时他看到他们都在敬畏地望着自己。很显然,他和费伦泽熟悉到能搭上话,使同学们佩服不已,他们好像觉

CHAPTER TWENTY-SEVEN The Centaur and the Sneak

speaking terms with Firenze, whom they seemed to find intimidating.

When the door was closed and the last student had sat down on a tree stump beside the wastepaper basket, Firenze gestured around the room.

'Professor Dumbledore has kindly arranged this classroom for us,' said Firenze, when everyone had settled down, 'in imitation of my natural habitat. I would have preferred to teach you in the Forbidden Forest, which was – until Monday – my home ... but that is no longer possible.'

'Please – er – sir –' said Parvati breathlessly, raising her hand, '– why not? We've been in there with Hagrid, we're not frightened!'

'It is not a question of your bravery,' said Firenze, 'but of my position. I cannot return to the forest. My herd has banished me.'

'Herd?' said Lavender in a confused voice, and Harry knew she was thinking of cows. 'What – oh!'

Comprehension dawned on her face. 'There are *more of you*?' she said, stunned.

'Did Hagrid breed you, like the Thestrals?' asked Dean eagerly.

Firenze turned his head very slowly to face Dean, who seemed to realise at once that he had said something very offensive.

'I didn't – I meant – sorry,' he finished in a hushed voice.

'Centaurs are not the servants or playthings of humans,' said Firenze quietly. There was a pause, then Parvati raised her hand again.

'Please, sir ... why have the other centaurs banished you?'

'Because I have agreed to work for Professor Dumbledore,' said Firenze. 'They see this as a betrayal of our kind.'

Harry remembered how, nearly four years ago, the centaur Bane had shouted at Firenze for allowing Harry to ride to safety on his back; he had called him a 'common mule'. He wondered whether it had been Bane who had kicked Firenze in the chest.

'Let us begin,' said Firenze. He swished his long palomino tail, raised his hand towards the leafy canopy overhead, then lowered it slowly, and as he did so, the light in the room dimmed, so that they now seemed to be sitting in a forest clearing by twilight, and stars appeared on the ceiling. There were

第27章 马人和告密生

得费伦泽怪吓人的。

门已经关好,最后一个学生坐在了废纸篓旁的树桩上,于是费伦泽朝教室四面做了个手势。

"邓布利多教授很能体谅人,为我们安排了这间教室,"大家都安静下来后,费伦泽说,"模拟出符合我生活习性的环境。我更喜欢在禁林里给你们上课,那里——直到星期一——还是我的家园……但是现在已经不可能了。"

"请问——呃——先生——"帕瓦蒂屏住呼吸,举起手说,"——为什么呢?我们和海格一起去过那里,我们不害怕!"

"这与你们的勇气无关,"费伦泽说,"而是关系到我的处境。我不能再返回禁林了。我的群落已经把我放逐了。"

"群落?"拉文德摸不着头脑地说,哈利知道,她一定是想到了牛群,"什么——噢!"

拉文德脸上露出醒悟过来的表情。"不止你一个吗?"她惊愕地问。

"海格也像喂养夜骐一样喂养你们吗?"迪安热切地问道。

费伦泽很慢很慢地转过头面对着迪安,迪安似乎立刻意识到,自己刚才说了非常失礼的话。

"我不是——我的意思是——对不起。"说到最后,迪安已经是细声细气了。

"马人并非人类的仆人或宠物。"费伦泽平和地说。沉默了一会儿,帕瓦蒂又举起了手。

"请问,先生……别的马人为什么要放逐你呢?"

"因为我同意为邓布利多教授工作,"费伦泽说,"他们认为这是对同胞的背叛。"

哈利想起将近四年前,马人贝恩朝费伦泽大声嚷嚷的情形,那是因为费伦泽允许哈利骑在自己背上,好把他驮到安全的地方;当时贝恩说费伦泽是头"普通的骡子"。哈利怀疑可能就是贝恩当胸踢了费伦泽一蹄子。

"我们开始吧。"费伦泽说。他甩了甩长长的银色尾巴,扬起一只手,指向头顶华盖似的茂密树叶,接着又把手缓缓地垂下来。随着他的动作,屋里的光线变得暗淡,现在他们就像坐在黄昏时分的林间空地中,

CHAPTER TWENTY-SEVEN The Centaur and the Sneak

oohs and gasps and Ron said audibly, 'Blimey!'

'Lie back on the floor,' said Firenze in his calm voice, 'and observe the heavens. Here is written, for those who can see, the fortune of our races.'

Harry stretched out on his back and gazed upwards at the ceiling. A twinkling red star winked at him from overhead.

'I know that you have learned the names of the planets and their moons in Astronomy,' said Firenze's calm voice, 'and that you have mapped the stars' progress through the heavens. Centaurs have unravelled the mysteries of these movements over centuries. Our findings teach us that the future may be glimpsed in the sky above us –'

'Professor Trelawney did astrology with us!' said Parvati excitedly, raising her hand in front of her so that it stuck up in the air as she lay on her back. 'Mars causes accidents and burns and things like that, and when it makes an angle to Saturn, like now –' she drew a right-angle in the air above her '– that means people need to be extra careful when handling hot things –'

'That,' said Firenze calmly, 'is human nonsense.'

Parvati's hand fell limply to her side.

'Trivial hurts, tiny human accidents,' said Firenze, as his hooves thudded over the mossy floor. 'These are of no more significance than the scurryings of ants to the wide universe, and are unaffected by planetary movements.'

'Professor Trelawney –' began Parvati, in a hurt and indignant voice.

'– is a human,' said Firenze simply. 'And is therefore blinkered and fettered by the limitations of your kind.'

Harry turned his head very slightly to look at Parvati. She looked very offended, as did several of the people surrounding her.

'Sybill Trelawney may have Seen, I do not know,' continued Firenze, and Harry heard the swishing of his tail again as he walked up and down before them, 'but she wastes her time, in the main, on the self-flattering nonsense humans call fortune-telling. I, however, am here to explain the wisdom of centaurs, which is impersonal and impartial. We watch the skies for the great tides of evil or change that are sometimes marked there. It may take ten years to be sure of what we are seeing.'

第27章 马人和告密生

星星呈现在天花板上。有人发出了嘚的赞叹声，还有人倒抽了一口气，罗恩则出声地叫了起来："天哪！"

"躺在地板上，"费伦泽平静地说，"然后观察天空。对于能读懂星相的人来说，那里已经描绘出了我们各个种族的命运。"

哈利摊开手脚躺了下来，注视着上面的天花板。一颗闪耀的红色星星在空中朝他眨了眨眼睛。

"我知道在天文课上，你们已经学习了这些行星及其卫星的名称，"费伦泽平缓地说，"你们还绘制了星辰在天空中的运行图。马人用几个世纪的时间，揭示出了这些运动的奥秘。我们的研究成果告诉我们，通过观察我们头顶上的天空，我们也许能窥测到未来——"

"特里劳尼教授教过我们占星术！"帕瓦蒂在胸前举起一只手——她躺在地上，这只手就立在了空中，她兴奋地说，"火星能引起意外事故、烫伤这一类的事情，当它和土星形成一个角度时，就像这样——"她在空中比画出一个直角，"——就意味着人们在处理热东西时要格外小心——"

"那些，"费伦泽平和地说，"是人类在胡说八道。"

帕瓦蒂那只手没精打采地垂了下去，落在自己身旁。

"无关紧要的伤痛，人类微不足道的意外事故，"费伦泽说，他的蹄子在长满苔藓的地板上发出了嗵嗵声，"和广阔的宇宙相比，这些事跟乱爬的蚂蚁一样无足轻重，不受行星运行的影响。"

"特里劳尼教授——"帕瓦蒂开口说，语气既委屈又愤愤不平。

"——是人类的一员，"费伦泽简洁地说，"因此被蒙住了双眼，而且被你们人类的缺陷所束缚。"

哈利稍微侧过脑袋看了看帕瓦蒂。帕瓦蒂显得很生气，她周围的几个人也一样。

"西比尔·特里劳尼也许能预见未来，这一点我不大清楚，"费伦泽接着说，哈利听见他在他们面前走来走去时又在甩动尾巴，"但是她的时间几乎都浪费在自吹自擂的废话上了，这种废话被人类称作算命。而我在这里要讲解的是马人客观、公允的见解。我们观察天空，要留心那些灾难或变故的重要动向，有时空中会标示出这些动向。也许要用十年时间才能确证我们所看到的。"

CHAPTER TWENTY-SEVEN The Centaur and the Sneak

Firenze pointed to the red star directly above Harry.

'In the past decade, the indications have been that wizardkind is living through nothing more than a brief calm between two wars. Mars, bringer of battle, shines brightly above us, suggesting that the fight must soon break out again. How soon, centaurs may attempt to divine by the burning of certain herbs and leaves, by the observation of fume and flame ...'

It was the most unusual lesson Harry had ever attended. They did indeed burn sage and mallowsweet there on the classroom floor, and Firenze told them to look for certain shapes and symbols in the pungent fumes, but he seemed perfectly unconcerned that not one of them could see any of the signs he described, telling them that humans were hardly ever good at this, that it took centaurs years and years to become competent, and finished by telling them that it was foolish to put too much faith in such things, anyway, because even centaurs sometimes read them wrongly. He was nothing like any human teacher Harry had ever had. His priority did not seem to be to teach them what he knew, but rather to impress upon them that nothing, not even centaurs' knowledge, was foolproof.

'He's not very definite on anything, is he?' said Ron in a low voice, as they put out their mallowsweet fire. 'I mean, I could do with a few more details about this war we're about to have, couldn't you?'

The bell rang right outside the classroom door and everyone jumped; Harry had completely forgotten they were still inside the castle, and quite convinced that he was really in the Forest. The class filed out, looking slightly perplexed.

Harry and Ron were on the point of following them when Firenze called, 'Harry Potter, a word, please.'

Harry turned. The centaur advanced a little towards him. Ron hesitated.

'You may stay,' Firenze told him. 'But close the door, please.'

Ron hastened to obey.

'Harry Potter, you are a friend of Hagrid's, are you not?' said the centaur.

'Yes,' said Harry.

'Then give him a warning from me. His attempt is not working. He would do better to abandon it.'

'His attempt is not working?' Harry repeated blankly.

第27章 马人和告密生

费伦泽指向哈利正上方那颗红色的星星。

"在过去的十年里,有种种迹象表明,巫师界的人们只是在度过两场战争之间短暂的和平时期。能带来战争的火星在我们头上明亮地闪耀,预示着不久以后肯定要再次爆发战争。至于还有多久,马人也许能通过燃烧几种药草和树叶,通过观察烟雾与火焰,试着预测一下……"

哈利从来没上过这么奇特的课。他们居然真的在教室地板上点燃了鼠尾草和香锦葵,费伦泽要求他们观察呛人的烟雾,从中找出某些形状和征象,虽然谁都看不出他描述的那些迹象,可他好像一点儿也不在乎。他对他们说,人类向来不怎么擅长做这种事,就连马人都是经过漫长的岁月才拥有了这种能力。最后他还告诉他们,反正有时连马人都会看走眼,所以过于相信这一类事物是很愚蠢的。他和哈利见过的人类老师没有一点相似之处。他优先考虑的好像并不是把自己的学识传授给他们,而是让他们牢牢记住,没有任何事物是万无一失的,即便马人的学问也不例外。

"他什么事都没讲清楚,对吧?"他们熄灭香锦葵的火焰时,罗恩低声说,"我的意思是,对这场我们将要进行的战争,我想多知道一些细节,你怎么想呢?"

铃声在教室门外响了起来,把大家吓了一跳;哈利一点儿也不记得他们还在城堡中,一心以为自己就是在禁林里。同学们一个接一个地走了出去,看起来都有点稀里糊涂。

哈利和罗恩正要跟上他们时,费伦泽大声说:"哈利·波特,请听我说句话。"

哈利转过身。马人朝他走过来。罗恩犹豫了一下。

"你可以留下,"费伦泽对罗恩说,"不过请关上门。"

罗恩赶忙照办了。

"哈利·波特,你是海格的朋友吗?"马人说。

"是啊。"哈利说。

"那就替我给他提个醒。他的努力没有用。他最好还是放弃。"

"他的努力没有用?"哈利茫然地重复道。

1005

CHAPTER TWENTY-SEVEN   The Centaur and the Sneak

'And he would do better to abandon it,' said Firenze, nodding. 'I would warn Hagrid myself, but I am banished – it would be unwise for me to go too near the Forest now – Hagrid has troubles enough, without a centaurs' battle.'

'But – what's Hagrid attempting to do?' said Harry nervously.

Firenze looked at Harry impassively.

'Hagrid has recently rendered me a great service,' said Firenze, 'and he has long since earned my respect for the care he shows all living creatures. I shall not betray his secret. But he must be brought to his senses. The attempt is not working. Tell him, Harry Potter. Good-day to you.'

The happiness Harry had felt in the aftermath of *The Quibbler* interview had long since evaporated. As a dull March blurred into a squally April, his life seemed to have become one long series of worries and problems again.

Umbridge had continued attending all Care of Magical Creatures lessons, so it had been very difficult to deliver Firenze's warning to Hagrid. At last, Harry had managed it by pretending he'd lost his copy of *Fantastic Beasts and Where to Find Them*, and doubling back after class one day. When he'd passed on Firenze's message, Hagrid gazed at him for a moment through his puffy, blackened eyes, apparently taken aback. Then he seemed to pull himself together.

'Nice bloke, Firenze,' he said gruffly, 'but he don' know what he's talkin' abou' on this. The attemp's comin' on fine.'

'Hagrid, what're you up to?' asked Harry seriously. 'Because you've got to be careful, Umbridge has already sacked Trelawney and, if you ask me, she's on a roll. If you're doing anything you shouldn't be, you'll be –'

'There's things more importan' than keepin' a job,' said Hagrid, though his hands shook slightly as he said this and a basin full of Knarl droppings crashed to the floor. 'Don' worry abou' me, Harry, jus' get along now, there's a good lad.'

Harry had no choice but to leave Hagrid mopping up the dung all over his floor, but he felt thoroughly dispirited as he trudged back up to the castle.

Meanwhile, as the teachers and Hermione persisted in reminding them, the O.W.L.s were drawing ever nearer. All the fifth-years were suffering from stress to some degree, but Hannah Abbott became the first to receive a Calming Draught from Madam Pomfrey after she burst into tears during Herbology and sobbed that she was too stupid to take exams and wanted to

第27章 马人和告密生

"还有他最好还是放弃。"费伦泽点点头说,"我本想亲自提醒海格,但是我已经被放逐了——对我来说,现在过于接近禁林太不明智——就算没有马人之间的争斗,海格的麻烦也够多了。"

"可是——海格在努力做什么呀?"哈利不安地说。

费伦泽毫无表情地看着哈利。

"海格最近帮了我很大的忙,"费伦泽说,"而且他关爱所有的动物,很久以前就赢得了我的尊敬。所以我不应该泄露他的秘密。但是他必须恢复理智。那种努力没有用。告诉他,哈利·波特。再见。"

接受《唱唱反调》的采访后,有一阵子哈利觉得很开心,可这种感觉老早以前就消失了。自从阴沉沉的三月黯然进入风雨迭起的四月后,他的生活似乎又变成了一长串的烦恼和麻烦。

乌姆里奇照旧旁听每一节保护神奇动物课,所以哈利很难把费伦泽的提醒转告给海格。后来哈利总算想出了办法。一天下课后,他假装落下了自己那本《神奇动物在哪里》,就原路折了回去。他转告了费伦泽的口信以后,海格用青肿的双眼盯了他好一会儿,显然吃了一惊。接着他似乎让自己镇定下来了。

"好小子,费伦泽,"海格粗声粗气地说,"可他根本不了解情况。这些努力就要见效了。"

"海格,你在搞什么名堂呀?"哈利严肃地说,"你一定要小心哪,乌姆里奇已经解雇了特里劳尼。依我看,她是不会罢手的。要是你做了什么不该做的事情,你会——"

"有些事比保住工作更重要,"海格说,但是说这句话的时候,他的双手在微微颤抖,手中满满一盆刺佬儿粪砰的一声落在了地上,"别为我担心了,哈利,现在走吧,好伙计。"

哈利别无选择,只好离开了正在清扫满地大粪的海格。当他步履沉重地回到城堡时,觉得真是丧气极了。

这段时间里,老师与赫敏在不断地提醒他们,O.W.L. 考试离得越来越近了。五年级学生都多多少少承受着压力,汉娜·艾博在草药课上突然大哭起来,呜咽着说自己笨得不配参加考试,现在就想离开学校,

CHAPTER TWENTY-SEVEN

The Centaur and the Sneak

leave school now.

If it had not been for the DA lessons, Harry thought he would have been extremely unhappy. He sometimes felt he was living for the hours he spent in the Room of Requirement, working hard but thoroughly enjoying himself at the same time, swelling with pride as he looked around at his fellow DA members and saw how far they had come. Indeed, Harry sometimes wondered how Umbridge was going to react when all the members of the DA received 'Outstanding' in their Defence Against the Dark Arts O.W.L.s.

They had finally started work on Patronuses, which everybody had been very keen to practise, though, as Harry kept reminding them, producing a Patronus in the middle of a brightly lit classroom when they were not under threat was very different from producing it when confronted by something like a Dementor.

'Oh, don't be such a killjoy,' said Cho brightly, watching her silvery swan-shaped Patronus soar around the Room of Requirement during their last lesson before Easter. 'They're so pretty!'

'They're not supposed to be pretty, they're supposed to protect you,' said Harry patiently. 'What we really need is a Boggart or something; that's how I learned, I had to conjure a Patronus while the Boggart was pretending to be a Dementor –'

'But that would be really scary!' said Lavender, who was shooting puffs of silver vapour out of the end of her wand. 'And I still – can't – do it!' she added angrily.

Neville was having trouble, too. His face was screwed up in concentration, but only feeble wisps of silver smoke issued from his wand-tip.

'You've got to think of something happy,' Harry reminded him.

'I'm trying,' said Neville miserably, who was trying so hard his round face was actually shining with sweat.

'Harry, I think I'm doing it!' yelled Seamus, who had been brought along to his first ever DA meeting by Dean. 'Look – ah – it's gone ... but it was definitely something hairy, Harry!'

Hermione's Patronus, a shining silver otter, was gambolling around her.

'They *are* sort of nice, aren't they?' she said, looking at it fondly.

The door of the Room of Requirement opened, and closed. Harry looked round to see who had entered, but there did not seem to be anybody

第27章 马人和告密生

结果她第一个收到了庞弗雷女士的镇静剂。

要不是有 D.A. 训练课,哈利真会觉得心烦透顶。他有时觉得,自己活着就是为了在有求必应屋里花上几个小时进行练习,虽然辛苦,但是非常愉快。他打量着周围的 D.A. 成员,看到他们的进步时,心里充满了自豪感。哈利有时真想知道,当所有 D.A. 成员在黑魔法防御术 O.W.L. 考试中成绩都达到"优秀"时,乌姆里奇会是什么反应。

他们终于开始练习守护神咒了,每个人都练得很起劲,不过哈利一再提醒大家,他们是在一间灯火明亮的教室中召唤守护神,并且没有受到威胁,而面对摄魂怪这类东西时可就是另一回事了。

"哎呀,别煞风景了,"秋·张在复活节前的最后一节课上愉快地说,她正望着自己银色的天鹅形守护神环绕有求必应屋飞翔,"它可真漂亮!"

"它用不着漂亮,它应该能够保护你。"哈利耐心地说,"其实我们需要博格特什么的;我就是那么学会的,我必须在博格特假扮成摄魂怪时召唤守护神——"

"那也太吓人了!"拉文德说,她的魔杖顶端正喷出一股股银色的气体,"我还是——不——行!"她恼火地加了一句。

纳威也不顺手。他全神贯注地紧皱着眉头,但是他的魔杖尖上只冒出几缕稀薄的银色烟雾。

"你必须想想高兴的事情。"哈利提醒他。

"我正想着呢。"纳威烦恼地说。他拼命地想,汗津津的圆脸上都闪闪发亮了。

"哈利,我觉得我成功了!"西莫喊道,他头一回参加 D.A. 聚会,是迪安带他来的,"看——唉——它不见了……不过它肯定是一种毛茸茸的东西,哈利!"

赫敏的守护神是一只亮闪闪的银色水獭,正绕着她欢蹦乱跳。

"它确实挺好看的,对吗?"赫敏满心欢喜地瞧着它说。

有求必应屋的门打开后又关上了。哈利扭过头,想看看是谁进来了,但是门口好像什么人也没有。过了一会儿,他才注意到靠近门的几个人不出声了。接着他感觉到,有什么东西正使劲拉扯他膝盖附近的袍子。

CHAPTER TWENTY-SEVEN The Centaur and the Sneak

there. It was a few moments before he realised that the people close to the door had fallen silent. Next thing he knew, something was tugging at his robes somewhere near the knee. He looked down and saw, to his very great astonishment, Dobby the house-elf peering up at him from beneath his usual eight woolly hats.

'Hi, Dobby!' he said. 'What are you – What's wrong?'

The elf's eyes were wide with terror and he was shaking. The members of the DA closest to Harry had fallen silent; everybody in the room was watching Dobby. The few Patronuses people had managed to conjure faded away into silver mist, leaving the room looking much darker than before.

'Harry Potter, sir ...' squeaked the elf, trembling from head to foot, 'Harry Potter, sir ... Dobby has come to warn you ... but the house-elves have been warned not to tell ...'

He ran head-first at the wall. Harry, who had some experience of Dobby's habits of self-punishment, made to seize him, but Dobby merely bounced off the stone, cushioned by his eight hats. Hermione and a few of the other girls let out squeaks of fear and sympathy.

'What's happened, Dobby?' Harry asked, grabbing the elf's tiny arm and holding him away from anything with which he might seek to hurt himself.

'Harry Potter ... she ... she ...'

Dobby hit himself hard on the nose with his free fist. Harry seized that, too.

'Who's "she", Dobby?'

But he thought he knew; surely only one 'she' could induce such fear in Dobby? The elf looked up at him, slightly cross-eyed, and mouthed wordlessly.

'Umbridge?' asked Harry, horrified.

Dobby nodded, then tried to bang his head on Harry's knees. Harry held him at arm's length.

'What about her? Dobby – she hasn't found out about this – about us – about the DA?'

He read the answer in the elf's stricken face. His hands held fast by Harry, Dobby tried to kick himself and sank to his knees.

'Is she coming?' Harry asked quietly.

Dobby let out a howl.

第27章 马人和告密生

他一低头,非常惊讶地看到,家养小精灵多比正仰头盯着他,脑袋上跟往常一样戴着八顶羊毛帽子。

"嘿,多比!"他说,"你怎么——出什么事情了?"

小精灵惊恐地睁大了双眼,而且还在发抖。哈利身旁的D.A.成员不作声了;屋子里的人都盯着多比。人们召唤出来的为数不多的几个守护神渐渐消退,变成了银色的薄雾,屋里显得比刚才暗多了。

"哈利·波特,先生……"小精灵全身哆嗦着尖声说,"哈利·波特,先生……多比来给你报信……但是家养小精灵被警告过,不能说出……"

他一头朝墙壁冲过去。哈利想抓住多比,因为他已经知道多比有自我惩罚的习惯,不过多比戴着八顶帽子,所以从石墙上弹了回来。赫敏和另外几个女生既害怕又同情地尖叫起来。

"出什么事了,多比?"哈利问道,他抓住小精灵一只纤细的胳膊,不让他靠近任何能用来伤害他自己的东西。

"哈利·波特……她……她……"

多比用另一只拳头使劲捶打着自己的鼻子。哈利把那只胳膊也抓住了。

"'她'是谁,多比?"

不过他认为自己知道那是谁;除了那个"她",还有谁能让多比这么害怕呢?小精灵抬头看着他,两只眼睛有点对在一起,然后不出声地说了出来。

"乌姆里奇?"哈利惊恐地问道。

多比点了点头,想用脑袋往哈利的膝盖上撞。哈利伸直手臂挡住了他。

"她怎么了?多比——她发现了这件事——发现了我们——发现了D.A.?"

他从小精灵愁眉苦脸的表情中看出了答案。多比的双手被哈利紧紧攥着。他想踢自己,结果双膝跪在了地板上。

"她就要来了?"哈利小声问道。

多比发出一声哭号。

CHAPTER TWENTY-SEVEN   The Centaur and the Sneak

'Yes, Harry Potter, yes!'

Harry straightened up and looked around at the motionless, terrified people gazing at the thrashing elf.

'WHAT ARE YOU WAITING FOR?' Harry bellowed. 'RUN!'

They all pelted towards the exit at once, forming a scrum at the door, then people burst through. Harry could hear them sprinting along the corridors and hoped they had the sense not to try and make it all the way to their dormitories. It was only ten to nine; if they just took refuge in the library or the Owlery, which were both nearer –

'Harry, come on!' shrieked Hermione from the centre of the knot of people now fighting to get out.

He scooped up Dobby, who was still attempting to do himself serious injury, and ran with the elf in his arms to join the back of the queue.

'Dobby – this is an order – get back down to the kitchen with the other elves and, if she asks you whether you warned me, lie and say no!' said Harry. 'And I forbid you to hurt yourself!' he added, dropping the elf as he made it over the threshold at last and slammed the door behind him.

'Thank you, Harry Potter!' squeaked Dobby, and he streaked off. Harry glanced left and right, the others were all moving so fast he caught only glimpses of flying heels at either end of the corridor before they vanished; he started to run right; there was a boys' bathroom up ahead, he could pretend he'd been in there all the time if he could just reach it –

'AAARGH!'

Something caught him around the ankles and he fell spectacularly, skidding along on his front for six feet before coming to a halt. Someone behind him was laughing. He rolled over on to his back and saw Malfoy concealed in a niche beneath an ugly dragon-shaped vase.

'Trip Jinx, Potter!' he said. 'Hey, Professor – PROFESSOR! I've got one!'

Umbridge came bustling round the far corner, breathless but wearing a delighted smile.

'It's him!' she said jubilantly at the sight of Harry on the floor. 'Excellent, Draco, excellent, oh, very good – fifty points to Slytherin! I'll take him from here ... stand up, Potter!'

Harry got to his feet, glaring at the pair of them. He had never seen

第27章 马人和告密生

"是的,哈利·波特,是的!"

哈利直起身子,扫视了一下吓得呆若木鸡的人们,他们正盯着拼命扑腾的小精灵。

"你们还等什么?"哈利吼道,"跑啊!"

他们全都立刻奔向出口,在门口挤成一团,接着有人突然冲了出去。哈利听见他们沿着走廊狂奔,心里希望他们脑子够用,不至于直接跑回自己的宿舍。现在才八点五十;图书馆和猫头鹰棚屋要近得多,只要他们能躲进去——

"哈利,快走!"赫敏在奋力向外挤的人群中尖声喊道。

多比仍然在想方设法伤害自己,哈利一把抄起小精灵,用双臂抱着他跑到了长队末尾。

"多比——这是个命令——回到下面的厨房和其他小精灵待在一起,要是她问你有没有给我报过信,你就撒谎说没有!"哈利说,"还有,我不准你伤害自己!"他补充了一句。总算跨过门槛后,他放下小精灵,砰的一声关上了身后的房门。

"谢谢你,哈利·波特!"多比尖声说,随后飞快地跑开了。哈利朝两旁扫了一眼,其他人跑得那么快,此刻正消失在走廊两端,他只能瞥见一些飞舞的脚后跟;他动身朝右边跑去;前面有一间男生盥洗室,只要他能跑到,就可以假装自己一直在那里——

"哎呀!"

什么东西绊住了他的脚,他猛地倒了下去,趴在地上滑行了六英尺才停住。有人在他身后笑起来。他翻过身,看见马尔福躲在一个丑陋的龙形装饰瓶下面的壁龛里。

"绊腿咒,波特!"马尔福说,"喂,教授——**教授**!我抓住了一个!"

乌姆里奇匆匆转过远处的拐角,她气喘吁吁,但是脸上挂着高兴的笑容。

"是他!"看到地板上的哈利时,她喜气洋洋地说,"好极了,德拉科,好极了,哈,太好了——给斯莱特林加五十分!我来把他带走……起来,波特!"

哈利站起来,瞪着他们两个。他从来没见乌姆里奇这么高兴过。

CHAPTER TWENTY-SEVEN   The Centaur and the Sneak

Umbridge looking so happy. She seized his arm in a vice-like grip and turned, beaming broadly, to Malfoy.

'You hop along and see if you can round up any more of them, Draco,' she said. 'Tell the others to look in the library – anybody out of breath – check the bathrooms, Miss Parkinson can do the girls' ones – off you go – and you,' she added in her softest, most dangerous voice, as Malfoy walked away, 'you can come with me to the Headmaster's office, Potter.'

They were at the stone gargoyle within minutes. Harry wondered how many of the others had been caught. He thought of Ron – Mrs Weasley would kill him – and of how Hermione would feel if she was expelled before she could take her O.W.L.s. And it had been Seamus's very first meeting ... and Neville had been getting so good ...

'Fizzing Whizzbee,' sang Umbridge; the stone gargoyle jumped aside, the wall behind split open, and they ascended the moving stone staircase. They reached the polished door with the griffin knocker, but Umbridge did not bother to knock, she strode straight inside, still holding tight to Harry.

The office was full of people. Dumbledore was sitting behind his desk, his expression serene, the tips of his long fingers together. Professor McGonagall stood rigidly beside him, her face extremely tense. Cornelius Fudge, Minister for Magic, was rocking backwards and forwards on his toes beside the fire, apparently immensely pleased with the situation; Kingsley Shacklebolt and a tough-looking wizard with very short wiry hair whom Harry did not recognise, were positioned either side of the door like guards, and the freckled, bespectacled form of Percy Weasley hovered excitedly beside the wall, a quill and a heavy scroll of parchment in his hands, apparently poised to take notes.

The portraits of old headmasters and headmistresses were not shamming sleep tonight. All of them were alert and serious, watching what was happening below them. As Harry entered, a few flitted into neighbouring frames and whispered urgently into their neighbour's ear.

Harry pulled himself free of Umbridge's grasp as the door swung shut behind them. Cornelius Fudge was glaring at him with a kind of vicious satisfaction on his face.

'Well,' he said. 'Well, well, well ...'

Harry replied with the dirtiest look he could muster. His heart drummed madly inside him, but his brain was oddly cool and clear.

第27章 马人和告密生

她的手像老虎钳似的紧紧抓住哈利的胳膊,笑容满面地朝马尔福转过身。

"你快去看看能不能再多抓几个,德拉科,"她说,"叫其他人去图书馆——查一查里面有没有上气不接下气的人——检查盥洗室,帕金森小姐可以检查女生盥洗室——你们去吧——至于你,"马尔福走开时,她用最温和最吓人的口气加了一句,"你跟我去校长办公室,波特。"

几分钟后,他们走到滴水嘴石兽那里。哈利想知道还有多少人被抓住了。他想到了罗恩——韦斯莱夫人会杀了他——还想到要是在O.W.L.考试之前被开除,赫敏会是什么感觉。这是西莫第一次参加聚会……纳威有了那么大的进步……

"滋滋蜜蜂糖。"乌姆里奇有节奏地说;石兽跳到一旁,后面的墙裂成了两半,他们走上正在移动的石头楼梯,来到了光亮的大门前,门上有一个狮身鹰首兽门环,但是乌姆里奇没有费工夫敲门,她紧紧抓着哈利,迈开步子径直闯了进去。

办公室里挤满了人。邓布利多表情安详地坐在桌子后面,修长的手指指尖合在一起。麦格教授直挺挺地站在他身旁,表情非常紧张。魔法部部长康奈利·福吉站在炉火旁,兴奋地前后轻轻摇晃着,显然很满意现在的局面。金斯莱·沙克尔和另一个巫师像警卫一样站在大门两旁,那个巫师外表粗野,硬直的头发留得很短,哈利从来没见过他。长着雀斑、戴着眼镜的珀西·韦斯莱在墙边激动地走来走去,手里拿着一支羽毛笔和一卷厚厚的羊皮纸,显然是随时准备记录。

今天晚上,男女老校长们的肖像都没有假装睡觉。他们都很警觉、严肃,正注视着下面的动静。哈利一进来,几个老校长就飞进邻近的相框,和邻居急切地咬起了耳朵。

身后的大门关上以后,哈利甩开了紧紧抓着他的乌姆里奇。康奈利·福吉怒气冲冲地瞪着他,脸上露出一种幸灾乐祸的表情。

"好啊,"他说,"好啊,好啊,好啊……"

哈利用他最狠毒的眼神瞪了福吉一眼。他的心脏跳得飞快,可是头脑却出奇地冷静、清醒。

CHAPTER TWENTY-SEVEN The Centaur and the Sneak

'He was heading back to Gryffindor Tower,' said Umbridge. There was an indecent excitement in her voice, the same callous pleasure Harry had heard as she watched Professor Trelawney dissolving with misery in the Entrance Hall. 'The Malfoy boy cornered him.'

'Did he, did he?' said Fudge appreciatively. 'I must remember to tell Lucius. Well, Potter ... I expect you know why you are here?'

Harry fully intended to respond with a defiant 'yes': his mouth had opened and the word was half-formed when he caught sight of Dumbledore's face. Dumbledore was not looking directly at Harry – his eyes were fixed on a point just over his shoulder – but as Harry stared at him, he shook his head a fraction of an inch to each side.

Harry changed direction mid-word.

'Ye—no.'

'I beg your pardon?' said Fudge.

'No,' said Harry, firmly.

'You *don't* know why you are here?'

'No, I don't,' said Harry.

Fudge looked incredulously from Harry to Professor Umbridge. Harry took advantage of his momentary inattention to steal another quick look at Dumbledore, who gave the carpet the tiniest of nods and the shadow of a wink.

'So you have no idea,' said Fudge, in a voice positively sagging with sarcasm, 'why Professor Umbridge has brought you to this office? You are not aware that you have broken any school rules?'

'School rules?' said Harry. 'No.'

'Or Ministry Decrees?' amended Fudge angrily.

'Not that I'm aware of,' said Harry blandly.

His heart was still hammering very fast. It was almost worth telling these lies to watch Fudge's blood pressure rising, but he could not see how on earth he would get away with them; if somebody had tipped off Umbridge about the DA then he, the leader, might as well be packing his trunk right now.

'So, it's news to you, is it,' said Fudge, his voice now thick with anger, 'that an illegal student organisation has been discovered within this school?'

第27章 马人和告密生

"他正在返回格兰芬多塔楼的路上。"乌姆里奇说。她的语气里有一股很邪恶的兴奋劲,当她在门厅里看着特里劳尼教授因为悲伤而崩溃的时候,哈利也听到过同样冷酷无情的快乐语气,"马尔福那孩子把他堵住了。"

"是吗,是吗?"福吉赞赏地说,"我得记着告诉卢修斯。好了,波特……我想你应该知道自己为什么在这儿吧?"

哈利拿定了主意,想要轻蔑地回答"知道",当他瞥见邓布利多的表情时,他已经张开嘴巴将这个词说出了一半。邓布利多没有直接看着哈利——他目不转睛地盯着哈利肩膀上方的一处地方——但是当哈利望着他时,他轻轻摇了摇头,动作小得几乎让人察觉不出来。

哈利说到一半改了口。

"知——不道。"

"对不起,你说什么?"福吉说。

"不知道。"哈利坚决地说。

"你不知道自己为什么在这儿?"

"对,我不知道。"哈利说。

福吉疑惑地看了看哈利,又瞧了瞧乌姆里奇教授。哈利利用他这一瞬间的疏忽,又偷偷瞥了一眼邓布利多,邓布利多用最轻微的动作朝地毯点了点头,稍稍挤了挤眼睛。

"那么你不清楚,"福吉用毫不掩饰的挖苦口气说,"为什么乌姆里奇教授带你来这间办公室吗?你没有发觉自己已经违反了校规吗?"

"校规?"哈利说,"没有。"

"那魔法部的法令呢?"福吉生气地换了个角度问道。

"起码没有违反我知道的法令。"哈利泰然自若地说。

他的心还在飞快地咚咚直跳。为了看看福吉血压上升的样子,说这些假话还是挺值得的,但是他看不出自己究竟怎样才能逃脱他们的处罚,要是已经有人对乌姆里奇泄露了D.A.的情况,那么他这个领头者也许马上就要收拾行李走人了。

"那么,你是头一次听说,"福吉说,现在他的语调充满了怒气,"在这所学校里发现了一个非法的学生组织?"

CHAPTER TWENTY-SEVEN   The Centaur and the Sneak

'Yes, it is,' said Harry, hoisting an unconvincing look of innocent surprise on to his face.

'I think, Minister,' said Umbridge silkily from beside him, 'we might make better progress if I fetch our informant.'

'Yes, yes, do,' said Fudge, nodding, and he glanced maliciously at Dumbledore as Umbridge left the room. 'There's nothing like a good witness, is there, Dumbledore?'

'Nothing at all, Cornelius,' said Dumbledore gravely, inclining his head.

There was a wait of several minutes, in which nobody looked at each other, then Harry heard the door open behind him. Umbridge moved past him into the room, gripping by the shoulder Cho's curly-haired friend, Marietta, who was hiding her face in her hands.

'Don't be scared, dear, don't be frightened,' said Professor Umbridge softly, patting her on the back, 'it's quite all right, now. You have done the right thing. The Minister is very pleased with you. He'll be telling your mother what a good girl you've been. Marietta's mother, Minister,' she added, looking up at Fudge, 'is Madam Edgecombe from the Department of Magical Transportation, Floo Network office – she's been helping us police the Hogwarts fires, you know.'

'Jolly good, jolly good!' said Fudge heartily. 'Like mother, like daughter, eh? Well, come on, now, dear, look up, don't be shy, let's hear what you've got to – galloping gargoyles!'

As Marietta raised her head, Fudge leapt backwards in shock, nearly landing himself in the fire. He cursed, and stamped on the hem of his cloak which had started to smoke. Marietta gave a wail and pulled the neck of her robes right up to her eyes, but not before everyone had seen that her face was horribly disfigured by a series of close-set purple pustules that had spread across her nose and cheeks to form the word 'SNEAK'.

'Never mind the spots now, dear,' said Umbridge impatiently, 'just take your robes away from your mouth and tell the Minister –'

But Marietta gave another muffled wail and shook her head frantically.

'Oh, very well, you silly girl, *I'll* tell him,' snapped Umbridge. She hitched her sickly smile back on to her face and said, 'Well, Minister, Miss Edgecombe here came to my office shortly after dinner this evening and told

第27章 马人和告密生

"是啊，没错。"哈利说，脸上露出了似乎一无所知、非常惊讶的表情，但并不太有说服力。

"部长，我觉得，"乌姆里奇在哈利身旁柔和地说，"如果我把检举人带来，也许我们的进展会快一些。"

"是的，是的，去吧。"福吉点点头说，乌姆里奇离开屋子时，他不怀好意地扫了邓布利多一眼，"什么都顶不上一个好证人，对吗，邓布利多？"

"对极了，康奈利。"邓布利多点点头，声音低沉地说。

大家等待了几分钟，谁也不看谁，然后哈利听到身后的门打开了。乌姆里奇从他身旁走进屋子，手里紧紧抓着秋·张那个鬈发朋友的肩膀，那是玛丽埃塔，她用双手捂住了脸颊。

"别慌，亲爱的，别害怕，"乌姆里奇教授轻轻拍着她的后背，柔和地说，"现在没事了。你做得很正确。部长对你很满意。他会告诉你妈妈，你是个乖女孩。部长，玛丽埃塔的母亲，"她抬眼望着福吉补充了一句，"是魔法交通司飞路网管理局的艾克莫夫人——你知道，她在帮助我们监视霍格沃茨的炉火。"

"太好了，太好了！"福吉热情地说，"有其母必有其女，嗯？好了，讲讲吧，快点儿，亲爱的，抬起头，别怕羞，让我们听听你——狂奔的滴水嘴石兽啊！"

玛丽埃塔抬起头时，福吉被吓得向后一跳，差点跌到炉火里。他骂骂咧咧，猛跺着自己开始冒烟的斗篷下摆。玛丽埃塔哀号一声，赶紧把长袍领子扯到了眼睛下，但是还没等她这么做，大家已经看到，一连串密密麻麻的紫色脓包爬过她的鼻子和脸颊，呈现出"**告密生**"这个词，让她的脸变得要多难看有多难看。

"现在别担心这些斑点了，亲爱的，"乌姆里奇不耐烦地说，"把袍子从嘴巴上拉下来，告诉部长——"

但是玛丽埃塔又闷声闷气地哀号了一声，拼命地摇着脑袋。

"哼，那好吧，你这个傻丫头，我来告诉他。"乌姆里奇没好气地说。她迅速换上令人作呕的笑脸，说道："是这样，部长，今天晚上，这位艾克莫小姐在晚饭后不久来到我的办公室，对我说她有些事情要告诉

CHAPTER TWENTY-SEVEN   The Centaur and the Sneak

me she had something she wanted to tell me. She said that if I proceeded to a secret room on the seventh floor, sometimes known as the Room of Requirement, I would find out something to my advantage. I questioned her a little further and she admitted that there was to be some kind of meeting there. Unfortunately, at that point this hex,' she waved impatiently at Marietta's concealed face, 'came into operation and upon catching sight of her face in my mirror the girl became too distressed to tell me any more.'

'Well, now,' said Fudge, fixing Marietta with what he evidently imagined was a kind and fatherly look, 'it is very brave of you, my dear, coming to tell Professor Umbridge. You did exactly the right thing. Now, will you tell me what happened at this meeting? What was its purpose? Who was there?'

But Marietta would not speak; she merely shook her head again, her eyes wide and fearful.

'Haven't we got a counter-jinx for this?' Fudge asked Umbridge impatiently, gesturing at Marietta's face. 'So she can speak freely?'

'I have not yet managed to find one,' Umbridge admitted grudgingly, and Harry felt a surge of pride in Hermione's jinxing ability. 'But it doesn't matter if she won't speak, I can take up the story from here.

'You will remember, Minister, that I sent you a report back in October that Potter had met a number of fellow students in the Hog's Head in Hogsmeade –'

'And what is your evidence for that?' cut in Professor McGonagall.

'I have testimony from Willy Widdershins, Minerva, who happened to be in the bar at the time. He was heavily bandaged, it is true, but his hearing was quite unimpaired,' said Umbridge smugly. 'He heard every word Potter said and hastened straight to the school to report to me –'

'Oh, so *that's* why he wasn't prosecuted for setting up all those regurgitating toilets!' said Professor McGonagall, raising her eyebrows. 'What an interesting insight into our justice system!'

'Blatant corruption!' roared the portrait of the corpulent, red-nosed wizard on the wall behind Dumbledore's desk. 'The Ministry did not cut deals with petty criminals in my day, no sir, they did not!'

'Thank you, Fortescue, that will do,' said Dumbledore softly.

'The purpose of Potter's meeting with these students,' continued Professor Umbridge, 'was to persuade them to join an illegal society, whose aim was to

第27章 马人和告密生

我。她说如果我进入八楼的一间密室,就会发现一些对我有好处的事情,据说这间密室有时被称作有求必应屋。我进一步盘问她时,她承认那里有某种聚会。遗憾的是,当时这些恶咒,"她朝玛丽埃塔藏在袍子里的脸不耐烦地挥了挥手,"开始起作用了,她在我的镜子里忽然看到自己的面孔后,就伤心得没办法再多跟我讲了。"

"哦,是这样,"福吉说,他带着一副自以为和蔼、慈祥的表情盯着玛丽埃塔,"你去通知了乌姆里奇教授,亲爱的,这么做可真勇敢。你的行为十分正确。好了,你愿意跟我讲讲在聚会中发生了什么事吗?聚会的目的是什么?有谁在场?"

可是玛丽埃塔不愿意开口;她只是又摇了摇脑袋,眼睛睁得大大的,充满恐惧。

"我们有没有破解咒对付这个?"福吉朝玛丽埃塔的脸打了个手势,不耐烦地问乌姆里奇,"好让她自由自在地讲话?"

"我还没能找到,"乌姆里奇不情愿地承认道,赫敏使用咒语的能力使哈利心里涌起了一阵自豪感,"不过她不开口也没关系,我可以替她说下去。"

"你也许还记得,部长,我在十月份向你报告过,波特曾经在霍格莫德的猪头酒吧和许多同学聚会——"

"这件事情你有证据吗?"麦格教授插了一句。

"我有威利·威德辛的证词,米勒娃,当时他正巧在酒吧里。他身上确实缠了很多绷带,但是他的听力完全没有受到损害,"乌姆里奇洋洋自得地说,"他听到了波特说过的每一句话,急忙直接赶到学校向我报告——"

"哦,原来就是为了这件事,他才被免除了对他制造的厕所污水回涌事件的起诉!"麦格教授扬起眉毛说,"我们的司法系统真是让人大开眼界啊!"

"无耻的堕落!"在邓布利多桌子后面的墙上,一幅红鼻子胖巫师的肖像吼道,"在我那个时代,魔法部从不和卑鄙的罪犯做交易,绝对不会,他们从不这么做!"

"谢谢你,福斯科,说这么多就够了。"邓布利多平和地说。

"波特与这些学生聚会,"乌姆里奇教授接着说,"是想说服他们加

CHAPTER TWENTY-SEVEN   The Centaur and the Sneak

learn spells and curses the Ministry has decided are inappropriate for school-age –'

'I think you'll find you're wrong there, Dolores,' said Dumbledore quietly, peering at her over the half-moon spectacles perched halfway down his crooked nose.

Harry stared at him. He could not see how Dumbledore was going to talk him out of this one; if Willy Widdershins had indeed heard every word he had said in the Hog's Head there was simply no escaping it.

'Oho!' said Fudge, bouncing up and down on the balls of his feet again. 'Yes, do let's hear the latest cock-and-bull story designed to pull Potter out of trouble! Go on, then, Dumbledore, go on – Willy Widdershins was lying, was he? Or was it Potter's identical twin in the Hog's Head that day? Or is there the usual simple explanation involving a reversal of time, a dead man coming back to life and a couple of invisible Dementors?'

Percy Weasley let out a hearty laugh.

'Oh, very good, Minister, very good!'

Harry could have kicked him. Then he saw, to his astonishment, that Dumbledore was smiling gently, too.

'Cornelius, I do not deny – and nor, I am sure, does Harry – that he was in the Hog's Head that day, nor that he was trying to recruit students to a Defence Against the Dark Arts group. I am merely pointing out that Dolores is quite wrong to suggest that such a group was, at that time, illegal. If you remember, the Ministry Decree banning all student societies was not put into effect until two days after Harry's Hogsmeade meeting, so he was not breaking any rules at all in the Hog's Head.'

Percy looked as though he had been struck in the face by something very heavy. Fudge remained motionless in mid-bounce, his mouth hanging open.

Umbridge recovered first.

'That's all very fine, Headmaster,' she said, smiling sweetly, 'but we are now nearly six months on from the introduction of Educational Decree Number Twenty-four. If the first meeting was not illegal, all those that have happened since most certainly are.'

'Well,' said Dumbledore, surveying her with polite interest over the top of his interlocked fingers, 'they certainly *would* be, if they *had* continued after the Decree came into effect. Do you have any evidence that any such meetings continued?'

第27章 马人和告密生

入一个非法团体,这个团体的目标是学习一些咒语,而魔法部已经将那些咒语裁定为不适合学生——"

"我认为,你会发现自己在这一点上搞错了,多洛雷斯。"邓布利多轻声说,半月形眼镜耷拉在他歪扭的鼻子上,他正从眼镜上方盯着乌姆里奇。

哈利望着邓布利多。他想不出邓布利多该怎么说才能替他解围;如果威利·威德辛确实听到了他在猪头酒吧里说过的每一句话,那自己就完全没有出路了。

"啊哈!"福吉说着又踮起脚蹦蹦跳跳,"好啊,为了给波特解围,又编出了新的奇谈怪论,请让我们听听吧!那就接着讲吧,邓布利多,接着讲啊——是威利·威德辛在撒谎吗?还是那天在猪头酒吧里的,是一个跟波特一模一样的双胞胎兄弟?要么就是往常那种简单的解释,说什么时间逆转了,一个死人复活了,还有两个无形的摄魂怪?"

珀西·韦斯莱放声大笑起来。

"哎呀,讲得真好,部长,讲得太好了!"

哈利真想踢他一脚。可他惊讶地看到,邓布利多也在温和地微笑。

"康奈利,我没有否认,相信哈利也不会否认,他那天是在猪头酒吧,是想招募学生参加黑魔法防御小组。我不过是想指出,多洛雷斯认为那样一个小组在当时是非法的,完全没有道理。如果你没忘记的话,直到哈利的霍格莫德聚会两天之后,魔法部取缔所有学生社团的法令才生效,所以他在猪头酒吧时没有违反任何规定。"

珀西看上去就像被很重的东西迎面敲了一下。福吉才跳了一半就张大嘴巴不动了。

乌姆里奇头一个回过神来。

"这些都不错,校长,"她亲切地笑着说,"但是如今我们实施《第二十四号教育令》已经将近六个月了。虽然第一次聚会没有违法,但从那以后所有的聚会肯定都是违法的。"

"这个嘛,"邓布利多一边说,一边从交叉在一起的手指上方既礼貌又感兴趣地打量着她,"如果他们确实在这项法令生效后继续聚会,那当然是违法的。你有什么证据能够证明后来还有这种聚会呢?"

CHAPTER TWENTY-SEVEN The Centaur and the Sneak

As Dumbledore spoke, Harry heard a rustle behind him and rather thought Kingsley whispered something. He could have sworn, too, that he felt something brush against his side, a gentle something like a draught or bird wings, but looking down he saw nothing there.

'Evidence?' repeated Umbridge, with that horrible wide toad-like smile. 'Have you not been listening, Dumbledore? Why do you think Miss Edgecombe is here?'

'Oh, can she tell us about six months' worth of meetings?' said Dumbledore, raising his eyebrows. 'I was under the impression that she was merely reporting a meeting tonight.'

'Miss Edgecombe,' said Umbridge at once, 'tell us how long these meetings have been going on, dear. You can simply nod or shake your head, I'm sure that won't make the spots worse. Have they been happening regularly over the last six months?'

Harry felt a horrible plummeting in his stomach. This was it, they had hit a dead end of solid evidence that not even Dumbledore would be able to shift aside.

'Just nod or shake your head, dear,' Umbridge said coaxingly to Marietta, 'come on, now, that won't reactivate the jinx.'

Everyone in the room was gazing at the top of Marietta's face. Only her eyes were visible between the pulled-up robes and her curly fringe. Perhaps it was a trick of the firelight, but her eyes looked oddly blank. And then – to Harry's utter amazement – Marietta shook her head.

Umbridge looked quickly at Fudge, then back at Marietta.

'I don't think you understood the question, did you, dear? I'm asking whether you've been going to these meetings for the past six months? You have, haven't you?'

Again, Marietta shook her head.

'What do you mean by shaking your head, dear?' said Umbridge in a testy voice.

'I would have thought her meaning was quite clear,' said Professor McGonagall harshly, 'there have been no secret meetings for the past six months. Is that correct, Miss Edgecombe?'

Marietta nodded.

'But there was a meeting tonight!' said Umbridge furiously. 'There was a meeting, Miss Edgecombe, you told me about it, in the Room of

第27章 马人和告密生

在邓布利多说话时,哈利听见身后响起了沙沙声,甚至还觉得金斯莱在小声嘀咕着什么。他可以发誓,自己感到有什么东西在身边扫过,这种东西非常轻柔,就像一阵风或者鸟的翅膀,但是当他低下头时,却什么也没看见。

"证据?"乌姆里奇重复说,她满面笑容,就像丑陋的癞蛤蟆,"你刚才一直没在听吗,邓布利多?你认为艾克莫小姐为什么会到这儿来呢?"

"噢,她能跟我们说说这六个月里的聚会吗?"邓布利多扬起眉毛说,"我记得她好像只告发了今晚的一次聚会。"

"艾克莫小姐,"乌姆里奇马上说,"告诉我们这些聚会延续了多长时间,亲爱的。你只要点头、摇头就行了,我能肯定,这么做不会让那些斑点更严重。在过去的六个月里,这样的聚会定期举行吗?"

哈利感到胃里猛地一沉。完了,他们找到了最确凿的证据,连邓布利多都没办法推脱了。

"只要点头、摇头就行了,亲爱的,"乌姆里奇哄劝玛丽埃塔说,"好了,快点,这样不会重新激活咒语的。"

屋里的人都盯着玛丽埃塔的上半张脸,在拉起的长袍和拳曲的刘海之间,只露出了她的双眼。也许仅仅是火光造成的错觉吧,她的眼神很古怪,显得非常迷茫。接着——哈利大吃一惊——玛丽埃塔居然摇了摇头。

乌姆里奇瞥了福吉一眼,然后又看着玛丽埃塔。

"我觉得你没听明白这个问题,对吗,亲爱的?我是问你在过去的六个月里是否经常参加这些聚会?你参加了,对不对?"

玛丽埃塔又摇了摇头。

"你摇头是什么意思啊,亲爱的?"乌姆里奇恼火地说。

"我认为她的意思很清楚,"麦格教授严厉地说,"在过去的六个月里,没有什么秘密聚会。是这样吗,艾克莫小姐?"

玛丽埃塔点了点头。

"可是今晚有一次聚会!"乌姆里奇气急败坏地说,"有一次聚会,艾克莫小姐,是你告诉我的,就在有求必应屋里!波特是头儿,没错,

CHAPTER TWENTY-SEVEN The Centaur and the Sneak

Requirement! And Potter was the leader, was he not, Potter organised it, Potter – *why are you shaking your head, girl?*'

'Well, usually when a person shakes their head,' said McGonagall coldly, 'they mean "no". So unless Miss Edgecombe is using a form of sign-language as yet unknown to humans –'

Professor Umbridge seized Marietta, pulled her round to face her and began shaking her very hard. A split second later Dumbledore was on his feet, his wand raised; Kingsley started forwards and Umbridge leapt back from Marietta, waving her hands in the air as though they had been burned.

'I cannot allow you to manhandle my students, Dolores,' said Dumbledore and, for the first time, he looked angry.

'You want to calm yourself, Madam Umbridge,' said Kingsley, in his deep, slow voice. 'You don't want to get yourself into trouble, now.'

'No,' said Umbridge breathlessly, glancing up at the towering figure of Kingsley. 'I mean, yes – you're right, Shacklebolt – I – I forgot myself.'

Marietta was standing exactly where Umbridge had released her. She seemed neither perturbed by Umbridge's sudden attack, nor relieved by her release; she was still clutching her robe up to her oddly blank eyes and staring straight ahead of her.

A sudden suspicion, connected to Kingsley's whisper and the thing he had felt shoot past him, sprang into Harry's mind.

'Dolores,' said Fudge, with the air of trying to settle something once and for all, 'the meeting tonight – the one we know definitely happened –'

'Yes,' said Umbridge, pulling herself together, 'yes ... well, Miss Edgecombe tipped me off and I proceeded at once to the seventh floor, accompanied by certain *trustworthy* students, so as to catch those in the meeting red-handed. It appears that they were forewarned of my arrival, however, because when we reached the seventh floor they were running in every direction. It does not matter, however. I have all their names here, Miss Parkinson ran into the Room of Requirement for me to see if they had left anything behind. We needed evidence and the room provided.'

And to Harry's horror, she withdrew from her pocket the list of names that had been pinned upon the Room of Requirement's wall and handed it to Fudge.

第27章 马人和告密生

是波特组织了聚会,波特——你为什么老是摇头啊,丫头?"

"这个嘛,通常人们摇头的时候,"麦格教授冷冷地说,"他们的意思是'不'。所以除非艾克莫小姐是在用一种人类不了解的肢体语言——"

乌姆里奇教授抓住玛丽埃塔,使劲把她扳过来面对自己,开始猛烈地摇晃她。眨眼之间,邓布利多已经站起来扬起了魔杖;金斯莱冲了上去,乌姆里奇向后一跳,放开了玛丽埃塔,她的双手在空中挥舞,就像被烫伤了似的。

"我不允许你粗暴地对待我的学生,多洛雷斯。"邓布利多说,他的脸上第一次显出了怒色。

"你应该冷静些,乌姆里奇夫人,"金斯莱用低沉缓慢的声音说,"现在你不该给自己惹麻烦。"

"不,"乌姆里奇气喘吁吁地说,抬起头瞥了一眼金斯莱高大的身影,"我的意思是,是的——你说得对,沙克尔——我——我失态了。"

玛丽埃塔就站在乌姆里奇放开她的地方。乌姆里奇突如其来的粗暴行为好像并没有吓着她,她也没有为自己被放开而松一口气;她的眼神还是那么古怪、迷茫,手里紧紧攥着拉到眼睛下面的袍子,直勾勾地盯着前方。

哈利突然想起,金斯莱刚才在小声嘀咕,而且自己还感到有什么东西从身旁掠过,这些事让他产生了怀疑。

"多洛雷斯,"福吉说,他摆出了要彻底解决问题的神态,"今晚的聚会——我们能肯定有这次聚会——"

"是的,"乌姆里奇镇静下来说,"是的……是这样,艾克莫小姐给我通风报信以后,我立刻前往八楼,同时带去了几个值得信赖的学生,以便当场抓到那些参加聚会的人。可是,看来在我到达以前,他们预先得到了警报,因为我们到达八楼时他们正在四下奔跑。不过没关系。他们的名字我都掌握了,帕金森小姐冲进了有求必应屋,替我看看他们是否落下了什么东西。这间屋子提供了我们所需要的证据。"

让哈利惊骇的是,她从衣袋里抽出了钉在有求必应屋墙上的名单,把它递给了福吉。

CHAPTER TWENTY-SEVEN — The Centaur and the Sneak

'The moment I saw Potter's name on the list, I knew what we were dealing with,' she said softly.

'Excellent,' said Fudge, a smile spreading across his face, 'excellent, Dolores. And ... by thunder ...'

He looked up at Dumbledore, who was still standing beside Marietta, his wand held loosely in his hand.

'See what they've named themselves?' said Fudge quietly. *'Dumbledore's Army.'*

Dumbledore reached out and took the piece of parchment from Fudge. He gazed at the heading scribbled by Hermione months before and for a moment seemed unable to speak. Then he looked up, smiling.

'Well, the game is up,' he said simply. 'Would you like a written confession from me, Cornelius – or will a statement before these witnesses suffice?'

Harry saw McGonagall and Kingsley look at each other. There was fear in both faces. He did not understand what was going on, and nor, apparently, did Fudge.

'Statement?' said Fudge slowly. 'What – I don't –?'

'Dumbledore's Army, Cornelius,' said Dumbledore, still smiling as he waved the list of names before Fudge's face. 'Not Potter's Army. *Dumbledore's Army.*'

'But – but –'

Understanding blazed suddenly in Fudge's face. He took a horrified step backwards, yelped, and jumped out of the fire again.

'You?' he whispered, stamping again on his smouldering cloak.

'That's right,' said Dumbledore pleasantly.

'You organised this?'

'I did,' said Dumbledore.

'You recruited these students for – for your army?'

'Tonight was supposed to be the first meeting,' said Dumbledore, nodding. 'Merely to see whether they would be interested in joining me. I see now that it was a mistake to invite Miss Edgecombe, of course.'

Marietta nodded. Fudge looked from her to Dumbledore, his chest swelling.

'Then you *have* been plotting against me!' he yelled.

第27章 马人和告密生

"一看到这份名单上有波特的名字,我就明白我们是在和谁打交道了。"她柔和地说。

"太棒了,"福吉说,脸上绽放出笑容,"太棒了,多洛雷斯。我来瞧瞧……天哪……"

他抬眼望着仍旧站在玛丽埃塔身旁,手里轻轻握着魔杖的邓布利多。

"看看他们给自己起了什么名字?"福吉轻声说,"邓布利多军。"

邓布利多伸出手,从福吉手里拿过那张羊皮纸。他注视着赫敏几个月前草草写下的标题,有一阵子似乎什么话都说不出来。然后他笑着抬起了眼睛。

"看来,一切都完了,"他简短地说,"请问你需要我写一份书面供词吗,康奈利——或者,在这些证人面前做一个陈述就够了?"

哈利看到麦格和金斯莱对望了一眼。两人的表情都很焦虑。他不明白眼前是怎么回事,福吉显然也不明白。

"陈述?"福吉缓慢地说,"什么——我不——?"

"邓布利多军,康奈利,"邓布利多说,他在福吉面前挥动着那份名单,脸上仍然挂着笑容,"不是波特军。而是邓布利多军。"

"可是——可是——"

福吉脸上突然闪现出醒悟的表情。他惊骇地向后退了一步,大叫一声,又从炉火旁跳开了。

"你?"他小声说着,又一次猛踩自己那件正在冒着烟闷烧的斗篷。

"没错。"邓布利多愉快地说。

"这是你组织的?"

"是我组织的。"邓布利多说。

"你招募这些学生参——参加你的军队?"

"本来今晚应该是第一次聚会,"邓布利多点点头说,"只是想看看他们是否愿意跟我合作。当然,现在我明白了,邀请艾克莫小姐是个错误。"

玛丽埃塔点了点头。福吉看了看她,又瞅了瞅邓布利多,他的胸脯在不停地起伏。

"那你确实在密谋反对我!"他嚷嚷道。

CHAPTER TWENTY-SEVEN   The Centaur and the Sneak

'That's right,' said Dumbledore cheerfully.

'NO!' shouted Harry.

Kingsley flashed a look of warning at him, McGonagall widened her eyes threateningly, but it had suddenly dawned on Harry what Dumbledore was about to do, and he could not let it happen.

'No – Professor Dumbledore –!'

'Be quiet, Harry, or I am afraid you will have to leave my office,' said Dumbledore calmly.

'Yes, shut up, Potter!' barked Fudge, who was still ogling Dumbledore with a kind of horrified delight. 'Well, well, well – I came here tonight expecting to expel Potter and instead –'

'Instead you get to arrest me,' said Dumbledore, smiling. 'It's like losing a Knut and finding a Galleon, isn't it?'

'Weasley!' cried Fudge, now positively quivering with delight, 'Weasley, have you written it all down, everything he's said, his confession, have you got it?'

'Yes, sir, I think so, sir!' said Percy eagerly, whose nose was splattered with ink from the speed of his note-taking.

'The bit about how he's been trying to build up an army against the Ministry, how he's been working to destabilise me?'

'Yes, sir, I've got it, yes!' said Percy, scanning his notes joyfully.

'Very well, then,' said Fudge, now radiant with glee, 'duplicate your notes, Weasley, and send a copy to the *Daily Prophet* at once. If we send a fast owl we should make the morning edition!' Percy dashed from the room, slamming the door behind him, and Fudge turned back to Dumbledore. 'You will now be escorted back to the Ministry, where you will be formally charged, then sent to Azkaban to await trial!'

'Ah,' said Dumbledore gently, 'yes. Yes, I thought we might hit that little snag.'

'Snag?' said Fudge, his voice still vibrating with joy. 'I see no snag, Dumbledore!'

'Well,' said Dumbledore apologetically, 'I'm afraid I do.'

'Oh, really?'

'Well – it's just that you seem to be labouring under the delusion that I am going to – what is the phrase? – *come quietly*. I am afraid I am not going

第27章 马人和告密生

"没错。"邓布利多高高兴兴地说。

"不!"哈利喊道。

金斯莱飞快地给他递了个警告的眼色,麦格教授睁大了眼睛告诫他,但是哈利突然领悟到了邓布利多的意图,他不能让他这么做。

"不——邓布利多教授——!"

"别出声,哈利,不然的话,恐怕我只好让你离开我的办公室了。"邓布利多平静地说。

"没错,闭嘴,波特!"福吉大声喊道,他还在惊喜交加地紧紧盯着邓布利多,"很好,很好,很好——我今晚来这里本想开除波特,可反倒——"

"反倒可以逮捕我了。"邓布利多笑着说,"丢了芝麻捡了西瓜,对吗?"

"韦斯莱!"福吉大声喊道,现在他高兴得直哆嗦,"韦斯莱,这些你都记下来了吗,他说过的话,他的口供,你记下了吗?"

"是的,先生,我想是的,先生!"珀西殷切地说,他飞快地做记录时,鼻子上都溅了墨水。

"他想建立一支军队对抗魔法部,他想推翻我,这一段记录了吗?"

"是的,先生,我记下了,是的!"珀西一边说一边高兴地浏览着记录。

"很好,那么,"福吉说,现在他高兴得容光焕发,"把你的记录复制一份,韦斯莱,马上把副本送给《预言家日报》。要是派一只速度快的猫头鹰,我们还能赶上早上那一版!"珀西飞快地跑出屋子,用力关上了身后的门,福吉朝邓布利多转过身。"你现在要被押送到魔法部,在那里你将被正式起诉,然后被送往阿兹卡班等待审判!"

"啊,"邓布利多轻轻地说,"是啊。不过,我觉得我们也许遇到了一个小小的困难。"

"困难?"福吉说,他的声音仍然高兴得直发抖,"我看不出有什么困难,邓布利多!"

"可是,"邓布利多抱歉地说,"恐怕我看到了。"

"哦,真的吗?"

"嗯——你好像误以为我会——那句话怎么说来着?——束手就擒。恐怕我是根本不会束手就擒的,康奈利。我一点儿也不想被送进

1031

CHAPTER TWENTY-SEVEN The Centaur and the Sneak

to come quietly at all, Cornelius. I have absolutely no intention of being sent to Azkaban. I could break out, of course – but what a waste of time, and frankly, I can think of a whole host of things I would rather be doing.'

Umbridge's face was growing steadily redder; she looked as though she was being filled with boiling water. Fudge stared at Dumbledore with a very silly expression on his face, as though he had just been stunned by a sudden blow and could not quite believe it had happened. He made a small choking noise, then looked round at Kingsley and the man with short grey hair, who alone of everyone in the room had remained entirely silent so far. The latter gave Fudge a reassuring nod and moved forwards a little, away from the wall. Harry saw his hand drift, almost casually, towards his pocket.

'Don't be silly, Dawlish,' said Dumbledore kindly. 'I'm sure you are an excellent Auror – I seem to remember that you achieved "Outstanding" in all your N.E.W.T.s – but if you attempt to – er – *bring me in* by force, I will have to hurt you.'

The man called Dawlish blinked rather foolishly. He looked towards Fudge again, but this time seemed to be hoping for a clue as to what to do next.

'So,' sneered Fudge, recovering himself, 'you intend to take on Dawlish, Shacklebolt, Dolores and myself single-handed, do you, Dumbledore?'

'Merlin's beard, no,' said Dumbledore, smiling, 'not unless you are foolish enough to force me to.'

'He will not be single-handed!' said Professor McGonagall loudly, plunging her hand inside her robes.

'Oh yes he will, Minerva!' said Dumbledore sharply. 'Hogwarts needs you!'

'Enough of this rubbish!' said Fudge, pulling out his own wand. 'Dawlish! Shacklebolt! *Take him!*'

A streak of silver light flashed around the room; there was a bang like a gunshot and the floor trembled; a hand grabbed the scruff of Harry's neck and forced him down on the floor as a second silver flash went off; several of the portraits yelled, Fawkes screeched and a cloud of dust filled the air. Coughing in the dust, Harry saw a dark figure fall to the ground with a crash in front of him; there was a shriek and a thud and somebody cried, 'No!'; then there was the sound of breaking glass, frantically scuffling footsteps, a groan ... and silence.

第27章 马人和告密生

阿兹卡班。当然了,我能逃出去——但是多浪费时间哪,而且坦率地说,我想起自己还有一大堆事呢,我倒是更愿意去做那些事。"

乌姆里奇的脸色越来越红;她看上去活像被灌满了滚烫的开水。福吉盯着邓布利多,脸上的表情傻乎乎的,就像突然被打蒙了,而且简直不能相信竟然发生了这种事。他轻轻发出一种哽咽似的声音,扭头看了看金斯莱和那个留着灰白短发的男人。到现在为止,在屋子里的人当中,只有这个男人始终一言不发。他朝福吉坚决地点了点头,离开墙壁向前走了几步。哈利看到,他的一只手漫不经心地伸向了自己的衣袋。

"别犯傻,德力士,"邓布利多和蔼地说,"我确信你是个出色的傲罗——我记得你的 N.E.W.T. 考试成绩好像都达到了'优秀'——不过你如果想——哦——用暴力逮捕我,我就只好对你不客气了。"

这个叫德力士的男人挺滑稽地眨了眨眼睛。他又看了看福吉,不过这回好像是希望得到下一步该怎么办的指示。

"这么说,"福吉冷笑一声,恢复了常态,"你打算单枪匹马对付德力士、沙克尔、多洛雷斯和我,是吗,邓布利多?"

"梅林的胡子啊,当然不是,"邓布利多笑着说,"除非你蠢到逼我这么做。"

"他不是单枪匹马!"麦格教授响亮地说,一只手伸进了长袍。

"哦,是单枪匹马,米勒娃!"邓布利多严厉地说,"霍格沃茨需要你!"

"废话说够了!"福吉说着抽出自己的魔杖,"德力士!沙克尔!抓住他!"

一道银色闪光在屋里飞旋;随着炮声似的一声巨响,地板抖动起来;一只手抓住了哈利的后脖颈,用力把他按倒在地板上,第二道银色闪光爆炸了;几幅肖像在喊叫,福克斯发出了尖叫声,空气中尘埃弥漫。哈利在尘埃中咳嗽着,看到面前有个模糊的身影轰隆一声倒在地上;响起了一声尖叫,接着是嘭的一声,有人喊道:"不!"随后传来玻璃碎裂的声音,拖着脚步拼命走动的声音,还有一声呻吟……接着是一阵平静。

CHAPTER TWENTY-SEVEN   The Centaur and the Sneak

Harry struggled around to see who was half strangling him and saw Professor McGonagall crouched beside him; she had forced both him and Marietta out of harm's way. Dust was still floating gently down through the air on to them. Panting slightly, Harry saw a very tall figure moving towards them.

'Are you all right?' Dumbledore asked.

'Yes!' said Professor McGonagall, getting up and dragging Harry and Marietta with her.

The dust was clearing. The wreckage of the office loomed into view: Dumbledore's desk had been overturned, all of the spindly tables had been knocked to the floor, their silver instruments in pieces. Fudge, Umbridge, Kingsley and Dawlish lay motionless on the floor. Fawkes the phoenix soared in wide circles above them, singing softly.

'Unfortunately, I had to hex Kingsley too, or it would have looked very suspicious,' said Dumbledore in a low voice. 'He was remarkably quick on the uptake, modifying Miss Edgecombe's memory like that while everyone was looking the other way – thank him, for me, won't you, Minerva?

'Now, they will all awake very soon and it will be best if they do not know that we had time to communicate – you must act as though no time has passed, as though they were merely knocked to the ground, they will not remember –'

'Where will you go, Dumbledore?' whispered Professor McGonagall. 'Grimmauld Place?'

'Oh no,' said Dumbledore, with a grim smile, 'I am not leaving to go into hiding. Fudge will soon wish he'd never dislodged me from Hogwarts, I promise you.'

'Professor Dumbledore ...' Harry began.

He did not know what to say first: how sorry he was that he had started the DA in the first place and caused all this trouble, or how terrible he felt that Dumbledore was leaving to save him from expulsion? But Dumbledore cut him off before he could say another word.

'Listen to me, Harry,' he said urgently. 'You must study Occlumency as hard as you can, do you understand me? Do everything Professor Snape tells you and practise it particularly every night before sleeping so that you can close your mind to bad dreams – you will understand why soon enough, but you must promise me –'

The man called Dawlish was stirring. Dumbledore seized Harry's wrist.

第27章 马人和告密生

哈利挣扎着翻过身,想瞧瞧是谁把自己勒得差点喘不过气来,他看到麦格教授蜷伏在他身旁;是她让哈利和玛丽埃塔摆脱了危险。飘浮在空中的尘埃轻轻地落在他们身上。哈利有点气喘吁吁,他看到一个非常高大的身影正朝他们走来。

"你们没事吧?"邓布利多问道。

"没事!"麦格教授说,她一边站起来,一边拉起哈利和玛丽埃塔。

尘埃在渐渐散去。一片狼藉的办公室隐隐约约地显现出来:邓布利多的办公桌翻了个底朝天,那些细长腿的桌子都被撞翻在地板上,桌上的银器也摔坏了。福吉、乌姆里奇、金斯莱和德力士躺在地板上一动不动。凤凰福克斯在他们头顶绕着大圈飞翔,轻柔地鸣叫。

"真遗憾,我不得不给金斯莱施魔法,不然就显得太可疑了,"邓布利多低声说,"他的理解力真出色,大家都看着另一个方向时,他修改了艾克莫小姐的记忆——替我谢谢他,好吗,米勒娃?"

"好了,他们很快都会醒过来的,最好不要让他们知道我们有时间交谈——你们必须装出这中间没有时间流逝的样子,就像他们刚刚是被打倒在地,他们不会记得——"

"你要去哪里啊,邓布利多?"麦格教授小声说,"格里莫广场?"

"噢,不,"邓布利多说着坚毅地笑了笑,"我不会跑得远远地躲起来。用不了多久福吉就会觉得,要是没把我从霍格沃茨赶走就好了,我敢向你保证。"

"邓布利多教授……"哈利开口说。

他不知道应该先说什么:是先说说自己真后悔创办了 D.A.,引来了这么大的麻烦呢?还是说说邓布利多为了使他不被开除而离开让他难受极了呢?可是没等他再开口,邓布利多就截住了他的话头。

"听我说,哈利,"他急切地说,"你必须尽全力学习大脑封闭术,你明白我的话吗?完全按照斯内普教授的盼咐去做,要练习大脑封闭术,特别是在每天晚上睡觉以前,那样你就可以封闭你自己的头脑,不再做噩梦——你很快就会知道原因,但是你必须向我保证——"

那个叫德力士的男人正在动弹。邓布利多握住了哈利的手腕。

CHAPTER TWENTY-SEVEN The Centaur and the Sneak

'Remember – close your mind –'

But as Dumbledore's fingers closed over Harry's skin, a pain shot through the scar on his forehead and he felt again that terrible, snake-like longing to strike Dumbledore, to bite him, to hurt him –

'– you will understand,' whispered Dumbledore.

Fawkes circled the office and swooped low over him. Dumbledore released Harry, raised his hand and grasped the phoenix's long golden tail. There was a flash of fire and the pair of them were gone.

'Where is he?' yelled Fudge, pushing himself up from the floor. '*Where is he?*'

'I don't know!' shouted Kingsley, also leaping to his feet.

'Well, he can't have Disapparated!' cried Umbridge. 'You can't do it from inside this school –'

'The stairs!' cried Dawlish, and he flung himself upon the door, wrenched it open and disappeared, followed closely by Kingsley and Umbridge. Fudge hesitated, then got slowly to his feet, brushing dust from his front. There was a long and painful silence.

'Well, Minerva,' said Fudge nastily, straightening his torn shirt-sleeve, 'I'm afraid this is the end of your friend Dumbledore.'

'You think so, do you?' said Professor McGonagall scornfully.

Fudge seemed not to hear her. He was looking around at the wrecked office. A few of the portraits hissed at him; one or two even made rude hand gestures.

'You'd better get those two off to bed,' said Fudge, looking back at Professor McGonagall with a dismissive nod towards Harry and Marietta.

Professor McGonagall said nothing, but marched Harry and Marietta to the door. As it swung closed behind them, Harry heard Phineas Nigellus's voice.

'You know, Minister, I disagree with Dumbledore on many counts … but you cannot deny he's got style …'

第27章 马人和告密生

"记住——封闭你的大脑——"

当邓布利多的手指接触到哈利的皮肤时，哈利额头上的伤疤突然一阵剧痛，他又感到了可怕的蛇一样的感觉，渴望去攻击邓布利多，咬他，伤害他——

"——你会明白的。"邓布利多低声说。

福克斯在办公室里盘旋了一圈，然后在邓布利多上空低飞。邓布利多松开哈利，举起一只手紧紧握住凤凰长长的金色尾巴。随着一道火焰，他们两个消失了。

"他在哪里？"福吉嚷嚷着，费劲地从地板上爬了起来，"他在哪里？"

"我不知道！"金斯莱大声说着一跃而起。

"不对，他不可能幻影移形！"乌姆里奇喊道，"在学校里不能这么做——"

"楼梯！"德力士喊道，他扑过去用力甩开房门，消失在门外，金斯莱和乌姆里奇紧跟在他身后。福吉犹豫了一下，然后慢慢站起身来，掸去胸前的尘土。大家难受地沉默了好一阵子。

"哼，米勒娃，"福吉恶狠狠地说，一边把撕裂的衬衫袖子弄平整，"我想你的朋友邓布利多这回恐怕完蛋了。"

"你这么认为吗？"麦格教授轻蔑地说。

福吉好像没有听见她说什么。他四下打量着被毁坏的办公室。几幅肖像朝他发出不满的嘘声；有一两幅甚至做出了粗鲁的手势。

"你最好带他们俩去睡觉。"福吉说，他回头望着麦格教授，不屑一顾地朝哈利和玛丽埃塔点了点头。

麦格教授什么也没说，带着哈利和玛丽埃塔走向门口。房门在他们身后关上时，哈利听到了菲尼亚斯·奈杰勒斯的声音。

"你知道，部长，我在很多问题上跟邓布利多的意见都不一样……但是你不能否认他很有个性……"

CHAPTER TWENTY-EIGHT

Snape's Worst Memory

BY ORDER OF THE MINISTRY OF MAGIC

Dolores Jane Umbridge (High Inquisitor) has replaced Albus Dumbledore as Head of Hogwarts School of Witchcraft and Wizardry.

The above is in accordance with Educational Decree Number Twenty-eight.

Signed:
*Cornelius Oswald Fudge,
Minister for Magic*

The notices had gone up all around the school overnight, but they did not explain how every single person within the castle seemed to know that Dumbledore had overcome two Aurors, the High Inquisitor, the Minister for Magic and his Junior Assistant to escape. No matter where Harry went within the castle, the sole topic of conversation was Dumbledore's flight, and though some of the details may have gone awry in the retelling (Harry overheard one second-year girl assuring another that Fudge was now lying in St Mungo's with a pumpkin for a head) it was surprising how accurate the rest of their information was. Everybody knew, for instance, that Harry and Marietta were the only students to have witnessed the scene in Dumbledore's office and, as Marietta was now in the hospital wing, Harry found himself besieged with requests to give a firsthand account.

'Dumbledore will be back before long,' said Ernie Macmillan confidently on the way back from Herbology, after listening intently to Harry's story.

第 28 章

斯内普最痛苦的记忆

魔法部令

兹由多洛雷斯·简·乌姆里奇（高级调查官）接替阿不思·邓布利多出任霍格沃茨魔法学校校长。

以上条例符合《第二十八号教育令》。

签名：

魔法部部长

康奈利·奥斯瓦尔德·福吉

这个告示一夜之间贴遍了整个学校，城堡里的人似乎都听说邓布利多在制服两名傲罗、那位高级调查官，还有魔法部部长和他的初级助理之后逃走了，可告示上却没有做出解释。哈利在城堡里无论走到什么地方，听到人们谈论的话题只有一个，那就是邓布利多的出逃，尽管一些细节可能被传得走了样（哈利无意中听到一个二年级女生深信不疑地对另一个二年级女生说，福吉眼下正躺在圣芒戈医院里，脑袋变成了南瓜），但是其他消息却出奇地准确。比如每个人都知道，在学生中，只有哈利和玛丽埃塔亲眼见过邓布利多办公室里的情形，现在玛丽埃塔还在学校医院里，所以哈利被那些想获得第一手消息的同学弄得应接不暇。

"邓布利多不久以后就会回来。"厄尼·麦克米兰聚精会神地听完哈利的描述，在上完草药课回来的路上自信地说，"我们上二年级时，

CHAPTER TWENTY-EIGHT   Snape's Worst Memory

'They couldn't keep him away in our second year and they won't be able to this time. The Fat Friar told me –' he dropped his voice conspiratorially, so that Harry, Ron and Hermione had to lean closer to him to hear '– that Umbridge tried to get back into his office last night after they'd searched the castle and grounds for him. Couldn't get past the gargoyle. The Head's office has sealed itself against her.' Ernie smirked. 'Apparently, she had a right little tantrum.'

'Oh, I expect she really fancied herself sitting up there in the Head's office,' said Hermione viciously, as they walked up the stone steps into the Entrance Hall. 'Lording it over all the other teachers, the stupid puffed-up, power-crazy old –'

'Now, do you *really* want to finish that sentence, Granger?'

Draco Malfoy had slid out from behind the door, followed by Crabbe and Goyle. His pale, pointed face was alight with malice.

'Afraid I'm going to have to dock a few points from Gryffindor and Hufflepuff,' he drawled.

'You can't take points from fellow prefects, Malfoy,' said Ernie at once.

'I know *prefects* can't dock points from each other,' sneered Malfoy. Crabbe and Goyle sniggered. 'But members of the Inquisitorial Squad –'

'The *what?*' said Hermione sharply.

'The Inquisitorial Squad, Granger,' said Malfoy, pointing towards a tiny silver 'I' on his robes just beneath his prefect's badge. 'A select group of students who are supportive of the Ministry of Magic, hand-picked by Professor Umbridge. Anyway, members of the Inquisitorial Squad *do* have the power to dock points ... so, Granger, I'll have five from you for being rude about our new Headmistress. Macmillan, five for contradicting me. Five because I don't like you, Potter. Weasley, your shirt's untucked, so I'll have another five for that. Oh yeah, I forgot, you're a Mudblood, Granger, so ten off for that.'

Ron pulled out his wand, but Hermione pushed it away, whispering, 'Don't!'

'Wise move, Granger,' breathed Malfoy. 'New Head, new times ... be good now, Potty ... Weasel King ...'

Laughing heartily, he strode away with Crabbe and Goyle.

'He was bluffing,' said Ernie, looking appalled. 'He can't be allowed to

第28章 斯内普最痛苦的记忆

他们没办法赶走他,这回他们照样办不到。胖修士告诉我——"他神秘兮兮地压低了嗓门,哈利、罗恩和赫敏只好探过身去靠近他才能听到他的话,"——昨天晚上他们在城堡和场地里搜索他,后来那个乌姆里奇想进入他的办公室。可是没办法通过滴水嘴石兽。校长办公室自动封闭了起来,她进不去。"厄尼得意地笑了,"看来,她很是发了一顿脾气。"

"哼,我看她是一心想坐进校长办公室,"他们登上石头台阶走进门厅时,赫敏厌恶地说,"骑在所有的老师头上作威作福,这个愚蠢的自大狂,权势熏心的老——"

"喂,你真要说完这句话吗,格兰杰?"

德拉科·马尔福从门背后溜了出来,身后跟着克拉布和高尔。他苍白的尖脸上闪现出恶毒的神色。

"恐怕我必须给格兰芬多和赫奇帕奇扣掉几分了。"他拖长了腔调说。

"你不能给级长扣分,马尔福。"厄尼马上说。

"我知道级长不能相互扣分。"马尔福挖苦说,克拉布和高尔嗾嗾地笑了起来,"但是调查行动组的成员——"

"什么?"赫敏尖声问。

"调查行动组,格兰杰,"马尔福说着指了指自己长袍上级长徽章下的一个很小的银色"I"符号,"是一群精选出来的学生,都支持魔法部,由乌姆里奇教授亲手挑选的。总之,调查行动组的成员确实有扣分的权力……所以,格兰杰,因为你不尊重我们的新校长,我要扣掉你五分。麦克米兰跟我顶嘴,扣掉五分。扣掉波特五分,因为我不喜欢你。韦斯莱,你的衬衫没掖好,所以我要再扣五分。哦,对了,我忘了,你是个泥巴种,格兰杰,所以扣掉你十分。"

罗恩抽出了魔杖,但是赫敏把它拨到一旁,小声说:"别!"

"很明智的举动,格兰杰。"马尔福低声说,"新校长,新时代……现在老实点吧,傻宝宝波特……鼬王……"

他放声大笑,和克拉布和高尔阔步走开了。

"他在吓唬人,"厄尼带着惊讶的表情说,"不可能给他扣分的权

dock points ... that would be ridiculous ... it would completely undermine the prefect system.'

But Harry, Ron and Hermione had turned automatically towards the giant hourglasses set in niches along the wall behind them, which recorded the house-points. Gryffindor and Ravenclaw had been neck and neck in the lead that morning. Even as they watched, stones flew upwards, reducing the amounts in the lower bulbs. In fact, the only glass that seemed unchanged was the emerald-filled one of Slytherin.

'Noticed, have you?' said Fred's voice.

He and George had just come down the marble staircase and joined Harry, Ron, Hermione and Ernie in front of the hourglasses.

'Malfoy just docked us all about fifty points,' said Harry furiously, as they watched several more stones fly upwards from the Gryffindor hourglass.

'Yeah, Montague tried to do us during break,' said George.

'What do you mean, "tried"?' said Ron quickly.

'He never managed to get all the words out,' said Fred, 'due to the fact that we forced him head-first into that Vanishing Cabinet on the first floor.'

Hermione looked very shocked.

'But you'll get into terrible trouble!'

'Not until Montague reappears, and that could take weeks, I dunno where we sent him,' said Fred coolly. 'Anyway ... we've decided we don't care about getting into trouble any more.'

'Have you ever?' asked Hermione.

'Course we have,' said George. 'Never been expelled, have we?'

'We've always known where to draw the line,' said Fred.

'We might have put a toe across it occasionally,' said George.

'But we've always stopped short of causing real mayhem,' said Fred.

'But now?' said Ron tentatively.

'Well, now –' said George.

'– what with Dumbledore gone –' said Fred.

'– we reckon a bit of mayhem –' said George.

'– is exactly what our dear new Head deserves,' said Fred.

第28章 斯内普最痛苦的记忆

力……这也太荒唐了……会彻底破坏级长制度的。"

可是哈利、罗恩和赫敏不由自主地朝身后巨大的沙漏转过身,那几个沙漏并排嵌在壁龛里,记录着各个学院的分数。今天早上,格兰芬多和拉文克劳还并驾齐驱处于领先地位。就在他们的注视下,宝石向上飞去,下半截沙漏里的宝石数量越来越少。实际上,好像只有装着绿宝石的斯莱特林沙漏没有变化。

"你们注意到了,是吧?"弗雷德的声音问。

他和乔治刚刚走下大理石楼梯,跟哈利、罗恩、赫敏和厄尼一起站在沙漏前。

"刚才马尔福几乎给我们扣掉了五十分。"哈利愤怒地说,这时他们看到格兰芬多的沙漏里又有几块宝石飞了上去。

"是啊,蒙太在课间休息时也打算扣我们的分。"乔治说。

"你是什么意思,'打算'?"罗恩马上问。

"他没能把话说完,"弗雷德说,"因为实际上,我们硬把他大头朝下塞进了二楼的消失柜里。"

赫敏看上去大吃了一惊。

"你们会惹上大麻烦的!"

"在蒙太重新露面以前不会的,那可能要几个星期以后呢,我不知道我们把他打发到什么地方去了。"弗雷德冷冷地说,"反正……我们决定再也不担心会不会惹麻烦了。"

"你们担心过吗?"赫敏问道。

"当然了,"乔治说,"我们不是一直没有被开除吗?"

"我们一直很明白要在哪里画个界线。"弗雷德说。

"我们偶尔也许会越过一个脚趾。"乔治说。

"但总是在惹出大乱子之前停下来。"弗雷德说。

"那现在呢?"罗恩没有把握地问道。

"嗯,现在嘛——"乔治说。

"——既然邓布利多已经走了——"弗雷德说。

"——我们认为出点大乱子——"乔治说。

"——正是我们亲爱的新校长罪有应得的。"弗雷德说。

CHAPTER TWENTY-EIGHT   Snape's Worst Memory

'You mustn't!' whispered Hermione. 'You really mustn't! She'd love a reason to expel you!'

'You don't get it, Hermione, do you?' said Fred, smiling at her. 'We don't care about staying any more. We'd walk out right now if we weren't determined to do our bit for Dumbledore first. So, anyway,' he checked his watch, 'phase one is about to begin. I'd get in the Great Hall for lunch, if I were you, that way the teachers will see you can't have had anything to do with it.'

'Anything to do with what?' said Hermione anxiously.

'You'll see,' said George. 'Run along, now.'

Fred and George turned away and disappeared into the swelling crowd descending the stairs towards lunch. Looking highly disconcerted, Ernie muttered something about unfinished Transfiguration homework and scurried away.

'I think we *should* get out of here, you know,' said Hermione nervously. 'Just in case ...'

'Yeah, all right,' said Ron, and the three of them moved towards the doors to the Great Hall, but Harry had barely glimpsed the day's ceiling of scudding white clouds when somebody tapped him on the shoulder and, turning, he found himself almost nose-to-nose with Filch the caretaker. He took several hasty steps backwards; Filch was best viewed at a distance.

'The Headmistress would like to see you, Potter,' he leered.

'I didn't do it,' said Harry stupidly, thinking of whatever Fred and George were planning. Filch's jowls wobbled with silent laughter.

'Guilty conscience, eh?' he wheezed. 'Follow me.'

Harry glanced back at Ron and Hermione, who were both looking worried. He shrugged, and followed Filch back into the Entrance Hall, against the tide of hungry students.

Filch seemed to be in an extremely good mood; he hummed creakily under his breath as they climbed the marble staircase. As they reached the first landing he said, 'Things are changing around here, Potter.'

'I've noticed,' said Harry coldly.

'Yerse ... I've been telling Dumbledore for years and years he's too soft with you all,' said Filch, chuckling nastily. 'You filthy little beasts would never have dropped Stink Pellets if you'd known I had it in my power to

第28章 斯内普最痛苦的记忆

"你们不能这么干！"赫敏小声说，"绝对不能！她巴不得有个理由开除你们呢！"

"你还没有听明白吧，赫敏？"弗雷德笑着对她说，"我们再也不关心能不能留在这里了。要不是决定先为邓布利多做些贡献，我们马上就退学。所以，总之，"他看了看自己的手表，"第一阶段即将开始了。如果我是你的话，就会去礼堂吃午饭，那样老师们就会看到你和那件事一点儿关系也没有。"

"和什么事一点儿关系也没有？"赫敏不安地问道。

"你会看到的，"乔治说，"现在快走吧。"

下楼去吃午饭的人越来越多，弗雷德和乔治转身离开，消失在人群里。厄尼表情很慌乱，嘴里嘟哝着变形课作业还没做完什么的，匆匆跑开了。

"你知道，我觉得我们必须离开这里，"赫敏紧张地说，"免得……"

"对，没错。"罗恩说。他们三个朝礼堂大门走去，但是哈利刚刚瞥见在白天的天花板上飞掠的白云，就有人在他肩膀上轻轻拍了一下。他一转身，发现自己几乎和管理员费尔奇脸对着脸。他急忙向后退了几步，觉得最好还是从远处看着费尔奇。

"校长想见你，波特。"费尔奇不怀好意地斜眼看着哈利。

"不是我干的。"哈利想着弗雷德和乔治的计划，傻乎乎地说。费尔奇无声地笑起来，下巴上的垂肉颤抖着。

"做贼心虚，是吧？"他喘息着说，"跟我来。"

哈利扭头瞥了一眼罗恩和赫敏，他们两个都显得很担心。他耸了耸肩膀，跟随费尔奇迎着潮水般涌来的饥肠辘辘的学生走回门厅。

费尔奇似乎心情特别好。他们走上大理石楼梯时，他断断续续地小声哼着歌。他们来到第一个楼梯平台上时，他说："这里的情况都在变，波特。"

"我看到了。"哈利冷冷地说。

"你知道……我跟邓布利多说了好多好多年，他对你们太宽厚了。"费尔奇说着，难听地轻声笑了起来，"要是知道我有权力用鞭子打得你们皮开肉绽，你们这些卑鄙的小畜生就再也不会扔臭弹了，是吧？要

CHAPTER TWENTY-EIGHT   Snape's Worst Memory

whip you raw, would you, now? Nobody would have thought of throwing Fanged Frisbees down the corridors if I could've strung you up by the ankles in my office, would they? But when Educational Decree Number Twenty-nine comes in, Potter, I'll be allowed to do them things ... *and* she's asked the Minister to sign an order for the expulsion of Peeves ... oh, things are going to be very different around here with *her* in charge ...'

Umbridge had obviously gone to some lengths to get Filch on her side, Harry thought, and the worst of it was that he would probably prove an important weapon; his knowledge of the school's secret passageways and hiding places was probably second only to that of the Weasley twins.

'Here we are,' he said, leering down at Harry as he rapped three times on Professor Umbridge's door and pushed it open. 'The Potter boy to see you, Ma'am.'

Umbridge's office, so very familiar to Harry from his many detentions, was the same as usual except for the large wooden block lying across the front of her desk on which golden letters spelled the word: HEADMISTRESS. Also, his Firebolt and Fred and George's Cleansweeps, which he saw with a pang, were chained and padlocked to a stout iron peg in the wall behind the desk.

Umbridge was sitting behind the desk, busily scribbling on some of her pink parchment, but she looked up and smiled widely at their entrance.

'Thank you, Argus,' she said sweetly.

'Not at all, Ma'am, not at all,' said Filch, bowing as low as his rheumatism would permit, and exiting backwards.

'Sit,' said Umbridge curtly, pointing towards a chair. Harry sat. She continued to scribble for a few moments. He watched some of the foul kittens gambolling around the plates over her head, wondering what fresh horror she had in store for him.

'Well, now,' she said finally, setting down her quill and looking like a toad about to swallow a particularly juicy fly. 'What would you like to drink?'

'What?' said Harry, quite sure he had misheard her.

'To drink, Mr Potter,' she said, smiling still more widely. 'Tea? Coffee? Pumpkin juice?'

As she named each drink, she gave her short wand a wave, and a cup or glass of it appeared on her desk.

'Nothing, thank you,' said Harry.

第28章 斯内普最痛苦的记忆

是我能吊住你们的脚脖子,把你们倒挂在我的办公室里,就再没人打算在走廊里扔狼牙飞碟了,是吧?等到《第二十九号教育令》一生效,波特,我就有权那么做了……她还请求部长签署一道命令,驱逐皮皮鬼……哈,由她来掌权,这里的情况会大不一样……"

乌姆里奇显然在不遗余力地把费尔奇拉到自己那一边,哈利想,最糟糕的是,费尔奇很可能会成为重要的威胁。论起对学校里秘密通道和躲藏处的熟悉程度,他可能仅次于韦斯莱家的双胞胎。

"我们到了。"费尔奇说,斜眼看着哈利,在乌姆里奇教授的房门上轻轻敲了三下,然后把门推开了,"波特那小子来见你了,夫人。"

哈利被关了那么多次禁闭,对乌姆里奇的办公室已经非常熟悉,一块木质的大姓名牌横放在她的桌子上,上面用金字写着**校长**这个词,除此以外,办公室里还是老样子。另外,他看见了自己的火弩箭,还有弗雷德与乔治的两把横扫,心里觉得一阵难过。在桌子后面的墙上钉着一根粗大、结实的铁栓,飞天扫帚被铁链捆在铁栓上,而且上了锁。

乌姆里奇坐在桌子后面,正忙着在粉红色的羊皮纸上写些什么,他们进来时,她满脸堆笑地抬起了眼睛。

"谢谢你,阿格斯。"她亲切地说。

"不必客气,夫人,不必客气。"患有风湿病的费尔奇一边说一边尽量地弯腰鞠躬,同时向外退去。

"坐下。"乌姆里奇指着一把椅子简短生硬地说。哈利坐下了。乌姆里奇又接着写了一会儿。在她头上的盘子里,几只画得难看的小猫正在乱蹦乱跳,哈利望着它们,心里猜不透自己又会遇到什么新麻烦。

"好了,"乌姆里奇终于说,她放下羽毛笔,脸上的表情就像一只癞蛤蟆正打算吞下一只美味多汁的苍蝇,"请问你想喝些什么?"

"什么?"哈利说,他觉得自己肯定听错了。

"喝什么,波特先生。"乌姆里奇说着,笑得更开心了,"茶?咖啡?南瓜汁?"

她在说出每种饮料时,都轻轻挥动自己的那根短魔杖,盛着饮料的茶杯或者玻璃杯就会出现在她的桌子上。

"不用了,谢谢。"哈利说。

CHAPTER TWENTY-EIGHT   Snape's Worst Memory

'I wish you to have a drink with me,' she said, her voice becoming dangerously sweet. 'Choose one.'

'Fine ... tea then,' said Harry, shrugging.

She got up and made quite a performance of adding milk with her back to him. She then bustled around the desk with it, smiling in a sinisterly sweet fashion.

'There,' she said, handing it to him. 'Drink it before it gets cold, won't you? Well, now, Mr Potter ... I thought we ought to have a little chat, after the distressing events of last night.'

He said nothing. She settled herself back into her seat and waited. When several long moments had passed in silence, she said gaily, 'You're not drinking up!'

He raised the cup to his lips and then, just as suddenly, lowered it. One of the horrible painted kittens behind Umbridge had great round blue eyes just like Mad-Eye Moody's magical one and it had just occurred to Harry what Mad-Eye would say if he ever heard that Harry had drunk anything offered by a known enemy.

'What's the matter?' said Umbridge, who was still watching him. 'Do you want sugar?'

'No,' said Harry.

He raised the cup to his lips again and pretended to take a sip, though keeping his mouth tightly closed. Umbridge's smile widened.

'Good,' she whispered. 'Very good. Now then ...' She leaned forwards a little. '*Where is Albus Dumbledore?*'

'No idea,' said Harry promptly.

'Drink up, drink up,' she said, still smiling. 'Now, Mr Potter, let us not play childish games. I know that you know where he has gone. You and Dumbledore have been in this together from the beginning. Consider your position, Mr Potter ...'

'I don't know where he is.'

Harry pretended to drink again.

'Very well,' said Umbridge, looking displeased. 'In that case, you will kindly tell me the whereabouts of Sirius Black.'

Harry's stomach turned over and his hand holding the teacup shook so that it rattled in its saucer. He tilted the cup to his mouth with his lips pressed together, so that some of the hot liquid trickled down on to his robes.

第28章 斯内普最痛苦的记忆

"我真希望你能跟我一起喝一杯。"乌姆里奇说,她的声调开始变得既吓人又悦耳,"选一杯。"

"好吧……那就喝茶吧。"哈利耸耸肩膀说。

乌姆里奇站起来,装模作样地背对着哈利加了些牛奶。然后她端着茶快步绕过桌子,脸上带着一种既阴险又亲切的笑容。

"给,"她说着把茶递给了哈利,"趁热喝了它,好吗?现在,波特先生……我觉得,在发生了昨晚那些不幸事件后,我们应该聊一聊。"

哈利什么也没说。乌姆里奇回到自己的座位上等待着。沉默了好一阵子后,她轻快地说:"你还没喝呢!"

哈利把茶杯举到唇边,突然又放了下来。乌姆里奇背后那些画得很丑陋的花猫中,有一只长着又大又圆的蓝眼睛,就像疯眼汉穆迪的那只魔眼一样,这让哈利想到,要是疯眼汉听说哈利喝下了敌人提供的东西,会说些什么呢。

"怎么了?"乌姆里奇说,她还在盯着哈利,"你要加糖吗?"

"不用。"哈利说。

他又把茶杯举到唇边,假装呷了一口,可他的嘴唇紧紧地抿在了一起。乌姆里奇笑得更开心了。

"很好,"她小声说,"太好了。那么……"她向前稍微倾了倾身子,"阿不思·邓布利多在哪儿?"

"不清楚。"哈利马上说。

"喝光,喝光,"她说,脸上仍然挂着笑容,"好了,波特先生,我们别玩小孩子的游戏了。我知道你很清楚他到什么地方去了。从一开始,你和邓布利多就是一伙的。考虑到你的处境,波特先生……"

"我不知道他在哪儿。"

哈利又装着喝茶。

"好极了,"乌姆里奇说,显得不太高兴,"既然如此,要是你能告诉我小天狼星布莱克的下落,那就太好了。"

哈利心中揪得好紧,端着茶杯的那只手抖了一下,茶杯咔嗒一声碰响了茶碟。他在嘴边斜过茶杯,嘴唇紧紧地抿在一起,一些热茶滴落在他的长袍上。

CHAPTER TWENTY-EIGHT   Snape's Worst Memory

'I don't know,' he said, a little too quickly.

'Mr Potter,' said Umbridge, 'let me remind you that it was I who almost caught the criminal Black in the Gryffindor fire in October. I know perfectly well it was you he was meeting and if I had had any proof neither of you would be at large today, I promise you. I repeat, Mr Potter ... where is Sirius Black?'

'No idea,' said Harry loudly. 'Haven't got a clue.'

They stared at each other so long that Harry felt his eyes watering. Then Umbridge stood up.

'Very well, Potter, I will take your word for it this time, but be warned: the might of the Ministry stands behind me. All channels of communication in and out of this school are being monitored. A Floo Network regulator is keeping watch over every fire in Hogwarts – except my own, of course. My Inquisitorial Squad is opening and reading all owl post entering and leaving the castle. And Mr Filch is observing all secret passages in and out of the castle. If I find a shred of evidence ...'

BOOM!

The very floor of the office shook. Umbridge slipped sideways, clutching her desk for support, and looking shocked.

'What was –?'

She was gazing towards the door. Harry took the opportunity to empty his almost-full cup of tea into the nearest vase of dried flowers. He could hear people running and screaming several floors below.

'Back to lunch you go, Potter!' cried Umbridge, raising her wand and dashing out of the office. Harry gave her a few seconds' start, then hurried after her to see what the source of all the uproar was.

It was not difficult to find. One floor down, pandemonium reigned. Somebody (and Harry had a very shrewd idea who) had set off what seemed to be an enormous crate of enchanted fireworks.

Dragons comprised entirely of green and gold sparks were soaring up and down the corridors, emitting loud fiery blasts and bangs as they went; shocking-pink Catherine wheels five feet in diameter were whizzing lethally through the air like so many flying saucers; rockets with long tails of brilliant silver stars were ricocheting off the walls; sparklers were writing swear

第28章 斯内普最痛苦的记忆

"我不知道。"他说,语调有点太急了。

"波特先生,"乌姆里奇说,"我来提醒你一下,在十月份,正是我本人在格兰芬多的炉火里差点抓到了那个罪犯布莱克。我非常清楚和他见面的人就是你,如果我有证据的话,今天你们两个谁都不能逍遥法外,我可以向你保证。我再说一遍,波特先生……小天狼星布莱克在什么地方?"

"不清楚,"哈利响亮地说,"我什么都不知道。"

他们久久地瞪着对方,哈利觉得自己都快流眼泪了。接着乌姆里奇站了起来。

"那好吧,波特,这一回我就相信你的话,不过提醒一下:我背后可有魔法部撑腰。学校内外的通讯渠道都在监控之下。一位飞路网管理员会始终监视霍格沃茨里的每一处炉火——当然了,我的炉火除外。我的调查行动组将拆阅所有进出城堡的猫头鹰邮件。而且费尔奇先生会留意城堡内外所有的秘密通道。如果我发现一丁点证据……"

轰隆!

办公室里的地板晃动起来。乌姆里奇朝旁边一歪,她紧紧抓着桌子撑住自己,一脸震惊的表情。

"怎么——?"

她注视着房门。哈利那杯茶几乎还是满的,他趁着这个机会,把它全都倒在了最近处插着干花的花瓶里。他听到在几层楼下面,人们正在奔跑、尖叫。

"你回去吃午饭,波特!"乌姆里奇喊着,扬起自己的魔杖冲出了办公室。哈利让乌姆里奇先跑上几秒钟,然后才快步跟上去寻找这些骚乱的来源。

一看就明白了。楼下一片混乱。有人(哈利立刻想到了是谁)好像点燃了一大箱施过魔法的烟火。

一些全身由绿色和金色火花构成的火龙正在走廊里飞来飞去,一路喷射出艳丽的火红色气流,发出巨大的爆炸声;颜色鲜艳的粉红色凯瑟琳车轮式烟火,直径有五英尺,带着可怕的嗖嗖声飞速转动着穿行在空中,就像许多飞碟;火箭拖着闪耀的由银星构成的长尾巴从墙

CHAPTER TWENTY-EIGHT   Snape's Worst Memory

words in midair of their own accord; firecrackers were exploding like mines everywhere Harry looked, and instead of burning themselves out, fading from sight or fizzling to a halt, these pyrotechnical miracles seemed to be gaining in energy and momentum the longer he watched.

Filch and Umbridge were standing, apparently transfixed in horror, halfway down the stairs. As Harry watched, one of the larger Catherine wheels seemed to decide that what it needed was more room to manoeuvre; it whirled towards Umbridge and Filch with a sinister '*wheeeeeeeeee*'. They both yelled with fright and ducked, and it soared straight out of the window behind them and off across the grounds. Meanwhile, several of the dragons and a large purple bat that was smoking ominously took advantage of the open door at the end of the corridor to escape towards the second floor.

'Hurry, Filch, hurry!' shrieked Umbridge, 'they'll be all over the school unless we do something – *Stupefy*!'

A jet of red light shot out of the end of her wand and hit one of the rockets. Instead of freezing in midair, it exploded with such force that it blasted a hole in a painting of a soppy-looking witch in the middle of a meadow; she ran for it just in time, reappearing seconds later squashed into the next painting, where a couple of wizards playing cards stood up hastily to make room for her.

'Don't Stun them, Filch!' shouted Umbridge angrily, for all the world as though it had been his incantation.

'Right you are, Headmistress!' wheezed Filch, who as a Squib could no more have Stunned the fireworks than swallowed them. He dashed to a nearby cupboard, pulled out a broom and began swatting at the fireworks in midair; within seconds the head of the broom was ablaze.

Harry had seen enough; laughing, he ducked down low, ran to a door he knew was concealed behind a tapestry a little way along the corridor and slipped through it to find Fred and George hiding just behind it, listening to Umbridge and Filch's yells and quaking with suppressed mirth.

'Impressive,' Harry said quietly, grinning. 'Very impressive ... you'll put Dr Filibuster out of business, no problem ...'

'Cheers,' whispered George, wiping tears of laughter from his face. 'Oh, I hope she tries Vanishing them next ... they multiply by ten every time you try.'

第28章 斯内普最痛苦的记忆

上反弹开；烟火棍在空中自动写出骂人的话；哈利看到，处处都有爆竹像地雷一样炸开，它们并没有烧光，渐渐从视线中消失或者发出嘶嘶声停下来，而是相反，时间越久，这些烟火奇迹似乎越有能量和动力。

费尔奇和乌姆里奇站在楼梯中间，显然是被吓呆了。哈利看见，一只个头比较大的凯瑟琳车轮式烟火好像认为自己需要更多的活动空间，发出恐怖的嗡——嗡——声，转动着朝乌姆里奇和费尔奇飞过去。他们俩都吓得大喊大叫，猛地弯下身子，凯瑟琳车轮式烟火径直飞出他们身后的窗户，穿过了场地。与此同时，几条火龙和一只冒出吓人烟雾的紫色大蝙蝠通过走廊尽头敞开的大门朝三楼逃去。

"快，费尔奇，赶快！"乌姆里奇尖声喊道，"我们得想点办法，不然它们要飞遍整个学校了——昏昏倒地！"

她的魔杖顶端突然喷出一道红光，击中了一枚火箭。火箭没有在空中停下来，反而猛烈地爆炸了。它在一幅画上炸出了一个洞，画中的草地上有一个表情多愁善感的女巫及时逃开，几秒钟后才重新露面。她挤进了隔壁的画，那里有几个正在打牌的巫师，他们急忙站起来为她腾出地方。

"不要对它们用昏迷咒，费尔奇！"乌姆里奇恼火地喊道，好像刚才是费尔奇念了这个咒语似的。

"你说得对，校长！"费尔奇喘息着说，其实他是个哑炮，与其让他击昏那些爆竹，倒不如让他把它们吞下去。费尔奇冲向附近的橱柜，拽出一把扫帚，开始用力拍打半空中的烟火；几秒钟内扫帚头就着火了。

哈利看够了；他笑着深深弯下腰，顺着走廊向不远处的一扇门跑去，他知道这扇门就隐藏在一幅挂毯后面。他悄悄溜进去，发现弗雷德和乔治正藏在门后，他们俩听着乌姆里奇和费尔奇大喊大叫，使劲憋住笑，憋得身上直发抖。

"了不起，"哈利轻轻地说，咧开嘴笑着，"真了不起……你们会把费力拔博士的生意挤垮的，没问题……"

"谢谢，"乔治低声说，一边抹去脸上笑出来的眼泪，"嘿，我希望她接下来对它们试试消失咒……只要你这么干，它们就会成十倍地增加。"

1053

CHAPTER TWENTY-EIGHT Snape's Worst Memory

The fireworks continued to burn and to spread all over the school that afternoon. Though they caused plenty of disruption, particularly the firecrackers, the other teachers didn't seem to mind them very much.

'Dear, dear,' said Professor McGonagall sardonically, as one of the dragons soared around her classroom, emitting loud bangs and exhaling flame. 'Miss Brown, would you mind running along to the Headmistress and informing her that we have an escaped firework in our classroom?'

The upshot of it all was that Professor Umbridge spent her first afternoon as Headmistress running all over the school answering the summonses of the other teachers, none of whom seemed able to rid their rooms of the fireworks without her. When the final bell rang and they were heading back to Gryffindor Tower with their bags, Harry saw, with immense satisfaction, a dishevelled and soot-blackened Umbridge tottering sweaty-faced from Professor Flitwick's classroom.

'Thank you so much, Professor!' said Professor Flitwick in his squeaky little voice. 'I could have got rid of the sparklers myself, of course, but I wasn't sure whether or not I had the *authority*.'

Beaming, he closed his classroom door in her snarling face.

Fred and George were heroes that night in the Gryffindor common room. Even Hermione fought her way through the excited crowd to congratulate them.

'They were wonderful fireworks,' she said admiringly.

'Thanks,' said George, looking both surprised and pleased. 'Weasleys' Wildfire Whiz-bangs. Only thing is, we used our whole stock; we're going to have to start again from scratch now.'

'It was worth it, though,' said Fred, who was taking orders from clamouring Gryffindors. 'If you want to add your name to the waiting list, Hermione, it's five Galleons for your Basic Blaze box and twenty for the Deflagration Deluxe …'

Hermione returned to the table where Harry and Ron were sitting staring at their schoolbags as though hoping their homework would spring out and start doing itself.

'Oh, why don't we have a night off?' said Hermione brightly, as a silver-tailed Weasley rocket zoomed past the window. 'After all, the Easter holidays start on Friday, we'll have plenty of time then.'

'Are you feeling all right?' Ron asked, staring at her in disbelief.

第28章 斯内普最痛苦的记忆

整个下午，烟火一直在燃烧，而且扩散到了学校里的每个地方。尽管这些烟火，尤其是那些爆竹引发了多处混乱，但别的老师好像并不是很在意。

"天哪，天哪，"麦格教授嘲讽地说，这时一条火龙正在她的教室里四处飞舞，发出响亮的爆炸声，喷出火焰，"布朗小姐，请问你能不能跑去告诉校长一声，我们教室里有一个漏网的烟火？"

结果乌姆里奇当上校长的第一个下午，全都用来在学校各处跑来跑去，应付其他老师的要求。离了她，这些老师好像谁都没办法清除自己教室里的烟火。放学的铃声响了起来，他们拿着书包朝格兰芬多塔楼走去，这时哈利非常满意地看到，衣冠不整、被烟火熏黑了的乌姆里奇正步履蹒跚、满脸是汗地走出弗立维教授的教室。

"非常感谢你，教授！"弗立维教授用尖细的声音说，"当然了，我自己能够清除这些烟火棍，但是我不能肯定自己是否有这个权力。"

他满脸笑容，当着脸上乌七八糟的乌姆里奇的面关上了教室的门。

那天晚上，在格兰芬多公共休息室里，弗雷德和乔治成了英雄。连赫敏都奋力挤过兴奋的人群去祝贺他们。

"这些烟火太奇妙了。"她钦佩地说。

"多谢，"乔治说，他显得既惊讶又高兴，"那是韦斯莱嗖嗖－嘭烟火。只不过，我们把存货全用光了；现在又得重新做了。"

"可是这么做很值得啊，"弗雷德说，他正在接受吵吵嚷嚷的格兰芬多学生的订单，"赫敏，如果你想把自己的名字列入订货名单，可以付五个加隆买简装火焰盒，付二十个加隆买豪华爆燃……"

赫敏回到桌子旁，哈利和罗恩正坐在那里盯着自己的书包，好像希望他们的作业能够跳出来自动完成似的。

"嘿，今晚我们为什么不休息一下呢？"赫敏欢快地说，这时候一枚拖着银色尾巴的韦斯莱火箭飞快地从窗户外掠过，"毕竟星期五就要开始复活节假期了，我们到时候有足够的时间。"

"你没生病吧？"罗恩怀疑地盯着她问道。

CHAPTER TWENTY-EIGHT   Snape's Worst Memory

'Now you mention it,' said Hermione happily, 'd'you know ... I think I'm feeling a bit ... *rebellious*.'

Harry could still hear the distant bangs of escaped firecrackers when he and Ron went up to bed an hour later; and as he got undressed a sparkler floated past the tower, still resolutely spelling out the word 'POO'.

He got into bed, yawning. With his glasses off, the occasional firework passing the window had become blurred, looking like sparkling clouds, beautiful and mysterious against the black sky. He turned on to his side, wondering how Umbridge was feeling about her first day in Dumbledore's job, and how Fudge would react when he heard that the school had spent most of the day in a state of advanced disruption. Smiling to himself, Harry closed his eyes ...

The whizzes and bangs of escaped fireworks in the grounds seemed to be growing more distant ... or perhaps he was simply speeding away from them ...

He had fallen right into the corridor leading to the Department of Mysteries. He was speeding towards the plain black door ... *let it open ... let it open* ...

It did. He was inside the circular room lined with doors ... he crossed it, placed his hand on an identical door and it swung inwards ...

Now he was in a long, rectangular room full of an odd mechanical clicking. There were dancing flecks of light on the walls but he did not pause to investigate ... he had to go on ...

There was a door at the far end ... it, too, opened at his touch ...

And now he was in a dimly lit room as high and wide as a church, full of nothing but rows and rows of towering shelves, each laden with small, dusty, spun-glass spheres ... now Harry's heart was beating fast with excitement ... he knew where to go ... he ran forwards, but his footsteps made no noise in the enormous, deserted room ...

There was something in this room he wanted very, very much ...

Something he wanted ... or somebody else wanted ...

His scar was hurting ...

BANG!

Harry awoke instantly, confused and angry. The dark dormitory was full of the sound of laughter.

第28章 斯内普最痛苦的记忆

"既然你这么说,"赫敏愉快地说,"是这样的……我想我找到了一点儿……叛逆的感觉。"

一小时后,当哈利和罗恩上楼去睡觉时,哈利仍能听到漏网的爆竹在远处发出的巨响;他脱去衣服后,一根烟火棍从塔楼旁飘过,还在不屈不挠地拼出"呸"字。

哈利打着哈欠上了床。摘掉自己的眼镜后,偶尔从窗户旁经过的烟火变得模糊起来,看上去就像闪闪发光的云朵,在黑色天空的映衬下显得既漂亮又神秘。他侧过身躺着,心里想道,不知乌姆里奇接替邓布利多职位的第一天是什么感受,还有当福吉听到整个学校在大半天的时间里,都处于严重的混乱状态时会有什么反应。哈利笑着闭上了眼睛……

场地上漏网烟火的嗖嗖声和嘭嘭声似乎越来越远……也许,只是哈利在迅速远离它们……

他一下子落入了通向神秘事务司的走廊。他正快步走向那扇黑色房门……打开它……打开它……

房门开了。他置身于圆形的房间里,周围环绕着房门……他穿过房间,把手搭在一扇跟其他门完全一样的门上,门朝里面转开了……

现在他进入了一间很长的长方形房间,满耳都是一种机械装置发出的古怪滴答声。一些光斑在四堵墙壁上跳跃,但是他没有停下来看个究竟……他必须往前走……

在屋子尽头有一扇门……他碰了碰这扇门,它也打开了……

现在他来到了一间灯火昏暗、像教堂一样高大宽敞的房间里,这里没有别的东西,只有一排排高大的架子,每个架子上都摆满了尘封的小玻璃球……现在哈利激动得心脏猛跳……他知道应该去哪里……他向前跑去,可是在空无一人的巨大房间里,他的脚步没有发出声响。

在这个房间里,有一件他非常非常想得到的东西……

他想得到这件东西……或者是别的什么人想得到它……

他的伤疤在疼痛……

砰!

哈利立刻被惊醒了,他既困惑又生气。黑暗的宿舍里充满了笑声。

CHAPTER TWENTY-EIGHT Snape's Worst Memory

'Cool!' said Seamus, who was silhouetted against the window. 'I think one of those Catherine wheels hit a rocket and it's like they mated, come and see!'

Harry heard Ron and Dean scramble out of bed for a better look. He lay quite still and silent while the pain in his scar subsided and disappointment washed over him. He felt as though a wonderful treat had been snatched from him at the very last moment ... he had got so close that time.

Glittering pink and silver winged piglets were now soaring past the windows of Gryffindor Tower. Harry lay and listened to the appreciative whoops of Gryffindors in the dormitories below them. His stomach gave a sickening jolt as he remembered that he had Occlumency the following evening.

Harry spent the whole of the next day dreading what Snape was going to say if he found out how much further into the Department of Mysteries Harry had penetrated during his last dream. With a surge of guilt he realised that he had not practised Occlumency once since their last lesson: there had been too much going on since Dumbledore had left; he was sure he would not have been able to empty his mind even if he had tried. He doubted, however, whether Snape would accept that excuse.

He attempted a little last-minute practice during classes that day, but it was no good. Hermione kept asking him what was wrong whenever he fell silent trying to rid himself of all thought and emotion and, after all, the best moment to empty his brain was not while teachers were firing revision questions at the class.

Resigned to the worst, he set off for Snape's office after dinner. Halfway across the Entrance Hall, however, Cho came hurrying up to him.

'Over here,' said Harry, glad of a reason to postpone his meeting with Snape, and beckoning her across to the corner of the Entrance Hall where the giant hourglasses stood. Gryffindor's was now almost empty. 'Are you OK? Umbridge hasn't been asking you about the DA, has she?'

'Oh, no,' said Cho hurriedly. 'No, it was only ... well, I just wanted to say ... Harry, I never dreamed Marietta would tell ...'

'Yeah, well,' said Harry moodily. He did feel Cho might have chosen her friends a bit more carefully; it was small consolation that the last he had heard, Marietta was still up in the hospital wing and Madam Pomfrey had

第28章 斯内普最痛苦的记忆

"酷!"西莫说,窗户映衬出他的黑色身影,"我觉得有个凯瑟琳车轮式烟火撞上了一枚火箭,它们好像连在一起了,过来看哪!"

哈利听见罗恩和迪安急忙从床上爬起来,好看得更清楚些。他还是静静地躺着默不作声,伤疤的疼痛渐渐消退了,失望的感觉笼罩着他。他觉得就像一件美妙的开心事在最后一刻被打断了……当时他已经离得那么近了。

现在,一些长着翅膀、发出闪耀的粉红色和银色的小猪正从格兰芬多塔楼旁飞过。哈利躺在床上,听见楼下宿舍里格兰芬多学生赞叹的叫喊声。他想起明天晚上要去学习大脑封闭术,胃里立刻难受地颤动了一下。

第二天,哈利一整天都在担心,要是斯内普发现自己在昨晚的梦中潜入神秘事务司后走了那么远,不知道会说些什么。伴随着一阵阵的内疚,哈利意识到在上一节课后,自己一次都没练习过大脑封闭术。自从邓布利多离开学校,发生了那么多的事情,他确信就算自己想清空头脑也办不到。不过他拿不准斯内普是否会接受这个借口。

这一天,他想在上课时临阵磨枪练习一下,但是毫无用处。每当他默不作声,想摒除自己所有的念头和思绪时,赫敏总要问他哪里不舒服,而且老师在课上连珠炮似的提问复习,这种时候确实不是清空头脑的最佳时刻。

晚饭后,哈利抱着听天由命的心情,动身前往斯内普的办公室。在穿过门厅的半路上,秋·张急匆匆地朝他走了过来。

"到这儿来。"哈利说,很高兴自己能有个理由晚些和斯内普见面。他招手示意秋·张到对面门厅的角落里去,那些巨大的沙漏就矗立在那里。格兰芬多的沙漏现在几乎已经见底了。"你还好吗?乌姆里奇没有向你问起 D.A. 的事吧?"

"哦,没有,"秋·张急促地说,"没有,只不过……嗯,我只是想说……哈利,我做梦也想不到玛丽埃塔会告……"

"是啊,嗯。"哈利闷闷不乐地说。他确实觉得秋·张在挑选朋友时也许应该更谨慎一些;玛丽埃塔仍然在校医院里,庞弗雷女士拿她

CHAPTER TWENTY-EIGHT   Snape's Worst Memory

not been able to make the slightest improvement to her pimples.

'She's a lovely person really,' said Cho. 'She just made a mistake –'

Harry looked at her incredulously.

'*A lovely person who made a mistake?* She sold us all out, including you!'

'Well ... we all got away, didn't we?' said Cho pleadingly. 'You know, her mum works for the Ministry, it's really difficult for her –'

'Ron's dad works for the Ministry too!' Harry said furiously. 'And in case you hadn't noticed, he hasn't got *sneak* written across *his* face –'

'That was a really horrible trick of Hermione Granger's,' said Cho fiercely. 'She should have told us she'd jinxed that list –'

'I think it was a brilliant idea,' said Harry coldly. Cho flushed and her eyes grew brighter.

'Oh yes, I forgot – of course, if it was darling *Hermione's* idea –'

'Don't start crying again,' said Harry warningly.

'I wasn't going to!' she shouted.

'Yeah ... well ... good,' he said. 'I've got enough to cope with at the moment.'

'Go and cope with it then!' Cho said furiously, turning on her heel and stalking off.

Fuming, Harry descended the stairs to Snape's dungeon and, though he knew from experience how much easier it would be for Snape to penetrate his mind if he arrived angry and resentful, he succeeded in nothing but thinking of a few more things he should have said to Cho about Marietta before reaching the dungeon door.

'You're late, Potter,' said Snape coldly, as Harry closed the door behind him.

Snape was standing with his back to Harry, removing, as usual, certain of his thoughts and placing them carefully in Dumbledore's Pensieve. He dropped the last silvery strand into the stone basin and turned to face Harry.

'So,' he said. 'Have you been practising?'

'Yes,' Harry lied, looking carefully at one of the legs of Snape's desk.

'Well, we'll soon find out, won't we?' said Snape smoothly. 'Wand out, Potter.'

第28章 斯内普最痛苦的记忆

的脓包一点儿办法也没有,哈利上次听到这个消息后,稍微消了消气。

"她这个人其实挺可爱的,"秋·张说,"她不过是犯了个错误——"

哈利难以置信地看着她。

"一个挺可爱的人犯了错误?她把我们全都出卖了,其中也包括你!"

"嗯……我们不是都没事吗?"秋·张辩解道,"你知道,她妈妈在魔法部工作,对她来说实在太难——"

"罗恩的爸爸也在魔法部工作!"哈利恼火地说,"而你也许没注意到,他的脸上可没写着告密生——"

"赫敏·格兰杰那个鬼把戏太可恶了,"秋·张不高兴地说,"她应该告诉我们她给那份名单施过咒语——"

"我倒认为那是个很高明的主意。"哈利冷冷地说。秋·张满脸通红,眼睛变得更亮了。

"噢,对啦,我忘了——当然了,那是亲爱的赫敏的主意——"

"别又哭鼻子。"哈利警告说。

"我刚才可没想哭!"她喊道。

"是啊……哈……很好,"哈利说,"眼前我要应付的事情够多的了。"

"那就去应付吧!"秋·张怒气冲冲地说,猛一转身,昂首阔步地走开了。

哈利气鼓鼓地走下通向斯内普地下教室的台阶,凭自己的经验,他很清楚如果自己到了那里还在生气,斯内普会更容易看透他的思想,可是在到达斯内普的门口以前,他一直在想应该和秋·张多讲几件玛丽埃塔的事情,除此以外,他什么都顾不上去想。

"你迟到了,波特。"哈利关上身后的门时,斯内普冷若冰霜地说。

斯内普背对哈利站着,正像往常一样把自己的某些思想抽出来,小心地放进邓布利多的冥想盆里。他把最后一缕银色物质加到了石盆里,转过身面对着哈利。

"那么,"他说,"你已经练习过了?"

"是的。"哈利撒了个谎,小心地望着斯内普那张桌子的一条腿。

"好吧,我们马上就能看出真假,对吗?"斯内普拿腔拿调地说,"拿出魔杖,波特。"

CHAPTER TWENTY-EIGHT   Snape's Worst Memory

Harry moved into his usual position, facing Snape with the desk between them. His heart was pumping fast with anger at Cho and anxiety about how much Snape was about to extract from his mind.

'On the count of three then,' said Snape lazily. 'One – two –'

Snape's office door banged open and Draco Malfoy sped in.

'Professor Snape, sir – oh – sorry –'

Malfoy was looking at Snape and Harry in some surprise.

'It's all right, Draco,' said Snape, lowering his wand. 'Potter is here for a little remedial Potions.'

Harry had not seen Malfoy look so gleeful since Umbridge had turned up to inspect Hagrid.

'I didn't know,' he said, leering at Harry, who knew his face was burning. He would have given a great deal to be able to shout the truth at Malfoy – or, even better, to hit him with a good curse.

'Well, Draco, what is it?' asked Snape.

'It's Professor Umbridge, sir – she needs your help,' said Malfoy. 'They've found Montague, sir, he's turned up jammed inside a toilet on the fourth floor.'

'How did he get in there?' demanded Snape.

'I don't know, sir, he's a bit confused.'

'Very well, very well. Potter,' said Snape, 'we shall resume this lesson tomorrow evening.'

He turned and swept from his office. Malfoy mouthed, '*Remedial Potions?*' at Harry behind Snape's back before following him.

Seething, Harry replaced his wand inside his robes and made to leave the room. At least he had twenty-four more hours in which to practise; he knew he ought to feel grateful for the narrow escape, though it was hard that it came at the expense of Malfoy telling the whole school that he needed remedial Potions.

He was at the office door when he saw it: a patch of shivering light dancing on the doorframe. He stopped, and stood looking at it, reminded of something ... then he remembered: it was a little like the lights he had seen in his dream last night, the lights in the second room he had walked through on his journey through the Department of Mysteries.

He turned around. The light was coming from the Pensieve sitting on

第28章 斯内普最痛苦的记忆

哈利走到老位置上，隔着桌子面对斯内普。他仍然在生秋·张的气，而且还担心斯内普看透自己的心思，所以心里扑通扑通跳得很快。

"那就数到三吧，"斯内普慢条斯理地说，"一——二——"

斯内普办公室的门砰的一声开了，德拉科·马尔福快步走了进来。

"斯内普教授，先生——哦——对不起——"

马尔福有几分惊讶地望着斯内普和哈利。

"没关系，德拉科，"斯内普说着垂下魔杖，"波特在补习一些魔药课。"

自从那次乌姆里奇突然袭击、审查海格之后，哈利还从没见过马尔福显得这么开心。

"我不知道这件事。"马尔福说，斜眼看着哈利，哈利感到自己脸上火辣辣的。他真愿意付出巨大的代价，只要能够向马尔福大声说出事实真相——也许，更好的办法是，用一个厉害的咒语打中他。

"那么，德拉科，有什么事吗？"斯内普问道。

"是乌姆里奇教授，先生——她需要你帮个忙。"马尔福说，"他们找到蒙太了，先生，他在五楼的一个马桶里被卡住了。"

"他怎么到那里去了？"斯内普问道。

"我不知道，先生，他有些昏头昏脑的。"

"很好，很好。波特，"斯内普说，"我们明天晚上再接着上这一课。"

他转身大模大样地离开了办公室。马尔福在斯内普背后用口形对哈利不出声地说："补习魔药课？"然后跟了上去。

哈利怒气冲冲地把魔杖放回长袍里，想要离开这间屋子。至少他又多出二十四个小时可以来进行练习了；他知道自己应该为侥幸逃脱感到庆幸，但他付出的沉重代价是马尔福告诉全校同学哈利需要补习魔药课。

他在办公室门口看到：一块颤动的光斑正在门框上跳跃。他停下脚步，站在那里望着它，想起了什么事情……他记起来了：这有点像他昨天晚上在梦中看到过的那些光斑，当他穿过神秘事务司时，那些光斑就出现在他走过的第二间屋子里。

他转过身。这块光斑是从摆在斯内普桌子上的冥想盆里发出来

CHAPTER TWENTY-EIGHT — Snape's Worst Memory

Snape's desk. The silver-white contents were ebbing and swirling within. Snape's thoughts ... things he did not want Harry to see if he broke through Snape's defences accidentally ...

Harry gazed at the Pensieve, curiosity welling inside him ... what was it that Snape was so keen to hide from Harry?

The silvery lights shivered on the wall ... Harry took two steps towards the desk, thinking hard. Could it possibly be information about the Department of Mysteries that Snape was determined to keep from him?

Harry looked over his shoulder, his heart now pumping harder and faster than ever. How long would it take Snape to release Montague from the toilet? Would he come straight back to his office afterwards, or accompany Montague to the hospital wing? Surely the latter ... Montague was Captain of the Slytherin Quidditch team, Snape would want to make sure he was all right.

Harry walked the remaining few feet to the Pensieve and stood over it, gazing into its depths. He hesitated, listening, then pulled out his wand again. The office and the corridor beyond were completely silent. He gave the contents of the Pensieve a small prod with the end of his wand.

The silvery stuff within began to swirl very fast. Harry leaned forwards over it and saw that it had become transparent. He was, once again, looking down into a room as though through a circular window in the ceiling ... in fact, unless he was much mistaken, he was looking down into the Great Hall.

His breath was actually fogging the surface of Snape's thoughts ... his brain seemed to be in limbo ... it would be insane to do the thing he was so strongly tempted to do ... he was trembling ... Snape could be back at any moment ... but Harry thought of Cho's anger, of Malfoy's jeering face, and a reckless daring seized him.

He took a great gulp of breath, and plunged his face into the surface of Snape's thoughts. At once, the floor of the office lurched, tipping Harry head-first into the Pensieve ...

He was falling through cold blackness, spinning furiously as he went, and then —

He was standing in the middle of the Great Hall, but the four house tables were gone. Instead, there were more than a hundred smaller tables, all facing the same way, at each of which sat a student, head bent low, scribbling on a roll of parchment. The only sound was the scratching of quills and the occasional rustle as somebody adjusted their parchment. It was clearly exam time.

第28章 斯内普最痛苦的记忆

的。冥想盆里银白色的物质正在旋转着下沉。那是斯内普的思想……如果哈利意外地突破了斯内普的防御，斯内普不想让哈利看到一些事情……

哈利注视着冥想盆，心中涌起一阵阵好奇……斯内普这样小心瞒着哈利的到底是什么呢？

银光在墙上颤动……哈利朝桌子迈了两步，用心地思考着。那会不会是斯内普决定瞒住他的，关于神秘事务司的事情呢？

哈利回头看了看，一颗心从未像现在跳得这么猛、这么快。斯内普把蒙太从马桶里解救出来要花多长时间呢？他会直接返回自己的办公室，还是会护送蒙太去校医院呢？当然是后者……蒙太是斯莱特林魁地奇队的队长，斯内普肯定想确保他没问题。

哈利朝冥想盆跨出最后几步，站在盆边俯视着盆底。他犹豫了一下，听了听，然后抽出魔杖。办公室和外面的走廊十分安静。他用魔杖尖轻轻戳了一下冥想盆里的物质。

盆里的银色物体开始飞快地旋转起来。哈利朝它俯下身，看到它变得透明了。他好像在通过一个圆形的天窗朝一间屋子里看。这已经是第二回了……假如他的判断没有出大错的话，那么他实际上正在俯视着礼堂。

他的呼吸给斯内普的思想表面蒙上了雾气……他觉得自己进退两难……他忍不住想做一件事，但那样太不理智……他颤抖起来……斯内普随时都可能回来……但是哈利想起了秋·张的怒气，想起了马尔福嘲笑的表情，一种鲁莽的勇气控制了他。

他吸了一大口气，把脸颊埋进了斯内普的思想。办公室的地板立刻倾侧过来，使哈利头朝下翻进了冥想盆……

他在一片冰冷的黑暗中飞快地旋转着向下坠落，然后——

他站在礼堂中央，可是四张学院桌不见了。取而代之的是一百多张面对同一方向的小桌子，每张桌旁都坐着一个学生，低着头在一卷羊皮纸上匆匆书写。只能听见羽毛笔的嚓嚓声，偶尔也会响起某人调整自己的羊皮纸时发出的沙沙声。这显然是在进行考试。

CHAPTER TWENTY-EIGHT   Snape's Worst Memory

Sunshine was streaming through the high windows on to the bent heads, which shone chestnut and copper and gold in the bright light. Harry looked around carefully. Snape had to be here somewhere ... this was *his* memory ...

And there he was, at a table right behind Harry. Harry stared. Snape-the-teenager had a stringy, pallid look about him, like a plant kept in the dark. His hair was lank and greasy and was flopping on to the table, his hooked nose barely half an inch from the surface of the parchment as he scribbled. Harry moved around behind Snape and read the heading of the examination paper: DEFENCE AGAINST THE DARK ARTS – ORDINARY WIZARDING LEVEL.

So Snape had to be fifteen or sixteen, around Harry's own age. His hand was flying across the parchment; he had written at least a foot more than his closest neighbours, and yet his writing was minuscule and cramped.

'Five more minutes!'

The voice made Harry jump. Turning, he saw the top of Professor Flitwick's head moving between the desks a short distance away.

Professor Flitwick was walking past a boy with untidy black hair ... very untidy black hair ...

Harry moved so quickly that, had he been solid, he would have knocked desks flying. Instead he seemed to slide, dreamlike, across two aisles and up a third. The back of the black-haired boy's head drew nearer and ... he was straightening up now, putting down his quill, pulling his roll of parchment towards him so as to reread what he had written ...

Harry stopped in front of the desk and gazed down at his fifteen-year-old father.

Excitement exploded in the pit of his stomach: it was as though he was looking at himself but with deliberate mistakes. James's eyes were hazel, his nose was slightly longer than Harry's and there was no scar on his forehead, but they had the same thin face, same mouth, same eyebrows; James's hair stuck up at the back exactly as Harry's did, his hands could have been Harry's and Harry could tell that, when James stood up, they would be within an inch of each other in height.

James yawned hugely and rumpled up his hair, making it even messier than it had been. Then, with a glance towards Professor Flitwick, he turned in his seat and grinned at a boy sitting four seats behind him.

第28章 斯内普最痛苦的记忆

阳光穿过高大的窗户,照射在那些低下去的脑袋上,在明亮的光线中,那些脑袋映现出灰褐色、红棕色和金色的光泽。哈利仔细地四下里看了看。斯内普一定就在这里的什么地方……这是他的记忆……

他在那里,就在哈利身后的一张桌子旁。哈利注视着他。十几岁的斯内普显得瘦长而结实,但脸色苍白,就像一株一直生长在黑暗中的植物。他的长发平直油腻,垂荡在桌子上,当他匆忙地书写时,他那只鹰钩鼻离羊皮纸几乎不到半英寸。哈利绕到斯内普背后,看了看试卷上的标题:**黑魔法防御术——普通巫师等级**。

这么说,斯内普一定是十五六岁,跟哈利现在的年龄差不多。那只手在羊皮纸上飞快地左右移动;他比身旁离他最近的那几个人至少多写了一英尺,而且他的字迹又小又密。

"还有五分钟!"

这个声音吓了哈利一跳。他转过身,看见弗立维教授的头顶正在不远处的桌子间移动。弗立维教授从一个长着乱蓬蓬黑头发的男生旁边走过……非常凌乱的黑发……

哈利移动得非常快,如果他有实在的形体,那他准会撞飞几张桌子。然而他好像是在滑行,就像梦中一样,横穿两条过道,顺着第三条过道向前滑去。那个黑发男生的后脑勺离得越来越近了,而且……他现在正直起身体,放下羽毛笔,把那卷羊皮纸拉向身前,好重新读一读自己写下的答案……

哈利停在这张桌子前,低头注视着十五岁时的父亲。

他的心窝里迸发出一阵兴奋:就像在看着一个有点走样的自己。詹姆的眼睛是浅褐色的,鼻子比哈利稍稍长一些,前额上没有伤疤,但是他们俩都长着一样的瘦削面孔,一样的嘴巴,一样的眉毛;詹姆的头发跟哈利的完全相同,也是在脑后支棱着,他的两只手简直就是哈利的手。哈利还能看出,如果詹姆站起来,他们俩的身高相差不会超过一英寸。

詹姆打了个大哈欠,揉了揉自己的头发,把它们弄得比刚才还要凌乱。然后,他朝弗立维教授瞥了一眼,接着在座位上转过身,向身后第四个座位上的男生咧嘴笑了笑。

CHAPTER TWENTY-EIGHT — Snape's Worst Memory

With another shock of excitement, Harry saw Sirius give James the thumbs-up. Sirius was lounging in his chair at his ease, tilting it back on two legs. He was very good-looking; his dark hair fell into his eyes with a sort of casual elegance neither James's nor Harry's could ever have achieved, and a girl sitting behind him was eyeing him hopefully, though he didn't seem to have noticed. And two seats along from this girl – Harry's stomach gave another pleasurable squirm – was Remus Lupin. He looked rather pale and peaky (was the full moon approaching?) and was absorbed in the exam: as he reread his answers, he scratched his chin with the end of his quill, frowning slightly.

So that meant Wormtail had to be around here somewhere, too ... and sure enough, Harry spotted him within seconds: a small, mousy-haired boy with a pointed nose. Wormtail looked anxious; he was chewing his fingernails, staring down at his paper, scuffing the ground with his toes. Every now and then he glanced hopefully at his neighbour's paper. Harry stared at Wormtail for a moment, then back at James, who was now doodling on a bit of scrap parchment. He had drawn a Snitch and was now tracing the letters 'L.E.'. What did they stand for?

'Quills down, please!' squeaked Professor Flitwick. 'That means you too, Stebbins! Please remain seated while I collect your parchment! *Accio!*'

Over a hundred rolls of parchment zoomed into the air and into Professor Flitwick's outstretched arms, knocking him backwards off his feet. Several people laughed. A couple of students at the front desks got up, took hold of Professor Flitwick beneath the elbows and lifted him back on to his feet.

'Thank you ... thank you,' panted Professor Flitwick. 'Very well, everybody, you're free to go!'

Harry looked down at his father, who had hastily crossed out the 'L.E.' he had been embellishing, jumped to his feet, stuffed his quill and the exam paper into his bag, which he slung over his back, and stood waiting for Sirius to join him.

Harry looked around and glimpsed Snape a short way away, moving between the tables towards the doors to the Entrance Hall, still absorbed in his own exam paper. Round-shouldered yet angular, he walked in a twitchy manner that recalled a spider, and his oily hair was jumping about his face.

第28章 斯内普最痛苦的记忆

又是一阵兴奋冲击着哈利,他看到小天狼星向詹姆跷起了大拇指。小天狼星懒洋洋地靠在椅子上,显得很自在,他的身体向后仰着,只用椅子的两条腿着地。他非常英俊,黑色的头发垂在眼前,不经意间带出几分典雅,不管是詹姆的头发还是哈利的头发,可从来都没有这份典雅。一个坐在小天狼星身后的女生正满怀期待地注视着他,可他好像没有注意到。在这个女生所在的那一排,隔着两个座位——哈利高兴得胃里又是一阵蠕动——是莱姆斯·卢平。他显得十分苍白、憔悴(是不是快到月圆的日子了?),正全神贯注地投入考试:他重新读了读自己的答案,用羽毛笔的笔头搔着下巴,微微皱着眉头。

这样看来,虫尾巴一定也在附近的什么地方……果然,哈利片刻之间就发现了他:那个体形矮小、长着灰褐色头发的尖鼻子男生。虫尾巴显得有些焦虑,他啃着手指甲,低头盯着自己的试卷,脚尖在地上蹭来蹭去。他还时不时满怀希望地瞟一眼邻桌学生的试卷。哈利盯着虫尾巴看了一会儿,然后又把目光转向了詹姆,现在他正在一小块羊皮纸上随手乱涂乱画。他已经画好了一个金色飞贼,正描画着"L.E."这两个字母。它们代表什么意思呢?

"请停笔!"弗立维教授尖声说,"也包括你,斯特宾斯!在我收羊皮纸的时候,请留在座位上!飞来!"

一百多卷羊皮纸猛地腾空而起,飞进弗立维教授伸出的双臂中,把他撞倒在地上。有些人笑了起来。几个坐在前排桌子旁的学生起身托住弗立维教授的两只胳膊,把他扶了起来。

"谢谢你们……谢谢你们。"弗立维教授气喘吁吁地说,"很好,各位,你们可以走了!"

哈利低头看着自己的父亲,只见他匆匆涂掉了自己刚才一直在修饰的两个字母"L.E.",跳起来把羽毛笔和试卷塞进书包,把书包往肩膀上一甩,站在那里等着小天狼星过来跟他会合。

哈利环顾四周,瞥见斯内普就在不远处,他在两排桌子之间朝通往门厅的大门走去,仍全神贯注地盯着自己的试卷。他拱背曲肩,动作僵硬,那种抽筋似的步伐让人想起了蜘蛛,油腻腻的头发在脸旁跳动。

CHAPTER TWENTY-EIGHT Snape's Worst Memory

A gang of chattering girls separated Snape from James, Sirius and Lupin, and by planting himself in their midst, Harry managed to keep Snape in sight while straining his ears to catch the voices of James and his friends.

'Did you like question ten, Moony?' asked Sirius as they emerged into the Entrance Hall.

'Loved it,' said Lupin briskly. '*Give five signs that identify the werewolf.* Excellent question.'

'D'you think you managed to get all the signs?' said James in tones of mock concern.

'Think I did,' said Lupin seriously, as they joined the crowd thronging around the front doors eager to get out into the sunlit grounds. 'One: he's sitting on my chair. Two: he's wearing my clothes. Three: his name's Remus Lupin.'

Wormtail was the only one who didn't laugh.

'I got the snout shape, the pupils of the eyes and the tufted tail,' he said anxiously, 'but I couldn't think what else –'

'How thick are you, Wormtail?' said James impatiently. 'You run round with a werewolf once a month –'

'Keep your voice down,' implored Lupin.

Harry looked anxiously behind him again. Snape remained close by, still buried in his exam questions – but this was Snape's memory and Harry was sure that if Snape chose to wander off in a different direction once outside in the grounds, he, Harry, would not be able to follow James any further. To his intense relief, however, when James and his three friends strode off down the lawn towards the lake, Snape followed, still poring over the exam paper and apparently with no fixed idea of where he was going. By keeping a little ahead of him, Harry managed to maintain a close watch on James and the others.

'Well, I thought that paper was a piece of cake,' he heard Sirius say. 'I'll be surprised if I don't get "Outstanding" on it at least.'

'Me too,' said James. He put his hand in his pocket and took out a struggling Golden Snitch.

'Where'd you get that?'

'Nicked it,' said James casually. He started playing with the Snitch, allowing it to fly as much as a foot away before seizing it again; his reflexes

第28章 斯内普最痛苦的记忆

一群叽叽喳喳的女生把斯内普跟詹姆、小天狼星和卢平他们隔开了，哈利把自己安插在他们之间，设法不让斯内普脱离自己的视野，同时竖起耳朵倾听詹姆和他的朋友们的对话。

"你喜欢第十题吗，月亮脸？"他们进入门厅后，小天狼星问道。

"太喜欢了，"卢平轻快地说，"举出五种识别狼人的征象。真是好题目。"

"你觉得你能举出所有的征象吗？"詹姆装出担心的口气说。

"我想可以，"卢平一本正经地说，这时人们在前门挤成了一团，急着到外面阳光照耀的场地上去，他们也走进了人群，"第一：他坐在我的座位上。第二：他穿着我的衣服。第三：他的名字叫莱姆斯·卢平。"

只有虫尾巴没有笑。

"我写上了口鼻的形状、眼睛的瞳孔和呈簇状的尾巴，"他焦虑不安地说，"但是我想不起来其他——"

"你怎么这么笨哪，虫尾巴？"詹姆不耐烦地说，"你每个月都要跟一个狼人到处跑上一回——"

"你小声点儿。"卢平恳求道。

哈利不放心地又看了看后面。斯内普仍旧在不远处，还在埋头看着自己的考试题目——不过这是斯内普的记忆，哈利能肯定，要是斯内普到了外面的场地上决定去别的方向溜达溜达，他——哈利，就没办法再跟着詹姆往前走了。不过，让他长长松了一口气的是，当詹姆和自己的三个朋友大步跨过草地、顺坡而下朝湖边走去时，还在钻研试卷的斯内普跟了上去，他显然没有确定自己要去哪里。哈利一直在斯内普前面不远的地方，设法紧紧地盯住詹姆和其他人。

"哼，我觉得那些试题是小菜一碟，"他听到小天狼星说，"我至少也能考个'优秀'，不然才怪呢。"

"我也是。"詹姆说。他把一只手伸进口袋，掏出了一个正在挣扎的金色飞贼。

"你从哪儿弄来的？"

"偷来的。"詹姆漫不经心地说。他开始耍弄那个飞贼，让它飞到差不多一英尺外，然后再抓住它；他的反应能力出色极了。虫尾巴敬

CHAPTER TWENTY-EIGHT   Snape's Worst Memory

were excellent. Wormtail watched him in awe.

They stopped in the shade of the very same beech tree on the edge of the lake where Harry, Ron and Hermione had once spent a Sunday finishing their homework, and threw themselves down on the grass. Harry looked over his shoulder yet again and saw, to his delight, that Snape had settled himself on the grass in the dense shadow of a clump of bushes. He was as deeply immersed in the O.W.L. paper as ever, which left Harry free to sit down on the grass between the beech and the bushes and watch the foursome under the tree. The sunlight was dazzling on the smooth surface of the lake, on the bank of which the group of laughing girls who had just left the Great Hall were sitting, with their shoes and socks off, cooling their feet in the water.

Lupin had pulled out a book and was reading. Sirius stared around at the students milling over the grass, looking rather haughty and bored, but very handsomely so. James was still playing with the Snitch, letting it zoom further and further away, almost escaping but always grabbed at the last second. Wormtail was watching him with his mouth open. Every time James made a particularly difficult catch, Wormtail gasped and applauded. After five minutes of this, Harry wondered why James didn't tell Wormtail to get a grip on himself, but James seemed to be enjoying the attention. Harry noticed that his father had a habit of rumpling up his hair as though to keep it from getting too tidy, and he also kept looking over at the girls by the water's edge.

'Put that away, will you,' said Sirius finally, as James made a fine catch and Wormtail let out a cheer, 'before Wormtail wets himself with excitement.'

Wormtail turned slightly pink, but James grinned.

'If it bothers you,' he said, stuffing the Snitch back in his pocket. Harry had the distinct impression that Sirius was the only one for whom James would have stopped showing off.

'I'm bored,' said Sirius. 'Wish it was full moon.'

'You might,' said Lupin darkly from behind his book. 'We've still got Transfiguration, if you're bored you could test me. Here ...' and he held out his book.

But Sirius snorted. 'I don't need to look at that rubbish, I know it all.'

'This'll liven you up, Padfoot,' said James quietly. 'Look who it is ...'

第28章 斯内普最痛苦的记忆

畏地看着他。

他们停在湖边那棵山毛榉树的树荫里，然后趴在草地上闲聊。就在同一棵树下，哈利、罗恩和赫敏曾经花了一个星期天写完作业。哈利又回头瞧了瞧，他高兴地看见，在灌木丛浓密的阴影下，斯内普已经坐在了草地上。跟刚才一样，他还在潜心钻研O.W.L.考试的试卷，于是哈利可以自由自在地坐在山毛榉树和灌木丛之间的草地上，望着树底下的那四个人。耀眼的阳光照射在平静的湖面上，照射在岸边，那里坐着一群刚从礼堂里出来的女生，她们欢笑着，脱下了鞋袜，把双脚浸在湖水中凉快着。

卢平抽出一本书，开始阅读。小天狼星盯着周围那些在草地上转悠的学生，他的神色很高傲、很厌倦，不过这样也显得非常帅气。詹姆还在耍弄那只飞贼，让它蹿得越来越远，几乎都要逃脱了，但是他总能在最后一刻一把抓住它。虫尾巴看着他，嘴巴都合不拢了。每当詹姆做出难度极高的动作擒住飞贼时，虫尾巴都会喘着大气拍手喝彩。就这样过去了五分钟，哈利不明白，詹姆为什么不让虫尾巴自己也来抓一抓飞贼，但是詹姆好像很享受被人关注的乐趣。哈利注意到，自己的父亲有揉乱头发的习惯，他好像始终不想让头发太整齐，而且他还老是望着水边的那些女生。

"把那玩意儿收起来吧，行吗？"在詹姆做了个漂亮的抓捕动作，虫尾巴发出了一声喝彩后，小天狼星终于开口说，"不然虫尾巴要激动得尿裤子了。"

虫尾巴微微有点脸红，可詹姆却咧开嘴笑了。

"打扰你了。"他说着把飞贼塞回了衣袋。哈利明显地感觉到，詹姆只有在小天狼星面前才会停止炫耀。

"我觉得真无聊，"小天狼星说，"今天要是满月就好了。"

"你没问题，"卢平在书本后面阴沉地说，"我们还要考变形术，要是你觉得无聊，你可以考考我。给你……"他把自己的那本书递了过去。

可是小天狼星用鼻子哼了一声："我用不着看这些垃圾，我全都知道。"

"这个能让你打起精神，大脚板，"詹姆低声说，"看看那是谁……"

1073

CHAPTER TWENTY-EIGHT Snape's Worst Memory

Sirius's head turned. He became very still, like a dog that has scented a rabbit.

'Excellent,' he said softly. '*Snivellus.*'

Harry turned to see what Sirius was looking at.

Snape was on his feet again, and was stowing the O.W.L. paper in his bag. As he left the shadows of the bushes and set off across the grass, Sirius and James stood up.

Lupin and Wormtail remained sitting: Lupin was still staring down at his book, though his eyes were not moving and a faint frown line had appeared between his eyebrows; Wormtail was looking from Sirius and James to Snape with a look of avid anticipation on his face.

'All right, Snivellus?' said James loudly.

Snape reacted so fast it was as though he had been expecting an attack: dropping his bag, he plunged his hand inside his robes and his wand was halfway into the air when James shouted, '*Expelliarmus!*'

Snape's wand flew twelve feet into the air and fell with a little thud in the grass behind him. Sirius let out a bark of laughter.

'*Impedimenta!*' he said, pointing his wand at Snape, who was knocked off his feet halfway through a dive towards his own fallen wand.

Students all around had turned to watch. Some of them had got to their feet and were edging nearer. Some looked apprehensive, others entertained.

Snape lay panting on the ground. James and Sirius advanced on him, wands raised, James glancing over his shoulder at the girls at the water's edge as he went. Wormtail was on his feet now, watching hungrily, edging around Lupin to get a clearer view.

'How'd the exam go, Snivelly?' said James.

'I was watching him, his nose was touching the parchment,' said Sirius viciously. 'There'll be great grease marks all over it, they won't be able to read a word.'

Several people watching laughed; Snape was clearly unpopular. Wormtail sniggered shrilly. Snape was trying to get up, but the jinx was still operating on him; he was struggling, as though bound by invisible ropes.

'You – wait,' he panted, staring up at James with an expression of purest loathing, 'you – wait!'

第28章 斯内普最痛苦的记忆

小天狼星扭过头。他突然变得一动不动了，就像一条嗅到了兔子的狗。

"太棒了，"他轻轻地说，"鼻涕精。"

哈利转过身去瞧小天狼星正在看什么。

斯内普又站了起来，把O.W.L.考试的试卷塞进书包里。当他离开灌木丛的阴影、想要穿过草地时，小天狼星和詹姆站了起来。

卢平和虫尾巴坐着没动：卢平还在低头盯着自己的书，但是他的眼睛没有移动，而且微微皱起了眉毛；虫尾巴看了看小天狼星和詹姆，又看了看斯内普，脸上显出一种狂热的期待。

"还好吗，鼻涕精？"詹姆大声说。

斯内普的反应真快，就像他已经料到会有一场攻击似的：他甩掉书包，一只手猛地探进长袍，可他的魔杖才举到一半，詹姆就吼道："除你武器！"

斯内普的魔杖朝空中飞上去十二英尺高，噗的一声轻轻落在他身后的草丛里。小天狼星短促清脆地笑了一声。

"障碍重重！"他说着用魔杖对准了斯内普，斯内普正扑向自己失落的魔杖，可在半路上就被撞倒了。

四周的学生都转身望着他们。一些人站起身，慢慢地凑拢过来。有些人露出疑惧的表情，另一些却觉得挺好玩儿。

斯内普气喘吁吁地躺在地上。詹姆和小天狼星向他步步逼近，扬起了魔杖，詹姆一边走，一边回头瞥着水边那些女生。虫尾巴现在站了起来，兴致勃勃地看着，并朝旁边挪了挪，避开了卢平，好看得更清楚些。

"考得怎么样啊，鼻涕精？"詹姆问。

"我盯着他呢，他的鼻子都碰到羊皮纸了。"小天狼星刻薄地说，"羊皮纸上肯定全都是大块的油渍，他们一个字儿别想看清楚。"

几个看热闹的人大声笑了起来；斯内普的人缘显然不怎么样。虫尾巴尖声地哧哧笑着。斯内普很想站起来，但是咒语还对他起着作用；他挣扎着，就像被无形的绳索捆住了似的。

"你——等着吧，"他喘息着，抬眼瞪着詹姆，脸上带着十足的憎恶表情，"你——等着吧！"

CHAPTER TWENTY-EIGHT   Snape's Worst Memory

'Wait for what?' said Sirius coolly. 'What're you going to do, Snivelly, wipe your nose on us?'

Snape let out a stream of mixed swear words and hexes, but with his wand ten feet away nothing happened.

'Wash out your mouth,' said James coldly. '*Scourgify!*'

Pink soap bubbles streamed from Snape's mouth at once; the froth was covering his lips, making him gag, choking him –

'Leave him ALONE!'

James and Sirius looked round. James's free hand immediately jumped to his hair.

It was one of the girls from the lake edge. She had thick, dark red hair that fell to her shoulders, and startlingly green almond-shaped eyes – Harry's eyes.

Harry's mother.

'All right, Evans?' said James, and the tone of his voice was suddenly pleasant, deeper, more mature.

'Leave him alone,' Lily repeated. She was looking at James with every sign of great dislike. 'What's he done to you?'

'Well,' said James, appearing to deliberate the point, 'it's more the fact that he exists, if you know what I mean ...'

Many of the surrounding students laughed, Sirius and Wormtail included, but Lupin, still apparently intent on his book, didn't, and nor did Lily.

'You think you're funny,' she said coldly. 'But you're just an arrogant, bullying toerag, Potter. Leave him *alone*.'

'I will if you go out with me, Evans,' said James quickly. 'Go on ... go out with me and I'll never lay a wand on old Snivelly again.'

Behind him, the Impediment Jinx was wearing off. Snape was beginning to inch towards his fallen wand, spitting out soapsuds as he crawled.

'I wouldn't go out with you if it was a choice between you and the giant squid,' said Lily.

'Bad luck, Prongs,' said Sirius briskly, and turned back to Snape. 'OI!'

第28章 斯内普最痛苦的记忆

"等什么呀?"小天狼星冷冷地说,"你想怎么样啊,鼻涕精,往我们身上蹭鼻涕吗?"

一连串夹杂在一起的粗话和恶咒从斯内普嘴里冒了出来,但是他的魔杖在十英尺以外,所以什么事也没发生。

"给你洗干净嘴巴,"詹姆冷冰冰地说,"清理一新!"

斯内普的嘴里立刻吐出了粉红色的肥皂泡;他的嘴唇上沾满了泡沫,他想呕吐,憋得透不过气来——

"放开他!"

詹姆和小天狼星扭头望去。詹姆的另一只手立即飞快地伸向自己的头发。

那是一个从湖边走来的女生。她有一头浓密的深红色长发,一直垂到肩膀上,还有一双绿得出奇的杏眼——哈利的眼睛。

哈利的母亲。

"你好吗,伊万斯?"詹姆说,他的语调突然友好起来,变得更深沉更成熟了。

"放开他。"莉莉重复道,她看着詹姆,露出极为厌恶的表情,"他怎么惹你了?"

"这个嘛,"詹姆说,摆出一副正在苦苦考虑要点的样子,"他根本就不应该存在,但愿你明白我的意思……"

许多围观的学生大声笑起来,小天狼星和虫尾巴也笑了,但是好像还在专注读书的卢平却没笑,莉莉也没有笑。

"你觉得自己挺风趣,"她冷冷地说,"可你只不过是个傲慢无礼、欺负弱小的下三烂,波特。放开他。"

"要是你愿意跟我好,我就放了他,伊万斯,"詹姆马上说,"说吧……跟我一起出去玩玩,我就再也不会用魔杖动老鼻涕精一根汗毛。"

在他身后,障碍咒的效力正在逐渐减弱。斯内普开始朝自己失落的魔杖慢慢挪动,他一边爬一边呕吐出带泡泡的肥皂水。

"就算是要在你和巨乌贼之间选一个,我也不会和你出去玩。"莉莉说。

"走背字了吧,尖头叉子。"小天狼星快活地说,朝斯内普转过身,"哎呀!"

CHAPTER TWENTY-EIGHT   Snape's Worst Memory

But too late; Snape had directed his wand straight at James; there was a flash of light and a gash appeared on the side of James's face, spattering his robes with blood. James whirled about: a second flash of light later, Snape was hanging upside-down in the air, his robes falling over his head to reveal skinny, pallid legs and a pair of greying underpants.

Many people in the small crowd cheered; Sirius, James and Wormtail roared with laughter.

Lily, whose furious expression had twitched for an instant as though she was going to smile, said, 'Let him down!'

'Certainly,' said James and he jerked his wand upwards; Snape fell into a crumpled heap on the ground. Disentangling himself from his robes he got quickly to his feet, wand up, but Sirius said, '*Petrificus Totalus!*' and Snape keeled over again, rigid as a board.

'LEAVE HIM ALONE!' Lily shouted. She had her own wand out now. James and Sirius eyed it warily.

'Ah, Evans, don't make me hex you,' said James earnestly.

'Take the curse off him, then!'

James sighed deeply, then turned to Snape and muttered the counter-curse.

'There you go,' he said, as Snape struggled to his feet. 'You're lucky Evans was here, Snivellus –'

'I don't need help from filthy little Mudbloods like her!'

Lily blinked.

'Fine,' she said coolly. 'I won't bother in future. And I'd wash your pants if I were you, *Snivellus*.'

'Apologise to Evans!' James roared at Snape, his wand pointed threateningly at him.

'I don't want *you* to make him apologise,' Lily shouted, rounding on James. 'You're as bad as he is.'

'What?' yelped James. 'I'd NEVER call you a – you-know-what!'

'Messing up your hair because you think it looks cool to look like you've just got off your broomstick, showing off with that stupid Snitch, walking down corridors and hexing anyone who annoys you just because you can – I'm surprised your broomstick can get off the ground with that fat head on it.

第28章 斯内普最痛苦的记忆

但是太晚了；斯内普已经把魔杖对准了詹姆，一道闪光，詹姆的一侧脸颊上出现了一道深深的伤口，鲜血溅落在他的长袍上。詹姆猛地转身：第二道闪光过后，斯内普被头朝下倒挂在空中，他的长袍垂落下去盖住了脑袋，露出了瘦得皮包骨头的苍白的双腿，还有一条快变成黑色的内裤。

在周围的一小群人里，有许多人在喝彩；小天狼星、詹姆和虫尾巴纵声大笑。

刹那间，莉莉愤怒的表情波动了一下，就像她也要微笑似的，但她说："把他放下来！"

"当然可以。"詹姆说，然后他猛地扬起魔杖；斯内普坠落到地上缩成了一团。他挣开自己的长袍，马上站起来，举起了魔杖，不料小天狼星说了声："统统石化！"斯内普又仰面朝天倒在地上，僵硬得像块木板。

"**放开他！**"莉莉喊道。现在她把自己的魔杖抽了出来。詹姆和小天狼星小心地盯着它。

"哎，伊万斯，别逼我对你施恶咒啊。"詹姆严肃地说。

"那就给他解开咒语！"

詹姆深深地叹了一口气，接着转身面对斯内普，低声说出了破解咒。

"你走吧，"他在斯内普挣扎着站起来时说，"算你走运，伊万斯在这里，鼻涕精——"

"我用不着她这种臭烘烘的小泥巴种来帮忙！"

莉莉眨了眨眼睛。

"很好，"她冷冷地说，"往后我再也不会操这个心了。还有，如果我是你的话，我会洗洗自己的内裤，鼻涕精。"

"向伊万斯道歉！"詹姆朝斯内普吼道，他的魔杖威胁地指着斯内普。

"我用不着你来逼着他道歉。"莉莉转身朝詹姆喊道，"你跟他一样讨厌。"

"什么？"詹姆大声喊道，"我**从来**没说过你是个——你知道是什么！"

"你认为摆出刚从飞天扫帚上下来的样子很酷，所以就把头发弄得乱七八糟，拿着那只傻乎乎的飞贼卖弄，在走廊里碰上谁惹你不高兴就给谁念咒语，就因为你能——我真奇怪，你的扫帚上有那么个大肥

CHAPTER TWENTY-EIGHT   Snape's Worst Memory

You make me SICK.'

She turned on her heel and hurried away.

'Evans!' James shouted after her. 'Hey, EVANS!'

But she didn't look back.

'What is it with her?' said James, trying and failing to look as though this was a throwaway question of no real importance to him.

'Reading between the lines, I'd say she thinks you're a bit conceited, mate,' said Sirius.

'Right,' said James, who looked furious now, 'right –'

There was another flash of light, and Snape was once again hanging upside-down in the air.

'Who wants to see me take off Snivelly's pants?'

But whether James really did take off Snape's pants, Harry never found out. A hand had closed tight over his upper arm, closed with a pincer-like grip. Wincing, Harry looked round to see who had hold of him, and saw, with a thrill of horror, a fully grown, adult-sized Snape standing right beside him, white with rage.

'Having fun?'

Harry felt himself rising into the air; the summer's day evaporated around him; he was floating upwards through icy blackness, Snape's hand still tight upon his upper arm. Then, with a swooping feeling as though he had turned head-over-heels in midair, his feet hit the stone floor of Snape's dungeon and he was standing again beside the Pensieve on Snape's desk in the shadowy, present-day Potion master's study.

'So,' said Snape, gripping Harry's arm so tightly Harry's hand was starting to feel numb. '*So* ... been enjoying yourself, Potter?'

'N-no,' said Harry, trying to free his arm.

It was scary: Snape's lips were shaking, his face was white, his teeth were bared.

'Amusing man, your father, wasn't he?' said Snape, shaking Harry so hard his glasses slipped down his nose.

'I – didn't –'

Snape threw Harry from him with all his might. Harry fell hard on to the dungeon floor.

脑袋居然还能离开地面。你让我**恶心**。"

她猛地一转身，飞快地跑开了。

"伊万斯！"詹姆在她身后喊道，"喂，**伊万斯**！"

可她没有回头。

"她怎么了？"詹姆问。他本想漫不经心地说出这个问题，就像这个问题对他来说无所谓一样，但是他失败了。

"从她话里的言外之意来看，我只能说，她觉得你有点傲慢自大，哥们儿。"小天狼星说。

"好吧，"詹姆说，现在他看上去真的来了火气，"好吧——"

又是一道闪光，斯内普又被头朝下倒挂在空中。

"谁想看看我把鼻涕精的内裤脱下来？"

但是，哈利永远不会知道詹姆是否真的脱下了斯内普的内裤。一只手紧紧抓住了他的上臂，紧得像用钳子夹住一样。哈利退缩着，扭头看是谁抓住了自己，这一看把他吓得哆嗦起来，一个已经长大成人的斯内普就站在他旁边，气得脸色煞白。

"玩得开心吗？"

哈利感到自己在升向空中；他周围的夏日景象消失了；他在冰冷的黑暗中向上飘去，斯内普那只手还在紧紧抓着他的上臂。然后，随着一种急速俯冲的感觉，就像他在半空中翻了个跟头，他的双脚撞在了斯内普地下教室的石头地板上，他又一次站在斯内普桌子上的冥想盆旁，置身于现实中的魔药课老师昏暗的书房里。

"那么，"斯内普说，他用力地抓着哈利的胳膊，哈利感到手开始麻木，"那么……很开心吧，波特？"

"没—没有。"哈利说着，想努力把胳膊挣脱出来。

太吓人了：斯内普双唇颤抖，脸色苍白，露出了牙齿。

"你父亲是个有趣的人，是吧？"斯内普说，使劲地摇晃着哈利，哈利的眼镜都从鼻子上滑落了下去。

"我——没有——"

斯内普使足全身的力气把哈利推了出去。哈利重重地摔在地下教室的地板上。

CHAPTER TWENTY-EIGHT — Snape's Worst Memory

'You will not tell anybody what you saw!' Snape bellowed.

'No,' said Harry, getting to his feet as far from Snape as he could. 'No, of course I w—'

'Get out, get out, I don't want to see you in this office ever again!'

And as Harry hurtled towards the door, a jar of dead cockroaches exploded over his head. He wrenched the door open and flew along the corridor, stopping only when he had put three floors between himself and Snape. There he leaned against the wall, panting, and rubbing his bruised arm.

He had no desire at all to return to Gryffindor Tower so early, nor to tell Ron and Hermione what he had just seen. What was making Harry feel so horrified and unhappy was not being shouted at or having jars thrown at him; it was that he knew how it felt to be humiliated in the middle of a circle of onlookers, knew exactly how Snape had felt as his father had taunted him, and that judging from what he had just seen, his father had been every bit as arrogant as Snape had always told him.

第28章 斯内普最痛苦的记忆

"不准你把看到的事告诉任何人!"斯内普怒吼道。

"不会。"哈利说着站起来,尽量离斯内普远一点儿,"不会,我当然——"

"滚出去,滚出去,我再也不想在这间办公室里看到你!"

当哈利朝门口猛冲过去时,一个盛着死蟑螂的罐子在他头顶上炸裂了。他用力甩开房门,顺着走廊一路飞奔,直到与斯内普隔了三层楼才停下来。他气喘吁吁地靠在墙上,揉搓着那只带瘀伤的胳膊。

他一点儿也不想这么早就回到格兰芬多塔楼,也不想把自己刚才看见的事情告诉罗恩和赫敏。哈利觉得那么恐惧、难过,这并不是因为斯内普冲他大喊大叫,也不是因为斯内普用罐子砸他,而是因为他深知在一群围观者中间受辱是什么滋味,他很清楚斯内普被他的父亲嘲弄时是什么心情。从他刚才的所见所闻来看,他的父亲确实是个傲慢自大的人,跟斯内普一直以来对他讲述的一模一样。

CHAPTER TWENTY-NINE

Careers Advice

'But why haven't you got Occlumency lessons any more?' said Hermione, frowning.

'I've *told* you,' Harry muttered. 'Snape reckons I can carry on by myself now I've got the basics.' 'So you've stopped having funny dreams?' said Hermione sceptically.

'Pretty much,' said Harry, not looking at her.

'Well, I don't think Snape should stop until you're absolutely sure you can control them!' said Hermione indignantly. 'Harry, I think you should go back to him and ask –'

'No,' said Harry forcefully. 'Just drop it, Hermione, OK?'

It was the first day of the Easter holidays and Hermione, as was her custom, had spent a large part of the day drawing up revision timetables for the three of them. Harry and Ron had let her do it; it was easier than arguing with her and, in any case, they might come in useful.

Ron had been startled to discover there were only six weeks left until their exams.

'How can that come as a shock?' Hermione demanded, as she tapped each little square on Ron's timetable with her wand so that it flashed a different colour according to its subject.

'I dunno,' said Ron, 'there's been a lot going on.'

'Well, there you are,' she said, handing him his timetable, 'if you follow that you should do fine.'

Ron looked down it gloomily, but then brightened.

'You've given me an evening off every week!'

'That's for Quidditch practice,' said Hermione.

The smile faded from Ron's face.

'What's the point?' he said. 'We've got about as much chance of winning

第29章

就业指导

"可是你为什么不再上大脑封闭术课了?"赫敏皱着眉头问。

"我跟你说过了,"哈利低声说道,"斯内普认为我已经掌握了基本规则,能够自己往下学了。"

"那么,你不再做怪梦了?"赫敏怀疑地说。

"差不多吧。"哈利躲着她的目光说。

"哼,我认为,在你完全有把握能够控制之前,斯内普不应该停课!"赫敏气愤地说,"哈利,我认为你应该回去找他请求——"

"不。"哈利斩钉截铁地说,"别再说这事儿了,赫敏,好吗?"

这是复活节假日的第一天,赫敏按照惯例,花了大半天时间给他们三人画了复习时间表。哈利和罗恩随她去画,这比跟她争论省事得多,而且,说不定那些时间表会派上用场呢。

罗恩发现离考试只有六个星期时,着实吃了一惊。

"这有什么可吃惊的?"赫敏问道,一边用魔杖敲了敲罗恩时间表上的每个小方块,使它们根据不同的科目闪出不同的颜色。

"不知道,"罗恩说,"最近发生的事情太多了。"

"好了,给你吧,"赫敏说着,把时间表递给罗恩,"只要照着做,就应该没问题。"

罗恩愁眉苦脸地低头看着时间表,突然喜笑颜开了。

"你让我每星期有一个晚上休息!"

"那是有魁地奇训练。"赫敏说。

罗恩脸上的笑容消失了。

"有什么用呢?"他说,"今年我们要想赢得魁地奇杯,就跟我爸

the Quidditch Cup this year as Dad's got of becoming Minister for Magic.'

Hermione said nothing; she was looking at Harry, who was staring blankly at the opposite wall of the common room while Crookshanks pawed at his hand, trying to get his ears scratched.

'What's wrong, Harry?'

'What?' he said quickly. 'Nothing.'

He seized his copy of *Defensive Magical Theory* and pretended to be looking something up in the index. Crookshanks gave him up as a bad job and slunk away under Hermione's chair.

'I saw Cho earlier,' said Hermione tentatively. 'She looked really miserable, too ... have you two had a row again?'

'Wha – oh, yeah, we have,' said Harry, seizing gratefully on the excuse.

'What about?'

'That sneak friend of hers, Marietta,' said Harry.

'Yeah, well, I don't blame you!' said Ron angrily, setting down his revision timetable. 'If it hadn't been for her ...'

Ron went into a rant about Marietta Edgecombe, which Harry found helpful; all he had to do was look angry, nod and say 'Yeah' and 'That's right' whenever Ron drew breath, leaving his mind free to dwell, ever more miserably, on what he had seen in the Pensieve.

He felt as though the memory of it was eating him from inside. He had been so sure his parents were wonderful people that he had never had the slightest difficulty in disbelieving the aspersions Snape cast on his father's character. Hadn't people like Hagrid and Sirius *told* Harry how wonderful his father had been? (*Yeah, well, look what Sirius was like himself,* said a nagging voice inside Harry's head ... *he was as bad, wasn't he?*) Yes, he had once overheard Professor McGonagall saying that his father and Sirius had been troublemakers at school, but she had described them as forerunners of the Weasley twins, and Harry could not imagine Fred and George dangling someone upside-down for the fun of it ... not unless they really loathed them ... perhaps Malfoy, or somebody who really deserved it ...

Harry tried to make a case for Snape having deserved what he had suffered at James's hands: but hadn't Lily asked, 'What's he done to you?' And hadn't James replied, 'It's more the fact that he exists, if you know what I mean.' Hadn't James started it all simply because Sirius had said he was

爸要当魔法部部长一样希望渺茫。"

赫敏什么也没说，她看着哈利，只见他呆呆地望着公共休息室的墙壁，克鲁克山用爪子扒拉着他的手，想让他给它挠挠耳朵。

"怎么啦，哈利？"

"什么？"他赶紧说道，"没什么。"

他一把抓起自己的《魔法防御理论》，假装在索引里查找什么。克鲁克山觉得自己是白费力气，就离开他，钻到了赫敏椅子底下。

"我刚才看见秋·张了，"赫敏试探地说，"她看上去脸色也很糟糕……你们俩又吵架了？"

"什——哦，是啊，吵架了。"哈利说，赶紧抓住这个借口。

"为什么吵呢？"

"还不是为了她那个告密的朋友，玛丽埃塔。"哈利说。

"对，没错，你做得对！"罗恩放下复习时间表，气呼呼地说，"要不是她……"

罗恩开始喋喋不休地大骂玛丽埃塔·艾克莫，哈利觉得这正好帮了他的忙。他只需显出生气的样子，在罗恩喘气的空当点点头，说一声"对啊""没错"就行了，而他的思绪则沉浸在冥想盆里看到的事情中，这使他心情更糟糕了。

这段往事啃噬着他的心灵。他一直那么坚信爸爸妈妈是出类拔萃的人，从不相信斯内普对他爸爸人品的恶意中伤。海格和小天狼星这些人不是对哈利说过他爸爸有多么优秀吗？（是啊，是啊，看看小天狼星自己的那副德性，哈利脑子里一个恼人的声音说……他也好不到哪儿去，不是吗？）不错，他有一次确实听见麦格教授说他爸爸和小天狼星在学校里专门惹是生非，可是麦格教授把他们说成是韦斯莱孪生兄弟的先驱，而哈利无法想象弗雷德和乔治会为了闹着玩儿把人头朝下倒挂起来……除非确实恨之入骨……比如马尔福，或者某个活该受此惩罚的人……

哈利想找出理由证明斯内普活该在詹姆手里遭受那样的折磨。然而，莉莉这样发问："他怎么惹着你们了？"詹姆这样回答，"他根本就不应该存在，但愿你明白我的意思。"仅仅因为小天狼星说了一声无

CHAPTER TWENTY-NINE   Careers Advice

bored? Harry remembered Lupin saying back in Grimmauld Place that Dumbledore had made him prefect in the hope that he would be able to exercise some control over James and Sirius ... but in the Pensieve, he had sat there and let it all happen ...

Harry kept reminding himself that Lily had intervened; his mother had been decent. Yet, the memory of the look on her face as she had shouted at James disturbed him quite as much as anything else; she had clearly loathed James, and Harry simply could not understand how they could have ended up married. Once or twice he even wondered whether James had forced her into it ...

For nearly five years the thought of his father had been a source of comfort, of inspiration. Whenever someone had told him he was like James, he had glowed with pride inside. And now ... now he felt cold and miserable at the thought of him.

The weather grew breezier, brighter and warmer as the Easter holidays passed, but Harry, along with the rest of the fifth- and seventh-years, was trapped inside, revising, traipsing back and forth to the library. Harry pretended his bad mood had no other cause but the approaching exams, and as his fellow Gryffindors were sick of studying themselves, his excuse went unchallenged.

'Harry, I'm talking to you, can you hear me?'

'Huh?'

He looked round. Ginny Weasley, looking very windswept, had joined him at the library table where he had been sitting alone. It was late on Sunday evening: Hermione had gone back to Gryffindor Tower to revise Ancient Runes, and Ron had Quidditch practice.

'Oh, hi,' said Harry, pulling his books towards him. 'How come you're not at practice?'

'It's over,' said Ginny. 'Ron had to take Jack Sloper up to the hospital wing.'

'Why?'

'Well, we're not sure, but we *think* he knocked himself out with his own bat.' She sighed heavily. 'Anyway ... a package just arrived, it's only just got through Umbridge's new screening process.'

She hoisted a box wrapped in brown paper on to the table; it had clearly been unwrapped and carelessly rewrapped. There was a scribbled note across it in red ink, reading:

第29章 就业指导

聊，詹姆就开始了这一切，不是吗？哈利记得卢平在格里莫广场说过，邓布利多选他做级长，就是希望他能对詹姆和小天狼星有所管束……可是在冥想盆里，他只是坐在那儿，袖手旁观……

哈利不断地提醒自己，莉莉出面干涉了。她妈妈是正直的。然而，想起她朝詹姆嚷嚷时脸上的表情，哈利同样也非常烦恼。她显然十分讨厌詹姆，哈利想不明白他们最后怎么会结婚，有一两次他甚至怀疑是詹姆强迫莉莉嫁给了他……

近五年来，哈利一想起爸爸，就能获得安慰和鼓励。每当有人对他说他长得像詹姆，他便会感到由衷的骄傲。然而现在……现在，他想起爸爸，只觉得心里发冷、难受。

复活节的假日一天天过去了，天气越来越晴朗、温暖，和风习习，可是哈利和其他五年级、七年级的同学一起困在屋里，复习功课，一趟趟地跑图书馆。哈利假装自己情绪不好不是别的原因，只是考试临近引起的。格兰芬多的其他同学也对学习产生了厌倦，所以他的说法没有引起怀疑。

"哈利，我在跟你说话呢，你能听见吗？"

"唔？"

哈利回过头来，金妮·韦斯莱已经来到图书馆里他独自孤坐的桌旁，她的头发被风吹得乱蓬蓬的。这是星期天晚上，时间已经很晚。赫敏去格兰芬多塔楼复习古代如尼文，罗恩有魁地奇训练。

"哦，你好，"哈利说着，把书本往跟前拖了拖，"你怎么没参加训练？"

"已经结束了，"金妮说，"罗恩不得不送杰克·斯劳珀去了医院。"

"为什么？"

"唉，我们也不清楚，我们觉得他是被自己的球棒打昏了。"她重重地叹了口气，"不说他了……刚才送来了一个包裹，它好歹通过了乌姆里奇的新审查程序。"

她把一个包着牛皮纸的盒子放在桌上，盒子显然被打开过，又被马马虎虎地重新包上了。上面贴着一张纸条，用红墨水潦草地写着：

CHAPTER TWENTY-NINE   Careers Advice

Inspected and Passed by the Hogwarty High Inquisitor.

'It's Easter eggs from Mum,' said Ginny. 'There's one for you ... there you go.'

She handed him a handsome chocolate egg decorated with small, iced Snitches and, according to the packaging, containing a bag of Fizzing Whizzbees. Harry looked at it for a moment, then, to his horror, felt a lump rise in his throat.

'Are you OK, Harry?' Ginny asked quietly.

'Yeah, I'm fine,' said Harry gruffly. The lump in his throat was painful. He did not understand why an Easter egg should have made him feel like this.

'You seem really down lately,' Ginny persisted. 'You know, I'm sure if you just *talked* to Cho ...'

'It's not Cho I want to talk to,' said Harry brusquely.

'Who is it, then?' asked Ginny.

'I ...'

He glanced around to make quite sure nobody was listening. Madam Pince was several shelves away, stamping out a pile of books for a frantic-looking Hannah Abbott.

'I wish I could talk to Sirius,' he muttered. 'But I know I can't.'

More to give himself something to do than because he really wanted any, Harry unwrapped his Easter egg, broke off a large bit and put it into his mouth.

'Well,' said Ginny slowly, helping herself to a bit of egg, too, 'if you really want to talk to Sirius, I expect we could think of a way to do it.'

'Come on,' said Harry hopelessly. 'With Umbridge policing the fires and reading all our mail?'

'The thing about growing up with Fred and George,' said Ginny thoughtfully, 'is that you sort of start thinking anything's possible if you've got enough nerve.'

Harry looked at her. Perhaps it was the effect of the chocolate – Lupin had always advised eating some after encounters with Dementors – or simply because he had finally spoken aloud the wish that had been burning inside him for a week, but he felt a bit more hopeful.

'WHAT DO YOU THINK YOU ARE DOING?'

'Oh damn,' whispered Ginny, jumping to her feet. 'I forgot –'

第29章 就业指导

经霍格沃茨高级调查官审查通过。

"是妈妈寄来的复活节彩蛋,"金妮说,"有一个是给你的……拿着。"

她递给哈利一个漂亮的巧克力蛋,上面装饰着一些糖霜做的小小的金飞贼,根据包装上的说明,里面还装着一袋滋滋蜜蜂糖。哈利盯着它看了一会儿,惊恐地感觉到喉头变得哽咽了。

"你没事吧,哈利?"金妮小声问。

"没事,我挺好的。"哈利声音沙哑地说。被哽住的喉头很疼。他不明白为什么一个复活节彩蛋会使他感觉这么强烈。

"你最近好像情绪很低落。"金妮追问道,"其实,我相信只要你跟秋·张好好谈谈……"

"我不想跟秋·张谈。"哈利唐突地说。

"那你想跟谁谈?"金妮问。

"我……"

他朝四周望望,确保没有人在偷听。平斯女士与他们隔着几排书架,正在给神情焦虑的汉娜·艾博往一大摞图书上盖章。

"我希望能跟小天狼星谈谈,"他低声说,"可是我知道办不到。"

哈利拆开复活节彩蛋的包装,掰下一大块巧克力放进嘴里,他其实并不想吃,只是为了让自己有点事情做。

"我看,"金妮慢慢地说,一边也给自己掰了一块巧克力,"如果你真的想跟小天狼星谈话,我们倒是可以想一个办法。"

"得了吧,"哈利绝望地说,"有乌姆里奇在那儿监视炉火,查看我们所有的信件呢!"

"跟弗雷德和乔治一起长大有一个好处,"金妮若有所思地说,"就是你会认为,只要有胆量就没有办不成的事。"

哈利看着金妮。兴许是巧克力的效果吧——卢平总是建议在遭遇摄魂怪后吃些巧克力——或者只是因为他终于说出了一星期来折磨他的想法,他觉得心里亮堂了一些。

"你们在这里干什么?"

"哦,该死,"金妮小声说,腾地站了起来,"我忘记了——"

CHAPTER TWENTY-NINE Careers Advice

Madam Pince was swooping down on them, her shrivelled face contorted with rage. '*Chocolate in the library!*' she screamed. 'Out – *out* – OUT!'

And whipping out her wand, she caused Harry's books, bag and ink bottle to chase him and Ginny from the library, whacking them repeatedly over the head as they ran.

As though to underline the importance of their upcoming examinations, a batch of pamphlets, leaflets and notices concerning various wizarding careers appeared on the tables in Gryffindor Tower shortly before the end of the holidays, along with yet another notice on the board, which read:

> CAREERS ADVICE
> All fifth-years are required to attend a short meeting with their Head of House during the first week of the summer term to discuss their future careers. Times of individual appointments are listed below.

Harry looked down the list and found that he was expected in Professor McGonagall's office at half past two on Monday, which would mean missing most of Divination. He and the other fifth-years spent a considerable part of the final weekend of the Easter break reading all the careers information that had been left there for their perusal.

'Well, I don't fancy Healing,' said Ron on the last evening of the holidays. He was immersed in a leaflet that carried the crossed bone-and-wand emblem of St Mungo's on its front. 'It says here you need at least "E" at N.E.W.T. level in Potions, Herbology, Transfiguration, Charms and Defence Against the Dark Arts. I mean ... blimey ... don't want much, do they?'

'Well, it's a very responsible job, isn't it?' said Hermione absently. She was poring over a bright pink and orange leaflet that was headed, 'SO YOU THINK YOU'D LIKE TO WORK IN MUGGLE RELATIONS?' 'You don't seem to need many qualifications to liaise with Muggles; all they want is an O.W.L. in Muggle Studies: *Much more important is your enthusiasm, patience and a good sense of fun!*'

'You'd need more than a good sense of fun to liaise with my uncle,' said Harry darkly. 'Good sense of when to duck, more like.' He was halfway through a pamphlet on wizard banking. 'Listen to this: *Are you seeking a challenging career involving travel, adventure and substantial, danger-related treasure*

第29章 就业指导

平斯女士朝他们俩扑了过来,一张皱巴巴的脸气得都扭曲了。

"在图书馆里吃巧克力!"她嚷道,"出去——出去——**出去**!"

她嗖地抽出魔杖,让哈利的课本、书包和墨水瓶一下下地砸着他和金妮的脑袋,把他们赶出了图书馆。

似乎是为了强调即将到来的考试的重要性,假期快结束时,格兰芬多塔楼的桌子上出现了一大堆关于各种巫师职业的小册子、传单和通知,布告栏里也贴着一张告示,上面写着:

就业指导

夏季学期的第一个星期内,所有五年级同学必须与其院长面谈将来的就业问题。每位同学的面谈时间见下表。

哈利看看列表,发现他要在星期一下午两点半到麦格教授的办公室去,这就意味着会错过大半堂占卜课。复活节的最后一个周末,他和五年级的其他同学花了大量时间阅读放在那里供他们浏览的所有就业资料。

"哦,我不喜欢当治疗师。"罗恩在假期的最后一天晚上说。他正在埋头研究一张传单,上面印着圣芒戈医院的骨头加魔杖的标志。"这上面说你在魔药学、草药学、变形术、魔咒学和黑魔法防御术的N.E.W.T.考试中成绩至少达到'E'。我是说……天哪……这要求还真不高呀,是不是?"

"那是一份责任非常重大的工作,不是吗?"赫敏漫不经心地说。她在钻研一张鲜艳的粉红色和橘黄色相间的传单,顶上印着:"**你认为自己愿意从事麻瓜联络的工作吗?**""跟麻瓜打交道倒似乎不需要许多资格,只需要一张麻瓜研究的O.W.L.证书:更重要的是你的热情、耐心和幽默感!"

"要跟我姨父打交道,光有幽默感可就不管用了,"哈利板着脸说,"恐怕还需要知道什么时候该躲闪。"他正在读一本关于巫师银行的小册子,"听听这个,你在寻找一份具有挑战性的工作,涉及旅游、冒险

bonuses? Then consider a position with Gringotts Wizarding Bank, who are currently recruiting Curse-Breakers for thrilling opportunities abroad ... They want Arithmancy, though; you could do it, Hermione!'

'I don't much fancy banking,' said Hermione vaguely, now immersed in: 'HAVE YOU GOT WHAT IT TAKES TO TRAIN SECURITY TROLLS?'

'Hey,' said a voice in Harry's ear. He looked round; Fred and George had come to join them. 'Ginny's had a word with us about you,' said Fred, stretching out his legs on the table in front of them and causing several booklets on careers with the Ministry of Magic to slide off on to the floor. 'She says you need to talk to Sirius?'

'What?' said Hermione sharply, freezing with her hand halfway towards picking up 'MAKE A BANG AT THE DEPARTMENT OF MAGICAL ACCIDENTS AND CATASTROPHES'.

'Yeah ...' said Harry, trying to sound casual, 'yeah, I thought I'd like –'

'Don't be so ridiculous,' said Hermione, straightening up and looking at him as though she could not believe her eyes. 'With Umbridge groping around in the fires and frisking all the owls?'

'Well, we think we can find a way around that,' said George, stretching and smiling. 'It's a simple matter of causing a diversion. Now, you might have noticed that we have been rather quiet on the mayhem front during the Easter holidays?'

'What was the point, we asked ourselves, of disrupting leisure time?' continued Fred. 'No point at all, we answered ourselves. And of course, we'd have messed up people's revision, too, which would be the very last thing we'd want to do.'

He gave Hermione a sanctimonious little nod. She looked rather taken aback by this thoughtfulness.

'But it's business as usual from tomorrow,' Fred continued briskly. 'And if we're going to be causing a bit of uproar, why not do it so that Harry can have his chat with Sirius?'

'Yes, but *still*,' said Hermione, with an air of explaining something very simple to somebody very obtuse, 'even if you *do* cause a diversion, how is Harry supposed to talk to him?'

'Umbridge's office,' said Harry quietly.

He had been thinking about it for a fortnight and could come up with no

第29章　就业指导

和大量与危险有关的财富吗？请考虑就职于古灵阁巫师银行，本行目前正在招聘解咒员，有令人激动的出国工作机会……可是需要学过算术占卜。赫敏，你能行！"

"我不太喜欢在银行工作。"赫敏淡淡地说。她现在研究的是：**你有培训巨怪保安所需要的资格吗**？

"喂。"一个声音在哈利耳边响起。他转过头，看见弗雷德和乔治也来了。"金妮跟我们谈了你的事。"弗雷德说着，把他两条腿伸在面前的桌上，几本介绍魔法部职业的小册子被碰得滑落在地，"她说你想跟小天狼星谈谈？"

"什么？"赫敏敏感地问，一只手正要去拿**"在魔法事故和灾害司找到乐趣"**，停在了半空。

"是啊……"哈利假装不经意地说，"是啊，我想——"

"别胡思乱想了。"赫敏说，挺起身子望着他，好像不敢相信自己的眼睛似的，"别忘了乌姆里奇在监视炉火，搜查所有的猫头鹰！"

"是这样，我们认为能找到办法摆脱这些。"乔治说着，笑眯眯地伸了个懒腰，"很简单，只要打一个掩护。对了，你们恐怕注意到我们在复活节一直比较安静，没搞什么破坏，是不是？"

"我们问自己，破坏休闲时间有什么意义呢？"弗雷德接着说，"我们的回答是：毫无意义。而且，那样我们肯定会扰乱别人的复习，这可是我们最不愿意做的事情。"

他假装一本正经地朝赫敏微微点点头。赫敏似乎为这种周到的考虑感到很吃惊。

"可是从明天起我们又走上正轨了，"弗雷德继续用轻快的语调说，"如果我们要制造一点混乱，为什么不让哈利趁这个机会跟小天狼星聊聊呢？"

"是啊，不过，"赫敏说，那架势好像在跟某个脑子迟钝的人解释一件非常简单的事，"即使你们打了掩护，哈利又怎么能跟他说上话呢？"

"乌姆里奇的办公室。"哈利轻声说。

两个星期来，他一直在考虑这件事，认为没有别的选择。乌姆里

CHAPTER TWENTY-NINE Careers Advice

alternative. Umbridge herself had told him that the only fire that was not being watched was her own.

'Are – you – insane?' said Hermione in a hushed voice.

Ron had lowered his leaflet on jobs in the Cultivated Fungus Trade and was watching the conversation warily.

'I don't think so,' said Harry, shrugging.

'And how are you going to get in there in the first place?'

Harry was ready for this question.

'Sirius's knife,' he said.

'Excuse me?'

'Christmas before last Sirius gave me a knife that'll open any lock,' said Harry. 'So even if she's bewitched the door so *Alohomora* won't work, which I bet she has –'

'What do you think about this?' Hermione demanded of Ron, and Harry was reminded irresistibly of Mrs Weasley appealing to her husband during Harry's first dinner in Grimmauld Place.

'I dunno,' said Ron, looking alarmed at being asked to give an opinion. 'If Harry wants to do it, it's up to him, isn't it?'

'Spoken like a true friend and Weasley,' said Fred, clapping Ron hard on the back. 'Right, then. We're thinking of doing it tomorrow, just after lessons, because it should cause maximum impact if everybody's in the corridors – Harry, we'll set it off in the east wing somewhere, draw her right away from her own office – I reckon we should be able to guarantee you, what, twenty minutes?' he said, looking at George.

'Easy,' said George.

'What sort of diversion is it?' asked Ron.

'You'll see, little bro',' said Fred, as he and George got up again. 'At least, you will if you trot along to Gregory the Smarmy's corridor round about five o'clock tomorrow.'

Harry awoke very early the next day, feeling almost as anxious as he had done on the morning of his disciplinary hearing at the Ministry of Magic. It was not only the prospect of breaking into Umbridge's office and using her fire to speak to Sirius that was making him feel nervous, though that was certainly bad enough; today also happened to be the first time Harry would be in close proximity to Snape since Snape had thrown him out of his office.

第29章 就业指导

奇亲自对他说过,唯一不受监视的是她自己的炉火。

"你——难道——疯了吗?"赫敏压低声音说。

罗恩放下了菌类种植业的就业传单,警惕地听着他们的谈话。

"我认为没有。"哈利耸耸肩膀说。

"首先你怎么进去呢?"

哈利对这个问题早有准备。

"小天狼星的刀子。"他说。

"你说什么?"

"前年圣诞节,小天狼星送给了我一把能开各种锁的刀子,"哈利说,"如果乌姆里奇给门施了魔法——我猜她肯定会这么做,阿拉霍洞开也不管用——"

"你对这件事怎么看?"赫敏质问罗恩,哈利不由自主地想起第一天在格里莫广场吃晚饭时韦斯莱夫人求助于丈夫时的模样。

"不知道。"罗恩说,他突然被问及自己的看法,显得很紧张,"如果哈利想这么做,就该由他自己决定,不是吗?"

"说得好,够朋友,不愧是韦斯莱家的人。"弗雷德说着,重重地拍了一下罗恩的后背,"好了,我们考虑就在明天行动,放在下课之后,因为大家都在走廊上时效果才最壮观——哈利,我们将在城堡东侧某个地方行动,把她从办公室里引出来——我估计我们可以保证你有,多少呢,二十分钟?"他看着乔治说。

"没问题。"乔治说。

"用什么方式打掩护呢?"罗恩问。

"你会看到的,老弟,"弗雷德说着,跟乔治一起站了起来,"如果你明天五点钟左右溜达到马屁精格雷戈里的走廊上,就会看到。"

第二天,哈利醒得很早,他的心情简直就跟去魔法部受审的那天早晨一样焦虑不安。他感到紧张,不仅是因为想到要闯进乌姆里奇的办公室,利用她的炉火跟小天狼星说话——这确实很冒险,而且还因为今天他要接近斯内普,自从斯内普把他赶出办公室后,这还是第一次。

CHAPTER TWENTY-NINE Careers Advice

After lying in bed for a while thinking about the day ahead, Harry got up very quietly and moved across to the window beside Neville's bed, and stared out on a truly glorious morning. The sky was a clear, misty, opalescent blue. Directly ahead of him, Harry could see the towering beech tree below which his father had once tormented Snape. He was not sure what Sirius could possibly say to him that would make up for what he had seen in the Pensieve, but he was desperate to hear Sirius's own account of what had happened, to know of any mitigating factors there might have been, any excuse at all for his father's behaviour ...

Something caught Harry's attention: movement on the edge of the Forbidden Forest. Harry squinted into the sun and saw Hagrid emerging from between the trees. He seemed to be limping. As Harry watched, Hagrid staggered to the door of his cabin and disappeared inside it. Harry watched the cabin for several minutes. Hagrid did not emerge again, but smoke furled from the chimney, so Hagrid could not be so badly injured that he was unequal to stoking the fire.

Harry turned away from the window, headed back to his trunk and started to dress.

With the prospect of forcing entry into Umbridge's office ahead, Harry had never expected the day to be a restful one, but he had not reckoned on Hermione's almost continual attempts to dissuade him from what he was planning to do at five o'clock. For the first time ever, she was at least as inattentive to Professor Binns in History of Magic as Harry and Ron were, keeping up a stream of whispered admonitions that Harry tried very hard to ignore.

'... and if she does catch you there, apart from being expelled, she'll be able to guess you've been talking to Snuffles and this time I expect she'll *force* you to drink Veritaserum and answer her questions ...'

'Hermione,' said Ron in a low and indignant voice, 'are you going to stop telling Harry off and listen to Binns, or am I going to have to take my own notes?'

'You take notes for a change, it won't kill you!'

By the time they reached the dungeons, neither Harry nor Ron was speaking to Hermione. Undeterred, she took advantage of their silence to maintain an uninterrupted flow of dire warnings, all uttered under her breath in a vehement hiss that caused Seamus to waste five whole minutes checking his cauldron for leaks.

Snape, meanwhile, seemed to have decided to act as though Harry were invisible. Harry was, of course, well-used to this tactic, as it was one of Uncle

第29章 就业指导

哈利躺在床上考虑着即将到来的一天，片刻之后，他悄悄起身，走到纳威床旁的窗前，望着外面堪称十分灿烂的早晨。天空是一片晴朗的、雾蒙蒙的乳白蓝色。正对着窗户，哈利看见了下面那棵高大的山毛榉树，他爸爸当年曾在那里欺负过斯内普。他不知道小天狼星能对他说什么来解释他在冥想盆里看到的情景，但是他迫切地想听听小天狼星对这件事的叙述，想知道有没有可以使他的痛苦大大缓和的因素，有没有为他爸爸的行为开脱的理由……

什么东西吸引了哈利的注意：禁林边缘有什么东西在动。哈利在阳光下眯起眼睛，看见海格从树丛中钻了出来。他看上去一瘸一拐的。哈利注视着他步履蹒跚地走进小屋的门，不见了。哈利盯着小屋看了几分钟，海格没有再出现，但烟囱里冒出了缕缕青烟，说明海格受伤不是很严重，还有力气自己烧火。

哈利离开窗户，走到自己的箱子前，开始穿衣服。

要强行闯进乌姆里奇的办公室，哈利知道这一天肯定不会过得很平静，但是他没有想到赫敏会这样喋喋不休、不依不饶地劝说他放弃五点钟的计划。破天荒地，她在魔法史课上像哈利和罗恩一样心不在焉，没有听宾斯教授讲课，而是不停地小声劝说，哈利硬着头皮不理不睬。

"……如果她真的把你逮住，不仅你会被开除，而且她肯定能猜到你是在跟伤风谈话，我估计这次她会强迫你喝下吐真剂，回答她的审问……"

"赫敏，"罗恩气愤地压低声音说，"你能不能别再数落哈利，好好听宾斯讲课，难道要我自己记笔记吗？"

"你就记一回笔记吧，这要不了你的命！"

当他们来到地下教室时，哈利和罗恩都不跟赫敏说话了。赫敏毫不妥协，她利用他们的沉默，继续喋喋不休，长篇大论地提出警告，而且一直压低声音，用情绪激烈的嘶嘶声说话，害得西莫浪费了整整五分钟时间检查他的坩埚是不是漏了。

斯内普呢，似乎拿定主意把哈利当成空气。哈利对这一策略早已司空见惯，因为这是弗农姨父惯用的伎俩之一，他还暗自庆幸用不着

CHAPTER TWENTY-NINE Careers Advice

Vernon's favourites, and on the whole was grateful he had to suffer nothing worse. In fact, compared to what he usually had to endure from Snape in the way of taunts and snide remarks, he found the new approach something of an improvement, and was pleased to find that when left well alone, he was able to concoct an Invigoration Draught quite easily. At the end of the lesson he scooped some of the potion into a flask, corked it and took it up to Snape's desk for marking, feeling that he might at last have scraped an 'E'.

He had just turned away when he heard a smashing noise. Malfoy gave a gleeful yell of laughter. Harry whipped around. His potion sample lay in pieces on the floor and Snape was watching him with a look of gloating pleasure.

'Whoops,' he said softly. 'Another zero, then, Potter.'

Harry was too incensed to speak. He strode back to his cauldron, intending to fill another flask and force Snape to mark it, but saw to his horror that the rest of the contents had vanished.

'I'm sorry!' said Hermione, with her hands over her mouth. 'I'm really sorry, Harry. I thought you'd finished, so I cleared up!'

Harry could not bring himself to answer. When the bell rang, he hurried out of the dungeon without a backwards glance, and made sure that he found himself a seat between Neville and Seamus for lunch so that Hermione could not start nagging him again about using Umbridge's office.

He was in such a bad mood by the time he got to Divination that he had quite forgotten his careers appointment with Professor McGonagall, remembering it only when Ron asked him why he wasn't in her office. He hurtled back upstairs and arrived out of breath, only a few minutes late.

'Sorry, Professor,' he panted, as he closed the door. 'I forgot.'

'No matter, Potter,' she said briskly, but as she spoke, somebody else sniffed from the corner. Harry looked round.

Professor Umbridge was sitting there, a clipboard on her knee, a fussy little pie-frill around her neck and a small, horribly smug smile on her face.

'Sit down, Potter,' said Professor McGonagall tersely. Her hands shook slightly as she shuffled the many pamphlets littering her desk.

Harry sat down with his back to Umbridge and did his best to pretend he could not hear the scratching of her quill on her clipboard.

'Well, Potter, this meeting is to talk over any career ideas you might have, and to help you decide which subjects you should continue into the sixth

第29章 就业指导

遭受更厉害的折磨。实际上，跟他平常忍受的斯内普那些恶意的冷嘲热讽比起来，这种新方式倒算得上是一种改善。他很高兴地发现，在不受干扰的情况下，他很轻松地就调制出了一锅活力滋补剂。快要下课的时候，他把一些药剂舀进瓶子，塞紧瓶塞，拿到斯内普的讲台上去让他打分，觉得自己总算勉强能捞到一个"E"了。

他刚转身离开，就听见哗啦一声响。马尔福爆发出开心的大笑。哈利赶紧回过身去。他的药剂样品在地板上摔成了碎片，斯内普带着一种幸灾乐祸的表情注视着他。

"哎哟，"他轻声说，"又是一个零分，波特。"

哈利气得说不出话来。他大步走回自己的坩埚，打算再装满一瓶子，强迫斯内普给他打分，可是他惊恐地看到剩下的药剂都没了。

"对不起！"赫敏用双手捂住嘴巴说道，"实在对不起，哈利。我以为你完事儿了呢，就把它清理掉了！"

哈利沮丧极了，没有心情做答。下课铃响了，他匆匆跑出地下教室，头也不回，想在吃午饭时能在纳威和西莫中间找到一个座位，这样赫敏就没法再跟他唠叨使用乌姆里奇办公室的事了。

去上占卜课时，他的心情糟透了，竟然忘记了跟麦格教授预约的就业问题指导。直到罗恩问他怎么没去麦格教授的办公室，他才突然想了起来。他赶紧冲上楼梯，跑得上气不接下气，还好，只迟到了几分钟。

"对不起，教授，"他气喘吁吁地关上房门说，"我忘记了。"

"没关系，波特。"麦格教授语气轻快地说，可是就在她说话的当儿，墙角里有人抽了一下鼻子。哈利扭过头望去。

乌姆里奇教授坐在那里，膝盖上放着写字板，脖子上围着花里胡哨的荷叶边，脸上带着一丝得意的笑容，难看极了。

"坐下吧，波特。"麦格教授简短地说。她挪动着散落在她桌上的许多小册子，双手微微颤抖。

哈利背对乌姆里奇坐了下来，努力假装听不见她的羽毛笔在写字板上发出的沙沙声。

"好了，波特，这次面谈是要讨论你对就业的一些想法，帮助你决

CHAPTER TWENTY-NINE Careers Advice

and seventh years,' said Professor McGonagall. 'Have you had any thoughts about what you would like to do after you leave Hogwarts?'

'Er –' said Harry.

He was finding the scratching noise from behind him very distracting.

'Yes?' Professor McGonagall prompted Harry.

'Well, I thought of, maybe, being an Auror,' Harry mumbled.

'You'd need top grades for that,' said Professor McGonagall, extracting a small, dark leaflet from under the mass on her desk and opening it. 'They ask for a minimum of five N.E.W.T.s, and nothing under "Exceeds Expectations" grade, I see. Then you would be required to undergo a stringent series of character and aptitude tests at the Auror office. It's a difficult career path, Potter, they only take the best. In fact, I don't think anybody has been taken on in the last three years.'

At this moment, Professor Umbridge gave a very tiny cough, as though she was trying to see how quietly she could do it. Professor McGonagall ignored her.

'You'll want to know which subjects you ought to take, I suppose?' she went on, talking a little louder than before.

'Yes,' said Harry. 'Defence Against the Dark Arts, I suppose?'

'Naturally,' said Professor McGonagall crisply. 'I would also advise –'

Professor Umbridge gave another cough, a little more audible this time. Professor McGonagall closed her eyes for a moment, opened them again, and continued as though nothing had happened.

'I would also advise Transfiguration, because Aurors frequently need to Transfigure or Untransfigure in their work. And I ought to tell you now, Potter, that I do not accept students into my N.E.W.T. classes unless they have achieved "Exceeds Expectations" or higher at Ordinary Wizarding Level. I'd say you're averaging "Acceptable" at the moment, so you'll need to put in some good hard work before the exams to stand a chance of continuing. Then you ought to do Charms, always useful, and Potions. Yes, Potter, Potions,' she added, with the merest flicker of a smile. 'Poisons and antidotes are essential study for Aurors. And I must tell you that Professor Snape absolutely refuses to take students who get anything other than "Outstanding" in their O.W.L.s, so –'

Professor Umbridge gave her most pronounced cough yet.

'May I offer you a cough drop, Dolores?' Professor McGonagall asked curtly, without looking at Professor Umbridge.

第29章 就业指导

定六、七年级应该继续学习哪些科目。"麦格教授说道,"你有没有考虑过,你离开霍格沃茨后想做什么呢?"

"呃——"哈利支吾着。

他发现身后羽毛笔的沙沙声很让人分神。

"说吧。"麦格教授催促哈利。

"我,我想,也许,当一名傲罗。"哈利小声嘟哝说。

"那你需要成绩优异才行。"麦格教授说着,从桌上乱糟糟的一堆东西下抽出一张黑色的小传单打开来,"他们要求至少五个 N.E.W.T. 证书,成绩都不能低于'良好'。此外你必须在傲罗办公室经受一系列严格的性格和才能测试。从事这种职业很不容易,波特,他们只接受最优秀的人才。事实上,我记得最近三年他们都没有接受新人。"

这时,乌姆里奇教授十分轻微地咳嗽了一声,似乎在试探她的咳嗽声能有多轻。麦格教授没有理会。

"你大概需要知道应该学习哪些科目吧?"麦格教授继续说道,声音比刚才略高了一些。

"是啊,"哈利说,"我猜有黑魔法防御术吧?"

"那是当然,"麦格教授干脆地说,"我还建议——"

乌姆里奇教授又咳嗽了一声,这次声音稍微大了一点儿。麦格教授把眼睛闭了闭又睁开了,仍然当什么事也没有发生似的。

"我还建议你学习变形术,因为傲罗在工作中需要频繁地变形和现形。我现在就应该告诉你,波特,我的 N.E.W.T. 班只接受在 O.W.L. 考试中获得'良'以上成绩的学生。你目前的平均成绩是'及格',所以需要在考试前格外用功,才有机会继续学习。此外你还需要学习魔咒学,它在任何时候都很有用,还有魔药学。是的,波特,魔药学,"她脸上闪过一丝若有若无的微笑,"魔药和解药是傲罗需要掌握的基本知识。我必须告诉你,斯内普教授断然拒绝接受魔药学 O.W.L. 考试成绩低于'优秀'的学生,所以——"

乌姆里奇教授发出了到目前为止最响的一声咳嗽。

"要我给你一点止咳药水吗,多洛雷斯?"麦格教授生硬地问,看也不看乌姆里奇教授。

CHAPTER TWENTY-NINE Careers Advice

'Oh, no, thank you very much,' said Umbridge, with that simpering laugh Harry hated so much. 'I just wondered whether I could make the teensiest interruption, Minerva?'

'I daresay you'll find you can,' said Professor McGonagall through tightly gritted teeth.

'I was just wondering whether Mr Potter has *quite* the temperament for an Auror?' said Professor Umbridge sweetly.

'Were you?' said Professor McGonagall haughtily. 'Well, Potter,' she continued, as though there had been no interruption, 'if you are serious in this ambition, I would advise you to concentrate hard on bringing your Transfiguration and Potions up to scratch. I see Professor Flitwick has graded you between "Acceptable" and "Exceeds Expectations" for the last two years, so your Charmwork seems satisfactory. As for Defence Against the Dark Arts, your marks have been generally high, Professor Lupin in particular thought you – *are you quite sure you wouldn't like a cough drop, Dolores?*'

'Oh, no need, thank you, Minerva,' simpered Professor Umbridge, who had just coughed her loudest yet. 'I was just concerned that you might not have Harry's most recent Defence Against the Dark Arts marks in front of you. I'm quite sure I slipped in a note.'

'What, this thing?' said Professor McGonagall in a tone of revulsion, as she pulled a sheet of pink parchment from between the leaves of Harry's folder. She glanced down it, her eyebrows slightly raised, then placed it back into the folder without comment.

'Yes, as I was saying, Potter, Professor Lupin thought you showed a pronounced aptitude for the subject, and obviously for an Auror –'

'Did you not understand my note, Minerva?' asked Professor Umbridge in honeyed tones, quite forgetting to cough.

'Of course I understood it,' said Professor McGonagall, her teeth clenched so tightly the words came out a little muffled.

'Well, then, I am confused ... I'm afraid I don't quite understand how you can give Mr Potter false hope that –'

'False hope?' repeated Professor McGonagall, still refusing to look round at Professor Umbridge. 'He has achieved high marks in all his Defence Against the Dark Arts tests –'

'I'm terribly sorry to have to contradict you, Minerva, but as you will see from my note, Harry has been achieving very poor results in his classes with me –'

第29章 就业指导

"哦,不用,太谢谢了。"乌姆里奇说,脸上挂着哈利恨之入骨的那种假笑,"我只是在考虑我能不能稍稍地打点儿小岔,米勒娃。"

"看来你已经发现自己能够打岔。"麦格教授从紧咬的牙缝里说。

"我刚才在考虑,波特先生是否具备一名傲罗所需要的气质呢?"乌姆里奇教授用甜甜的声音说。

"是吗?"麦格教授高傲地说。"听我说,波特,"她继续往下说,就好像根本没有被打断似的,"如果你真有这个抱负,我建议你集中精力让你的变形术和魔药学达到标准。我看到近两年弗立维教授给你的成绩在'及格'和'良'之间,看来你的魔咒学还符合要求。至于黑魔法防御术,你的成绩一向很好,特别是卢平教授认为你——你真的不想喝点止咳药水吗,多洛雷斯?"

"哦,不必了,谢谢你,米勒娃,"乌姆里奇教授假笑着说,她刚才发出了一声更加响亮的咳嗽,"我只是担心你恐怕没有看到哈利最近的黑魔法防御术的成绩。我相信我塞了一张纸条。"

"什么,是这东西吗?"麦格教授用反感的语气说,从哈利的档案夹里抽出一张粉红色的羊皮纸。她扫了一眼,微微扬起了眉毛。她没作评论,又把它放回了档案夹里。

"是的,就像我刚才说的,波特,卢平教授认为你在这门课上表现出了出色的才能,对于成为一名傲罗——"

"你没有看懂我的纸条吗,米勒娃?"乌姆里奇教授用甜腻腻的声音问,她居然忘记了咳嗽。

"当然看懂了。"麦格教授说,她牙齿咬得真紧,说话的声音都有点儿发闷了。

"那就好,我只是感到困惑……我恐怕不能理解你怎么能给波特先生不切实际的希望——"

"不切实际的希望?"麦格教授重复了一遍,仍然不肯回头看看乌姆里奇教授,"他在黑魔法防御术的所有考试中都拿到了高分——"

"非常抱歉,我不得不对你提出异议,米勒娃,你从我的纸条上可以看出,哈利在我班上的成绩很糟糕——"

CHAPTER TWENTY-NINE Careers Advice

'I should have made my meaning plainer,' said Professor McGonagall, turning at last to look Umbridge directly in the eyes. 'He has achieved high marks in all Defence Against the Dark Arts tests set by a competent teacher.'

Professor Umbridge's smile vanished as suddenly as a light bulb blowing. She sat back in her chair, turned a sheet on her clipboard and began scribbling very fast indeed, her bulging eyes rolling from side to side. Professor McGonagall turned back to Harry, her thin nostrils flared, her eyes burning.

'Any questions, Potter?'

'Yes,' said Harry. 'What sort of character and aptitude tests do the Ministry do on you, if you get enough N.E.W.T.s?'

'Well, you'll need to demonstrate the ability to react well to pressure and so forth,' said Professor McGonagall, 'perseverance and dedication, because Auror training takes a further three years, not to mention very high skills in practical Defence. It will mean a lot more study even after you've left school, so unless you're prepared to –'

'I think you'll also find,' said Umbridge, her voice very cold now, 'that the Ministry looks into the records of those applying to be Aurors. Their criminal records.'

'– unless you're prepared to take even more exams after Hogwarts, you should really look at another –'

'Which means that this boy has as much chance of becoming an Auror as Dumbledore has of ever returning to this school.'

'A very good chance, then,' said Professor McGonagall.

'Potter has a criminal record,' said Umbridge loudly.

'Potter has been cleared of all charges,' said McGonagall, even more loudly.

Professor Umbridge stood up. She was so short that this did not make a great deal of difference, but her fussy, simpering demeanour had given place to a hard fury that made her broad, flabby face look oddly sinister.

'Potter has no chance whatsoever of becoming an Auror!'

Professor McGonagall got to her feet, too, and in her case this was a much more impressive move; she towered over Professor Umbridge.

'Potter,' she said in ringing tones, 'I will assist you to become an Auror if

第29章 就业指导

"我应该把我的意思说得更清楚一些,"麦格教授说,终于回过头直视着乌姆里奇的眼睛,"在每一位称职的老师安排的所有黑魔法防御术考试中,他都拿到了高分。"

乌姆里奇教授的笑容突然消失了,就像一只灯泡突然爆掉了一样。她靠回到椅背上,在写字板上翻过一页,开始速度很快地写着什么,一对鼓凸的眼睛左右转动。麦格教授转向哈利,她的鼻翼翕动,眼睛里冒着怒火。

"还有什么问题吗,波特?"

"有,"哈利说,"如果 N.E.W.T. 考试的成绩够了,魔法部会做什么样的性格和才能测试呢?"

"是这样,你需要在承受压力方面展示出良好的反应能力,"麦格教授说,"还有毅力和献身精神,因为傲罗培训还需要三年时间,更不用说非常高超的防御术实践技巧。这意味着离开学校之后还要学习很多东西,因此,除非你有心理准备——"

"我认为你还会发现,"乌姆里奇说,现在她的语气变得很冷了,"魔法部要调查那些申请成为傲罗的人的记录。违法记录。"

"——除非你有心理准备,在离开霍格沃茨后还要参加更多的考试,不然你真的应该考虑考虑别的——"

"这就意味着,这个男孩成为傲罗的希望,就像邓布利多重返这所学校的希望一样。"

"那就希望很大了。"麦格教授说。

"波特有违法记录。"乌姆里奇大声说。

"对波特的所有指控都已澄清。"麦格的声音比她的还大。

乌姆里奇教授站了起来。她个子太矮了,站起来和坐着没有多大区别,但是她原先那副假惺惺的、大惊小怪的做派,已经变成了实实在在的愤恨,这使得她那张皮肉松弛的胖脸显得特别狰狞可怕。

"波特绝对没有可能成为傲罗!"

麦格教授也站了起来,而她的这个举动就很有威慑力了。她和乌姆里奇教授站在一起,明显高出了许多。

"波特,"她说,声音清脆响亮,"我会帮助你成为一名傲罗,哪怕

CHAPTER TWENTY-NINE   Careers Advice

it is the last thing I do! If I have to coach you nightly, I will make sure you achieve the required results!'

'The Minister for Magic will never employ Harry Potter!' said Umbridge, her voice rising furiously.

'There may well be a new Minister for Magic by the time Potter is ready to join!' shouted Professor McGonagall.

'Aha!' shrieked Professor Umbridge, pointing a stubby finger at McGonagall. 'Yes! Yes, yes, yes! Of course! That's what you want, isn't it, Minerva McGonagall? You want Cornelius Fudge replaced by Albus Dumbledore! You think you'll be where I am, don't you: Senior Undersecretary to the Minister and Headmistress to boot!'

'You are raving,' said Professor McGonagall, superbly disdainful. 'Potter, that concludes our careers consultation.'

Harry swung his bag over his shoulder and hurried out of the room, not daring to look at Professor Umbridge. He could hear her and Professor McGonagall continuing to shout at each other all the way back along the corridor.

Professor Umbridge was still breathing as though she had just run a race when she strode into their Defence Against the Dark Arts lesson that afternoon.

'I hope you've thought better of what you were planning to do, Harry,' Hermione whispered, the moment they had opened their books to 'Chapter Thirty-four, Non-Retaliation and Negotiation'. 'Umbridge looks like she's in a really bad mood already ...'

Every now and then Umbridge shot glowering looks at Harry, who kept his head down, staring at *Defensive Magical Theory*, his eyes unfocused, thinking ...

He could just imagine Professor McGonagall's reaction if he was caught trespassing in Professor Umbridge's office mere hours after she had vouched for him ... there was nothing to stop him simply going back to Gryffindor Tower and hoping that some time during the next summer holidays he would have a chance to ask Sirius about the scene he had witnessed in the Pensieve ... nothing, except that the thought of taking this sensible course of action made him feel as though a lead weight had dropped into his stomach ... and then there was the matter of Fred and George, whose diversion was already planned, not to mention the knife Sirius had given him, which was currently residing in his schoolbag along with his father's old Invisibility Cloak.

But the fact remained that if he was caught ...

第29章 就业指导

这是我生前做的最后一件事！哪怕需要我每天晚上给你补课，我也会保证你获得需要的成绩！"

"魔法部部长绝对不会雇用哈利·波特！"乌姆里奇恼羞成怒地提高了声音。

"等到波特准备加入时，魔法部也该换部长了！"麦格教授嚷道。

"啊哈！"乌姆里奇教授尖叫起来，用一根粗短的手指指着麦格，"对了！对了，对了，对了！当然啦！这就是你想要的，是不是，米勒娃·麦格？你想要阿不思·邓布利多取代康奈利·福吉！你想坐到我的位置上，是不是：魔法部高级副部长兼校长！"

"真是胡言乱语。"麦格教授极端蔑视地说，"波特，我们的就业咨询结束了。"

哈利把书包甩上肩头，没敢看乌姆里奇教授一眼，冲出了办公室。他在走廊里飞跑，一路都能听见乌姆里奇和麦格教授还在互相嚷嚷。

这天下午，乌姆里奇教授大步走进黑魔法防御术的课堂时，仍然气喘吁吁，就好像刚刚参加完赛跑。

"哈利，我希望你慎重考虑过了你打算做的事情。"赫敏小声说，这时他们把课本翻到了第三十四章，非报复手段和谈判，"看上去乌姆里奇的情绪已经很糟糕了……"

乌姆里奇不时朝哈利投来愤怒的目光，哈利一直低着脑袋，盯着《魔法防御理论》，但他的眼睛是失神的，心里在思索……

他可以想象出，如果他擅自闯入乌姆里奇教授办公室时被抓住，麦格教授会有什么反应，就在几小时前，她还为哈利做了担保……他完全可以返回格兰芬多塔楼，希望在暑假某个时候有机会跟小天狼星打听他在冥想盆里看到的一幕……然而，一想起要采取这种理智的行为，他就觉得心头压上了一块沉甸甸的东西……而且还有弗雷德和乔治，他们已经在策划着打掩护了，更不用说小天狼星给他的那把刀子，此刻就放在他的书包里，跟他父亲的那件旧隐形衣在一起。

可是，万一他被抓住……

CHAPTER TWENTY-NINE   Careers Advice

'Dumbledore sacrificed himself to keep you in school, Harry!' whispered Hermione, raising her book to hide her face from Umbridge. 'And if you get thrown out today it will all have been for nothing!'

He could abandon the plan and simply learn to live with the memory of what his father had done on a summer's day more than twenty years ago ...

And then he remembered Sirius in the fire upstairs in the Gryffindor common room ...

You're less like your father than I thought ... the risk would've been what made it fun for James ...

But did he want to be like his father any more?

'Harry, don't do it, please don't do it!' Hermione said in anguished tones as the bell rang at the end of the class.

He did not answer; he did not know what to do.

Ron seemed determined to give neither his opinion nor his advice; he would not look at Harry, though when Hermione opened her mouth to try dissuading Harry some more, he said in a low voice, 'Give it a rest, OK? He can make up his own mind.'

Harry's heart beat very fast as he left the classroom. He was halfway along the corridor outside when he heard the unmistakeable sounds of a diversion going off in the distance. There were screams and yells reverberating from somewhere above them; people exiting the classrooms all around Harry were stopping in their tracks and looking up at the ceiling fearfully –

Umbridge came pelting out of her classroom as fast as her short legs would carry her. Pulling out her wand, she hurried off in the opposite direction: it was now or never.

'Harry – please!' Hermione pleaded weakly.

But he had made up his mind; hitching his bag more securely on to his shoulder, he set off at a run, weaving in and out of students now hurrying in the opposite direction to see what all the fuss was about in the east wing.

Harry reached the corridor to Umbridge's office and found it deserted. Dashing behind a large suit of armour whose helmet creaked around to watch him, he pulled open his bag, seized Sirius's knife and donned the Invisibility Cloak. He then crept slowly and carefully back out from behind the suit of armour and along the corridor until he reached Umbridge's door.

He inserted the blade of the magical knife into the crack around it and

"为了让你留在学校,邓布利多做出了牺牲,哈利!"赫敏小声说,她把课本举起来挡住脸,不让乌姆里奇看见,"如果你今天被赶出学校,他的牺牲就白费了!"

他可以放弃这个计划,努力忍受那段记忆,他父亲二十多年前一个夏天做的事情……

接着他想起了小天狼星在楼上格兰芬多公共休息室的炉火里……

你不如我想的那样像你父亲……对詹姆来说,只有冒险才有乐趣……

然而,他还愿意像他父亲吗?

"哈利,别干了,求求你别干了!"下课铃响起时,赫敏用苦恼的声音说。

哈利没有回答,他不知道该怎么办。

罗恩似乎拿定主意不发表意见,不提出忠告,他躲着不看哈利,但每当赫敏又开口劝说哈利时,他会轻声说一句:"你歇歇吧,好吗?他可以自己做决定的。"

离开教室时,哈利的心跳得很快。他顺着走廊走到一半,就听到远处传来了确凿无疑的打掩护的声音。尖叫声和大喊声在上面什么地方回荡着。哈利周围,从教室里出来的人们都停下脚步,忧心忡忡地抬头望着天花板——

乌姆里奇拼命摆动着两条短腿,从教室里冲了出来。她抽出魔杖,朝另一个方向奔了过去:要么现在行动,要么就没机会了。

"哈利——求求你!"赫敏无力地央求道。

可是他的主意已定。他把书包稳稳地背在肩上,在人群中撒腿奔跑,此刻人们都匆匆地朝相反的方向奔去,想看看城堡东侧闹出了什么风波。

哈利来到乌姆里奇办公室所在的走廊,发现那里空无一人。他冲到一套巨大的铠甲后面,铠甲的头盔吱吱嘎嘎地转过来望着他。哈利打开书包,掏出小天狼星的刀子,把隐形衣披在身上。然后他慢慢地、小心翼翼地从铠甲后面溜出来,顺着走廊来到乌姆里奇办公室的门前。

他把魔法刀塞进门缝,轻轻地上下移动,然后拔了出来。随着咔

CHAPTER TWENTY-NINE Careers Advice

moved it gently up and down, then withdrew it. There was a tiny click, and the door swung open. He ducked inside the office, closed the door quickly behind him and looked around.

Nothing was moving except the horrible kittens that were still frolicking on the wall plates above the confiscated broomsticks.

Harry pulled off his Cloak and, striding over to the fireplace, found what he was looking for within seconds: a small box containing glittering Floo powder.

He crouched down in front of the empty grate, his hands shaking. He had never done this before, though he thought he knew how it must work. Sticking his head into the fireplace, he took a large pinch of powder and dropped it on to the logs stacked neatly beneath him. They exploded at once into emerald green flames.

'Number twelve, Grimmauld Place!' Harry said loudly and clearly.

It was one of the most curious sensations he had ever experienced. He had travelled by Floo powder before, of course, but then it had been his entire body that had spun around and around in the flames through the network of wizarding fireplaces that stretched over the country. This time, his knees remained firm upon the cold floor of Umbridge's office, and only his head hurtled through the emerald fire …

And then, as abruptly as it had begun, the spinning stopped. Feeling rather sick and as though he were wearing an exceptionally hot muffler around his head, Harry opened his eyes to find that he was looking up out of the kitchen fireplace at the long, wooden table, where a man sat poring over a piece of parchment.

'Sirius?'

The man jumped and looked around. It was not Sirius, but Lupin.

'Harry!' he said, looking thoroughly shocked. 'What are you – what's happened, is everything all right?'

'Yeah,' said Harry. 'I just wondered – I mean, I just fancied a – a chat with Sirius.'

'I'll call him,' said Lupin, getting to his feet, still looking perplexed, 'he went upstairs to look for Kreacher, he seems to be hiding in the attic again …'

And Harry saw Lupin hurry out of the kitchen. Now he was left with nothing to look at but the chair and table legs. He wondered why Sirius had never mentioned how very uncomfortable it was to speak out of the fire; his knees were already objecting painfully to their prolonged contact with Umbridge's hard stone floor.

第29章 就业指导

嗒一声轻响,门开了。他猫腰闪进办公室,迅速关上身后的门,环顾着四周。

唯一有动静的是那些难看的猫,它们仍旧在那几把被没收的扫帚上方的盘子里嬉笑打闹。

哈利脱掉隐形衣,三步并作两步走到壁炉前,几秒钟就找到了他要的东西:一个小盒子,里面装着亮闪闪的飞路粉。

他蹲在空荡荡的炉栅前,双手在颤抖。他以前从没做过这种事,不过他认为自己知道该怎么办。他把脑袋钻进壁炉,捻起一大撮粉末,丢进下面一堆整整齐齐的木头上。顿时,木头爆出了艳绿色的火苗。

"格里莫广场12号!"哈利响亮、清晰地说。

这是他体验过的最奇怪的感觉之一。当然啦,他以前也通过飞路粉旅行过,但那时他的整个身体都在火焰中一圈圈地旋转,在遍布全国的巫师壁炉网络中穿行。这次,他的膝盖还稳稳地跪在乌姆里奇办公室冰冷的地面上,只有他的脑袋在艳绿色的火苗中飞转……

旋转猛地停止,就像开始时那样突然。哈利觉得很难受,就像脑袋上裹着一条特别闷热的围巾。他睁开眼睛,发现自己正从厨房的壁炉里往外看着一张木头长桌,桌旁坐着一个男人,正在研究一张羊皮纸。

"小天狼星?"

那人惊跳起来,环顾四周。他不是小天狼星,是卢平。

"哈利!"他说,看上去完全惊呆了,"你怎么——出什么事了,一切都好吗?"

"都好,"哈利说,"我只是想知道——我是说,我只想——跟小天狼星谈谈。"

"我去叫他,"卢平说着站了起来,仍然一脸迷惑,"他到楼上去找克利切了,克利切好像又躲在阁楼里了……"

哈利看见卢平匆匆走出了厨房。现在,除了椅子和桌腿,没有什么可看的了。他不明白小天狼星为什么从没提到过透过炉火说话有多么难受。他的膝盖在乌姆里奇办公室坚硬的石头地面上跪得太久,已经开始发痛。

CHAPTER TWENTY-NINE   Careers Advice

Lupin returned with Sirius at his heels moments later.

'What is it?' said Sirius urgently, sweeping his long dark hair out of his eyes and dropping to the ground in front of the fire, so that he and Harry were on a level. Lupin knelt down too, looking very concerned. 'Are you all right? Do you need help?'

'No,' said Harry, 'it's nothing like that ... I just wanted to talk ... about my dad.'

They exchanged a look of great surprise, but Harry did not have time to feel awkward or embarrassed; his knees were becoming sorer by the second and he guessed five minutes had already passed from the start of the diversion; George had only guaranteed him twenty. He therefore plunged immediately into the story of what he had seen in the Pensieve.

When he had finished, neither Sirius nor Lupin spoke for a moment. Then Lupin said quietly, 'I wouldn't like you to judge your father on what you saw there, Harry. He was only fifteen –'

'I'm fifteen!' said Harry heatedly.

'Look, Harry,' said Sirius placatingly, 'James and Snape hated each other from the moment they set eyes on each other, it was just one of those things, you can understand that, can't you? I think James was everything Snape wanted to be – he was popular, he was good at Quidditch – good at pretty much everything. And Snape was just this little oddball who was up to his eyes in the Dark Arts, and James – whatever else he may have appeared to you, Harry – always hated the Dark Arts.'

'Yeah,' said Harry, 'but he just attacked Snape for no good reason, just because – well, just because you said you were bored,' he finished, with a slightly apologetic note in his voice.

'I'm not proud of it,' said Sirius quickly.

Lupin looked sideways at Sirius, then said, 'Look, Harry, what you've got to understand is that your father and Sirius were the best in the school at whatever they did – everyone thought they were the height of cool – if they sometimes got a bit carried away –'

'If we were sometimes arrogant little berks, you mean,' said Sirius.

Lupin smiled.

'He kept messing up his hair,' said Harry in a pained voice.

Sirius and Lupin laughed.

'I'd forgotten he used to do that,' said Sirius affectionately.

第29章 就业指导

片刻之后，卢平回来了，身后跟着小天狼星。

"怎么啦？"小天狼星急切地问，一边拂去挡住眼睛的长长黑发，扑通跪在炉火前的地上，让自己跟哈利处在同样高度。卢平也跪了下来，神情十分担忧。"你没事儿吧？需要帮助吗？"

"不，"哈利说，"不是那样的事……我只是想谈谈……谈谈我爸爸。"

他们交换了一个十分惊奇的目光，可是哈利没有时间感到尴尬或难为情了，他的膝盖疼得越来越厉害，而且他猜想双胞胎替他打掩护的时间已经过去了五分钟。乔治只给了他二十分钟。于是，他直奔主题，立刻说起了他在冥想盆里看见的那段往事。

他说完后，一时间小天狼星和卢平都没有说话。然后卢平轻声说道："我不希望你根据在那里看见的事情来评判你父亲，哈利。他当时只有十五岁——"

"我也十五岁！"哈利激动地说。

"你听我说，哈利，"小天狼星息事宁人地说，"詹姆和斯内普自打第一眼看到对方就互相仇视，这种事情没法儿解释，你明白的，对吧？我认为詹姆拥有斯内普梦寐以求的一切——他人缘好，魁地奇打得好——几乎什么都好。斯内普是个古里古怪的小家伙，整天忙着研究黑魔法，而詹姆——哈利，不管你认为他别的方面怎么样——他一向很讨厌黑魔法。"

"是啊，"哈利说，"可是他无缘无故就攻击斯内普，就因为——就因为你说你觉得有些无聊。"他的语气里微微透着一丝歉意。

"我确实做得不对。"小天狼星立刻说了一句。

卢平侧眼看看小天狼星，说道："是这样，哈利，你必须明白，你父亲和小天狼星不管做什么都是全校最棒的——大伙儿认为他们酷极了——如果他们偶尔有点忘乎所以——"

"你的意思是，我们偶尔变成狂傲的小笨蛋。"小天狼星说。

卢平微微笑了笑。

"他总是把头发弄得乱糟糟的。"哈利用痛苦的语气说。

小天狼星和卢平笑了起来。

"我倒忘记他经常这么做了。"小天狼星充满深情地说。

1115

CHAPTER TWENTY-NINE Careers Advice

'Was he playing with the Snitch?' said Lupin eagerly.

'Yeah,' said Harry, watching uncomprehendingly as Sirius and Lupin beamed reminiscently. 'Well ... I thought he was a bit of an idiot.'

'Of course he was a bit of an idiot!' said Sirius bracingly, 'we were all idiots! Well – not Moony so much,' he said fairly, looking at Lupin.

But Lupin shook his head. 'Did I ever tell you to lay off Snape?' he said. 'Did I ever have the guts to tell you I thought you were out of order?'

'Yeah, well,' said Sirius, 'you made us feel ashamed of ourselves sometimes ... that was something ...'

'And,' said Harry doggedly, determined to say everything that was on his mind now he was here, 'he kept looking over at the girls by the lake, hoping they were watching him!'

'Oh, well, he always made a fool of himself whenever Lily was around,' said Sirius, shrugging, 'he couldn't stop himself showing off whenever he got near her.'

'How come she married him?' Harry asked miserably. 'She hated him!'

'Nah, she didn't,' said Sirius.

'She started going out with him in seventh year,' said Lupin.

'Once James had deflated his head a bit,' said Sirius.

'And stopped hexing people just for the fun of it,' said Lupin.

'Even Snape?' said Harry.

'Well,' said Lupin slowly, 'Snape was a special case. I mean, he never lost an opportunity to curse James so you couldn't really expect James to take that lying down, could you?'

'And my mum was OK with that?'

'She didn't know too much about it, to tell you the truth,' said Sirius. 'I mean, James didn't take Snape on dates with her and jinx him in front of her, did he?'

Sirius frowned at Harry, who was still looking unconvinced.

'Look,' he said, 'your father was the best friend I ever had and he was a good person. A lot of people are idiots at the age of fifteen. He grew out of it.'

'Yeah, OK,' said Harry heavily. 'I just never thought I'd feel sorry for Snape.'

第29章 就业指导

"他当时在玩弄金飞贼吗?"卢平热切地问。

"是的。"哈利说,他不理解地望着小天狼星和卢平,他们都笑眯眯地沉浸在回忆中,"我……我觉得他有点像个傻瓜。"

"他当然有点像个傻瓜!"小天狼星情绪激动地说,"我们都是傻瓜!不过——月亮脸不算太傻。"他看着卢平,说了句公道话。

可是卢平摇了摇头:"我什么时候叫你们放过斯内普了?我什么时候有勇气对你们说我认为你们闹得过分了?"

"是啊,是啊,"小天狼星说,"你让我们有时候为自己感到难为情……这就够了……"

"还有,"哈利不依不饶地说,他想,既然到了这里,索性就把心里所有的话都吐出来吧,"他在湖边老是打量那些姑娘,希望她们都看他!"

"哦,是啊,每次有莉莉在,他都表现得像个傻瓜,"小天狼星耸了耸肩说,"只要在莉莉旁边,他就忍不住要显摆一下。"

"她怎么会嫁给他的?"哈利苦恼地问,"她讨厌他!"

"不,她不讨厌他。"小天狼星说。

"她七年级的时候就开始跟他谈恋爱了。"卢平说。

"那时詹姆的脑子就不那么膨胀了。"小天狼星说。

"不再为了寻开心而给别人下恶咒了。"卢平说。

"包括斯内普?"哈利说。

"是这样,"卢平语速很慢地说,"斯内普是个特殊情况。我是说,他只要一有机会就对詹姆施咒,所以你不可能指望詹姆放他一马,是不是?"

"我妈妈对这些事没有意见吗?"

"实话告诉你吧,她对这些事知道得并不多,"小天狼星说,"我是说,詹姆跟她约会时并没有带着斯内普,然后当着她的面给斯内普念咒语,对不对?"

小天狼星皱起眉头看着哈利,哈利似乎并没有被说服。

"你听我说,"小天狼星说,"你父亲是我这辈子最好的朋友,同时他也是个好人。许多人在十五岁时都会犯傻。他后来长大了就好了。"

"是啊,好吧,"哈利语气沉重地说,"只是,我从没想到我会为斯内普感到难过。"

CHAPTER TWENTY-NINE   Careers Advice

'Now you mention it,' said Lupin, a faint crease between his eye-brows, 'how did Snape react when he found you'd seen all this?'

'He told me he'd never teach me Occlumency again,' said Harry indifferently, 'like that's a big disappoint—'

'He WHAT?' shouted Sirius, causing Harry to jump and inhale a mouthful of ashes.

'Are you serious, Harry?' said Lupin quickly. 'He's stopped giving you lessons?'

'Yeah,' said Harry, surprised at what he considered a great overreaction. 'But it's OK, I don't care, it's a bit of a relief to tell you the —'

'I'm coming up there to have a word with Snape!' said Sirius forcefully, and he actually made to stand up, but Lupin wrenched him back down again.

'If anyone's going to tell Snape it will be me!' he said firmly. 'But Harry, first of all, you're to go back to Snape and tell him that on no account is he to stop giving you lessons — when Dumbledore hears —'

'I can't tell him that, he'd kill me!' said Harry, outraged. 'You didn't see him when we got out of the Pensieve.'

'Harry, there is nothing so important as you learning Occlumency!' said Lupin sternly. 'Do you understand me? Nothing!'

'OK, OK,' said Harry, thoroughly discomposed, not to mention annoyed. 'I'll … I'll try and say something to him … but it won't be —'

He fell silent. He could hear distant footsteps.

'Is that Kreacher coming downstairs?'

'No,' said Sirius, glancing behind him. 'It must be somebody your end.'

Harry's heart skipped several beats.

'I'd better go!' he said hastily and pulled his head backwards out of the Grimmauld Place fire. For a moment his head seemed to be revolving on his shoulders, then he found himself kneeling in front of Umbridge's fire with it firmly back on and watching the emerald flames flicker and die.

'Quickly, quickly!' he heard a wheezy voice mutter right outside the office door. 'Ah, she's left it open —'

Harry dived for the Invisibility Cloak and had just managed to pull it back over himself when Filch burst into the office. He looked absolutely delighted about something and was talking to himself feverishly as he crossed the

第29章 就业指导

"既然你提到了,"卢平说着,眉心间显出一道浅浅的皱纹,"斯内普发现你看见了这些,他是什么反应呢?"

"他对我说,他再也不教我大脑封闭术了,"哈利不当回事地说,"就好像我会感到失望似的——"

"他说*什么*?"小天狼星大叫一声,哈利吃了一惊,吸进一大口炉灰。

"你没开玩笑吧,哈利?"卢平迅速问道,"他真的不给你上课了?"

"是啊。"哈利说,惊讶地认为他们俩的反应太过度了,"可是没关系,我不在乎,说句实话,这倒让我松了口——"

"我要去跟斯内普谈谈!"小天狼星气冲冲地说,他说着就要站起来,卢平把他又按了回去。

"如果需要有人去告诉斯内普,那也应该是我!"他坚决地说,"可是哈利,首先,你回去找斯内普,对他说无论如何不能停止给你上课——要是邓布利多知道了——"

"我不能跟他这么说,他会杀了我的!"哈利愤怒地说,"你们没有看见我从冥想盆里出来时他的那副模样。"

"哈利,什么也比不上你学习大脑封闭术重要啊!"卢平严肃地说,"你明白我的意思吗?什么也比不上!"

"好吧,好吧,"哈利说,他不仅生气,而且心里十分慌乱,"我……我去试着跟他说说……但恐怕不能——"

他停住话头。他听见远处传来了脚步声。

"是克利切下楼来了吗?"

"不是,"小天狼星扭头望了望说,"肯定是你那边的什么人。"

哈利的心狂跳了几下。

"我得走了!"他匆匆地说,把脑袋从格里莫广场的炉火中抽了回去。一时间,他的脑袋似乎在肩膀上打转儿,然后他发现自己跪在乌姆里奇的炉火前,脑袋牢牢地回到了脖子上,注视着艳绿色的火苗一闪一闪地熄灭了。

"快!快!"他听见办公室门外一个呼哧带喘的声音在嘟哝,"啊,她的门没关——"

哈利赶紧俯身去拿隐形衣,他刚把它披在身上,费尔奇就冲进了

CHAPTER TWENTY-NINE Careers Advice

room, pulled open a drawer in Umbridge's desk and began rifling through the papers inside it.

'Approval for Whipping ... Approval for Whipping ... I can do it at last ... they've had it coming to them for years ...'

He pulled out a piece of parchment, kissed it, then shuffled rapidly back out of the door, clutching it to his chest.

Harry leapt to his feet and, making sure he had his bag and that the Invisibility Cloak was completely covering him, he wrenched open the door and hurried out of the office after Filch, who was hobbling along faster than Harry had ever seen him go.

One landing down from Umbridge's office, Harry thought it was safe to become visible again. He pulled off the Cloak, shoved it in his bag and hurried onwards. There was a great deal of shouting and movement coming from the Entrance Hall. He ran down the marble staircase and found what looked like most of the school assembled there.

It was just like the night when Trelawney had been sacked. Students were standing all around the walls in a great ring (some of them, Harry noticed, covered in a substance that looked very like Stinksap); teachers and ghosts were also in the crowd. Prominent among the onlookers were members of the Inquisitorial Squad, who were all looking exceptionally pleased with themselves, and Peeves, who was bobbing overhead, gazed down at Fred and George, who stood in the middle of the floor with the unmistakeable look of two people who had just been cornered.

'So!' said Umbridge triumphantly. Harry realised she was standing just a few stairs in front of him, once more looking down upon her prey. 'So – you think it amusing to turn a school corridor into a swamp, do you?'

'Pretty amusing, yeah,' said Fred, looking up at her without the slightest sign of fear.

Filch elbowed his way closer to Umbridge, almost crying with happiness.

'I've got the form, Headmistress,' he said hoarsely, waving the piece of parchment Harry had just seen him take from her desk. 'I've got the form and I've got the whips waiting ... oh, let me do it now ...'

'Very good, Argus,' she said. 'You two,' she went on, gazing down at Fred and George, 'are about to learn what happens to wrongdoers in my school.'

'You know what?' said Fred. 'I don't think we are.'

第29章 就业指导

办公室。他好像为什么事情高兴得要命,一边激动地喃喃自语,一边走过来打开乌姆里奇办公桌的一个抽屉,开始在里面的文件中翻找。

"《鞭刑批准令》……《鞭刑批准令》……我终于能动手了……他们几年前就该尝尝这滋味了……"

他抽出一张羊皮纸,亲了亲,然后把它贴在胸口,拖着步子迅速走出门去。

哈利一跃而起,把书包拿在手里,用隐形衣把自己遮得严严实实,拧开房门,跟着费尔奇冲出了办公室。费尔奇在前面一瘸一拐的,哈利从没见他走得这么快过。

来到乌姆里奇办公室那层的楼梯平台上,哈利认为危险已经过去,可以让自己显形了。他脱下隐形衣塞进书包,匆匆往前走去。门厅里传来很大的喧嚣和骚动声。他跑下大理石楼梯,发现好像全校大部分师生都集聚在那里了。

眼前的情景就像特里劳妮被解雇的那天夜里。同学们都围成一个大圆圈站在墙边(哈利注意到,有些人身上还沾着像是臭汁的东西),老师和幽灵也在人群中。在旁观者中引人注目的是调查行动组的成员,他们都显出特别得意的样子。皮皮鬼在头顶上蹿来蹿去,低头看着站在门厅中央的弗雷德和乔治。从他们俩的样子看,刚才无疑是被逼得走投无路了。

"好啊!"乌姆里奇得意地说。哈利这才发现她就站在他前面几级楼梯下,低头望着她的猎物。"这么说——你们认为把学校走廊变成沼泽地很好玩,是不是?"

"确实很好玩,没错。"弗雷德说,他抬头望着她,没有一丝畏惧。

费尔奇用胳膊肘开路,凑到乌姆里奇身边,高兴得几乎带着哭腔。

"我找到文件了,校长。"他用沙哑的声音说,挥舞着哈利刚才看见他从乌姆里奇书桌里拿来的那张羊皮纸,"文件有了,鞭子也准备好了……哦,现在就让我动手吧……"

"很好,阿格斯。"乌姆里奇说。"你们俩,"她低头望着弗雷德和乔治继续说,"将要领教在我的学校为非作歹会受到什么样的惩罚。"

"你知道吗?"弗雷德说,"我认为我们不会领教了。"

CHAPTER TWENTY-NINE — Careers Advice

He turned to his twin.

'George,' said Fred, 'I think we've outgrown full-time education.'

'Yeah, I've been feeling that way myself,' said George lightly.

'Time to test our talents in the real world, d'you reckon?' asked Fred.

'Definitely,' said George.

And before Umbridge could say a word, they raised their wands and said together:

'*Accio brooms!*'

Harry heard a loud crash somewhere in the distance. Looking to his left, he ducked just in time. Fred and George's broomsticks, one still trailing the heavy chain and iron peg with which Umbridge had fastened them to the wall, were hurtling along the corridor towards their owners; they turned left, streaked down the stairs and stopped sharply in front of the twins, the chain clattering loudly on the flagged stone floor.

'We won't be seeing you,' Fred told Professor Umbridge, swinging his leg over his broomstick.

'Yeah, don't bother to keep in touch,' said George, mounting his own.

Fred looked around at the assembled students, at the silent, watchful crowd.

'If anyone fancies buying a Portable Swamp, as demonstrated upstairs, come to number ninety-three, Diagon Alley – Weasleys' Wizard Wheezes,' he said in a loud voice. 'Our new premises!'

'Special discounts to Hogwarts students who swear they're going to use our products to get rid of this old bat,' added George, pointing at Professor Umbridge.

'STOP THEM!' shrieked Umbridge, but it was too late. As the Inquisitorial Squad closed in, Fred and George kicked off from the floor, shooting fifteen feet into the air, the iron peg swinging dangerously below. Fred looked across the hall at the poltergeist bobbing on his level above the crowd.

'Give her hell from us, Peeves.'

And Peeves, who Harry had never seen take an order from a student before, swept his belled hat from his head and sprang to a salute as Fred and George wheeled about to tumultuous applause from the students below and sped out of the open front doors into the glorious sunset.

第29章 就业指导

他转向自己的孪生兄弟。

"乔治,"弗雷德说,"我认为我们已经不再适合全日制教育了。"

"是啊,我也有同感。"乔治轻快地说。

"应该到现实世界里去试试我们的才能了,你认为呢?"弗雷德问。

"完全正确。"乔治说。

乌姆里奇还没来得及说话,他们俩就举起魔杖,异口同声地说:

"扫帚飞来!"

哈利听见远处什么地方传来一声爆响。他往左边一看,及时地猫腰躲过。弗雷德和乔治的飞天扫帚从走廊上飞来,奔向它们的主人,其中一把扫帚上还拖着沉甸甸的链条和铁栓,因为乌姆里奇一直把它们固定在墙上。它们向左一拐,快速冲下楼梯,猛地停在孪生兄弟面前,链条砸在石板地面上,发出响亮的哗啦哗啦声。

"我们不会再看见你了。"弗雷德对乌姆里奇教授说,一边抬腿跨上了扫帚。

"是啊,不用费事儿跟我们联系了。"乔治说着,也骑上了他的扫帚。

弗雷德看看聚集在周围的同学,看看那些沉默而戒备的人群。

"如果你们想买楼上演示的那种便携式沼泽,请来对角巷93号——韦斯莱魔法把戏坊,"他大声说,"我们的新店铺!"

"只要霍格沃茨学生发誓要用我们的产品赶走这只老蝙蝠,就可享受特殊折扣。"乔治指着乌姆里奇教授说。

"**拦住他们!**"乌姆里奇尖叫道,可是已经晚了。就在调查行动组包围过来的当儿,弗雷德和乔治使劲一蹬地面,蹿到了十五英尺高的空中,那根大铁钉危险地挂在下面晃来晃去。弗雷德看着门厅那边的恶作剧精灵——皮皮鬼悬在人群上空,跟弗雷德同样高度。

"皮皮鬼,替我们教训她。"

哈利从没见过皮皮鬼听从哪个学生的吩咐,此刻皮皮鬼却快速脱下头上的钟形帽子,敏捷地向弗雷德和乔治行了个礼。孪生兄弟在下面同学们暴风雨般的喝彩声中,飞出敞开的大门,融入了辉煌夺目的夕阳之中。

CHAPTER THIRTY

Grawp

The story of Fred and George's flight to freedom was retold so often over the next few days that Harry could tell it would soon become the stuff of Hogwarts legend: within a week, even those who had been eye-witnesses were half convinced they had seen the twins dive-bomb Umbridge on their brooms and pelt her with Dungbombs before zooming out of the doors. In the immediate aftermath of their departure there was a great wave of talk about copying them. Harry frequently heard students saying things like, 'Honestly, some days I just feel like jumping on my broom and leaving this place,' or else, 'One more lesson like that and I might just do a Weasley.'

Fred and George had made sure nobody was likely to forget them too soon. For one thing, they had not left instructions on how to remove the swamp that now filled the corridor on the fifth floor of the east wing. Umbridge and Filch had been observed trying different means of removing it but without success. Eventually, the area was roped off and Filch, gnashing his teeth furiously, was given the task of punting students across it to their classrooms. Harry was certain that teachers like McGonagall or Flitwick could have removed the swamp in an instant but, just as in the case of Fred and George's Wildfire Whiz-bangs, they seemed to prefer to watch Umbridge struggle.

Then there were the two large broom-shaped holes in Umbridge's office door, through which Fred and George's Cleansweeps had smashed to rejoin their masters. Filch fitted a new door and removed Harry's Firebolt to the dungeons where, it was rumoured, Umbridge had set an armed security troll to guard it. However, her troubles were far from over.

Inspired by Fred and George's example, a great number of students were now vying for the newly vacant positions of Troublemakers-in-Chief. In spite of the new door, somebody managed to slip a hairy-snouted Niffler

第30章

格洛普

在接下来的几天里,弗雷德和乔治奔向自由的故事被复述了一遍又一遍,哈利断定它很快就会成为霍格沃茨的经典传奇。一星期内,就连那些亲眼目睹这一幕的同学,也隐约相信他们真的看见孪生兄弟骑着扫帚冲向乌姆里奇,朝她投掷了粪弹,然后才飞出门去的。弗雷德和乔治刚离开那段时间,大家纷纷说要模仿他们。哈利经常听见同学们说:"说实在的,有朝一日我真想跳上扫帚,离开这个鬼地方",或"再上一堂这样的课,我就去做韦斯莱了"。

弗雷德和乔治确保不让任何人很快忘记他们。比如,他们没有留下指示,告诉别人怎么清除现在淤积在城堡东侧六楼走廊上的那些沼泽。人们看到乌姆里奇和费尔奇试了各种办法清除沼泽都无济于事。最后,那片地方用绳子隔开了,费尔奇负责用平底船载同学们渡过沼泽去教室上课,他为此气得直咬牙。哈利相信,麦格和弗立维这样的教师有办法一眨眼间就把沼泽清除干净,但是他们的态度就像对待弗雷德和乔治的嗖嗖—嘭烟火时一样,似乎更愿意袖手旁观乌姆里奇的狼狈样儿。

乌姆里奇办公室的门上有两个扫帚形状的大洞,那是弗雷德和乔治的两把横扫冲出去寻找主人时留下的。费尔奇给乌姆里奇的办公室新换了一扇门,并把哈利的火弩箭转移到地下教室,据说乌姆里奇还派了全副武装的巨怪保安在那里看守。然而,她的麻烦还远远没有结束。

在弗雷德和乔治这两个榜样的感召下,许多同学都在竞争新近空缺的捣蛋大王的位置。虽然乌姆里奇的办公室换了新门,但不知是谁

CHAPTER THIRTY   Grawp

into Umbridge's office, which promptly tore the place apart in its search for shiny objects, leapt on Umbridge when she entered and tried to gnaw the rings off her stubby fingers. Dungbombs and Stink Pellets were dropped so frequently in the corridors that it became the new fashion for students to perform Bubble-Head Charms on themselves before leaving lessons, which ensured them a supply of fresh air, even though it gave them all the peculiar appearance of wearing upside-down goldfish bowls on their heads.

Filch prowled the corridors with a horsewhip ready in his hands, desperate to catch miscreants, but the problem was that there were now so many of them he never knew which way to turn. The Inquisitorial Squad was attempting to help him, but odd things kept happening to its members. Warrington of the Slytherin Quidditch team reported to the hospital wing with a horrible skin complaint that made him look as though he had been coated in cornflakes; Pansy Parkinson, to Hermione's delight, missed all her lessons the following day as she had sprouted antlers.

Meanwhile, it became clear just how many Skiving Snackboxes Fred and George had managed to sell before leaving Hogwarts. Umbridge only had to enter her classroom for the students assembled there to faint, vomit, develop dangerous fevers or else spout blood from both nostrils. Shrieking with rage and frustration, she attempted to trace the mysterious symptoms to their source, but the students told her stubbornly they were suffering from 'Umbridge-itis'. After putting four successive classes in detention and failing to discover their secret, she was forced to give up and allow the bleeding, swooning, sweating and vomiting students to leave her classes in droves.

But not even the users of the Snackboxes could compete with that master of chaos, Peeves, who seemed to have taken Fred's parting words deeply to heart. Cackling madly, he soared through the school, upending tables, bursting out of blackboards, toppling statues and vases; twice he shut Mrs Norris inside a suit of armour, from which she was rescued, yowling loudly, by the furious caretaker. Peeves smashed lanterns and snuffed out candles, juggled burning torches over the heads of screaming students, caused neatly stacked piles of parchment to topple into fires or out of windows; flooded the second floor when he pulled off all the taps in the bathrooms, dropped a bag of tarantulas in the middle of the Great Hall during breakfast and, whenever he fancied a break, spent hours at a time floating along after Umbridge and blowing loud raspberries every time she spoke.

第30章 格洛普

竟然把一个毛鼻子的嗅嗅塞了进去。嗅嗅到处寻找发亮的东西，很快就把屋子里翻得乱七八糟。乌姆里奇一进门，它就扑了上去，想把她粗短的手指上的那些戒指咬下来。粪弹和臭弹频频在走廊里爆炸，同学们开始流行在离开教室前给自己念一个泡头咒，确保能呼吸到新鲜空气，虽然头上反扣着一个金鱼缸的样子非常滑稽。

费尔奇手里拿着马鞭在走廊里巡视，迫不及待地想抓到肇事者，可问题是现在肇事的人太多，他总是不知道该到哪边去找。调查行动组也想帮他，可是行动组成员身上不断发生一些怪事。斯莱特林魁地奇队的沃林顿被送进了医院，他得了一种可怕的皮肤病，看上去好像全身覆盖着一层玉米片；潘西·帕金森第二天一直没来上课，因为她脑袋上长出了鹿角，这使赫敏暗自高兴。

另外，人们这才开始弄清弗雷德和乔治在离开霍格沃茨前卖出了多少速效逃课糖。只要乌姆里奇一走进教室，那里的同学就会昏迷、呕吐、发起危险的高烧，或者两个鼻孔同时喷血。乌姆里奇愤怒而烦恼地尖声大叫，试图查出这些神秘症状的根源，但同学们一口咬定他们是患了"乌姆里奇综合征"。她接连关了四个班的禁闭，却没有弄清他们的秘密，最后只好作罢，允许那些流血、昏厥、大汗淋漓、呕吐不止的同学成群结队地离开她的教室。

然而，就连那些使用速效逃课糖的同学，跟捣蛋大王皮皮鬼比起来也是小巫见大巫。皮皮鬼似乎把弗雷德的临别嘱托牢记在了心里。他呱呱狂笑着在学校里飞来飞去，掀翻课桌，从黑板里蹿出来，把雕像和花瓶全部推倒。有两次他把洛丽丝夫人关在一套铠甲里面，洛丽丝夫人高声惨叫，才被气得发疯的管理员解救出来。皮皮鬼还把灯打碎，把蜡烛熄灭，在同学们头上抛接燃烧的火把，吓得他们惊慌尖叫；他还把一摞摞整整齐齐的羊皮纸丢进火里或扔到窗外；把盥洗室的所有水龙头拔掉，弄得三楼发起了大水；并在吃早饭的时候把一袋狼蛛扔在礼堂中央。此外，每当他消停一会儿，就会花上几个小时跟在乌姆里奇身后飘荡，她一开口说话就大声地呸她。

CHAPTER THIRTY — Grawp

None of the staff but Filch seemed to be stirring themselves to help her. Indeed, a week after Fred and George's departure Harry witnessed Professor McGonagall walking right past Peeves, who was determinedly loosening a crystal chandelier, and could have sworn he heard her tell the poltergeist out of the corner of her mouth, 'It unscrews the other way.'

To cap matters, Montague had still not recovered from his sojourn in the toilet; he remained confused and disorientated and his parents were to be observed one Tuesday morning striding up the front drive, looking extremely angry.

'Should we say something?' said Hermione in a worried voice, pressing her cheek against the Charms window so that she could see Mr and Mrs Montague marching inside. 'About what happened to him? In case it helps Madam Pomfrey cure him?'

'Course not, he'll recover,' said Ron indifferently.

'Anyway, more trouble for Umbridge, isn't it?' said Harry in a satisfied voice.

He and Ron both tapped the teacups they were supposed to be charming with their wands. Harry's spouted four very short legs that could not reach the desk and wriggled pointlessly in midair. Ron's grew four very thin spindly legs that hoisted the cup off the desk with great difficulty, trembled for a few seconds, then folded, causing the cup to crack into two.

'*Reparo*,' said Hermione quickly, mending Ron's cup with a wave of her wand. 'That's all very well, but what if Montague's permanently injured?'

'Who cares?' said Ron irritably, while his teacup stood up drunkenly again, trembling violently at the knees. 'Montague shouldn't have tried to take all those points from Gryffindor, should he? If you want to worry about anyone, Hermione, worry about me!'

'You?' she said, catching her teacup as it scampered happily away across the desk on four sturdy little willow-patterned legs, and replacing it in front of her. 'Why should I be worried about you?'

'When Mum's next letter finally gets through Umbridge's screening process,' said Ron bitterly, now holding his cup up while its frail legs tried feebly to support its weight, 'I'm going to be in deep trouble. I wouldn't be surprised if she's sent another Howler.'

'But —'

'It'll be my fault Fred and George left, you wait,' said Ron darkly. 'She'll

第30章 格洛普

除了费尔奇,教员们似乎谁也不出来帮她。而且,在弗雷德和乔治离开一星期后,哈利亲眼看见麦格教授走过皮皮鬼身边,皮皮鬼正在起劲地拧松一个枝形水晶吊灯的螺丝,哈利可以发誓他听见麦格教授几乎不动嘴唇地说:"你拧反了。"

最可怕的是,蒙太还没有从被卡在马桶的惊吓中恢复过来。他仍然神志恍惚,思维混乱。一个星期二的早晨,人们看见他的父母大步流星地走在城堡前的车道上,看上去火冒三丈。

"我们是不是应该出来说句话?"赫敏用担忧的语气说,她把脸贴在魔咒课教室的窗户上,看见蒙太夫妇大步走进了城堡,"说说他是怎么回事,没准儿能帮助庞弗雷女士把他治好呢。"

"当然不用,他会好起来的。"罗恩漫不经心地说。

"反正给乌姆里奇添了麻烦,不是吗?"哈利用满意的口吻说。

他和罗恩都用魔杖敲着需要施魔咒的茶杯。哈利的茶杯冒出了四条小短腿,却够不到桌面,只是徒劳地悬在半空中扭动。罗恩的茶杯长出了四条长长的细腿,十分吃力地把茶杯从桌上举了起来,颤颤巍巍地坚持了几秒钟,终于支撑不住,茶杯摔成了两半。

"恢复如初。"赫敏赶紧说道,一挥魔杖,把罗恩的茶杯修好了,"那倒是挺好,可是万一蒙太的伤永远好不了呢?"

"管他呢?"罗恩不耐烦地说,他的茶杯又摇摇晃晃地站了起来,膝盖颤抖得特别厉害,"蒙太就不应该试图给格兰芬多减去那么多分,不是吗?赫敏,如果你硬要替人操心,就操心操心我吧!"

"你?"赫敏说,她那个茶杯迈动四条柳叶花纹的结实小腿,在桌面上快活地跑来跑去,她把它抓起来重新放在自己面前,"我凭什么要替你操心呀?"

"等妈妈的下一封信通过了乌姆里奇的审查程序,"罗恩气恼地说,用手扶着他的杯子,那些软弱的细腿正挣扎着支撑茶杯的重量,"我的麻烦可就大了。即使她再寄一封吼叫信来,我也不会感到意外。"

"可是——"

"你等着吧,弗雷德和乔治离开都是我的错,"罗恩闷闷不乐地说,

CHAPTER THIRTY · Grawp

say I should've stopped them leaving, I should've grabbed the ends of their brooms and hung on or something ... yeah, it'll be all my fault.'

'Well, if she *does* say that it'll be very unfair, you couldn't have done anything! But I'm sure she won't, I mean, if it's really true they've got premises in Diagon Alley, they must have been planning this for ages.'

'Yeah, but that's another thing, how did they get premises?' said Ron, hitting his teacup so hard with his wand that its legs collapsed again and it lay twitching before him. 'It's a bit dodgy, isn't it? They'll need loads of Galleons to afford the rent on a place in Diagon Alley. She'll want to know what they've been up to, to get their hands on that sort of gold.'

'Well, yes, that occurred to me, too,' said Hermione, allowing her teacup to jog in neat little circles around Harry's, whose stubby little legs were still unable to touch the desktop, 'I've been wondering whether Mundungus has persuaded them to sell stolen goods or something awful.'

'He hasn't,' said Harry curtly.

'How do you know?' said Ron and Hermione together.

'Because –' Harry hesitated, but the moment to confess finally seemed to have come. There was no good to be gained in keeping silent if it meant anyone suspected that Fred and George were criminals. 'Because they got the gold from me. I gave them my Triwizard winnings last June.'

There was a shocked silence, then Hermione's teacup jogged right over the edge of the desk and smashed on the floor.

'Oh, Harry, you *didn't!*' she said.

'Yes, I did,' said Harry mutinously. 'And I don't regret it, either. I didn't need the gold and they'll be great at running a joke shop.'

'But this is excellent!' said Ron, looking thrilled. 'It's all your fault, Harry – Mum can't blame me at all! Can I tell her?'

'Yeah, I suppose you'd better,' said Harry dully, ''specially if she thinks they're receiving stolen cauldrons or something.'

Hermione said nothing at all for the rest of the lesson, but Harry had a shrewd suspicion that her self-restraint was bound to crack before long. Sure enough, once they had left the castle for break and were standing around in the weak May sunshine, she fixed Harry with a beady eye and opened her mouth with a determined air.

第30章 格洛普

"她会说我应该把他们拦住,我应该抓住他们的扫帚尾巴死死不放什么的……没错,什么都是我的错。"

"她如果真的那么说,就太不公平了,你根本就无能为力!但我相信她不会怪你的,我是说,如果他们真的在对角巷弄到了门面,那肯定是蓄谋已久的了。"

"没错,可是又一个问题来了,他们是怎么弄到门面的?"罗恩说着,用魔杖敲了一下茶杯,但敲得太重了,那四条腿又瘫软下去,茶杯躺在他面前抽搐,"有点儿可疑,是不是?他们需要有大把的金加隆才能在对角巷租到一个门面。妈妈肯定想知道他们都做了些什么才弄到那么多金子的。"

"是啊,是啊,我也想到了。"赫敏说,一边让自己的茶杯在哈利茶杯周围绕着圈儿小跑,而哈利茶杯的那几条短腿还是够不着桌面,"我一直在想,是不是蒙顿格斯在怂恿他们贩卖赃物什么的。"

"没有。"哈利断然否认。

"你怎么知道?"罗恩和赫敏异口同声地问。

"因为——"哈利迟疑着,但似乎终于到了该说实话的时候了。如果有人怀疑弗雷德和乔治犯了法,那么他再保持沉默就没有任何好处了。"因为他们是从我这里得到的金子。我把去年六月三强争霸赛的奖金给了他们。"

一阵惊愕的沉默,赫敏的茶杯跑到桌子边缘,掉在地上摔碎了。

"哦,哈利,不会吧!"她说。

"没错,就是这样,"哈利倔强地说,"而且我不后悔。我不需要那些金子,它们用来开笑话店再合适不过了。"

"太棒了!"罗恩说,一副激动的样子,"这事儿都怪你,哈利——妈妈不会来责怪我了!我可以告诉她吗?"

"可以,我想你最好告诉她,"哈利淡淡地说,"特别是她可能以为他们在接受偷来的坩埚什么的。"

赫敏一直到下课都没有说话,但是哈利敏锐地怀疑她用不了多久就会克制不住自己。果然,课间休息时他们刚离开城堡,站在微弱的五月阳光下,赫敏就用严厉的目光瞪着哈利,带着一种决绝的神情张开了嘴巴。

CHAPTER THIRTY   Grawp

Harry interrupted her before she had even started.

'It's no good nagging me, it's done,' he said firmly. 'Fred and George have got the gold – spent a good bit of it, too, by the sounds of it – and I can't get it back from them and I don't want to. So save your breath, Hermione.'

'I wasn't going to say anything about Fred and George!' she said in an injured voice.

Ron snorted disbelievingly and Hermione threw him a very dirty look.

'No, I wasn't!' she said angrily. 'As a matter of fact, I was going to ask Harry when he's going to go back to Snape and ask for more Occlumency lessons!'

Harry's heart sank. Once they had exhausted the subject of Fred and George's dramatic departure, which admittedly had taken many hours, Ron and Hermione had wanted to hear news of Sirius. As Harry had not confided in them the reason he had wanted to talk to Sirius in the first place, it had been hard to think of what to tell them; he had ended up saying, truthfully, that Sirius wanted Harry to resume Occlumency lessons. He had been regretting this ever since; Hermione would not let the subject drop and kept reverting to it when Harry least expected it.

'You can't tell me you've stopped having funny dreams,' Hermione said now, 'because Ron told me you were muttering in your sleep again last night.'

Harry threw Ron a furious look. Ron had the grace to look ashamed of himself.

'You were only muttering a bit,' he mumbled apologetically. 'Something about "just a bit further".'

'I dreamed I was watching you lot play Quidditch,' Harry lied brutally. 'I was trying to get you to stretch out a bit further to grab the Quaffle.'

Ron's ears went red. Harry felt a kind of vindictive pleasure; he had not, of course, dreamed anything of the sort.

Last night, he had once again made the journey along the Department of Mysteries corridor. He had passed through the circular room, then the room full of clicking and dancing light, until he found himself again inside that cavernous room full of shelves on which were ranged dusty glass spheres.

He had hurried straight towards row number ninety-seven, turned left and run along it ... it had probably been then that he had spoken aloud ... *just a bit further* ... for he felt his conscious self struggling to wake ... and before

第30章 格洛普

哈利没等她开口，就打断了她。

"跟我唠叨也没用，事情已经做了。"他语气坚决地说，"弗雷德和乔治拿到了金子——听起来已经花了不少——我没法从他们那儿再要回来，我也不想这么做。你就省省力气吧，赫敏。"

"我根本没打算说弗雷德和乔治的事！"她用一种委屈的口吻说。

罗恩不相信地哼了一声，赫敏恶狠狠地白了他一眼。

"不是那回事！"她气呼呼地说，"实际上，我是想问哈利什么时候去找斯内普要求再上大脑封闭术课！"

哈利的心一沉。他们谈够了弗雷德和乔治戏剧性的离别之后——必须承认，这占去了好几个小时——罗恩和赫敏就想听听小天狼星的消息。哈利没有把他想跟小天狼星谈话的原因告诉他们，所以想不出该跟他们说些什么。最后他只好说小天狼星希望他继续上大脑封闭术课，这倒是实话。结果，话一出口他就一直在后悔。赫敏不肯放过这个话题，总是在哈利最没提防的时候提起这件事。

"你别跟我说你已经不再做怪梦了，"赫敏说道，"因为罗恩告诉我，你昨晚又说梦话了。"

哈利气恼地瞪了罗恩一眼。罗恩通情达理地显出羞愧的样子。

"你只是嘟哝了几句，"他充满歉意地低声说，"好像是说'再往前一点'。"

"我梦见我在观看你们那帮人打魁地奇，"哈利狠狠心撒谎说，"我想让你把胳膊再伸长一些，抓住鬼飞球。"

罗恩的耳朵红了。哈利感到一种报复性的快感。当然啦，他根本没有梦见这一类事情。

昨天夜里，他又一次穿行在神秘事务司的走廊里。他走过圆形房间，走过那个充满了滴答声和跳动灯光的房间，最后发现自己又来到了那间大屋子里，一排排架子上摆着许多灰扑扑的玻璃球。

他快步走向第九十七排，往左一拐，顺着架子往前跑……他大概就是在那个时候说出声来了……再往前一点……因为他感觉到自己的意识挣扎着要醒过来了……没等他跑到那排架子的尽头，他就发现自

CHAPTER THIRTY   Grawp

he had reached the end of the row, he had found himself lying in bed again, gazing up at the canopy of his four-poster.

'You are *trying* to block your mind, aren't you?' said Hermione, looking beadily at Harry. 'You are keeping going with your Occlumency?'

'Of course I am,' said Harry, trying to sound as though this question was insulting, but not quite meeting her eye. The truth was he was so intensely curious about what was hidden in that room full of dusty orbs, that he was quite keen for the dreams to continue.

The problem was that with just under a month to go until the exams and every free moment devoted to revision, his mind seemed so saturated with information when he went to bed he found it very difficult to get to sleep at all; and when he did, his overwrought brain presented him most nights with stupid dreams about the exams. He also suspected that part of his mind – the part that often spoke in Hermione's voice – now felt guilty on the occasions it strayed down that corridor ending in the black door, and sought to wake him before he could reach the journey's end.

'You know,' said Ron, whose ears were still flaming red, 'if Montague doesn't recover before Slytherin play Hufflepuff, we might be in with a chance of winning the Cup.'

'Yeah, I s'pose so,' said Harry, glad of a change of subject.

'I mean, we've won one, lost one – if Slytherin lose to Hufflepuff next Saturday –'

'Yeah, that's right,' said Harry, losing track of what he was agreeing to. Cho Chang had just walked across the courtyard, determinedly not looking at him.

The final match of the Quidditch season, Gryffindor versus Ravenclaw, was to take place on the last weekend of May. Although Slytherin had been narrowly defeated by Hufflepuff in their last match, Gryffindor were not daring to hope for victory, due mainly (though of course nobody said it to him) to Ron's abysmal goal-keeping record. He, however, seemed to have found a new optimism.

'I mean, I can't get any worse, can I?' he told Harry and Hermione grimly over breakfast on the morning of the match. 'Nothing to lose now, is there?'

'You know,' said Hermione, as she and Harry walked down to the pitch

第30章 格洛普

己又躺在床上，望着四柱床帷帐的帐顶。

"你正在试着封闭你的意识，对吗？"赫敏严厉地望着哈利说，"你在继续练习大脑封闭术，对吗？"

"那还用说。"哈利说，努力假装这个问题对他来说是一种侮辱，却不敢面对赫敏的目光。事实上，他对那间装满灰扑扑玻璃球的屋子里藏着什么感到非常好奇，迫不及待地想让梦境继续下去。

问题是，离考试只有不到一个月的时间，余暇都用来复习功课了，他脑子里塞满了知识，上床以后，他发现连入睡都很困难。等真的睡着了，大多数夜晚，他紧张过度的大脑向他呈现的是关于考试的无聊梦境。他还怀疑自己的一部分大脑——这部分大脑经常用赫敏的声音说话——为徘徊在黑门走廊上感到内疚，总是想办法在他到达旅程终点之前把他唤醒。

"你知道，"罗恩说，他的耳朵仍然红通通的，"如果蒙太不能在斯莱特林跟赫奇帕奇比赛之前恢复健康，我们说不定还有机会赢得奖杯呢。"

"是啊，我也是这样想的。"哈利说，很高兴能够改变话题。

"我的意思是，我们赢了一场，输了一场——如果下个星期六斯莱特林输给了赫奇帕奇——"

"是啊，没错。"哈利说，却忘记了自己在赞同什么。秋·张刚刚从院子里走过，故意没有看他。

魁地奇赛季的最后一场比赛，格兰芬多对拉文克劳，将在五月的最后一个周末举行。虽然斯莱特林在上次比赛中以微弱比分输给了赫奇帕奇，但格兰芬多并不敢奢望能够获胜，这主要是因为罗恩糟糕的守门成绩（当然啦，没有人对他当面点破）。不过，他自己似乎又找到了一种乐观的理由。

"我的意思是，我不可能更糟糕了，是不是？"比赛那天吃早饭时，他严肃地对哈利和赫敏说，"现在没有什么可失去的了，是不是？"

"知道吗，"赫敏说，这时她正和哈利裹在兴奋的人群中朝球场走去，

CHAPTER THIRTY   Grawp

a little later in the midst of a very excitable crowd, 'I think Ron might do better without Fred and George around. They never exactly gave him a lot of confidence.'

Luna Lovegood overtook them with what appeared to be a live eagle perched on top of her head.

'Oh, gosh, I forgot!' said Hermione, watching the eagle flapping its wings as Luna walked serenely past a group of cackling and pointing Slytherins. 'Cho will be playing, won't she?'

Harry, who had not forgotten this, merely grunted.

They found seats in the second topmost row of the stands. It was a fine, clear day; Ron could not wish for better, and Harry found himself hoping against hope that Ron would not give the Slytherins cause for more rousing choruses of 'Weasley is our King'.

Lee Jordan, who had been very dispirited since Fred and George had left, was commentating as usual. As the teams zoomed out on to the pitch he named the players with something less than his usual gusto.

'... Bradley ... Davies ... Chang,' he said, and Harry felt his stomach perform, less of a back flip, more a feeble lurch as Cho walked out on to the pitch, her shiny black hair rippling in the slight breeze. He was not sure what he wanted to happen any more, except that he could not stand any more rows. Even the sight of her chatting animatedly to Roger Davies as they prepared to mount their brooms caused him only a slight twinge of jealousy.

'And they're off!' said Lee. 'And Davies takes the Quaffle immediately, Ravenclaw Captain Davies with the Quaffle, he dodges Johnson, he dodges Bell, he dodges Spinnet as well ... he's going straight for goal! He's going to shoot – and – and –' Lee swore very loudly. 'And he's scored.'

Harry and Hermione groaned with the rest of the Gryffindors. Predictably, horribly, the Slytherins on the other side of the stands began to sing:

> *'Weasley cannot save a thing*
> *He cannot block a single ring ...'*

'Harry,' said a hoarse voice in Harry's ear. 'Hermione ...'

第30章 格洛普

"我认为弗雷德和乔治不在，罗恩可能会表现得更好。他们从来没有给过他多少信心。"

卢娜·洛夫古德赶上了他们，她头顶上似乎栖息着一只活生生的老鹰。

"哦，糟了，我给忘了！"赫敏说，一边注视着老鹰扑扇翅膀，卢娜旁若无人地走过一群喊喊喳喳、指指点点的斯莱特林，"秋·张也参加比赛，是不是？"

哈利可没有忘记，他只是嘟哝了一句。

他们在看台最高处的第二排找到了座位。这是一个晴朗、明媚的日子，罗恩肯定很满意，哈利发现自己内心存着一丝希望，这次罗恩不会再给斯莱特林高唱"韦斯莱是我们的王"的理由了。

李·乔丹自从弗雷德和乔治走后一直情绪低落，他和往常一样担任比赛解说员。球队快速进场时，他报出每位队员的名字，但热情远不如以前。

"……布拉德利……戴维斯……张。"他说。哈利看到秋·张走进球场，一头闪闪发亮的黑发在微风中飘动，他感到自己的心十分微妙地悸动了一下。他不知道自己希望怎样，只知道再也受不了争吵。即使看到秋·张在准备骑上扫帚时跟罗杰·戴维斯亲热交谈，哈利也只感到一丝丝妒意。

"比赛开始了！"李说，"戴维斯立刻得球，拉文克劳队队长戴维斯拿到了鬼飞球，他闪过约翰逊，闪过贝尔，又闪过斯平内特……他朝球门直冲过去！他要投了——结果——结果——"李大声骂了一句，"他得分了。"

哈利和赫敏跟格兰芬多的其他同学一起唉声叹气。不出所料，看台另一边的斯莱特林们令人恐惧地唱了起来：

韦斯莱那个小傻样
他一个球也不会挡……

"哈利，"一个沙哑的声音在哈利耳边响起，"赫敏……"

CHAPTER THIRTY Grawp

Harry looked round and saw Hagrid's enormous bearded face sticking between the seats. Apparently, he had squeezed his way all along the row behind, for the first- and second-years he had just passed had a ruffled, flattened look about them. for some reason, Hagrid was bent double as though anxious not to be seen, though he was still at least four feet taller than everybody else.

'Listen,' he whispered, 'can yeh come with me? Now? While ev'ryone's watchin' the match?'

'Er ... can't it wait, Hagrid?' asked Harry. 'Till the match is over?'

'No,' said Hagrid. 'No, Harry, it's gotta be now ... while ev'ryone's lookin' the other way ... please?'

Hagrid's nose was gently dripping blood. His eyes were both blackened. Harry had not seen him this close-up since his return to the school; he looked utterly woebegone.

'Course,' said Harry at once, 'course we'll come.'

He and Hermione edged back along their row of seats, causing much grumbling among the students who had to stand up for them. The people in Hagrid's row were not complaining, merely attempting to make themselves as small as possible.

'I 'ppreciate this, you two, I really do,' said Hagrid as they reached the stairs. He kept looking around nervously as they descended towards the lawn below. 'I jus' hope she doesn' notice us goin'.'

'You mean Umbridge?' said Harry. 'She won't, she's got her whole Inquisitorial Squad sitting with her, didn't you see? She must be expecting trouble at the match.'

'Yeah, well, a bit o' trouble wouldn' hurt,' said Hagrid, pausing to peer around the edge of the stands to make sure the stretch of lawn between there and his cabin was deserted. 'Give us more time.'

'What is it, Hagrid?' said Hermione, looking up at him with a concerned expression on her face as they hurried across the grass towards the edge of the Forest.

'Yeh – yeh'll see in a mo',' said Hagrid, looking over his shoulder as a great roar rose from the stands behind them. 'Hey – did someone jus' score?'

'It'll be Ravenclaw,' said Harry heavily.

'Good ... good ...' said Hagrid distractedly. 'Tha's good ...'

第30章 格洛普

哈利回过头,看见海格胡子拉碴的大脸庞从两个座位间探了出来。显然,他刚才顺着后面一排座位挤了过来,被他挤过的那些一二年级学生看上去都衣冠不整,好像被压扁了似的。不知为什么,海格把身子弯得很低,似乎特别担心被人看见,其实他仍然比别人至少高出四英尺。

"听着,"他小声说,"你们能跟我来一趟吗?就现在?趁别人都在看比赛?"

"呃……就不能等等吗,海格?"哈利问,"等比赛结束了再说?"

"不行,"海格说,"不行,哈利,必须现在……趁别人都看着另一边……求你了。"

海格的鼻子微微有些流血,两个眼圈都黑了。自从海格回到学校后,哈利还没有这么近距离地看过他,他完全是一副落魄相。

"行,"哈利赶紧说,"我们当然可以去。"

他和赫敏顺着那排座位往外挤,那些同学不得不站起来让他们通过,都不满地抱怨着。海格那排座位上的人倒是没有抱怨,只是尽量把自己缩得越小越好。

"太感谢你们俩了,真的。"走到楼梯口时,海格说。他们朝下面的草坪走去,海格一直紧张地东张西望。"但愿她没有注意到我们走了。"

"你是说乌姆里奇?"哈利说,"不会的,她的调查行动组都跟她坐在一起呢,你没看见吗?她肯定以为比赛中会出乱子。"

"是啊,是啊,出点儿乱子没什么坏处,"海格说着,停下来从看台边缘向外张望,确保从那里到他小屋间的草地上没有人,"可以多给我们一些时间。"

"怎么回事,海格?"赫敏抬头望着他问,脸上是一副担忧的表情,这时他们匆匆穿过草地朝禁林边缘走去。

"你们——你们很快就会明白的,"海格说,后面的看台上突然一阵喧哗,他扭头看了看,"哟——有人进球了吗?"

"肯定是拉文克劳。"哈利闷闷不乐地说。

"好……好……"海格心不在焉地说,"那就好……"

CHAPTER THIRTY   Grawp

They had to jog to keep up with him as he strode across the lawn, looking around with every other step. When they reached his cabin, Hermione turned automatically left towards the front door. Hagrid, however, walked straight past it into the shade of the trees on the outermost edge of the Forest, where he picked up a crossbow that was leaning against a tree. When he realised they were no longer with him, he turned.

'We're goin' in here,' he said, jerking his shaggy head behind him.

'Into the Forest?' said Hermione, perplexed.

'Yeah,' said Hagrid. 'C'mon now, quick, before we're spotted!'

Harry and Hermione looked at each other, then ducked into the cover of the trees behind Hagrid, who was already striding away from them into the green gloom, his crossbow over his arm. Harry and Hermione ran to catch up with him.

'Hagrid, why are you armed?' said Harry.

'Jus' a precaution,' said Hagrid, shrugging his massive shoulders.

'You didn't bring your crossbow the day you showed us the Thestrals,' said Hermione timidly.

'Nah, well, we weren' goin' in so far then,' said Hagrid. 'An' anyway, tha' was before Firenze left the Forest, wasn' it?'

'Why does Firenze leaving make a difference?' asked Hermione curiously.

''Cause the other centaurs are good an' riled at me, tha's why,' said Hagrid quietly, glancing around. 'They used ter be – well, yeh couldn' call 'em friendly – but we got on all righ'. Kept 'emselves to 'emselves, bu' always turned up if I wanted a word. Not any more.'

He sighed deeply.

'Firenze said they're angry because he went to work for Dumbledore,' Harry said, tripping on a protruding root because he was busy watching Hagrid's profile.

'Yeah,' said Hagrid heavily. 'Well, angry doesn' cover it. Ruddy livid. If I hadn' stepped in, I reckon they'd've kicked Firenze ter death –'

'They attacked him?' said Hermione, sounding shocked.

'Yep,' said Hagrid gruffly, forcing his way through several low-hanging branches. 'He had half the herd on to him.'

'And you stopped it?' said Harry, amazed and impressed. 'By yourself?'

'Course I did, couldn't stand by an' watch 'em kill 'im, could I?' said Hagrid.

第30章 格洛普

他在草地上迈着大步,每走两步就回头张望一眼,哈利和赫敏不得不小跑着跟上他。到了小屋跟前,赫敏习惯性地左拐,朝屋门走去。可是海格直接走了过去,走进禁林最外围的树荫,拿起靠在树上的一把弩箭。他发现他们没有跟过来,就转回身。

"我们进这里面。"他说,把乱蓬蓬的脑袋朝后面摆了一下。

"进禁林?"赫敏迷惑地问。

"是啊,"海格说,"来吧,快点,趁别人没有发现!"

哈利和赫敏交换了一下目光,然后跟着海格钻进了树丛。海格已经大步走进昏暗的树影中,胳膊上挎着弩。哈利和赫敏奔跑着追上了他。

"海格,你为什么拿着武器?"哈利问。

"以防万一吧。"海格说着,耸了耸宽阔的肩膀。

"你给我们看夜骐的那天并没有带着弩啊。"赫敏小心翼翼地说。

"是啊,因为,我们那次不用走得这么远,"海格说,"而且,那是在费伦泽离开禁林之前,不是吗?"

"和费伦泽离开禁林有什么关系?"赫敏好奇地问。

"因为别的马人都对我特别生气,"海格东张西望地小声说,"他们以前都很——是啊,也不能说他们友好——但我们相处得还不错。从来不打扰我,每当我想跟他们谈谈的时候,他们总会出现。现在不了。"

他重重地叹了一口气。

"费伦泽说,他们生气是因为他去为邓布利多工作。"哈利说,他只顾盯着海格的身影,不小心被一块突出的树根绊了一下。

"是啊,"海格语气沉重地说,"唉,说生气远远不够,简直是大怒。要不是我进去干预,他们恐怕会把费伦泽踢死——"

"他们居然攻击他?"赫敏用震惊的口吻说。

"可不是吗,"海格粗声说,费力地穿过几根低垂的树枝,"一半的马人都扑在他身上。"

"你阻止了?"哈利又惊讶又佩服地说,"你一个人?"

"那还用说,总不能眼睁睁地看着他们把他弄死吧,是不是?"海

CHAPTER THIRTY   Grawp

'Lucky I was passin', really ... an' I'd've thought Firenze mighta remembered tha' before he started sendin' me stupid warnin's!' he added hotly and unexpectedly.

Harry and Hermione looked at each other, startled, but Hagrid, scowling, did not elaborate.

'Anyway,' he said, breathing a little more heavily than usual, 'since then the other centaurs've bin livid with me, an' the trouble is they've got a lot of influence in the Forest ... cleverest creatures in here.'

'Is that why we're here, Hagrid?' asked Hermione. 'The centaurs?'

'Ah, no,' said Hagrid, shaking his head dismissively, 'no, it's not them. Well, o' course, they could complicate the problem, yeah ... but yeh'll see what I mean in a bit.'

On this incomprehensible note he fell silent and forged a little ahead, taking one stride for every three of theirs, so that they had great trouble keeping up with him.

The path was becoming increasingly overgrown and the trees grew so closely together as they walked further and further into the Forest that it was as dark as dusk. They were soon a long way past the clearing where Hagrid had shown them the Thestrals, but Harry felt no sense of unease until Hagrid stepped unexpectedly off the path and began wending his way in and out of trees towards the dark heart of the Forest.

'Hagrid!' said Harry, fighting his way through thickly knotted brambles, over which Hagrid had stepped with ease, and remembering very vividly what had happened to him on the other occasion he had stepped off the Forest path. 'Where are we going?'

'Bit further,' said Hagrid over his shoulder. 'C'mon, Harry ... we need ter keep together now.'

It was a great struggle to keep up with Hagrid, what with branches and thickets of thorn through which Hagrid marched as easily as if they were cobwebs, but which snagged Harry and Hermione's robes, frequently entangling them so severely that they had to stop for minutes at a time to free themselves. Harry's arms and legs were soon covered in small cuts and scratches. They were so deep in the Forest now that sometimes all Harry could see of Hagrid in the gloom was a massive dark shape ahead of him. Any sound seemed threatening in the muffled silence. The breaking of a twig echoed loudly and the tiniest rustle of movement, even though it might have been made by an innocent

第30章 格洛普

格说,"幸亏我路过那里……我还以为费伦泽会记我点儿好呢,没想到他竟给我发了一些愚蠢的警告!"他出人意料地动了怒气。

哈利和赫敏交换了一下目光,都很惊讶,但海格皱着眉头没有多说。

"反正,"海格说,他的呼吸比平常粗重一些,"从那以后,别的马人都对我很恼火,麻烦的是他们在禁林里很有影响力……马人是这里最聪明的动物。"

"这是我们来这里的原因吗,海格?"赫敏问,"为了马人?"

"啊,不是,"海格说着,轻蔑地摇摇头,"不是,不是为了他们。当然啦,他们可能会把事情搞得更复杂,是啊……但你们很快就会明白我的意思。"

说完这句令人费解的话,他就沉默下来,领头往前走去,一步就顶他们三步,他们费了九牛二虎之力才跟上他。

他们在禁林里越走越深,小路上逐渐杂草丛生,树木十分茂密,光线如黄昏一般黑暗。很快他们就远远离开了海格给他们看夜骐的那片空地,但哈利并没有感到不安。后来,海格出人意料地离开小路,开始在树丛中蜿蜒穿行,朝黑黢黢的禁林中央走去,他这才觉得不对劲儿。

"海格!"哈利非常清晰地记得上次他偏离禁林小路后发生的事情,他一边说,一边费力地穿过茂密、纠结的荆棘——海格倒是一抬脚就跨了过去,"我们去哪儿?"

"再往前一点儿,"海格扭头说道,"快走,哈利……现在我们需要聚在一起。"

要跟上海格真是不容易,到处都是树枝和带刺的灌木,海格穿过它们就像穿过蜘蛛网,毫不费力。但它们却钩住了哈利和赫敏的袍子,而且老是缠住他们不放,害得他们不得不停下脚步,花几分钟把自己解脱出来。哈利的胳膊和腿上很快就布满了伤痕和划痕。现在已经进入禁林最深处,在昏暗的光线中,哈利只能看见前面海格的巨大黑影。密林里一片寂静,每一点声音都显得那么吓人。树枝折断的回声令人心惊,任何一点小小的动静,哪怕只是一只无辜的麻雀发出的响动,也会使哈利警惕地在黑暗中寻找声音的源头。他想起他每次进入禁林

CHAPTER THIRTY Grawp

sparrow, caused Harry to peer through the gloom for a culprit. It occurred to him that he had never managed to get this far into the Forest without meeting some kind of creature; their absence struck him as rather ominous.

'Hagrid, would it be all right if we lit our wands?' said Hermione quietly.

'Er ... all righ',' Hagrid whispered back. 'In fact –'

He stopped suddenly and turned around; Hermione walked right into him and was knocked over backwards. Harry caught her just before she hit the Forest floor.

'Maybe we bes' jus' stop fer a momen', so I can ... fill yeh in,' said Hagrid. 'Before we ge' there, like.'

'Good!' said Hermione, as Harry set her back on her feet. They both murmured '*Lumos!*' and their wand-tips ignited. Hagrid's face swam through the gloom by the light of the two wavering beams and Harry saw again that he looked nervous and sad.

'Righ',' said Hagrid. 'Well ... see ... the thing is ...'

He took a great breath.

'Well, there's a good chance I'm goin' ter be gettin' the sack any day now,' he said.

Harry and Hermione looked at each other, then back at him.

'But you've lasted this long –' Hermione said tentatively. 'What makes you think –'

'Umbridge reckons it was me that put tha' Niffler in her office.'

'And was it?' said Harry, before he could stop himself.

'No, it ruddy well wasn'!' said Hagrid indignantly. 'On'y anythin' ter do with magical creatures an' she thinks it's got somethin' ter do with me. Yeh know she's bin lookin' fer a chance ter get rid of me ever since I got back. I don' wan' ter go, o' course, but if it wasn' fer ... well ... the special circumstances I'm abou' ter explain to yeh, I'd leave righ' now, before she's go' the chance ter do it in front o' the whole school, like she did with Trelawney.'

Harry and Hermione both made noises of protest, but Hagrid overrode them with a wave of one of his enormous hands.

'It's not the end o' the world, I'll be able ter help Dumbledore once I'm outta here, I can be useful ter the Order. An' you lot'll have Grubbly Plank, yeh'll – yeh'll get through yer exams fine ...'

His voice trembled and broke.

'Don' worry abou' me,' he said hastily, as Hermione made to pat his

第30章 格洛普

深处都会遇到某种动物。而现在却不见它们的踪影,他感到十分不祥。

"海格,我们可不可以把魔杖点亮?"赫敏轻声说。

"呃……好吧,"海格压低声音回答,"实际上——"

他突然停住脚步,打量着周围。赫敏撞到他身上,撞得踉跄后退。哈利在赫敏跌倒之前扶住了她。

"也许我们最好停一停,让我……把情况跟你们说说,"海格说,"然后再去那儿。"

"好啊!"赫敏说,哈利扶她站稳了脚跟。两人低声念了一句荧光闪烁!魔杖尖就亮了起来。海格的脸在黑暗中浮动,被两束摇曳的光柱照着,哈利又一次发现他显得紧张而忧伤。

"好了,"海格说,"嗯……知道吗……事情是这样……"

他深深地吸了一口气。

"唉,现在我随时都可能被解雇。"海格说。

哈利和赫敏互相看看,然后又看着海格。

"可是你已经撑了这么长时间——"赫敏小心翼翼地说,"你怎么又会想到——"

"乌姆里奇认为是我把那个嗅嗅放进她办公室的。"

"是不是呢?"哈利的话脱口而出。

"不是,当然不是!"海格气愤地说,"只要是跟神奇动物有关的事,她就会怀疑到我头上。你们知道,自打我回来以后,她就一直在找机会把我赶走。当然啦,我不想走,但如果不是为了……唉……为了我将要给你们解释的特殊情况,我会立刻就走,不等她有机会当着全校师生解雇我,就像她对特里劳妮那样。"

哈利和赫敏都出声地表示反对,但海格一挥大手,阻止了他们。

"这并不是世界末日,我离开了这里,可以去帮助邓布利多,可以为凤凰社出力。而且会有格拉普兰给你们上课,你们会——你们会顺利通过考试的……"

他声音颤抖,说不下去了。

"别为我担心。"看到赫敏伸手来拍他的胳膊,他赶紧说道。他从

1145

CHAPTER THIRTY Grawp

arm. He pulled his enormous spotted handkerchief from the pocket of his waistcoat and mopped his eyes with it. 'Look, I wouldn' be tellin' yer this at all if I didn' have ter. See, if I go ... well, I can' leave withou' ... withou' tellin' someone ... because I'll – I'll need you two ter help me. An' Ron, if he's willin'.'

'Of course we'll help you,' said Harry at once. 'What do you want us to do?'

Hagrid gave a great sniff and patted Harry wordlessly on the shoulder with such force Harry was knocked sideways into a tree.

'I knew yeh'd say yes,' said Hagrid into his handkerchief, 'but I won' ... never ... forget ... well ... c'mon ... jus' a little bit further through here ... watch yerselves, now, there's nettles ...'

They walked on in silence for another fifteen minutes; Harry had opened his mouth to ask how much further they had to go when Hagrid threw out his right arm to signal that they should stop.

'Really easy,' he said softly. 'Very quiet, now ...'

They crept forwards and Harry saw that they were facing a large, smooth mound of earth nearly as tall as Hagrid that he thought, with a jolt of dread, was sure to be the lair of some enormous animal. Trees had been ripped up at the roots all around the mound, so that it stood on a bare patch of ground surrounded by heaps of trunks and boughs that formed a kind of fence or barricade, behind which Harry, Hermione and Hagrid now stood.

'Sleepin',' breathed Hagrid.

Sure enough, Harry could hear a distant, rhythmic rumbling that sounded like a pair of enormous lungs at work. He glanced sideways at Hermione, who was gazing at the mound with her mouth slightly open. She looked utterly terrified.

'Hagrid,' she said in a whisper barely audible over the sound of the sleeping creature, 'who is he?'

Harry found this an odd question ... 'What is it?' was the one he had been planning on asking.

'Hagrid, you told us –' said Hermione, her wand now shaking in her hand, 'you told us none of them wanted to come!'

Harry looked from her to Hagrid and then, as realisation hit him, he looked back at the mound with a small gasp of horror.

第30章 格洛普

背心口袋里掏出那块圆点点的大手帕擦了擦眼睛。"要知道,如果不是万不得已,我根本不会把这事告诉你们。明白吗,如果我走了……唉,我必须……必须告诉某个人……因为我——我需要你们俩帮助我。还有罗恩,如果他愿意的话。"

"我们当然会帮你,"哈利立刻说,"你需要我们做什么呢?"

海格响亮地抽了一下鼻子,无言地拍了拍哈利的肩膀。他的力气太大了,哈利被拍得撞到了旁边的一棵树上。

"我就知道你们会同意的,"海格用手帕捂着脸说,"我不会……永远不会……忘记……好吧……来吧……往这里面再走一些……留神,有荨麻……"

他们又默默地走了十五分钟。哈利刚要张嘴询问还有多远,海格突然举起右臂,示意他们停下。

"慢一点,"他轻声说,"静悄悄地……"

他们蹑手蹑脚地凑上前,哈利看见前面是一个几乎跟海格一般高的光滑的大土堆,他猜想肯定是某种庞然大物的巢穴,不由得感到一阵恐惧。土堆周围的树都被连根拔掉了,因此土堆是在一片光秃秃的土地上,许多大树干和大树枝落在周围,构成了某种栅栏或屏障,哈利、赫敏和海格此刻就站在这栅栏后面。

"睡着了。"海格压低声音说。

果然,哈利听见一种模糊的、有节奏的隆隆声,像是一副十分庞大的肺在呼吸。他侧眼看看赫敏,赫敏盯着土堆,嘴巴微微张着,看上去完全吓呆了。

"海格,"她说,声音在熟睡的动物的鼾声中勉强能够听见,"这是谁?"

哈利觉得她问得好奇怪……他本来打算问的是:"这是什么?"

"海格,你对我们说过——"赫敏说,魔杖在手中颤抖,"你对我们说过,他们谁都不愿意来!"

哈利看看她又看看海格,突然明白过来。他惊恐地抽了一口冷气,回过头再去看那个土堆。

CHAPTER THIRTY   Grawp

The great mound of earth, on which he, Hermione and Hagrid could easily have stood, was moving slowly up and down in time with the deep, grunting breathing. It was not a mound at all. It was the curved back of what was clearly –

'Well – no – he didn' want ter come,' said Hagrid, sounding desperate. 'But I had ter bring him, Hermione, I had ter!'

'But why?' asked Hermione, who sounded as though she wanted to cry. 'Why – what – oh, *Hagrid*!'

'I knew if I jus' got him back,' said Hagrid, sounding close to tears himself, 'an' – an' taught him a few manners – I'd be able ter take him outside an' show ev'ryone he's harmless!'

'Harmless!' said Hermione shrilly, and Hagrid made frantic hushing noises with his hands as the enormous creature before them grunted loudly and shifted in its sleep. 'He's been hurting you all this time, hasn't he? That's why you've had all these injuries!'

'He don' know his own strength!' said Hagrid earnestly. 'An' he's gettin' better, he's not fightin' so much any more –'

'So, this is why it took you two months to get home!' said Hermione distractedly. 'Oh, Hagrid, why did you bring him back if he didn't want to come? Wouldn't he have been happier with his own people?'

'They were all bullyin' him, Hermione, 'cause he's so small!' said Hagrid.

'Small?' said Hermione. '*Small?*'

'Hermione, I couldn' leave him,' said Hagrid, tears now trickling down his bruised face into his beard. 'See – he's my brother!'

Hermione simply stared at him, her mouth open.

'Hagrid, when you say "brother",' said Harry slowly, 'do you mean –?'

'Well – half-brother,' amended Hagrid. 'Turns out me mother took up with another giant when she left me dad, an' she went an' had Grawp here –'

'Grawp?' said Harry.

'Yeah ... well, tha's what it sounds like when he says his name,' said Hagrid anxiously. 'He don' speak a lot of English ... I've bin tryin' ter teach him ... anyway, she don' seem ter have liked him much more'n she liked me. See, with giantesses, what counts is producin' good big kids, and he's always been a bit on the runty side fer a giant – on'y sixteen foot –'

第30章 格洛普

土堆很大,他和赫敏、海格三个人站在上面也绰绰有余,它随着粗重的呼吸声缓缓地上下起伏。那根本不是什么土堆,而是弯曲的后背,那显然是——

"唉——是啊——他不想来,"海格焦急地说,"但我必须把他带来,赫敏,必须!"

"可是为什么呢?"赫敏问,听声音好像快要哭了,"为什么——干吗——哦,海格!"

"我知道只要我把他带回来,"海格说,似乎也快要流泪了,"再——再教他一些规矩——我就能把他带出去,让大家看到他是没有危险的!"

"没有危险!"赫敏尖声道,海格赶紧用双手示意她安静,这时他们面前的庞然大物很响地咕哝着,在睡梦中翻了个身,"他一直在伤害你,对吗?所以你才遍体鳞伤!"

"他不知道自己的力气有多大!"海格热切地说,"他已经好多了,不再那么爱打架了——"

"怪不得你回家花了两个月的时间!"赫敏心烦意乱地说,"哦,海格,他不想来,你干吗硬要把他带来呢?他跟自己人待在一起不是更快乐吗?"

"他们都欺负他,赫敏,就因为他个子太小!"海格说。

"太小?"赫敏说,"太小?"

"赫敏,我不能撇下他,"海格说,泪水顺着伤痕累累的脸流进了胡子里,"明白吗——他是我弟弟!"

赫敏张大嘴巴瞪着他。

"海格,你说的'弟弟',"哈利语速很慢地说,"难道是指——?"

"其实——是同母异父的弟弟。"海格纠正道,"我后来发现,我妈妈离开我爸后,又跟了另一个巨人,后来就有了格洛普——"

"格洛普?"哈利说。

"是啊……他说自己名字时,听起来像是这个音。"海格焦虑地说,"他不怎么会说话……我一直在试着教他——我妈妈好像不怎么喜欢他,就像当初不喜欢我一样。要知道,对女巨人来说,最要紧的是生出高大体面的孩子,而他作为一个巨人就显得有点矮小——只有十六英尺高——"

1149

'Oh, yes, tiny!' said Hermione, with a kind of hysterical sarcasm. 'Absolutely minuscule!'

'He was bein' kicked aroun' by all o' them – I jus' couldn' leave him –'

'Did Madame Maxime want to bring him back?' asked Harry.

'She – well, she could see it was right importan' ter me,' said Hagrid, twisting his enormous hands. 'Bu' – bu' she got a bit tired o' him after a while, I must admit ... so we split up on the journey home ... she promised not ter tell anyone, though ...'

'How on earth did you get him back without anyone noticing?' said Harry.

'Well, tha's why it took so long, see,' said Hagrid. 'Could on'y travel by nigh' an' through wild country an' stuff. Course, he covers the ground pretty well when he wants ter, but he kep' wantin' ter go back.'

'Oh, Hagrid, why on earth didn't you let him!' said Hermione, flopping down on to a ripped-up tree and burying her face in her hands. 'What do you think you're going to do with a violent giant who doesn't even want to be here!'

'Well, now – "violent" – tha's a bit harsh,' said Hagrid, still twisting his hands agitatedly. 'I'll admit he mighta taken a couple o' swings at me when he's bin in a bad mood, but he's gettin' better, loads better, settlin' down well.'

'What are those ropes for, then?' Harry asked.

He had just noticed ropes thick as saplings stretching from around the trunks of the largest nearby trees towards the place where Grawp lay curled on the ground with his back to them.

'You have to keep him tied up?' said Hermione faintly.

'Well ... yeah ...' said Hagrid, looking anxious. 'See – it's like I say – he doesn' really know 'is own strength.'

Harry understood now why there had been such a suspicious lack of any other living creature in this part of the Forest.

'So, what is it you want Harry and Ron and me to do?' Hermione asked apprehensively.

'Look after him,' said Hagrid croakily. 'After I'm gone.'

Harry and Hermione exchanged miserable looks, Harry uncomfortably aware that he had already promised Hagrid that he would do whatever he asked.

'What – what does that involve, exactly?' Hermione enquired.

'Not food or anythin'!' said Hagrid eagerly. 'He can get his own food, no

第30章 格洛普

"哦，是啊，是够小的！"赫敏带着一种歇斯底里的嘲讽说，"简直就是个小不点儿！"

"他被那些人驱来赶去——我怎么也不能撇下他不管——"

"马克西姆女士愿意带他回来吗？"哈利问。

"她——唉，她看出这对我来说很重要。"海格说，一边绞着两只大手，"可是——可是我必须承认，过了一阵子，她就对他厌烦了……回家的路上我们就分了手……但她答应不告诉任何人……"

"你把他带回来，怎么可能不引起别人的注意呢？"哈利说。

"是啊，所以才花了这么长时间，"海格说，"只能夜里赶路，只能走荒郊野外。当然啦，他愿意的时候倒是走得挺快的，可就是老想回去。"

"哦，海格，你干吗不让他回去呢！"赫敏说着，扑通一声坐在一棵连根拔起的树上，用双手捂住了脸，"一个根本不肯来的凶猛的巨人，你准备拿他怎么办呢？"

"要我说——'凶猛'——这个词有点过了，"海格说，仍然痛苦地绞着双手，"我承认，他心情不好的时候，会冲我来那么几下，但他正在变得越来越好，好多了，适应得不错。"

"那么，那些绳子是做什么用的？"哈利问。

他刚注意到有几根小树那么粗的绳子，从近旁最粗的树干上拉出来，伸向格洛普背对他们蜷伏的地方。

"你必须把他绑起来吗？"赫敏无奈地问。

"说起来……是啊……"海格说，显得有些不安，"是这样——就像我说的——他不知道自己力气有多大。"

哈利这才明白为什么禁林的这片地方不见了别的动物。

"那么，你想要哈利、罗恩和我做什么呢？"赫敏忧心忡忡地问。

"照看他，"海格声音嘶哑地说，"在我走了之后。"

哈利和赫敏苦恼地交换了一下目光，哈利不安地想到他已经答应海格去做他提出的任何事情。

"那——那具体要做什么呢？"赫敏问。

"不用提供食物什么的！"海格热切地说，"他自己能弄到吃的，

CHAPTER THIRTY Grawp

problem. Birds an' deer an' stuff ... no, it's company he needs. If I jus' knew someone was carryin' on tryin' ter help him a bit ... teach-in' him, yeh know.'

Harry said nothing, but turned to look back at the gigantic form lying asleep on the ground in front of them. Unlike Hagrid, who simply looked like an oversized human, Grawp looked strangely misshapen. What Harry had taken to be a vast mossy boulder to the left of the great earthen mound he now recognised as Grawp's head. It was much larger in proportion to the body than a human head, and was almost perfectly round and covered with tightly curling, close-growing hair the colour of bracken. The rim of a single large, fleshy ear was visible on top of the head, which seemed to sit, rather like Uncle Vernon's, directly upon the shoulders with little or no neck in between. The back, under what looked like a dirty brownish smock comprised of animal skins sewn roughly together, was very broad; and as Grawp slept, it seemed to strain a little at the rough seams of the skins. The legs were curled up under the body. Harry could see the soles of enormous, filthy, bare feet, large as sledges, resting one on top of the other on the earthy Forest floor.

'You want us to teach him,' Harry said in a hollow voice. He now understood what Firenze's warning had meant. *His attempt is not working. He would do better to abandon it.* Of course, the other creatures who lived in the Forest would have heard Hagrid's fruitless attempts to teach Grawp English.

'Yeah – even if yeh jus' talk ter him a bit,' said Hagrid hopefully. ''Cause I reckon, if he can talk ter people, he'll understand more that we all like 'im really, an' want 'im ter stay.'

Harry looked at Hermione, who peered back at him from between the fingers over her face.

'Kind of makes you wish we had Norbert back, doesn't it?' he said, and she gave a very shaky laugh.

'Yeh'll do it, then?' said Hagrid, who did not seem to have caught what Harry had just said.

'We'll ...' said Harry, already bound by his promise. 'We'll try, Hagrid.'

'I knew I could count on yeh, Harry,' Hagrid said, beaming in a very watery way and dabbing at his face with his handkerchief again. 'An' I don' wan' yeh ter put yerself out too much, like ... I know yeh've got exams ... if yeh could jus' nip down here in yer Invisibility Cloak maybe once a week an' have a little chat with 'im. I'll wake 'im up, then – introduce yeh –'

第30章 格洛普

没有问题。鸟，鹿，等等，他需要的是同伴。我只想知道有人会继续过来帮帮他……教教他，你们知道。"

哈利什么也没说，只是回头望着躺在地上的那个熟睡的庞然大物。海格看上去只是一个体格超大的人类，而格洛普的模样却显得有些畸形。大土堆左边，哈利本以为是一块巨大的布满青苔的岩石，现在才辨认出是格洛普的脑袋。它跟身体的比例比人脑袋大得多，几乎是滚圆的，覆盖着浓密的羊齿草色的小鬈发。脑袋顶上可见一只巨大的、肉嘟嘟的耳朵，他的脑袋像弗农姨父的一样，好像直接坐在肩膀上，中间几乎没有脖子。后背非常宽阔，穿着像是用动物皮粗粗缝就的肮脏的灰褐色罩衫。格洛普睡觉时，动物皮的粗糙接缝似乎都绷紧了。他的两条腿蜷缩在身子下。哈利看见两只脏兮兮的光脚，大得像雪橇一样，互相交叠着放在禁林的地面上。

"你想让我们教他。"哈利声音空洞地说。他这才明白费伦泽的警告是什么意思。他的努力没有用。他最好还是放弃。不用说，生活在禁林里的其他动物肯定听说了海格正在徒劳地教格洛普说话。

"是啊——哪怕你们跟他说说话也好。"海格满怀希望地说，"我估摸着，如果他能跟人交谈，他就会明白我们其实都很喜欢他，愿意他留下来。"

哈利看着赫敏，她透过手指的缝隙望着他。

"我们还不如盼望诺伯回来呢，是不是？"他说，赫敏声音发颤地笑了笑。

"你们会做到的，是不？"海格说，他似乎没有听见哈利的话。

"我们……"哈利说，他被自己的承诺约束住了，"我们试试吧，海格。"

"我就知道我可以指望你们，哈利，"海格说着，眼泪汪汪地笑了起来，又用手帕擦了擦脸，"我也不愿意太麻烦你们……我知道你们快要考试了……如果，每星期有那么一次，你们穿着隐形衣偷偷溜下来，跟他稍微聊聊天就可以了。我去把他叫醒，给你们——介绍介绍——"

CHAPTER THIRTY Grawp

'Wha— no!' said Hermione, jumping up. 'Hagrid, no, don't wake him, really, we don't need —'

But Hagrid had already stepped over the great tree trunk in front of them and was proceeding towards Grawp. When he was about ten feet away, he lifted a long, broken bough from the ground, smiled reassuringly over his shoulder at Harry and Hermione, then poked Grawp hard in the middle of the back with the end of the bough.

The giant gave a roar that echoed around the silent Forest; birds in the treetops overhead rose twittering from their perches and soared away. In front of Harry and Hermione, meanwhile, the gigantic Grawp was rising from the ground, which shuddered as he placed an enormous hand upon it to push himself on to his knees. He turned his head to see who and what had disturbed him.

'All righ', Grawpy?' said Hagrid, in a would-be cheery voice, backing away with the long bough raised, ready to poke Grawp again. 'Had a nice sleep, eh?'

Harry and Hermione retreated as far as they could while still keeping the giant within their sights. Grawp knelt between two trees he had not yet uprooted. They looked up into his startlingly huge face that resembled a grey full moon swimming in the gloom of the clearing. It was as though the features had been hewn on to a great stone ball. The nose was stubby and shapeless, the mouth lopsided and full of misshapen yellow teeth the size of half-bricks; the eyes, small by giant standards, were a muddy greenish-brown and just now were half gummed together with sleep. Grawp raised dirty knuckles, each as big as a cricket ball, to his eyes, rubbed vigorously, then, without warning, pushed himself to his feet with surprising speed and agility.

'Oh my!' Harry heard Hermione squeal, terrified, beside him.

The trees to which the other ends of the ropes around Grawp's wrists and ankles were attached creaked ominously. He was, as Hagrid had said, at least sixteen feet tall. Gazing blearily around, Grawp reached out a hand the size of a beach umbrella, seized a bird's nest from the upper branches of a towering pine and turned it upside-down with a roar of apparent displeasure that there was no bird in it; eggs fell like grenades towards the ground and Hagrid threw his arms over his head to protect himself.

'Anyway, Grawpy,' shouted Hagrid, looking up apprehensively in case of further falling eggs, 'I've brought some friends ter meet yeh. Remember, I

第30章 格洛普

"什么——别！"赫敏说着一跃而起，"海格，别，别叫醒他，真的，我们不需要——"

可是海格已经跨过他们面前的那根大树干，朝格洛普走去。离格洛普还有大约十英尺的时候，海格从地上捡起一根长长的断枝，回头朝哈利和赫敏笑笑，似乎想消除他们的顾虑，然后用树枝使劲捅了捅格洛普的后背中央。

巨人发出一声咆哮，声音在寂静的禁林里久久地回荡。栖息在树梢上的鸟儿叽叽喳喳地被惊起，向远处飞去。与此同时，在哈利和赫敏面前，巨人格洛普从地上起身。他跪起时把一只大手往地上一撑，震得大地都在颤抖。他转过脑袋看是谁打搅了他。

"没事儿吧，格洛普？"海格用他自以为欢快的声音说，举着长树枝后退了几步，准备再去捅格洛普，"睡得挺香，是不？"

哈利和赫敏尽量退得远远的，同时又让巨人留在他们的视线内。格洛普跪在两棵还没有被他拔起的树中间。他们抬头望着他那张大得吓人的脸，觉得很像一轮灰蒙蒙的满月，飘浮在昏暗的林中空地上。他的五官似乎是刻在一块球形大石头上的。鼻子又短又粗，不成形状，嘴巴歪着，里面满是半块砖头那么大的、歪歪倒倒的黄牙。他的眼睛，按照巨人的标准算是比较小的，是一种混浊的绿褐色，因为刚刚睡醒，眼皮半睁半闭。格洛普举起两个脏兮兮的、像板球那么大的指关节，使劲擦了擦眼睛，然后突然以惊人的速度和敏捷，一骨碌从地上爬了起来。

"哦，天哪！"哈利听见赫敏在身边惊恐地尖叫起来。

格洛普的手脚都被绳子拴着，绳子的另一端绑在树上，那些树发出吱吱嘎嘎的不祥的声音。就像海格说的，格洛普至少有十六英尺高。他睡眼惺忪地瞪着四周，伸出遮阳伞那么大的一只手，从一棵高大的松树梢上抓起一个鸟窝，看到里面没有鸟，气呼呼地大吼一声，把它翻了过来。鸟蛋像手榴弹一样撒向地面，海格赶紧用双臂护住脑袋。

"没事儿，格洛普，"海格大声说，一边心有余悸地抬头看着，生怕再有鸟蛋落下来，"我带来几个朋友让你认识。记得吗，我跟你说过

CHAPTER THIRTY Grawp

told yeh I might? Remember, when I said I might have ter go on a little trip an' leave them ter look after yeh fer a bit? Remember that, Grawpy?'

But Grawp merely gave another low roar; it was hard to say whether he was listening to Hagrid or whether he even recognised the sounds Hagrid was making as speech. He had now seized the top of the pine tree and was pulling it towards him, evidently for the simple pleasure of seeing how far it would spring back when he let go.

'Now, Grawpy, don' do that!' shouted Hagrid. 'Tha's how you ended up pullin' up the others –'

And sure enough, Harry could see the earth around the tree's roots beginning to crack.

'I got company for yeh!' Hagrid shouted. 'Company, see! Look down, yeh big buffoon, I brought yeh some friends!'

'Oh, Hagrid, don't,' moaned Hermione, but Hagrid had already raised the bough again and gave Grawp's knee a sharp poke.

The giant let go of the top of the tree, which swayed alarmingly and deluged Hagrid with a rain of pine needles, and looked down.

'*This*,' said Hagrid, hastening over to where Harry and Hermione stood, 'is Harry, Grawp! Harry Potter! He migh' be comin' ter visit yeh if I have ter go away, understand?'

The giant had only just realised that Harry and Hermione were there. They watched, in great trepidation, as he lowered his huge boulder of a head so that he could peer blearily at them.

'An' this is Hermione, see? Her–' Hagrid hesitated. Turning to Hermione, he said, 'Would yeh mind if he called yeh Hermy, Hermione? On'y it's a difficult name fer him ter remember.'

'No, not at all,' squeaked Hermione.

'This is Hermy, Grawp! An' she's gonna be comin' an' all! Is'n' tha' nice? Eh? Two friends fer yeh ter – GRAWPY, NO!'

Grawp's hand had shot out of nowhere towards Hermione; Harry seized her and pulled her backwards behind the tree, so that Grawp's fist scraped the trunk but closed on thin air.

'BAD BOY, GRAWPY!' they heard Hagrid yelling, as Hermione clung to Harry behind the tree, shaking and whimpering. 'VERY BAD BOY! YEH DON' GRAB – OUCH!'

第30章 格洛普

的？记得吗，我说我可能要出去走走，暂时让他们来照顾你？你还记得吗，格洛普？"

然而格洛普只是又发出一声低吼。很难说清他是不是在听海格说话，甚至是不是听得出海格在说话。只见他抓住松树梢，使劲往自己那边拉，显然只是想给自己找点乐子，看看一松手它能弹回去多远。

"我说，格洛普，别这么做！"海格喊道，"你就是这样把那些树拔掉的——"

果然，哈利看见树根周围的土壤裂开了。

"我带了人来陪你！"海格喊道，"同伴，看见了吗？低头看看，你这个大块头小丑，我给你带来了几个朋友！"

"哦，海格，别！"赫敏哀求道，可是海格已经又把树枝举起来，狠狠地捅了一下格洛普的膝盖。

巨人松开树梢，大树吓人地摇晃着，把阵雨般的松针撒向海格，格洛普低下了头。

"这位，"海格说着，匆匆走到哈利和赫敏站的地方，"是哈利，格洛普！哈利·波特！如果我必须离开，他会来看你的，明白吗？"

巨人这才意识到哈利和赫敏的存在。他们怀着巨大的恐惧，注视着他垂下巨石般的大脑袋，用浑浊的目光望着他们。

"这是赫敏，看见了吗？赫——"海格迟疑着。他转向赫敏说："让他叫你赫米行吗，赫敏？你的名字太难，他恐怕记不住。"

"行，怎么都行。"赫敏尖声说。

"这是赫米，格洛普！她会来看你的！是不是很棒？嗯？给你两个朋友——**格洛普，别！**"

格洛普的手突然凭空朝赫敏伸来，哈利赶紧抓住赫敏往后一拉，躲到了树后。格洛普的拳头擦过树干，抓了个空。

"**坏孩子，格洛普！**"他们听见海格在叫喊，赫敏在树后紧紧地抓住哈利，浑身发抖，低声呜咽。海格说："**真是坏孩子！不许抓人——哎哟！**"

CHAPTER THIRTY   Grawp

Harry poked his head out from around the trunk and saw Hagrid lying on his back, his hand over his nose. Grawp, apparently losing interest, had straightened up and was again engaged in pulling back the pine as far as it would go.

'Righ',' said Hagrid thickly, getting up with one hand pinching his bleeding nose and the other grasping his crossbow, 'well … there yeh are … yeh've met him an' – an' now he'll know yeh when yeh come back. Yeah … well …'

He looked up at Grawp, who was now pulling back the pine with an expression of detached pleasure on his boulderish face; the roots were creaking as he ripped them away from the ground.

'Well, I reckon tha's enough fer one day,' said Hagrid. 'We'll – er – we'll go back now, shall we?'

Harry and Hermione nodded. Hagrid shouldered his crossbow again and, still pinching his nose, led the way back into the trees.

Nobody spoke for a while, not even when they heard the distant crash that meant Grawp had pulled over the pine tree at last. Hermione's face was pale and set. Harry could not think of a single thing to say. What on earth was going to happen when somebody found out that Hagrid had hidden Grawp in the Forbidden Forest? And he had promised that he, Ron and Hermione would continue Hagrid's totally pointless attempts to civilise the giant. How could Hagrid, even with his immense capacity to delude himself that fanged monsters were loveably harmless, fool himself that Grawp would ever be fit to mix with humans?

'Hold it,' said Hagrid abruptly, just as Harry and Hermione were struggling through a patch of thick knotgrass behind him. He pulled an arrow out of the quiver over his shoulder and fitted it into the crossbow. Harry and Hermione raised their wands; now that they had stopped walking, they, too, could hear movement close by.

'Oh, blimey,' said Hagrid quietly.

'I thought we told you, Hagrid,' said a deep male voice, 'that you are no longer welcome here?'

A man's naked torso seemed for an instant to be floating towards them through the dappled green half-light; then they saw that his waist joined smoothly into a horse's chestnut body. This centaur had a proud, high-cheekboned face and long black hair. Like Hagrid, he was armed; a quiverful of arrows and a longbow were slung over his shoulders.

第30章 格洛普

哈利从树干后面探出脑袋,看见海格仰面躺在地上,手捂着鼻子。格洛普似乎觉得没意思了,直起身子,又开始把松树尽量朝自己拉过来。

"好吧,"海格瓮声瓮气地说,从地上站了起来,一只手捏着流血的鼻子,另一只手抓住弩,"好吧……就这样吧……你们已经见过他了——你们再来,他就会认识了。是啊……是啊……"

他抬头望着格洛普,格洛普使劲拉扯松树,巨石般的脸上显出一种呆滞的喜悦。树根嘎嘎响着,被他从地里拔了出来。

"好吧,我想今天就到这儿吧,"海格说,"我们——呃——我们现在回去吧,行吗?"

哈利和赫敏点点头。海格又把弩扛在肩上,仍然用手捏着鼻子,领头走进了树丛。

他们谁也没有说话,后来听见远处传来哗啦啦一声巨响,知道格洛普终于把那棵松树拔了起来,他们依然沉默不语。赫敏的脸苍白而僵硬。哈利想不出一句话来说。如果有人发现海格把格洛普藏在禁林里会怎么样呢?而且哈利还答应过,他跟罗恩、赫敏要继续像海格那样徒劳地教导这位巨人。海格虽说一向喜欢欺骗自己,认为长着獠牙的怪物是可爱的、没有危险的,但他怎么能自欺欺人地指望格洛普会跟人类打成一片呢?

"慢着。"海格突然说道,他身后的哈利和赫敏正费力地穿过一片茂密的两耳草。他从肩上的箭筒里抽出一支箭,搭在弓上。哈利和赫敏举起魔杖,现在他们停住脚步,便也听见了近旁有动静。

"哦,天哪。"海格轻声说。

"我们好像对你说过,"一个低沉的男声说道,"你在这里已经不受欢迎了。"

一时间,一个男子赤裸的躯干似乎在斑斑驳驳的绿色柔光中朝他们飘来,接着他们看见他的腰部自然地与栗色的马身连在一起。这个马人有一张骄傲的、高颧骨的脸,一头乌黑的长发。他像海格一样也带着武器,肩上挂着一筒箭和一把长弓。

CHAPTER THIRTY — Grawp

'How are yeh, Magorian?' said Hagrid warily.

The trees behind the centaur rustled and four or five more centaurs emerged behind him. Harry recognised the black-bodied and bearded Bane, whom he had met nearly four years ago on the same night he had met Firenze. Bane gave no sign that he had ever seen Harry before.

'So,' he said, with a nasty inflection in his voice, before turning immediately to Magorian. 'We agreed, I think, what we would do if this human ever showed his face in the Forest again?'

'"This human" now, am I?' said Hagrid testily. 'Jus' fer stoppin' all of yeh committin' murder?'

'You ought not to have meddled, Hagrid,' said Magorian. 'Our ways are not yours, nor are our laws. Firenze has betrayed and dishonoured us.'

'I dunno how yeh work that out,' said Hagrid impatiently. 'He's done nothin' except help Albus Dumbledore –'

'Firenze has entered into servitude to humans,' said a grey centaur with a hard, deeply lined face.

'*Servitude!*' said Hagrid scathingly. 'He's doin' Dumbledore a favour is all –'

'He is peddling our knowledge and secrets among humans,' said Magorian quietly. 'There can be no return from such disgrace.'

'If yeh say so,' said Hagrid, shrugging, 'but personally I think yeh're makin' a big mistake –'

'As are you, human,' said Bane, 'coming back into our Forest when we warned you –'

'Now, yeh listen ter me,' said Hagrid angrily. 'I'll have less of the "our" Forest, if it's all the same ter yeh. It's not up ter yeh who comes an' goes in here –'

'No more is it up to you, Hagrid,' said Magorian smoothly. 'I shall let you pass today because you are accompanied by your young –'

'They're not his!' interrupted Bane contemptuously. 'Students, Magorian, from up at the school! They have probably already profited from the traitor Firenze's teachings.'

'Nevertheless,' said Magorian calmly, 'the slaughter of foals is a terrible crime – we do not touch the innocent. Today, Hagrid, you pass. Henceforth, stay away from this place. You forfeited the friendship of the centaurs when

第30章 格洛普

"你好吗，玛格瑞？"海格警惕地说。

马人身后的树木沙沙作响，又有四五个马人出现了。哈利认出了黑身体、留着胡子的贝恩，他在约四年前遇见费伦泽的那天夜里见到过他。贝恩没有显露出曾经见过哈利的样子。

"够了。"贝恩说，声音里带着难听的变调，随即转向玛格瑞，"我们已经商定，如果这个人再在禁林露面，我们该怎么对付，是吗？"

"现在我成了'这个人'？"海格脾气暴躁地说，"就因为我阻止了你们杀人？"

"你不应该插手的，海格。"玛格瑞说，"我们的习惯跟你们的不同，法律也跟你们的不同。费伦泽背叛和侮辱了我们。"

"我不明白你是怎么想的，"海格不耐烦地说，"他并没有做什么，只是帮助阿不思·邓布利多——"

"费伦泽做了人类的奴隶。"一个表情冷酷、脸上布满皱纹的灰色马人说。

"奴隶！"海格尖刻地说，"他只是帮邓布利多一点忙——"

"他在人类中间散播我们的知识和秘密，"玛格瑞轻声说，"这种耻辱无法清除。"

"随你怎么说吧，"海格耸耸肩膀说，"但我个人认为，你们犯了一个大错误——"

"你也是，人类，"贝恩说，"我们已经提醒过你，可你还是闯进了我们的林子——"

"哼，你给我听着，"海格气愤地说，"如果你们不介意的话，我不想再听到什么'我们的'林子。谁来谁去，并不由你们决定——"

"可也不由你决定，海格。"玛格瑞心平气和地说，"我今天放你一马，因为你身边有你的幼——"

"不是他的！"贝恩轻蔑地打断了他，"是学生，玛格瑞，是上面那所学校的学生！他们大概已经从叛徒费伦泽的教学中受益了。"

"不管怎么说，"玛格瑞平静地说，"杀害幼崽是一种可怕的罪孽——我们不伤害无辜。海格，今天放你过去。从今以后，别再来这个地方。"

CHAPTER THIRTY   Grawp

you helped the traitor Firenze escape us.'

'I won' be kept outta the Fores' by a bunch o' old mules like yeh!' said Hagrid loudly.

'Hagrid,' said Hermione in a high-pitched and terrified voice, as both Bane and the grey centaur pawed at the ground, 'let's go, please let's go!'

Hagrid moved forwards, but his crossbow was still raised and his eyes were still fixed threateningly upon Magorian.

'We know what you are keeping in the Forest, Hagrid!' Magorian called after them, as the centaurs slipped out of sight. 'And our tolerance is waning!'

Hagrid turned and gave every appearance of wanting to walk straight back to Magorian.

'Yeh'll tolerate 'im as long as he's here, it's as much his Forest as yours!' he yelled, as Harry and Hermione both pushed with all their might against Hagrid's moleskin waistcoat in an effort to keep him moving forwards. Still scowling, he looked down; his expression changed to mild surprise at the sight of them both pushing him; he seemed not to have felt it.

'Calm down, you two,' he said, turning to walk on while they panted along behind him. 'Ruddy old mules, though, eh?'

'Hagrid,' said Hermione breathlessly, skirting the patch of nettles they had passed on their way there, 'if the centaurs don't want humans in the Forest, it doesn't really look as though Harry and I will be able —'

'Ah, you heard what they said,' said Hagrid dismissively, 'they wouldn't hurt foals — I mean, kids. Anyway, we can' let ourselves be pushed aroun' by that lot.'

'Nice try,' Harry murmured to Hermione, who looked crestfallen.

At last they rejoined the path and, after another ten minutes, the trees began to thin; they were able to see patches of clear blue sky again and, in the distance, the definite sounds of cheering and shouting.

'Was that another goal?' asked Hagrid, pausing in the shelter of the trees as the Quidditch stadium came into view. 'Or d'yeh reckon the match is over?'

'I don't know,' said Hermione miserably. Harry saw that she looked much the worse for wear; her hair was full of twigs and leaves, her robes were ripped in several places and there were numerous scratches on her face and arms. He knew he must look little better.

'I reckon it's over, yeh know!' said Hagrid, still squinting towards the stadium. 'Look — there's people comin' out already — if yeh two hurry yeh'll

第30章 格洛普

你帮助叛徒费伦泽从我们手里逃走,已经失去了我们的友谊。"

"我不会因为你们这群老骡子就不进林子的!"海格大声说。

"海格,"赫敏说,声音尖利而恐惧,因为贝恩和那个灰色马人都用蹄子刨着地面,"我们走吧,求求你,快走吧!"

海格迈步向前,但手里仍然举着弩,眼睛仍然气势汹汹地盯着玛格瑞。

"我们知道你在林子里养了什么,海格!"玛格瑞冲着他们的背影喊道,这时马人们逐渐从视线中消失了,"我们的忍耐快到尽头了!"

海格转过身,看样子要返回到玛格瑞那里去。

"只要他在这儿,你们就得忍着,这是你们的林子,也是他的林子!"他嚷道,哈利和赫敏用吃奶的力气推着海格的鼹鼠皮背心,努力阻止他往回走。海格仍然皱着眉头,低头一看,发现他们都在推他,表情微微有些吃惊,他似乎根本就没有感觉到。

"镇静,你们俩。"他说完转身继续赶路,他们跟在后面气喘吁吁,"这帮该死的老骡子,是不?"

"海格,"赫敏上气不接下气地说,绕过刚才来的时候经过的那片荨麻,"如果马人不让人类进林子,我和哈利恐怕就不可能——"

"啊,你听见他们刚才的话了,"海格不当回事地说,"他们不会伤害幼崽——我是说孩子。总之,我们不能让自己受那帮家伙的摆布。"

"看来没有退路了。"哈利低声对赫敏说,赫敏一副垂头丧气的样子。

他们终于回到了小路上,又走了十分钟,树木开始变得稀疏起来。他们又能看见一片片清澈的蓝天了,远处传来了清晰的欢呼声和叫嚷声。

"又得分了吗?"海格问,在树荫下停住了脚步,这时他们已经看得见魁地奇球场了,"还是比赛已经结束了?"

"不知道。"赫敏气恼地说。哈利看到她一副狼狈样,头发上粘着叶子和小树枝,袍子撕破了好几处,脸上和胳膊上伤痕累累。他知道自己也好不到哪儿去。

"我猜是结束了!"海格说,仍然眯着眼睛朝球场眺望,"看——人们已经出来了——如果你们俩跑快点,就能混进人群,就没有人会

be able ter blend in with the crowd an' no one'll know yeh weren't there!'

'Good idea,' said Harry. 'Well ... see you later, then, Hagrid.'

'I don't believe him,' said Hermione in a very unsteady voice, the moment they were out of earshot of Hagrid. 'I don't believe him. I *really* don't believe him.'

'Calm down,' said Harry.

'Calm down!' she said feverishly. 'A giant! A giant in the Forest! And we're supposed to give him English lessons! Always assuming, of course, we can get past the herd of murderous centaurs on the way in and out! I – don't – *believe* – him!'

'We haven't got to do anything yet!' Harry tried to reassure her in a quiet voice, as they joined a stream of jabbering Hufflepuffs heading back towards the castle. 'He's not asking us to do anything unless he gets chucked out and that might not even happen.'

'Oh, come off it, Harry!' said Hermione angrily, stopping dead in her tracks so that the people behind had to swerve to avoid her. 'Of course he's going to be chucked out and, to be perfectly honest, after what we've just seen, who can blame Umbridge?'

There was a pause in which Harry glared at her, and her eyes filled slowly with tears.

'You didn't mean that,' said Harry quietly.

'No ... well ... all right ... I didn't,' she said, wiping her eyes angrily. 'But why does he have to make life so difficult for himself – for *us*?'

'I dunno –'

>*'Weasley is our King,*
>*Weasley is our King,*
>*He didn't let the Quaffle in,*
>*Weasley is our King ...'*

'And I wish they'd stop singing that stupid song,' said Hermione miserably, 'haven't they gloated enough?'

A great tide of students was moving up the sloping lawns from the pitch.

'Oh, let's get in before we have to meet the Slytherins,' said Hermione.

第30章 格洛普

发现你们溜出来过！"

"好主意！"哈利说，"好吧……那就再见了，海格。"

"真不敢相信他，"估摸着海格听不见了，赫敏用颤颤抖抖的声音说，"真不敢相信他。我真的不敢相信他。"

"平静点儿。"哈利说。

"平静！"赫敏激动地说，"一个巨人！禁林里有一个巨人！我们还要给他上语文课！当然还得假设我们每次进进出出都能通过那群凶残的马人！我——真的——不敢相信他！"

"我们暂时还用不着做什么！"哈利压低声音安慰她说，这时他们汇入了一群叽叽喳喳返回城堡的赫奇帕奇同学中，"如果他不被赶走，我们就不需要做什么，他还不一定被解雇呢。"

"哦，别胡扯了，哈利！"赫敏气呼呼地说，突然停下脚步，害得后面的人不得不绕过她去，"他肯定会被解雇的，而且，说句实话，有了我们刚才看见的东西，谁还能责怪乌姆里奇呢？"

一阵沉默，哈利没好气地瞪着赫敏，泪水慢慢地涌进了她的眼眶。

"你不是真的这么想吧？"哈利轻声说。

"不……唉……是啊……不是，"说着，她气呼呼地擦干眼泪，"可是他为什么要把生活弄得这么艰难，害了自己——也害了我们？"

"不知道——"

> 韦斯莱是我们的王，
> 韦斯莱是我们的王，
> 绝不把球往门里放，
> 韦斯莱是我们的王……

"我希望他们别再唱那首愚蠢的歌了，"赫敏难过地说，"他们幸灾乐祸得还不够吗？"

一大群学生潮水般地从球场拥上了草坡。

"哦，我们快进去，免得碰上斯莱特林的人。"赫敏说。

CHAPTER THIRTY — Grawp

*'Weasley can save anything,
He never leaves a single ring,
That's why Gryffindors all sing:
Weasley is our King.'*

'Hermione ...' said Harry slowly.

The song was growing louder, but it was issuing not from a crowd of green-and-silver-clad Slytherins, but from a mass of red and gold moving slowly towards the castle, bearing a solitary figure upon its many shoulders.

*'Weasley is our King,
Weasley is our King,
He didn't let the Quaffle in,
Weasley is our King ...'*

'No?' said Hermione in a hushed voice.

'YES!' said Harry loudly.

'HARRY! HERMIONE!' yelled Ron, waving the silver Quidditch cup in the air and looking quite beside himself. 'WE DID IT! WE WON!'

They beamed up at him as he passed. There was a scrum at the door of the castle and Ron's head got rather badly bumped on the lintel, but nobody seemed to want to put him down. Still singing, the crowd squeezed itself into the Entrance Hall and out of sight. Harry and Hermione watched them go, beaming, until the last echoing strains of 'Weasley is our King' died away. Then they turned to each other, their smiles fading.

'We'll save our news till tomorrow, shall we?' said Harry.

'Yes, all right,' said Hermione wearily. 'I'm not in any hurry.'

They climbed the steps together. At the front doors both instinctively looked back at the Forbidden Forest. Harry was not sure whether or not it was his imagination, but he rather thought he saw a small cloud of birds erupting into the air over the treetops in the distance, almost as though the tree in which they had been nesting had just been pulled up by the roots.

第30章 格洛普

韦斯莱真真是好样,
一个球都不往门里放,
格兰芬多人放声唱:
韦斯莱是我们的王。

"赫敏……"哈利慢慢地说。

歌声越来越响,但不是从身穿绿色和银色衣服的斯莱特林同学中传出来的,而是从缓缓朝城堡移动的穿红色和金色衣服的人群中传出来的,许多人的肩膀上扛着一个身影。

韦斯莱是我们的王,
韦斯莱是我们的王,
绝不把球往门里放,
韦斯莱是我们的王……

"不可能吧?"赫敏压低声音说。

"赢了!"哈利大声说。

"哈利!赫敏!"罗恩喊道,在空中挥舞着银色的魁地奇杯,看上去高兴得发了狂,"我们赢了!我们赢了!"

他们笑眯眯地看着他经过。城堡门口一片混乱,罗恩的脑袋重重地撞在门楣上,但似乎谁也不愿意把他放下。那群人仍然唱着歌,挤进了门厅,消失在视线中。哈利和赫敏笑容满面地注视着他们,直到"韦斯莱是我们的王"的最后一缕余音也消失了。然后他们互相看着对方,笑容隐去了。

"我们把这个消息留到明天再说吧?"哈利说。

"好的,"赫敏疲倦地说,"我反正不着急。"

他们一起走上台阶。到了门口,两人都本能地扭头看着禁林。哈利不知道是不是自己的幻觉,他似乎看见远处的树梢上飞起一群鸟,就好像它们栖息的那棵树刚刚被连根拔起。

CHAPTER THIRTY-ONE

O.W.L.s

Ron's euphoria at helping Gryffindor scrape the Quidditch cup was such that he couldn't settle to anything next day. All he wanted to do was talk over the match, so Harry and Hermione found it very difficult to find an opening in which to mention Grawp. Not that either of them tried very hard; neither was keen to be the one to bring Ron back to reality in quite such a brutal fashion. As it was another fine, warm day, they persuaded him to join them in revising under the beech tree at the edge of the lake, where they had less chance of being overheard than in the common room. Ron was not particularly keen on this idea at first – he was thoroughly enjoying being patted on the back by every Gryffindor who walked past his chair, not to mention the occasional outbursts of 'Weasley is our King' – but after a while he agreed that some fresh air might do him good.

They spread their books out in the shade of the beech tree and sat down while Ron talked them through his first save of the match for what felt like the dozenth time.

'Well, I mean, I'd already let in that one of Davies's, so I wasn't feeling all that confident, but I dunno, when Bradley came towards me, just out of nowhere, I thought – *you can do this*! And I had about a second to decide which way to fly, you know, because he looked like he was aiming for the right goalhoop – my right, obviously, his left – but I had a funny feeling that he was feinting, and so I took the chance and flew left – his right, I mean – and – well – you saw what happened,' he concluded modestly, sweeping his hair back quite unnecessarily so that it looked interestingly windswept and glancing around to see whether the people nearest to them – a bunch of gossiping third-year Hufflepuffs – had heard him. 'And then, when Chambers came at me about five minutes later – What?' Ron asked, having stopped

第 31 章

O.W.L. 考试

罗恩帮助格兰芬多夺得魁地奇杯,心里别提多兴奋了,第二天也没法静下心来做任何事情。他只想谈论比赛,哈利和赫敏发现很难开口跟他说格洛普的事。其实他们俩都没有努力尝试,都不急于用这种残酷的方式把罗恩拉回到现实中来。这又是一个晴朗、温暖的日子,他们说服罗恩跟他们一起在湖边的山毛榉树下复习功课,在这里说话不像在公共休息室里容易被人听见。罗恩起先对这个主意不太热情——每个格兰芬多同学走过他的椅子都要拍拍他的后背,更不用说还会不时爆发出"韦斯莱是我们的王"的歌声,他太陶醉于这样的感觉了——可是过了一会儿,他承认呼吸一点儿新鲜空气对他会有好处。

他们坐了下来,把书本摊在山毛榉树的树荫下,罗恩滔滔不绝地跟他们讲他救起比赛中第一个球的情景,他恐怕已经讲了十多遍了。

"我的意思是,我已经漏掉了戴维斯的那个球,所以信心不是很足,但我也不知道是怎么回事,布拉德利突然从什么地方朝我冲来,我想——这次准能行!我用一秒钟左右的时间决定往哪边扑,你们知道,他那样子好像瞄准的是右边的圆环——我的右边,他的左边——但我有一种奇怪的感觉,觉得他是在伪装,于是我冒险往左边飞去——我是指他的右边——然后——嘿——后来的事情你们都看到了。"他谦逊地结束了自己的讲话,同时毫无必要地把头发往后一甩,使它显得像是被风吹乱了似的,很有风度,然后他望望四周,看离他们最近的那些人——一群叽叽喳喳的赫奇帕奇三年级学生——是不是听见了他的话,"后来,大约五分钟后,钱伯斯朝我冲来——你怎么啦?"罗恩看

mid-sentence at the look on Harry's face. 'Why are you grinning?'

'I'm not,' said Harry quickly, and looked down at his Transfiguration notes, attempting to straighten his face. The truth was that Ron had just reminded Harry forcibly of another Gryffindor Quidditch player who had once sat rumpling his hair under this very tree. 'I'm just glad we won, that's all.'

'Yeah,' said Ron slowly, savouring the words, '*we won*. Did you see the look on Chang's face when Ginny got the Snitch right out from under her nose?'

'I suppose she cried, did she?' said Harry bitterly.

'Well, yeah – more out of temper than anything, though ...' Ron frowned slightly. 'But you saw her chuck her broom away when she got back to the ground, didn't you?'

'Er –' said Harry.

'Well, actually ... no, Ron,' said Hermione with a heavy sigh, putting down her book and looking at him apologetically. 'As a matter of fact, the only bit of the match Harry and I saw was Davies's first goal.'

Ron's carefully ruffled hair seemed to wilt with disappointment. 'You didn't watch?' he said faintly, looking from one to the other. 'You didn't see me make any of those saves?'

'Well – no,' said Hermione, stretching out a placatory hand towards him. 'But Ron, we didn't want to leave – we had to!'

'Yeah?' said Ron, whose face was growing rather red. 'How come?'

'It was Hagrid,' said Harry. 'He decided to tell us why he's been covered in injuries ever since he got back from the giants. He wanted us to go into the Forest with him, we had no choice, you know how he gets. Anyway ...'

The story was told in five minutes, by the end of which Ron's indignation had been replaced by a look of total incredulity.

'*He brought one back and hid it in the Forest?*'

'Yep,' said Harry grimly.

'No,' said Ron, as though by saying this he could make it untrue. 'No, he can't have.'

'Well, he has,' said Hermione firmly. 'Grawp's about sixteen feet tall, enjoys ripping up twenty-foot pine trees, and knows me,' she snorted, 'as *Hermy*.'

第31章 O.W.L.考试

到哈利脸上的表情,突然停住了话头,"你笑什么?"

"我没笑。"哈利赶紧说道,低头去看他的变形课笔记,努力让脸上的表情严肃起来。事实上,罗恩刚才的样子,使哈利不由自主地想起了另一位格兰芬多魁地奇球员,他也曾经在这棵树下把自己的头发弄得乱糟糟的。"我只是高兴我们赢了。"

"是啊,"罗恩慢悠悠地说,品味着哈利的话,"我们赢了。金妮从秋·张的鼻子底下抓到飞贼时,你们看到秋·张脸上的表情了吗?"

"我猜她哭了,是不是?"哈利苦涩地说。

"是啊,没错——不过更像在发脾气……"罗恩微微皱起眉头,"你们看到她回到地面后,把她的飞天扫帚扔到了一边,是不是?"

"呃——"哈利支吾着说。

"唉,实际上……没有,罗恩,"赫敏沉沉地叹了一口气,放下书本,满怀歉意地望着罗恩,"实际上,我和哈利只看到了戴维斯的第一个进球。"

罗恩故意弄乱的头发似乎失望地耷拉了下来。"你们没看到?"他轻轻地问,挨个儿看着他们两人,"我扑出去的那些球,你们一个都没看到?"

"唉——是啊,"赫敏说着,伸出一只手去安慰他,"可是罗恩,我们也不想离开——不走不行啊!"

"是吗?"罗恩说,他的脸涨得通红,"怎么回事?"

"是海格,"哈利说,"他决定告诉我们为什么他从巨人那里回来后一直遍体鳞伤。他要我们跟他一起进入禁林,我们没有办法,你知道他那副样子。反正……"

哈利花了五分钟把事情讲了一遍,最后,罗恩的愤怒被一种完全难以置信的表情取代了。

"他带了一个巨人回来,藏在禁林里?"

"是啊。"哈利严肃地说。

"不可能。"罗恩说,似乎他这样一说,事情就不是真的了,"不,他不可能这么做。"

"他就这么做了。"赫敏毫不含糊地说,"格洛普身高大约十六英尺,喜欢把二十英尺高的松树连根拔起,而且以为我叫,"她从鼻子里哼了一声,"我叫赫米。"

1171

CHAPTER THIRTY-ONE — O.W.L.s

Ron gave a nervous laugh.

'And Hagrid wants us to ...?'

'Teach him English, yeah,' said Harry.

'He's lost his mind,' said Ron in an almost awed voice.

'Yes,' said Hermione irritably, turning a page of *Intermediate Transfiguration* and glaring at a series of diagrams showing an owl turning into a pair of opera glasses. 'Yes, I'm starting to think he has. But, unfortunately, he made Harry and me promise.'

'Well, you're just going to have to break your promise, that's all,' said Ron firmly. 'I mean, come on ... we've got exams and we're about that far –' he held up his hand to show thumb and forefinger almost touching '– from being chucked out as it is. And anyway ... remember Norbert? Remember Aragog? Have we ever come off better for mixing with any of Hagrid's monster mates?'

'I know, it's just that – we promised,' said Hermione in a small voice.

Ron smoothed his hair flat again, looking preoccupied.

'Well,' he sighed, 'Hagrid hasn't been sacked yet, has he? He's hung on this long, maybe he'll hang on till the end of term and we won't have to go near Grawp at all.'

The castle grounds were gleaming in the sunlight as though freshly painted; the cloudless sky smiled at itself in the smoothly sparkling lake; the satin green lawns rippled occasionally in a gentle breeze. June had arrived, but to the fifth-years this meant only one thing: their O.W.L.s were upon them at last.

Their teachers were no longer setting them homework; lessons were devoted to revising those topics the teachers thought most likely to come up in the exams. The purposeful, feverish atmosphere drove nearly everything but the O.W.L.s from Harry's mind, though he did wonder occasionally during Potions lessons whether Lupin had ever told Snape that he must continue giving Harry Occlumency tuition. If he had, then Snape had ignored Lupin as thoroughly as he was now ignoring Harry. This suited Harry very well; he was quite busy and tense enough without extra classes with Snape, and to his relief Hermione was much too preoccupied these days to badger him about Occlumency; she was spending a lot of time muttering to herself, and had not laid out any elf clothes for days.

第31章 O.W.L.考试

罗恩局促地笑了一声。

"海格想要我们……？"

"教他说话，没错。"哈利说。

"他疯了。"罗恩用近乎畏惧的口吻说。

"是啊，"赫敏不耐烦地说，把《中级变形术》翻过一页，眼睛瞪着把猫头鹰变成一副小型望远镜的一系列图标，"是啊，我也有点怀疑他疯了。然而，不幸的是，他强迫我和哈利做了保证。"

"那没办法，你们只能食言了，"罗恩坚决地说，"我的意思是……我们还要考试，而且我们就差这么一点——"他举起手，大拇指和食指几乎碰在一起，"就被开除了。不管怎么说……记得诺伯吗？记得阿拉戈克吗？跟海格的怪物伙伴打交道，我们什么时候有过好下场？"

"我知道，但就是——我们已经答应了呀。"赫敏用很小的声音说。

罗恩又把头发抚平，显得心事重重。

"我说，"他叹了一口气，"海格还没有被解雇，不是吗？他坚持了这么久，说不定能坚持到学期结束，那样我们就根本用不着接近格洛普了。"

城堡的场地在阳光下闪闪发亮，好像刚刚油漆过一样。万里无云的天空对着波光粼粼的湖面中的倒影微笑。丝缎般光滑的绿茵在微风中轻柔地起伏。六月到了，对于五年级同学来说，这只意味着一件事：O.W.L.考试终于来临了。

老师不再给他们布置家庭作业，课堂上也全部用来复习那些老师认为考试中最有可能出现的题目。这种狂热拼搏的气氛，使哈利满脑子都是O.W.L.，几乎顾不上考虑其他事。不过在魔药课上，他时不时会猜想卢平有没有跟斯内普谈过他必须继续教自己大脑封闭术。如果卢平已经说了，那么斯内普完全未予理睬，正如他现在不理睬哈利一样。哈利正巴不得这样呢。没有斯内普的课外辅导，他已经够忙碌、够紧张的了。令他宽慰的是，赫敏这些日子忙得要命，没有工夫缠着他说大脑封闭术的事。赫敏许多时间都在喃喃自语，已经好些天没有给家养小精灵发放衣服了。

CHAPTER THIRTY-ONE — O.W.L.s

She was not the only person acting oddly as the O.W.L.s drew steadily nearer. Ernie Macmillan had developed an irritating habit of interrogating people about their revision practices.

'How many hours d'you think you're doing a day?' he demanded of Harry and Ron as they queued outside Herbology, a manic gleam in his eyes.

'I dunno,' said Ron. 'A few.'

'More or less than eight?'

'Less, I s'pose,' said Ron, looking slightly alarmed.

'I'm doing eight,' said Ernie, puffing out his chest. 'Eight or nine. I'm getting an hour in before breakfast every day. Eight's my average. I can do ten on a good weekend day. I did nine and a half on Monday. Not so good on Tuesday – only seven and a quarter. Then on Wednesday –'

Harry was deeply thankful that Professor Sprout ushered them into greenhouse three at that point, forcing Ernie to abandon his recital.

Meanwhile, Draco Malfoy had found a different way to induce panic.

'Of course, it's not what you know,' he was heard to tell Crabbe and Goyle loudly outside Potions a few days before the exams were to start, 'it's who you know. Now, Father's been friendly with the head of the Wizarding Examinations Authority for years – old Griselda Marchbanks – we've had her round for dinner and everything ...'

'Do you think that's true?' Hermione whispered in alarm to Harry and Ron.

'Nothing we can do about it if it is,' said Ron gloomily.

'I don't think it's true,' said Neville quietly from behind them. 'Because Griselda Marchbanks is a friend of my gran's, and she's never mentioned the Malfoys.'

'What's she like, Neville?' asked Hermione at once. 'Is she strict?'

'Bit like Gran, really,' said Neville in a subdued voice.

'Knowing her won't hurt your chances, though, will it?' Ron told him encouragingly.

'Oh, I don't think it will make any difference,' said Neville, still more miserably. 'Gran's always telling Professor Marchbanks I'm not as good as my dad ... well ... you saw what she's like at St Mungo's ...'

Neville looked fixedly at the floor. Harry, Ron and Hermione glanced at each other, but didn't know what to say. It was the first time Neville had acknowledged that they had met at the wizarding hospital.

Meanwhile, a flourishing black-market trade in aids to concentration,

第31章 O.W.L.考试

O.W.L.考试日益临近,行为怪异的人不止她一个。厄尼·麦克米兰养成了一个恼人的习惯,总喜欢盘问别人的复习情况。

"你们认为自己一天复习多少时间?"在草药课堂外排队的时候,他问哈利和罗恩,眼睛里闪着焦虑的光芒。

"我不知道,"罗恩说,"几个小时吧。"

"比八个小时多还是少?"

"我猜是少吧。"罗恩说,显得有点儿惊慌。

"我是八个小时,"厄尼得意地说道,"八到九个小时。我每天早饭前复习一个小时。平均是八个小时。周末一般十个小时。星期一九个半小时。星期二就不太好了——只有七小时一刻钟。星期三——"

就在这个时候,斯普劳特教授把他们领进了三号温室,厄尼才不得不停止他的叙述,哈利觉得如释重负。

可是德拉科·马尔福发现了另一种引起恐慌的办法。

"其实,"考试前几天,有人听见他在魔药课堂外大声告诉克拉布和高尔,"重要的不是你知道什么,而是你认识什么人。我爸爸跟巫师考试管理局的头儿有好多年的交情——格丝尔达·玛奇班那老太太——我们还请她吃过饭什么的……"

"你们认为他说的是真的吗?"赫敏紧张地轻声问哈利和罗恩。

"即使是真的,我们也没办法。"罗恩闷闷不乐地说。

"我认为不是真的,"纳威在他们身后小声说,"因为格丝尔达·玛奇班是我奶奶的朋友,她从来没提到过马尔福一家。"

"她什么样儿,纳威?"赫敏立刻问道,"严厉吗?"

"说实在的,有点像我奶奶。"纳威用郁闷的口吻说。

"认识她也不会妨碍你什么,不是吗?"罗恩给他鼓劲道。

"哦,我认为也没什么区别。"纳威说,仍然显得可怜巴巴的,"奶奶经常对玛奇班教授说我没有我爸爸那么好……唉……你们在圣芒戈医院见过我奶奶是什么样子……"

纳威的目光盯着地面。哈利、罗恩和赫敏交换了一下目光,却不知道说什么才好。这是纳威第一次承认他们在巫师医院见过面。

这段时间,五年级和七年级同学中间的黑市交易十分兴隆,交易

CHAPTER THIRTY-ONE   O.W.L.s

mental agility and wakefulness had sprung up among the fifth- and seventh-years. Harry and Ron were much tempted by the bottle of Baruffio's Brain Elixir offered to them by Ravenclaw sixth-year Eddie Carmichael, who swore it was solely responsible for the nine 'Outstanding' O.W.L.s he had gained the previous summer and was offering a whole pint for a mere twelve Galleons. Ron assured Harry he would reimburse him for his half the moment he left Hogwarts and got a job, but before they could close the deal, Hermione had confiscated the bottle from Carmichael and poured the contents down a toilet.

'Hermione, we wanted to buy that!' shouted Ron.

'Don't be stupid,' she snarled. 'You might as well take Harold Dingle's powdered dragon claw and have done with it.'

'Dingle's got powdered dragon claw?' said Ron eagerly.

'Not any more,' said Hermione. 'I confiscated that, too. None of these things actually work, you know.'

'Dragon claw does work!' said Ron. 'It's supposed to be incredible, really gives your brain a boost, you come over all cunning for a few hours – Hermione, let me have a pinch, go on, it can't hurt –'

'This stuff can,' said Hermione grimly. 'I've had a look at it, and it's actually dried Doxy droppings.'

This information took the edge off Harry and Ron's desire for brain stimulants.

They received their examination timetables and details of the procedure for O.W.L.s during their next Transfiguration lesson.

'As you can see,' Professor McGonagall told the class as they copied down the dates and times of their exams from the blackboard, 'your O.W.L.s are spread over two successive weeks. You will sit the theory papers in the mornings and the practice in the afternoons. Your practical Astronomy examination will, of course, take place at night.

'Now, I must warn you that the most stringent anti-cheating charms have been applied to your examination papers. Auto-Answer Quills are banned from the examination hall, as are Remembralls, Detachable Cribbing Cuffs and Self-Correcting Ink. Every year, I am afraid to say, seems to harbour at least one student who thinks that he or she can get around the Wizarding Examinations Authority's rules. I can only hope that it is nobody in Gryffindor. Our new – Headmistress –' Professor McGonagall pronounced the word with the same look on her face that Aunt Petunia had whenever she was contemplating a particularly

第31章 O.W.L.考试

的都是一些可以让人集中精力、提神醒脑、保持清醒的东西。哈利和罗恩看到拉文克劳六年级同学埃迪·卡米切尔拿给他们的那瓶巴费醒脑剂，非常动心。埃迪一口咬定他去年夏天 O.W.L. 考试拿了九个"优秀"全靠这玩意儿，并提出一品脱只卖十二个金加隆。罗恩向哈利保证，他毕业一找到工作就还清他的那一半，可是没等他们成交，赫敏就把瓶子从卡米切尔手里没收了，把里面的东西全都倒进了抽水马桶。

"赫敏，我们还想买呢！"罗恩嚷道。

"别犯傻了，"赫敏恶声恶气地说，"你还不如吃点哈罗德·丁戈的龙爪粉凑合一下呢。"

"丁戈弄到了龙爪粉？"罗恩很感兴趣地说。

"已经没有了，"赫敏说，"也被我没收了。其实这些东西都根本不管用。"

"龙爪粉是管用的！"罗恩说，"据说它特别神奇，确实能让你精神振奋，在几个小时里脑瓜特别好使——赫敏，给我来一点儿吧，求求你了，没有害处的——"

"那可不一定，"赫敏板着脸说，"我仔细看过了，实际上它就是风干了的狐媚子粪便。"

这话让哈利和罗恩对大脑兴奋剂的渴望大大减弱了。

下一节变形课上，他们拿到了考试的时间表和具体要求。

"正如你们看到的，"麦格教授对全班同学说，他们正忙着把黑板上的考试日期和时间记下来，"你们的 O.W.L. 考试将持续两周。上午考理论，下午考实践。当然啦，天文学的实践考试将在夜里进行。"

"我还必须提醒你们，每一份考卷上都加了特别严厉的防作弊咒。自动答题羽毛笔不许带进考场，还有记忆球、小抄活页袖和自动纠错墨水。我很遗憾地告诉你们，每年似乎都至少有一位同学自认为能躲过巫师考试管理局的规定。我只能希望这个人不是格兰芬多的。我们的新任——校长——"麦格教授说这个词时的神情，就像佩妮姨妈注视一块特别顽固的污垢时一样，"——要求院长告诉本院学生，作弊将

CHAPTER THIRTY-ONE O.W.L.s

stubborn bit of dirt '– has asked the Heads of House to tell their students that cheating will be punished most severely – because, of course, your examination results will reflect upon the Headmistress's new regime at the school –'

Professor McGonagall gave a tiny sigh; Harry saw the nostrils of her sharp nose flare.

'– however, that is no reason not to do your very best. You have your own futures to think about.'

'Please, Professor,' said Hermione, her hand in the air, 'when will we find out our results?'

'An owl will be sent to you some time in July,' said Professor McGonagall.

'Excellent,' said Dean Thomas in an audible whisper, 'so we don't have to worry about it till the holidays.'

Harry imagined sitting in his bedroom in Privet Drive in six weeks' time, waiting for his O.W.L. results. Well, he thought, at least he would be sure of one bit of post that summer.

Their first examination, Theory of Charms, was scheduled for Monday morning. Harry agreed to test Hermione after lunch on Sunday, but regretted it almost at once; she was very agitated and kept snatching the book back from him to check that she had got the answer completely right, finally hitting him hard on the nose with the sharp edge of *Achievements in Charming*.

'Why don't you just do it yourself?' he said firmly, handing the book back to her, his eyes watering.

Meanwhile, Ron was reading two years' worth of Charms notes with his fingers in his ears, his lips moving soundlessly; Seamus Finnigan was lying flat on his back on the floor, reciting the definition of a Substantive Charm while Dean checked it against *The Standard Book of Spells, Grade 5*; and Parvati and Lavender, who were practising basic Locomotion Charms, were making their pencil-cases race each other around the edge of the table.

Dinner was a subdued affair that night. Harry and Ron did not talk much, but ate with gusto, having studied hard all day. Hermione, on the other hand, kept putting down her knife and fork and diving under the table for her bag, from which she would seize a book to check some fact or figure. Ron was just telling her that she ought to eat a decent meal or she would not sleep that night, when her fork slid from her limp fingers and landed with a loud tinkle on her plate.

'Oh, my goodness,' she said faintly, staring into the Entrance Hall. 'Is that them? Is that the examiners?'

第31章 O.W.L.考试

受到最为严厉的惩罚——不用说,你们的考试成绩将会反映校长对学校的新的管理制度——"

麦格教授轻轻叹了一口气,哈利看见她尖鼻子的鼻翼在翕动。

"——不过,你们不能因为这个就不刻苦努力。你们要考虑的是自己的未来。"

"请问,教授,"赫敏举着手问,"我们什么时候能知道成绩?"

"七月里会有猫头鹰给你们送信。"麦格教授说。

"太棒了,"迪安·托马斯用别人能够听见的耳语声说,"这样我们放假前都不用为它担心了。"

哈利想象着六星期后自己坐在女贞路的卧室里,等候 O.W.L. 考试的成绩。也好,他想,至少他暑假肯定能收到一封邮件。

第一场考试是魔咒理论,定于星期一上午。哈利答应星期天吃过午饭给赫敏提问,可是几乎立刻就后悔了。赫敏焦躁不安,不停地夺过哈利手里的课本,查看自己是不是答得一字不差,最后《魔咒成就》尖锐的书角重重地撞到了哈利的鼻子。

"你干吗不自己复习呢?"哈利坚决地说,把课本还给赫敏,他的眼睛在流泪。

与此同时,罗恩用手指堵着耳朵,嘴唇不出声地嚅动着,在恶补整整两年的魔咒课笔记。西莫·斐尼甘仰面躺在地板上,背诵一种存在咒的定义,迪安对照着《标准咒语,五级》看西莫背得对不对。帕瓦蒂和拉文德在练习最基本的移动咒,让她们的铅笔盒绕着桌边互相追逐。

那天吃晚饭的时候气氛压抑。哈利和罗恩没有怎么说话,但因为用功了一整天,倒是吃得津津有味。赫敏却不停地放下刀叉,钻到桌子底下去拿书包,抽出一本书核对某个数字或知识点。罗恩刚要对她说应该好好吃饭,不然夜里会睡不着觉的,突然赫敏的叉子从无力的手指间滑落,当啷一声掉在盘子里。

"哦,天哪,"她盯着门厅轻声说道,"那是他们吗?是主考官吗?"

CHAPTER THIRTY-ONE — O.W.L.s

Harry and Ron whipped around on their bench. Through the doors to the Great Hall they could see Umbridge standing with a small group of ancient-looking witches and wizards. Umbridge, Harry was pleased to see, looked rather nervous.

'Shall we go and have a closer look?' said Ron.

Harry and Hermione nodded and they hastened towards the double doors into the Entrance Hall, slowing down as they stepped over the threshold to walk sedately past the examiners. Harry thought Professor Marchbanks must be the tiny, stooped witch with a face so lined it looked as though it had been draped in cobwebs; Umbridge was speaking to her deferentially. Professor Marchbanks seemed to be a little deaf; she was answering Professor Umbridge very loudly considering they were only a foot apart.

'Journey was fine, journey was fine, we've made it plenty of times before!' she said impatiently. 'Now, I haven't heard from Dumbledore lately!' she added, peering around the Hall as though hopeful he might suddenly emerge from a broom cupboard. 'No idea where he is, I suppose?'

'None at all,' said Umbridge, shooting a malevolent look at Harry, Ron and Hermione, who were now dawdling around the foot of the stairs as Ron pretended to do up his shoelace. 'But I daresay the Ministry of Magic will track him down soon enough.'

'I doubt it,' shouted tiny Professor Marchbanks, 'not if Dumbledore doesn't want to be found! I should know ... examined him personally in Transfiguration and Charms when he did N.E.W.T.s ... did things with a wand I'd never seen before.'

'Yes ... well ...' said Professor Umbridge as Harry, Ron and Hermione dragged their feet up the marble staircase as slowly as they dared, 'let me show you to the staff room. I daresay you'd like a cup of tea after your journey.'

It was an uncomfortable sort of an evening. Everyone was trying to do some last-minute revising but nobody seemed to be getting very far. Harry went to bed early but then lay awake for what felt like hours. He remembered his careers consultation and McGonagall's furious declaration that she would help him become an Auror if it was the last thing she did. He wished he had expressed a more achievable ambition now that exam time was here. He knew he was not the only one lying awake, but none of the others in the

第31章 O.W.L.考试

哈利和罗恩在板凳上转过身子。透过礼堂大门，他们看见乌姆里奇跟一小群老态龙钟的男女巫师站在一起。哈利高兴地看到乌姆里奇显得十分紧张。

"我们过去仔细看看？"罗恩问。

哈利和赫敏点点头，三人快步朝通向门厅的双扇门走去。跨过门槛后，他们放慢脚步，镇定自若地经过那些主考官身边。哈利认为玛奇班教授肯定是那个驼背的小个子女巫，脸上皱纹密布，像蒙着一层蜘蛛网。乌姆里奇正在毕恭毕敬地跟她说话。玛奇班教授似乎有点耳背，用很大的声音回答乌姆里奇教授，其实她们之间只隔着一英尺。

"旅途很愉快，旅途很愉快，我们以前来过许多次了！"她不耐烦地说，"我说，我最近一直没有得到邓布利多的消息！"她说着就在门厅里四处张望，似乎指望着邓布利多会突然从某个扫帚间里冒出来似的，"怎么，还没弄清他在哪儿？"

"还没弄清。"乌姆里奇说着，恶狠狠地瞪了哈利、罗恩和赫敏一眼，他们此刻在楼梯脚下故意磨蹭，罗恩假装系鞋带，"但是我敢发誓，魔法部很快就能把他抓获。"

"那可不一定，"小个子的玛奇班教授大声说，"如果邓布利多不想让人发现，那就没戏！我应该知道的……当年他参加N.E.W.T.考试时，我亲自考他的变形术和魔咒学……他用魔杖变出的花样，是我以前从没见过的。"

"是啊……是啊……"乌姆里奇教授说，哈利、罗恩和赫敏正往大理石楼梯上走，尽量把脚步拖得很慢很慢，"我领你们到教工休息室去吧。你们一路辛苦，肯定很想喝杯茶。"

这个晚上大家过得很不自在。每个人都想抓紧最后的时间复习，但似乎谁也没有取得多少进展。哈利早早就上了床，但很长时间没有睡着，感觉辗转反侧了好几个小时。他想起了他在接受就业指导时，麦格教授愤怒地宣称要帮助他成为一名傲罗，哪怕这是她这辈子做的最后一件事情。现在考试迫在眉睫，他后悔自己没有提出一种比较容易实现的理想。他知道不止他一个人难以入睡，但宿舍里的其他人都没有说话。

CHAPTER THIRTY-ONE   O.W.L.s

dormitory spoke and finally, one by one, they fell asleep.

None of the fifth-years talked very much at breakfast next day, either: Parvati was practising incantations under her breath while the salt cellar in front of her twitched; Hermione was rereading *Achievements in Charming* so fast that her eyes appeared blurred; and Neville kept dropping his knife and fork and knocking over the marmalade.

Once breakfast was over, the fifth- and seventh-years milled around in the Entrance Hall while the other students went off to lessons; then, at half past nine, they were called forwards class by class to re-enter the Great Hall, which had been rearranged exactly as Harry had seen it in the Pensieve when his father, Sirius and Snape had been taking their O.W.L.s; the four house tables had been removed and replaced instead with many tables for one, all facing the staff-table end of the Hall where Professor McGonagall stood facing them. When they were all seated and quiet, she said, 'You may begin,' and turned over an enormous hourglass on the desk beside her, on which there were also spare quills, ink bottles and rolls of parchment.

Harry turned over his paper, his heart thumping hard – three rows to his right and four seats ahead Hermione was already scribbling – and lowered his eyes to the first question: *a) Give the incantation and b) describe the wand movement required to make objects fly.*

Harry had a fleeting memory of a club soaring high into the air and landing loudly on the thick skull of a troll ... smiling slightly, he bent over the paper and began to write.

'Well, it wasn't too bad, was it?' asked Hermione anxiously in the Entrance Hall two hours later, still clutching the exam paper. 'I'm not sure I did myself justice on Cheering Charms, I just ran out of time. Did you put in the counter-charm for hiccoughs? I wasn't sure whether I ought to, it felt like too much – and on question twenty-three –'

'Hermione,' said Ron sternly, 'we've been through this before ... we're not going through every exam afterwards, it's bad enough doing them once.'

The fifth-years ate lunch with the rest of the school (the four house tables had reappeared for the lunch hour), then they trooped off into the small chamber beside the Great Hall, where they were to wait until called for their practical examination. As small groups of students were called forwards in alphabetical order, those left behind muttered incantations and practised wand movements, occasionally poking each other in the back or eye by mistake.

第31章 O.W.L.考试

最后，终于一个个都睡着了。

第二天吃早饭的时候，五年级同学都没怎么交谈。帕瓦蒂不出声地练习咒语，她面前的盐瓶在急速扭动。赫敏又在复习《魔咒成就》，她读得可真快，眼神看上去都模糊了。纳威手里的刀叉不停地掉落，还把橘子酱给打翻了。

吃完早饭，其他同学去上课了，五年级和七年级同学就在门厅里转悠。九点半，他们一个班一个班地被叫进礼堂。礼堂里已经重新做了布置，跟哈利在冥想盆里看到的他父亲、小天狼星和斯内普参加O.W.L.考试的情形一模一样。四张学院桌子被搬走了，取而代之的是许多单人课桌，都面朝礼堂尽头的教工桌摆放着，麦格教授面对着他们站在前面。大家坐定，安静下来后，麦格教授说："可以开始了。"她把旁边桌上一只巨大的沙漏翻转过来，那张桌上还有备用的羽毛笔、墨水瓶和一卷卷羊皮纸。

哈利翻过自己的考卷，心怦怦地狂跳着——坐在他右边第三排、向前第四个座位上的赫敏，已经开始奋笔疾书——哈利低头看着第一个问题：1）写出让物体飞起来的咒语；2）描述挥动魔杖的动作。

哈利脑海中闪出一根棍子，它嗖地飞到高空，然后重重地落在一个巨怪的厚脑壳上……他微微笑了笑，埋头写了起来。

"唉，还不算太糟糕，是吧？"两个小时后，赫敏在门厅里担忧地问，手里仍然抓着试题，"我不敢说我的快乐咒考出了水平，我只是把时间耗完了。你们把打嗝的破解咒写出来了吗？我不知道到底该不该写，我写得好像太多了——还有第二十三个问题——"

"赫敏，"罗恩板着脸说，"已经考完了……我们不想每门考试结束后再考一遍，考一遍就够糟糕的了。"

五年级同学跟全校其他同学一起吃午饭（四张学院桌子在午饭时间又出现了），然后排着队走进礼堂旁边的那个小房间，等着被叫去参加实践考试。一小群同学按照字母顺序被叫走了，留下来的同学喃喃地念着咒语，练习魔杖动作，不时误捅了别人的后背或眼睛。

CHAPTER THIRTY-ONE

O.W.L.s

Hermione's name was called. Trembling, she left the chamber with Anthony Goldstein, Gregory Goyle and Daphne Greengrass. Students who had already been tested did not return afterwards, so Harry and Ron had no idea how Hermione had done.

'She'll be fine, remember she got a hundred and twelve per cent on one of our Charms tests?' said Ron.

Ten minutes later, Professor Flitwick called, 'Parkinson, Pansy – Patil, Padma – Patil, Parvati – Potter, Harry.'

'Good luck,' said Ron quietly. Harry walked into the Great Hall, clutching his wand so tightly his hand shook.

'Professor Tofty is free, Potter,' squeaked Professor Flitwick, who was standing just inside the door. He pointed Harry towards what looked like the very oldest and baldest examiner who was sitting behind a small table in a far corner, a short distance from Professor Marchbanks, who was halfway through testing Draco Malfoy.

'Potter, is it?' said Professor Tofty, consulting his notes and peering over his pince-nez at Harry as he approached. 'The famous Potter?'

Out of the corner of his eye, Harry distinctly saw Malfoy throw a scathing look over at him; the wine-glass Malfoy had been levitating fell to the floor and smashed. Harry could not suppress a grin; Professor Tofty smiled back at him encouragingly.

'That's it,' he said in his quavery old voice, 'no need to be nervous. Now, if I could ask you to take this egg cup and make it do some cartwheels for me.'

On the whole, Harry thought it went rather well. His Levitation Charm was certainly much better than Malfoy's had been, though he wished he had not mixed up the incantations for Colour Change and Growth Charms, so that the rat he was supposed to be turning orange swelled shockingly and was the size of a badger before Harry could rectify his mistake. He was glad Hermione had not been in the Hall at the time and neglected to mention it to her afterwards. He could tell Ron, though; Ron had caused a dinner plate to mutate into a large mushroom and had no idea how it had happened.

There was no time to relax that night; they went straight to the common room after dinner and submerged themselves in revision for Transfiguration next day; Harry went to bed with his head buzzing with complex spell models and theories.

第31章 O.W.L.考试

赫敏的名字被叫到了。她浑身颤抖着，跟安东尼·戈德斯坦、格雷戈里·高尔和达芙妮·格林格拉斯一起离开了小房间。已经考完的同学没有再返回来，所以哈利和罗恩不知道赫敏考得怎么样。

"她肯定没事！记得吗，有一次考魔咒，她得了一百一十二分呢！"罗恩说。

十分钟后，弗立维教授喊道："潘西·帕金森——帕德玛·佩蒂尔——帕瓦蒂·佩蒂尔——哈利·波特。"

"祝你好运。"罗恩轻声说。哈利走进礼堂，手里攥着魔杖，但攥得太紧，手都在发抖。

"托福迪教授有空，波特。"站在门口的弗立维教授尖声说。他给哈利指了指远处角落里一张小桌子后面的主考官，那人看上去年纪最大、脑袋最秃，离正在考德拉科·马尔福的玛奇班教授不远。

"是波特吗？"托福迪教授说，他看看笔记，又从夹鼻眼镜上方注视着哈利走近，"大名鼎鼎的波特？"

哈利从眼角清清楚楚地看到马尔福朝他投来恶毒的目光。马尔福正在让一个酒杯飘浮起来，结果酒杯掉在地上摔得粉碎。哈利忍不住笑了起来。托福迪教授也鼓励地朝他露出了微笑。

"这就对了，"他用苍老的、颤颤抖抖的声音说，"没必要紧张。好了，我想请你把这个蛋杯拿去，让它做几个侧身翻给我看看。"

总的来说，哈利觉得自己做得还不错。他的飘浮咒肯定比马尔福的好得多，不过他后悔不该把变色咒和生长咒弄混，结果那只本该变成橘黄色的老鼠惊人地膨胀起来，一直变成了獾那么大，哈利才纠正了自己的错误。他庆幸赫敏当时没在礼堂，后来也没把这事告诉她。不过他可以告诉罗恩，罗恩把一个盘子变成了大蘑菇，自己还不知道是怎么回事呢。

那天晚上根本没有时间休息。他们吃过晚饭就去了公共休息室，埋头复习第二天要考的变形术。哈利上床时，脑袋里嗡嗡响着各种复杂的咒语范例和理论。

CHAPTER THIRTY-ONE O.W.L.s

He forgot the definition of a Switching Spell during his written paper next morning but thought his practical could have been a lot worse. At least he managed to Vanish the whole of his iguana, whereas poor Hannah Abbott lost her head completely at the next table and somehow managed to multiply her ferret into a flock of flamingos, causing the examination to be halted for ten minutes while the birds were captured and carried out of the Hall.

They had their Herbology exam on Wednesday (other than a small bite from a Fanged Geranium, Harry felt he had done reasonably well); and then, on Thursday, Defence Against the Dark Arts. Here, for the first time, Harry felt sure he had passed. He had no problem with any of the written questions and took particular pleasure, during the practical examination, in performing all the counter-jinxes and defensive spells right in front of Umbridge, who was watching coolly from near the doors into the Entrance Hall.

'Oh, bravo!' cried Professor Tofty, who was examining Harry again, when Harry demonstrated a perfect Boggart banishing spell. 'Very good indeed! Well, I think that's all, Potter … unless …'

He leaned forwards a little.

'I heard, from my dear friend Tiberius Ogden, that you can produce a Patronus? For a bonus point …?'

Harry raised his wand, looked directly at Umbridge and imagined her being sacked.

'*Expecto patronum!*'

His silver stag erupted from the end of his wand and cantered the length of the Hall. All of the examiners looked around to watch its progress and when it dissolved into silver mist Professor Tofty clapped his veined and knotted hands enthusiastically.

'Excellent!' he said. 'Very well, Potter, you may go!'

As Harry passed Umbridge beside the door, their eyes met. There was a nasty smile playing around her wide, slack mouth, but he did not care. Unless he was very much mistaken (and he was not planning on telling anybody, in case he was), he had just achieved an 'Outstanding' O.W.L.

On Friday, Harry and Ron had a day off while Hermione sat her Ancient Runes exam, and as they had the whole weekend in front of them they permitted themselves a break from revision. They stretched and yawned beside the open window, through which warm summer air was wafting as

第31章 O.W.L.考试

第二天上午的书面考试中，他忘记了转换咒的定义，但是实践考试远不像他预想的那样糟糕。他至少让他的鬣蜥完全消失了，而邻桌的汉娜·艾博真是不幸，她完全晕了头，竟然把她那只白鼬变成了一大群火烈鸟，导致考试中断了十分钟，人们才把那些鸟抓住送出了礼堂。

星期三进行的是草药课考试（哈利觉得自己考得还算不错，只是被一株毒牙天竺葵咬了一小口），星期四考黑魔法防御术。哈利第一次觉得自己肯定有把握过关。笔试没有任何问题，实践考试中，他当着乌姆里奇的面操练各种破解咒和防御咒，感到特别过瘾；乌姆里奇站在通往门厅的门边，冷冷地注视着他。

"哦，太好了！"托福迪教授喊道，这次又是他考哈利，哈利刚才展示了无懈可击的博格特驱逐咒，"确实很好！好了，我认为可以了，波特……除非……"

他把身子往前探了一点儿。

"我听我亲爱的朋友提贝卢斯·奥格登说，你能变出一个守护神，是吗？作为加分……？"

哈利举起魔杖，直视着乌姆里奇，想象着她被解雇的情景。

"呼神护卫！"

银色的牡鹿从他的魔杖尖上蹿了出来，一直跑到礼堂那头。所有的主考官都扭头注视着它，最后它变成一团银雾消失了，托福迪教授兴奋地拍了拍骨节粗大、青筋毕露的手。

"太棒了！"他说，"很好，波特，你可以走了！"

哈利经过门边乌姆里奇身旁时，两人的目光相遇了。乌姆里奇那肥阔、松弛的嘴巴露出一丝狞笑，但哈利没有在意。他觉得自己刚才得了个"优秀"，除非他的判断存在严重错误（他不打算告诉任何人，生怕自己果真判断失误）。

星期五，赫敏参加古代如尼文的考试，哈利和罗恩休息，因为接下来就是周末，所以他们就让自己暂时把复习放在了一边。他们懒洋洋地坐在敞开的窗边，打着哈欠下巫师棋，夏日的和风在窗口轻轻吹拂。

they played wizard chess. Harry could see Hagrid in the distance, teaching a class on the edge of the Forest. He was trying to guess what creatures they were examining – he thought it must be unicorns, because the boys seemed to be standing back a little – when the portrait hole opened and Hermione clambered in, looking thoroughly bad-tempered.

'How were the Runes?' said Ron, yawning and stretching.

'I mistranslated *ehwaz*,' said Hermione furiously. 'It means *partnership*, not *defence*; I mixed it up with *eihwaz*.'

'Ah well,' said Ron lazily, 'that's only one mistake, isn't it, you'll still get –'

'Oh, shut up!' said Hermione angrily. 'It could be the one mistake that makes the difference between a pass and a fail. And what's more, someone's put another Niffler in Umbridge's office. I don't know how they got it through that new door, but I just walked past there and Umbridge is shrieking her head off – by the sound of it, it tried to take a chunk out of her leg –'

'Good,' said Harry and Ron together.

'It is *not* good!' said Hermione hotly. 'She thinks it's Hagrid doing it, remember? And we do *not* want Hagrid chucked out!'

'He's teaching at the moment; she can't blame him,' said Harry, gesturing out of the window.

'Oh, you're so *naïve* sometimes, Harry. You really think Umbridge will wait for proof?' said Hermione, who seemed determined to be in a towering temper, and she swept off towards the girls' dormitories, banging the door behind her.

'Such a lovely, sweet-tempered girl,' said Ron, very quietly, prodding his queen forward to beat up one of Harry's knights.

Hermione's bad mood persisted for most of the weekend, though Harry and Ron found it quite easy to ignore as they spent most of Saturday and Sunday revising for Potions on Monday, the exam which Harry had been looking forward to least – and which he was sure would be the downfall of his ambitions to become an Auror. Sure enough, he found the written paper difficult, though he thought he might have got full marks on the question about Polyjuice Potion; he could describe its effects accurately, having taken it illegally in his second year.

The afternoon practical was not as dreadful as he had expected it to be. With Snape absent from the proceedings, he found that he was much more relaxed than he usually was while making potions. Neville, who was sitting very

第31章 O.W.L.考试

哈利看见海格在远处的禁林边上教课。他努力猜想他们在研究什么动物——肯定是独角兽，因为男生好像都站在后面——就在这时，肖像洞口打开了，赫敏爬了进来，看上去情绪十分暴躁。

"如尼文考得怎么样？"罗恩打着哈欠、伸着懒腰问。

"我把 ehwaz 翻译错了，"赫敏气恼地说，"它的意思是合作，不是防御，我把它跟 eihwaz 搞混了。"

"好了好了，"罗恩懒洋洋地说，"不就错了一个嘛，你仍然能拿到——"

"哦，闭嘴！"赫敏气冲冲地说，"这个错误可能就关系到及格还是不及格。而且，有人又把一只嗅嗅放进了乌姆里奇的办公室，不知道他们是怎么让它进入那扇新门的。我刚从那里经过，乌姆里奇正在一迭声地尖叫——听她的叫声，好像嗅嗅想从她腿上咬下一大块肉来——"

"太好了。"哈利和罗恩异口同声地说。

"才不好呢！"赫敏激动地说，"她认为是海格干的，记得吗？我们可不愿意海格被解雇！"

"海格正在教课呢，她不可能怪到他头上。"哈利说着，朝窗外做了个手势。

"哦，哈利，你有的时候真是太天真了。你真的以为乌姆里奇会等着拿到证据吗？"赫敏说，她似乎打定主意要发脾气，说完就快步朝女生宿舍走去，把身后的门重重地关上了。

"多么可爱的好脾气的姑娘。"罗恩声音很轻地说，把他的王后推向前，吃掉了哈利的一个骑士。

赫敏的坏脾气几乎持续了整个周末，不过哈利和罗恩觉得很容易不理会她，因为星期六和星期天的大部分时间他们都在复习，准备星期一的魔药课考试。这是哈利最不愿参加的一门考试——他相信这门考试肯定会挫败他当一名傲罗的理想。果然，他发现笔试很难，不过他认为关于复方汤剂的题目他能拿到满分，二年级的时候，他曾违反校规服用过这种药剂，所以能精确地描绘它的药效。

下午的实践考试不像他想象得那样可怕。斯内普不在场，哈利发现自己调制药剂比平时轻松自如多了。纳威的位置距哈利很近，哈利

CHAPTER THIRTY-ONE O.W.L.s

near Harry, also looked happier than Harry had ever seen him during a Potions class. When Professor Marchbanks said, 'Step away from your cauldrons, please, the examination is over,' Harry corked his sample flask feeling that he might not have achieved a good grade but he had, with luck, avoided a fail.

'Only four exams left,' said Parvati Patil wearily as they headed back to Gryffindor common room.

'Only!' said Hermione snappishly. '*I've* got Arithmancy and it's probably the toughest subject there is!'

Nobody was foolish enough to snap back, so she was unable to vent her spleen on any of them and was reduced to telling off some first-years for giggling too loudly in the common room.

Harry was determined to perform well in Tuesday's Care of Magical Creatures exam so as not to let Hagrid down. The practical examination took place in the afternoon on the lawn on the edge of the Forbidden Forest, where students were required to correctly identify the Knarl hidden among a dozen hedgehogs (the trick was to offer them all milk in turn: Knarls, highly suspicious creatures whose quills had many magical properties, generally went berserk at what they saw as an attempt to poison them); then demonstrate correct handling of a Bowtruckle; feed and clean out a Fire Crab without sustaining serious burns; and choose, from a wide selection of food, the diet they would give a sick unicorn.

Harry could see Hagrid watching anxiously out of his cabin window. When Harry's examiner, a plump little witch this time, smiled at him and told him he could leave, Harry gave Hagrid a fleeting thumbs-up before heading back to the castle.

The Astronomy theory paper on Wednesday morning went well enough. Harry was not convinced he had got the names of all Jupiter's moons right, but was at least confident that none of them was inhabited by mice. They had to wait until evening for their practical Astronomy; the afternoon was devoted instead to Divination.

Even by Harry's low standards in Divination, the exam went very badly. He might as well have tried to see moving pictures on the desktop as in the stubbornly blank crystal ball; he lost his head completely during tea-leaf reading, saying it looked to him as though Professor Marchbanks would shortly be meeting a round, dark, soggy stranger, and rounded off the whole fiasco by mixing up the life and head lines on her palm and informing her that she ought to have died the previous Tuesday.

第31章 O.W.L.考试

也从没见他在魔药课上这么开心过。后来，玛奇班教授说："请离开你们的坩埚，考试结束了。"哈利把他的样品装进瓶里，觉得虽然不一定能拿到好成绩，但如果顺利的话，应该不会不及格。

"只剩下四门考试了。"他们返回格兰芬多公共休息室时，帕瓦蒂·佩蒂尔疲惫地说。

"只有四门！"赫敏咄咄逼人地说，"我还有算术占卜呢，这恐怕是最难的一门课！"

谁也不会傻乎乎地去反驳她，所以她没能把自己的怒气发泄到任何人身上，只好去教训几个在公共休息室里笑得太响的一年级新生。

哈利拿定主意要在星期二的保护神奇动物课的考试中好好表现，不让海格失望。下午的实践考试是在禁林边的草地上进行的，同学们需要准确认出藏在十几只刺猬中的刺佬儿（诀窍是挨个儿喂它们牛奶，刺佬儿是一种十分多疑的动物，身上的刺有多种魔法特性，每当怀疑有人试图给它们下毒就会气得发狂）；接着演示怎样对付护树罗锅，怎样给火螃蟹喂食和清扫而不被严重烧伤，然后从一大堆东西中挑选喂养病中独角兽的食物。

哈利看见海格在小屋里担忧地看着窗外。这次哈利的主考官是一位胖胖的小个子女巫，她笑眯眯地看着哈利，说他可以离开了。哈利朝海格竖起两个大拇指，回身朝城堡走去。

星期三上午的天文学理论考得还算顺利。哈利虽然没有把握把木星所有卫星的名字都写对了，但他至少可以肯定没有一颗卫星上住着老鼠。天文学实践考试要到晚上才进行，下午考占卜。

哈利本来就对占卜课期望不高，但还是觉得考得一塌糊涂。该死的水晶球里一片空白，他还不如看看桌面上活动的图像。解读茶叶的时候，他完全昏了头，说他认为茶叶显示玛奇班教授很快会遇到一个又黑又胖的讨厌的陌生人，最后他还弄混了玛奇班教授的生命线和智慧线，说她应该死于上个星期二，至此，他的占卜课算是彻底考砸了。

CHAPTER THIRTY-ONE O.W.L.s

'Well, we were always going to fail that one,' said Ron gloomily as they ascended the marble staircase. He had just made Harry feel rather better by telling him how he had told the examiner in detail about the ugly man with a wart on his nose in his crystal ball, only to look up and realise he had been describing his examiner's reflection.

'We shouldn't have taken the stupid subject in the first place,' said Harry.

'Still, at least we can give it up now.'

'Yeah,' said Harry. 'No more pretending we care what happens when Jupiter and Uranus get too friendly.'

'And from now on, I don't care if my tea-leaves spell *die, Ron, die* – I'm just chucking them in the bin where they belong.'

Harry laughed just as Hermione came running up behind them. He stopped laughing at once, in case it annoyed her.

'Well, I think I've done all right in Arithmancy,' she said, and Harry and Ron both sighed with relief. 'Just time for a quick look over our star-charts before dinner, then …'

When they reached the top of the Astronomy Tower at eleven o'clock, they found a perfect night for stargazing, cloudless and still. The grounds were bathed in silvery moonlight and there was a slight chill in the air. Each of them set up his or her telescope and, when Professor Marchbanks gave the word, proceeded to fill in the blank star-chart they had been given.

Professors Marchbanks and Tofty strolled among them, watching as they entered the precise positions of the stars and planets they were observing. All was quiet except for the rustle of parchment, the occasional creak of a telescope as it was adjusted on its stand, and the scribbling of many quills. Half an hour passed, then an hour; the little squares of reflected gold light flickering on the ground below started to vanish as lights in the castle windows were extinguished.

As Harry completed the constellation Orion on his chart, however, the front doors of the castle opened directly below the parapet where he was standing, so that light spilled down the stone steps a little way across the lawn. Harry glanced down as he made a slight adjustment to the position of his telescope and saw five or six elongated shadows moving over the brightly lit grass before the doors swung shut and the lawn became a sea of darkness once more.

Harry put his eye back to his telescope and refocused it, now examining Venus. He looked down at his chart to enter the planet there, but something

第31章 O.W.L.考试

"唉，这门课我们本来也没指望能及格。"他们走上大理石楼梯时，罗恩郁闷地说。他刚才对哈利说，他详详细细地告诉主考官，他在水晶球里看到的是一个鼻子上有疣的丑八怪，结果一抬头，发现自己描绘的是主考官映在水晶球里的影子。

"我们本来就不应该学这门无聊的课。"哈利说。

"还好，现在放弃还来得及。"

"是啊，"哈利说，"我们别再假装关心木星和天王星过于靠近会发生什么事情了。"

"从今往后，我再也不管我的茶叶是不是拼出死亡，罗恩，死亡的字样——我要把它们扔进垃圾桶，那才是它们应该待的地方。"

哈利笑了起来，这时赫敏从他们身后跑了过来，哈利赶紧止住笑，生怕又会惹恼了她。

"知道吗，我觉得我算术占卜考得挺好的。"她说，哈利和罗恩这才放心地松了口气，"赶紧在吃晚饭前再看看星象图，然后……"

夜里十一点，他们来到天文塔顶上，发现这是一个观察天体的理想夜晚，没有云，也没有风。场地沐浴在银色的月光下，空气里微微有一丝凉意。每人都架好自己的望远镜，等玛奇班教授一发话，就开始填写发给他们的空白星象图。

玛奇班和托福迪教授在他们中间走来走去，看着他们填写观察到的恒星和行星的精确位置。四下里静悄悄的，只有羊皮纸的摩擦声，偶尔还有调整架子上望远镜的吱嘎声，还有许多支羽毛笔写字的沙沙声。半个小时过去了，一个小时过去了，城堡窗口的灯一盏接一盏地熄灭，映在场地上的一方方金色亮光也逐渐消失了。

哈利正在图表上填写猎户星座，突然城堡的大门开了。大门就在他所站的矮墙下面，一道亮光洒向石头台阶，映在前方的草坪上。哈利微微调整了一下望远镜的位置，看见五六个拉长的影子在被照亮的草地上移动，接着门关上了，草地又变得一片漆黑。

哈利重新把眼睛贴在望远镜上，调整焦距，现在他观察的是金星。他低头看着图表准备填写这颗行星，但什么东西分散了他的注意力。

CHAPTER THIRTY-ONE O.W.L.s

distracted him; pausing with his quill suspended over the parchment, he squinted down into the shadowy grounds and saw half a dozen figures walking over the lawn. If they had not been moving, and the moonlight had not been gilding the tops of their heads, they would have been indistinguishable from the dark ground on which they walked. Even at this distance, Harry had a funny feeling he recognised the walk of the squattest of them, who seemed to be leading the group.

He could not think why Umbridge would be taking a stroll outside after midnight, much less accompanied by five others. Then somebody coughed behind him, and he remembered that he was halfway through an exam. He had quite forgotten Venus's position. Jamming his eye to his telescope, he found it again and was once more about to enter it on his chart when, alert for any odd sound, he heard a distant knock which echoed through the deserted grounds, followed immediately by the muffled barking of a large dog.

He looked up, his heart hammering. There were lights on in Hagrid's windows and the people he had observed crossing the lawn were now silhouetted against them. The door opened and he distinctly saw six sharply defined figures walk over the threshold. The door closed again and there was silence.

Harry felt very uneasy. He glanced around to see whether Ron or Hermione had noticed what he had, but Professor Marchbanks came walking behind him at that moment and, not wanting to look as though he was sneaking looks at anyone else's work, Harry hastily bent over his star-chart and pretended to be adding notes to it while really peering over the top of the parapet towards Hagrid's cabin. Figures were now moving across the cabin windows, temporarily blocking the light.

He could feel Professor Marchbanks's eyes on the back of his neck and pressed his eye again to his telescope, staring up at the moon though he had marked its position an hour ago, but as Professor Marchbanks moved on he heard a roar from the distant cabin that echoed through the darkness right to the top of the Astronomy Tower. Several of the people around Harry ducked out from behind their telescopes and peered instead in the direction of Hagrid's cabin.

Professor Tofty gave another dry little cough.

'Try and concentrate, now, boys and girls,' he said softly.

Most people returned to their telescopes. Harry looked to his left. Hermione was gazing transfixed at Hagrid's cabin.

第31章 O.W.L.考试

他的羽毛笔悬在羊皮纸上,他眯起眼睛看着下面幽暗的场地,只见六个人影在草地上行走。如果他们不是在移动,如果没有月光掠过他们的头顶,可能他们就会与漆黑的场地融为一体,难以分辨。虽然离得很远,哈利有一种奇怪的感觉,他好像从打头那个最矮胖的人的步态中认出了那是谁。

他不明白乌姆里奇为什么过了午夜还出来闲逛,而且身边还跟着另外五个人。就在这时,身后有人咳嗽,他才想起自己正在考试。他已经把金星的位置忘记了。他赶紧把眼睛贴到望远镜上,重新找到金星,正要往图表上填,突然他警惕的耳朵听见远处传来敲门声,声音在空寂的场地上回荡,接着是一条大狗发出的闷叫。

哈利抬起目光,心跳得像打鼓一样。海格的窗户里透出灯光,映出了哈利刚才看见穿过草坪的那几个人的身影。门开了,哈利清清楚楚地看见六个轮廓分明的人影跨过门槛。门又关上了,一片寂静。

哈利觉得心里很不安。他环顾四周,想看看罗恩和赫敏是不是像他一样注意到了这一幕,可是玛奇班教授正好从他身后走来,哈利不想让人觉得他在偷看别人的考卷,就赶紧低头去看自己的图表,假装在上面填写着什么,实际上他的目光正越过矮墙窥视着海格的小屋。几个人影在小屋窗口晃动,不时把灯光遮住。

哈利感觉到玛奇班教授的目光正注视着自己的后脖颈,便赶紧把眼睛贴到望远镜上,盯视着天空的月亮,其实他一个小时前就标出了月亮的位置。玛奇班教授走开时,哈利听见远处小屋里传来一声咆哮,回声穿透黑夜,一直传到了天文塔顶上。哈利周围的几个同学从望远镜后面闪了出来,朝海格小屋的方向望去。

托福迪教授又轻轻干咳了一声。

"同学们,请集中思想。"他轻声说。

大部分同学都回到自己的望远镜前。哈利看看左边。赫敏呆呆地盯着海格的小屋。

CHAPTER THIRTY-ONE O.W.L.s

'Ahem – twenty minutes to go,' said Professor Tofty.

Hermione jumped and returned at once to her star-chart; Harry looked down at his own and noticed that he had mis-labelled Venus as Mars. He bent to correct it.

There was a loud BANG from the grounds. Several people cried 'Ouch!' when they poked themselves in the face with the ends of their telescopes as they hastened to see what was going on below.

Hagrid's door had burst open and by the light flooding out of the cabin they saw him quite clearly, a massive figure roaring and brandishing his fists, surrounded by six people, all of whom, judging by the tiny threads of red light they were casting in his direction, seemed to be attempting to Stun him.

'No!' cried Hermione.

'My dear!' said Professor Tofty in a scandalised voice. 'This is an examination!'

But nobody was paying the slightest attention to their star-charts any more. Jets of red light were still flying about beside Hagrid's cabin, yet somehow they seemed to be bouncing off him; he was still upright and still, as far as Harry could see, fighting. Cries and yells echoed across the grounds; a man yelled, 'Be reasonable, Hagrid!'

Hagrid roared, 'Reasonable be damned, yeh won' take me like this, Dawlish!'

Harry could see the tiny outline of Fang, attempting to defend Hagrid, leaping repeatedly at the wizards surrounding him until a Stunning Spell caught him and he fell to the ground. Hagrid gave a howl of fury, lifted the culprit bodily from the ground and threw him; the man flew what looked like ten feet and did not get up again. Hermione gasped, both hands over her mouth; Harry looked round at Ron and saw that he, too, was looking scared. None of them had ever seen Hagrid in a real temper before.

'Look!' squealed Parvati, who was leaning over the parapet and pointing to the foot of the castle where the front doors had opened again; more light was spilling out on to the dark lawn and a single long black shadow was now rippling across the lawn.

'Now, really!' said Professor Tofty anxiously. 'Only sixteen minutes left, you know!'

But nobody paid him the slightest attention: they were watching the person now sprinting towards the battle beside Hagrid's cabin.

'How dare you!' the figure shouted as she ran. 'How *dare* you!'

第31章 O.W.L.考试

"咳咳——还有二十分钟。"托福迪教授说。

赫敏吓了一跳,赶紧去看她的图表。哈利也低头看着图表,发现他把金星写成了火星,便俯身改了过来。

场地上传来砰的一声巨响。几个同学急于看清下面发生了什么事情,被望远镜的尾端戳痛了脸,哎哟哎哟地叫了起来。

海格的门突然被撞开了,在小屋透出的灯光中,他们清楚地看见一个庞大的身影挥着拳头在咆哮,有六个人把他围在中间,从他们射向他的一道道细细的红光看,他们是想给他施昏迷咒。

"不!"赫敏叫了起来。

"天哪!"托福迪教授用震惊的声音说,"这是考试!"

可是,谁都不再理会自己的图表了。海格的小屋旁仍然飞出一道道红光,但不知怎的,它们似乎都从他身上弹了回去。他仍然稳稳地站着,而且,从哈利看到的情形看,他仍然在反击。叫喊声、咆哮声在场地上回荡,一个声音嚷道:"海格,理智点儿!"

海格吼道:"去你的理智吧,你们休想这样把我带走,德力士!"

哈利看见了牙牙小小的身影,它为了保护海格,一次次朝海格周围的那些巫师扑去,最后被一个昏迷咒击中,倒在了地上。海格怒吼一声,把那个念咒者整个儿从地上拎起来扔了出去。那人飞出去足有十英尺,再也没有站起来。赫敏抽了一口冷气,用双手捂住了嘴巴。哈利扭头看看罗恩,发现他也是满脸惊恐。他们以前都没看见过海格真正发脾气。

"看!"帕瓦蒂尖叫起来,她靠在矮墙上,指着城堡脚下。大门又被打开了,又有亮光洒在黑黢黢的草坪上,一个长长的黑影在草坪上快速走动。

"请注意!"托福迪教授焦急地说,"请注意,只剩十六分钟了!"

但是谁都没有理睬他的话。他们都注视着那个身影冲向海格小屋旁打斗的那些人。

"你们怎么敢这样!"那个身影边跑边喊,"你们怎么敢!"

CHAPTER THIRTY-ONE O.W.L.s

'It's McGonagall!' whispered Hermione.

'Leave him alone! *Alone*, I say!' said Professor McGonagall's voice through the darkness. 'On what grounds are you attacking him? He has done nothing, nothing to warrant such –'

Hermione, Parvati and Lavender all screamed. The figures around the cabin had shot no fewer than four Stunners at Professor McGonagall. Halfway between cabin and castle the red beams collided with her; for a moment she looked luminous and glowed an eerie red, then she lifted right off her feet, landed hard on her back, and moved no more.

'Galloping gargoyles!' shouted Professor Tofty, who also seemed to have forgotten the exam completely. 'Not so much as a warning! Outrageous behaviour!'

'COWARDS!' bellowed Hagrid; his voice carried clearly to the top of the tower, and several lights flickered back on inside the castle. 'RUDDY COWARDS! HAVE SOME O' THAT – AN' THAT –'

'Oh my –' gasped Hermione.

Hagrid took two massive swipes at his closest attackers; judging by their immediate collapse, they had been knocked cold. Harry saw Hagrid double over, and thought he had finally been overcome by a spell. But, on the contrary, next moment Hagrid was standing again with what appeared to be a sack on his back – then Harry realised that Fang's limp body was draped around his shoulders.

'Get him, get him!' screamed Umbridge, but her remaining helper seemed highly reluctant to go within reach of Hagrid's fists; indeed, he was backing away so fast he tripped over one of his unconscious colleagues and fell over. Hagrid had turned and begun to run with Fang still hung around his neck. Umbridge sent one last Stunning Spell after him but it missed; and Hagrid, running full-pelt towards the distant gates, disappeared into the darkness.

There was a long minute's quivering silence as everybody gazed open-mouthed into the grounds. Then Professor Tofty's voice said feebly, 'Um … five minutes to go, everybody.'

Though he had only filled in two-thirds of his chart, Harry was desperate for the exam to end. When it came at last he, Ron and Hermione forced their telescopes haphazardly back into their holders and dashed back down the spiral staircase. None of the students were going to bed; they were all talking loudly and excitedly at the foot of the stairs about what they had witnessed.

'That evil woman!' gasped Hermione, who seemed to be having difficulty

第31章 O.W.L.考试

"是麦格！"赫敏小声说。

"放开他！我说，放开！"麦格教授的声音穿透了黑夜，"你们有什么理由攻击他？他没做什么，没做什么，不该受到这样——"

赫敏、帕瓦蒂和拉文德都尖叫起来。小屋周围的人影同时朝麦格教授射出至少四个昏迷咒。那几道红光在小屋和城堡之间击中了她。刹那间，她好像是个发光体，周身透出一种诡异的红光，然后她双脚离地，重重地仰面摔倒在地上，不再动弹。

"狂奔的滴水嘴石兽啊！"托福迪教授喊道，他似乎也把考试忘在了脑后，"连个警告也没有！真是无耻的行径！"

"**胆小鬼！**"海格吼道，他的声音清晰地传到塔楼顶上，城堡里又亮起了几盏灯，"**该死的胆小鬼！尝尝这个——再尝尝这个——**"

"哦，天哪——"赫敏吃惊地说。

海格挥起大手朝两个离他最近的进攻者捆去，他们立刻瘫倒在地上，看来是被打昏了。哈利看见海格弯下腰，以为他终于被咒语击中。不料海格立刻又站了起来，背上似乎扛着一个口袋——哈利接着意识到那是牙牙毫无生气的身体挂在他肩头。

"抓住他，抓住他！"乌姆里奇嚷道，但她剩下来的那名助手似乎极不情愿走近海格拳头够得到的地方。他快步地连连后退，被一名昏迷不醒的同伙一绊，摔倒在地。海格转过身，拔腿就跑，牙牙仍然挂在他的脖子上。乌姆里奇对着他的背影又发了最后一个昏迷咒，但没有击中。海格全速朝远处的大门奔去，消失在黑暗中。

接下来是长时间的心惊胆战的沉默，每个人都目瞪口呆地望着下面的场地。托福迪教授有气无力地说："唔……同学们，还有五分钟。"

虽然图表只填了三分之二，哈利却巴不得考试赶紧结束。终于考完了，他和罗恩、赫敏把望远镜胡乱放回架子上，飞快地冲下旋转楼梯。同学们都没有去睡觉，都聚集在楼梯脚下激动地大声议论着刚才目睹的事情。

"那个坏女人！"赫敏气喘吁吁地嚷道，她似乎愤怒得连话也说不

CHAPTER THIRTY-ONE O.W.L.s

talking due to rage. 'Trying to sneak up on Hagrid in the dead of night!'

'She clearly wanted to avoid another scene like Trelawney's,' said Ernie Macmillan sagely, squeezing over to join them.

'Hagrid did well, didn't he?' said Ron, who looked more alarmed than impressed. 'How come all the spells bounced off him?'

'It'll be his giant blood,' said Hermione shakily. 'It's very hard to Stun a giant, they're like trolls, really tough ... but poor Professor McGonagall ... four Stunners straight in the chest and she's not exactly young, is she?'

'Dreadful, dreadful,' said Ernie, shaking his head pompously. 'Well, I'm off to bed. Night, all.'

People around them were drifting away, still talking excitedly about what they had just seen.

'At least they didn't get to take Hagrid off to Azkaban,' said Ron. 'I 'spect he's gone to join Dumbledore, hasn't he?'

'I suppose so,' said Hermione, who looked tearful. 'Oh, this is awful, I really thought Dumbledore would be back before long, but now we've lost Hagrid too.'

They traipsed back to the Gryffindor common room to find it full. The commotion out in the grounds had woken several people, who had hastened to rouse their friends. Seamus and Dean, who had arrived ahead of Harry, Ron and Hermione, were now telling everyone what they had seen and heard from the top of the Astronomy Tower.

'But why sack Hagrid now?' asked Angelina Johnson, shaking her head. 'It's not like Trelawney; he's been teaching much better than usual this year!'

'Umbridge hates part-humans,' said Hermione bitterly, flopping down into an armchair. 'She was always going to try and get Hagrid out.'

'And she thought Hagrid was putting Nifflers in her office,' piped up Katie Bell.

'Oh, blimey,' said Lee Jordan, covering his mouth. 'It's me who's been putting the Nifflers in her office. Fred and George left me a couple; I've been levitating them in through her window.'

'She'd have sacked him anyway,' said Dean. 'He was too close to Dumbledore.'

'That's true,' said Harry, sinking into an armchair beside Hermione's.

第31章 O.W.L.考试

连贯了,"竟然在半夜三更偷袭海格!"

"她显然是想避免再出现特里劳尼的那一幕。"厄尼·麦克米兰的口气像位智者,他说着挤到了他们中间。

"海格真是好样的,不是吗?"罗恩说,他与其说是佩服,不如说是惊恐,"那些咒语怎么都从他身上弹开了呢?"

"可能是因为他的巨人血统,"赫敏声音发颤地说,"要把巨人击昏是很难的,他们就像巨怪,特别结实……但是可怜的麦格教授……四个昏迷咒击中了她的胸口,而她已经不年轻了,是不是?"

"可怕,可怕。"厄尼说,煞有介事地摇着脑袋,"好了,我要去睡觉了。诸位晚安。"

周围的人逐渐散去,离开时仍在激动地谈论着刚才看见的事。

"至少他们没能把海格弄到阿兹卡班去。"罗恩说,"我怀疑他去找邓布利多了,对吗?"

"我想是的。"赫敏说,眼泪都快掉下来了,"哦,太可怕了,我还以为邓布利多很快就会回来呢,现在我们连海格也没有了。"

他们拖着疲惫的脚步回到格兰芬多公共休息室,发现里面挤满了人。场地上的骚动惊醒了几个同学,他们又急忙叫醒各自的朋友。西莫和迪安在哈利、罗恩和赫敏之前赶到,正在给大伙儿讲述他们在天文塔顶上看到和听到的情形。

"为什么现在解雇海格呢?"安吉利娜·约翰逊摇着头问,"他不像特里劳尼,他这学期教课比以前强多了!"

"乌姆里奇讨厌半人类,"赫敏恨恨地说,一屁股坐在一把扶手椅上,"她一直在想办法把海格赶走。"

"她还以为是海格把嗅嗅放进她办公室的。"凯蒂·贝尔插嘴道。

"哦,天哪,"李·乔丹捂着嘴叫了起来,"是我把嗅嗅放进她办公室的呀。弗雷德和乔治给我留了两只。我让它们飘起来钻进了她的窗户。"

"不管怎样她都会把海格解雇的,"迪安说,"海格跟邓布利多走得太近了。"

"这倒是的。"哈利说着,跌坐在赫敏旁边的一把扶手椅上。

1201

CHAPTER THIRTY-ONE

O.W.L.s

'I just hope Professor McGonagall's all right,' said Lavender tearfully.

'They carried her back up to the castle, we watched through the dormitory window,' said Colin Creevey. 'She didn't look very well.'

'Madam Pomfrey will sort her out,' said Alicia Spinnet firmly. 'She's never failed yet.'

It was nearly four in the morning before the common room cleared. Harry felt wide awake; the image of Hagrid sprinting away into the dark was haunting him; he was so angry with Umbridge he could not think of a punishment bad enough for her, though Ron's suggestion of having her fed to a box of starving Blast-Ended Skrewts had its merits. He fell asleep contemplating hideous revenges and arose from bed three hours later feeling distinctly unrested.

Their final exam, History of Magic, was not to take place until that afternoon. Harry would very much have liked to go back to bed after breakfast, but he had been counting on the morning for a spot of last-minute revision, so instead he sat with his head in his hands by the common-room window, trying hard not to doze off as he read through some of the three-and-a-half-feet-high stack of notes that Hermione had lent him.

The fifth-years entered the Great Hall at two o'clock and took their places in front of their face-down examination papers. Harry felt exhausted. He just wanted this to be over, so that he could go and sleep; then tomorrow, he and Ron were going to go down to the Quidditch pitch – he was going to have a fly on Ron's broom – and savour their freedom from revision.

'Turn over your papers,' said Professor Marchbanks from the front of the Hall, flicking over the giant hourglass. 'You may begin.'

Harry stared fixedly at the first question. It was several seconds before it occurred to him that he had not taken in a word of it; there was a wasp buzzing distractingly against one of the high windows. Slowly, tortuously, he at last began to write an answer.

He was finding it very difficult to remember names and kept confusing dates. He simply skipped question four (*In your opinion, did wand legislation contribute to, or lead to better control of, goblin riots of the eighteenth century?*), thinking that he would go back to it if he had time at the end. He had a stab at question five (*How was the Statute of Secrecy breached in 1749 and what measures were introduced to prevent a recurrence?*) but had a nagging suspicion that he had missed several important points; he had a feeling vampires had come into the story somewhere.

第31章 O.W.L.考试

"我只是希望麦格教授没事。"拉文德眼泪汪汪地说。

"他们把她抬进了城堡,我们透过宿舍窗户看见的,"科林·克里维说,"她看上去情况不太好。"

"庞弗雷女士会把她治好的,"艾丽娅·斯平内特肯定地说,"她还从来没有失败过呢。"

直到将近凌晨四点,同学们才离开了公共休息室。哈利毫无睡意,脑海里总是浮现出海格冲进黑暗的身影。他恨透了乌姆里奇,想不出怎样惩罚她才足以解恨,不过罗恩提出的拿她去喂一箱饥饿的炸尾螺的建议倒值得考虑。他想着各种可怕的报复方式,不知不觉间就睡着了。三个小时后他就起床了,觉得自己根本没有休息好。

最后一门考试是魔法史,要到下午才进行。哈利很想吃过早饭再上床睡一觉,可是又指望用上午的时间最后抱抱佛脚,所以他坐在公共休息室的窗口,两手抱着脑袋,强忍着瞌睡,硬着头皮阅读赫敏借给他的那一摞高达三英尺半的笔记。

下午两点,五年级同学走进礼堂,面对反扣着的试卷坐了下来。哈利觉得心力交瘁,巴不得考试赶紧结束,可以回去睡一觉。明天他和罗恩就能到下面的魁地奇球场去了——他要骑一骑罗恩的扫帚——尽情享受摆脱复习后的自由。

"请把试卷翻过来,"玛奇班教授在礼堂前面说,并把那个大沙漏翻转过来,"可以开始了。"

哈利呆呆地盯着第一道题。几秒钟后,他才发现自己一个字也没有看进去。高高的窗户外面有一只黄蜂在嗡嗡叫,干扰了他的注意力。最后,他好不容易才慢慢写出了一个答案。

他发现许多人名都想不起来了,而且他总是把日期搞混。他干脆跳过第四题(在你看来,魔杖立法是推动了十八世纪的妖精叛乱,还是有助于更好地控制它?),他想最后有时间再回来答它。他试着做第五题(《保密法》在一七四九年怎样被违反,后又采取了什么措施以防止这类事件再次发生?),但他怀疑自己漏掉了几个要点,总觉得什么地方应该出现吸血鬼的内容。

CHAPTER THIRTY-ONE

O.W.L.s

He looked ahead for a question he could definitely answer and his eyes alighted upon number ten: *Describe the circumstances that led to the formation of the International Confederation of Wizards and explain why the warlocks of Liechtenstein refused to join.*

I know this, Harry thought, though his brain felt torpid and slack. He could visualise a heading, in Hermione's handwriting: *The formation of the International Confederation of Wizards* ... he had read those notes only this morning.

He began to write, looking up now and again to check the large hourglass on the desk beside Professor Marchbanks. He was sitting right behind Parvati Patil, whose long dark hair fell below the back of her chair. Once or twice he found himself staring at the tiny golden lights that glistened in it when she moved her head slightly, and had to give his own head a little shake to clear it.

> *...the first Supreme Mugwump of the International Confederation of Wizards was Pierre Bonaccord, but his appointment was contested by the wizarding community of Liechtenstein, because -*

All around Harry quills were scratching on parchment like scurrying, burrowing rats. The sun was very hot on the back of his head. What was it that Bonaccord had done to offend the wizards of Liechtenstein? Harry had a feeling it had something to do with trolls ... he gazed blankly at the back of Parvati's head again. If he could only perform Legilimency and open a window in the back of her head and see what it was about trolls that had caused the breach between Pierre Bonaccord and Liechtenstein ...

Harry closed his eyes and buried his face in his hands, so that the glowing red of his eyelids grew dark and cool. Bonaccord had wanted to stop troll-hunting and give the trolls rights ... but Liechtenstein was having problems with a tribe of particularly vicious mountain trolls ... that was it.

He opened his eyes; they stung and watered at the sight of the blazing white parchment. Slowly, he wrote two lines about the trolls, then read through what he had done so far. It did not seem very informative or detailed, yet he was sure Hermione's notes on the Confederation had gone on for pages and pages.

第31章 O.W.L.考试

他往后寻找一个他有把握回答的题目，最后把目光落在第十题上：请陈述是哪些事件导致了国际巫师联合会的成立，并解释列支敦士登的巫师拒绝加入的原因。

这我知道。哈利想，尽管他的大脑迟钝、发木。他脑海里浮现出赫敏的笔迹写的标题：国际巫师联合会的成立……他就在今天上午刚看过。

他写了起来，不时抬头看看玛奇班教授旁边桌上的那个大沙漏。他坐在帕瓦蒂·佩蒂尔身后，她一头乌黑的长发一直垂落到椅背下，脑袋微微一动，头发里就闪烁出金灿灿的小光点。有那么一两次，哈利发现自己呆呆地盯着那些光点，不得不轻轻摇晃脑袋使自己摆脱出来。

……国际巫师联合会第一任会长是

皮埃尔·波拿库德，

但列支敦士登魔法界对这个任命提出了质疑，因为——

哈利周围都是羽毛笔在羊皮纸上书写的沙沙声，像许多老鼠在奔跑挖洞。太阳照得他的后脑勺火辣辣的。波拿库德做了什么事得罪了列支敦士登的巫师呢？哈利隐约感觉好像跟巨怪有关……他又盯着帕瓦蒂的后脑勺发呆了。但愿他能用摄神取念，打开她后脑勺里的一扇窗户，看看巨怪到底是怎么引起了皮埃尔·波拿库德和列支敦士登之间的决裂……

哈利闭上眼睛，把脸埋在双手里，让红得发烫的眼皮逐渐变暗、冷却。波拿库德想要停止追捕巨怪，让巨怪拥有自己的权益……列支敦士登跟一支特别凶恶的山地巨怪关系紧张……对，就是这个。

他睁开眼睛，面对白得耀眼的羊皮纸，眼睛被刺得酸痛，流出了眼泪。他慢慢地写了两行关于巨怪的内容，然后把他的答题从头到尾读了一遍。感觉似乎不是很详实、具体，他相信赫敏关于联合会的笔记有好多好多页呢。

CHAPTER THIRTY-ONE O.W.L.s

He closed his eyes again, trying to see them, trying to remember ... the Confederation had met for the first time in France, yes, he had written that already ...

Goblins had tried to attend and been ousted ... he had written that, too ...

And nobody from Liechtenstein had wanted to come ...

Think, he told himself, his face in his hands, while all around him quills scratched out never-ending answers and the sand trickled through the hourglass at the front ...

He was walking along the cool, dark corridor to the Department of Mysteries again, walking with a firm and purposeful tread, breaking occasionally into a run, determined to reach his destination at last ... the black door swung open for him as usual, and here he was in the circular room with its many doors ...

Straight across the stone floor and through the second door ... patches of dancing light on the walls and floor and that odd mechanical clicking, but no time to explore, he must hurry ...

He jogged the last few feet to the third door, which swung open just like the others ...

Once again he was in the cathedral-sized room full of shelves and glass spheres ... his heart was beating very fast now ... he was going to get there this time ... when he reached number ninety-seven he turned left and hurried along the aisle between two rows ...

But there was a shape on the floor at the very end, a black shape moving on the floor like a wounded animal ... Harry's stomach contracted with fear ... with excitement ...

A voice issued from his own mouth, a high, cold voice empty of any human kindness ...

'Take it for me ... lift it down, now ... I cannot touch it ... but you can ...'

The black shape on the floor shifted a little. Harry saw a long-fingered white hand clutching a wand rise at the end of his own arm ... heard the high, cold voice say '*Crucio!*'

The man on the floor let out a scream of pain, attempted to stand but fell back, writhing. Harry was laughing. He raised his wand, the curse lifted and the figure groaned and became motionless.

'Lord Voldemort is waiting ...'

第31章 O.W.L.考试

他又闭上眼睛,努力回忆,拼命回忆……联合会第一次会议是在法国召开的,对,这一点他已经写过了……

妖精也想参加,被赶了出去……这一点他也写过了……

列支敦士登没有人愿意参加……

再想想,他对自己说,脸埋在双手里,周围羽毛笔的沙沙声不绝于耳,前面沙漏里的沙粒不断漏下去……

他又走在神秘事务司那昏暗、凉爽的走廊上,步子坚决、果断,偶尔小跑几步,相信这次终于要到达目的地……黑门像往常一样为他打开了,他站在有许多扇门的圆形房间里……

径直走过石板地面,穿过第二道门……一块块光斑在墙壁和地板上跳动,古怪的仪器在滴滴作响,但没有时间细看了,他必须抓紧……

哈利紧跑几步,来到第三道门前,它也像另外几扇门一样打开了……

他又一次置身于满是架子和圆球的大教堂般的房间里……此刻他的心跳得特别快……这次肯定能走到那儿……走到第九十七排架子前,他往左一拐,顺着两排架子间的过道匆匆往前走……

可是在过道顶头的地板上有个东西,一个黑乎乎的东西正在地上蠕动,像一只受伤的动物……哈利的心抽紧了,因为恐惧……因为兴奋……

一个声音从他自己的嘴里发了出来,一个冰冷、高亢的声音,没有丝毫人性的善意……

"给我去拿……快,拿下来……我不能碰它……你可以碰……"

地板上黑乎乎的东西微微动了动。哈利看见自己的胳膊前端伸出了一只苍白、修长的手,手里抓着魔杖……听见那个冰冷、高亢的声音说:"钻心剜骨!"

地板上的男人发出痛苦的尖叫,努力想站起来,却倒了下去,在地上扭动。哈利在大笑。他举起魔杖,咒语停止了,那身影呻吟着,不再动弹。

"伏地魔大人在等着呢……"

CHAPTER THIRTY-ONE O.W.L.s

Very slowly, his arms trembling, the man on the ground raised his shoulders a few inches and lifted his head. His face was bloodstained and gaunt, twisted in pain yet rigid with defiance ...

'You'll have to kill me,' whispered Sirius.

'Undoubtedly I shall in the end,' said the cold voice. 'But you will fetch it for me first, Black ... you think you have felt pain thus far? Think again ... we have hours ahead of us and nobody to hear you scream ...'

But somebody screamed as Voldemort lowered his wand again; somebody yelled and fell sideways off a hot desk on to the cold stone floor; Harry awoke as he hit the ground, still yelling, his scar on fire, as the Great Hall erupted all around him.

第31章 O.W.L.考试

地板上的男人双臂颤抖,很慢很慢地把肩膀从地面上支撑起几英寸,抬起头来。他的脸憔悴,血迹斑斑,因痛苦而扭曲,却带着不屈的刚毅……

"除非你杀了我。"小天狼星轻声说。

"最后肯定会这么做的,"那个冰冷的声音说,"但你先要给我把它拿下来,布莱克……你认为已经感觉到疼痛了?好好想想……我们有的是时间,谁也听不见你的尖叫……"

可是,就在伏地魔放下魔杖的时候,有人尖叫起来,有人尖叫着从滚烫的桌子上摔下来,倒在冰冷的石板地上。哈利撞在地上就醒过来了,嘴里仍在尖叫,伤疤像着了火似的,礼堂在他周围突然出现了。

CHAPTER THIRTY-TWO

Out of the Fire

'I'm not going ... I don't need the hospital wing ... I don't want ...'

He was gibbering as he tried to pull away from Professor Tofty, who was looking at Harry with much concern after helping him out into the Entrance Hall with the students all around them staring.

'I'm – I'm fine, sir,' Harry stammered, wiping the sweat from his face. 'Really ... I just fell asleep ... had a nightmare ...'

'Pressure of examinations!' said the old wizard sympathetically, patting Harry shakily on the shoulder. 'It happens, young man, it happens! Now, a cooling drink of water, and perhaps you will be ready to return to the Great Hall? The examination is nearly over, but you may be able to round off your last answer nicely?'

'Yes,' said Harry wildly. 'I mean ... no ... I've done – done as much as I can, I think ...'

'Very well, very well,' said the old wizard gently. 'I shall go and collect your examination paper and I suggest that you go and have a nice lie down.'

'I'll do that,' said Harry, nodding vigorously. 'Thanks very much.'

The second that the old man's heels disappeared over the threshold into the Great Hall, Harry ran up the marble staircase, hurtled along the corridors so fast the portraits he passed muttered reproaches, up more flights of stairs, and finally burst like a hurricane through the double doors of the hospital wing, causing Madam Pomfrey – who had been spooning some bright blue liquid into Montague's open mouth – to shriek in alarm.

'Potter, what do you think you're doing?'

'I need to see Professor McGonagall,' gasped Harry, the breath tearing his lungs. 'Now ... it's urgent!'

第 32 章

从火中归来

"我不去……我不需要去校医院……我不想去……"

哈利语无伦次地说着,想从托福迪教授手里挣脱出来。托福迪教授已经扶着他离开礼堂走进门厅,正十分关切地望着他,同学们都在周围看着。

"我——我没事,先生。"哈利结结巴巴地说,擦去脸上的汗水,"真的……我只是睡着了……做了个噩梦……"

"考试压力!"老巫师深表同情地说,用颤抖的手拍了拍哈利的肩膀,"确实会有这种事,年轻人,会有这种事!好了,喝杯水清醒清醒,也许你就可以再进礼堂去?考试马上就要结束了,你也许可以好好地完成最后的答题,是不是?"

"是的,"哈利胡乱地说,"我的意思是……不……我已经答完了——能答的都答完了,我想……"

"很好,很好,"老巫师温和地说,"我去把你的考卷收起来,我建议你躺下来好好休息一下。"

"我会的,"哈利拼命点着头说,"非常感谢。"

老人的双脚刚跨过门槛走进礼堂,哈利就奔上大理石楼梯,顺着走廊飞跑起来,惹得旁边那些肖像都低声责骂他。他又跑上几段楼梯,最后像一阵风似的冲进校医院的双扇门,庞弗雷女士正用勺子把一种蓝晶晶的液体喂进蒙太张开的嘴里,她惊得尖叫起来。

"波特,你这是在做什么?"

"我需要见麦格教授。"哈利上气不接下气地说,感觉肺都要爆炸了,"快……情况紧急!"

CHAPTER THIRTY-TWO Out of the Fire

'She's not here, Potter,' said Madam Pomfrey sadly. 'She was transferred to St Mungo's this morning. Four Stunning Spells straight to the chest at her age? It's a wonder they didn't kill her.'

'She's ... gone?' said Harry, shocked.

The bell rang just outside the dormitory and he heard the usual distant rumbling of students starting to flood out into the corridors above and below him. He remained quite still, looking at Madam Pomfrey. Terror was rising inside him.

There was nobody left to tell. Dumbledore had gone, Hagrid had gone, but he had always expected Professor McGonagall to be there, irascible and inflexible, perhaps, but always dependably, solidly present ...

'I don't wonder you're shocked, Potter,' said Madam Pomfrey, with a kind of fierce approval in her face. 'As if one of them could have Stunned Minerva McGonagall face-on by daylight! Cowardice, that's what it was ... despicable cowardice ... if I wasn't worried what would happen to you students without me, I'd resign in protest.'

'Yes,' said Harry blankly.

He strode blindly from the hospital wing into the teeming corridor where he stood, buffeted by the crowd, panic expanding inside him like poison gas so that his head swam and he could not think what to do ...

Ron and Hermione, said a voice in his head.

He was running again, pushing students out of the way, oblivious to their angry protests. He sprinted back down two floors and was at the top of the marble staircase when he saw them hurrying towards him.

'Harry!' said Hermione at once, looking very frightened. 'What happened? Are you all right? Are you ill?'

'Where have you been?' demanded Ron.

'Come with me,' Harry said quickly. 'Come on, I've got to tell you something.'

He led them along the first-floor corridor, peering through doorways, and at last found an empty classroom into which he dived, closing the door behind Ron and Hermione the moment they were inside, and leaned against it, facing them.

'Voldemort's got Sirius.'

'*What?*'

第32章 从火中归来

"她不在这儿,"庞弗雷女士难过地说,"今天上午她被转到圣芒戈医院去了。这把年纪了,怎么经得起被四个昏迷咒击中胸口?没要了她的命就算奇迹了。"

"她……走了?"哈利震惊地说。

病房外面的铃声响了,他听见远处楼上楼下的同学们像往常一样拥进走廊时发出的喧闹声。他一动不动地站着,望着庞弗雷女士,心头袭来一阵恐惧。

没有人可以告诉了。邓布利多走了,海格走了,他原以为还有麦格教授,虽然她脾气暴躁、态度强硬,但总是可以信赖,总是在他们身边……

"你感到震惊,我一点儿也不奇怪,波特,"庞弗雷女士说,脸上现出一种强烈赞同的神情,"他们别以为在大白天也能当面击昏米勒娃·麦格!懦夫行为,不是别的……纯粹是卑鄙的懦夫行为……要不是担心我走了以后你们学生会出事,我早就用辞职来抗议了。"

"是啊。"哈利茫然地说。

他漫无目的地走出校医院,走进拥挤的走廊,站在那里,被人群冲得东倒西歪,恐慌像毒气一样在他体内弥漫。他觉得大脑晕乎乎的,无法考虑该怎么办……

罗恩和赫敏,一个声音在他脑海里说。

他又跑了起来,推开那些挡路的同学,不理会他们愤怒的抗议。他冲下两层楼,来到大理石楼梯顶上,只见罗恩和赫敏正匆匆朝他走来。

"哈利!"赫敏立刻叫道,看上去非常害怕,"出什么事了?你没事吧?你病了吗?"

"你去哪儿了?"罗恩问道。

"跟我来,"哈利赶紧说道,"快,我有件事要告诉你们。"

他领着他们跑过二楼的走廊,朝一扇扇门里张望,最后找到了一间空教室,一头钻了进去。等罗恩和赫敏一走进教室,他就关上门,靠在上面,望着他们俩。

"伏地魔抓住了小天狼星。"

"什么?"

CHAPTER THIRTY-TWO

Out of the Fire

'How d'you –?'

'Saw it. Just now. When I fell asleep in the exam.'

'But – but where? How?' said Hermione, whose face was white.

'I dunno how,' said Harry. 'But I know exactly where. There's a room in the Department of Mysteries full of shelves covered in these little glass balls and they're at the end of row ninety-seven ... he's trying to use Sirius to get whatever it is he wants from in there ... he's torturing him ... says he'll end by killing him!'

Harry found his voice was shaking, as were his knees. He moved over to a desk and sat down on it, trying to master himself.

'How're we going to get there?' he asked them.

There was a moment's silence. Then Ron said, 'G-get there?'

'Get to the Department of Mysteries, so we can rescue Sirius!' Harry said loudly.

'But – Harry ...' said Ron weakly.

'What? *What?*' said Harry.

He could not understand why they were both gaping at him as though he was asking them something unreasonable.

'Harry,' said Hermione in a rather frightened voice, 'er ... how ... how did Voldemort get into the Ministry of Magic without anybody realising he was there?'

'How do I know?' bellowed Harry. 'The question is how *we're* going to get in there!'

'But ... Harry, think about this,' said Hermione, taking a step towards him, 'it's five o'clock in the afternoon ... the Ministry of Magic must be full of workers ... how would Voldemort and Sirius have got in without being seen? Harry ... they're probably the two most wanted wizards in the world ... you think they could get into a building full of Aurors undetected?'

'I dunno, Voldemort used an Invisibility Cloak or something!' Harry shouted. 'Anyway, the Department of Mysteries has always been completely empty whenever I've been –'

'You've never been there, Harry,' said Hermione quietly. 'You've dreamed about the place, that's all.'

'They're not normal dreams!' Harry shouted in her face, standing up

第32章 从火中归来

"你怎么会——？"

"我看见了。就在刚才。我考试时睡着了看见的。"

"可是——可是在哪儿呢？怎么抓住的？"赫敏说，她的脸都白了。

"不知道，"哈利说，"但我很清楚是在哪儿。神秘事务司里有一个房间，里面都是架子，架子上放着那些小小的玻璃球，他们在第九十七排架子的尽头……他想利用小天狼星从那里拿到他想要的东西……他在折磨小天狼星……说最后要杀掉他！"

哈利发现自己的声音在颤抖，膝盖也在颤抖。他走到一张桌子旁坐了下来，努力让自己镇静。

"我们怎么去那儿呢？"他问罗恩和赫敏。

片刻的沉默。接着罗恩说："去—去哪儿？"

"去神秘事务司呀，去了才能救小天狼星！"哈利大声说。

"可是——哈利……"罗恩底气不足地说。

"什么？什么？"哈利说。

他不明白他们俩为什么都呆呆地望着他，就好像他叫他们做的是一件不合情理的事。

"哈利，"赫敏用战战兢兢的声音说，"呃……伏……伏地魔怎么可能进入魔法部而不被人发现呢？"

"我怎么知道？"哈利吼道，"问题是我们怎么去那儿！"

"可是……哈利，好好想想吧，"赫敏说着，朝哈利面前跨了一步，"现在是下午五点……魔法部里肯定到处都是工作人员……伏地魔和小天狼星怎么可能进去而不被人看见呢？哈利……他们大概是全世界被头号通缉的两个巫师了……你认为他们能神不知鬼不觉地溜进一座满是傲罗的大楼吗？"

"我不知道，也许伏地魔是用了隐形衣什么的！"哈利大声说，"反正，神秘事务司里总是空无一人，每次我去——"

"你从来没去过那儿，哈利，"赫敏小声说，"你不过是梦见了那个地方。"

"不是普通的梦！"哈利冲她嚷道，站起来也朝她跨了一步。他真想抓住她使劲晃一晃。"那你怎么解释罗恩的爸爸那件事，那又是怎么

CHAPTER THIRTY-TWO Out of the Fire

and taking a step closer to her in turn. He wanted to shake her. 'How d'you explain Ron's dad then, what was all that about, how come I knew what had happened to him?'

'He's got a point,' said Ron quietly, looking at Hermione.

'But this is just – just so *unlikely*!' said Hermione desperately. 'Harry, how on earth could Voldemort have got hold of Sirius when he's been in Grimmauld Place all the time?'

'Sirius might've cracked and just wanted some fresh air,' said Ron, sounding worried. 'He's been desperate to get out of that house for ages –'

'But why,' Hermione persisted, 'why on earth would Voldemort want to use *Sirius* to get the weapon, or whatever the thing is?'

'I dunno, there could be loads of reasons!' Harry yelled at her. 'Maybe Sirius is just someone Voldemort doesn't care about seeing hurt –'

'You know what, I've just thought of something,' said Ron in a hushed voice. 'Sirius's brother was a Death Eater, wasn't he? Maybe he told Sirius the secret of how to get the weapon!'

'Yeah – and that's why Dumbledore's been so keen to keep Sirius locked up all the time!' said Harry.

'Look, I'm sorry,' cried Hermione, 'but neither of you is making sense, and we've got no proof for any of this, no proof Voldemort and Sirius are even there –'

'Hermione, Harry's seen them!' said Ron, rounding on her.

'OK,' she said, looking frightened yet determined, 'I've just got to say this –'

'What?'

'You ... this isn't a criticism, Harry! But you do ... sort of ... I mean – don't you think you've got a bit of a – a – *saving-people thing*?' she said.

He glared at her.

'And what's that supposed to mean, a "saving-people thing"?'

'Well ... you ...' She looked more apprehensive than ever. 'I mean ... last year, for instance ... in the lake ... during the Tournament ... you shouldn't have ... I mean, you didn't need to save that little Delacour girl ... you got a bit ... carried away ...'

A wave of hot, prickly anger swept through Harry's body; how could she remind him of that blunder now?

第32章 从火中归来

回事？我怎么会知道他出了意外？"

"他说得有道理。"罗恩看着赫敏轻声说。

"可是这太——太不可思议了！"赫敏烦躁地说，"哈利，小天狼星一直都在格里莫广场，伏地魔怎么可能抓住他呢？"

"小天狼星大概吃不消了，想出来透透新鲜空气。"罗恩说，声音里透着担忧，"他一直想逃离那座房子，有好长时间了——"

"可是为什么，"赫敏追问道，"为什么伏地魔要利用小天狼星去拿那件武器，或是别的什么东西呢？"

"不知道，可以有一大堆理由！"哈利冲她嚷道，"可能伏地魔不在乎小天狼星是不是会受伤——"

"你知道吗，我突然想起一件事，"罗恩压低声音说，"小天狼星的弟弟是食死徒，对吗？说不定他把怎么拿到那件武器的秘密告诉了小天狼星！"

"是啊——所以邓布利多才一直坚持把小天狼星锁在家里！"哈利说。

"原谅我这么说，"赫敏喊道，"但我认为你们俩说的都没道理，我们根本没有任何证据，没有证据证明伏地魔和小天狼星确实在那儿——"

"赫敏，哈利看见他们了！"罗恩冲她吼道。

"好吧，"赫敏说，看上去又害怕又坚决，"我不得不说——"

"什么？"

"你……我不是在批评你，哈利！可是你确实……有点儿……我的意思是——你不认为自己有点儿——有点儿——救人上瘾吗？"她说。

哈利狠狠地瞪着她。

"'救人上瘾'，这是什么意思？"

"就是……你……"赫敏看上去更加惶恐了，"我的意思是……比如去年……在湖里……三强争霸赛的时候……你不该……我的意思是，根本用不着救那个姓德拉库尔的小姑娘……你有点……头脑发热……"

一股滚烫的怒火在哈利的身体里涌动。她怎么能在这个时候重提他那个愚蠢的错误呢？

CHAPTER THIRTY-TWO Out of the Fire

'I mean, it was really great of you and everything,' said Hermione quickly, looking positively petrified at the look on Harry's face, 'everyone thought it was a wonderful thing to do –'

'That's funny,' said Harry in a trembling voice, 'because I definitely remember Ron saying I'd wasted time *acting the hero* ... is that what you think this is? You reckon I want to act the hero again?'

'No, no, no!' said Hermione, looking aghast. 'That's not what I mean at all!'

'Well, spit out what you've got to say, because we're wasting time here!' Harry shouted.

'I'm trying to say – Voldemort knows you, Harry! He took Ginny down into the Chamber of Secrets to lure you there, it's the kind of thing he does, he knows you're the – the sort of person who'd go to Sirius's aid! What if he's just trying to get *you* into the Department of Myst–?'

'Hermione, it doesn't matter if he's done it to get me there or not – they've taken McGonagall to St Mungo's, there isn't anyone from the Order left at Hogwarts who we can tell, and if we don't go, Sirius is dead!'

'But Harry – what if your dream was – was just that, a dream?' Harry let out a roar of frustration. Hermione actually stepped back from him, looking alarmed.

'You don't get it!' Harry shouted at her, 'I'm not having nightmares, I'm not just dreaming! What d'you think all the Occlumency was for, why d'you think Dumbledore wanted me prevented from seeing these things? Because they're REAL, Hermione – Sirius is trapped, I've seen him. Voldemort's got him, and no one else knows, and that means we're the only ones who can save him, and if you don't want to do it, fine, but I'm going, understand? And if I remember rightly, you didn't have a problem with my *saving-people thing* when it was you I was saving from the Dementors, or –' he rounded on Ron '– when it was your sister I was saving from the Basilisk –'

'I never said I had a problem!' said Ron heatedly.

'But Harry, you've just said it,' said Hermione fiercely, 'Dumbledore wanted you to learn to shut these things out of your mind, if you'd done Occlumency properly you'd never have seen this –'

'IF YOU THINK I'M JUST GOING TO ACT LIKE I HAVEN'T SEEN –'

'Sirius told you there was nothing more important than you learning to close your mind!'

第32章 从火中归来

"我的意思是，你那样做确实很不简单，"赫敏赶紧说道，似乎被哈利的脸色吓坏了，"大家都认为你的做法很了不起——"

"这就怪了，"哈利用颤抖的声音说，"我明明记得罗恩说我浪费时间去逞英雄……你是不是也这样看待这件事的？你认为我又想逞英雄？"

"不，不，不！"赫敏神色惊恐地说，"我根本不是那个意思！"

"好吧，你有什么话就快说吧，我们在这里是浪费时间！"哈利喊道。

"我想说的是——伏地魔了解你，哈利！他把金妮带到下面的密室，引诱你去那儿，这就是他做的事情，他知道你——你会去帮助小天狼星！如果他只是想把你引进神秘事务司——"

"赫敏，他是不是想把我引去并不重要——他们已经把麦格转到了圣芒戈医院，霍格沃茨没有凤凰社的人可以告诉了，如果我们不去，小天狼星就死定了！"

"可是，哈利——如果你的梦只是——只是一个梦呢？"

哈利气恼地吼了一声，赫敏吓得后退一步，满脸惊恐。

"你没听明白！"哈利冲她嚷道，"我没做噩梦，我根本没有做梦！你认为我学大脑封闭术是做什么用的？你认为邓布利多为什么不让我再看见那些东西？就因为它们是**真的**，赫敏——小天狼星中了圈套，我看见了。伏地魔抓住了他，别人谁都不知道，也就是说，只有我们才能救他；如果你不想去，可以，但我要去，明白吗？如果我记得不错，当我从摄魂怪手里把你救出来的时候，你对我的救人上瘾可没有意见，还有——"他向罗恩吼道，"——我把你妹妹从蛇怪手里救出来的时候——"

"我从来没说过对你有意见！"罗恩激动地说。

"可是，哈利，你自己也说了，"赫敏语气激烈地说，"邓布利多希望你学会关闭大脑，不让这些东西进来，如果你大脑封闭术做得到位，就根本不会看到这些——"

"如果你认为我应该假装什么都没看见——"

"小天狼星对你说过，没有什么比你学会关闭大脑更重要的了！"

CHAPTER THIRTY-TWO Out of the Fire

'WELL, I EXPECT HE'D SAY SOMETHING DIFFERENT IF HE KNEW WHAT I'D JUST –'

The classroom door opened. Harry, Ron and Hermione whipped around. Ginny walked in, looking curious, followed by Luna, who as usual looked as though she had drifted in accidentally.

'Hi,' said Ginny uncertainly. 'We recognised Harry's voice. What are you yelling about?'

'Never you mind,' said Harry roughly.

Ginny raised her eyebrows.

'There's no need to take that tone with me,' she said coolly, 'I was only wondering whether I could help.'

'Well, you can't,' said Harry shortly.

'You're being rather rude, you know,' said Luna serenely.

Harry swore and turned away. The very last thing he wanted now was a conversation with Luna Lovegood.

'Wait,' said Hermione suddenly. 'Wait … Harry, they *can* help.'

Harry and Ron looked at her.

'Listen,' she said urgently, 'Harry, we need to establish whether Sirius really has left Headquarters.'

'I've told you, I saw –'

'Harry, I'm begging you, please!' said Hermione desperately. 'Please let's just check that Sirius isn't at home before we go charging off to London. If we find out he's not there, then I swear I won't try to stop you. I'll come, I'll d – do whatever it takes to try and save him.'

'Sirius is being tortured NOW!' shouted Harry. 'We haven't got time to waste.'

'But if this is a trick of Voldemort's, Harry, we've got to check, we've got to.'

'How?' Harry demanded. 'How're we going to check?'

'We'll have to use Umbridge's fire and see if we can contact him,' said Hermione, who looked positively terrified at the thought. 'We'll draw Umbridge away again, but we'll need lookouts, and that's where we can use Ginny and Luna.'

Though clearly struggling to understand what was going on, Ginny said immediately, 'Yeah, we'll do it,' and Luna said, 'When you say "Sirius", are you talking about Stubby Boardman?'

第32章 从火中归来

"是啊,如果他知道我刚才看见了什么,我猜他就不会那么说了——"

教室的门开了。哈利、罗恩和赫敏赶紧转过身。金妮走了进来,满脸好奇,后面跟着卢娜,她还像往常一样,好像是不经意间飘进屋来的。

"你们好,"金妮迟疑地说,"我们听出了哈利的声音。你们在嚷嚷什么?"

"不用你管。"哈利粗暴地说。

金妮吃惊地扬起眉毛。

"犯不着用这种口气跟我说话,"她冷冷地说,"我只是在想我能不能帮上点忙。"

"你帮不了。"哈利一口回绝。

"你的态度相当粗鲁啊。"卢娜平静地说。

哈利骂了一句,转过身去。他现在最不想做的事就是跟卢娜·洛夫古德说话。

"等等,"赫敏突然说,"等等……哈利,她们可以帮忙的。"

哈利和罗恩都看着她。

"听我说,"赫敏急切地说,"哈利,我们需要确定小天狼星是不是真的离开了总部。"

"我告诉过你,我看见——"

"哈利,求求你了!"赫敏焦急地说,"在我们赶往伦敦之前,请先核实一下小天狼星在不在家。如果发现他真的不在,我发誓我绝不会阻拦你。我也会去,我会做——做什么都行,只要能够救他。"

"小天狼星眼下就在受折磨!"哈利嚷道,"我们没有时间可以浪费。"

"但如果这是伏地魔的诡计呢?哈利,我们必须核实一下,必须。"

"怎么核实?"哈利问道,"我们怎么核实?"

"我们利用乌姆里奇的炉火,看能不能联系到小天狼星。"赫敏说,她似乎一想到这个念头就怕得要命,"我们再一次把乌姆里奇引开,但需要有人放哨,这就可以用到金妮和卢娜了。"

金妮仍在努力弄清是怎么回事,但立刻说道:"对啊,我们能办到。"卢娜则说:"你们说的'小天狼星',就是胖墩勃德曼吗?"

CHAPTER THIRTY-TWO Out of the Fire

Nobody answered her.

'OK,' Harry said aggressively to Hermione, 'OK, if you can think of a way of doing this quickly, I'm with you, otherwise I'm going to the Department of Mysteries right now.'

'The Department of Mysteries?' said Luna, looking mildly surprised. 'But how are you going to get there?'

Again, Harry ignored her.

'Right,' said Hermione, twisting her hands together and pacing up and down between the desks. 'Right ... well ... one of us has to go and find Umbridge and – and send her off in the wrong direction, keep her away from her office. They could tell her – I don't know – that Peeves is up to something awful as usual ...'

'I'll do it,' said Ron at once. 'I'll tell her Peeves is smashing up the Transfiguration department or something, it's miles away from her office. Come to think of it, I could probably persuade Peeves to do it if I met him on the way.'

It was a mark of the seriousness of the situation that Hermione made no objection to the smashing up of the Transfiguration department.

'OK,' she said, her brow furrowed as she continued to pace. 'Now, we need to keep students right away from her office while we force entry, or some Slytherin's bound to go and tip her off.'

'Luna and I can stand at either end of the corridor,' said Ginny promptly, 'and warn people not to go down there because someone's let off a load of Garrotting Gas.' Hermione looked surprised at the readiness with which Ginny had come up with this lie; Ginny shrugged and said, 'Fred and George were planning to do it before they left.'

'OK,' said Hermione. 'Well then, Harry, you and I will be under the Invisibility Cloak and we'll sneak into the office and you can talk to Sirius –'

'He's not there, Hermione!'

'I mean, you can – can check whether Sirius is at home or not while I keep watch, I don't think you should be in there alone, Lee's already proved the window's a weak spot, sending those Nifflers through it.'

Even through his anger and impatience, Harry recognised Hermione's offer to accompany him into Umbridge's office as a sign of solidarity and loyalty.

第32章 从火中归来

谁也没有回答。

"好吧,"哈利咄咄逼人地对赫敏说,"好吧,如果你能想个办法速战速决,我就同意,不然,我现在就去神秘事务司。"

"神秘事务司?"卢娜说,看上去微微有些吃惊,"可是你怎么去那儿呢?"

哈利还是没有理她。

"好,"赫敏说,她绞着双手,在课桌间走来走去,"好……就这样……我们中间要有一个人去找到乌姆里奇——把她引到另一个方向,让她一直远离自己的办公室。可以对她说——怎么说呢——说皮皮鬼又像平常一样做坏事了……"

"我去吧,"罗恩立刻说道,"我去告诉她,皮皮鬼把变形课教室砸得稀巴烂什么的,那儿离她的办公室好远呢。对了,如果在路上碰到皮皮鬼,我还可以劝他真的那么做。"

赫敏听到要把变形课教室砸得稀巴烂,竟然没有提出反对,可见形势有多么严峻了。

"好吧。"她说,紧蹙着眉头,继续来回踱着步,"还有,我们闯进她的办公室时,还需要防止学生靠近那里,不然肯定会有斯莱特林的学生去向她报告。"

"我和卢娜可以站在走廊两头,"金妮不假思索地说,"警告人们不要往前走,因为有人放了好多锁喉毒气。"金妮的假话张口就来,赫敏显得很吃惊。金妮耸了耸肩说:"弗雷德和乔治走之前就打算这么做来着。"

"好吧,"赫敏说,"就这样,哈利,我和你披上隐形衣,溜进办公室,你就可以跟小天狼星谈话——"

"他不在那儿,赫敏!"

"我的意思是,你就可以——可以核实一下小天狼星是否在家,我在一旁放哨,我认为不应该让你一个人在那儿,李·乔丹把那些嗅嗅通过窗户放了进去,已经证明窗户是个薄弱环节。"

哈利虽然怒气冲冲,很不耐烦,但他承认赫敏提出陪他一起去乌姆里奇办公室是一种关心和忠诚的表示。

CHAPTER THIRTY-TWO Out of the Fire

'I ... OK, thanks,' he muttered.

'Right, well, even if we do all of that, I don't think we're going to be able to bank on more than five minutes,' said Hermione, looking relieved that Harry seemed to have accepted the plan, 'not with Filch and the wretched Inquisitorial Squad floating around.'

'Five minutes'll be enough,' said Harry. 'C'mon, let's go –'

'*Now?*' said Hermione, looking shocked.

'Of course now!' said Harry angrily. 'What did you think, we're going to wait until after dinner or something? Hermione, Sirius is being tortured *right now!*'

'I – oh, all right,' she said desperately. 'You go and get the Invisibility Cloak and we'll meet you at the end of Umbridge's corridor, OK?'

Harry didn't answer, but flung himself out of the room and began to fight his way through the milling crowds outside. Two floors up he met Seamus and Dean, who hailed him jovially and told him they were planning a dusk-till-dawn end-of-exams celebration in the common room. Harry barely heard them. He scrambled through the portrait hole while they were still arguing about how many black-market Butterbeers they would need and was climbing back out of it, the Invisibility Cloak and Sirius's knife secure in his bag, before they noticed he had left them.

'Harry, d'you want to chip in a couple of Galleons? Harold Dingle reckons he could sell us some Firewhisky –'

But Harry was already tearing away back along the corridor, and a couple of minutes later was jumping the last few stairs to join Ron, Hermione, Ginny and Luna, who were huddled together at the end of Umbridge's corridor.

'Got it,' he panted. 'Ready to go, then?'

'All right,' whispered Hermione as a gang of loud sixth-years passed them. 'So Ron – you go and head Umbridge off ... Ginny, Luna, if you can start moving people out of the corridor ... Harry and I will get the Cloak on and wait until the coast is clear ...'

Ron strode away, his bright-red hair visible right to the end of the passage; meanwhile Ginny's equally vivid head bobbed between the jostling students surrounding them in the other direction, trailed by Luna's blonde one.

第32章 从火中归来

"我……好吧，谢谢了。"他低声说。

"好，我说，即使这些我们都做到了，恐怕也最多只能有五分钟，"赫敏说，她似乎为哈利接受了这个计划而松了一口气，"要知道有费尔奇和讨厌的调查行动组在四处转悠呢。"

"五分钟就够了，"哈利说，"快，我们走吧——"

"现在？"赫敏说，似乎很惊讶。

"当然是现在！"哈利生气地说，"你认为什么时候，我们要等到吃过晚饭以后吗？赫敏，小天狼星此刻正在受折磨！"

"我——哦，好吧。"赫敏无奈地说，"你去拿隐形衣，我们在乌姆里奇办公室的走廊尽头会合，好吗？"

哈利没有回答，转身冲出教室，在外面拥挤的人群中奋力穿行。上了两层楼，他遇到了西莫和迪安，他们快活地跟哈利打了声招呼，然后告诉他，他们正计划要在公共休息室里通宵达旦地庆祝考试结束。哈利几乎没听见他们说些什么。他跌跌撞撞地钻过肖像洞口时，他们仍在争论需要在黑市买多少黄油啤酒。他把隐形衣和小天狼星的刀子装在书包里，重新爬出肖像洞口时，他们都没发现他刚才离开过。

"哈利，你愿意捐助两个金加隆吗？哈罗德·丁戈认为他可以卖给我们一些火焰威士忌——"

哈利已经顺着走廊往回跑了，两分钟后，他跳下最后几级楼梯，来到罗恩、赫敏、金妮和卢娜中间，他们都聚集在乌姆里奇办公室外的走廊尽头。

"拿到了。"他气喘吁吁地说，"可以走了吧？"

"好吧，"赫敏轻声说，这时一群叽叽喳喳的六年级学生从他们身旁走过，"罗恩——你去把乌姆里奇引开……金妮，卢娜，你们可以开始把人们赶出走廊了……我和哈利披上隐形衣，等到四下没人的时候……"

罗恩大步走开了，红色的头发在走廊尽头清晰可见。与此同时，金妮那同样耀眼的红发在周围拥挤的同学们中间跳跃着，朝相反方向移去，后面跟着卢娜的一头金发。

CHAPTER THIRTY-TWO   Out of the Fire

'Get over here,' muttered Hermione, tugging at Harry's wrist and pulling him back into a recess where the ugly stone head of a medieval wizard stood muttering to itself on a column. 'Are – are you sure you're OK, Harry? You're still very pale.'

'I'm fine,' he said shortly, tugging the Invisibility Cloak from out of his bag. In truth, his scar was aching, but not so badly that he thought Voldemort had yet dealt Sirius a fatal blow; it had hurt much worse than this when Voldemort had been punishing Avery ...

'Here,' he said; he threw the Invisibility Cloak over both of them and they stood listening carefully over the Latin mumblings of the bust in front of them.

'You can't come down here!' Ginny was calling to the crowd. 'No, sorry, you're going to have to go round by the swivelling staircase, someone's let off Garrotting Gas just along here –'

They could hear people complaining; one surly voice said, 'I can't see no gas.'

'That's because it's colourless,' said Ginny in a convincingly exasperated voice, 'but if you want to walk through it, carry on, then we'll have your body as proof for the next idiot who doesn't believe us.'

Slowly, the crowd thinned. The news about the Garrotting Gas seemed to have spread; people were not coming this way any more. When at last the surrounding area was quite clear, Hermione said quietly, 'I think that's as good as we're going to get, Harry – come on, let's do it.'

They moved forwards, covered by the Cloak. Luna was standing with her back to them at the far end of the corridor. As they passed Ginny, Hermione whispered, 'Good one ... don't forget the signal.'

'What's the signal?' muttered Harry, as they approached Umbridge's door.

'A loud chorus of "Weasley is our King" if they see Umbridge coming,' replied Hermione, as Harry inserted the blade of Sirius's knife in the crack between door and wall. The lock clicked open and they entered the office.

The garish kittens were basking in the late-afternoon sunshine that was warming their plates, but otherwise the office was as still and unoccupied as last time. Hermione breathed a sigh of relief.

'I thought she might have added extra security after the second Niffler.'

They pulled off the Cloak; Hermione hurried over to the window and stood out of sight, peering down into the grounds with her wand out. Harry dashed

第32章 从火中归来

"快过来。"赫敏轻声说,拽着哈利的手腕,把他拉进一个壁龛里,一个中世纪男巫的丑陋石制头像立在柱子上喃喃自语,"你——你真的没事吗,哈利?你的脸色好苍白。"

"我没事。"哈利简短地说,从书包里抽出了隐形衣。实际上,他的伤疤正在疼痛,但疼得不算严重,因此他认为伏地魔还没有给小天狼星以致命的一击。伏地魔惩罚埃弗里的时候,伤疤疼得比这厉害得多……

"给。"哈利把隐形衣披在他和赫敏身上,两人站在那里,在面前这座胸像喋喋不休的拉丁语中,仔细听着周围的动静。

"你们不能过来!"金妮对人群大声喊道,"不行,对不起,你们必须从旋转楼梯绕过去,有人在这里放了锁喉毒气——"

他们听见人们在抱怨,一个阴沉沉的声音说:"我没看见什么毒气。"

"因为它是无色的,"金妮用令人信服的焦急口吻说,"但如果你想从这里走,那就请便,我们就会把你的尸体当成证据,拿给下一个不相信我们的白痴看。"

人群慢慢散去了。锁喉毒气的消息似乎传开了,人们不再往这边来。最后,周围终于没人了,赫敏轻声说:"我觉得差不多了,哈利——快,我们行动吧。"

他们在隐形衣的遮蔽下往前移动。卢娜背对着他们站在走廊尽头。他们走过金妮身旁时,赫敏悄声说:"好样的……别忘了信号。"

"信号是什么?"哈利低声问,一边朝乌姆里奇办公室的门口走去。

"她们一看见乌姆里奇过来,就齐声高唱'韦斯莱是我们的王'。"赫敏说。哈利把小天狼星的刀子插进门和墙壁之间的缝隙,咔嗒一声,锁开了,他们走进了办公室。

那些难看的小猫,正在夕阳映照的它们盘子上晒着暖儿,除此之外,办公室里跟上次一样寂静无声,空无一人。赫敏放心地松了一口气。

"我还以为,在第二只嗅嗅放进来之后,她加强了安全措施呢。"

他们脱掉隐形衣,赫敏快步走到窗前,躲在外面的人看不见的地方,举着魔杖窥视下面的场地。哈利冲到壁炉前,抓起飞路粉的罐子,捻

CHAPTER THIRTY-TWO   Out of the Fire

over to the fireplace, seized the pot of Floo powder and threw a pinch into the grate, causing emerald flames to burst into life there. He knelt down quickly, thrust his head into the dancing fire and cried, 'Number twelve, Grimmauld Place!'

His head began to spin as though he had just got off a fairground ride though his knees remained firmly planted on the cold office floor. He kept his eyes screwed up against the whirling ash and when the spinning stopped he opened them to find himself looking out at the long, cold kitchen of Grimmauld Place.

There was nobody there. He had expected this, yet was not prepared for the molten wave of dread and panic that seemed to burst through his stomach at the sight of the deserted room.

'Sirius?' he shouted. 'Sirius, are you there?'

His voice echoed around the room, but there was no answer except a tiny scuffing sound to the right of the fire.

'Who's there?' he called, wondering whether it was just a mouse.

Kreacher the house-elf crept into view. He looked highly delighted about something, though he seemed to have recently sustained a nasty injury to both hands, which were heavily bandaged.

'It's the Potter boy's head in the fire,' Kreacher informed the empty kitchen, stealing furtive, oddly triumphant glances at Harry. 'What has he come for, Kreacher wonders?'

'Where's Sirius, Kreacher?' Harry demanded.

The house-elf gave a wheezy chuckle.

'Master has gone out, Harry Potter.'

'Where's he gone? *Where's he gone, Kreacher?*'

Kreacher merely cackled.

'I'm warning you!' said Harry, fully aware that his scope for inflicting punishment upon Kreacher was almost non-existent in this position. 'What about Lupin? Mad-Eye? Any of them, are any of them there?'

'Nobody here but Kreacher!' said the elf gleefully, and turning away from Harry he began to walk slowly towards the door at the end of the kitchen. 'Kreacher thinks he will have a little chat with his mistress now, yes, he hasn't had a chance in a long time, Kreacher's master has been keeping him away from her –'

'Where has Sirius gone?' Harry yelled after the elf. '*Kreacher, has he gone to*

第32章 从火中归来

起一些扔进炉栅，炉膛里顿时迸出艳绿色的火苗。他迅速跪下身，把脑袋伸进跳动的火焰，大声喊道："格里莫广场12号！"

他的脑袋开始旋转，就好像刚从游乐设施上下来，虽然他的膝盖还牢牢地跪在办公室冰冷的地面上。他在旋舞的炉灰中把眼睛闭得紧紧的，最后，旋转停止了。他睁开眼睛，发现自己从炉子里注视着格里莫广场12号那间狭长的、冷冰冰的厨房。

厨房里没有人，这在他的意料之中，但是看着空无一人的厨房，他内心还是突然产生了一种强烈的紧张和恐惧，令他猝不及防。

"小天狼星？"他喊道，"小天狼星，你在吗？"

他的声音在屋子里回荡，但没有人回答，只是炉火右侧传来一种踢踢踏踏的小声音。

"是谁？"哈利大声问，怀疑那不过是一只老鼠。

家养小精灵克利切蹑手蹑脚地出现了。他好像为什么事情特别高兴，但两只手似乎最近受了重伤，缠着厚厚的绷带。

"火焰里是男孩波特的脑袋。"克利切对着空荡荡的厨房说，一边鬼鬼祟祟地朝哈利瞥了几眼，神情里透着奇怪的得意，"克利切纳闷，他来做什么呢？"

"克利切，小天狼星在哪里？"哈利问道。

家养小精灵发出呼哧带喘的笑声。

"主人出去了，哈利·波特。"

"他去哪儿了？他去哪儿了，克利切？"

克利切只是咯咯地笑着。

"我警告你！"哈利说，但他完全明白，以他现在的处境要对克利切施行惩罚几乎是不可能的，"卢平呢？疯眼汉呢？谁都行，有人在吗？"

"这里除了克利切没有别人！"小精灵高兴地说，转身离开哈利，慢慢地朝厨房那头的门走去，"克利切想跟他的女主人聊一会儿，是的，他已经很长时间没有这种机会了，克利切的主人一直不让他接近女主人——"

"小天狼星去哪儿了？"哈利冲着小精灵的背影嚷道，"克利切，

CHAPTER THIRTY-TWO Out of the Fire

the Department of Mysteries?'

Kreacher stopped in his tracks. Harry could just make out the back of his bald head through the forest of chair legs before him.

'Master does not tell poor Kreacher where he is going,' said the elf quietly.

'But you know!' shouted Harry. 'Don't you? You know where he is!'

There was a moment's silence, then the elf let out his loudest cackle yet.

'Master will not come back from the Department of Mysteries!' he said gleefully. 'Kreacher and his mistress are alone again!'

And he scurried forwards and disappeared through the door to the hall.

'You –!'

But before he could utter a single curse or insult, Harry felt a great pain at the top of his head; he inhaled a lot of ash and, choking, found himself being dragged backwards through the flames, until with a horrible abruptness he was staring up into the wide, pallid face of Professor Umbridge, who had dragged him backwards out of the fire by the hair and was now bending his neck back as far as it would go, as though she were going to slit his throat.

'You think,' she whispered, bending Harry's neck back even further, so that he was looking up at the ceiling, 'that after two Nifflers I was going to let one more foul, scavenging little creature enter my office without my knowledge? I had Stealth Sensoring Spells placed all around my doorway after the last one got in, you foolish boy. Take his wand,' she barked at someone he could not see, and he felt a hand grope inside the chest pocket of his robes and remove the wand. 'Hers, too.'

Harry heard a scuffle over by the door and knew that Hermione had also just had her wand wrested from her.

'I want to know why you are in my office,' said Umbridge, shaking the fist clutching his hair so that he staggered.

'I was – trying to get my Firebolt!' Harry croaked.

'Liar.' She shook his head again. 'Your Firebolt is under strict guard in the dungeons, as you very well know, Potter. You had your head in my fire. With whom have you been communicating?'

'No one –' said Harry, trying to pull away from her. He felt several hairs part company with his scalp.

第32章 从火中归来

他是不是去了神秘事务司？"

克利切停住了脚步。哈利透过面前丛林般的椅子腿，只能勉强看见他光秃秃的后脑勺。

"主人没有告诉可怜的克利切他要去哪儿。"小精灵轻声说。

"可是你知道！"哈利喊道，"是不是？你知道他在哪儿！"

片刻的沉默，然后小精灵发出了从没有过的最响亮的笑声。

"主人不会从神秘事务司回来了！"他开心地说，"克利切又可以和他的女主人独自相守了！"

说完，他快速迈动脚步，出门到厅里去了。

"你——！"

可是，没等哈利发出诅咒或辱骂，他突然感到头顶一阵剧痛。他吸进一大口烟灰，呛住了。他发现自己从火焰里被拉了回去，在那恐怖的一瞬间，他眼前竟突然出现了乌姆里奇教授那张苍白的阔脸，正是她揪着哈利的头发把他拖了出来。此刻她正竭力把哈利的脑袋往后扯，就好像准备割断他的喉咙似的。

"你们以为，"她压低声音说，一边又把哈利的脖子往后扯，使哈利仰头望着天花板，"有了两只嗅嗅之后，我还会再让一个肮脏的、捡垃圾的小动物擅自闯进我的办公室吗？第二只嗅嗅进来后，我就在门口施了窃贼感应咒，你这个傻瓜。拿掉他的魔杖，"她朝哈利看不见的某个人吼道，哈利感到一只手伸进他长袍胸前的口袋，掏走了他的魔杖，"还有她的。"

哈利听到门边传来扭打声，知道赫敏的魔杖也被夺走了。

"我想知道你们在我的办公室里干什么。"乌姆里奇说着，晃了晃揪着哈利头发的拳头，哈利打了个趔趄。

"我——我想拿我的火弩箭！"哈利用嘶哑的声音说。

"撒谎，"乌姆里奇又扯着他的脑袋摇晃起来，"你的火弩箭在地下教室里受到严密监视，这点你很清楚，波特。你把脑袋伸进了我的炉火里。你刚才在跟谁交谈？"

"没有谁——"哈利说，拼命想从她的手里挣脱出来。他感到好几根头发离开了他的头皮。

CHAPTER THIRTY-TWO   Out of the Fire

'*Liar!*' shouted Umbridge. She threw him from her and he slammed into the desk. Now he could see Hermione pinioned against the wall by Millicent Bulstrode. Malfoy was leaning on the window sill, smirking as he threw Harry's wand into the air one-handed and caught it again.

There was a commotion outside and several large Slytherins entered, each gripping Ron, Ginny, Luna and – to Harry's bewilderment – Neville, who was trapped in a stranglehold by Crabbe and looked in imminent danger of suffocation. All four of them had been gagged.

'Got 'em all,' said Warrington, shoving Ron roughly forwards into the room. '*That* one,' he poked a thick finger at Neville, 'tried to stop me taking *her*,' he pointed at Ginny, who was trying to kick the shins of the large Slytherin girl holding her, 'so I brought him along too.'

'Good, good,' said Umbridge, watching Ginny's struggles. 'Well, it looks as though Hogwarts will shortly be a Weasley-free zone, doesn't it?'

Malfoy laughed loudly and sycophantically. Umbridge gave her wide, complacent smile and settled herself into a chintz-covered armchair, blinking up at her captives like a toad in a flowerbed.

'So, Potter,' she said. 'You stationed lookouts around my office and you sent this buffoon,' she nodded at Ron – Malfoy laughed even louder – 'to tell me the poltergeist was wreaking havoc in the Transfiguration department when I knew perfectly well that he was busy smearing ink on the eyepieces of all the school telescopes – Mr Filch having just informed me so.

'Clearly, it was very important for you to talk to somebody. Was it Albus Dumbledore? Or the half-breed, Hagrid? I doubt it was Minerva McGonagall, I hear she is still too ill to talk to anyone.'

Malfoy and a few of the other members of the Inquisitorial Squad laughed some more at that. Harry found he was so full of rage and hatred he was shaking.

'It's none of your business who I talk to,' he snarled.

Umbridge's slack face seemed to tighten.

'Very well,' she said in her most dangerous and falsely sweet voice. 'Very well, Mr Potter … I offered you the chance to tell me freely. You refused. I have no alternative but to force you. Draco – fetch Professor Snape.'

Malfoy stowed Harry's wand inside his robes and left the room smirking, but

第32章 从火中归来

"撒谎!"乌姆里奇喊道。她把哈利甩了出去,哈利砰地撞到桌上。他这才看见赫敏被米里森·伯斯德摁在墙上,动弹不得。马尔福靠在窗台上,一边单手抛接着哈利的魔杖,一边得意地傻笑着。

外面一阵骚动,几个大块头的斯莱特林学生走了进来,分别抓着罗恩、金妮、卢娜,还有纳威——这令哈利感到迷惑不解。纳威被克拉布死死卡着脖子,眼看随时都有窒息的危险。四个人的嘴都被塞住了。

"都抓到了。"沃林顿说着,把罗恩粗暴地推进了屋子。"那个家伙,"他用一根粗粗的手指点着纳威,"不让我抓她,"他指指金妮,金妮正拼命去踢抓住她的那个大块头斯莱特林女生的小腿,"所以我把他也带来了。"

"很好,很好,"乌姆里奇注视着金妮的挣扎,说道,"好啊,看样子过不了多久,霍格沃茨就会成为没有韦斯莱的地方了,是不是?"

马尔福讨好地高声大笑。乌姆里奇张开大嘴,露出她那得意扬扬的笑容,在一把蒙着印花布的扶手椅上坐了下来,眨巴着眼睛打量着她的俘虏,那样子活像花圃里的一只癞蛤蟆。

"如此说来,波特,"她说,"你在我的办公室周围安了岗哨,还派这个小丑,"她朝罗恩点了点头——马尔福笑得更响了——"跑来对我说,皮皮鬼正在变形课教室里大搞破坏,其实我知道得很清楚,皮皮鬼正忙着往学校所有望远镜的镜片上涂墨水呢——费尔奇先生刚刚告诉我的。

"显然,你想跟人谈话,这件事很重要。是阿不思·邓布利多吗?还是那个杂种海格?我不相信会是米勒娃·麦格,我听说她还没有力气跟人说话。"

听了这话,马尔福和调查行动组的另外几位成员又笑了起来。哈利发现自己因为愤怒和仇恨而浑身发抖。

"我跟谁说话,你管不着。"他怒吼道。

乌姆里奇松弛的脸庞似乎绷紧了。

"很好,"她用她最阴险的假惺惺的甜腻声音说,"很好,波特先生……我给你机会主动告诉我,但你拒绝了。我没有选择,只能强行撬开你的嘴了。德拉科——去把斯内普教授找来。"

马尔福把哈利的魔杖插进袍子,傻笑着离开了房间,但哈利几乎没

CHAPTER THIRTY-TWO   Out of the Fire

Harry hardly noticed. He had just realised something; he could not believe he had been so stupid as to forget it. He had thought that all the members of the Order, all those who could help him save Sirius, were gone – but he had been wrong. There was still a member of the Order of the Phoenix at Hogwarts – Snape.

There was silence in the office except for the fidgetings and scufflings resulting from the Slytherins' efforts to keep Ron and the others under control. Ron's lip was bleeding on to Umbridge's carpet as he struggled against Warrington's half-nelson; Ginny was still trying to stamp on the feet of the sixth-year girl who had both her upper arms in a tight grip; Neville was turning steadily more purple in the face while tugging at Crabbe's arms; and Hermione was attempting, in vain, to throw Millicent Bulstrode off her. Luna, however, stood limply by the side of her captor, gazing vaguely out of the window as though rather bored by the proceedings.

Harry looked back at Umbridge, who was watching him closely. He kept his face deliberately smooth and blank as footsteps were heard in the corridor outside and Draco Malfoy came back into the room, holding open the door for Snape.

'You wanted to see me, Headmistress?' said Snape, looking around at all the pairs of struggling students with an expression of complete indifference.

'Ah, Professor Snape,' said Umbridge, smiling widely and standing up again. 'Yes, I would like another bottle of Veritaserum, as quick as you can, please.'

'You took my last bottle to interrogate Potter,' he said, observing her coolly through his greasy curtains of black hair. 'Surely you did not use it all? I told you that three drops would be sufficient.'

Umbridge flushed.

'You can make some more, can't you?' she said, her voice becoming more sweetly girlish as it always did when she was furious. 'Certainly,' said Snape, his lip curling. 'It takes a full moon-cycle to mature, so I should have it ready for you in around a month.'

'A month?' squawked Umbridge, swelling toadishly. 'A *month*? But I need it this evening, Snape! I have just found Potter using my fire to communicate with a person or persons unknown!'

'Really?' said Snape, showing his first, faint sign of interest as he looked round at Harry. 'Well, it doesn't surprise me. Potter has never shown much inclination to follow school rules.'

第32章 从火中归来

有注意。他突然想起了什么,他不敢相信自己竟然愚蠢到忘记了这一点。他以为凤凰社的所有成员,所有能帮助他去救小天狼星的人,都不在了——其实他错了。霍格沃茨还有一位凤凰社的成员——斯内普。

办公室里一片寂静,只有那些斯莱特林学生在使劲制服罗恩和其他人,发出一些骚动和扭打的声音。鲜血从罗恩的嘴唇滴到乌姆里奇的地毯上,但他仍然挣扎着想摆脱沃林顿的控制。金妮还在努力去踩那个紧紧拧住她双臂的六年级女生的脚。纳威在克拉布怀里扭动着,脸色变得越来越青。赫敏拼命想把米里森·伯斯德从身上甩掉,可是怎么也甩不掉。卢娜站在抓她的人旁边,一副无所谓的样子,目光迷蒙地望着窗外,似乎觉得眼前发生的事情怪无聊的。

哈利回头看着乌姆里奇,只见她正仔细地端详着自己。他努力让自己神色镇静,面无表情,这时门外的走廊上传来脚步声。德拉科·马尔福走进房间,扶着门让斯内普进来。

"校长,你想见我?"斯内普说,他望着屋里那一对对扭打的学生,表情十分冷漠。

"啊,斯内普教授,"乌姆里奇咧开大嘴笑着,重又站了起来,"是的,我想再要一瓶吐真剂,拜托你了,越快越好。"

"你拿走了我的最后一瓶去审问波特,"斯内普说,目光从乌黑油腻的头发间冷冷地端详着她,"肯定没有用完吧?我告诉过你三滴就够了。"

乌姆里奇的脸红了。

"你可以再调制一些,是不是?"她说,声音变得更加甜腻,像小姑娘的一样,每次她动怒时都是这样。

"当然可以,"斯内普说,嘴角微微扭曲着,"需要一个月亮周期才能酿熟,所以,我会在一个月左右给你调制好。"

"一个月?"乌姆里奇粗声大叫起来,显出癞蛤蟆一般自命不凡的样子,"一个月?可是我今天晚上就要用,斯内普!我刚才发现波特利用我的炉火在跟不知什么人交谈!"

"真的?"斯内普说,这才第一次显出一丝兴趣,转头望着哈利,"这倒并不令我吃惊。波特一向不太遵守学校的规章制度。"

CHAPTER THIRTY-TWO   Out of the Fire

His cold, dark eyes were boring into Harry's, who met his gaze unflinchingly, concentrating hard on what he had seen in his dream, willing Snape to read it in his mind, to understand ...

'I wish to interrogate him!' shouted Umbridge angrily, and Snape looked away from Harry back into her furiously quivering face. 'I wish you to provide me with a potion that will force him to tell me the truth!'

'I have already told you,' said Snape smoothly, 'that I have no further stocks of Veritaserum. Unless you wish to poison Potter – and I assure you I would have the greatest sympathy with you if you did – I cannot help you. The only trouble is that most venoms act too fast to give the victim much time for truth-telling.'

Snape looked back at Harry, who stared at him, frantic to communicate without words.

Voldemort's got Sirius in the Department of Mysteries, he thought desperately. *Voldemort's got Sirius –*

'You are on probation!' shrieked Professor Umbridge, and Snape looked back at her, his eyebrows slightly raised. 'You are being deliberately unhelpful! I expected better, Lucius Malfoy always speaks most highly of you! Now get out of my office!'

Snape gave her an ironic bow and turned to leave. Harry knew his last chance of letting the Order know what was going on was walking out of the door.

'He's got Padfoot!' he shouted. 'He's got Padfoot at the place where it's hidden!'

Snape had stopped with his hand on Umbridge's door handle.

'Padfoot?' cried Professor Umbridge, looking eagerly from Harry to Snape. 'What is Padfoot? Where what is hidden? What does he mean, Snape?'

Snape looked round at Harry. His face was inscrutable. Harry could not tell whether he had understood or not, but he did not dare speak more plainly in front of Umbridge.

'I have no idea,' said Snape coldly. 'Potter, when I want nonsense shouted at me I shall give you a Babbling Beverage. And Crabbe, loosen your hold a little. If Longbottom suffocates it will mean a lot of tedious paperwork and I am afraid I shall have to mention it on your reference if ever you apply for a job.'

第32章 从火中归来

他那双冷冰冰的黑眼睛锥子一般瞪着哈利，哈利毫不退缩地迎着他的目光，集中意念回忆他在梦里看到的情景，努力让斯内普去读他的思想，让他理解……

"我想审问他！"乌姆里奇气愤地嚷道，斯内普把目光从哈利身上挪开了，重新盯着她那张气得发颤的脸，"我想要你给我一剂药，能强迫他把实话告诉我！"

"我已经告诉过你，"斯内普语调平和地说，"我的吐真剂没有存货了。我对你爱莫能助，除非你想给波特下毒——我向你保证，我会非常赞同你这么做。难就难在大多数毒药都发作得太快，受害者根本没有多少时间交代问题。"

斯内普又回头看着哈利，哈利盯着他，迫不及待地想跟他做无声的交流。

伏地魔把小天狼星弄到了神秘事务司里，他焦急地想，伏地魔把小天狼星——

"你还在试用期！"乌姆里奇教授尖叫道，斯内普回头看着她，微微扬起了眉毛，"你是故意不肯帮忙！你太让我失望了，卢修斯·马尔福一向对你评价很高！你可以离开我的办公室了！"

斯内普讥讽地朝她鞠了一躬，转身离开。哈利知道，他把情报通知给凤凰社的最后一点儿机会正在走出门去。

"他抓住了大脚板！"他喊了起来，"他抓住了大脚板，在藏那个东西的地方！"

斯内普停住脚步，手放在乌姆里奇的门把手上。

"大脚板？"乌姆里奇教授大声说，急切地看看哈利又看看斯内普，"大脚板是什么？什么东西藏在什么地方？他的话是什么意思，斯内普？"

斯内普扭头看着哈利。他脸上的神情深不可测。哈利看不出他是不是听懂了，但当着乌姆里奇的面，他又不敢把话说得更清楚。

"我不明白。"斯内普冷冷地说，"波特，如果我想要你冲我嚷嚷废话，我会给你服一剂唠叨汤剂。还有克拉布，你把手松开一点儿。如果隆巴顿窒息而死，可就要准备一大堆繁琐的书面材料，以后等你申请工作的时候，恐怕我还要在你的推荐信里提到这件事。"

CHAPTER THIRTY-TWO   Out of the Fire

He closed the door behind him with a snap, leaving Harry in a state of worse turmoil than before: Snape had been his very last hope. He looked at Umbridge, who seemed to be feeling the same way; her chest was heaving with rage and frustration.

'Very well,' she said, and she pulled out her wand. 'Very well ... I am left with no alternative ... this is more than a matter of school discipline ... this is an issue of Ministry security ... yes ... yes ...'

She seemed to be talking herself into something. She was shifting her weight nervously from foot to foot, staring at Harry, beating her wand against her empty palm and breathing heavily. As he watched her, Harry felt horribly powerless without his own wand.

'You are forcing me, Potter ... I do not want to,' said Umbridge, still moving restlessly on the spot, 'but sometimes circumstances justify the use ... I am sure the Minister will understand that I had no choice ...'

Malfoy was watching her with a hungry expression on his face.

'The Cruciatus Curse ought to loosen your tongue,' said Umbridge quietly.

'No!' shrieked Hermione. 'Professor Umbridge – it's illegal.'

But Umbridge took no notice. There was a nasty, eager, excited look on her face that Harry had never seen before. She raised her wand.

'The Minister wouldn't want you to break the law, Professor Umbridge!' cried Hermione.

'What Cornelius doesn't know won't hurt him,' said Umbridge, who was now panting slightly as she pointed her wand at different parts of Harry's body in turn, apparently trying to decide where it would hurt most. 'He never knew I ordered Dementors to go after Potter last summer, but he was delighted to be given the chance to expel him, all the same.'

'It was *you*?' gasped Harry. '*You* sent the Dementors after me?'

'*Somebody* had to act,' breathed Umbridge, as her wand came to rest pointing directly at Harry's forehead. 'They were all bleating about silencing you somehow – discrediting you – but I was the one who actually *did* something about it ... only you wriggled out of that one, didn't you, Potter? Not today though, not now –' And taking a deep breath, she cried, '*Cruc*–'

'NO!' shouted Hermione in a cracked voice from behind Millicent Bulstrode. 'No – Harry – we'll have to tell her!'

第32章 从火中归来

他走了出去，砰地把门关上了，哈利心里更是乱成了一团麻。斯内普曾是他的最后一线希望。他看着乌姆里奇，乌姆里奇似乎也是同样的感觉，她因为气愤和失望，胸脯剧烈地起伏着。

"很好，"她说着抽出了魔杖，"很好……这样我就没有选择了……这件事不仅关系到学校的纪律……还涉及魔法部的安全……没错……没错……"

她似乎在说服自己。她紧张地把身体重心从一只脚移到另一只脚上，眼睛盯着哈利，用魔杖敲击着另一只手掌，呼吸粗重。哈利注视着她，觉得自己没有了魔杖，真是束手无策。

"你在逼我，波特……我也不想这么做，"乌姆里奇说，仍在原地焦躁不安地挪动，"可是有的时候，形势所迫……我相信部长会理解我的别无选择……"

马尔福脸上带着贪婪的表情注视着她。

"钻心咒应该能把你的嘴巴撬开吧。"乌姆里奇轻声说。

"不！"赫敏尖叫起来，"乌姆里奇教授——这是违法的。"

可是乌姆里奇不予理会。她脸上带着哈利以前从没见过的丑陋、急切、兴奋的神情。她举起了魔杖。

"部长不会允许你违反法律的，乌姆里奇教授！"赫敏嚷道。

"只要康奈利不知道就没关系，"乌姆里奇说，她微微喘息着，用魔杖轮流指着哈利身体的不同部位，似乎想判断哪里会疼得最厉害，"他从不知道去年夏天是我命令摄魂怪追击波特的，但他还是很高兴能有机会把波特开除。"

"是你？"哈利吃惊地说，"是你派摄魂怪追我的？"

"必须有人采取行动，"乌姆里奇喘着粗气说，用魔杖瞄准了哈利的脑门，"他们都在嚷嚷着要想办法让你闭嘴——让你名声扫地——只有我真正采取了行动……可惜那次让你逃脱了，是不是，波特？但今天不会了，现在不会了——"她深深吸了一口气，大喊，"钻心——"

"不！"赫敏在米里森·伯斯德身后用嘶哑的声音喊道，"不——哈利——我们只能告诉她了！"

CHAPTER THIRTY-TWO Out of the Fire

'No way!' yelled Harry, staring at the little of Hermione he could see.

'We'll have to, Harry, she'll force it out of you anyway, what's ... what's the point?'

And Hermione began to cry weakly into the back of Millicent Bulstrode's robes. Millicent stopped trying to squash her against the wall immediately and dodged out of her way looking disgusted.

'Well, well, well!' said Umbridge, looking triumphant. 'Little Miss Question-all is going to give us some answers! Come on then, girl, come on!'

'Er – my – nee – no!' shouted Ron through his gag.

Ginny was staring at Hermione as though she had never seen her before. Neville, still choking for breath, was gazing at her, too. But Harry had just noticed something. Though Hermione was sobbing desperately into her hands, there was no trace of a tear.

'I'm – I'm sorry everyone,' said Hermione. 'But – I can't stand it –'

'That's right, that's right, girl!' said Umbridge, seizing Hermione by the shoulders, thrusting her into the abandoned chintz chair and leaning over her. 'Now then ... with whom was Potter communicating just now?'

'Well,' gulped Hermione into her hands, 'well, he was *trying* to speak to Professor Dumbledore.'

Ron froze, his eyes wide; Ginny stopped trying to stamp on her Slytherin captor's toes; and even Luna looked mildly surprised. Fortunately, the attention of Umbridge and her minions was focused too exclusively upon Hermione to notice these suspicious signs.

'Dumbledore?' said Umbridge eagerly. 'You know where Dumbledore is, then?'

'Well ... no!' sobbed Hermione. 'We've tried the Leaky Cauldron in Diagon Alley and the Three Broomsticks and even the Hog's Head –'

'Idiot girl – Dumbledore won't be sitting in a pub when the whole Ministry's looking for him!' shouted Umbridge, disappointment etched in every sagging line of her face.

'But – but we needed to tell him something important!' wailed Hermione, holding her hands more tightly over her face, not, Harry knew, out of anguish, but to disguise the continued absence of tears.

'Yes?' said Umbridge with a sudden resurgence of excitement. 'What was

第32章 从火中归来

"绝对不行!"哈利嚷道,盯着几乎被遮得看不见的赫敏。

"只能这样了,哈利,她反正也会逼你说出来的,还有……还有什么用呢?"

赫敏伏在米里森·伯斯德长袍的后背上呜呜哭泣,米里森原本把她挤压在墙上,现在赶紧松开身子,闪到一旁,脸上露出厌恶的表情。

"好啊,好啊,好啊!"乌姆里奇得意扬扬地说,"这位问题多小姐要告诉我们一些答案了!说吧,姑娘,快说吧!"

"呃——我——别——不!"嘴被堵住的罗恩挣扎着嚷道。

金妮呆呆地盯着赫敏,好像以前从没见过她似的。纳威也瞪着赫敏,他仍然被勒得喘不过气来。只有哈利注意到了一丝异样。虽然赫敏用手捂着脸哭得很伤心,却看不见一丝泪痕。

"我——我很抱歉,诸位,"赫敏说,"可是——我忍受不了了——"

"这就对了,这就对了,姑娘!"乌姆里奇说着,抓住赫敏的肩膀,把她塞到刚才她自己坐过的那把蒙着印花布的椅子上,俯身对她说道,"说吧……刚才波特是在跟谁交谈?"

"是这样,"赫敏双手捂脸哽咽着说,"是这样,他是想跟邓布利多教授说话。"

罗恩呆住了,眼睛睁得大大的。金妮不再一跳一跳地去踩那个斯莱特林学生的脚趾。就连卢娜也显得微微有些吃惊。幸好,乌姆里奇和她那些跟班的注意力全都集中在赫敏身上,没有注意到这些可疑的迹象。

"邓布利多?"乌姆里奇急切地说,"这么说,你们知道邓布利多在哪儿喽?"

"哦……不知道!"赫敏抽抽搭搭地说,"我们试了对角巷的破釜酒吧,试了三把扫帚,还试了猪头——"

"你这傻瓜——邓布利多不会坐在酒吧里的,要知道整个魔法部都在找他呢!"乌姆里奇喊道,脸上每一道松弛的皱纹里都刻着失望。

"可是——可是我们有重要的事情要告诉他!"赫敏叫道,双手把脸捂得更紧了,哈利知道她不是因为痛苦,而是要掩饰她眼里仍然没有泪水。

"是吗?"乌姆里奇带着突然重新燃起的兴奋说,"你们想告诉他

CHAPTER THIRTY-TWO   Out of the Fire

it you wanted to tell him?'

'We ... we wanted to tell him it's r – ready!' choked Hermione.

'What's ready?' demanded Umbridge, and now she grabbed Hermione's shoulders again and shook her slightly. 'What's ready, girl?'

'The ... the weapon,' said Hermione.

'Weapon? Weapon?' said Umbridge, and her eyes seemed to pop with excitement. 'You have been developing some method of resistance? A weapon you could use against the Ministry? On Professor Dumbledore's orders, of course?'

'Y – y – yes,' gasped Hermione, 'but he had to leave before it was finished and n – n – now we've finished it for him, and we c – c – can't find him t – t – to tell him!'

'What kind of weapon is it?' said Umbridge harshly, her stubby hands still tight on Hermione's shoulders.

'We don't r – r – really understand it,' said Hermione, sniffing loudly. 'We j – j – just did what P – P – Professor Dumbledore told us t – t – to do.'

Umbridge straightened up, looking exultant.

'Lead me to the weapon,' she said.

'I'm not showing ... *them*,' said Hermione shrilly, looking around at the Slytherins through her fingers.

'It is not for you to set conditions,' said Professor Umbridge harshly.

'Fine,' said Hermione, now sobbing into her hands again. 'Fine ... let them see it, I hope they use it on you! In fact, I wish you'd invite loads and loads of people to come and see! Th – that would serve you right – oh, I'd love it if the wh – whole school knew where it was, and how to u – use it, and then if you annoy any of them they'll be able to s – sort you out!'

These words had a powerful impact on Umbridge: she glanced swiftly and suspiciously around at her Inquisitorial Squad, her bulging eyes resting for a moment on Malfoy, who was too slow to disguise the look of eagerness and greed that had appeared on his face.

Umbridge contemplated Hermione for another long moment, then spoke in what she clearly thought was a motherly voice.

'All right, dear, let's make it just you and me ... and we'll take Potter, too, shall we? Get up, now.'

第32章 从火中归来

什么呢？"

"我们……我们想告诉他，东西已经准—准备好了！"赫敏哽咽地说。

"什么准备好了？"乌姆里奇追问道，又抓住了赫敏的肩膀，轻轻摇晃着，"什么准备好了，姑娘？"

"那件……那件武器。"赫敏说。

"武器？武器？"乌姆里奇说，兴奋得眼珠子都要突出来了，"你们一直在研究某种抵抗措施？一件你们可以用来反抗魔法部的武器？肯定是邓布利多教授吩咐的，对吗？"

"是—是—是的，"赫敏喘着粗气说，"可是没等完成，他就被迫离开了，现—现—现在，我们替他完成了，却找—找—找不到他跟—跟他说！"

"那是什么武器？"乌姆里奇用刺耳的声音说，粗短的双手仍然牢牢地抓着赫敏的肩膀。

"我们也—也—也不太明白，"赫敏说，大声抽着鼻子，"我们只—只—只是按照邓布利多教授的吩咐去做。"

乌姆里奇直起身子，神情狂喜。

"带我去看那件武器。"她说。

"我不想让……让他们看到。"赫敏用尖细的声音说，从手指缝里看着周围那些斯莱特林的学生。

"轮不到你来提条件。"乌姆里奇教授声音刺耳地说。

"好吧，"赫敏又把脸埋在双手里哭泣着说，"好吧……就让他们看吧，我希望他们用它来对付你！实际上，我巴不得你邀请好多好多的人来看！那—那才是你应得的惩罚——哦，我真巴不得全—全校同学都知道它在哪儿，怎么使—使用，那样的话，只要你惹了他们中间的谁，他们就—就能狠狠地教训你！"

这些话对乌姆里奇很管用，她迅速地、疑神疑鬼地望了望她的调查行动组，一双鼓凸的眼睛盯在马尔福身上。马尔福反应迟钝，没有及时掩饰住脸上露出的急切和贪婪的神情。

乌姆里奇又打量了赫敏很长时间，然后用她显然认为是慈母般的声音说话了。

"好吧，亲爱的，就你和我……再带上波特，好吗？快，起来吧。"

'Professor,' said Malfoy eagerly, 'Professor Umbridge, I think some of the Squad should come with you to look after –'

'I am a fully qualified Ministry official, Malfoy, do you really think I cannot manage two wandless teenagers alone?' asked Umbridge sharply. 'In any case, it does not sound as though this weapon is something that schoolchildren should see. You will remain here until I return and make sure none of these –' she gestured around at Ron, Ginny, Neville and Luna '– escape.'

'All right,' said Malfoy, looking sulky and disappointed.

'And you two can go ahead of me and show me the way,' said Umbridge, pointing at Harry and Hermione with her wand. 'Lead on.'

第32章 从火中归来

"教授,"马尔福急切地说,"乌姆里奇教授,我认为应该让几名行动组成员陪你一起去,照顾——"

"我是一名完全称职的魔法部官员,马尔福,你难道认为我连两个没拿魔杖的毛头小孩都对付不了吗?"乌姆里奇厉声问道,"而且,听起来这件武器是不应该让学生看见的。你们留在这里等我回来,注意别让这些家伙——"她指指周围的罗恩、金妮、纳威和卢娜,"——逃走了。"

"好的。"马尔福说,看上去大失所望,很不高兴。

"你们两个在前面走,给我带路,"乌姆里奇用魔杖指着哈利和赫敏,说道,"走吧……"

CHAPTER THIRTY-THREE

Fight and Flight

Harry had no idea what Hermione was planning, or even whether she had a plan. He walked half a pace behind her as they headed down the corridor outside Umbridge's office, knowing it would look very suspicious if he appeared not to know where they were going. He did not dare attempt to talk to her; Umbridge was walking so closely behind them that he could hear her ragged breathing.

Hermione led the way down the stairs into the Entrance Hall. The din of loud voices and the clatter of cutlery on plates echoed from out of the double doors to the Great Hall – it seemed incredible to Harry that twenty feet away were people who were enjoying dinner, celebrating the end of exams, not a care in the world …

Hermione walked straight out of the oak front doors and down the stone steps into the balmy evening air. The sun was falling towards the tops of the trees in the Forbidden Forest now, and as Hermione marched purposefully across the grass – Umbridge jogging to keep up – their long dark shadows rippled over the grass behind them like cloaks.

'It's hidden in Hagrid's hut, is it?' said Umbridge eagerly in Harry's ear.

'Of course not,' said Hermione scathingly. 'Hagrid might have set it off accidentally.'

'Yes,' said Umbridge, whose excitement seemed to be mounting. 'Yes, he would have done, of course, the great half-breed oaf.'

She laughed. Harry felt a strong urge to swing round and seize her by the throat, but resisted. His scar was throbbing in the soft evening air but it had not yet burned white-hot, as he knew it would if Voldemort had moved in for the kill.

'Then … where is it?' asked Umbridge, with a hint of uncertainty in her voice as Hermione continued to stride towards the Forest.

'In there, of course,' said Hermione, pointing into the dark trees. 'It had

第 33 章

战斗与飞行

哈利不知道赫敏的计划是什么,甚至不知道她到底有没有计划。他们顺着乌姆里奇办公室外的走廊往前走,他跟在赫敏身后半步。他知道,如果他显出不知道要去哪里的样子,肯定会令人生疑。他不敢冒险跟赫敏说话,乌姆里奇就跟在他后面,他能听见她呼哧呼哧的喘息声。

赫敏领头走下楼梯,进入门厅。喧闹的说话声和刀叉碰撞盘子的叮当声从礼堂的双扇门里传了出来。就在二十英尺之外,人们正在津津有味地享用晚餐,庆祝考试结束,没有任何操心的事……

赫敏径直走出橡木大门,走下石阶,来到傍晚温暖宜人的空气中。太阳在禁林的树梢上缓缓坠落,赫敏胸有成竹地大步走过草地——乌姆里奇小跑着跟在后面——他们长长的黑影像斗篷一样拖曳在身后的草地上。

"藏在海格的小屋里吗?"乌姆里奇急切地在哈利耳边问。

"当然不是。"赫敏尖刻地说,"海格会不小心把它放出来的。"

"是的,"乌姆里奇说,她的兴奋劲儿似乎有增无减,"是的,他肯定会这么做的,那个傻大个儿杂种。"

她大笑起来。哈利恨不得转过身去掐住她的喉咙,但他克制住了这种冲动。他的伤疤在柔和的晚风中一跳一跳地疼,他知道如果伏地魔开始杀戮,伤疤会是一种火辣辣的剧痛,而现在还不是。

"那么……是在哪儿呢?"乌姆里奇问,声音里透着一丝犹疑,赫敏继续大步流星地朝禁林走去。

"当然是在那里面,"赫敏指着黑黢黢的树丛说,"必须是在学生们

CHAPTER THIRTY-THREE   Fight and Flight

to be somewhere that students weren't going to find it accidentally, didn't it?'

'Of course,' said Umbridge, though she sounded a little apprehensive now. 'Of course ... very well, then ... you two stay ahead of me.'

'Can we have your wand, then, if we're going first?' Harry asked her.

'No, I don't think so, Mr Potter,' said Umbridge sweetly, poking him in the back with it. 'The Ministry places a rather higher value on my life than yours, I'm afraid.'

As they reached the cool shade of the first trees, Harry tried to catch Hermione's eye; walking into the Forest without wands seemed to him to be more foolhardy than anything they had done so far this evening. She, however, merely gave Umbridge a contemptuous glance and plunged straight into the trees, moving at such a pace that Umbridge, with her shorter legs, had difficulty in keeping up.

'Is it very far in?' Umbridge asked, as her robe ripped on a bramble.

'Oh yes,' said Hermione, 'yes, it's well hidden.'

Harry's misgivings increased. Hermione was not taking the path they had followed to visit Grawp, but the one he followed three years ago to the lair of the monster Aragog. Hermione had not been with him on that occasion; he doubted she had any idea what danger lay at the end of it.

'Er – are you sure this is the right way?' he asked her pointedly.

'Oh yes,' she said in a steely voice, crashing through the undergrowth with what he thought was a wholly unnecessary amount of noise. Behind them, Umbridge tripped over a fallen sapling. Neither of them paused to help her up again; Hermione merely strode on, calling loudly over her shoulder, 'It's a bit further in!'

'Hermione, keep your voice down,' Harry muttered, hurrying to catch up with her. 'Anything could be listening in here –'

'I want us heard,' she answered quietly, as Umbridge jogged noisily after them. 'You'll see ...'

They walked on for what seemed a long time, until they were once again so deep into the Forest that the dense tree canopy blocked out all light. Harry had the feeling he had had before in the Forest, one of being watched by unseen eyes.

'How much further?' demanded Umbridge angrily from behind him.

'Not far now!' shouted Hermione, as they emerged into a dim, dank

第33章 战斗与飞行

不可能无意中发现的地方，是不是？"

"那当然，"乌姆里奇说，不过她的语气听上去有点担忧，"那当然……很好……你们俩走在我前面。"

"如果我们走在前面，能不能拿着你的魔杖？"哈利问她。

"不行，我认为不行，波特同学，"乌姆里奇声音甜腻地说，一边用魔杖捅了捅他的后背，"恐怕魔法部把我生命的价值看得比你的高得多。"

当他们来到禁林外围凉爽的树荫下时，哈利试图捕捉赫敏的目光。在他看来，不带魔杖走进禁林似乎比他们今晚做的所有事情都更鲁莽。但赫敏只是轻蔑地扫了乌姆里奇一眼，径直走进了树丛。她的步子很快，乌姆里奇迈着一双小短腿，吃力地跟在后面。

"在里面很深的地方吗？"乌姆里奇问，她的袍子被刺藤刮破了。

"噢，是的，"赫敏说，"没错，藏得很隐蔽。"

哈利的担忧在增加。赫敏走的不是他们去看格洛普的路线，而是三年前他进入巨蜘蛛阿拉戈克老巢的那条路。那次，赫敏没有跟他在一起，所以他怀疑赫敏根本不知道前面会有什么危险。

"呃——你肯定这么走没错吗？"他直截了当地问。

"没错。"赫敏斩钉截铁地说，她哗啦哗啦地在灌木丛中穿行，发出在哈利看来完全没有必要的响声。在他们身后，乌姆里奇被一棵倒地的小树绊倒了。他们俩都没有停下脚步去扶她。赫敏只顾大步往前走，一边扭头大声叫道："再往里走一点儿就到了！"

"赫敏，你小声点儿，"哈利低声说，加快脚步赶上了她，"这里会有东西在偷听——"

"我就想让它们听见。"赫敏小声说，乌姆里奇小跑着追了上来，发出很响的动静，"你待会儿就明白了……"

他们似乎走了很长时间，又一次来到禁林深处，头顶上浓密的树荫挡住了所有的光线。哈利又产生了他以前在禁林里的那种感觉，似乎有看不见的眼睛在监视着他们。

"还要走多远？"乌姆里奇在他身后气呼呼地问。

"已经不远了！"赫敏大声说，这时他们进入了一片昏暗、潮湿的

CHAPTER THIRTY-THREE Fight and Flight

clearing. 'Just a little bit –'

An arrow flew through the air and landed with a menacing thud in the tree just over her head. The air was suddenly full of the sound of hooves; Harry could feel the Forest floor trembling; Umbridge gave a little scream and pushed him in front of her like a shield –

He wrenched himself free of her and turned. Around fifty centaurs were emerging on every side, their bows raised and loaded, pointing at Harry, Hermione and Umbridge. They backed slowly into the centre of the clearing, Umbridge uttering odd little whimpers of terror. Harry looked sideways at Hermione. She was wearing a triumphant smile.

'Who are you?' said a voice.

Harry looked left. The chestnut-bodied centaur called Magorian was walking towards them out of the circle: his bow, like those of the others, was raised. On Harry's right, Umbridge was still whimpering, her wand trembling violently as she pointed it at the advancing centaur.

'I asked you who are you, human,' said Magorian roughly.

'I am Dolores Umbridge!' said Umbridge in a high-pitched, terrified voice. 'Senior Undersecretary to the Minister for Magic and Headmistress and High Inquisitor of Hogwarts!'

'You are from the Ministry of Magic?' said Magorian, as many of the centaurs in the surrounding circle shifted restlessly.

'That's right!' said Umbridge, in an even higher voice, 'so be very careful! By the laws laid down by the Department for the Regulation and Control of Magical Creatures, any attack by half-breeds such as yourselves on a human –'

'*What* did you call us?' shouted a wild-looking black centaur, whom Harry recognised as Bane. There was a great deal of angry muttering and tightening of bowstrings around them.

'Don't call them that!' Hermione said furiously, but Umbridge did not appear to have heard her. Still pointing her shaking wand at Magorian, she continued, 'Law Fifteen "B" states clearly that "any attack by a magical creature who is deemed to have near-human intelligence, and therefore considered responsible for its actions –"'

'"Near-human intelligence"?' repeated Magorian, as Bane and several others roared with rage and pawed the ground. 'We consider that a great insult, human! Our intelligence, thankfully, far outstrips your own.'

林中空地,"再往前走一点儿——"

一支箭从空中飞过,随着令人胆寒的一声闷响,射中了赫敏头顶上方的树干。空气里突然充满了杂乱的马蹄声。哈利感觉到禁林的地面都在颤抖,乌姆里奇尖叫一声,把他拖在面前当作挡箭牌——

哈利使劲摆脱了她,转身望去。大约五十个马人从四面八方奔来,手里都拿着弓箭,引弓待发地瞄准了哈利、赫敏和乌姆里奇。他们退到空地中央,乌姆里奇惊恐地发出怪异的小声呜咽。哈利侧眼看着赫敏。赫敏脸上露出一丝得意的微笑。

"你们是谁?"一个声音问。

哈利往左看去。那个名叫玛格瑞的栗色身体的马人,离开包围圈朝他们走来。他像其他马人一样,手里也举着弓箭。在哈利右边,乌姆里奇仍在呜咽,她用魔杖指着向她逼近的马人,手颤抖得厉害。

"我在问你们是谁,人类。"玛格瑞粗暴地说。

"我是多洛雷斯·乌姆里奇!"乌姆里奇用尖厉、恐惧的声音说,"魔法部高级副部长,霍格沃茨的校长兼高级调查官!"

"你是魔法部的?"玛格瑞问,包围圈里的许多马人不安地挪动着脚步。

"没错!"乌姆里奇提高了声音说,"所以你们要多多留神!根据神奇动物管理控制司的法律,凡是像你们这样的杂种攻击人类——"

"你管我们叫什么?"一个模样粗野的黑色马人喊道,哈利认出他是贝恩。周围传来一片愤怒的低语声和弓弦拉紧的声音。

"不要这么叫他们!"赫敏气愤地说,可是乌姆里奇似乎没有听见她的话。她仍然用颤抖的魔杖指着玛格瑞,说道:"第十五条法令的第二款明确指出,'被认为拥有接近人类的智力,因而能为自己行为负责的神奇动物,若是攻击——'"

"'接近人类的智力'?"玛格瑞重复了一句,贝恩和另外几个马人气得大吼,用蹄子刨着地面,"我们认为那是一种极大的侮辱,人类!值得欣慰的是,我们的智力远远超过你们人类。"

CHAPTER THIRTY-THREE   Fight and Flight

'What are you doing in our Forest?' bellowed the hard-faced grey centaur Harry and Hermione had seen on their last trip into the Forest. 'Why are you here?'

'*Your* Forest?' said Umbridge, shaking now not only with fright but also, it seemed, with indignation. 'I would remind you that you live here only because the Ministry of Magic permits you certain areas of land –'

An arrow flew so close to her head that it caught at her mousy hair in passing: she let out an ear-splitting scream and threw her hands over her head, while some of the centaurs bellowed their approval and others laughed raucously. The sound of their wild, neighing laughter echoing around the dimly lit clearing and the sight of their pawing hooves was extremely unnerving.

'Whose Forest is it now, human?' bellowed Bane.

'Filthy half-breeds!' she screamed, her hands still tight over her head. 'Beasts! Uncontrolled animals!'

'Be quiet!' shouted Hermione, but it was too late: Umbridge pointed her wand at Magorian and screamed, '*Incarcerous!*'

Ropes flew out of midair like thick snakes, wrapping themselves tightly around the centaur's torso and trapping his arms: he gave a cry of rage and reared on to his hind legs, attempting to free himself, while the other centaurs charged.

Harry grabbed Hermione and pulled her to the ground; face down on the Forest floor, he knew a moment of terror as hooves thundered around him, but the centaurs leapt over and around them, bellowing and screaming with rage.

'Nooooo!' he heard Umbridge shriek. 'Noooooo ... I am Senior Undersecretary ... you cannot – Unhand me, you animals ... nooooo!'

Harry saw a flash of red light and knew she had attempted to Stun one of them; then she screamed very loudly. Lifting his head a few inches, Harry saw that Umbridge had been seized from behind by Bane and lifted high into the air, wriggling and yelling with fright. Her wand fell from her hand to the ground, and Harry's heart leapt. If he could just reach it –

But as he stretched out a hand towards it, a centaur's hoof descended upon the wand and it broke cleanly in half.

'Now!' roared a voice in Harry's ear and a thick hairy arm descended from thin air and dragged him upright. Hermione, too, had been pulled

第33章 战斗与飞行

"你们在我们的林子里干什么？"哈利和赫敏上次进林子看见的那个表情冷酷的灰色马人吼道，"你们来干什么？"

"你们的林子？"乌姆里奇说，她浑身颤抖，似乎不仅因为恐惧，还因为愤怒，"我要提醒你们，你们能在这里生活，是因为魔法部允许你们占据一些地盘——"

一支箭贴着她的脑袋飞过，钩住了她灰褐色的头发。她发出一声震耳欲聋的尖叫，赶紧用双手捂住脑袋。几个马人赞许地吼叫着，其他马人粗声大笑起来。他们狂野的、马嘶般的笑声在光线昏暗的林中空地间回荡，他们用蹄子刨地的样子看上去令人心惊胆战。

"人类，现在这是谁的林子？"贝恩咆哮道。

"肮脏的杂种！"乌姆里奇叫喊着说，双手仍然紧紧捂着脑袋，"畜生！无法无天的畜生！"

"别说了！"赫敏喊道，可是已经来不及了。乌姆里奇用魔杖指着玛格瑞，大喊一声："速速绑缚！"

像粗蛇一样的绳索从半空中飞来，结结实实地捆住马人的身体，使他的双臂无法动弹。他狂怒地大吼一声，两条后腿直立起来，拼命想挣脱绳索，其他马人冲了过来。

哈利抓住赫敏，把她拉倒在地。他把脸贴在禁林的地面上，周围都是轰隆隆的马蹄声，一阵恐惧袭上他的心头，可是马人跳过他们的身体，围着他们愤怒地呐喊、狂吼。

"不——！"他听见乌姆里奇在尖叫，"不……我是高级副部长……你们不能——放开我，你们这些畜生……不——！"

哈利看见红光一闪，知道乌姆里奇想把其中一个马人击昏，接着听到她撕心裂肺地尖叫起来。哈利把脑袋抬起了几英寸，看见乌姆里奇被贝恩从后面抓起来拎到半空，她惊恐地扭动着身体狂叫。她手里的魔杖掉在地上，哈利的心狂跳起来。如果他能拿到它——

可是，他刚把手伸向魔杖，一个马人的蹄子便踩了下来，魔杖断成了两截。

"好了！"一个声音在哈利耳边吼道，一只汗毛粗重的大手凌空而降，把哈利拽了起来。赫敏也被拖了起来。哈利透过那些迅速奔窜的

1253

CHAPTER THIRTY-THREE Fight and Flight

to her feet. Over the plunging, many-coloured backs and heads of the centaurs, Harry saw Umbridge being borne away through the trees by Bane. Screaming non-stop, her voice grew fainter and fainter until they could no longer hear it over the trampling of hooves surrounding them.

'And these?' said the hard-faced, grey centaur holding Hermione.

'They are young,' said a slow, doleful voice from behind Harry. 'We do not attack foals.'

'They brought her here, Ronan,' replied the centaur who had such a firm grip on Harry. 'And they are not so young ... he is nearing man-hood, this one.'

He shook Harry by the neck of his robes.

'Please,' said Hermione breathlessly, 'please, don't attack us, we don't think like her, we aren't Ministry of Magic employees! We only came in here because we hoped you'd drive her off for us.'

Harry knew at once, from the look on the face of the grey centaur holding Hermione, that she had made a terrible mistake in saying this. The grey centaur threw back his head, his back legs stamping furiously, and bellowed, 'You see, Ronan? They already have the arrogance of their kind! So we were to do your dirty work, were we, human girl? We were to act as your servants, drive away your enemies like obedient hounds?'

'No!' said Hermione in a horrorstruck squeak. 'Please – I didn't mean that! I just hoped you'd be able to – to help us –'

But she seemed to be going from bad to worse.

'We do not help humans!' snarled the centaur holding Harry, tightening his grip and rearing a little at the same time, so that Harry's feet left the ground momentarily. 'We are a race apart and proud to be so. We will not permit you to walk from here, boasting that we did your bidding!'

'We're not going to say anything like that!' Harry shouted. 'We know you didn't do what you did because we wanted you to –'

But nobody seemed to be listening to him.

A bearded centaur towards the back of the crowd shouted, 'They came here unasked, they must pay the consequences!'

A roar of approval met these words and a dun-coloured centaur shouted, 'They can join the woman!'

第33章 战斗与飞行

马人杂色的后背和脑袋,看见乌姆里奇被贝恩抓进了密林深处。她一声接一声地惨叫着,声音越来越远。最后,在周围杂乱的马蹄声中,他们再也听不见她的叫声了。

"这些家伙怎么办?"揪着赫敏的那个表情冷酷的灰色马人问道。

"他们还小,"哈利身后一个缓慢、忧郁的声音说,"我们不攻击幼崽。"

"是他们把她带来的,罗南,"紧紧抓着哈利的那个马人回答道,"而且他们也不小了……这一个差不多是成人了。"

他揪着哈利的长袍领子晃了晃。

"求求你们,"赫敏上气不接下气地说,"求求你们,不要攻击我们,我们的想法跟她不一样,我们不是魔法部的雇员!我们到这里来,是希望你们能替我们把她赶走。"

哈利看见那个抓着赫敏的灰色马人的脸色,立刻知道赫敏这么说是犯了一个可怕的错误。灰色马人把脑袋往后一仰,后腿愤怒地踏着地面,吼道:"看见了吗,罗南?他们已经有了那种人类的傲慢!这么说,我们要替你们做下三烂的事情,是吗,人类女孩?我们要做你们的奴仆,像忠实的猎狗一样,替你们把敌人赶走?"

"不!"赫敏用惊恐、尖厉的声音说道,"求求你——我不是这个意思!我只是希望你们能够——能够帮助我们——"

可是她似乎把事情越弄越糟了。

"我们不会帮助人类!"抓住哈利的那个马人恶狠狠地说,他加大手上的力度,同时抬起前腿,哈利的双脚立刻离开了地面,"我们是一个独特的种族,我们为此感到自豪。我们不会允许你们从这里出去后吹嘘说我们服从了你们的吩咐!"

"我们不会说这种话的!"哈利喊道,"我们知道,你们刚才那么做并不是因为我们想要你们——"

然而似乎没有人在听他说话。

一个有胡子的马人朝后排的马人大声说道:"他们不请自来,必须承担后果!"

他的话引起一片赞同的吼声,一个暗褐色的马人叫道:"把他们弄到那个女人那儿去!"

1255

CHAPTER THIRTY-THREE   Fight and Flight

'You said you didn't hurt the innocent!' shouted Hermione, real tears sliding down her face now. 'We haven't done anything to hurt you, we haven't used wands or threats, we just want to go back to school, please let us go back –'

'We are not all like the traitor Firenze, human girl!' shouted the grey centaur, to more neighing roars of approval from his fellows. 'Perhaps you thought us pretty talking horses? We are an ancient people who will not stand wizard invasions and insults! We do not recognise your laws, we do not acknowledge your superiority, we are –'

But they did not hear what else centaurs were, for at that moment there came a crashing noise on the edge of the clearing so loud that all of them, Harry, Hermione and the fifty or so centaurs filling the clearing, looked around. Harry's centaur let him fall to the ground again as his hands flew to his bow and quiver of arrows. Hermione had been dropped, too, and Harry hurried towards her as two thick tree trunks parted ominously and the monstrous form of Grawp the giant appeared in the gap.

The centaurs nearest him backed into those behind; the clearing was now a forest of bows and arrows waiting to be fired, all pointing upwards at the enormous greyish face now looming over them from just beneath the thick canopy of branches. Grawp's lopsided mouth was gaping stupidly; they could see his bricklike yellow teeth glimmering in the half-light, his dull sludge-coloured eyes narrowed as he squinted down at the creatures at his feet. Broken ropes trailed from both ankles.

He opened his mouth even wider.

'Hagger.'

Harry did not know what 'hagger' meant, or what language it was from, nor did he much care; he was watching Grawp's feet, which were almost as long as Harry's whole body. Hermione gripped his arm tightly; the centaurs were quite silent, staring up at the giant, whose huge, round head moved from side to side as he continued to peer amongst them as though looking for something he had dropped.

'*Hagger!*' he said again, more insistently.

'Get away from here, giant!' called Magorian. 'You are not welcome among us!'

These words seemed to make no impression whatsoever on Grawp. He stooped a little (the centaurs' arms tensed on their bows), then bellowed, 'HAGGER!'

A few of the centaurs looked worried now. Hermione, however, gave a gasp.

第33章 战斗与飞行

"你们说过不伤害无辜的！"赫敏喊道，此刻她脸上真的有泪水在流淌了，"我们没有做任何伤害你们的事情，我们没有使用魔杖，也没有威胁你们，我们只想回学校去，请放我们回去吧——"

"我们可不像那个叛徒费伦泽，人类女孩！"灰色马人大声说，其他马人嘶吼着表示赞同，"你们大概以为我们只是漂亮的会说话的马吧？我们是一个古老的民族，不能忍受巫师的侵略和侮辱！我们不认可你们的法律，也不认可你们的优越感，我们——"

然而，他们没有听到马人还有什么特点，因为就在这时，空地边缘突然传来一声石破天惊的巨响，哈利、赫敏和约莫五十个马人都扭头望去。抓着哈利的马人立刻伸手去拿弓和箭筒，哈利扑通掉落在地，赫敏也被扔在地上。哈利快步朝她奔去，这时两根粗大的树干吓人地分开了，缝隙中露出巨人格洛普那庞大的身躯。

哈利身边的马人倒退几步，跟后面的那些马人站在一起。空地上现在满是丛林般的、准备发射的弓箭，都向上瞄准着那张灰色的大脸。那张脸在头顶遮天蔽日的密密树枝间赫然浮现，令人生畏。格洛普的歪嘴傻乎乎地咧着，他们看见那些砖头般的黄牙在昏暗的微光中闪烁。他眯起呆滞的、泥浆色的眼睛，打量着脚边的那些生物。他的两个脚脖子上拖着挣断的绳索。

他把嘴张得更大了。

"哈格。"

哈利不知道"哈格"是什么意思，是哪种语言。他也不想知道。他注视着格洛普的脚，它们几乎跟哈利的身体一样长。赫敏紧紧地抓住哈利的胳膊，马人都安静下来，抬头望着巨人。巨人圆溜溜的大脑袋左右摆动，继续朝他们中间张望，似乎在寻找他掉落的什么东西。

"哈格！"他又说了一遍，口气更急切了。

"快从这里滚开，巨人！"玛格瑞喊道，"你在我们这里不受欢迎！"

他的话对格洛普不起任何作用。格洛普把身子弯下一点儿（马人们绷紧了拉着弓弦的胳膊），大吼一声："**哈格！**"

几个马人露出担忧的神情。赫敏却倒抽了一口冷气。

CHAPTER THIRTY-THREE   Fight and Flight

'Harry!' she whispered. 'I think he's trying to say "Hagrid"!'

At this precise moment Grawp caught sight of them, the only two humans in a sea of centaurs. He lowered his head another foot or so, staring intently at them. Harry could feel Hermione shaking as Grawp opened his mouth wide again and said, in a deep, rumbling voice, 'Hermy.'

'Goodness,' said Hermione, gripping Harry's arm so tightly it was growing numb and looking as though she was about to faint, 'he – he remembered!'

'HERMY!' roared Grawp. 'WHERE HAGGER?'

'I don't know!' squealed Hermione, terrified. 'I'm sorry, Grawp, I don't know!'

'GRAWP WANT HAGGER!'

One of the giant's massive hands reached down. Hermione let out a real scream, ran a few steps backwards and fell over. Wandless, Harry braced himself to punch, kick, bite or whatever else it took as the hand swooped towards him and knocked a snow-white centaur off his legs.

It was what the centaurs had been waiting for – Grawp's out-stretched fingers were a foot from Harry when fifty arrows soared through the air at the giant, peppering his enormous face, causing him to howl with pain and rage and straighten up, rubbing his face with his enormous hands, breaking off the arrow shafts but forcing the arrowheads in still deeper.

He yelled and stamped his enormous feet and the centaurs scattered out of the way; pebble-sized droplets of Grawp's blood showered Harry as he pulled Hermione to her feet and the pair of them ran as fast as they could for the shelter of the trees. Once there they looked back; Grawp was snatching blindly at the centaurs as blood ran down his face; they were retreating in disorder, galloping away through the trees on the other side of the clearing. Harry and Hermione watched Grawp give another roar of fury and plunge after them, smashing more trees aside as he went.

'Oh no,' said Hermione, quaking so badly that her knees gave way. 'Oh, that was horrible. And he might kill them all.'

'I'm not that fussed, to be honest,' said Harry bitterly.

The sounds of the galloping centaurs and the blundering giant grew fainter and fainter. As Harry listened to them, his scar gave another great throb and a wave of terror swept over him.

They had wasted so much time – they were even further from rescuing Sirius than they had been when he had had the vision. Not only had Harry managed to lose his wand but they were stuck in the middle of the Forbidden

第33章 战斗与飞行

"哈利!"她小声说,"我认为他想说的是'海格'!"

就在这时,格洛普看见了他们,一大群马人中仅有的两个人类。他把脑袋又低下一英尺左右,专注地盯着他们。哈利感觉到赫敏在发抖,格洛普又把嘴张得大大的,用低沉、浑厚的声音说:"赫米。"

"天哪,"赫敏说着,使劲抓住哈利的胳膊,抓得他的胳膊直发麻,她看上去快要晕倒了,"他——他还记得!"

"**赫米!**"格洛普声如洪钟地说,"**哈格在哪?**"

"我不知道!"赫敏惊恐地尖声说道,"对不起,格洛普,我不知道!"

"**格洛普要哈格!**"

巨人的一只大手向他们伸了下来。赫敏发出一声惨叫,接连后退几步,摔倒了。这只手猛地向哈利扫来,把一个雪白色的马人撞翻在地。哈利没有魔杖,只能鼓起勇气拳打脚踢,连抓带咬。

马人们正等着呢——格洛普伸出的手指离哈利还有一英尺时,五十支箭掠过空中,射向巨人,雨点般扎入他那张大脸。巨人又痛又怒,连声吼叫,直起身来,用两只大手搓着脸庞,折断了那些箭杆,但箭头却往肉里扎得更深了。

巨人惨叫着,使劲跺着一双大脚,马人纷纷四下逃窜。卵石大的血珠从格洛普的脸上落下来,洒在哈利身上。哈利把赫敏从地上拽起来,两人以最快的速度跑到树荫下躲了起来。他们回头张望,格洛普胡乱地去抓那些马人,鲜血顺着他的脸庞往下流淌。马人们毫无秩序地撤退,跑进了空地另一边的树丛里。哈利和赫敏看到格洛普又发出一声怒吼,拔脚朝他们追去,一路又扯断了许多大树。

"哦,真糟糕。"赫敏说,她抖得特别厉害,膝盖都软了,"哦,太可怕了。他会把他们都杀死的。"

"说句实话,我可不操那份心。"哈利怨恨地说。

马人奔跑的声音和巨人跌跌撞撞的声音越来越远。哈利仔细听着这些声音,突然伤疤一阵剧烈的疼痛,他心里顿时充满惶恐。

他们浪费了这么多时间——和他做那个梦时相比,现在要救小天狼星更困难了。不仅哈利把魔杖给丢了,而且他们还被困在了禁林中央,

CHAPTER THIRTY-THREE — Fight and Flight

Forest with no means of transport whatsoever.

'Smart plan,' he spat at Hermione, having to release some of his fury. 'Really smart plan. Where do we go from here?'

'We need to get back up to the castle,' said Hermione faintly.

'By the time we've done that, Sirius'll probably be dead!' said Harry, kicking a nearby tree in temper. A high-pitched chattering started up overhead and he looked up to see an angry Bowtruckle flexing its long twiglike fingers at him.

'Well, we can't do anything without wands,' said Hermione hopelessly, dragging herself up again. 'Anyway, Harry, how exactly were you planning to get all the way to London?'

'Yeah, we were just wondering that,' said a familiar voice from behind her.

Harry and Hermione moved together instinctively and peered through the trees.

Ron came into sight with Ginny, Neville and Luna hurrying along behind him. All of them looked a little the worse for wear — there were several long scratches running the length of Ginny's cheek; a large purple lump was swelling above Neville's right eye; Ron's lip was bleeding worse than ever — but all were looking rather pleased with themselves.

'So,' said Ron, pushing aside a low-hanging branch and holding out Harry's wand, 'had any ideas?'

'How did you get away?' asked Harry in amazement, taking his wand from Ron.

'Couple of Stunners, a Disarming Charm, Neville brought off a really nice little Impediment Jinx,' said Ron airily, now handing back Hermione's wand, too. 'But Ginny was best, she got Malfoy — Bat-Bogey Hex — it was superb, his whole face was covered in the great flapping things. Anyway, we saw you out of the window heading into the Forest and followed. What've you done with Umbridge?'

'She got carried away,' said Harry. 'By a herd of centaurs.'

'And they left you behind?' asked Ginny, looking astonished.

'No, they got chased off by Grawp,' said Harry.

'Who's Grawp?' Luna asked interestedly.

'Hagrid's little brother,' said Ron promptly. 'Anyway, never mind that now. Harry, what did you find out in the fire? Has You-Know-Who got Sirius or —?'

'Yes,' said Harry, as his scar gave another painful prickle, 'and I'm sure

第33章 战斗与飞行

没有任何交通工具。

"好主意,"他必须发泄一下自己的怒火,就冲赫敏不满地说,"真是好主意。我们现在怎么办?"

"我们得回城堡去。"赫敏的声音细若游丝。

"等我们回到城堡,小天狼星恐怕已经死了!"哈利说,气呼呼地踢着旁边的树。头顶上传来一阵刺耳的唧唧叫声,他一抬头,看见一只怒气冲冲的护树罗锅正冲他挥舞着树枝般的长手指。

"可是,没有魔杖,我们什么也干不了。"赫敏绝望地说,挣扎着从地上站了起来,"而且,哈利,你打算怎么去伦敦呢?"

"是啊,我们也想知道这一点呢。"她身后传来一个熟悉的声音。

哈利和赫敏本能地靠在一起,透过树丛望去。

罗恩出现了,金妮、纳威和卢娜匆匆跟在他后面。几个人的模样看上去都很狼狈——金妮的面颊上有几道长长的抓痕;纳威的右眼上方肿起一个大紫包;罗恩的嘴唇在流血,流得比以前任何时候都厉害——但他们一个个都显得很得意。

"怎么样,"罗恩说,他拨开一根低垂的树枝,把哈利的魔杖递了过去,"有办法了吗?"

"你们是怎么逃出来的?"哈利惊讶地问,从罗恩手里接过魔杖。

"两个昏迷咒,一个缴械咒,纳威施了一个相当精彩的障碍咒,"罗恩得意地说,把赫敏的魔杖也递了过去,"不过最棒的是金妮,她搞定了马尔福——蝙蝠精咒——真是妙极了,马尔福整张脸都被扑扇着翅膀的大怪物覆盖了。反正,我们从窗口看见你们走进禁林,就跟了过来。你们把乌姆里奇怎么样了?"

"她被架走了,"哈利说,"被一群马人架走了。"

"他们竟然把你们留下了?"金妮问,显得很吃惊。

"不,他们被格洛普赶走了。"哈利说。

"格洛普是谁?"卢娜饶有兴趣地问。

"海格的弟弟。"罗恩立刻回答,"好了,别管那个了。哈利,你在炉火里弄清了什么?神秘人真的抓住了小天狼星,还是——?"

"是的,"哈利说,他的伤疤又是一阵剧烈的刺痛,"我相信小天狼

CHAPTER THIRTY-THREE Fight and Flight

Sirius is still alive, but I can't see how we're going to get there to help him.'

They all fell silent, looking rather scared; the problem facing them seemed insurmountable.

'Well, we'll have to fly, won't we?' said Luna, in the closest thing to a matter-of-fact voice Harry had ever heard her use.

'OK,' said Harry irritably, rounding on her. 'First of all, "*we*" aren't doing anything if you're including yourself in that, and second of all, Ron's the only one with a broomstick that isn't being guarded by a security troll, so –'

'I've got a broom!' said Ginny.

'Yeah, but you're not coming,' said Ron angrily.

'Excuse me, but I care what happens to Sirius as much as you do!' said Ginny, her jaw set so that her resemblance to Fred and George was suddenly striking.

'You're too –' Harry began, but Ginny said fiercely, 'I'm three years older than you were when you fought You-Know-Who over the Philosopher's Stone, and it's because of me that Malfoy's stuck back in Umbridge's office with giant flying bogies attacking him –'

'Yeah, but –'

'We were all in the DA together,' said Neville quietly. 'It was all supposed to be about fighting You-Know-Who, wasn't it? And this is the first chance we've had to do something real – or was that all just a game or something?'

'No – of course it wasn't –' said Harry impatiently.

'Then we should come too,' said Neville simply. 'We want to help.'

'That's right,' said Luna, smiling happily.

Harry's eyes met Ron's. He knew Ron was thinking exactly what he was: if he could have chosen any members of the DA, in addition to himself, Ron and Hermione, to join him in the attempt to rescue Sirius, he would not have picked Ginny, Neville or Luna.

'Well, it doesn't matter, anyway,' said Harry frustratedly, 'because we still don't know how to get there –'

'I thought we'd settled that,' said Luna maddeningly. 'We're flying!'

'Look,' said Ron, barely containing his anger, 'you might be able to fly without a broomstick but the rest of us can't sprout wings whenever we –'

第33章 战斗与飞行

星还活着,但我不知道我们怎么去那儿救他。"

大家都沉默了,看上去神色惊恐,他们面对的困难似乎无法克服。

"看来,我们只能飞了,是不是?"卢娜说,哈利还从没听过她用这样务实的口吻说话呢。

"好吧。"哈利不耐烦地冲她发火道,"第一,如果你把自己也包括在内,那'我们'什么也办不成;第二,只有罗恩的扫帚没有巨怪保安看守,所以——"

"我有一把扫帚!"金妮说。

"是啊,但你不许去。"罗恩生气地说。

"对不起,我跟你一样关心小天狼星的遭遇!"金妮说,她的下巴一抬,突然显得那么酷似弗雷德和乔治。

"你太——"哈利话还没说完,金妮就激烈地说:"我比你当年为魔法石跟神秘人搏斗的时候还大三岁,而且,多亏了我,马尔福才会被困在乌姆里奇的办公室里,遭受大飞妖们的袭击——"

"是啊,不过——"

"我们都是D.A.的成员,"纳威轻声说,"都应该跟神秘人斗争的,对吗?而且,这是我们第一次有机会做点像样的事——难道那只是做做游戏什么的吗?"

"不——当然不是——"哈利不耐烦地说。

"那我们也应该去,"纳威直截了当地说,"我们也想帮忙。"

"没错。"卢娜愉快地微笑着说。

哈利的目光与罗恩相遇。他知道罗恩的想法跟他完全一样。如果除了他、罗恩和赫敏,还要在D.A.里挑选几个人一起去救小天狼星,他是绝不会挑上金妮、纳威和卢娜的。

"唉,反正也没什么关系,"哈利沮丧地说,"因为我们还是不知道怎么去——"

"我认为这个问题已经解决了,"卢娜用让人恼火的口气说,"我们飞去好了!"

"好啊,"罗恩说,简直控制不住自己的怒火,"你或许不骑扫帚就能飞,但我们其他人可没法长出翅膀来——"

CHAPTER THIRTY-THREE Fight and Flight

'There are ways of flying other than with broomsticks,' said Luna serenely.

'I s'pose we're going to ride on the back of the Kacky Snorgle or whatever it is?' Ron demanded.

'The Crumple-Horned Snorkack can't fly,' said Luna in a dignified voice, 'but *they* can, and Hagrid says they're very good at finding places their riders are looking for.'

Harry whirled round. Standing between two trees, their white eyes gleaming eerily, were two Thestrals, watching the whispered conversation as though they understood every word.

'Yes!' he whispered, moving towards them. They tossed their reptilian heads, throwing back long black manes, and Harry stretched out his hand eagerly and patted the nearest one's shining neck; how could he ever have thought them ugly?

'Is it those mad horse things?' said Ron uncertainly, staring at a point slightly to the left of the Thestral Harry was patting. 'Those ones you can't see unless you've watched someone snuff it?'

'Yeah,' said Harry.

'How many?'

'Just two.'

'Well, we need three,' said Hermione, who was still looking a little shaken, but determined just the same.

'Four, Hermione,' said Ginny, scowling.

'I think there are six of us, actually,' said Luna calmly, counting.

'Don't be stupid, we can't all go!' said Harry angrily. 'Look, you three –' he pointed at Neville, Ginny and Luna, 'you're not involved in this, you're not –'

They burst into more protests. His scar gave another, more painful, twinge. Every moment they delayed was precious; he did not have time to argue.

'OK, fine, it's your choice,' he said curtly, 'but unless we can find more Thestrals you're not going to be able –'

'Oh, more of them will come,' said Ginny confidently, who like Ron was squinting in quite the wrong direction, apparently under the impression that she was looking at the horses.

'What makes you think that?'

'Because, in case you hadn't noticed, you and Hermione are both covered

第33章 战斗与飞行

"除了骑扫帚，还有别的办法可以飞呀。"卢娜心平气和地说。

"我猜我们可以骑弯弯鼾之类的东西吧？"罗恩问道。

"弯角鼾兽不会飞，"卢娜用高傲的口吻说，"但是它们会，而且海格说它们善于找到骑手想要寻找的地方。"

哈利转过身。站在两棵树之间的是两匹夜骐，白色的眼睛里闪着诡秘的光，正注视着他们窃窃私语，似乎能听懂每一个字。

"太好了！"他轻声说，拔腿朝它们走去。它们仰起爬行动物般的脑袋，把长长的黑色鬃毛甩到脑后。哈利急切地伸出手，拍了拍离他最近的那匹夜骐的闪亮的脖子。他以前怎么会认为它们模样丑陋呢？

"就是那些像马一样的怪家伙吗？"罗恩迟疑地说，盯着哈利轻拍的那匹夜骐左边一点的地方，"只有见过死人的人才能看见的？"

"是啊。"哈利说。

"有几匹？"

"只有两匹。"

"唉，我们需要三匹呢。"赫敏说，她看上去仍然惊魂未定，同时又很坚决。

"四匹，赫敏。"金妮皱着眉头说。

"实际上我认为我们是六个人。"卢娜心平气和地点着人数说。

"别说傻话了，我们不能都去！"哈利气冲冲地说，"听着，你们三个——"他指着纳威、金妮和卢娜，"你们跟这件事无关，你们不——"

他们又吵吵着表示反对。哈利的伤疤又是一阵更强烈的剧痛。他们耽误的每分每秒都很宝贵。他没有时间争论了。

"好吧，好吧，这是你们自己选择的，"他粗暴地说，"可是，除非能找到更多的夜骐，不然你们没办法——"

"哦，会有更多夜骐的。"金妮自信地说，她跟罗恩一样，也眯眼看着另一个方向，显然以为自己是在望着夜骐。

"你凭什么这么想？"

"因为，难道你没有注意到吗，你和赫敏身上都是血迹，"金妮冷

CHAPTER THIRTY-THREE Fight and Flight

in blood,' she said coolly, 'and we know Hagrid lures Thestrals with raw meat. That's probably why these two turned up in the first place.'

Harry felt a soft tug on his robes at that moment and looked down to see the closest Thestral licking his sleeve, which was damp with Grawp's blood.

'OK, then,' he said, a bright idea occurring, 'Ron and I will take these two and go ahead, and Hermione can stay here with you three and she'll attract more Thestrals –'

'I'm not staying behind!' said Hermione furiously.

'There's no need,' said Luna, smiling. 'Look, here come more now ... you two must really smell ...'

Harry turned: no fewer than six or seven Thestrals were picking their way through the trees, their great leathery wings folded tight to their bodies, their eyes gleaming through the darkness. He had no excuse now.

'All right,' he said angrily, 'pick one and get on, then.'

第33章 战斗与飞行

静地说,"而我们知道海格是用生肉引诱夜骐的。大概这两匹夜骐就是因为这个才出现的。"

就在这时,哈利觉得袍子被轻轻地扯了一下,他低头一看,只见离他最近的那匹夜骐正舔着自己被格洛普鲜血浸透的衣袖。

"那好吧,"他说,突然想起一个绝妙的主意,"我和罗恩骑两匹夜骐先走,赫敏和你们三个留在这里,她可以引来更多的夜骐——"

"我不想留下来!"赫敏气愤地说。

"没有必要,"卢娜笑眯眯地说,"看,又来了几匹……你们俩的气味真够冲的……"

哈利转过身,只见足有六七匹夜骐正穿过树丛走来,它们巨大的、皮革般坚韧的翅膀紧收在身体两侧,眼睛在黑暗中闪闪发亮。他现在没有借口了。

"好吧,"他没好气地说,"每人挑一匹骑上吧。"

CHAPTER THIRTY-FOUR

The Department of Mysteries

Harry wound his hand tightly into the mane of the nearest Thestral, placed a foot on a stump nearby and scrambled clumsily on to the horse's silken back. It did not object, but twisted its head around, fangs bared, and attempted to continue its eager licking of his robes.

He found there was a way of lodging his knees behind the wing joints that made him feel more secure, then looked around at the others. Neville had heaved himself over the back of the next Thestral and was now attempting to swing one short leg over the creature's back. Luna was already in place, sitting side-saddle and adjusting her robes as though she did this every day. Ron, Hermione and Ginny, however, were still standing motionless on the spot, open-mouthed and staring.

'What?' he said.

'How're we supposed to get on?' said Ron faintly. 'When we can't see the things?'

'Oh, it's easy,' said Luna, sliding obligingly from her Thestral and marching over to him, Hermione and Ginny. 'Come here …'

She pulled them over to the other Thestrals standing around and one by one managed to help them on to the back of their mount. All three looked extremely nervous as she wound their hands into their horse's mane and told them to grip tightly before she got back on to her own steed.

'This is mad,' Ron murmured, moving his free hand gingerly up and down his horse's neck. 'Mad … if I could just see it –'

'You'd better hope it stays invisible,' said Harry darkly. 'We all ready, then?'

They all nodded and he saw five pairs of knees tighten beneath their robes.

'OK …'

第34章

神秘事务司

哈利用手紧紧揪住离他最近的那匹夜骐的鬃毛,把脚踏在旁边的一个树桩上,笨拙地爬上了缎子般光滑的马背。夜骐没有反抗,只是扭过脑袋,露出牙齿,还想继续舔哈利的袍子。

哈利发现,把膝盖放在翅膀的关节后面可以使自己感觉更稳当,接着他望了望周围的其他人。纳威爬上了另一匹夜骐,正使劲把一条短腿抡过马背。卢娜已经坐好了,她侧着身子骑在夜骐的背上,正在整理自己的袍子,就好像她每天都骑夜骐似的。罗恩、赫敏和金妮仍然一动不动地站在原地,张着嘴巴,呆呆地望着。

"怎么啦?"哈利说。

"我们怎么骑上去呢?"罗恩底气不足地说,"我们根本看不见那玩意儿!"

"哦,很容易。"卢娜说着,热心地从她那匹夜骐上滑下来,大步走向罗恩、赫敏和金妮,"到这儿来……"

她把他们拉到周围另外几匹夜骐身旁,一个接一个地扶他们骑了上去。她手把手地引导他们揪住鬃毛,嘱咐他们抓紧,然后才走回自己的坐骑。那三个人看上去紧张得要命。

"这真不可思议,"罗恩喃喃地说,用另一只手小心翼翼地抚摸他那匹夜骐的脖子,"不可思议……如果我能看见它——"

"你最好希望永远都别看见它。"哈利表情凝重地说,"都准备好了,是吗?"

大家都点了点头,哈利看见五对膝盖在各自的袍子下绷紧了。

"好吧……"

CHAPTER THIRTY-FOUR   The Department of Mysteries

He looked down at the back of his Thestral's glossy black head and swallowed.

'Ministry of Magic, visitors' entrance, London, then,' he said uncertainly. 'Er ... if you know ... where to go ...'

For a moment Harry's Thestral did nothing at all; then, with a sweeping movement that nearly unseated him, the wings on either side extended; the horse crouched slowly, then rocketed upwards so fast and so steeply that Harry had to clench his arms and legs tightly around the horse to avoid sliding backwards over its bony rump. He closed his eyes and pressed his face down into the horse's silky mane as they burst through the topmost branches of the trees and soared out into a blood-red sunset.

Harry did not think he had ever moved so fast: the Thestral streaked over the castle, its wide wings hardly beating; the cooling air was slapping Harry's face; eyes screwed up against the rushing wind, he looked round and saw his five fellows soaring along behind him, each of them bent as low as possible into the neck of their Thestral to protect themselves from his slipstream.

They were over the Hogwarts grounds, they had passed Hogsmeade; Harry could see mountains and gullies below them. As the daylight began to fail, Harry saw small collections of lights as they passed over more villages, then a winding road on which a single car was beetling its way home through the hills ...

'This is bizarre!' Harry barely heard Ron yell from somewhere behind him, and he imagined how it must feel to be speeding along at this height with no visible means of support.

Twilight fell: the sky was turning to a light, dusky purple littered with tiny silver stars, and soon only the lights of Muggle towns gave them any clue of how far from the ground they were, or how very fast they were travelling. Harry's arms were wrapped tightly around his horse's neck as he willed it to go even faster. How much time had elapsed since he had seen Sirius lying on the Department of Mysteries floor? How much longer would Sirius be able to resist Voldemort? All Harry knew for sure was that his godfather had neither done as Voldemort wanted, nor died, for he was convinced that either outcome would have caused him to feel Voldemort's jubilation or fury course through his own body, making his scar sear as painfully as it had on the night Mr Weasley was attacked.

On they flew through the gathering darkness; Harry's face felt stiff and

第34章 神秘事务司

他低头看着夜骐乌黑光亮的后脑勺，咽了口唾沫。

"伦敦，魔法部，来宾入口，"他迟疑地说，"呃……如果你知道……该怎么走……"

有那么一会儿，哈利的夜骐没有一点儿动静，接着它的翅膀忽地向两边伸开，动作太突然了，哈利差点从它的背上摔了下去。夜骐慢慢伏下身子，又猛地向上冲去，速度之快，角度之陡，哈利不得不把腿和胳膊紧紧地箍在它身上，以免自己滑向它瘦骨嶙峋的臀部。哈利闭上眼睛，把脸贴在夜骐丝缎般的鬃毛上。他们冲出禁林的树梢，飞进了血红色的残阳。

哈利不记得自己什么时候以这么快的速度飞过。夜骐闪电般掠过城堡上空，宽大的翅膀几乎没有扇动。清凉的气流拍打着哈利的脸。在呼呼的风中，哈利眯起眼睛，扭头张望，看见五个同伴都跟在他身后飞着，每个人都把身子低低地伏在夜骐脖子上，以免自己被气流冲落。

他们飞过了霍格沃茨场地上空，飞过了霍格莫德村。哈利看见了下面起伏的山峦和溪谷。日光渐渐暗淡，他们飞过一些村庄，哈利看见了片片灯火，接着是一条蜿蜒的道路，上面只有一辆汽车在疾驰，穿行在山岭之间……

"这太古怪了！"哈利隐约听见罗恩在他后面什么地方喊道，于是他想象着在这样的高度急速飞行却看不见自己的交通工具，该是一种什么感觉。

夜幕降临了，天空变成了一种柔和的黛紫色，点缀着一些银色的小星星。不一会儿，他们只能从麻瓜城镇的灯光看出他们离地面有多远，飞行的速度有多快。哈利的双臂紧紧搂住夜骐的脖子，他用意志的力量催促它飞得再快一些。从他看到小天狼星躺在神秘事务司的地板上之后，已经过去了多少时间？小天狼星还能抵抗伏地魔多少时间？哈利只是相信他的教父没有做伏地魔叫他做的事，也没有死。因为他知道，不管是哪种结果，他都会通过自己的身体感受到伏地魔的狂喜或暴怒，他的伤疤都会像韦斯莱先生被袭的那天夜里一样剧痛难忍。

他们在越来越浓的夜色中继续飞行。哈利感到自己的脸冰冷、僵

CHAPTER THIRTY-FOUR   The Department of Mysteries

cold, his legs numb from gripping the Thestral's sides so tightly, but he did not dare shift his position lest he slip ... he was deaf from the thundering rush of air in his ears, and his mouth was dry and frozen from the cold night wind. He had lost all sense of how far they had come; all his faith was in the beast beneath him, still streaking purposefully through the night, barely flapping its wings as it sped ever onwards.

If they were too late ...

He's still alive, he's still fighting, I can feel it ...

If Voldemort decided Sirius was not going to crack ...

I'd know ...

Harry's stomach gave a jolt; the Thestral's head was suddenly pointing towards the ground and he actually slid forwards a few inches along its neck. They were descending at last ... he thought he heard a shriek behind him and twisted around dangerously, but could see no sign of a falling body ... presumably they had all received a shock from the change of direction, just as he had.

And now bright orange lights were growing larger and rounder on all sides; they could see the tops of buildings, streams of headlights like luminous insect eyes, squares of pale yellow that were windows. Quite suddenly, it seemed, they were hurtling towards the pavement; Harry gripped the Thestral with every last ounce of his strength, braced for a sudden impact, but the horse touched the dark ground as lightly as a shadow and Harry slid from its back, looking around at the street where the overflowing skip still stood a short way from the vandalised telephone box, both drained of colour in the flat orange glare of the streetlights.

Ron landed a short way off and toppled immediately from his Thestral on to the pavement.

'Never again,' he said, struggling to his feet. He made as though to stride away from his Thestral, but, unable to see it, collided with its hindquarters and almost fell over again. 'Never, ever again ... that was the worst –'

Hermione and Ginny touched down on either side of him: both slid off their mounts a little more gracefully than Ron, though with similar expressions of relief at being back on firm ground; Neville jumped down, shaking; and Luna dismounted smoothly.

'Where do we go from here, then?' she asked Harry in a politely interested

第34章 神秘事务司

硬,双腿因为紧紧夹住夜骐的身体而变得麻木,但他不敢改变一下姿势,生怕滑落下去……风在他耳边呼呼作响,他什么都听不见,夜晚的寒风吹得他嘴巴发干发僵。他已经不知道他们飞了多远。他所有的信念都寄托在胯下的坐骑上。夜骐仍然十分果断地在夜空中迅速穿行,翅膀几乎不见扇动。

如果已经晚了……

他还活着,他还在反抗,我可以感觉到……

如果伏地魔断定小天狼星不会屈服……

我会知道的……

哈利的心悸动了一下。夜骐的脑袋突然朝地面的方向伸去,哈利顺着它的脖子向前滑了几英寸。他们终于开始降落了……他隐约听见身后传来一声尖叫,便冒险扭过头去,但并没有看见有人坠落的迹象……大概他们都像他一样,因为方向突然改变而受到了惊吓。

四周明亮的橘黄色的光变得更大更圆,他们看见了建筑物的顶部,看见了流动的车灯像亮晶晶的昆虫眼睛,看见了一扇扇窗户映出的四四方方的淡黄色灯光。突然,他们好像是在向人行道冲去。哈利使出全身的力气抓住夜骐,硬着头皮等待突然着地时的冲力,没想到夜骐像影子一般轻盈地落在黑暗的地面上。哈利从它的背上滑下来,扭头朝街道望去,那个满得快要溢出来的垃圾转运箱仍然在那里,离破旧的电话亭不远。在路灯刺眼的黄光映照下,翻斗车和电话亭都好像失去了颜色。

罗恩在近旁不远处降落,随即从夜骐背上滚到了人行道上。

"再也不了。"他挣扎着站起来说道。他拔腿想要离开他的夜骐,但是因为看不见,正好撞在它的后腿上,差点儿又摔倒在地,"再也不了,再也不了……简直太可怕了——"

赫敏和金妮分别在他两边落地,她们俩从夜骐背上滑落的姿势比罗恩略微优雅一点儿,但脸上带着与他同样如释重负的表情,因为她们的双脚终于踏上了坚实的地面。纳威跳下来时浑身发抖。卢娜倒是十分利索地下了夜骐的脊背。

"我们从这儿再去哪儿呢?"她用礼貌的、饶有兴趣的口吻问哈利,

CHAPTER THIRTY-FOUR The Department of Mysteries

voice, as though this was all a rather interesting day-trip.

'Over here,' he said. He gave his Thestral a quick, grateful pat, then led the way quickly to the battered telephone box and opened the door. 'Come on!' he urged the others, as they hesitated.

Ron and Ginny marched in obediently; Hermione, Neville and Luna squashed themselves in after them; Harry took one glance back at the Thestrals, now foraging for scraps of rotten food inside the skip, then forced himself into the box after Luna.

'Whoever's nearest the receiver, dial six two four four two!' he said.

Ron did it, his arm bent bizarrely to reach the dial; as it whirred back into place the cool female voice sounded inside the box.

'Welcome to the Ministry of Magic. Please state your name and business.'

'Harry Potter, Ron Weasley, Hermione Granger,' Harry said very quickly, 'Ginny Weasley, Neville Longbottom, Luna Lovegood ... we're here to save someone, unless your Ministry can do it first!'

'Thank you,' said the cool female voice. 'Visitors, please take the badges and attach them to the front of your robes.'

Half a dozen badges slid out of the metal chute where returned coins normally appeared. Hermione scooped them up and handed them mutely to Harry over Ginny's head; he glanced at the topmost one, *Harry Potter, Rescue Mission.*

'Visitors to the Ministry, you are required to submit to a search and present your wands for registration at the security desk, which is located at the far end of the Atrium.'

'Fine!' Harry said loudly, as his scar gave another throb. 'Now can we *move*?'

The floor of the telephone box shuddered and the pavement rose up past its glass windows; the scavenging Thestrals were sliding out of sight; blackness closed over their heads and with a dull grinding noise they sank down into the depths of the Ministry of Magic.

A chink of soft golden light hit their feet and, widening, rose up their bodies. Harry bent his knees and held his wand as ready as he could in such cramped conditions as he peered through the glass to see whether anybody was waiting for them in the Atrium, but it seemed to be completely empty. The light was dimmer than it had been by day; there were no fires burning under the mantelpieces set into the walls, but as the lift slid smoothly to a halt he saw that golden symbols continued to twist sinuously in the dark blue ceiling.

第34章 神秘事务司

似乎这不过是一次很有趣味的旅行。

"就在这儿。"哈利说。他感激地拍了拍他的夜骐,然后领头快步走向那个破破烂烂的电话亭,把门打开了。"快!"他看到其他人还在迟疑,便催促道。

罗恩和金妮顺从地大步走进电话亭,赫敏、纳威和卢娜也在他们后面挤了进来。哈利回头看了一眼那些夜骐,见它们正在垃圾转运箱里寻找腐烂的食物,然后他跟着卢娜费力地挤进了电话亭。

"谁最靠近电话,请拨六——二——四——四——二!"他说。

罗恩的胳膊别扭地弯曲着够到拨号盘,拨了号码。随着拨号盘呼呼地转回到原来的位置,电话亭里响起了一个女人冷漠的声音。

"欢迎来到魔法部,请说出您的姓名和来办事宜。"

"哈利·波特、罗恩·韦斯莱、赫敏·格兰杰,"哈利语速很快地说,"金妮·韦斯莱、纳威·隆巴顿、卢娜·洛夫古德……我们来这里救人,除非你们魔法部已经把人救了!"

"谢谢,"那个冷漠的女声说,"来宾,请拿起徽章,别在您的衣服前。"

哈利看见六个徽章从平常用来退出硬币的金属斜槽里滑了出来。赫敏把它们拿起来,默不作声地越过金妮头顶递给了哈利。哈利看了一眼最上面的那个:哈利·波特,救援任务。

"魔法部的来宾,您需要在安检台接受检查,并登记您的魔杖。安检台位于正厅的尽头。"

"好的!"哈利大声说,他的伤疤又疼了一下,"我们可以动身了吗?"

电话亭的地面突然颤抖起来,玻璃窗外的人行道越升越高,那些寻找食物的夜骐从视野中消失了。最后他们头顶上一片黑暗,哈利什么也看不见了。随着单调、刺耳的摩擦声,他们下到了魔法部深处。

一道细细的、柔和的金光照到他们的脚,随后金光逐渐变宽,扩大到他们的身体上。哈利半蹲下身,在狭窄的电话亭里尽量举起魔杖做好准备,一边透过玻璃观察正厅里是不是有人在等他们,但那里似乎空无一人。这里的光线比白天昏暗一些,镶嵌在四壁里的壁炉也没有生火,但是当升降梯缓缓停下来时,哈利看见在深蓝色的天花板上,那些金色符号仍然在不停地活动着、变化着。

CHAPTER THIRTY-FOUR   The Department of Mysteries

'The Ministry of Magic wishes you a pleasant evening,' said the woman's voice.

The door of the telephone box burst open; Harry toppled out of it, followed by Neville and Luna. The only sound in the Atrium was the steady rush of water from the golden fountain, where jets from the wands of the witch and wizard, the point of the centaur's arrow, the tip of the goblin's hat and the house-elf's ears continued to gush into the surrounding pool.

'Come on,' said Harry quietly and the six of them sprinted off down the hall, Harry in the lead, past the fountain towards the desk where the watchwizard who had weighed Harry's wand had sat, and which was now deserted.

Harry felt sure there ought to be a security person there, sure their absence was an ominous sign, and his feeling of foreboding increased as they passed through the golden gates to the lifts. He pressed the nearest 'down' button and a lift clattered into sight almost immediately, the golden grilles slid apart with a great, echoing clanking and they dashed inside. Harry stabbed the number nine button; the grilles closed with a bang and the lift began to descend, jangling and rattling. Harry had not realised how noisy the lifts were on the day he had come with Mr Weasley; he was sure the din would raise every security person within the building, yet when the lift halted, the cool female voice said, 'Department of Mysteries,' and the grilles slid open. They stepped out into the corridor where nothing was moving but the nearest torches, flickering in the rush of air from the lift.

Harry turned towards the plain black door. After months and months of dreaming about it, he was here at last.

'Let's go,' he whispered, and he led the way down the corridor, Luna right behind him, gazing around with her mouth slightly open.

'OK, listen,' said Harry, stopping again within six feet of the door. 'Maybe ... maybe a couple of people should stay here as a – as a lookout, and –'

'And how're we going to let you know something's coming?' asked Ginny, her eyebrows raised. 'You could be miles away.'

'We're coming with you, Harry,' said Neville.

'Let's get on with it,' said Ron firmly.

Harry still did not want to take them all with him, but it seemed he had no choice. He turned to face the door and walked forwards ... just as it had in his dream, it swung open and he marched forwards, leading the others over

第34章 神秘事务司

"魔法部希望您今晚过得愉快。"那个女人的声音说。

电话亭的门猛地打开了,哈利从里面跌了出来,后面跟着纳威和卢娜。正厅里只有金色喷泉发出的不绝于耳的水声,一道道闪亮的水柱从巫师的魔杖顶端、从马人的箭头上、从妖精的帽子尖、从家养小精灵的两只耳朵里喷射出来,落在近旁的水潭里。

"快走。"哈利轻声说。然后哈利领头,六个人飞快地在大厅里奔跑起来,经过喷泉,跑向上次检查哈利魔杖的那位巫师所坐的桌子,可是现在桌旁没有人。

哈利觉得这是一个不祥之兆,他认为这里肯定应该有保安的。他们穿过金色栅栏门朝升降梯走去时,他的预感越来越强烈了。他摁了摁离他最近的按钮"下",立刻就有一架升降梯哐啷啷地出现了。随着一阵巨大的、带着回响的叮当声,金色栅栏门轻轻地滑开了,他们一拥而入。哈利戳了一下第九个按钮,栅栏门砰的一声关上,升降梯开始降落,链条咔啦啦作响。哈利上次白天跟韦斯莱先生来的时候并没有发现升降梯的声音这么响。他认为这噪音肯定会惊动大楼里的每位保安人员,结果升降梯停下了,那个冷漠的女声说:"神秘事务司。"栅栏门轻轻滑开。他们来到外面的走廊上。四下里没有动静,只有离他们最近的火把被升降梯搅起的气流吹得左右摇晃。

哈利转向那扇全黑色的门。多少个月来他一直在梦中看见它,现在他终于来到了这里。

"我们走吧。"他小声说,领头在走廊里往前走,卢娜紧跟在他身后,微微张着嘴巴东张西望。

"好了,听我说。"哈利在距离黑门不到六英尺的地方又停了下来,说道,"也许……也许应该派两个人留在这里——望望风,然后——"

"如果有什么动静,我们怎么让你们知道呢?"金妮扬起眉毛问道,"你们可能在好远的地方呢。"

"我们跟你一起去,哈利。"纳威说。

"我们接着走吧。"罗恩坚决地说。

哈利仍然不愿意把他们都带去,但似乎已经没有别的选择。他转身面对着那扇门,走上前去……就像在梦里一样,门开了,他领头大

CHAPTER THIRTY-FOUR The Department of Mysteries

the threshold.

They were standing in a large, circular room. Everything in here was black including the floor and ceiling; identical, unmarked, handleless black doors were set at intervals all around the black walls, interspersed with branches of candles whose flames burned blue; their cool, shimmering light reflected in the shining marble floor made it look as though there was dark water underfoot.

'Someone shut the door,' Harry muttered.

He regretted giving this order the moment Neville had obeyed it. Without the long chink of light from the torchlit corridor behind them, the place became so dark that for a moment the only things they could see were the bunches of shivering blue flames on the walls and their ghostly reflections in the floor.

In his dream, Harry had always walked purposefully across this room to the door immediately opposite the entrance and walked on. But there were around a dozen doors here. Just as he was gazing ahead at the doors opposite him, trying to decide which was the right one, there was a great rumbling noise and the candles began to move sideways. The circular wall was rotating.

Hermione grabbed Harry's arm as though frightened the floor might move, too, but it did not. For a few seconds, the blue flames around them were blurred to resemble neon lines as the wall sped around; then, quite as suddenly as it had started, the rumbling stopped and everything became stationary once again.

Harry's eyes had blue streaks burned into them; it was all he could see.

'What was that about?' whispered Ron fearfully.

'I think it was to stop us knowing which door we came in through,' said Ginny in a hushed voice.

Harry realised at once she was right: he could no sooner identify the exit door than locate an ant on the jet-black floor; *and* the door through which they needed to proceed could be any one of the dozen surrounding them.

'How're we going to get back out?' said Neville uncomfortably.

'Well, that doesn't matter now,' said Harry forcefully, blinking to try to erase the blue lines from his vision, and clutching his wand tighter than ever, 'we won't need to get out till we've found Sirius –'

'Don't go calling for him, though!' Hermione said urgently; but Harry had never needed her advice less, his instinct was to keep as quiet as possible.

第34章 神秘事务司

步跨过了门槛。

他们站在一个很大的圆形房间里。这里的每样东西都是黑的，包括地面和天花板。周围的黑墙上镶嵌着许多黑门，全都一模一样，没有标记，也没有把手。门与门之间点缀着几支蜡烛，火苗是蓝色的，摇曳的冷光投在锃亮的大理石地面上，使人觉得脚下是黝黑的水面。

"谁把门关上。"哈利轻声说。

纳威照办了，但哈利立刻就后悔下了这道命令。刚才点着火把的走廊从他们身后射进一道长长的亮光，现在这道亮光没有了，房间里顿时变暗，他们只能看见墙上那一束束颤抖的蓝色火苗，以及它们映在地面的阴森恐怖的影子。

在梦中，哈利总是胸有成竹地穿过这个房间，走向正对着入口的那扇门。可是现在周围有十二扇门。他打量着自己对面的那些门，想判断究竟应该进哪一扇。就在这时，随着一阵隆隆巨响，蜡烛开始往旁边移动。圆形的墙壁旋转起来。

赫敏一把抓住哈利的胳膊，似乎害怕地板也会移动，还好没有。几秒钟里，墙壁飞快地旋转着，蓝色的火苗在他们周围模糊成一片，像霓虹灯光带一样。接着，就像开始时那样突然，隆隆声停止了，每样东西又恢复了平静。

哈利眼睛里闪着一道道蓝色光带，除此之外看不见别的。

"这是怎么回事？"罗恩害怕地小声问。

"我想是为了不让我们知道是从哪扇门进来的。"金妮压低声音说。

哈利立刻意识到她说对了。他无法分辨出口，就像无法在漆黑的地板上找到一只蚂蚁一样。而他们需要进入的那扇门，可以是周围十二扇门中的任何一扇。

"我们怎么从这里出去呢？"纳威不安地问。

"噢，那个暂时不重要，"哈利坚决地说，一边使劲眨巴着眼睛，消除眼里的那一道道蓝光，他把魔杖抓得更紧了，"我们先不需要出去，要等找到小天狼星——"

"别叫他的名字！"赫敏焦急地说，但哈利从没有像现在这样不需要她的忠告，他凭直觉就知道应该暂时尽量保持安静。

1279

CHAPTER THIRTY-FOUR The Department of Mysteries

'Where do we go, then, Harry?' Ron asked.

'I don't –' Harry began. He swallowed. 'In the dreams I went through the door at the end of the corridor from the lifts into a dark room – that's this one – and then I went through another door into a room that kind of ... glitters. We should try a few doors,' he said hastily, 'I'll know the right way when I see it. C'mon.'

He marched straight at the door now facing him, the others following close behind him, set his left hand against its cool, shining surface, raised his wand ready to strike the moment it opened, and pushed.

It swung open easily.

After the darkness of the first room, the lamps hanging low on golden chains from this ceiling gave the impression that this long rectangular room was much brighter, though there were no glittering, shimmering lights as Harry had seen in his dreams. The place was quite empty except for a few desks and, in the very middle of the room, an enormous glass tank of deep green liquid, big enough for all of them to swim in; a number of pearly-white objects were drifting around lazily in it.

'What're those things?' whispered Ron.

'Dunno,' said Harry.

'Are they fish?' breathed Ginny.

'Aquavirius Maggots!' said Luna excitedly. 'Dad said the Ministry were breeding –'

'No,' said Hermione. She sounded odd. She moved forward to look through the side of the tank. 'They're brains.'

'*Brains?*'

'Yes ... I wonder what they're doing with them?'

Harry joined her at the tank. Sure enough, there could be no mistake now he saw them at close quarters. Glimmering eerily, they drifted in and out of sight in the depths of the green liquid, looking something like slimy cauliflowers.

'Let's get out of here,' said Harry. 'This isn't right, we need to try another door.'

'There are doors here, too,' said Ron, pointing around the walls. Harry's heart sank; how big was this place?

'In my dream I went through that dark room into the second one,' he said.

第34章 神秘事务司

"那我们往哪儿走呢,哈利?"罗恩问。

"不知——"哈利没有把话说完,他咽了口唾沫,"在梦里,我出了升降梯,穿过那道走廊尽头的那扇门,进入了一间黑屋子——就是这间——然后我又穿过一扇门,进入了一个像是……像是会发光的屋子。我们应该找几扇门试试,"他急速地说,"找对了我会知道的。快。"

哈利大步走向他对面的那扇门,其他人紧紧跟在后面。他把左手放在冰冷发亮的门上,举起魔杖,准备门一开就出手攻击,然后用力一推。

门一下子就开了。

经过第一个房间的黑暗之后,他们觉得天花板上用金链子吊着的几盏灯使这个长方形房间看上去亮多了,可是并没有哈利梦中见过的那些闪烁、摇曳的灯光。房间里空荡荡的,只有几张桌子,中央有一个巨大的、足够他们几个在里面游泳的玻璃水箱,里面是深绿色的液体,许多珍珠白色的物质在里面懒洋洋地漂来漂去。

"这些是什么东西?"罗恩小声问。

"不知道。"哈利说。

"是鱼吗?"金妮轻声轻气地问。

"颤颤蛆!"卢娜兴奋地说,"爸爸说魔法部在培育——"

"不是,"赫敏说。她的声音有些异样,她凑上前,透过箱壁往里看,"是大脑。"

"大脑?"

"是啊……不知道他们拿它们做什么用?"

哈利跟她一起凑到水箱边。现在离得这么近,不会看错的。那些东西闪着诡异的光,在绿色液体的深处漂来漂去,忽隐忽现,看上去就像黏糊糊的花椰菜。

"我们离开这里吧,"哈利说,"这里不对,我们需要再找一扇门试试。"

"这里也有一些门呢。"罗恩指着周围的墙壁说。哈利的心往下一沉。这地方到底有多大?

"在我梦里,我穿过那间黑屋子,就进入了第二个房间,"他说,"我

CHAPTER THIRTY-FOUR   The Department of Mysteries

'I think we should go back and try from there.'

So they hurried back into the dark, circular room; the ghostly shapes of the brains were now swimming before Harry's eyes instead of the blue candle flames.

'Wait!' said Hermione sharply, as Luna made to close the door of the brain room behind them. '*Flagrate!*'

She drew with her wand in midair and a fiery 'X' appeared on the door. No sooner had the door clicked shut behind them than there was a great rumbling, and once again the wall began to revolve very fast, but now there was a great red-gold blur in amongst the faint blue and, when all became still again, the fiery cross still burned, showing the door they had already tried.

'Good thinking,' said Harry. 'OK, let's try this one –'

Again, he strode directly at the door facing him and pushed it open, his wand still raised, the others at his heels.

This room was larger than the last, dimly lit and rectangular, and the centre of it was sunken, forming a great stone pit some twenty feet deep. They were standing on the topmost tier of what seemed to be stone benches running all around the room and descending in steep steps like an amphitheatre, or the courtroom in which Harry had been tried by the Wizengamot. Instead of a chained chair, however, there was a raised stone dais in the centre of the pit, on which stood a stone archway that looked so ancient, cracked and crumbling that Harry was amazed the thing was still standing. Unsupported by any surrounding wall, the archway was hung with a tattered black curtain or veil which, despite the complete stillness of the cold surrounding air, was fluttering very slightly as though it had just been touched.

'Who's there?' said Harry, jumping down on to the bench below. There was no answering voice, but the veil continued to flutter and sway.

'Careful!' whispered Hermione.

Harry scrambled down the benches one by one until he reached the stone bottom of the sunken pit. His footsteps echoed loudly as he walked slowly towards the dais. The pointed archway looked much taller from where he now stood than it had when he'd been looking down on it from above. Still the veil swayed gently, as though somebody had just passed through it.

'Sirius?' Harry spoke again, but more quietly now that he was nearer.

He had the strangest feeling that there was someone standing right behind the veil on the other side of the archway. Gripping his wand very tightly, he

第34章 神秘事务司

认为我们应该回去，从那里再试。"

于是他们匆匆回到那个黑乎乎的圆形房间。那些阴森恐怖的大脑在哈利眼前游动，代替了刚才蓝色的烛焰。

"等等！"赫敏突然说道，卢娜正要关上他们身后大脑屋的门，"标记显现！"

她用魔杖在空中比画着，门上出现了一个火红的X。门咔嗒一声关上了，随即又是一阵响亮的隆隆声，墙壁又开始迅速旋转。但是这一次，在一片蓝色中间还有一大团模糊的金红色。等一切都固定不动了，那个火红的X还在燃烧，显示着那扇门他们已经试过了。

"想得真妙。"哈利说，"好了，我们试试这一扇——"

他又直接走向对面的那扇门，其他人紧跟其后。他仍然举着魔杖，把门推开了。

这个房间比刚才的那个还要大，光线昏暗，呈长方形，中间凹陷，形成一个大约二十英尺深的巨大石坑。房间四周是阶梯式的一排排石头长凳，他们站在最顶上一排，那些石凳以很陡的角度向下延伸，很像一个环形剧场，又像哈利接受威森加摩审判时的那个审判室。但石坑中央并没有带锁链的椅子，只有一个高高的石台，上面竖着一个石头拱门，看上去非常古老、破旧、衰败，哈利很惊讶它居然还能竖在那里。拱门周围没有墙壁支撑，上面挂着一道破破烂烂的黑色帘子或帷幔，虽然寒冷的空气里没有一丝微风，但帷幔在轻轻地飘动，好像被人刚刚碰过一样。

"谁在那儿？"哈利问，跳到下一级的石凳上。没有人回答，帷幔仍在飘动、摇曳。

"小心！"赫敏轻声说。

哈利快步跳下一排排石凳，来到深坑的石头底部。他慢慢地朝高台走去，脚步发出了很响的回声。从这里再看尖尖的拱门，比刚才从上面往下看时显得高多了。帷幔仍在轻轻摇摆，似乎有人刚刚从中穿过。

"小天狼星？"哈利叫道，现在离帷幔近了，他的声音放得更低。

他有一种十分奇怪的感觉，似乎有人就站在拱门另一边的帷幔后

CHAPTER THIRTY-FOUR The Department of Mysteries

edged around the dais, but there was nobody there; all that could be seen was the other side of the tattered black veil.

'Let's go,' called Hermione from halfway up the stone steps. 'This isn't right, Harry, come on, let's go.'

She sounded scared, much more scared than she had in the room where the brains swam, yet Harry thought the archway had a kind of beauty about it, old though it was. The gently rippling veil intrigued him; he felt a very strong inclination to climb up on the dais and walk through it.

'Harry, let's go, OK?' said Hermione more forcefully.

'OK,' he said, but did not move. He had just heard something. There were faint whispering, murmuring noises coming from the other side of the veil.

'What are you saying?' he said, very loudly, so that his words echoed all around the stone benches.

'Nobody's talking, Harry!' said Hermione, now moving over to him.

'Someone's whispering behind there,' he said, moving out of her reach and continuing to frown at the veil. 'Is that you, Ron?'

'I'm here, mate,' said Ron, appearing around the side of the archway.

'Can't anyone else hear it?' Harry demanded, for the whispering and murmuring was becoming louder; without really meaning to put it there, he found his foot was on the dais.

'I can hear them too,' breathed Luna, joining them around the side of the archway and gazing at the swaying veil. 'There are people *in there*!'

'What do you mean, "*in there*"?' demanded Hermione, jumping down from the bottom step and sounding much angrier than the occasion warranted. 'There isn't any "*in there*", it's just an archway, there's no room for anybody to be there. Harry, stop it, come away –'

She grabbed his arm and pulled, but he resisted.

'Harry, we are supposed to be here for Sirius!' she said in a high-pitched, strained voice.

'Sirius,' Harry repeated, still gazing, mesmerised, at the continuously swaying veil. 'Yeah ...'

Something finally slid back into place in his brain; *Sirius*, captured, bound and tortured, and he was staring at this archway ...

He took several paces back from the dais and wrenched his eyes from the veil.

'Let's go,' he said.

第34章 神秘事务司

面。他紧紧地抓住魔杖,侧身绕过高台,然而那儿没人。他只能看见破破烂烂的黑色帷幔的另一边。

"我们走吧,"赫敏从石阶的半腰处喊道,"这里不对,哈利,快,我们走吧。"

她的声音里透着恐惧,比刚才在大脑游动的房间里时要恐惧多了,但哈利觉得拱门虽然古旧,却自有一种美感。那微微飘动的帷幔令他着迷,他有一种很强烈的冲动,想要爬上高台,穿过帷幔。

"哈利,我们走吧,好吗?"赫敏更坚决地说。

"好吧。"他说,但身子并没有动弹。他听到了动静。隐隐约约地,有喃喃的低语声从帷幔的另一边传来。

"你在说什么?"他声音很大地问,他的话在周围的石凳间回荡。

"没有人说话,哈利!"赫敏说,拔腿朝他走来。

"有人在那后面小声说话。"哈利说着,闪身躲开她,继续紧锁眉头看着帷幔,"是你吗,罗恩?"

"我在这儿呢,哥们儿。"罗恩说着,从拱门侧面绕了过来。

"你们谁也没听见吗?"哈利问道,喃喃的低语声越来越响了。他发现自己莫名其妙地把一只脚踏上了高台。

"我也能听见。"卢娜屏住呼吸说,她绕过拱门来到他们身边,盯着飘动的帷幔,"里面有人!"

"你说什么,里面?"赫敏问道,跳下最底层石阶,声音里透着不必要的怒气,"根本就没有什么里面,这只是个拱门,没地方可以待人。哈利,别闹了,快走——"

她抓住哈利的胳膊拉他,但哈利不肯动弹。

"哈利,我们来这里是为了救小天狼星的!"她扯着嗓子尖声说。

"小天狼星,"哈利跟着说了一遍,目光仍然痴迷般地盯着不断飘动的帷幔,"是啊……"

什么东西终于回到了他的脑海里:小天狼星,被囚禁、束缚,遭受着折磨,而自己却傻乎乎地盯着这道拱门……

他从高台前倒退了几步,强迫目光离开了帷幔。

"我们走吧。"他说。

CHAPTER THIRTY-FOUR The Department of Mysteries

'That's what I've been trying to – well, come on, then!' said Hermione, and she led the way back around the dais. On the other side, Ginny and Neville were staring, apparently entranced, at the veil too. Without speaking, Hermione took hold of Ginny's arm, Ron grabbed Neville's, and they marched them firmly back to the lowest stone bench and clambered all the way back up to the door.

'What d'you reckon that arch was?' Harry asked Hermione as they regained the dark circular room.

'I don't know, but whatever it was, it was dangerous,' she said firmly, again inscribing a fiery cross on the door.

Once more, the wall spun and became still again. Harry approached another door at random and pushed. It did not move.

'What's wrong?' said Hermione.

'It's ... locked ...' said Harry, throwing his weight at the door, but it didn't budge.

'This is it, then, isn't it?' said Ron excitedly, joining Harry in the attempt to force the door open. 'Bound to be!'

'Get out of the way!' said Hermione sharply. She pointed her wand at the place where a lock would have been on an ordinary door and said, '*Alohomora!*'

Nothing happened.

'Sirius's knife!' said Harry. He pulled it out from inside his robes and slid it into the crack between the door and the wall. The others all watched eagerly as he ran it from top to bottom, withdrew it and then flung his shoulder again at the door. It remained as firmly shut as ever. What was more, when Harry looked down at the knife, he saw the blade had melted.

'Right, we're leaving that room,' said Hermione decisively.

'But what if that's the one?' said Ron, staring at it with a mixture of apprehension and longing.

'It can't be, Harry could get through all the doors in his dream,' said Hermione, marking the door with another fiery cross as Harry replaced the now-useless handle of Sirius's knife in his pocket.

'You know what could be in there?' said Luna eagerly, as the wall started to spin yet again.

'Something blibbering, no doubt,' said Hermione under her breath and Neville gave a nervous little laugh.

第34章 神秘事务司

"早该走了——好吧,那就走吧!"赫敏说完,领头绕过高台往回走。在石台的另一边,金妮和纳威也都呆呆地盯着帷幔,如同着了迷似的。赫敏与罗恩什么也没说,赫敏一把抓住金妮的胳膊,罗恩则抓住了纳威,不由分说地押着他们回到最底层的石凳,一路往上爬到了门口。

"你说那道拱门是什么呢?"返回那间黑暗的圆形房间时,哈利问赫敏。

"不知道,但不管是什么,都是危险的。"她坚决地说,又在门上印了一个燃烧的 X。

墙壁再一次开始旋转,然后又静止下来。哈利随意走到一扇门前,推了推门。没有推动。

"怎么啦?"赫敏说。

"是……是锁着的……"哈利说着,用全身的重量去撞门,但门还是纹丝不动。

"看来就是它了,对不对?"罗恩兴奋地说,跟哈利一起试着强行把门撞开,"肯定对了!"

"闪开!"赫敏厉声说。她用魔杖指着普通门锁所在的位置,说了一声:"阿拉霍洞开!"

没有反应。

"小天狼星的刀子!"哈利说。他把刀子从衣袍里抽了出来,插进门和墙壁间的缝隙。另外几个人都在一旁急切地注视着,哈利把刀子从上到下划了一遍,然后拔出刀子,又用肩膀去撞门。门还和刚才一样关得死死的,不仅如此,哈利低头一看,发现刀刃熔化掉了。

"好啦,我们离开这个房间吧。"赫敏果断地说。

"但如果就是这间呢?"罗恩说,既恐惧又渴望地盯着这扇门。

"不可能,哈利在梦里能穿过所有的门。"赫敏说着,也在这扇门上印了一个燃烧的 X。小天狼星的刀子只剩下了没用的刀柄,哈利把它放回了口袋。

"你知道那里面可能会有什么?"卢娜兴致很浓地问,这时墙壁又开始旋转了。

"肯定是一些唠唠叨叨的东西。"赫敏压低声音说,纳威紧张地笑了一声。

CHAPTER THIRTY-FOUR

The Department of Mysteries

The wall slid to a halt and Harry, with a feeling of increasing desperation, pushed the next door open.

'*This is it!*'

He knew it at once by the beautiful, dancing, diamond-sparkling light. As Harry's eyes became accustomed to the brilliant glare, he saw clocks gleaming from every surface, large and small, grandfather and carriage, hanging in spaces between the bookcases or standing on desks ranging the length of the room, so that a busy, relentless ticking filled the place like thousands of minuscule, marching footsteps. The source of the dancing, diamond-bright light was a towering crystal bell jar that stood at the far end of the room.

'This way!'

Harry's heart was pumping frantically now that he knew they were on the right track; he led the way down the narrow space between the lines of desks, heading, as he had done in his dream, for the source of the light, the crystal bell jar quite as tall as he was that stood on a desk and appeared to be full of a billowing, glittering wind.

'Oh, *look*!' said Ginny, as they drew nearer, pointing at the very heart of the bell jar.

Drifting along in the sparkling current inside was a tiny, jewel-bright egg. As it rose in the jar, it cracked open and a humming-bird emerged, which was carried to the very top of the jar, but as it fell on the draught its feathers became bedraggled and damp again, and by the time it had been borne back to the bottom of the jar it had been enclosed once more in its egg.

'Keep going!' said Harry sharply, because Ginny showed signs of wanting to stop and watch the egg's progress back into a bird.

'You dawdled enough by that old arch!' she said crossly, but followed him past the bell jar to the only door behind it.

'This is it,' Harry said again, and his heart was now pumping so hard and fast he felt it must interfere with his speech, 'it's through here –'

He glanced around at them all; they had their wands out and looked suddenly serious and anxious. He looked back at the door and pushed. It swung open.

They were there, they had found the place: high as a church and full of nothing but towering shelves covered in small, dusty, glass orbs. They glimmered dully in the light issuing from more candle-brackets set at intervals along the shelves. Like those in the circular room behind them, their flames

第34章 神秘事务司

墙壁慢慢停止了旋转,哈利怀着越来越焦虑的心情,推开了旁边的一扇门。

"就是这儿!"

他一看到那美丽的、如钻石般闪亮的跳动的光,就知道这次选对了。哈利的眼睛适应了耀眼的光线后,看见了各种各样的钟,大钟小钟,老爷钟和旅行钟,挂在书架间的空隙处,或放在那些有房间那么长的桌子上,钟面上闪着亮光,四下里响着一片持续不断的繁忙的滴答声,就像有成千上万细小的、行进中的脚步声。而发出那跳动的、钻石般光亮的,是位于房间尽头的一个高大的钟形水晶罩。

"这边走!"

哈利知道现在走对了,激动得心怦怦狂跳。他领头顺着桌子间狭窄的空隙往前走,就像在梦里一样,走向那个光源。那个几乎跟他一样高的钟形水晶罩,立在一张桌子上,看上去里面似乎弥漫着一股翻腾的、闪烁发光的气流。

"哦,快看!"他们靠近罩子时,金妮指着水晶罩的中心说。

在罩子里闪闪发亮的气流中,飘浮着一个小小的、宝石般明亮的蛋。它在罩子里浮起,裂开,一只蜂鸟出现了,被托到罩子顶部。可是碰到那股气流后,它的羽毛就变得脏兮兮、湿漉漉的了;等它被送回罩子底部时,便又被包进了蛋壳里。

"快走啊!"哈利严厉地说,因为金妮似乎想停下来观看那个蛋重新变成小鸟。

"你在破拱门那儿耽搁的时间也够长的!"金妮气呼呼地说,但还是跟着哈利走过钟形水晶罩,来到后面仅有的一扇门前。

"就是这儿。"哈利又说了一遍。他的心跳得又快又猛,觉得连说话都会受影响了,"从这里穿过去——"

他扭头看了看大家。他们都拿出了魔杖,一下子显得十分严肃和紧张。他转过头,把门一推。门开了。

他们进去了,他们找到了:这里像教堂一样高,里面摆满了高高的架子,架子上是许多小小的、灰扑扑的玻璃球。在顺着架子排列的那些烛台的映照下,玻璃球闪着暗淡的光。这里就像刚才那个圆形房

CHAPTER THIRTY-FOUR The Department of Mysteries

were burning blue. The room was very cold.

Harry edged forward and peered down one of the shadowy aisles between two rows of shelves. He could not hear anything or see the slightest sign of movement.

'You said it was row ninety-seven,' whispered Hermione.

'Yeah,' breathed Harry, looking up at the end of the closest row. Beneath the branch of blue-glowing candles protruding from it glimmered the silver figure fifty-three.

'We need to go right, I think,' whispered Hermione, squinting to the next row. 'Yes ... that's fifty-four ...'

'Keep your wands ready,' Harry said softly.

They crept forward, glancing behind them as they went on down the long alleys of shelves, the further ends of which were in near-total darkness. Tiny, yellowing labels had been stuck beneath each glass orb on the shelves. Some of them had a weird, liquid glow; others were as dull and dark within as blown light bulbs.

They passed row eighty-four ... eighty-five ... Harry was listening hard for the slightest sound of movement, but Sirius might be gagged now, or else unconscious ... *or*, said an unbidden voice inside his head, *he might already be dead ...*

I'd have felt it, he told himself, his heart now hammering against his Adam's apple, I'd already know ...

'Ninety-seven!' whispered Hermione.

They stood grouped around the end of the row, gazing down the alley beside it. There was nobody there.

'He's right down at the end,' said Harry, whose mouth had become slightly dry. 'You can't see properly from here.'

And he led them between the towering rows of glass balls, some of which glowed softly as they passed ...

'He should be near here,' whispered Harry, convinced that every step was going to bring the ragged form of Sirius into view on the darkened floor. 'Anywhere here ... really close ...'

'Harry?' said Hermione tentatively, but he did not want to respond. His mouth was very dry.

'Somewhere about ... here ...' he said.

They had reached the end of the row and emerged into more dim

第34章 神秘事务司

间里一样，烛火也是蓝色的。房间里非常寒冷。

哈利小心翼翼地向前移动，注视着两排架子之间昏暗的通道。他什么也听不见，也看不见任何动静。

"你说在第九十七排。"赫敏小声说。

"是的。"哈利轻轻应了一声，抬头看着最近一排架子的顶端。从架子里伸出的一支闪着蓝光的蜡烛下，一个银色的数字在闪烁：53。

"我想应该往右边走，"赫敏轻声说，眯起眼睛望着旁边那排架子，"没错……那是五十四……"

"都把魔杖准备好。"哈利压低声音说。

他们顺着架子之间长长的过道，蹑手蹑脚地往前走，不时地回头张望，过道尽头几乎一片漆黑。架子上的每只玻璃球下都插着泛黄的小标签。有的玻璃球闪烁着一种诡异的、液体般的光芒，也有的里面暗淡无光，就像灯丝烧断了的灯泡一样。

他们经过了第八十四排……第八十五排……哈利侧耳倾听每一丝细小的动静，但是什么也听不到。小天狼星可能已经被堵住了嘴巴，或者昏迷不醒……或者，他脑子里一个自作主张的声音说，他可能已经死了……

我会感觉到的，哈利对自己说，这时他的心都快跳到嗓子眼儿了，我会知道的……

"九十七！"赫敏小声说。

他们聚集在那排架子尽头，望着旁边的那条过道。那里没有人。

"他就在这尽头的，"哈利说，他的嘴微微发干，"你们从这里看不清楚。"

他领头在摆放着玻璃球的高架间穿行，几只玻璃球在他们经过时闪烁出柔和的光……

"他应该就在这附近，"哈利轻声说，他相信每走一步，地板上都可能出现小天狼星那衣衫褴褛的身影，"就在这儿……真的很近了……"

"哈利？"赫敏迟疑地叫了一声，但哈利不想回答，他的嘴很干。

"就在这里的……什么地方……"他说。

他们已经来到这排架子的另一头，又进入了昏暗的烛光下。这里

CHAPTER THIRTY-FOUR   The Department of Mysteries

candlelight. There was nobody there. All was echoing, dusty silence.

'He might be ...' Harry whispered hoarsely, peering down the next alley. 'Or maybe ...' He hurried to look down the one beyond that.

'Harry?' said Hermione again.

'What?' he snarled.

'I ... I don't think Sirius is here.'

Nobody spoke. Harry did not want to look at any of them. He felt sick. He did not understand why Sirius was not here. He had to be here. This was where he, Harry, had seen him ...

He ran up the space at the end of the rows, staring down them. Empty aisle after empty aisle flickered past. He ran the other way, back past his staring companions. There was no sign of Sirius anywhere, nor any hint of a struggle.

'Harry?' Ron called.

'What?'

He did not want to hear what Ron had to say; did not want to hear Ron tell him he had been stupid or suggest that they ought to go back to Hogwarts, but the heat was rising in his face and he felt as though he would like to skulk down here in the darkness for a long while before facing the brightness of the Atrium above and the others' accusing stares ...

'Have you seen this?' said Ron.

'What?' said Harry, but eagerly this time – it had to be a sign that Sirius had been there, a clue. He strode back to where they were all standing, a little way down row ninety-seven, but found nothing except Ron staring at one of the dusty glass spheres on the shelf.

'What?' Harry repeated glumly.

'It's – it's got your name on,' said Ron.

Harry moved a little closer. Ron was pointing at one of the small glass spheres that glowed with a dull inner light, though it was very dusty and appeared not to have been touched for many years.

'My name?' said Harry blankly.

He stepped forwards. Not as tall as Ron, he had to crane his neck to read the yellowish label affixed to the shelf right beneath the dusty glass ball. In spidery writing was written a date of some sixteen years previously, and below that:

第34章 神秘事务司

也没有人。只有一片尘封的、回音缭绕的寂静。

"他可能……"哈利望着旁边一条过道,声音嘶哑地说,"也许……"他匆匆走过去查看前面的那条过道。

"哈利?"赫敏又叫了一声。

"怎么啦?"哈利凶巴巴地说。

"我……我认为小天狼星不在这里。"

没有人说话。哈利不想看他们中间的任何一个。他觉得很难受。他不明白小天狼星为什么不在这里。他必须在这里的。哈利就是看见他在这里呀……

他顺着过道尽头那块地方往前跑,朝一排排架子间张望。他眼前闪过一条又一条空空的过道。然后他又掉过头来跑,从那些目瞪口呆的朋友们身边跑过。没有小天狼星的影子,也没有任何搏斗的痕迹。

"哈利?"罗恩喊道。

"怎么啦?"

他不想听罗恩说什么,不想听罗恩告诉他做了傻事,或者听罗恩建议大家返回霍格沃茨,但他的脸在发烧,他巴不得能够久久地躲在这黑黢黢的地方,不去面对楼上正厅的亮光,不去面对别人指责的目光……

"你看见这个了吗?"罗恩问。

"什么?"哈利说,这次的语气比较积极了——肯定是小天狼星来过这里的某个迹象,某个线索。他大步回到其他人身边,回到第九十七排架子往里一点儿的地方,但他什么也没发现,只看见罗恩盯着架子上一个灰扑扑的玻璃球。

"什么?"哈利又闷闷不乐地问了一遍。

"这上面——这上面有你的名字。"罗恩说。

哈利凑近了一些。罗恩指着那个小玻璃球,它虽然落满灰尘,好像许多年无人触摸过,但却从里面透出一种淡淡的光。

"我的名字?"哈利茫然地问。

他走上前去。他个头比罗恩矮,不得不伸长脖子去看尘封的玻璃球下面的架子上插着的泛黄的标签。标签上用细长的字迹写着大约十六年前的一个日期,接着是:

CHAPTER THIRTY-FOUR   The Department of Mysteries

> *S.P.T. to A.P.W.B.D.*
> *Dark Lord*
> *and (?) Harry Potter*

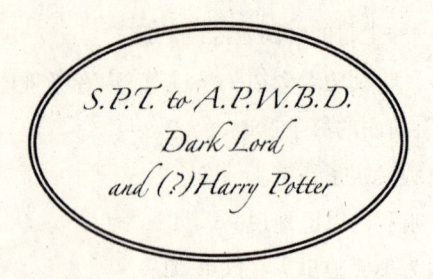

Harry stared at it.

'What is it?' Ron asked, sounding unnerved. 'What's your name doing down here?'

He glanced along at the other labels on that stretch of shelf.

'I'm not here,' he said, sounding perplexed. 'None of the rest of us are here.'

'Harry, I don't think you should touch it,' said Hermione sharply, as he stretched out his hand.

'Why not?' he said. 'It's something to do with me, isn't it?'

'Don't, Harry,' said Neville suddenly. Harry looked at him. Neville's round face was shining slightly with sweat. He looked as though he could not take much more suspense.

'It's got my name on,' said Harry.

And feeling slightly reckless, he closed his fingers around the dusty ball's surface. He had expected it to feel cold, but it did not. On the contrary, it felt as though it had been lying in the sun for hours, as though the glow of light within was warming it. Expecting, even hoping, that something dramatic was going to happen, something exciting that might make their long and dangerous journey worthwhile after all, Harry lifted the glass ball down from its shelf and stared at it.

Nothing whatsoever happened. The others moved in closer around Harry, gazing at the orb as he brushed it free of the clogging dust.

And then, from right behind them, a drawling voice spoke.

'Very good, Potter. Now turn around, nice and slowly, and give that to me.'

第34章 神秘事务司

S.P.T. to A.P.W.B.D.
黑魔头
和（？）哈利·波特

哈利呆呆地望着。

"这是什么呢？"罗恩问，声音里透着胆怯，"你的名字怎么会在这上面？"

他扫了一眼那排架子上的其他标签。

"没有我，"他困惑不解地说，"也没有我们其他人。"

"哈利，我认为你不应该去碰它。"赫敏看到哈利伸出了手，严厉地说。

"为什么？"哈利说，"这东西跟我有关系，不是吗？"

"别碰，哈利。"纳威突然说道。哈利看着他，纳威的圆脸汗津津的，看上去似乎再也不能承受更多的焦虑了。

"这上面写着我的名字呢。"哈利说。

哈利带着有点鲁莽的感觉，用手指握住了那个灰扑扑的玻璃球。他本以为球面摸上去是凉的，然而正相反，玻璃球就好像在太阳底下晒了好几个小时，就好像球内的光亮把球面烤暖了。哈利猜想——甚至希望——会发生一件戏剧性的事，一件惊心动魄的事，使他们漫长而危险的旅程最终有些价值。他怀着这样的心情，把玻璃球从架子上拿下来，仔细端详着。

什么也没有发生。其他人都聚拢在哈利身边，注视着圆球，哈利拂去了它上面的积尘。

就在这时，他们身后一个拖着长腔的声音说话了。

"很好，波特。现在转过身来，慢慢地转过身来，把它给我。"

CHAPTER THIRTY-FIVE

Beyond the Veil

Black shapes were emerging out of thin air all around them, blocking their way left and right; eyes glinted through slits in hoods, a dozen lit wand-tips were pointing directly at their hearts; Ginny gave a gasp of horror.

'To me, Potter,' repeated the drawling voice of Lucius Malfoy as he held out his hand, palm up.

Harry's insides plummeted sickeningly. They were trapped, and outnumbered two to one.

'To me,' said Malfoy yet again.

'Where's Sirius?' Harry said.

Several of the Death Eaters laughed; a harsh female voice from the midst of the shadowy figures to Harry's left said triumphantly, 'The Dark Lord always knows!'

'Always,' echoed Malfoy softly. 'Now, give me the prophecy, Potter.'

'I want to know where Sirius is!'

'*I want to know where Sirius is!*' mimicked the woman to his left. She and her fellow Death Eaters had closed in so that they were mere feet away from Harry and the others, the light from their wands dazzling Harry's eyes.

'You've got him,' said Harry, ignoring the rising panic in his chest, the dread he had been fighting since they had first entered the ninety-seventh row. 'He's here. I know he is.'

'*The little baby woke up fwightened and fort what it dweamed was twoo,*' said the woman in a horrible, mock baby voice. Harry felt Ron stir beside him.

'Don't do anything,' Harry muttered. 'Not yet –'

The woman who had mimicked him let out a raucous scream of laughter.

第35章

帷幔那边

突然,周围凭空出现了许多黑压压的身影,把左右两边的路都挡住了。那些人的眼睛从兜帽的狭缝里射出光芒,十几根发亮的魔杖直指他们的心脏。金妮惊恐地倒抽了一口冷气。

"给我,波特。"卢修斯·马尔福用拖着长腔的声音又说了一遍,一边伸出手来,掌心向上。

哈利的心陡地往下一沉。他们被困住了,对方人数是他们的两倍。

"给我。"马尔福又说。

"小天狼星在哪儿?"哈利问。

几个食死徒大笑起来。在哈利左边那片黑乎乎的人影中间,一个粗哑的女声得意洋洋地说:"黑魔王真是神机妙算!"

"没错。"马尔福轻声附和,"好了,把预言球给我吧,波特。"

"我想知道小天狼星在哪儿!"

"我想知道小天狼星在哪儿!"左边那个女人学着他的声音说。

她和那些食死徒围拢过来,距哈利和其他人只有几英尺了,他们的魔杖发出的亮光刺得哈利睁不开眼睛。

"你们抓住了他,"哈利说,努力不去理会内心泛起的紧张,不去理会自从他走进第九十七排架子后就一直在克服的恐惧,"他在这儿,我知道。"

"小宝宝醒过来吓坏了,以为梦里的事情都是真的呢。"那女人难听地模仿着婴儿的声音说。哈利感觉到身边的罗恩动了一下。

"什么也别做,"哈利压低声音说,"暂时不要——"

刚才学他说话的那个女人发出一阵粗声狂笑。

CHAPTER THIRTY-FIVE Beyond the Veil

'You hear him? *You hear him?* Giving instructions to the other children as though he thinks of fighting us!'

'Oh, you don't know Potter as I do, Bellatrix,' said Malfoy softly. 'He has a great weakness for heroics; the Dark Lord understands this about him. *Now give me the prophecy, Potter.*'

'I know Sirius is here,' said Harry, though panic was causing his chest to constrict and he felt as though he could not breathe properly. 'I know you've got him!'

More of the Death Eaters laughed, though the woman laughed loudest of all.

'It's time you learned the difference between life and dreams, Potter,' said Malfoy. 'Now give me the prophecy, or we start using wands.'

'Go on, then,' said Harry, raising his own wand to chest height. As he did so, the five wands of Ron, Hermione, Neville, Ginny and Luna rose on either side of him. The knot in Harry's stomach tightened. If Sirius really was not here, he had led his friends to their deaths for no reason at all ...

But the Death Eaters did not strike.

'Hand over the prophecy and no one need get hurt,' said Malfoy coolly.

It was Harry's turn to laugh.

'Yeah, right!' he said. 'I give you this – prophecy, is it? And you'll just let us skip off home, will you?'

The words were hardly out of his mouth when the female Death Eater shrieked: '*Accio proph—*'

Harry was just ready for her: he shouted '*Protego!*' before she had finished her spell, and though the glass sphere slipped to the tips of his fingers he managed to cling on to it.

'Oh, he knows how to play, little bitty baby Potter,' she said, her mad eyes staring through the slits in her hood. 'Very well, then –'

'I TOLD YOU, NO!' Lucius Malfoy roared at the woman. 'If you smash it –!'

Harry's mind was racing. The Death Eaters wanted this dusty spun-glass sphere. He had no interest in it. He just wanted to get them all out of this alive, to make sure none of his friends paid a terrible price for his stupidity ...

The woman stepped forward, away from her fellows, and pulled off her

第35章 帷幔那边

"听见了吗？听见了吗？他在给别的孩子下指令，好像打算跟我们搏斗呢！"

"哦，贝拉特里克斯，你不如我了解波特，"马尔福轻声说，"他有一个很大的弱点：个人英雄主义。黑魔王了解他这一点。好了，把预言球给我吧，波特。"

"我知道小天狼星就在这儿。"哈利说，紧张的感觉使他胸口发紧，似乎连呼吸也不舒畅了，"我知道你们抓住了他！"

更多的食死徒放声大笑，但笑得最响的是那个女人。

"你应该学会分清现实和梦境了，波特。"马尔福说，"快把预言球给我，不然我们就动用魔杖了。"

"那就请便吧。"哈利说着，把自己的魔杖举到胸前。与此同时，罗恩、赫敏、纳威、金妮和卢娜的五根魔杖也在他周围举了起来。哈利的内心更加紧缩成一团。如果小天狼星确实不在这儿，他就等于无缘无故地把朋友们带来送死……

但是食死徒们并没有出击。

"乖乖地把预言球递过来，谁也不会受伤。"马尔福冷冷地说。

这次是哈利放声大笑了。

"是啊，没错！"哈利说，"我给你这个——它叫预言球，对吗？然后你就会让我们赶紧回家，对吗？"

他的话刚一出口，就听见那个女食死徒尖叫一声："预言球飞——"

哈利早有防备，不等她念完咒语就喊了一声："盔甲护身！"虽然玻璃球滑到了他的指尖，但他总算把它又抓住了。

"哦，他还挺会玩儿的呢，这个小不点儿波特。"女人说，一双疯狂的眼睛从兜帽的狭缝中往外瞪着，"很好，那么——"

"**我跟你说了，不行！**"卢修斯·马尔福冲那女人吼道，"万一你把它打碎——！"

哈利的大脑在迅速转动。食死徒想要得到这个灰扑扑的玻璃球。可他对这玩意儿毫无兴趣。他只想让大家安然无恙地离开这里，确保他的朋友们没有一个会因他的愚蠢而付出惨重的代价……

女人上前几步，离开她的那些同伙，摘掉了兜帽。阿兹卡班的牢

CHAPTER THIRTY-FIVE   Beyond the Veil

hood. Azkaban had hollowed Bellatrix Lestrange's face, making it gaunt and skull-like, but it was alive with a feverish, fanatical glow.

'You need more persuasion?' she said, her chest rising and falling rapidly. 'Very well – take the smallest one,' she ordered the Death Eaters beside her. 'Let him watch while we torture the little girl. I'll do it.'

Harry felt the others close in around Ginny; he stepped sideways so that he was right in front of her, the prophecy held up to his chest.

'You'll have to smash this if you want to attack any of us,' he told Bellatrix. 'I don't think your boss will be too pleased if you come back without it, will he?'

She did not move; she merely stared at him, the tip of her tongue moistening her thin mouth.

'So,' said Harry, 'what kind of prophecy are we talking about, anyway?'

He could not think what to do but to keep talking. Neville's arm was pressed against his, and he could feel him shaking; he could feel one of the others' quickened breath on the back of his head. He was hoping they were all thinking hard about ways to get out of this, because his mind was blank.

'What kind of prophecy?' repeated Bellatrix, the grin fading from her face. 'You jest, Harry Potter.'

'Nope, not jesting,' said Harry, his eyes flicking from Death Eater to Death Eater, looking for a weak link, a space through which they could escape. 'How come Voldemort wants it?'

Several of the Death Eaters let out low hisses.

'You dare speak his name?' whispered Bellatrix.

'Yeah,' said Harry, maintaining his tight grip on the glass ball, expecting another attempt to bewitch it from him. 'Yeah, I've got no problem with saying Vol–'

'Shut your mouth!' Bellatrix shrieked. 'You dare speak his name with your unworthy lips, you dare besmirch it with your half-blood's tongue, you dare –'

'Did you know he's a half-blood too?' said Harry recklessly. Hermione gave a little moan in his ear. 'Voldemort? Yeah, his mother was a witch but his dad was a Muggle – or has he been telling you lot he's pure-blood?'

'*STUPEF–*'

第35章 帷幔那边

狱生活使贝拉特里克斯·莱斯特兰奇面颊凹陷，形容枯槁，看上去像骷髅一样，但她脸上闪动着一种热烈而疯狂的光芒。

"你想敬酒不吃吃罚酒吗？"她说，胸脯急速地起伏着。"很好——抓住那个最小的，"她吩咐身边的那个食死徒，"让他看着我们折磨那个小姑娘。我来办。"

哈利感觉到其他人都围拢在金妮身边，他往旁边跨了一步，正好挡在金妮前面，并把预言球举在自己的胸前。

"要想对我们中间任何一个人下手，就必须先打碎这个。"他对贝拉特里克斯说，"如果你们空手而返，恐怕你们的主子会不高兴的，是不是？"

贝拉特里克斯没有动弹，只是盯着哈利，同时用舌尖舔着薄薄的嘴唇。

"那么，"哈利说，"我们谈论的到底是什么样的预言呢？"

除了不停地说话，他想不出还能做什么。纳威的胳膊紧贴着他，他能感觉到纳威在发抖。他还感觉到了他脑袋后面某个人的急促呼吸。他希望他们都在使劲思索如何逃脱这个险境，因为他的脑子里一片空白。

"什么样的预言？"贝拉特里克斯学说了一遍，脸上的狞笑消失了，"你在开玩笑吧，哈利·波特。"

"不，不是开玩笑，"哈利说，他的眼睛在那些食死徒之间来回扫视，想寻找一个薄弱环节，一个能让他们逃脱的突破口，"伏地魔为什么想要它？"

几个食死徒发出低哑的嘶嘶声。

"你敢说他的名字？"贝拉特里克斯轻声说。

"是啊，"哈利说，他紧紧抓着玻璃球不放，以防对方再次施魔法把它夺走，"是啊，我完全能说伏地——"

"闭嘴！"贝拉特里克斯尖叫起来，"你竟敢用你卑贱的嘴巴说出他的名字，你竟敢用你杂种的舌头玷污它，你竟敢——"

"你知道他也是个杂种吗？"哈利不顾一切地说。赫敏在他耳边轻轻地呻吟了一声。"伏地魔？没错，他母亲是个女巫，但他爸爸是个麻瓜——难道他一直对你们说他是个纯血种？"

"**昏昏——**"

CHAPTER THIRTY-FIVE   Beyond the Veil

'*NO!*'

A jet of red light had shot from the end of Bellatrix Lestrange's wand, but Malfoy had deflected it; his spell caused hers to hit the shelf a foot to the left of Harry and several of the glass orbs there shattered.

Two figures, pearly-white as ghosts, fluid as smoke, unfurled themselves from the fragments of broken glass upon the floor and each began to speak; their voices vied with each other, so that only fragments of what they were saying could be heard over Malfoy and Bellatrix's shouts.

'... *at the solstice will come a new* ...' said the figure of an old, bearded man.

'DO NOT ATTACK! WE NEED THE PROPHECY!'

'He dared – he dares –' shrieked Bellatrix incoherently, 'he stands there – filthy half-blood –'

'WAIT UNTIL WE'VE GOT THE PROPHECY!' bawled Malfoy.

'... *and none will come after* ...' said the figure of a young woman.

The two figures that had burst from the shattered spheres had melted into thin air. Nothing remained of them or their erstwhile homes but fragments of glass upon the floor. They had, however, given Harry an idea. The problem was going to be conveying it to the others.

'You haven't told me what's so special about this prophecy I'm supposed to be handing over,' he said, playing for time. He moved his foot slowly sideways, feeling around for someone else's.

'Do not play games with us, Potter,' said Malfoy.

'I'm not playing games,' said Harry, half his mind on the conversation, half on his wandering foot. And then he found someone's toes and pressed down upon them. A sharp intake of breath behind him told him they were Hermione's.

'What?' she whispered.

'Dumbledore never told you the reason you bear that scar was hidden in the bowels of the Department of Mysteries?' Malfoy sneered.

'I – what?' said Harry. And for a moment he quite forgot his plan. 'What about my scar?'

'*What?*' whispered Hermione more urgently behind him.

'Can this be?' said Malfoy, sounding maliciously delighted; some of the Death Eaters were laughing again, and under cover of their laughter, Harry

第35章 帷幔那边

"不!"

一道红光从贝拉特里克斯·莱斯特兰奇的杖尖射出,但马尔福使它改变了方向。他的咒语使贝拉特里克斯的咒语撞上了哈利左边一英尺处的那个架子,几个玻璃球被砸碎了。

两个像烟雾一样飘动,像幽灵一样泛白的身影,从地板上的玻璃碎片中浮现出来,开始说话。他们的声音彼此冲撞,在马尔福和贝拉特里克斯的叫喊声中,只能听得清他们的只言片语。

"……到了至日,会出现一个新的……"一个长胡子老人的身影说。

"不要出击!我们需要预言球!"

"他竟敢——他竟敢——"贝拉特里克斯语无伦次地叫道,"他就站在那儿——肮脏的杂种——"

"等我们拿到预言球再说!"马尔福大嚷。

"……之后便无人出现……"一个年轻女人的身影说。

随后,这两个从玻璃球碎片中迸出的身影消融不见了。他们,以及他们原先的居所都消失了,只剩下了地板上的玻璃残片。不过,这使哈利有了一个主意。问题是怎么把自己的主意告诉另外几个人。

"你叫我把这个预言球给你们,却没有告诉我它有什么特别之处。"哈利说,他只是为了拖延时间。他慢慢地把一只脚往旁边挪动着,想触碰到另一个人的脚。

"别跟我们耍花招,波特。"马尔福说。

"我不是耍花招。"波特说,他用一半心思跟他们对话,另一半心思则放在那只探索的脚上。他探到了某个人的脚尖,用力踩了上去。他的身后传来倒抽冷气的声音,他知道那只脚是赫敏的。

"怎么了?"赫敏轻声问。

"邓布利多从来没跟你说过,你之所以带着那道伤疤,原因就藏在神秘事务司里吗?"马尔福讥笑着说。

"我——什么?"哈利说,他一时几乎忘记了自己的计划,"我的伤疤怎么了?"

"怎么了?"赫敏在他身后更加焦急地小声问。

"这可能吗?"马尔福说,声音里透着恶毒的快意。几个食死徒又大笑起来,哈利在他们笑声的掩护下,压低声音、尽量不动嘴唇地对

CHAPTER THIRTY-FIVE Beyond the Veil

hissed to Hermione, moving his lips as little as possible, 'Smash shelves –'

'Dumbledore never told you?' Malfoy repeated. 'Well, this explains why you didn't come earlier, Potter, the Dark Lord wondered why –'

'– when I say *now* –'

'– you didn't come running when he showed you the place where it was hidden in your dreams. He thought natural curiosity would make you want to hear the exact wording ...'

'Did he?' said Harry. Behind him he felt rather than heard Hermione passing his message to the others and he sought to keep talking, to distract the Death Eaters. 'So he wanted me to come and get it, did he? Why?'

'*Why?*' Malfoy sounded incredulously delighted. 'Because the only people who are permitted to retrieve a prophecy from the Department of Mysteries, Potter, are those about whom it was made, as the Dark Lord discovered when he attempted to use others to steal it for him.'

'And why did he want to steal a prophecy about me?'

'About both of you, Potter, about both of you ... haven't you ever wondered why the Dark Lord tried to kill you as a baby?'

Harry stared into the slitted eye-holes through which Malfoy's grey eyes were gleaming. Was this prophecy the reason Harry's parents had died, the reason he carried his lightning-bolt scar? Was the answer to all of this clutched in his hand?

'Someone made a prophecy about Voldemort and me?' he said quietly, gazing at Lucius Malfoy, his fingers tightening over the warm glass sphere in his hand. It was hardly larger than a Snitch and still gritty with dust. 'And he's made me come and get it for him? Why couldn't he come and get it himself?'

'Get it himself?' shrieked Bellatrix, over a cackle of mad laughter. 'The Dark Lord, walk into the Ministry of Magic, when they are so sweetly ignoring his return? The Dark Lord, reveal himself to the Aurors, when at the moment they are wasting their time on my dear cousin?'

'So, he's got you doing his dirty work for him, has he?' said Harry. 'Like he tried to get Sturgis to steal it – and Bode?'

'Very good, Potter, very good ...' said Malfoy slowly. 'But the Dark Lord knows you are not unintell–'

第35章 帷幔那边

赫敏说："把架子砸烂——"

"邓布利多从来没跟你说过吗？"马尔福又问了一遍，"是啊，怪不得你没有早一点儿过来，波特，黑魔王不明白为什么——"

"——等我说开始——"

"——他在你梦里显示了这东西所藏的地方之后，你没有马上跑过来。他以为，你出于本能的好奇心，会想听听它到底是怎么说的……"

"是吗？"哈利说。他听到，更准确地说是感觉到，身后的赫敏正在把他的话传给另外几个人。于是他想办法不停地说话，转移食死徒们的注意力："这么说，他希望我过来拿它，是吗？为什么呢？"

"为什么？"马尔福的声音听上去开心极了，"因为只有预言涉及的人，才可以从神秘事务司拿取预言球。波特，这是黑魔王想利用别人为他偷取预言球的时候发现的。"

"他为什么要偷一个关于我的预言呢？"

"是关于你们俩的，波特，关于你们俩……你难道从来没有想过，为什么黑魔王想要杀死襁褓中的你吗？"

哈利盯着那两道狭缝，马尔福一双灰眼睛从狭缝里射出光芒。莫非就是因为这个预言，哈利的父母才双双死去，他脑门上才留下了这道闪电形的伤疤？莫非他手里捏着所有这些问题的答案？

"有人做了一个关于我和伏地魔的预言？"他盯着卢修斯·马尔福轻声说，手指把热乎乎的玻璃球握得更紧了。它比金飞贼大不了多少，上面仍然布满灰尘，"所以他就把我弄来，替他拿预言球？他为什么不自己来拿呢？"

"自己来拿？"贝拉特里克斯在一片嘎嘎的狂笑声中尖声嚷道，"在大家刚好都忽视黑魔王已经回来的时候，黑魔王自己走进魔法部？在傲罗们都在我亲爱的堂弟身上浪费时间的时候，黑魔王自己暴露在他们面前？"

"所以，他就让你们替他完成这个卑鄙的勾当，是吗？"哈利说，"比如他想让斯多吉来偷——还有博德？"

"很好，波特，很好……"马尔福慢悠悠地说，"但是黑魔王知道你并不愚蠢——"

CHAPTER THIRTY-FIVE   Beyond the Veil

'NOW!' yelled Harry.

Five different voices behind him bellowed, '*REDUCTO!*' Five curses flew in five different directions and the shelves opposite them exploded as they hit; the towering structure swayed as a hundred glass spheres burst apart, pearly-white figures unfurled into the air and floated there, their voices echoing from who knew what long-dead past amid the torrent of crashing glass and splintered wood now raining down upon the floor –

'RUN!' Harry yelled, as the shelves swayed precariously and more glass spheres began to fall from above. He seized a handful of Hermione's robes and dragged her forwards, holding one arm over his head as chunks of shelf and shards of glass thundered down upon them. A Death Eater lunged forwards through the cloud of dust and Harry elbowed him hard in the masked face; they were all yelling, there were cries of pain, and thunderous crashes as the shelves collapsed upon themselves, weirdly echoing fragments of the Seers unleashed from their spheres –

Harry found the way ahead clear and saw Ron, Ginny and Luna sprint past him, their arms over their heads; something heavy struck him on the side of the face but he merely ducked his head and sprinted onwards; a hand caught him by the shoulder; he heard Hermione shout, '*Stupefy!*' The hand released him at once –

They were at the end of row ninety-seven; Harry turned right and began to sprint in earnest; he could hear footsteps right behind him and Hermione's voice urging Neville on; straight ahead, the door through which they had come was ajar; Harry could see the glittering light of the bell jar; he pelted through the doorway, the prophecy still clutched tight and safe in his hand, and waited for the others to hurtle over the threshold before slamming the door behind them –

'*Colloportus!*' gasped Hermione and the door sealed itself with an odd squelching noise.

'Where – where are the others?' gasped Harry.

He had thought Ron, Luna and Ginny were ahead of them, that they would be waiting in this room, but there was nobody there.

'They must have gone the wrong way!' whispered Hermione, terror in her face.

'Listen!' whispered Neville.

Footsteps and shouts echoed from behind the door they had just sealed;

第35章 帷幔那边

"**开始！**"哈利大喊一声。

他身后五个声音同时喊道："**粉身碎骨！**"五个咒语射向五个不同的方向，被咒语击中的架子纷纷爆炸。整个高耸的结构摇摇欲坠，上百个玻璃球被炸成碎片，浮现出一个个乳白色的身影，在空中飘来飘去，他们的声音在雨点般洒落的碎玻璃和碎木片中回荡，传出不知多么久远的往昔话语——

"**快跑！**"哈利大喊一声，那些架子危险地摇晃着，更多的玻璃球从上面跌落下来。哈利揪住赫敏的袍子，拖着她往前跑，另一只胳膊护住脑袋，遮挡如阵雨般坠落的碎木头和玻璃片。一个食死徒从尘雾中扑了过来，哈利用胳膊肘使劲撞向他戴着面具的脸。各种声音响成一片，有痛苦的惨叫声，有架子坍塌时震耳欲聋的轰隆声，还有从玻璃球里释放出来的那些先知们的只言片语，在空气中发出诡异的回音——

哈利发现前面没人，接着看见罗恩、金妮和卢娜从自己身边冲过，每个人都用胳膊护着脑袋。什么东西重重地砸在他的面颊上，但他只顾埋下头来往前冲。突然一只手抓住了他的肩膀，他听见赫敏大喊："昏昏倒地！"那只手立刻松开了——

他们来到第九十七排架子的尽头，哈利往右一转，开始全速飞奔。他听见身后传来脚步声，还有赫敏催促纳威快跑的声音。在他前方，他们刚才进来的那扇门开着一道缝。哈利能看见钟形玻璃罩闪烁的亮光。他用最快的速度跑出了那扇门，预言球仍然稳稳地攥在他手里。他等其他人冲过门槛，便重重地关上了门——

"**快快禁锢！**"赫敏气喘吁吁地说，随着一阵古怪的吱嘎声，门自动封死了。

"其他人——其他人在哪儿？"哈利喘着粗气问。

他以为罗恩、卢娜和金妮跑在他们前面，以为他们就在这个房间里等着，然而这里一个人也没有。

"他们肯定走错了路！"赫敏小声说，满脸惊恐。

"听！"纳威轻声道。

脚步声和叫喊声从他们刚刚封死的门后面传来。哈利把耳朵贴在

CHAPTER THIRTY-FIVE   Beyond the Veil

Harry put his ear close to the door to listen and heard Lucius Malfoy roar, 'Leave Nott, *leave him, I say* – his injuries will be nothing to the Dark Lord compared to losing that prophecy. Jugson, come back here, we need to organise! We'll split into pairs and search, and don't forget, be gentle with Potter until we've got the prophecy, you can kill the others if necessary – Bellatrix, Rodolphus, you take the left; Crabbe, Rabastan, go right – Jugson, Dolohov, the door straight ahead – Macnair and Avery, through here – Rookwood, over there – Mulciber, come with me!'

'What do we do?' Hermione asked Harry, trembling from head to foot.

'Well, we don't stand here waiting for them to find us, for a start,' said Harry. 'Let's get away from this door.'

They ran as quietly as they could, past the shimmering bell jar where the tiny egg was hatching and unhatching, towards the exit into the circular hallway at the far end of the room. They were almost there when Harry heard something large and heavy collide with the door Hermione had charmed shut.

'Stand aside!' said a rough voice. '*Alohomora!*'

As the door flew open, Harry, Hermione and Neville dived under desks. They could see the bottom of the two Death Eaters' robes drawing nearer, their feet moving rapidly.

'They might've run straight through to the hall,' said the rough voice.

'Check under the desks,' said another.

Harry saw the knees of the Death Eaters bend; poking his wand out from under the desk, he shouted, '*STUPEFY!*'

A jet of red light hit the nearest Death Eater; he fell backwards into a grandfather clock and knocked it over; the second Death Eater, however, had leapt aside to avoid Harry's spell and was pointing his own wand at Hermione, who was crawling out from under the desk to get a better aim.

'*Avada* –'

Harry launched himself across the floor and grabbed the Death Eater around the knees, causing him to topple and his aim to go awry. Neville overturned a desk in his anxiety to help; and pointing his wand wildly at the struggling pair, he cried:

'*EXPELLIARMUS!*'

Both Harry's and the Death Eater's wands flew out of their hands and soared

第35章 帷幔那边

门上,听见卢修斯·马尔福在吼叫,"别管诺特,别管他了,听见没有——跟丢掉预言球相比,他的伤在黑魔王眼里一钱不值。加格森,过来,我们需要组织一下!我们分成两人一组去搜查,别忘了,在拿到预言球之前对波特手下留情,如果需要的话可以把其他人干掉——贝拉特里克斯、罗道夫斯,你们负责左边;克拉布、拉巴斯坦,往右边去——加格森、多洛霍夫,去前面那扇门——麦克尼尔和埃弗里,从这里走——卢克伍德,去那儿——穆尔塞伯,跟我来!"

"我们怎么办?"赫敏问哈利,她从头到脚都在发抖。

"嗯,反正不能站在这里干等着他们找到我们。"哈利说,"首先,快离开这扇门。"

他们尽量蹑手蹑脚地往前跑,经过那个闪闪发亮的钟形玻璃罩(那个小小的蛋仍然在那里孵出鸟儿再变回去),奔向房间那头通往圆形门厅的出口。快要跑到的时候,哈利听见什么沉重的大家伙在撞击赫敏刚才用魔法封死的门。

"闪开!"一个粗暴的声音说,"阿拉霍洞开!"

门一下子开了,哈利、赫敏和纳威赶紧钻到桌子底下。他们看见两个食死徒的长袍下摆离他们越来越近,脚步挪动得很快。

"他们大概直接跑到门厅去了。"那个粗暴的声音说。

"看看桌子底下。"另一个声音说。

哈利看见两个食死徒的膝盖弯了下来,他把魔杖从桌子底下伸出去,大喊一声:"**昏昏倒地!**"

一道红光击中了离得最近的那个食死徒,他往后倒在一个落地式大摆钟上,把钟撞翻了。另一个食死徒往旁边一跳,躲过了哈利的咒语,用自己的魔杖指着赫敏。赫敏为了瞄准,正从桌子底下爬出来。

"阿瓦达——"

哈利贴地扑了过去,一把抱住那个食死徒的双膝,把他掀翻在地,咒语打偏了。纳威急忙过来帮忙,撞翻了一张桌子,慌慌张张地用魔杖指着那两个扭打在一起的人,喊了声:

"**除你武器!**"

哈利和那个食死徒的魔杖都脱手而出,飞回了预言厅的入口。两

CHAPTER THIRTY-FIVE   Beyond the Veil

back towards the entrance to the Hall of Prophecy; both scrambled to their feet and charged after them, the Death Eater in front, Harry hot on his heels, and Neville bringing up the rear, plainly horrorstruck by what he had done.

'Get out of the way, Harry!' yelled Neville, clearly determined to repair the damage.

Harry flung himself sideways as Neville took aim again and shouted:

'*STUPEFY!*'

The jet of red light flew right over the Death Eater's shoulder and hit a glass-fronted cabinet on the wall full of variously shaped hourglasses; the cabinet fell to the floor and burst apart, glass flying everywhere, sprang back up on to the wall, fully mended, then fell down again, and shattered –

The Death Eater had snatched up his wand, which lay on the floor beside the glittering bell jar. Harry ducked down behind another desk as the man turned; his mask had slipped so that he couldn't see. He ripped it off with his free hand and shouted: 'STUP–'

'*STUPEFY!*' screamed Hermione, who had just caught up with them. The jet of red light hit the Death Eater in the middle of his chest: he froze, his arm still raised, his wand fell to the floor with a clatter and he collapsed backwards towards the bell jar. Harry expected to hear a *clunk*, for the man to hit solid glass and slide off the jar on to the floor, but instead, his head sank through the surface of the bell jar as though it were nothing but a soap bubble and he came to rest, sprawled on his back on the table, with his head lying inside the jar full of glittering wind.

'*Accio wand!*' cried Hermione. Harry's wand flew from a dark corner into her hand and she threw it to him.

'Thanks,' he said. 'Right, let's get out of –'

'Look out!' said Neville, horrified. He was staring at the Death Eater's head in the bell jar.

All three of them raised their wands again, but none of them struck: they were all gazing, open-mouthed, appalled, at what was happening to the man's head.

It was shrinking very fast, growing balder and balder, the black hair and stubble retracting into his skull; his cheeks becoming smooth, his skull round and covered with a peachlike fuzz ...

A baby's head now sat grotesquely on top of the thick, muscled neck of

第35章 帷幔那边

人都挣扎着站起来去追魔杖,食死徒在前,哈利紧随其后,跑在最后的是纳威,他似乎被自己做的事情吓呆了。

"快闪开,哈利!"纳威嚷道,显然想要将功补过。

哈利赶紧闪到一旁,纳威再次瞄准,喊道:

"**昏昏倒地!**"

红光擦着食死徒的肩膀掠过,击中了墙上的一个玻璃门吊柜,那里面摆着各种各样的沙漏。柜子掉在地上,裂开了,玻璃迸溅得到处都是,随即柜子又弹回到墙上,变得完好如初,然后又落下来,摔成碎片——

那个食死徒的魔杖掉在闪闪发亮的钟形玻璃罩旁的地板上,他一把抓了起来。在他转身时,哈利一猫腰躲到了另一张桌子后面。食死徒的面具滑了下来,什么也看不见了。他用另一只手扯掉面具,大喊:

"**昏昏——**"

"**昏昏倒地!**"正好赶来的赫敏大声嚷道。红光击中了食死徒的胸膛中央,他顿时僵住,胳膊仍然举着,魔杖啪嗒一声掉到地上,随后他仰面倒向了钟形玻璃罩。哈利以为会听见咣的一声,因为那人是撞向厚实的玻璃,再顺着玻璃罩滑到地上,然而他的脑袋却穿过玻璃罩表面陷了进去,就好像那只是一个肥皂泡似的,然后他不动了,四肢摊开仰面倒在桌上,脑袋扎进充满闪光气流的玻璃罩里。

"魔杖飞来!"赫敏喊道。哈利的魔杖从一个黑暗的角落飞到她手里,她把它扔给了哈利。

"谢谢,"哈利说,"好吧,我们离开——"

"快看!"纳威惊恐万状地说。他盯着食死徒陷在玻璃罩里的脑袋。

三个人又都把魔杖举起来,但谁也没有出击。他们都张着嘴巴,十分惊骇地盯着那人脑袋的变化。

那颗脑袋在迅速地缩小,而且越来越秃,黑色的头发和胡子楂儿缩进了脑袋里。他的面颊变得光滑起来,脑壳变得圆溜溜的,像桃子一般覆盖着一层茸毛……

此刻,在这个挣扎着想站起来的食死徒肌肉发达的粗脖子上,怪

CHAPTER THIRTY-FIVE   Beyond the Veil

the Death Eater as he struggled to get up again; but even as they watched, their mouths open, the head began to swell to its previous proportions again; thick black hair was sprouting from the pate and chin ...

'It's Time,' said Hermione in an awestruck voice. '*Time* ...'

The Death Eater shook his ugly head again, trying to clear it, but before he could pull himself together it began to shrink back to babyhood once more ...

There was a shout from a room nearby, then a crash and a scream.

'RON?' Harry yelled, turning quickly from the monstrous transformation taking place before them. 'GINNY? LUNA?'

'Harry!' Hermione screamed.

The Death Eater had pulled his head out of the bell jar. His appearance was utterly bizarre, his tiny baby's head bawling loudly while his thick arms flailed dangerously in all directions, narrowly missing Harry, who had ducked. Harry raised his wand but to his amazement Hermione seized his arm.

'You can't hurt a baby!'

There was no time to argue the point; Harry could hear more footsteps growing louder from the Hall of Prophecy and knew, too late, that he ought not to have shouted and given away their position.

'Come on!' he said, and leaving the ugly baby-headed Death Eater staggering behind them they took off for the door that stood open at the other end of the room, leading back into the black hallway.

They had run halfway towards it when Harry saw through the open door two more Death Eaters running across the black room towards them; veering left, he burst instead into a small, dark, cluttered office and slammed the door behind them.

'*Collo*–' began Hermione, but before she could complete the spell the door had burst open and the two Death Eaters had come hurtling inside.

With a cry of triumph, both yelled:

'*IMPEDIMENTA!*'

Harry, Hermione and Neville were all knocked backwards off their feet; Neville was thrown over the desk and disappeared from view; Hermione smashed into a bookcase and was promptly deluged in a cascade of heavy books; the back of Harry's head slammed into the stone wall behind him, tiny lights burst in front of his eyes and for a moment he was too dizzy and bewildered to react.

第35章 帷幔那边

异地顶着一颗婴儿的脑袋。而就在他们目瞪口呆的注视下,那颗脑袋又开始膨胀成原来的大小,浓密的黑色毛发又从头皮和下巴上冒了出来……

"是时间,"赫敏用敬畏的声音说,"时间……"

食死徒又晃了晃他丑陋的脑袋,想让自己清醒一些,可是没等他重新振作起来,那颗脑袋又开始缩回到婴儿时代……

附近一个房间里传来喊叫,接着是碎裂声和尖叫声。

"**罗恩?**"哈利嚷道,迅速转过身,离开眼前那令人毛骨悚然的变形过程,"**金妮?卢娜?**"

"哈利!"赫敏尖叫一声。

那个食死徒把脑袋从玻璃罩里拔了出来。他的模样古怪之极,一颗婴儿的小脑袋在声嘶力竭地大叫,而两条粗胳膊却在危险地四下拍打,差点儿打到了哈利,但哈利一弯腰躲过去了。哈利举起魔杖,可是赫敏一把抓住了他的胳膊。他吃了一惊。

"你不能伤害一个婴儿!"

没时间争论了。哈利听见预言厅那边的脚步声越来越响,他意识到刚才不应该叫喊,暴露他们的位置,但是后悔也来不及了。

"快!"他说,然后他们拔腿奔向房间那头那扇开着的通向黑色大厅的门,长着丑陋的婴儿脑袋的食死徒跟跟跄跄地跟在后面。

跑到半路,哈利看见开着的门里又有两个食死徒穿过黑色房间朝他们跑来。他们赶紧往左一拐,冲进一个黑黢黢的、拥挤杂乱的小办公室,回身砰地关上了门。

"快快——"赫敏的咒语没有念完,门就被撞开了,两个食死徒冲了进来。

这两个人得意地大喊一声,叫道:

"**障碍重重!**"

哈利、赫敏和纳威都被撞得向后飞去。纳威从桌子上滑过,消失了踪影。赫敏撞在一个书架上,顿时就被纷纷掉落的大部头书掩埋了。哈利的后脑勺撞在后面的石墙上,眼前直冒金星,一时间头晕眼花,不知所措。

CHAPTER THIRTY-FIVE   Beyond the Veil

'WE'VE GOT HIM!' yelled the Death Eater nearest Harry. 'IN AN OFFICE OFF—'

'*Silencio!*' cried Hermione and the man's voice was extinguished. He continued to mouth through the hole in his mask, but no sound came out. He was thrust aside by his fellow Death Eater.

'*Petrificus Totalus!*' shouted Harry, as the second Death Eater raised his wand. His arms and legs snapped together and he fell forwards, face down on to the rug at Harry's feet, stiff as a board and unable to move.

'Well done, Ha—'

But the Death Eater Hermione had just struck dumb made a sudden slashing movement with his wand; a streak of what looked like purple flame passed right across Hermione's chest. She gave a tiny 'Oh!' as though of surprise and crumpled on to the floor, where she lay motionless.

'HERMIONE!'

Harry fell to his knees beside her as Neville crawled rapidly towards her from under the desk, his wand held up in front of him. The Death Eater kicked out hard at Neville's head as he emerged – his foot broke Neville's wand in two and connected with his face. Neville gave a howl of pain and recoiled, clutching his mouth and nose. Harry twisted around, his own wand held high, and saw that the Death Eater had ripped off his mask and was pointing his wand directly at Harry, who recognised the long, pale, twisted face from the *Daily Prophet*: Antonin Dolohov, the wizard who had murdered the Prewetts.

Dolohov grinned. With his free hand, he pointed from the prophecy still clutched in Harry's hand, to himself, then at Hermione. Though he could no longer speak, his meaning could not have been clearer. Give me the prophecy, or you get the same as her …

'Like you won't kill us all anyway, the moment I hand it over!' said Harry.

A whine of panic inside his head was preventing him thinking properly: he had one hand on Hermione's shoulder, which was still warm, yet did not dare look at her properly. *Don't let her be dead, don't let her be dead, it's my fault if she's dead …*

'Whaddever you do, Harry,' said Neville fiercely from under the desk, lowering his hands to show a clearly broken nose and blood pouring down his mouth and chin, 'don'd gib it to him!'

第35章 帷幔那边

"我们抓住他了!"离哈利最近的那个食死徒喊道,"在一间办公室里,就在——"

"无声无息!"赫敏喊道,那人的声音立刻就哑了。他的嘴巴继续在面具上的窟窿里一张一合,却发不出一点声音。他被另一个食死徒推搡到了一边。

"统统石化!"哈利见到第二个食死徒举起魔杖,赶紧大喊一声。食死徒的腿和胳膊啪地合在一起,身子向前扑倒,脸朝下摔在哈利脚边的地毯上,像木板一样僵硬,动弹不得。

"干得好,哈——"

可是,刚才被赫敏击哑的那个食死徒突然挥舞着魔杖左右劈砍起来,赫敏的胸口像是掠过一道紫色的火焰。她似乎有些吃惊地轻唤了一声"哦",便瘫倒在地,一动不动了。

"赫敏!"

哈利扑通跪倒在她身边,举着魔杖的纳威迅速从桌子底下朝她爬来。纳威刚钻出桌子,食死徒就朝他的脑袋狠狠地踢了一脚——把纳威的魔杖踢成了两截,又踢中了他的脸。纳威痛得惨叫一声,蜷缩起来,用手捂住了嘴和鼻子。哈利扭过身,高举起魔杖,看见食死徒扯掉了面具,正用魔杖直指着自己。哈利认出了这张曾在《预言家日报》上出现过的苍白、扭曲的长脸:安东宁·多洛霍夫,就是他杀害了普威特兄弟俩。

多洛霍夫露出了狞笑。他用那只没拿魔杖的手指指哈利手里仍然紧攥着的预言球,指指自己,又指指赫敏。尽管他再也说不出话来,但他的意思再明显不过了:把预言球给我,否则你的下场跟她一样……

"其实只要我把它一交出去,你就会把我们全干掉!"哈利说。

哈利的脑子紧张得嗡嗡直叫,使他无法好好思索。他一只手搭在赫敏的肩膀上,肩膀还是热的,但是他不敢仔细看她。千万不能让她死,千万不能让她死,如果她死了,都是我的错……

"不管你怎么做,哈利,"纳威在桌子底下激动地说,他垂下双手,露出了明显被打断的鼻子,鲜血顺着嘴巴和下巴哗哗地往下流,"都别把东西给他!"

CHAPTER THIRTY-FIVE   Beyond the Veil

Then there was a crash outside the door and Dolohov looked over his shoulder – the baby-headed Death Eater had appeared in the doorway, his head bawling, his great fists still flailing uncontrollably at everything around him. Harry seized his chance:

'*PETRIFICUS TOTALUS!*'

The spell hit Dolohov before he could block it and he toppled forwards across his comrade, both of them rigid as boards and unable to move an inch.

'Hermione,' Harry said at once, shaking her as the baby-headed Death Eater blundered out of sight again. 'Hermione, wake up ...'

'Whaddid he do to her?' said Neville, crawling out from under the desk to kneel at her other side, blood streaming from his rapidly swelling nose.

'I dunno ...'

Neville groped for Hermione's wrist.

'Dat's a pulse, Harry, I'b sure id is.'

Such a powerful wave of relief swept through Harry that for a moment he felt light-headed.

'She's alive?'

'Yeah, I dink so.'

There was a pause in which Harry listened hard for the sound of more footsteps, but all he could hear were the whimpers and blunderings of the baby-headed Death Eater in the next room.

'Neville, we're not far from the exit,' Harry whispered, 'we're right next to that circular room ... if we can just get you across it and find the right door before any more Death Eaters come, I'll bet you can get Hermione up the corridor and into the lift ... then you could find someone ... raise the alarm ...'

'And whad are you going do do?' said Neville, mopping his bleeding nose with his sleeve and frowning at Harry.

'I've got to find the others,' said Harry.

'Well, I'b going do find dem wid you,' said Neville firmly.

'But Hermione –'

'We'll dake her wid us,' said Neville firmly. 'I'll carry her – you're bedder at fighding dem dan I ab –'

1316

第35章 帷幔那边

门外传来哗啦一声,多洛霍夫扭头看去——那个长着婴儿脑袋的食死徒出现在门口,他的脑袋在声嘶力竭地大叫,两只大拳头仍在不受控制地击打着周围的一切。哈利抓住这个机会:

"统统石化!"

多洛霍夫没来得及抵挡,咒语击中了他。他向前摔倒在同伴身上,两人都变得像木板一样僵硬,再也动弹不得了。

"赫敏,"哈利看到那个长着婴儿脑袋的食死徒又跌跌撞撞地走远了,便立刻摇晃着赫敏叫道,"赫敏,醒醒……"

"他对她做了什么?"纳威说着从桌子底下钻出来,跪在赫敏的另一边,迅速肿胀的鼻子还在一个劲儿地往外流血。

"不知道……"

纳威摸索着赫敏的手腕。

"还有脉搏,哈利,肯定还有脉搏。"

一阵强烈的如释重负的感觉袭上哈利心头,使他一时间感到有点眩晕。

"她还活着?"

"对,我认为还活着。"

一阵静默,哈利仔细倾听有没有更多的脚步声,但只能听见那个长着婴儿脑袋的食死徒在隔壁房间里横冲直撞,呜呜咽咽。

"纳威,我们离出口不远了,"哈利轻声说,"我们就在那个圆形房间隔壁……只要你能在别的食死徒赶来之前走过去,找到那扇门,我相信你肯定能把赫敏弄到走廊里,进入升降梯……然后你就会找到人……拉响警报……"

"那你打算怎么办?"纳威说,他用袖子擦擦流血的鼻子,皱着眉头看着哈利。

"我要去把其他人找到。"哈利说。

"那好,我跟你一起去找他们。"纳威坚决地说。

"可是赫敏——"

"我们带着她,"纳威坚定地说,"我来背她——你对付他们比我厉害——"

1317

CHAPTER THIRTY-FIVE   Beyond the Veil

He stood up and seized one of Hermione's arms, glaring at Harry, who hesitated, then grabbed the other and helped hoist Hermione's limp form over Neville's shoulders.

'Wait,' said Harry, snatching up Hermione's wand from the floor and shoving it into Neville's hand, 'you'd better take this.'

Neville kicked aside the broken fragments of his own wand as they walked slowly towards the door.

'My gran's going do kill be,' said Neville thickly, blood spattering from his nose as he spoke, 'dat was by dad's old wand.'

Harry stuck his head out of the door and looked around cautiously. The baby-headed Death Eater was screaming and banging into things, toppling grandfather clocks and overturning desks, bawling and confused, while the glass-fronted cabinet that Harry now suspected had contained Time-Turners continued to fall, shatter and repair itself on the wall behind them.

'He's never going to notice us,' he whispered. 'C'mon ... keep close behind me ...'

They crept out of the office and back towards the door into the black hallway, which now seemed completely deserted. They walked a few steps forwards, Neville tottering slightly due to Hermione's weight; the door of the Time Room swung shut behind them and the walls began to rotate once more. The recent blow on the back of Harry's head seemed to have unsteadied him; he narrowed his eyes, swaying slightly, until the walls stopped moving again. With a sinking heart, Harry saw that Hermione's fiery crosses had faded from the doors.

'So which way d'you reck–?'

But before they could make a decision as to which way to try, a door to their right sprang open and three people fell out of it.

'Ron!' croaked Harry, dashing towards them. 'Ginny – are you all –?'

'Harry,' said Ron, giggling weakly, lurching forwards, seizing the front of Harry's robes and gazing at him with unfocused eyes, 'there you are ... ha ha ha ... you look funny, Harry ... you're all messed up ...'

Ron's face was very white and something dark was trickling from the corner of his mouth. Next moment his knees had given way, but he still clutched the front of Harry's robes, so that Harry was pulled into a kind of bow.

第35章 帷幔那边

纳威站起来,抓住赫敏的一只胳膊,盯着迟疑不决的哈利,于是哈利抓起赫敏的另一只胳膊,帮着把她毫无生气的身体背上纳威的肩头。

"等等,"哈利说,他从地上抓起赫敏的魔杖,塞进纳威手里,"你最好拿上。"

他们慢慢地朝门口走去,纳威一脚踢开自己那根断裂的魔杖。

"我奶奶准会要了我的命,"纳威瓮声瓮气地说,说话时鲜血从鼻子里喷溅出来,"这是我爸爸的旧魔杖。"

哈利把脑袋探出门外,小心翼翼地四下张望。那个婴儿脑袋的食死徒尖叫着横冲直撞,撞翻了落地式大摆钟,撞翻了桌子。他声嘶力竭地大叫,困惑得摸不着头脑,那个玻璃门的吊柜——现在哈利怀疑里面装着时间转换器——仍然从他们身后的墙上掉落、摔成碎片,又自动修复。

"他不会注意到我们的,"他小声说,"快……紧紧跟着我……"

他们轻手轻脚地溜出办公室,朝通向黑色大厅的门走去,大厅里现在似乎空无一人。他们走了几步,纳威被赫敏的重量压得微微摇晃起来。时间屋的门在他们身后关上了,墙壁又开始旋转。哈利后脑勺上刚才遭了那一下撞击,到现在似乎都站立不稳。他眯起眼睛,身体微微地左右摇晃,直到墙壁停止了转动。哈利看到赫敏在门上刻的那些燃烧的X已经消失,心不由得往下一沉。

"你认为该往哪边——?"

没等他们决定往哪边尝试,右边的一扇门突然打开,跌出三个人来。

"罗恩!"哈利声音嘶哑地说,朝他们冲了过去,"金妮——你们都——?"

"哈利,"罗恩说,声音发虚地咯咯笑着,扑上前来,一把抓住哈利的袍子前襟,用聚不成焦的眼睛盯着他,"是你啊……哈哈哈……你看上去好滑稽,哈利……你整个儿乱糟糟的……"

罗恩的脸色十分苍白,某种黑乎乎的东西从嘴角流了出来。接着,他双膝一软瘫倒了,但仍然揪着哈利的前襟不放,哈利被他拉得像在鞠躬一样。

CHAPTER THIRTY-FIVE Beyond the Veil

'Ginny?' Harry said fearfully. 'What happened?'

But Ginny shook her head and slid down the wall into a sitting position, panting and holding her ankle.

'I think her ankle's broken, I heard something crack,' whispered Luna, who was bending over her and who alone seemed to be unhurt. 'Four of them chased us into a dark room full of planets; it was a very odd place, some of the time we were just floating in the dark –'

'Harry, we saw Uranus up close!' said Ron, still giggling feebly. 'Get it, Harry? We saw Uranus – ha ha ha –'

A bubble of blood grew at the corner of Ron's mouth and burst.

'– anyway, one of them grabbed Ginny's foot, I used the Reductor Curse and blew up Pluto in his face, but ...'

Luna gestured hopelessly at Ginny, who was breathing in a very shallow way, her eyes still closed.

'And what about Ron?' said Harry fearfully, as Ron continued to giggle, still hanging off the front of Harry's robes.

'I don't know what they hit him with,' said Luna sadly, 'but he's gone a bit funny, I could hardly get him along at all.'

'Harry,' said Ron, pulling Harry's ear down to his mouth and still giggling weakly, 'you know who this girl is, Harry? She's Loony ... Loony Lovegood ... ha ha ha ...'

'We've got to get out of here,' said Harry firmly. 'Luna, can you help Ginny?'

'Yes,' said Luna, sticking her wand behind her ear for safekeeping, then putting an arm around Ginny's waist and pulling her up.

'It's only my ankle, I can do it myself!' said Ginny impatiently, but next moment she had collapsed sideways and grabbed Luna for support. Harry pulled Ron's arm over his shoulder just as, so many months ago, he had pulled Dudley's. He looked around: they had a one in twelve chance of getting the exit right first time –

He heaved Ron towards a door; they were within a few feet of it when another door across the hall burst open and three Death Eaters sped in, led by Bellatrix Lestrange.

'*There they are!*' she shrieked.

第35章 帷幔那边

"金妮?"哈利恐惧地说,"出了什么事?"

可是金妮摇摇头,贴着墙出溜下去,坐在了地上,气喘吁吁地捏着自己的脚脖子。

"我认为她的脚脖子断了,我听见咔嚓一声。"卢娜俯身看着金妮轻声说,似乎只有她一个人毫发未伤,"他们四个人把我们赶进了一间满是行星的黑屋子。那地方特别古怪,有时候我们就在黑暗中飘着——"

"哈利,我们近距离看到了天王星!"罗恩说,仍然声音发虚地咯咯笑着,"明白吗,哈利?我们看到了天王星——哈哈哈——"

罗恩的嘴角鼓起一个血泡,然后破裂了。

"——反正,有个人抓住了金妮的脚,我用了粉碎咒,让冥王星在那人脸上爆炸了,可是……"

卢娜无奈地指了指金妮,金妮仍然闭着双眼,呼吸很虚弱。

"罗恩是怎么回事?"哈利害怕地问。罗恩还是咯咯笑个不停,揪着哈利的前襟不放。

"我也不知道他们用什么击中了他,"卢娜难过地说,"他变得有点不正常了,我差点儿没法把他带过来。"

"哈利,"罗恩拽着哈利,让哈利的耳朵贴近他的嘴,仍然声音发虚地咯咯笑着说,"你知道这个女孩是谁吗,哈利?她是疯姑娘……疯姑娘洛夫古德……哈哈哈……"

"我们必须离开这儿。"哈利坚决地说,"卢娜,你能扶着金妮吗?"

"没问题。"卢娜说,她把魔杖在耳朵后面插好,用一只胳膊搂住金妮的腰,拽她起来。

"只是脚脖子的问题,我自己能行!"金妮不耐烦地说,可她随即就往一边倒去,赶紧抓住卢娜稳住身子。哈利把罗恩的胳膊搭在自己肩膀上,就像好几个月前扶着达力那样。他看看四周,他们一下子找到正确出口的概率只有十二分之一——

他扶着罗恩朝一扇门走去,离门还差几步的时候,大门对面的另一扇门猛地打开了,三个食死徒冲了进来,领头的是贝拉特里克斯·莱斯特兰奇。

"他们在这儿!"她尖叫道。

CHAPTER THIRTY-FIVE   Beyond the Veil

Stunning Spells shot across the room: Harry smashed his way through the door ahead, flung Ron unceremoniously from him and ducked back to help Neville in with Hermione: they were all over the threshold just in time to slam the door against Bellatrix.

'*Colloportus!*' shouted Harry, and he heard three bodies slam into the door on the other side.

'It doesn't matter!' said a man's voice. 'There are other ways in – WE'VE GOT THEM, THEY'RE HERE!'

Harry spun round; they were back in the Brain Room and, sure enough, there were doors all around the walls. He could hear footsteps in the hall behind them as more Death Eaters came running to join the first.

'Luna – Neville – help me!'

The three of them tore around the room, sealing the doors as they went; Harry crashed into a table and rolled over the top of it in his haste to reach the next door:

'*Colloportus!*'

There were footsteps running along behind the doors, every now and then another heavy body would launch itself against one, so it creaked and shuddered; Luna and Neville were bewitching the doors along the opposite wall – then, as Harry reached the very top of the room, he heard Luna cry:

'*Collo*– aaaaaaaaargh ...'

He turned in time to see her flying through the air; five Death Eaters were surging into the room through the door she had not reached in time; Luna hit a desk, slid over its surface and on to the floor on the other side where she lay sprawled, as still as Hermione.

'Get Potter!' shrieked Bellatrix, and she ran at him; he dodged her and sprinted back up the room; he was safe as long as they thought they might hit the prophecy –

'Hey!' said Ron, who had staggered to his feet and was now tottering drunkenly towards Harry, giggling. 'Hey, Harry, there are *brains* in here, ha ha ha, isn't that weird, Harry?'

'Ron, get out of the way, get down –'

But Ron had already pointed his wand at the tank.

'Honest, Harry, they're brains – look – *Accio brain!*'

The scene seemed momentarily frozen. Harry, Ginny and Neville and

第35章 帷幔那边

昏迷咒在房间里嗖嗖地穿梭。哈利一路冲撞着穿过那扇门,匆匆把罗恩从自己身上甩掉,又弯腰跑回来帮纳威把赫敏弄进去。他们及时跨过门槛,正好在贝拉特里克斯赶来时把门关上了。

"快快禁锢!"哈利大喊,接着听见三具身体重重地撞在门的另一边。

"没关系!"一个男人的声音说,"还有别的路可以进去——**我们找到他们了,他们跑不了啦!**"

哈利迅速转过身,他们又回到了大脑屋。没错,周围的墙上有好几扇门。他听见身后的大厅里传来脚步声,更多的食死徒跑来跟先前那几个人会合了。

"卢娜——纳威——帮帮我!"

三个人绕着屋子飞跑,把一扇扇门全部封死了。哈利撞在一张桌子上,匆忙间就势滚过桌面,赶向另一扇门。

"快快禁锢!"

门后传来飞奔的脚步声,不时有沉重的身体在冲撞某一扇门,门颤抖着,发出吱吱嘎嘎的声音。卢娜和纳威顺着对面的墙给门施魔法——然后,就在哈利快要跑到屋子另一端时,他听见了卢娜的叫声:

"快快——啊……"

哈利赶紧转身,看见卢娜腾空飞了起来,五个食死徒从她刚才没来得及封死的那扇门一拥而入。卢娜摔在一张桌子上,滑过桌面,落在另一边的地上,四仰八叉地躺在那里,像赫敏那样一动不动了。

"抓住波特!"贝拉特里克斯尖叫着朝哈利跑来。哈利躲过她,返身在屋子里飞跑,只要他们顾忌着不敢砸坏预言球,他就没有危险——

"喂!"罗恩说,他已经跟跟跄跄地站了起来,正像醉汉一样摇摇摆摆地朝哈利走来,嘴里仍然咯咯笑着,"喂,哈利,这里有大脑呢,哈哈哈,是不是很古怪,哈利?"

"罗恩,闪开,趴下——"

可是罗恩已经用魔杖指着那个水箱。

"真的,哈利,真的是大脑——你看——大脑飞来!"

场面似乎在瞬间凝固了。哈利、金妮和纳威,还有每个食死徒都

1323

CHAPTER THIRTY-FIVE Beyond the Veil

each of the Death Eaters turned in spite of themselves to watch the top of the tank as a brain burst from the green liquid like a leaping fish: for a moment it seemed suspended in midair, then it soared towards Ron, spinning as it came, and what looked like ribbons of moving images flew from it, unravelling like rolls of film –

'Ha ha ha, Harry, look at it –' said Ron, watching it disgorge its gaudy innards, 'Harry, come and touch it; bet it's weird –'

'RON, NO!'

Harry did not know what would happen if Ron touched the tentacles of thought now flying behind the brain, but he was sure it would not be anything good. He darted forwards but Ron had already caught the brain in his outstretched hands.

The moment they made contact with his skin, the tentacles began wrapping themselves around Ron's arms like ropes.

'Harry, look what's happen– No – no – I don't like it – no, stop – *stop* –'

But the thin ribbons were spinning around Ron's chest now; he tugged and tore at them as the brain was pulled tight against him like an octopus's body.

'*Diffindo!*' yelled Harry, trying to sever the feelers wrapping themselves tightly around Ron before his eyes, but they would not break. Ron fell over, still thrashing against his bonds.

'Harry, it'll suffocate him!' screamed Ginny, immobilised by her broken ankle on the floor – then a jet of red light flew from one of the Death Eater's wands and hit her squarely in the face. She keeled over sideways and lay there unconscious.

'*STUBEFY!*' shouted Neville, wheeling around and waving Hermione's wand at the oncoming Death Eaters, '*STUBEFY, STUBEFY!*'

But nothing happened.

One of the Death Eaters shot their own Stunning Spell at Neville; it missed him by inches. Harry and Neville were now the only two left fighting the five Death Eaters, two of whom sent off streams of silver light like arrows which missed but left craters in the wall behind them. Harry ran for it as Bellatrix Lestrange raced right at him: holding the prophecy high above his head, he sprinted back up the room; all he could think of doing was to draw the Death Eaters away from the others.

第 35 章　帷幔那边

不由自主地转过身，注视着水箱顶部，只见一个大脑像条鱼一样，从绿色的液体中跳了出来。它似乎在空中悬了一会儿，然后一路旋转着朝罗恩飞去，如同由活动图像构成的丝带，从大脑里蹿出来，像一卷卷胶片似的散开了——

"哈哈哈，哈利，你看啊——"罗恩说，一边注视着大脑吐出的那些五颜六色的脑浆，"哈利，过来摸一摸，肯定特别古怪——"

"**罗恩，不要！**"

哈利不知道罗恩碰到那些飘散在大脑后面的思想触须会怎么样，但知道肯定不会有什么好结果。他冲上前去，可是罗恩已经伸出双手抓住了大脑。

那些触须一碰到罗恩的皮肤，就开始像绳索一样缠住他的胳膊。

"哈利，快看怎么回事——不——不——我不喜欢——不，停下——停下——"

那些细细的丝带已在缠绕罗恩的胸脯了。他使劲地又扯又拽，可大脑像章鱼的身体一样用触须把他勒紧了。

"四分五裂！"哈利大喊一声，想斩断那些在他眼前把罗恩紧紧缠住的触须，可是触须没有断。罗恩跌倒在地，仍然不断地扭动着身体想摆脱束缚。

"哈利，他会被勒死的！"金妮喊道，受伤的脚脖子使她在地上动弹不得——这时一道红光从一个食死徒的魔杖射出，不偏不倚地击中了金妮的脸。她往旁边一倒，躺在那里不省人事了。

"**昏昏倒地！**"纳威喊道，迅速转身，朝那些逼近的食死徒挥舞着赫敏的魔杖，"**昏昏倒地！昏昏倒地！**"

可是没有任何反应。

一个食死徒朝纳威射来昏迷咒，但射偏了几英寸，没有击中。现在，只剩下哈利和纳威两个人对付五个食死徒了，其中两个食死徒射出利箭般的道道银光，但都没有击中目标，只在他们身后的墙上留下了凹坑。贝拉特里克斯直朝哈利冲来，哈利赶紧躲避。他把预言球举过头顶，返身在房间里奔跑，一心只想把食死徒从朋友们身边引开。

CHAPTER THIRTY-FIVE   Beyond the Veil

It seemed to have worked; they streaked after him, knocking chairs and tables flying but not daring to bewitch him in case they hurt the prophecy, and he dashed through the only door still open, the one through which the Death Eaters themselves had come; inwardly praying that Neville would stay with Ron and find some way of releasing him. He ran a few feet into the new room and felt the floor vanish –

He was falling down steep stone step after steep stone step, bouncing on every tier until at last, with a crash that knocked all the breath out of his body, he landed flat on his back in the sunken pit where the stone archway stood on its dais. The whole room was ringing with the Death Eaters' laughter: he looked up and saw the five who had been in the Brain Room descending towards him, while as many more emerged through other doorways and began leaping from bench to bench towards him. Harry got to his feet though his legs were trembling so badly they barely supported him: the prophecy was still miraculously unbroken in his left hand, his wand clutched tightly in his right. He backed away, looking around, trying to keep all the Death Eaters within his sight. The back of his legs hit something solid: he had reached the dais where the archway stood. He climbed backwards onto it.

The Death Eaters all halted, gazing at him. Some were panting as hard as he was. One was bleeding badly; Dolohov, freed of the Body-Bind Curse, was leering, his wand pointing straight at Harry's face.

'Potter, your race is run,' drawled Lucius Malfoy, pulling off his mask, 'now hand me the prophecy like a good boy.'

'Let – let the others go, and I'll give it to you!' said Harry desperately.

A few of the Death Eaters laughed.

'You are not in a position to bargain, Potter,' said Lucius Malfoy, his pale face flushed with pleasure. 'You see, there are ten of us and only one of you … or hasn't Dumbledore ever taught you how to count?'

'He's dot alone!' shouted a voice from above them. 'He's still god be!'

Harry's heart sank: Neville was scrambling down the stone benches towards them, Hermione's wand held fast in his trembling hand.

'Neville – no – go back to Ron –'

'*STUBEFY!*' Neville shouted again, pointing his wand at each Death Eater

第35章　帷幔那边

看来这招奏效了。食死徒们纷纷追了过来，撞得桌子椅子四下乱飞，却不敢给哈利施魔法，生怕会把预言球弄坏。哈利冲出了唯一开着的那扇门，也就是食死徒冲进来的那扇。他暗自祈祷纳威能陪在罗恩身边，想办法使他挣脱束缚。他在这间他们没有进来过的屋子里刚跑了几步，就感到地板消失了——

他顺着一级又一级陡峭的石头台阶滚落下去，砰砰地撞在每一级台阶上。"砰！"最后的那一下猛烈撞击，几乎把他肺里的空气都挤了出去。他仰面平躺在那个深坑里，深坑的高台上就矗立着那道石头拱门。食死徒的笑声在整个房间里回荡。哈利往上一看，发现刚才在大脑屋里的五个食死徒正朝他奔下来，还有更多的食死徒从别的门里拥出，跳过一级级石阶朝他逼近。虽然双腿抖得厉害，几乎支撑不住身体，哈利还是勉强站了起来。预言球仍然奇迹般地握在他的左手里，完好无损；他的右手紧紧攥着魔杖。他一步步后退，同时环顾四周，让所有的食死徒都处在自己的视线中。突然，他的大腿后部撞在某个坚实的东西上，他碰到了那个矗立着拱门的高台。他后退着爬了上去。

食死徒们都停住了脚步，盯着他。有几个像他一样气喘吁吁，还有一个血流不止。摆脱了全身束缚咒的多洛霍夫，正斜眼瞥着哈利，用魔杖直指他的面门。

"波特，你完蛋了，"卢修斯·马尔福扯掉面具，拖着长腔说道，"乖乖地把预言球交给我吧。"

"让——让其他人离开，我就把它给你！"哈利孤注一掷地说。

几个食死徒笑了起来。

"你根本没资格讨价还价，波特。"卢修斯·马尔福说，惨白的脸因高兴而泛出红晕，"看到没有，我们十个人，你只有一个人……怎么，难道邓布利多没有教会你怎么数数吗？"

"他不是一个人！"上面一个声音喊道，"还有我呢！"

哈利的心往下一沉。纳威跌跌撞撞地跨过一级级石阶朝他跑来，颤抖的手里紧紧抓着赫敏的魔杖。

"纳威——不要——回到罗恩身边去——"

"**昏昏落地！**"纳威又大喊一声，用魔杖挨个儿指着每个食死徒，"**昏**

CHAPTER THIRTY-FIVE   Beyond the Veil

in turn. '*STUBEFY! STUBE–*'

One of the largest Death Eaters seized Neville from behind, pinioning his arms to his sides. He struggled and kicked; several of the Death Eaters laughed.

'It's Longbottom, isn't it?' sneered Lucius Malfoy. 'Well, your grandmother is used to losing family members to our cause ... your death will not come as a great shock.'

'Longbottom?' repeated Bellatrix, and a truly evil smile lit her gaunt face. 'Why, I have had the pleasure of meeting your parents, boy.'

'I DOE YOU HAB!' roared Neville, and he fought so hard against his captor's encircling grip that the Death Eater shouted, 'Someone Stun him!'

'No, no, no,' said Bellatrix. She looked transported, alive with excitement as she glanced at Harry, then back at Neville. 'No, let's see how long Longbottom lasts before he cracks like his parents ... unless Potter wants to give us the prophecy.'

'DON'D GIB ID DO DEM!' roared Neville, who seemed beside himself, kicking and writhing as Bellatrix drew nearer to him and his captor, her wand raised. 'DON'D GIB ID DO DEM, HARRY!'

Bellatrix raised her wand. '*Crucio!*'

Neville screamed, his legs drawn up to his chest so that the Death Eater holding him was momentarily holding him off the ground. The Death Eater dropped him and he fell to the floor, twitching and screaming in agony.

'That was just a taster!' said Bellatrix, raising her wand so that Neville's screams stopped and he lay sobbing at her feet. She turned and gazed up at Harry. 'Now, Potter, either give us the prophecy, or watch your little friend die the hard way!'

Harry did not have to think; there was no choice. The prophecy was hot with the heat of his clutching hand as he held it out. Malfoy jumped forwards to take it.

Then, high above them, two more doors burst open and five more people sprinted into the room: Sirius, Lupin, Moody, Tonks and Kingsley.

Malfoy turned, and raised his wand, but Tonks had already sent a Stunning Spell right at him. Harry did not wait to see whether it had made contact, but dived off the dais out of the way. The Death Eaters were completely distracted by the appearance of the members of the Order, who were now raining spells down upon them as they jumped from step to step

第35章 帷幔那边

昏落地！昏昏——"

一个块头最大的食死徒从后面抓住纳威，把他的双臂缚在身体两侧。纳威拼命挣扎，又踢又蹬。几个食死徒大笑起来。

"是隆巴顿，对吗？"卢修斯·马尔福用讥讽的声音说，"啊，你奶奶已经习惯了为我们的事业失去亲人……你的死不会令她特别震惊的。"

"隆巴顿？"贝拉特里克斯也跟着说道，憔悴的脸上绽开一个十分邪恶的笑容，"哎呀，小子，我有幸见过你的父母呀。"

"**我知道你见过！**"纳威吼道，他拼命挣脱那个抱住他的食死徒，那人连忙大喊，"有谁快把他击昏！"

"别、别、别，"贝拉特里克斯说。她扫了一眼哈利，然后又看着纳威，看上去欣喜若狂，兴奋得要命，"别，让我们看看隆巴顿能坚持多久才会像他父母那样变疯……除非波特愿意把预言球交给我们。"

"**别给他们！**"纳威咆哮道，贝拉特里克斯举着魔杖，一步步逼近他和那个食死徒，纳威似乎失去了常态，拼命扭动、踢蹬，"**别给他们，哈利！**"

贝拉特里克斯一举魔杖："钻心剜骨！"

纳威失声惨叫，双腿缩到胸前，那个食死徒一下子就悬空拎着他。食死徒把他一扔，纳威落在地上，痛苦地抽搐、尖叫。

"只是让你尝尝滋味！"贝拉特里克斯说着又举起魔杖，纳威停止了惨叫，躺在她的脚下啜泣着。她转过身盯着哈利。"好了，波特，要么把预言球给我们，要么就眼睁睁地看着你的小伙伴惨死！"

哈利根本用不着考虑，他没有别的选择。预言球被他的手攥得滚烫，他把它递了过去。马尔福冲上前来想拿走预言球。

就在这时，上面高处又有两扇门突然打开了，五个人冲进了房间：小天狼星、卢平、穆迪、唐克斯和金斯莱。

马尔福转身举起魔杖，但唐克斯已经朝他射去一个昏迷咒。哈利等不及看咒语有没有击中目标，赶紧跳下高台躲避。食死徒完全被凤凰社成员的出现搞乱了阵脚，那些人一边跳过一级级石阶，奔向下面的深坑，一边朝食死徒们射来雨点般的咒语。哈利在飞奔的人影和闪

CHAPTER THIRTY-FIVE   Beyond the Veil

towards the sunken floor. Through the darting bodies, the flashes of light, Harry could see Neville crawling along. He dodged another jet of red light and flung himself flat on the ground to reach Neville.

'Are you OK?' he yelled, as another spell soared inches over their heads.

'Yes,' said Neville, trying to pull himself up.

'And Ron?'

'I dink he's all righd – he was still fighding de brain when I lefd –'

The stone floor between them exploded as a spell hit it, leaving a crater right where Neville's hand had been only seconds before; both scrambled away from the spot, then a thick arm came out of nowhere, seized Harry around the neck and pulled him upright, so that his toes were barely touching the floor.

'Give it to me,' growled a voice in his ear, 'give me the prophecy –'

The man was pressing so tightly on Harry's windpipe that he could not breathe. Through watering eyes he saw Sirius duelling with a Death Eater some ten feet away; Kingsley was fighting two at once; Tonks, still halfway up the tiered seats, was firing spells down at Bellatrix – nobody seemed to realise that Harry was dying. He turned his wand backwards towards the man's side, but had no breath to utter an incantation, and the man's free hand was groping towards the hand in which Harry was grasping the prophecy –

'AARGH!'

Neville had come lunging out of nowhere; unable to articulate a spell, he had jabbed Hermione's wand hard into the eyehole of the Death Eater's mask. The man relinquished Harry at once with a howl of pain. Harry whirled around to face him and gasped:

'*STUPEFY!*'

The Death Eater keeled over backwards and his mask slipped off: it was Macnair, Buckbeak's would-be killer, one of his eyes now swollen and bloodshot.

'Thanks!' Harry said to Neville, pulling him aside as Sirius and his Death Eater lurched past, duelling so fiercely that their wands were blurs; then Harry's foot made contact with something round and hard and he slipped. For a moment he thought he had dropped the prophecy, but then he saw Moody's magical eye spinning away across the floor.

Its owner was lying on his side, bleeding from the head, and his attacker

第35章 帷幔那边

烁的光柱中看见纳威在地上蠕动。哈利又躲过一道红光,扑倒在地,朝纳威爬去。

"你没事吧?"他喊道,又一道咒语在他们头顶上几英寸的地方嗖地飞过。

"没事。"纳威说,挣扎着想站起来。

"罗恩呢?"

"我想他不会有事——我离开时他还在跟大脑搏斗呢——"

他们之间的石板地被一个咒语击中后炸开了,留下一个大坑,纳威的手几秒钟前就在那个地方。两人赶紧从那里爬开,这时一只粗胳膊从天而降,抓住哈利的脖子把他拎了起来,他的双脚几乎离开了地面。

"把它给我,"一个声音在哈利耳边吼道,"把预言球给我——"

那人死死地掐着哈利的喉咙,掐得他喘不过气来。哈利透过迷蒙的泪水,看见小天狼星正在大约十英尺外跟一个食死徒搏斗,金斯莱同时对付两个,唐克斯还在石阶的半腰处,朝下面的贝拉特里克斯发射咒语——似乎谁也没有发现哈利快要死了。他把魔杖转过去,朝身后指着那人的身体,却喘不上气来念咒语,而那人的另一只手,正摸索着来抓哈利握着预言球的那只手——

"啊!"

纳威不知从什么地方蹿了出来。他无法念出咒语,就用赫敏的魔杖狠狠地戳进了那个食死徒面具上的眼洞。那人惨叫一声,立刻松开了哈利。哈利迅速转过身对着他,喘着气喊道:

"昏昏倒地!"

食死徒往后一倒,面具滑落了:是差点杀死巴克比克的麦克尼尔。他的一只眼睛又红又肿。

"谢谢!"哈利对纳威说,并一把将他拖到一边,这时小天狼星和他的食死徒对手跟跄着从他们身边蹿过,搏斗得十分激烈,双方挥动的魔杖变成了一片模糊的影子。接着,哈利的脚触到一个圆圆的硬东西,滑了一下。他起初以为是预言球掉了,接着便看见穆迪的魔眼在地上滴溜溜地滚远了。

魔眼的主人侧身躺在地上,脑袋在流血,袭击他的人此刻正朝哈

1331

CHAPTER THIRTY-FIVE Beyond the Veil

was now bearing down upon Harry and Neville: Dolohov, his long pale face twisted with glee.

'*Tarantallegra!*' he shouted, his wand pointing at Neville, whose legs went immediately into a kind of frenzied tap-dance, unbalancing him and causing him to fall to the floor again. 'Now, Potter –'

He made the same slashing movement with his wand that he had used on Hermione just as Harry yelled, '*Protego!*'

Harry felt something streak across his face like a blunt knife; the force of it knocked him sideways and he fell over Neville's jerking legs, but the Shield Charm had stopped the worst of the spell.

Dolohov raised his wand again. '*Accio proph*–'

Sirius had hurtled out of nowhere, rammed Dolohov with his shoulder and sent him flying out of the way. The prophecy had again flown to the tips of Harry's fingers but he had managed to cling on to it. Now Sirius and Dolohov were duelling, their wands flashing like swords, sparks flying from their wand-tips –

Dolohov drew back his wand to make the same slashing movement he had used on Harry and Hermione. Springing up, Harry yelled, '*Petrificus Totalus!*' Once again, Dolohov's arms and legs snapped together and he keeled over backwards, landing with a crash on his back.

'Nice one!' shouted Sirius, forcing Harry's head down as a pair of Stunning Spells flew towards them. 'Now I want you to get out of –'

They both ducked again; a jet of green light had narrowly missed Sirius. Across the room Harry saw Tonks fall from halfway up the stone steps, her limp form toppling from stone seat to stone seat and Bellatrix, triumphant, running back towards the fray.

'Harry, take the prophecy, grab Neville and run!' Sirius yelled, dashing to meet Bellatrix. Harry did not see what happened next: Kingsley swayed across his field of vision, battling with the pockmarked and no longer masked Rookwood; another jet of green light flew over Harry's head as he launched himself towards Neville –

'Can you stand?' he bellowed in Neville's ear, as Neville's legs jerked and twitched uncontrollably. 'Put your arm round my neck –'

Neville did so – Harry heaved – Neville's legs were still flying in every direction, they would not support him, and then, out of nowhere, a man

第35章 帷幔那边

利和纳威冲来：是多洛霍夫，他苍白的长脸兴奋地抽搐着。

"塔朗泰拉舞！"他用魔杖指着纳威喊道，纳威的双腿立刻像是跳起了疯狂的踢踏舞，身体失去了平衡，再次摔倒在地。"现在，波特——"

多洛霍夫像刚才对付赫敏一样，挥舞着魔杖劈砍过来，哈利大叫一声："盔甲护身！"

哈利觉得什么东西像钝刀子一样在脸上划过，那股力量撞得他往旁边一倒，摔在纳威不断舞动的腿上，幸好铁甲咒挡住了这道咒语最强烈的威力。

多洛霍夫又举起了魔杖："预言球飞——"

小天狼星从什么地方蹿了出来，用肩膀一撞多洛霍夫，撞得他飞了出去。预言球又一次滑到哈利的指尖，但他好歹又把它抓紧了。现在小天狼星和多洛霍夫在决斗，魔杖像剑一样上下飞舞，杖尖迸出火星——

多洛霍夫抽回魔杖，做出对付哈利和赫敏时的那种劈砍动作。哈利一跃而起，喊道："统统石化！"多洛霍夫的腿和胳膊再次合在一起，他仰面向后倒去，砰的一声摔在地上。

"精彩！"小天狼星喊道，一边把哈利的脑袋往下一按，躲过了两个迎面射来的昏迷咒，"现在我要你离开这——"

两人同时又弯下身，一道绿光险些击中小天狼星。哈利看见在房间那头，唐克斯从石头台阶的半腰摔下来，软绵绵的身体从一个石座滚向另一个石座，贝拉特里克斯得意扬扬地跑回去加入战斗。

"哈利，拿好预言球，带上纳威，快跑！"小天狼星喊道，冲过去迎战贝拉特里克斯。哈利没有看见接下来的情形，金斯莱摇摇摆摆地闯入了他的视线，正跟摘了面具、满脸麻子的卢克伍德在搏斗。哈利朝纳威扑去时，又一道绿光从他头顶掠过——

"你能站起来吗？"他对着纳威的耳朵喊道，纳威的双腿不受控制地摆动、抽搐着，"用胳膊搂住我的脖子——"

纳威照办了——哈利使劲架起他——纳威的双腿仍然不停地四下甩动，无法支撑他的身体。这时，一个人不知从什么地方朝他们扑来，两人都向后摔倒了，纳威就像肚皮朝天的甲虫一样，双腿在

CHAPTER THIRTY-FIVE   Beyond the Veil

lunged at them: both fell backwards, Neville's legs waving wildly like an overturned beetle's, Harry with his left arm held up in the air to try to save the small glass ball from being smashed.

'The prophecy, give me the prophecy, Potter!' snarled Lucius Malfoy's voice in his ear, and Harry felt the tip of Malfoy's wand pressing hard between his ribs.

'No – get – off – me ... Neville – catch it!'

Harry flung the prophecy across the floor, Neville spun himself around on his back and scooped the ball to his chest. Malfoy pointed the wand instead at Neville, but Harry jabbed his own wand back over his shoulder and yelled, '*Impedimenta!*'

Malfoy was blasted off his back. As Harry scrambled up again he looked around and saw Malfoy smash into the dais on which Sirius and Bellatrix were now duelling. Malfoy aimed his wand at Harry and Neville again, but before he could draw breath to strike, Lupin had jumped between them.

'Harry, round up the others and GO!'

Harry seized Neville by the shoulder of his robes and lifted him bodily on to the first tier of stone steps; Neville's legs twitched and jerked and would not support his weight; Harry heaved again with all the strength he possessed and they climbed another step –

A spell hit the stone bench at Harry's heel; it crumbled away and he fell back to the step below. Neville sank on to the bench above, his legs still jerking and thrashing, and he thrust the prophecy into his pocket.

'Come on!' said Harry desperately, hauling at Neville's robes. 'Just try and push with your legs –'

He gave another stupendous heave and Neville's robes tore all along the left seam – the small spun-glass ball dropped from his pocket and, before either of them could catch it, one of Neville's floundering feet kicked it: it flew some ten feet to their right and smashed on the step beneath them. As both of them stared at the place where it had broken, appalled at what had happened, a pearly-white figure with hugely magnified eyes rose into the air, unnoticed by any but them. Harry could see its mouth moving, but in all the crashes and screams and yells surrounding them, not one word of the prophecy could he hear. The figure stopped speaking and dissolved into nothingness.

'Harry, I'b sorry!' cried Neville, his face anguished as his legs continued to

第35章 帷幔那边

空中胡乱摆动；哈利把左臂高高地举在空中，保护着小玻璃球，以防被摔碎。

"预言球，把预言球给我，波特！"卢修斯·马尔福贴着他的耳朵恶声恶气地说，哈利感觉到对方的魔杖尖用力抵着自己的肋骨。

"不！——放——开——我……纳威——接着！"

哈利把预言球贴地滚了出去，平躺在地的纳威转了个圈，把球揽在怀里。马尔福又用魔杖指着纳威，这时哈利用自己的魔杖越过肩头往后一捅，大喊一声："障碍重重！"

马尔福被炸飞了。哈利又挣扎着爬了起来，左右张望，只见马尔福撞在了小天狼星和贝拉特里克斯正在决斗的高台上。马尔福又用魔杖瞄准了哈利和纳威，可是没等他吸口气念出咒语，卢平就跳过来挡在了他们中间。

"哈利，把其他人召集起来，**快走**！"

哈利抓住纳威袍子的肩部，把他的身体拖上第一级石阶。纳威的双腿在抽搐、摆动，无法支撑自己的身体。哈利用尽全身的力气，他们又往上爬了一级——

一个咒语击中了哈利脚下的石头长凳，长凳被炸碎了，哈利跌落到下一层台阶上。纳威落在台阶上的石头长凳上面，双腿仍然在胡乱地抽搐、摆动，他把预言球塞进了口袋。

"快！"哈利焦急地说，使劲拽着纳威的袍子，"试着用腿蹬一蹬——"

哈利又使出吃奶的力气一拉，纳威的袍子沿着左边的接缝绽开了——小玻璃球从口袋里滚落出来，没等他们伸手去接，纳威一只胡乱摆动的脚踢中了它。预言球飞到了右边十英尺外，在他们下面的石阶上撞碎了。两人被眼前的情景吓坏了，呆呆地望着预言球碎裂的地方，只见一个双眼被放大了很多倍的乳白色身影升到空中，而周围除了他们俩，没有人注意到。哈利看见那身影的嘴在说话，可是四周充满了撞击声、呐喊声、尖叫声，预言说的是什么，他一个字也听不清。那身影说完话，就消失在了虚空中。

"哈利，对不起！"纳威大声说道，他满脸痛苦，双腿还在乱摆乱动，

CHAPTER THIRTY-FIVE   Beyond the Veil

flounder. 'I'b so sorry, Harry, I didn'd bean do –'

'It doesn't matter!' Harry shouted. 'Just try and stand, let's get out of –'

'*Dubbledore!*' said Neville, his sweaty face suddenly transported, staring over Harry's shoulder.

'What?'

'DUBBLEDORE!'

Harry turned to look where Neville was staring. Directly above them, framed in the doorway from the Brain Room, stood Albus Dumbledore, his wand aloft, his face white and furious. Harry felt a kind of electric charge surge through every particle of his body – *they were saved*.

Dumbledore had already sped past Neville and Harry, who had no more thoughts of leaving, when the Death Eaters nearest realised Dumbledore was there and yelled to the others. One of the Death Eaters ran for it, scrabbling like a monkey up the stone steps opposite. Dumbledore's spell pulled him back as easily and effortlessly as though he had hooked him with an invisible line –

Only one pair was still battling, apparently unaware of the new arrival. Harry saw Sirius duck Bellatrix's jet of red light: he was laughing at her.

'Come on, you can do better than that!' he yelled, his voice echoing around the cavernous room.

The second jet of light hit him squarely on the chest.

The laughter had not quite died from his face, but his eyes widened in shock.

Harry released Neville, though he was unaware of doing so. He jumped to the ground, pulling out his wand, as Dumbledore, too, turned towards the dais.

It seemed to take Sirius an age to fall: his body curved in a graceful arc as he sank backwards through the ragged veil hanging from the arch.

Harry saw the look of mingled fear and surprise on his godfather's wasted, once-handsome face as he fell through the ancient doorway and disappeared behind the veil, which fluttered for a moment as though in a high wind, then fell back into place.

Harry heard Bellatrix Lestrange's triumphant scream, but knew it meant nothing – Sirius had only just fallen through the archway, he would reappear from the other side any second ...

But Sirius did not reappear.

第35章 帷幔那边

"真对不起,哈利,我不是故意——"

"没关系!"哈利大声喊道,"试着站起来,我们快离开——"

"邓布利多!"纳威喊道,目光越过哈利的肩头瞪着,汗津津的脸突然变得欣喜若狂。

"什么?"

"**邓布利多!**"

哈利转身循着纳威的目光望去。就在他们上方,在大脑屋的门口,站着阿不思·邓布利多。他举着魔杖,脸色苍白,满是怒容。哈利觉得有一股电流突然涌过全身的每个细胞——他们得救了。

邓布利多快步走下石阶,经过纳威和哈利身边,此时他们俩不再想着离开了。邓布利多近旁的食死徒发现了他,赶紧嚷嚷着告诉别人。一个食死徒抱头逃窜,像猴子一样手脚并用爬上对面的石阶。邓布利多的咒语轻飘飘地把他拽了回来,就好像用一根看不见的钓线把他钩住了——

只有两个人还在打斗,似乎没有发现有人到来。哈利看见小天狼星躲过贝拉特里克斯射出的红光:他在大声嘲笑她。

"来吧,这不是你的水平!"他喊道,声音在巨大的房间里回荡。

第二道光正中他的胸膛。

笑容还没有完全从他脸上消失,他的眼睛惊骇地瞪圆。

哈利松开了纳威,但自己并没有意识到这一点。他再次跳下一级级石阶,一边抽出魔杖,邓布利多也转身看着高台。

小天狼星坠落的过程似乎十分缓慢:他的身体弯成一个优美的弧线,向后跌入了挂在拱门上的破烂的帷幔。

哈利看见,他的教父坠入那道古老的拱门时,那张曾经英俊、现已消瘦憔悴的脸上混杂着恐惧和惊讶。他消失在了帷幔后面,帷幔像被大风吹着一样飘摆片刻,又恢复了原样。

哈利听见了贝拉特里克斯·莱斯特兰奇得意的尖叫,但他知道这没有任何意义——小天狼星只是跌到了拱门里,随时都会在另一边重新出现……

可是小天狼星没有出现。

CHAPTER THIRTY-FIVE Beyond the Veil

'SIRIUS!' Harry yelled. 'SIRIUS!'

Harry's breath was coming in searing gasps. Sirius must be just behind the curtain, he, Harry, would pull him back out …

But as he sprinted towards the dais, Lupin grabbed Harry around the chest, holding him back.

'There's nothing you can do, Harry –'

'Get him, save him, he's only just gone through!'

'– it's too late, Harry.'

'We can still reach him –' Harry struggled hard and viciously, but Lupin would not let go …

'There's nothing you can do, Harry … nothing … he's gone.'

第35章　帷幔那边

"小天狼星!"哈利喊道,"小天狼星!"

他急促的呼吸如烧灼一般。小天狼星肯定就在帷幔后面,哈利要把他拉出来……

哈利刚拔腿朝高台跑去,卢平一把抱住他,把他拖了回来。

"你做不了什么,哈利——"

"去找他,救他,他不过是跌进去了!"

"——来不及了,哈利。"

"我们还是可以找到他——"哈利不顾一切地拼命挣扎,但卢平就是不放手……

"你做不了什么的,哈利……做不了什么……他死了。"

CHAPTER THIRTY-SIX

The Only One He Ever Feared

'He hasn't gone!' Harry yelled.

He did not believe it; he would not believe it; still he fought Lupin with every bit of strength he had. Lupin did not understand; people hid behind that curtain; Harry had heard them whispering the first time he had entered the room. Sirius was hiding, simply lurking out of sight –

'SIRIUS!' he bellowed. 'SIRIUS!'

'He can't come back, Harry,' said Lupin, his voice breaking as he struggled to contain Harry. 'He can't come back, because he's d–'

'He – IS – NOT – DEAD!' roared Harry. 'SIRIUS!'

There was movement going on around them, pointless bustling, the flashes of more spells. To Harry it was meaningless noise, the deflected curses flying past them did not matter, nothing mattered except that Lupin should stop pretending that Sirius – who was standing feet from them behind that old curtain – was not going to emerge at any moment, shaking back his dark hair and eager to re-enter the battle.

Lupin dragged Harry away from the dais. Harry, still staring at the archway, was angry at Sirius now for keeping him waiting –

But some part of him realised, even as he fought to break free from Lupin, that Sirius had never kept him waiting before ... Sirius had risked everything, always, to see Harry, to help him ... if Sirius was not reappearing out of that archway when Harry was yelling for him as though his life depended on it, the only possible explanation was that he could not come back ... that he really was –

Dumbledore had most of the remaining Death Eaters grouped in the middle of the room, seemingly immobilised by invisible ropes; Mad-Eye

第36章

他唯一害怕的人

"**不**，他没有死！"哈利嚷道。

他不相信，他怎么也不肯相信。他仍然用全身的力气跟卢平搏斗。卢平不明白，那帷幔后面藏着人呢。哈利第一次进入这个房间时就听见他们在喃喃低语。小天狼星躲起来了，藏在别人看不见的地方——

"小天狼星！"他大声喊道，"小天狼星！"

"他回不来了，哈利。"卢平说，他拼命制止着哈利，声音哽咽了，"他回不来了，因为他已经死——"

"他——没——有——死！"哈利吼道，"小天狼星！"

周围乱哄哄的。没有头绪的喧嚷，来回穿梭的咒语，这些对哈利来说，都是毫无意义的噪音。那些从他们身边飞过、被挡开的咒语都无关紧要，什么都无关紧要，只要卢平别再假说小天狼星不会再随时出现，不会再甩甩一头黑发，渴望着重新投入战斗。此刻小天狼星站在几英尺外的那个破帘子后面呢。

卢平把哈利拖下高台。哈利仍然盯着拱门，心里在生小天狼星的气，他为什么让自己等了这么久——

然而，他虽然挣扎着摆脱卢平，但内心的某个角落隐约意识到，小天狼星以前从没让他等待……小天狼星总是冒着一切危险来见哈利，来帮助哈利……现在，哈利这么没命地大声呼唤他，他都没有出现，那只能有一种解释，就是他再也回不来了……他真的已经——

邓布利多把剩下来的大多数食死徒都集中在房间中央，似乎用无形的绳索束缚住了他们，使他们动弹不得。疯眼汉穆迪爬到房间那头

CHAPTER THIRTY-SIX   The Only One He Ever Feared

Moody had crawled across the room to where Tonks lay, and was attempting to revive her; behind the dais there were still flashes of light, grunts and cries – Kingsley had run forward to continue Sirius's duel with Bellatrix.

'Harry?'

Neville had slid down the stone benches one by one to the place where Harry stood. Harry was no longer struggling against Lupin, who maintained a precautionary grip on his arm nevertheless.

'Harry ... I'b really sorry ...' said Neville. His legs were still dancing uncontrollably. 'Was dad man – was Sirius Black a – a friend of yours?'

Harry nodded.

'Here,' said Lupin quietly, and pointing his wand at Neville's legs he said, '*Finite.*' The spell was lifted: Neville's legs fell back to the floor and remained still. Lupin's face was pale. 'Let's – let's find the others. Where are they all, Neville?'

Lupin turned away from the archway as he spoke. It sounded as though every word was causing him pain.

'Dey're all back dere,' said Neville. 'A brain addacked Ron bud I dink he's all righd – and Herbione's unconscious, bud we could feel a bulse –'

There was a loud bang and a yell from behind the dais. Harry saw Kingsley hit the ground yelling in pain: Bellatrix Lestrange turned tail and ran as Dumbledore whipped around. He aimed a spell at her but she deflected it; she was halfway up the steps now –

'Harry – no!' cried Lupin, but Harry had already ripped his arm from Lupin's slackened grip.

'SHE KILLED SIRIUS!' bellowed Harry. 'SHE KILLED HIM – I'LL KILL HER!'

And he was off, scrambling up the stone benches; people were shouting behind him but he did not care. The hem of Bellatrix's robes whipped out of sight ahead and they were back in the room where the brains were swimming ...

She aimed a curse over her shoulder. The tank rose into the air and tipped. Harry was deluged in the foul-smelling potion within: the brains slipped and slid over him and began spinning their long coloured tentacles, but he shouted, '*Wingardium Leviosa!*' and they flew off him up into the air. Slipping and sliding, he ran on towards the door; he leapt over Luna, who

第36章 他唯一害怕的人

唐克斯的身边,努力想使她苏醒过来。高台后面仍然强光飞射,咒骂声、呐喊声不绝于耳——金斯莱早已挺身而出,代替小天狼星跟贝拉特里克斯继续决斗。

"哈利?"

纳威滑下一级又一级石头长凳,来到哈利站着的地方。哈利不再挣扎,但卢平仍然警惕地抓着他的胳膊。

"哈利……真对不起……"纳威说,他的腿还在不受控制地胡乱舞动着,"那个人——小天狼星·布莱克——是你的朋友?"

哈利点了点头。

"来。"卢平轻声说着,用魔杖指着纳威的双腿,念了句"终了结束"。咒语被消除了:纳威的腿落回地面,稳住不动了。卢平脸色苍白。"我们——我们快找到其他人。他们都在哪儿,纳威?"

卢平说着转身不去看那道拱门,似乎每说一个字都使他感到很痛苦。

"他们都在后面,"纳威说,"一个大脑缠住了罗恩,但我认为他不会有事的——赫敏昏过去了,但还能摸到脉搏——"

高台后面传来一声巨响和一声叫喊。哈利看见金斯莱惨叫着倒在地上:邓布利多猛地转过身,贝拉特里克斯·莱斯特兰奇想逃跑。邓布利多朝她射出一个咒语,但被她挡开了。她已经跑到石阶的半腰处——

"哈利——不要!"卢平喊道,但哈利已经把胳膊从卢平放松警惕的手里挣了出来。

"**她杀死了小天狼星!**"哈利吼道,"**她杀死了他——我要干掉她!**"

他飞快地爬上一级级石头长凳,人们在后面大声喊他,但他不予理会。贝拉特里克斯的长袍下摆在前面一闪就不见了,他们又来到了大脑游动的房间……

她从肩头向身后射来一个咒语。水箱蹿到空中,翻倒了。水箱里恶臭难闻的液体倾倒在哈利身上:大脑在他身上滑来滑去,并开始用长长的五颜六色的触须缠绕他。哈利大喊一声:"羽加迪姆 勒维奥萨!"那些触须就离开了他,飞到空中。他一步一滑地朝门口跑去。他从卢娜身上跳过,卢娜躺在地上呻吟;他跑过金妮,金妮说:"哈利——

CHAPTER THIRTY-SIX   The Only One He Ever Feared

was groaning on the floor, past Ginny, who said, 'Harry – what –?', past Ron, who giggled feebly, and Hermione, who was still unconscious. He wrenched open the door into the circular black hall and saw Bellatrix disappearing through a door on the other side of the room; beyond her was the corridor leading back to the lifts.

He ran, but she had slammed the door behind her and the walls were already rotating. Once more, he was surrounded by streaks of blue light from the whirling candelabra.

'Where's the exit?' he shouted desperately, as the wall rumbled to a halt again. 'Where's the way out?'

The room seemed to have been waiting for him to ask. The door right behind him flew open and the corridor towards the lifts stretched ahead of him, torch-lit and empty. He ran …

He could hear a lift clattering ahead; he sprinted up the passageway, swung around the corner and slammed his fist on to the button to call a second lift. It jangled and banged lower and lower; the grilles slid open and Harry dashed inside, now hammering the button marked *Atrium*. The doors slid shut and he was rising …

He forced his way out of the lift before the grilles were fully open and looked around. Bellatrix was almost at the telephone lift at the other end of the hall, but she looked back as he sprinted towards her and aimed another spell at him. He dodged behind the Fountain of Magical Brethren: the spell zoomed past him and hit the wrought-gold gates at the other end of the Atrium so that they rang like bells. There were no more footsteps. She had stopped running. He crouched behind the statues, listening.

'*Come out, come out, little Harry!*' she called in her mock baby voice, which echoed off the polished wooden floors. 'What did you come after me for, then? I thought you were here to avenge my dear cousin!'

'I am!' shouted Harry, and a score of ghostly Harrys seemed to chorus *I am! I am! I am!* All around the room.

'Aaaaaah … did you *love* him, little baby Potter?'

Hatred rose in Harry such as he had never known before; he flung himself out from behind the fountain and bellowed, '*Crucio!*'

Bellatrix screamed: the spell had knocked her off her feet, but she did not

第36章 他唯一害怕的人

怎么——?"他跑过罗恩,罗恩声音发虚地咯咯笑着;他又跑过赫敏,赫敏仍然昏迷不醒。他拧开门,冲进黑色的圆形大厅,看见贝拉特里克斯蹿出了房间对面的一扇门,而她前面便是那道通向升降梯的走廊。

哈利拼命奔跑,但是贝拉特里克斯出去后把门重重地关上了,墙壁又开始旋转。哈利又一次被旋转的大枝形烛台上的一道道蓝光包围。

"出口在哪儿?"墙壁隆隆地停止了旋转,哈利绝望地喊道,"出去的路在哪儿?"

那个房间似乎正等着他发问呢。他身后的那扇门突然打开,出现了那道通向升降梯的走廊,那里亮着火把,空无一人。他拔腿向前冲去……

他听见前面一架升降梯哐啷哐啷地响,他在过道里飞奔,转过拐角,用拳头使劲砸着按钮,召唤第二架升降梯。升降梯叮叮当当、咔啦咔啦地降落下来,栅栏门滑开,哈利冲了进去,又用拳头使劲砸着正厅的按钮。门关上了,他在上升……

没等栅栏门完全打开,他就挤出升降梯,左右张望。贝拉特里克斯已经跑到大厅另一头的电话亭升降梯那儿,哈利冲过去,贝拉特里克斯回头看看,又射出一个咒语。哈利闪身躲到魔法兄弟喷泉后面,咒语从他身边嗖地掠过,击中了正厅另一边的金色大门,发出铃铛般的响亮声音。脚步声没有了,贝拉特里克斯不再奔跑。哈利伏身躲在雕像后面,留神倾听。

"出来,出来,小哈利!"贝拉特里克斯又模仿着婴儿的声音喊道,声音在光洁的木板地上回荡,"你来追我做什么呢,嗯?我还以为你是来给我亲爱的堂弟报仇的呢!"

"没错!"哈利喊道,房间里似乎有二十个幽灵般的哈利在齐声回应,没错!没错!没错!

"啊……难道你爱他吗,小宝宝波特?"

哈利心头涌起一股他从没体验过的仇恨,他从喷泉后面冲出来,大吼一声:"钻心剜骨!"

贝拉特里克斯叫了起来:咒语把她打翻在地,但她没有像纳威那样痛苦地扭动、惨叫——她很快又站了起来,气喘吁吁,不再放声大笑。

CHAPTER THIRTY-SIX The Only One He Ever Feared

writhe and shriek with pain as Neville had – she was already back on her feet, breathless, no longer laughing. Harry dodged behind the golden fountain again. Her counter-spell hit the head of the handsome wizard, which was blown off and landed twenty feet away, gouging long scratches into the wooden floor.

'Never used an Unforgivable Curse before, have you, boy?' she yelled. She had abandoned her baby voice now. 'You need to *mean* them, Potter! You need to really want to cause pain – to enjoy it – righteous anger won't hurt me for long – I'll show you how it is done, shall I? I'll give you a lesson –'

Harry was edging around the fountain on the other side when she screamed, '*Crucio!*' and he was forced to duck down again as the centaur's arm, holding its bow, spun off and landed with a crash on the floor a short distance from the golden wizard's head.

'Potter, you cannot win against me!' she cried.

He could hear her moving to the right, trying to get a clear shot of him. He backed around the statue away from her, crouching behind the centaur's legs, his head level with the house-elf's.

'I was and am the Dark Lord's most loyal servant. I learned the Dark Arts from him, and I know spells of such power that you, pathetic little boy, can never hope to compete –'

'*Stupefy!*' yelled Harry. He had edged right around to where the goblin stood beaming up at the now headless wizard and taken aim at her back as she peered around the fountain. She reacted so fast he barely had time to duck.

'*Protego!*'

The jet of red light, his own Stunning Spell, bounced back at him. Harry scrambled back behind the fountain and one of the goblin's ears went flying across the room.

'Potter, I'm going to give you one chance!' shouted Bellatrix. 'Give me the prophecy – roll it out towards me now – and I may spare your life!'

'Well, you're going to have to kill me, because it's gone!' Harry roared and, as he shouted it, pain seared across his forehead; his scar was on fire again, and he felt a surge of fury that was quite unconnected with his own rage. 'And he knows!' said Harry, with a mad laugh to match Bellatrix's own. 'Your dear old mate Voldemort knows it's gone! He's not going to be happy with you, is he?'

第36章 他唯一害怕的人

哈利又闪身躲到金色喷泉后面。贝拉特里克斯的破解咒正中那位英俊男巫的脑袋,脑袋被炸掉了,落到二十英尺外,在木地板上留下一道又长又深的划痕。

"以前没有使用过不可饶恕咒吧,小子?"贝拉特里克斯嚷道,她已经放弃了那种婴儿般的声音,"你需要发自内心,波特!你需要真的希望造成痛苦——并且享受这种感觉——正当的愤怒不会伤害我多久的——我来给你演示一下,好吗?我来教教你——"

哈利侧身绕着喷泉的另一边挪动,只听她大喊一声:"钻心剜骨!"哈利不得不再次猫下腰,马人举着弓箭的胳膊飞了出去,砰的一声落在地上,距那金色男巫的脑袋不远。

"波特,你赢不了我的!"贝拉特里克斯喊道。

哈利听得出她正在往右边挪动,想瞄准他朝他出击。哈利赶紧绕到雕像后面,躲在马人的腿后,脑袋跟家养小精灵的脑袋相齐。

"我是黑魔王最忠实的奴仆,过去是,现在也是。我从他那里学到了黑魔法,知道许多威力强大的咒语,你这个可怜的小男孩做梦也别想跟我较量——"

"昏昏倒地!"哈利大喊一声。他已经悄悄绕到了妖精站的地方,那妖精笑眯眯地抬头望着已经没有脑袋的男巫。哈利趁贝拉特里克斯朝喷泉窥望的当儿,瞄准了她的后背。贝拉特里克斯反应极快,哈利几乎来不及躲避。

"盔甲护身!"

一道红光,是哈利自己发出的昏迷咒,朝他反弹回来。他赶紧爬到喷泉后面,妖精的一只耳朵飞到房间那头去了。

"波特,我给你一个机会!"贝拉特里克斯大声喊道,"把预言球给我——现在就把它滚过来——我就饶你一条小命!"

"唉,恐怕你只能把我杀死了,因为预言球没了!"哈利吼道,这时他的额头突然剧痛难忍,伤疤又好像着了火一般,而且心头涌起一阵狂怒,但这怒火似乎与他自己的愤怒没有关联。"他知道了!"哈利说着,发出了跟贝拉特里克斯一样的狂笑,"你亲爱的老伙伴伏地魔知道球没了!他对你不会满意的,是吗?"

CHAPTER THIRTY-SIX The Only One He Ever Feared

'What? What do you mean?' she cried, and for the first time there was fear in her voice.

'The prophecy smashed when I was trying to get Neville up the steps! What do you think Voldemort'll say about that, then?'

His scar seared and burned ... the pain of it was making his eyes stream ...

'LIAR!' she shrieked, but he could hear the terror behind the anger now. 'YOU'VE GOT IT, POTTER, AND YOU WILL GIVE IT TO ME! *Accio prophecy! ACCIO PROPHECY!*'

Harry laughed again because he knew it would incense her, the pain building in his head so badly he thought his skull might burst. He waved his empty hand from behind the one-eared goblin and withdrew it quickly as she sent another jet of green light flying at him.

'Nothing there!' he shouted. 'Nothing to summon! It smashed and nobody heard what it said, tell your boss that!'

'No!' she screamed. 'It isn't true, you're lying! MASTER, I TRIED, I TRIED – DO NOT PUNISH ME –'

'Don't waste your breath!' yelled Harry, his eyes screwed up against the pain in his scar, now more terrible than ever. 'He can't hear you from here!'

'Can't I, Potter?' said a high, cold voice.

Harry opened his eyes.

Tall, thin and black-hooded, his terrible snakelike face white and gaunt, his scarlet, slit-pupilled eyes staring ... Lord Voldemort had appeared in the middle of the hall, his wand pointing at Harry who stood frozen, quite unable to move.

'So, you smashed my prophecy?' said Voldemort softly, staring at Harry with those pitiless red eyes. 'No, Bella, he is not lying ... I see the truth looking at me from within his worthless mind ... months of preparation, months of effort ... and my Death Eaters have let Harry Potter thwart me again ...'

'Master, I am sorry, I knew not, I was fighting the Animagus Black!' sobbed Bellatrix, flinging herself down at Voldemort's feet as he paced slowly nearer. 'Master, you should know –'

'Be quiet, Bella,' said Voldemort dangerously. 'I shall deal with you in a moment. Do you think I have entered the Ministry of Magic to hear your

1348

第36章 他唯一害怕的人

"什么？你是什么意思？"贝拉特里克斯喊道，声音里第一次透出了恐惧。

"我使劲把纳威拖上台阶时，预言球摔碎了！你认为伏地魔对此会怎么说呢，嗯？"

他的伤疤火烧火燎地剧痛……疼得他眼里涌出了泪水……

"**撒谎！**"贝拉特里克斯尖叫道，但哈利听出她此刻的愤怒后面藏着恐惧，"**它在你手里，波特，你快把它给我！**预言球飞来！**预言球飞来！**"

哈利再次放声大笑，他知道这会激怒她。脑袋里的疼痛十分强烈，他觉得脑壳快要爆炸了。他从独耳妖精后面挥了挥空空的手，又赶紧把手缩回来，贝拉特里克斯又朝他射来一道绿光。

"什么也没有了！"哈利喊道，"没什么可召唤的！它摔碎了，没有人听见它说了什么，快跟你的主子汇报去吧！"

"不！"她尖叫道，"这不是真的，你在说谎！**主人，我尽力了，我尽力了——别惩罚我——**"

"别再浪费口舌了！"哈利嚷道，伤疤比任何时候疼得都厉害了，他闭紧了眼睛强忍着，"他可听不见你在这里说话！"

"是吗，波特？"一个冰冷、高亢的声音说。

哈利睁开了眼睛。

瘦高的身条，戴着黑色的兜帽，可怖的蛇一般的面孔苍白而憔悴，瞪着一双瞳仁细长的红眼睛……伏地魔出现在大厅中央，他的魔杖指着哈利，哈利呆呆地站着，几乎动弹不得。

"这么说，你把我的预言球给摔碎了？"伏地魔用那双冷酷的红眼睛盯着哈利，轻声说道，"不，贝拉，他没有说谎……我从他的废物脑子里看到了事情的真相……多少个月的准备，多少个月的努力……我的食死徒们又一次让哈利·波特妨碍了我……"

"主人，对不起，我不知道，我当时在跟阿尼马格斯布莱克搏斗！"贝拉特里克斯哭泣着说，扑倒在慢慢走近的伏地魔脚下，"主人，你知道的——"

"别说了，贝拉，"伏地魔令人胆寒地说，"我待会儿再跟你算账。

CHAPTER THIRTY-SIX   The Only One He Ever Feared

snivelling apologies?'

'But Master – he is here – he is below –'

Voldemort paid no attention.

'I have nothing more to say to you, Potter,' he said quietly. 'You have irked me too often, for too long. *AVADA KEDAVRA!*'

Harry had not even opened his mouth to resist; his mind was blank, his wand pointing uselessly at the floor.

But the headless golden statue of the wizard in the fountain had sprung alive, leaping from its plinth to land with a crash on the floor between Harry and Voldemort. The spell merely glanced off its chest as the statue flung out its arms to protect Harry.

'What –?' cried Voldemort, staring around. And then he breathed, '*Dumbledore!*'

Harry looked behind him, his heart pounding. Dumbledore was standing in front of the golden gates.

Voldemort raised his wand and another jet of green light streaked at Dumbledore, who turned and was gone in a whirling of his cloak. Next second, he had reappeared behind Voldemort and waved his wand towards the remnants of the fountain. The other statues sprang to life. The statue of the witch ran at Bellatrix, who screamed and sent spells streaming uselessly off its chest, before it dived at her, pinning her to the floor. Meanwhile, the goblin and the house-elf scuttled towards the fireplaces set along the wall and the one-armed centaur galloped at Voldemort, who vanished and reappeared beside the pool. The headless statue thrust Harry backwards, away from the fight, as Dumbledore advanced on Voldemort and the golden centaur cantered around them both.

'It was foolish to come here tonight, Tom,' said Dumbledore calmly. 'The Aurors are on their way –'

'By which time I shall be gone, and you will be dead!' spat Voldemort. He sent another killing curse at Dumbledore but missed, instead hitting the security guard's desk, which burst into flame.

Dumbledore flicked his own wand: the force of the spell that emanated from it was such that Harry, though shielded by his golden guard, felt his hair stand on end as it passed and this time Voldemort was forced to conjure a shining silver shield out of thin air to deflect it. The spell, whatever it

第36章 他唯一害怕的人

你以为我进入魔法部就是为了听你哭哭啼啼地道歉吗？"

"可是主人——他在这儿——就在下面——"

伏地魔未予理会。

"我没有什么话可对你说了，波特，"他轻声地说，"你三番五次地惹恼我，次数太多，时间太久了。**阿瓦达索命！**"

哈利甚至没有张嘴抵抗，他大脑一片空白，魔杖软绵绵地指着地面。

然而，喷泉里那个没有脑袋的金色男巫雕像突然活了起来，从底座上跳起，啪的一声落在哈利和伏地魔之间的地上，伸开双臂保护着哈利，咒语从它的胸前擦过。

"什么——？"伏地魔四下张望着喊道，接着他倒吸了一口冷气，"邓布利多！"

哈利的心怦怦狂跳着，他看看身后。邓布利多站在金色的大门前。

伏地魔举起魔杖，又一道绿光朝邓布利多飞去，邓布利多转过身，长袍忽地一旋，他不见了。随即他又在伏地魔身后出现了，朝喷泉里剩下的那些雕像挥舞魔杖。雕像们顿时活了过来。女巫雕像朝贝拉特里克斯冲去，贝拉特里克斯尖叫着发射出一个个咒语，但那些咒语都从雕像胸口擦过，不起作用，最后雕像扑过去把她压在了地上。与此同时，妖精和家养小精灵快步奔向周围墙上的那些壁炉，独臂马人朝伏地魔冲去。伏地魔突然消失，接着又出现在水池旁。邓布利多一步步逼近伏地魔，金色马人绕着他们俩奔跑。无头雕像把哈利推到后面，让他离开了激战现场。

"今晚到这里来是愚蠢的，汤姆，"邓布利多平静地说，"傲罗们就要来了——"

"等他们赶来，我已经走了，你已经死了！"伏地魔恶狠狠地说。他又朝邓布利多发射了一个杀戮咒，但没有击中，打在了保安的桌子上，桌子顿时燃起火苗。

邓布利多轻轻挥动着魔杖：魔杖射出的咒语威力太强大了，哈利虽然有金色男巫挡着，咒语飞过时也感到他的头发都竖了起来。伏地魔这次不得不凭空变出一个闪亮的银盾来抵挡。不知这是什么咒语，似乎并没有看见它给银盾造成什么破坏，但银盾里发出一种锣一般低

CHAPTER THIRTY-SIX The Only One He Ever Feared

was, caused no visible damage to the shield, though a deep, gong-like note reverberated from it – an oddly chilling sound.

'You do not seek to kill me, Dumbledore?' called Voldemort, his scarlet eyes narrowed over the top of the shield. 'Above such brutality, are you?'

'We both know that there are other ways of destroying a man, Tom,' Dumbledore said calmly, continuing to walk towards Voldemort as though he had not a fear in the world, as though nothing had happened to interrupt his stroll up the hall. 'Merely taking your life would not satisfy me, I admit –'

'There is nothing worse than death, Dumbledore!' snarled Voldemort.

'You are quite wrong,' said Dumbledore, still closing in upon Voldemort and speaking as lightly as though they were discussing the matter over drinks. Harry felt scared to see him walking along, undefended, shieldless; he wanted to cry out a warning, but his headless guard kept shunting him backwards towards the wall, blocking his every attempt to get out from behind it. 'Indeed, your failure to understand that there are things much worse than death has always been your greatest weakness –'

Another jet of green light flew from behind the silver shield. This time it was the one-armed centaur, galloping in front of Dumbledore, that took the blast and shattered into a hundred pieces, but before the fragments had even hit the floor, Dumbledore had drawn back his wand and waved it as though brandishing a whip. A long thin flame flew from the tip; it wrapped itself around Voldemort, shield and all. For a moment, it seemed Dumbledore had won, but then the fiery rope became a serpent, which relinquished its hold on Voldemort at once and turned, hissing furiously, to face Dumbledore.

Voldemort vanished; the snake reared from the floor, ready to strike –

There was a burst of flame in midair above Dumbledore just as Voldemort reappeared, standing on the plinth in the middle of the pool where so recently the five statues had stood.

'*Look out!*' Harry yelled.

But even as he shouted, another jet of green light flew at Dumbledore from Voldemort's wand and the snake struck –

Fawkes swooped down in front of Dumbledore, opened his beak wide and swallowed the jet of green light whole: he burst into flame and fell to the floor, small, wrinkled and flightless. At the same moment, Dumbledore brandished his wand in one long, fluid movement – the snake, which had

第36章 他唯一害怕的人

沉的颤音——这异样的声音令人胆寒。

"你不是想要我的命吧,邓布利多?"伏地魔大声说,在银盾上方眯起一双血红的眼睛,"你不屑于做这种残忍的事,对吗?"

"我们都知道还有其他方式可以摧毁一个人,汤姆,"邓布利多平静地说,一边继续朝伏地魔走去,似乎他在世上没有任何畏惧,似乎什么也不能打扰他的闲庭信步,"我承认,仅仅取你的性命,不会让我满足——"

"没有什么比死亡更糟糕的,邓布利多!"伏地魔恶狠狠地说。

"这你可就错了。"邓布利多说,他仍然一步步逼近伏地魔,说话的语气轻松随意,就好像他们是在喝酒聊天。哈利看到他没有防御、无遮无拦地向前走去,感到非常害怕。哈利想大喊一声提醒邓布利多,可是那个无头警卫不断赶着他往墙边退去,他每次想从它身后逃出去都被它挡住了。"是的,一直以来,你的最大弱点就是不能理解有些事情比死亡糟糕得多——"

又一道绿光从银盾后面射出。这次是独臂马人冲到邓布利多前面,被咒语击中,炸成了碎片。没等那些碎片落到地上,邓布利多就抽回魔杖,像挥鞭子一样四下挥舞起来。杖尖上蹿出一道细细长长的火焰,把伏地魔和他的银盾都缠绕起来。一时间,邓布利多似乎赢了,可是接着火绳变成了一条大蛇,它立刻放开伏地魔,转过来对着邓布利多,嘴里发出愤怒的咝咝声。

伏地魔消失了;蛇从地上竖起身子,准备出击——

邓布利多头顶上空爆出火焰,与此同时伏地魔又出现了,站在刚才矗立着五座雕像的水池中央的底座上。

"小心!"哈利喊道。

话音未落,又一道绿光从伏地魔的魔杖射向邓布利多,大蛇也发起进攻——

这时,凤凰福克斯俯冲到邓布利多身前,嘴巴张得大大的,把那道绿光整个儿吞了下去。它全身腾起火焰,落在地上,缩成了皱巴巴的一小团,飞不起来了。这时,邓布利多用流畅的动作大幅度地挥了一下魔杖——眼看就要把毒牙扎进他身体里的那条大蛇,突然被高高

CHAPTER THIRTY-SIX The Only One He Ever Feared

been an instant from sinking its fangs into him, flew high into the air and vanished in a wisp of dark smoke; and the water in the pool rose up and covered Voldemort like a cocoon of molten glass.

For a few seconds Voldemort was visible only as a dark, rippling, faceless figure, shimmering and indistinct upon the plinth, clearly struggling to throw off the suffocating mass –

Then he was gone and the water fell with a crash back into its pool, slopping wildly over the sides, drenching the polished floor.

'MASTER!' screamed Bellatrix.

Sure it was over, sure Voldemort had decided to flee, Harry made to run out from behind his statue guard, but Dumbledore bellowed: 'Stay where you are, Harry!'

For the first time, Dumbledore sounded frightened. Harry could not see why: the hall was quite empty but for themselves, the sobbing Bellatrix still trapped under the witch statue, and the baby phoenix Fawkes croaking feebly on the floor –

Then Harry's scar burst open and he knew he was dead: it was pain beyond imagining, pain past endurance –

He was gone from the hall, he was locked in the coils of a creature with red eyes, so tightly bound that Harry did not know where his body ended and the creature's began: they were fused together, bound by pain, and there was no escape –

And when the creature spoke, it used Harry's mouth, so that in his agony he felt his jaw move ...

'*Kill me now, Dumbledore ...*'

Blinded and dying, every part of him screaming for release, Harry felt the creature use him again ...

'*If death is nothing, Dumbledore, kill the boy ...*'

Let the pain stop, thought Harry ... let him kill us ... end it, Dumbledore ... death is nothing compared to this ...

And I'll see Sirius again ...

And as Harry's heart filled with emotion, the creature's coils loosened, the pain was gone; Harry was lying face down on the floor, his glasses gone, shivering as though he lay upon ice, not wood ...

And there were voices echoing through the hall, more voices than there

第36章 他唯一害怕的人

地抛到空中,变成一股黑烟消失了。池里的水升了起来,像一个由熔化的玻璃做成的茧一样罩住了伏地魔。

有那么几秒钟,只能看见伏地魔一个面目不清的波动的黑影,在底座上模模糊糊地闪动,似乎在挣扎着摆脱这团令他窒息的东西——

接着,他不见了,水哗啦一声落回池子里,大量地泼溅出来,打湿了光滑明亮的地板。

"主人!"贝拉特里克斯尖叫道。

哈利相信战斗已经结束,伏地魔已经决定逃跑。哈利刚要从雕像警卫身后冲出来,却听见邓布利多大吼一声:"待在那里别动,哈利!"

邓布利多的声音第一次透出了恐惧,哈利不明白这是为什么:正厅里除了他们没有别人,贝拉特里克斯呜咽着,仍然被女巫雕像压在身下,幼雏福克斯在地板上微弱地鸣叫着——

接着,哈利的伤疤爆裂开来,他知道他死了。这疼痛超乎想象,这疼痛无法忍受——

他离开了正厅,他被锁在了一个红眼睛怪物盘成的圆圈里,他被缠得那么紧,简直不知道他的身体在哪里结束,怪物的身体又从哪里开始。他们融为一体,被痛苦捆在了一起,无处可逃——

接着那怪物说话了,用的是哈利的嘴,于是哈利在痛苦中感到自己的下巴在动……

"快杀死我吧,邓布利多……"

哈利眼睛看不见,奄奄一息,身体的每一部分都在渴望着松绑,他觉得那个怪物又在利用他了……

"如果死亡不算什么,邓布利多,那就杀死这男孩……"

让疼痛停止吧,哈利想……让他杀死我们两个吧……邓布利多,结束这一切吧……死亡跟这个相比不算什么……

而且我又能见到小天狼星了。

当哈利心中充满感情时,那个怪物的缠绕放松了,疼痛也消失了。哈利面朝下躺在地上,浑身发抖,感觉不像躺在地板上,而像躺在冰上,眼镜不见了……

正厅里回响着许多声音,按说不应该有这么多声音的……哈利睁

CHAPTER THIRTY-SIX The Only One He Ever Feared

should have been ... Harry opened his eyes, saw his glasses lying by the heel of the headless statue that had been guarding him, but which now lay flat on its back, cracked and immobile. He put them on and raised his head a little to find Dumbledore's crooked nose inches from his own.

'Are you all right, Harry?'

'Yes,' said Harry, shaking so violently he could not hold his head up properly. 'Yeah, I'm – where's Voldemort, where – who are all these – what's –'

The Atrium was full of people; the floor was reflecting the emerald green flames that had burst into life in all the fireplaces along one wall; and streams of witches and wizards were emerging from them. As Dumbledore pulled him back to his feet, Harry saw the tiny gold statues of the house-elf and the goblin, leading a stunned-looking Cornelius Fudge forward.

'He was there!' shouted a scarlet-robed man with a ponytail, who was pointing at a pile of golden rubble on the other side of the hall, where Bellatrix had lain trapped only moments before. 'I saw him, Mr Fudge, I swear it was You-Know-Who, he grabbed a woman and Disapparated!'

'I know, Williamson, I know, I saw him too!' gibbered Fudge, who was wearing pyjamas under his pinstriped cloak and was gasping as though he had just run miles. 'Merlin's beard – here – *here*! – in the Ministry of Magic! – great heavens above – it doesn't seem possible – my word – how can this be –?'

'If you proceed downstairs into the Department of Mysteries, Cornelius,' said Dumbledore – apparently satisfied that Harry was all right, and walking forwards so that the newcomers realised he was there for the first time (a few of them raised their wands; others simply looked amazed; the statues of the elf and goblin applauded and Fudge jumped so much that his slipper-clad feet left the floor) – 'you will find several escaped Death Eaters contained in the Death Chamber, bound by an Anti-Disapparition Jinx and awaiting your decision as to what to do with them.'

'Dumbledore!' gasped Fudge, beside himself with amazement. 'You – here – I – I –'

He looked wildly around at the Aurors he had brought with him and it could not have been clearer that he was in half a mind to cry, 'Seize him!'

'Cornelius, I am ready to fight your men – and win, again!' said Dumbledore in a thunderous voice. 'But a few minutes ago you saw proof, with your own eyes, that I have been telling you the truth for a year. Lord

第36章 他唯一害怕的人

开眼睛,看见自己的眼镜就在那个无头雕像的脚边。刚才雕像一直守护着他,此刻却仰面躺在地上,碎裂了,一动不动。哈利戴上眼镜,把头抬起一些,发现邓布利多那歪扭的鼻子近在咫尺。

"你没事吧,哈利?"

"没事。"哈利回答,他抖得那么厉害,连脑袋都不能稳稳地抬起,"是啊,我没事——伏地魔呢——这些人是谁——怎么——"

正厅里挤满了人。一面墙上的那些壁炉都突然燃起了旺火,鲜绿色的火焰映在地板上。众多男女巫师潮水般地从壁炉里涌了出来。邓布利多拉着哈利站起身,哈利看见家养小精灵和妖精的金色小雕像领着一脸惊愕的康奈利·福吉走了过来。

"他刚才就在这儿!"一个梳马尾辫、穿红袍子的男人大声喊道,指着大厅另一边的一堆金色碎石,贝拉特里克斯刚才就是被压在这里的,"我看见他了,福吉先生,我发誓那就是神秘人,他抓起一个女人,幻影移形了!"

"我知道,威廉森,我知道,我也看见他了!"福吉含糊不清地说,他的细条纹斗篷下穿着睡衣,像刚刚长跑完似的气喘吁吁,"梅林的胡子啊——这儿——就在这儿——在魔法部里!——我的老天爷啊——这简直不可思议——哎呀——这怎么可能呢——?"

"如果你下楼到神秘事务司去看一看,康奈利,"邓布利多说——他看到哈利平安无事似乎很欣慰,迈步走上前去,那些新来的人这才发现邓布利多的存在(有些人举起了魔杖,另一些人只是露出惊异的神情。小精灵和妖精的雕像鼓起掌来,福吉大吃一惊,穿着拖鞋的脚跳离了地面)——"就会发现死刑厅里有几个逃跑的食死徒,被反幻影移形咒束缚着,等待着你的发落呢。"

"邓布利多!"福吉喘着粗气说,惊讶得失去了控制,"你——在这儿——我——我——"

他慌乱地看着周围他带来的那些傲罗,毫无疑问,他几乎想大喊一声:"把他抓起来!"

"康奈利,我准备跟你的人搏斗——并且再次获胜!"邓布利多用雷鸣般洪亮的声音说,"但是就在几分钟前,你亲眼看见了证据,说明

CHAPTER THIRTY-SIX The Only One He Ever Feared

Voldemort has returned, you have been chasing the wrong man for twelve months, and it is time you listened to sense!'

'I – don't – well –' blustered Fudge, looking around as though hoping somebody was going to tell him what to do. When nobody did, he said, 'Very well – Dawlish! Williamson! Go down to the Department of Mysteries and see ... Dumbledore, you – you will need to tell me exactly – the fountain of Magical Brethren – what happened?' he added in a kind of whimper, staring around at the floor, where the remains of the statues of the witch, wizard and centaur now lay scattered.

'We can discuss that after I have sent Harry back to Hogwarts,' said Dumbledore.

'Harry – *Harry Potter?*'

Fudge spun round and stared at Harry, who was still standing against the wall beside the fallen statue that had guarded him during Dumbledore and Voldemort's duel.

'He – here?' said Fudge. 'Why – what's all this about?'

'I shall explain everything,' repeated Dumbledore, 'when Harry is back at school.'

He walked away from the pool to the place where the golden wizard's head lay on the floor. He pointed his wand at it and muttered, '*Portus.*' The head glowed blue and trembled noisily against the wooden floor for a few seconds, then became still once more.

'Now see here, Dumbledore!' said Fudge, as Dumbledore picked up the head and walked back to Harry carrying it. 'You haven't got authorisation for that Portkey! You can't do things like that right in front of the Minister for Magic, you – you –'

His voice faltered as Dumbledore surveyed him magisterially over his half-moon spectacles.

'You will give the order to remove Dolores Umbridge from Hogwarts,' said Dumbledore. 'You will tell your Aurors to stop searching for my Care of Magical Creatures teacher so that he can return to work. I will give you ...' Dumbledore pulled a watch with twelve hands from his pocket and glanced at it '... half an hour of my time tonight, in which I think we shall be more than able to cover the important points of what has happened here. After that, I shall need to return to my school. If you need more help from me you are, of course, more than welcome to contact me at Hogwarts. Letters addressed to the Headmaster will find me.'

第36章 他唯一害怕的人

我一年来告诉你的都是事实。伏地魔回来了，你们在这十二个月里追错了人，现在你应该听听理智的声音了！"

"我——我不——哼——"福吉气冲冲地咆哮着，环顾四周，似乎指望有人告诉他该怎么做。见没人开口，他又说："很好——德力士！威廉森！下楼到神秘事务司去看看……邓布利多，你——你需要明明白白地告诉我——魔法兄弟喷泉——是怎么回事？"他用一种近乎呜咽的声音加了一句，望着地板上男巫、女巫和马人雕像的四分五裂的残骸。

"等我把哈利送回霍格沃茨后，我们再谈论这件事。"邓布利多说。

"哈利——哈利·波特？"

福吉猛地转过身盯着哈利，哈利仍然站在墙边，站在那座雕像旁，雕像在邓布利多和伏地魔搏斗中保护过他，此刻躺倒在地。

"他——在这儿？"福吉说，"为什么——这都是怎么回事？"

"等哈利回到学校之后，"邓布利多又说了一遍，"我会把一切都解释清楚的。"

他离开水池，来到金色男巫的脑袋坠落的地方。他用魔杖指着男巫的脑袋，低声念道："门托斯。"男巫的脑袋透出蓝光，在地板上颤抖着，发出很响的声音，几秒钟后又归于平静。

"你听我说，邓布利多！"福吉说，这时邓布利多捡起男巫的脑袋，拿着它走回哈利面前，"没有人批准你使用那个门钥匙！你不能在魔法部部长面前这样胡作非为，你——你——"

邓布利多从半月形眼镜上威严地审视着福吉，福吉的声音支吾了。

"你要下一道命令让多洛雷斯·乌姆里奇离开霍格沃茨。"邓布利多说，"你要告诉你的傲罗别再搜捕我的保护神奇动物课教师，好让他回来工作。今天晚上我给你……"邓布利多从口袋里掏出一只十二根指针的怀表看了看，"……半个小时，我认为这足够我们说清这里发生的事情的要点。毕竟，我还要回到我的学校去。如果你仍需要我的帮助，当然啦，非常欢迎你写信到霍格沃茨跟我联系。信上写校长，我就能收到。"

CHAPTER THIRTY-SIX The Only One He Ever Feared

Fudge goggled worse than ever; his mouth was open and his round face grew pinker under his rumpled grey hair.

'I – you –'

Dumbledore turned his back on him.

'Take this Portkey, Harry.'

He held out the golden head of the statue and Harry placed his hand on it, past caring what he did next or where he went.

'I shall see you in half an hour,' said Dumbledore quietly. 'One ... two ... three ...'

Harry felt the familiar sensation of a hook being jerked behind his navel. The polished wooden floor was gone from beneath his feet; the Atrium, Fudge and Dumbledore had all disappeared and he was flying forwards in a whirlwind of colour and sound ...

第36章 他唯一害怕的人

福吉的眼睛瞪得更大了,他嘴巴张着,那张圆脸在乱糟糟的灰头发下涨得更红了。

"我——你——"

邓布利多转身背对着他。

"拿着这个门钥匙,哈利。"

他递过雕像的金色脑袋,哈利把手放了上去,没再考虑下面要做什么,要去哪里。

"半小时后见,"邓布利多轻声说,"一……二……三……"

哈利又有了那种熟悉的感觉,似乎有钩子在他的肚脐眼后面使劲一拉。他脚下亮锃锃的木地板消失了,正厅、福吉和邓布利多也都消失了,他在一片旋舞的色彩和声音中,向前飞去……

CHAPTER THIRTY-SEVEN

The Lost Prophecy

Harry's feet hit solid ground; his knees buckled a little and the golden wizard's head fell with a resounding *clunk* to the floor. He looked around and saw that he had arrived in Dumbledore's office.

Everything seemed to have repaired itself during the Headmaster's absence. The delicate silver instruments stood once more on the spindle-legged tables, puffing and whirring serenely. The portraits of the headmasters and headmistresses were snoozing in their frames, heads lolling back in armchairs or against the edge of the picture. Harry looked through the window. There was a cool line of pale green along the horizon: dawn was approaching.

The silence and the stillness, broken only by the occasional grunt or snuffle of a sleeping portrait, was unbearable to him. If his surroundings could have reflected the feelings inside him, the pictures would have been screaming in pain. He walked around the quiet, beautiful office, breathing quickly, trying not to think. But he had to think ... there was no escape ...

It was his fault Sirius had died; it was all his fault. If he, Harry, had not been stupid enough to fall for Voldemort's trick, if he had not been so convinced that what he had seen in his dream was real, if he had only opened his mind to the possibility that Voldemort was, as Hermione had said, banking on Harry's *love of playing the hero* ...

It was unbearable, he would not think about it, he could not stand it ... there was a terrible hollow inside him he did not want to feel or examine, a dark hole where Sirius had been, where Sirius had vanished; he did not want to have to be alone with that great, silent space, he could not stand it –

A picture behind him gave a particularly loud grunting snore, and a cool voice said, 'Ah ... Harry Potter ...'

第37章

丢失的预言

哈利的脚撞到了坚实的地面；他膝盖有点打弯，金色男巫的脑袋喀的一声落在地上，发出回响。他环顾四周，发现来到了邓布利多的办公室。

校长不在的这段时间，这里似乎所有的东西都自动修复了。那些精美的银器又摆在细长腿的桌子上，静静地旋转着，喷着烟雾。昔日男女校长的肖像都在相框里打着盹，脑袋懒洋洋地仰靠在扶手椅上或倚在相框边上。哈利透过窗户朝外望去，地平线上有一道淡淡的浅绿色：天快亮了。

房间里一片寂静，只有某个睡梦中的肖像偶尔发出嘟哝声或哼哼声，这寂静令哈利无法忍受。如果周围的环境能够反映他内心的感受，那么这些肖像应该都在痛苦地尖叫。他在安静、漂亮的办公室里走动着，呼吸十分急促，努力克制着不去思考。可是他不得不思考……他没有办法逃避……

小天狼星的死都是他的错，完完全全都是他的错。如果不是哈利愚蠢地中了伏地魔的圈套，如果不是他那么相信梦里看到的一切都是真的，如果他哪怕稍微考虑一下伏地魔有可能——像赫敏说的那样——利用哈利喜欢逞英雄……

这太令人无法忍受了，他不愿意去想，他无法承受……他的内心有一个他不愿去感觉或探究的可怕的空洞，一个漆黑的窟窿，那是小天狼星所在的地方，那是小天狼星消失的地方。他不愿意被迫独自面对那个巨大而寂静的空间，他无法承受——

他身后的一幅肖像发出一声特别响的呼噜，接着一个冷冷的声音说道："啊……哈利·波特……"

CHAPTER THIRTY-SEVEN The Lost Prophecy

Phineas Nigellus gave a long yawn, stretching his arms as he watched Harry with shrewd, narrow eyes.

'And what brings you here in the early hours of the morning?' said Phineas eventually. 'This office is supposed to be barred to all but the rightful Headmaster. Or has Dumbledore sent you here? Oh, don't tell me …' He gave another shuddering yawn. 'Another message for my worthless great-great-grandson?'

Harry could not speak. Phineas Nigellus did not know that Sirius was dead, but Harry could not tell him. To say it aloud would be to make it final, absolute, irretrievable.

A few more of the portraits had stirred now. Terror of being interrogated made Harry stride across the room and seize the doorknob.

It would not turn. He was shut in.

'I hope this means,' said the corpulent, red-nosed wizard who hung on the wall behind the Headmaster's desk, 'that Dumbledore will soon be back among us?'

Harry turned. The wizard was eyeing him with great interest. Harry nodded. He tugged again on the doorknob behind his back, but it remained immovable.

'Oh good,' said the wizard. 'It has been very dull without him, very dull indeed.'

He settled himself on the throne-like chair on which he had been painted and smiled benignly upon Harry.

'Dumbledore thinks very highly of you, as I am sure you know,' he said comfortably. 'Oh yes. Holds you in great esteem.'

The guilt filling the whole of Harry's chest like some monstrous, weighty parasite, now writhed and squirmed. Harry could not stand this, he could not stand being himself any more … he had never felt more trapped inside his own head and body, never wished so intensely that he could be somebody, anybody, else …

The empty fireplace burst into emerald green flame, making Harry leap away from the door, staring at the man spinning inside the grate. As Dumbledore's tall form unfolded itself from the fire, the wizards and witches on the surrounding walls jerked awake, many of them giving cries of welcome.

'Thank you,' said Dumbledore softly.

第37章 丢失的预言

菲尼亚斯·奈杰勒斯伸展双臂，打了一个长长的哈欠，一边用犀利的小眼睛打量着哈利。

"一大早的，是什么风把你给吹来了？"菲尼亚斯终于说，"这间办公室，除了合法的校长谁也进不来。莫非是邓布利多送你来的？哦，别跟我说……"他又哆嗦着打了一个哈欠，"又是我那个没出息的玄孙派你来送信的？"

哈利说不出话来。菲尼亚斯·奈杰勒斯还不知道小天狼星已经死了，但哈利没法告诉他。如果把这件事大声说出来就会使它铁板钉钉，无法挽回。

又有几个肖像开始动弹了。遭受审问的恐惧使哈利大步走过房间，抓住了门的球形把手。

门把手转不动。他被关在这里了。

"我希望这意味着，"挂在校长办公桌后面的那个红鼻子胖男巫说，"邓布利多很快就要回到我们中间了？"

哈利转过身。男巫饶有兴趣地端详着他。哈利点了点头，又拽了拽身后的球形门把手，还是没有拽动。

"哦，太好了，"男巫说，"没有他，日子非常乏味，确实非常乏味。"

他在画中那把宝座般的椅子上舒舒服服地坐好，对哈利露出了慈祥的微笑。

"邓布利多一向很看重你，我想你肯定知道，"他和颜悦色地说，"是啊，他对你评价很高。"

负罪感像一种巨大的、沉甸甸的寄生虫一样挤满了哈利的整个胸膛，扭曲着、蠕动着。哈利无法承受，他无法承受再做他自己……他从没像现在这样感到被束缚在自己的大脑和身体里，从没像现在这样强烈地希望能够成为另一个人，不管是谁都行……

空空的壁炉里突然蹿出艳绿色的火苗，哈利惊得从门边跳开，呆呆地望着那个在炉栅里旋转的人。当邓布利多高高的身影从炉火中显现时，周围墙上的男女巫师都惊醒过来，许多人都大喊着表示欢迎。

"谢谢。"邓布利多轻声说。

CHAPTER THIRTY-SEVEN The Lost Prophecy

He did not look at Harry at first, but walked over to the perch beside the door and withdrew, from an inside pocket of his robes, the tiny, ugly, featherless Fawkes, whom he placed gently on the tray of soft ashes beneath the golden post where the full-grown Fawkes usually stood.

'Well, Harry,' said Dumbledore, finally turning away from the baby bird, 'you will be pleased to hear that none of your fellow students are going to suffer lasting damage from the night's events.'

Harry tried to say, 'Good,' but no sound came out. It seemed to him that Dumbledore was reminding him of the amount of damage he had caused, and although Dumbledore was for once looking at him directly, and although his expression was kindly rather than accusatory, Harry could not bear to meet his eyes.

'Madam Pomfrey is patching everybody up,' said Dumbledore. 'Nymphadora Tonks may need to spend a little time in St Mungo's, but it seems she will make a full recovery.'

Harry contented himself with nodding at the carpet, which was growing lighter as the sky outside grew paler. He was sure all the portraits around the room were listening eagerly to every word Dumbledore spoke, wondering where Dumbledore and Harry had been, and why there had been injuries.

'I know how you're feeling, Harry,' said Dumbledore very quietly.

'No, you don't,' said Harry, and his voice was suddenly loud and strong; white-hot anger leapt inside him; Dumbledore knew *nothing* about his feelings.

'You see, Dumbledore?' said Phineas Nigellus slyly. 'Never try to understand the students. They hate it. They would much rather be tragically misunderstood, wallow in self-pity, stew in their own –'

'That's enough, Phineas,' said Dumbledore.

Harry turned his back on Dumbledore and stared determinedly out of the window. He could see the Quidditch stadium in the distance. Sirius had appeared there once, disguised as the shaggy black dog, so he could watch Harry play ... he had probably come to see whether Harry was as good as James had been ... Harry had never asked him ...

'There is no shame in what you are feeling, Harry,' said Dumbledore's voice. 'On the contrary ... the fact that you can feel pain like this is your greatest strength.'

Harry felt the white-hot anger lick his insides, blazing in the terrible

第37章 丢失的预言

他最初并没有看哈利,而是走到门边的栖枝旁,从长袍里面的口袋里掏出弱小、丑陋、没有羽毛的福克斯,把它轻轻地放在金色栖枝下那盘细软的灰烬里,往常成年福克斯就栖息在那根栖枝上。

"好了,哈利,"邓布利多终于离开那只雏鸟,说道,"你会很高兴听到你的同学没有一个在昨晚的事件中遭受难以治愈的伤害。"

哈利很想说出一个"好"字,可是没有发出声音。他觉得邓布利多似乎在提醒他造成的破坏有多严重,尽管邓布利多的目光第一次直视着他,尽管他的表情很慈祥,并没有责备的意思,但哈利却无法承受与他对视。

"庞弗雷女士正在对他们每个人进行治疗,"邓布利多说,"尼法朵拉·唐克斯可能需要在圣芒戈医院待上一段时间,但看来她也能完全康复。"

哈利只是冲着地毯点了点头,随着外面天空逐渐泛白,地毯也在变亮。他相信周围那些肖像都在关切地听着邓布利多说的每个字,并猜想邓布利多和哈利去了哪里,为什么会有人受伤。

"我知道你现在的感受,哈利。"邓布利多声音很轻地说。

"不,你不知道。"哈利说,声音突然变得很响,火气很冲。强烈的怒火在他心头蹿动。邓布利多根本不知道他内心的感受。

"看到没有,邓布利多?"菲尼亚斯·奈杰勒斯诙谐地说,"永远不要试图去理解学生。他们讨厌这个。他们宁愿遭到可悲的误解,沉湎于自怜自艾之中,自我折磨——"

"够了,菲尼亚斯。"邓布利多说。

哈利转过身,背对着邓布利多,倔强地望着窗外。他看见了远处的魁地奇球场。小天狼星曾经出现在那里,变成一条毛蓬蓬的大黑狗,就为了能看到哈利比赛……他也许是来看哈利是否跟詹姆一样出色……哈利从来没有问过他……

"你有这样的感受并不丢人,哈利,"邓布利多说,"恰恰相反……你能感觉到这么痛苦,这正是你最强大的力量。"

哈利觉得熊熊的怒火舔噬着他的五脏六腑,在那个可怕的虚空中

CHAPTER THIRTY-SEVEN The Lost Prophecy

emptiness, filling him with the desire to hurt Dumbledore for his calmness and his empty words.

'My greatest strength, is it?' said Harry, his voice shaking as he stared out at the Quidditch stadium, no longer seeing it. 'You haven't got a clue ... you don't know ...'

'What don't I know?' asked Dumbledore calmly.

It was too much. Harry turned around, shaking with rage.

'I don't want to talk about how I feel, all right?'

'Harry, suffering like this proves you are still a man! This pain is part of being human –'

'THEN – I – DON'T – WANT – TO – BE – HUMAN!' Harry roared, and he seized the delicate silver instrument from the spindle-legged table beside him and flung it across the room; it shattered into a hundred tiny pieces against the wall. Several of the pictures let out yells of anger and fright, and the portrait of Armando Dippet said, '*Really!*'

'I DON'T CARE!' Harry yelled at them, snatching up a lunascope and throwing it into the fireplace. 'I'VE HAD ENOUGH, I'VE SEEN ENOUGH, I WANT OUT, I WANT IT TO END, I DON'T CARE ANY MORE –'

He seized the table on which the silver instrument had stood and threw that, too. It broke apart on the floor and the legs rolled in different directions.

'You do care,' said Dumbledore. He had not flinched or made a single move to stop Harry demolishing his office. His expression was calm, almost detached. 'You care so much you feel as though you will bleed to death with the pain of it.'

'I – DON'T!' Harry screamed, so loudly that he felt his throat might tear, and for a second he wanted to rush at Dumbledore and break him, too; shatter that calm old face, shake him, hurt him, make him feel some tiny part of the horror inside himself.

'Oh, yes, you do,' said Dumbledore, still more calmly. 'You have now lost your mother, your father, and the closest thing to a parent you have ever known. Of course you care.'

'YOU DON'T KNOW HOW I FEEL!' Harry roared. 'YOU – STANDING THERE – YOU –'

But words were no longer enough, smashing things was no more help; he wanted to run, he wanted to keep running and never look back, he wanted

第37章 丢失的预言

燃烧着,使他内心充满冲动,想要去伤害邓布利多。就因为他的若无其事,因为他的这些空洞的话语。

"我最强大的力量,是吗?"哈利说,他声音颤抖,眼睛望着窗外的魁地奇球场,但心思已不在那里,"你根本就不明白……根本就不知道……"

"我不知道什么?"邓布利多平静地问。

太过分了。哈利转过身来,气得浑身发抖。

"我不想讨论我的感受,好吗?"

"哈利,这种折磨证明你还是个人!这种痛苦是人性的一部分——"

"那——我——就——不——想——当——人!"哈利吼道,他抓起身边细长腿桌上的一件精致的银器,朝房间那头扔去。银器撞在墙上摔成了碎片。几幅肖像发出愤怒和恐惧的尖叫,阿芒多·迪佩特的肖像说:"真不像话!"

"我不管!"哈利朝他们嚷道,又抓起一个观月镜扔进了壁炉,"**我受够了,我看够了,我要摆脱,我要结束这一切,我什么也不在乎了——**"

他抓起放银器的桌子,把它也扔了出去。桌子摔在地上裂开了,几条桌腿朝不同的方向滚去。

"你在乎。"邓布利多说。他不动声色,也没有试图阻止哈利毁坏他的办公室。他的表情很平静,几乎可以说是漠然,"你太在乎了,你觉得这痛苦会使你流血而死。"

"我——没有!"哈利嚷了起来,声音那么响,他觉得喉咙都要撕裂了。那一瞬间,他真想冲向邓布利多,把他也撕碎,砸烂那张苍老、平静的脸,摇晃他,伤害他,让他也稍稍感受到一点哈利内心的这种恐惧。

"哦,没错,你在乎,"邓布利多更加心平气和地说,"你失去了你的母亲、父亲,还失去了一位你认识的最像是父母的人。你当然在乎。"

"你不知道我的感受!"哈利咆哮道,"你——站在那里——你——"

但是怒吼已经不够,砸东西也不再管用。他想跑,他想不停地跑,再也不回头;他想跑到一个地方,再也看不见那双盯着自己的清澈的

CHAPTER THIRTY-SEVEN   The Lost Prophecy

to be somewhere he could not see the clear blue eyes staring at him, that hatefully calm old face. He ran to the door, seized the doorknob again and wrenched at it.

But the door would not open.

Harry turned back to Dumbledore.

'Let me out,' he said. He was shaking from head to foot.

'No,' said Dumbledore simply.

For a few seconds they stared at each other.

'Let me out,' Harry said again.

'No,' Dumbledore repeated.

'If you don't – if you keep me in here – if you don't let me –'

'By all means continue destroying my possessions,' said Dumbledore serenely. 'I daresay I have too many.'

He walked around his desk and sat down behind it, watching Harry.

'Let me out,' Harry said yet again, in a voice that was cold and almost as calm as Dumbledore's.

'Not until I have had my say,' said Dumbledore.

'Do you – do you think I want to – do you think I give a – I DON'T CARE WHAT YOU'VE GOT TO SAY!' Harry roared. 'I don't want to hear *anything* you've got to say!'

'You will,' said Dumbledore steadily. 'Because you are not nearly as angry with me as you ought to be. If you are to attack me, as I know you are close to doing, I would like to have thoroughly earned it.'

'What are you talking –?'

'It is *my* fault that Sirius died,' said Dumbledore clearly. 'Or should I say, almost entirely my fault – I will not be so arrogant as to claim responsibility for the whole. Sirius was a brave, clever and energetic man, and such men are not usually content to sit at home in hiding while they believe others to be in danger. Nevertheless, you should never have believed for an instant that there was any necessity for you to go to the Department of Mysteries tonight. If I had been open with you, Harry, as I should have been, you would have known a long time ago that Voldemort might try and lure you to the Department of Mysteries, and you would never have been tricked into going there tonight. And Sirius would not have had to come after you. That blame lies with me, and with me alone.'

第37章　丢失的预言

蓝眼睛，再也看不见那张可恨的、苍老而平静的脸。他跑到门口，再一次抓住球形把手，使劲拧着。

可是房门打不开。

哈利扭头望着邓布利多。

"放我出去。"他说。他从头到脚都在发抖。

"不行。"邓布利多简单地说。

他们对视了几秒钟。

"放我出去。"哈利又说。

"不行。"邓布利多重复着刚才的话。

"如果你不——如果你把我关在这里——如果你不放我——"

"尽管继续毁坏我的财物吧，"邓布利多安详地说，"我认为我的财物太多了。"

他绕到桌后坐了下来，注视着哈利。

"放我出去。"哈利又说，声音冷冰冰的，几乎像邓布利多一样平静。

"等我讲完了话再说。"邓布利多说。

"难道——难道你以为我想——难道你以为我在乎——**我根本不关心你要说什么！**"哈利吼道，"我不想听你说的任何话！"

"你会听的，"邓布利多语调平稳地说，"因为实际上你应该更生我的气。我知道你差点对我动手，如果你真的那么做了，那也完全是我咎由自取。"

"你在说什么——？"

"小天狼星的死是我的错，"邓布利多清清楚楚地说，"或者我应该说，几乎完全是我的错——我不会狂傲到想承担事情的全部责任。小天狼星是一个勇敢、机智、精力充沛的人，这样的人，当他们相信别人身处险境的时候，一般不会安心躲藏在家里。但是，你不应该认为昨晚你有必要去神秘事务司。如果我以前跟你开诚布公地谈谈，哈利，唉，我完全应该那么做的，那么你早就会知道伏地魔会试图把你引到神秘事务司去，你昨晚也就绝不会被骗到那里。小天狼星也就不会过去找你。过错都在我身上，都在我一个人身上。"

CHAPTER THIRTY-SEVEN   The Lost Prophecy

Harry was still standing with his hand on the doorknob but was unaware of it. He was gazing at Dumbledore, hardly breathing, listening yet barely understanding what he was hearing.

'Please sit down,' said Dumbledore. It was not an order, it was a request.

Harry hesitated, then walked slowly across the room now littered with silver cogs and fragments of wood, and took the seat facing Dumbledore's desk.

'Am I to understand,' said Phineas Nigellus slowly from Harry's left, 'that my great-great-grandson – the last of the Blacks – is dead?'

'Yes, Phineas,' said Dumbledore.

'I don't believe it,' said Phineas brusquely.

Harry turned his head in time to see Phineas marching out of his portrait and knew that he had gone to visit his other painting in Grimmauld Place. He would walk, perhaps, from portrait to portrait, calling for Sirius through the house ...

'Harry, I owe you an explanation,' said Dumbledore. 'An explanation of an old man's mistakes. For I see now that what I have done, and not done, with regard to you, bears all the hallmarks of the failings of age. Youth cannot know how age thinks and feels. But old men are guilty if they forget what it was to be young ... and I seem to have forgotten, lately ...'

The sun was rising properly now; there was a rim of dazzling orange visible over the mountains and the sky above it was colourless and bright. The light fell upon Dumbledore, upon the silver of his eyebrows and beard, upon the lines gouged deeply into his face.

'I guessed, fifteen years ago,' said Dumbledore, 'when I saw the scar on your forehead, what it might mean. I guessed that it might be the sign of a connection forged between you and Voldemort.'

'You've told me this before, Professor,' said Harry bluntly. He did not care about being rude. He did not care about anything very much any more.

'Yes,' said Dumbledore apologetically. 'Yes, but you see – it is necessary to start with your scar. For it became apparent, shortly after you rejoined the magical world, that I was correct, and that your scar was giving you warnings when Voldemort was close to you, or else feeling powerful emotion.'

'I know,' said Harry wearily.

'And this ability of yours – to detect Voldemort's presence, even when he is disguised, and to know what he is feeling when his emotions are roused – has

第37章 丢失的预言

哈利站在那里,手仍然握着球形门把手,但自己已浑然不觉。他盯着邓布利多,几乎屏住了呼吸,他听着,却几乎不明白对方在说什么。

"请坐下吧。"邓布利多说。这不是命令,而是请求。

哈利迟疑了一下,慢慢走过散落着银齿轮和碎木片的房间,坐在邓布利多办公桌对面的椅子上。

"我是不是应该理解为,"菲尼亚斯·奈杰勒斯在哈利左边语速很慢地说,"我的玄孙——布莱克家族的最后一位——已经死了?"

"是的,菲尼亚斯。"邓布利多说。

"我不信。"菲尼亚斯粗暴地说。

哈利转过头,正好看见菲尼亚斯大步走出肖像,哈利知道他是去拜访他在格里莫广场的另一幅肖像了。也许,他会从一幅肖像走到另一幅肖像,在整个房子里呼唤小天狼星……

"哈利,我需要给你一个解释,"邓布利多说,"解释一个老年人犯的错误。我现在明白了,我所做的事情,以及我因为关心你而没有做的事情,都显示出衰老的迹象。年轻人无法了解老人的思想感情。但是老人如果忘记年轻时是什么滋味,罪过可就大了……而我,最近似乎忘记了……"

太阳正在冉冉升起,山峦上呈现出一道耀眼的橘黄色光边,天空一片亮白。亮光照在邓布利多身上,照在他银色的眉毛和胡须上,照在他脸部深深的皱纹上。

"十五年前,"邓布利多说,"当我看见你额头上的伤疤时,我就猜想它会意味着什么。我猜想它可能是你和伏地魔之间拥有某种联系的记号。"

"你以前已经跟我说过了,教授。"哈利生硬地说,他不管自己是不是态度粗鲁。他已经什么都不在乎了。

"是的,"邓布利多带着歉意说道,"是的,可是你看——必须从你的伤疤说起。你重归魔法世界后不久,就证明了我是对的,每当伏地魔靠近你或每当他情绪激烈时,你的伤疤都会向你发出警告。"

"我知道。"哈利疲惫地说。

"你的这种能力——能够感知他的存在,即使他做了伪装,也能够

CHAPTER THIRTY-SEVEN   The Lost Prophecy

become more and more pronounced since Voldemort returned to his own body and his full powers.'

Harry did not bother to nod. He knew all of this already.

'More recently,' said Dumbledore, 'I became concerned that Voldemort might realise that this connection between you exists. Sure enough, there came a time when you entered so far into his mind and thoughts that he sensed your presence. I am speaking, of course, of the night when you witnessed the attack on Mr Weasley.'

'Yeah, Snape told me,' Harry muttered.

'*Professor* Snape, Harry,' Dumbledore corrected him quietly. 'But did you not wonder why it was not I who explained this to you? Why I did not teach you Occlumency? Why I had not so much as looked at you for months?'

Harry looked up. He could see now that Dumbledore looked sad and tired.

'Yeah,' Harry mumbled. 'Yeah, I wondered.'

'You see,' Dumbledore continued, 'I believed it could not be long before Voldemort attempted to force his way into your mind, to manipulate and misdirect your thoughts, and I was not eager to give him more incentives to do so. I was sure that if he realised that our relationship was – or had ever been – closer than that of headmaster and pupil, he would seize his chance to use you as a means to spy on me. I feared the uses to which he would put you, the possibility that he might try and possess you. Harry, I believe I was right to think that Voldemort would have made use of you in such a way. On those rare occasions when we had close contact, I thought I saw a shadow of him stir behind your eyes ...'

Harry remembered the feeling that a dormant snake had risen in him, ready to strike, in those moments when he and Dumbledore had made eye-contact.

'Voldemort's aim in possessing you, as he demonstrated tonight, would not have been my destruction. It would have been yours. He hoped, when he possessed you briefly a short while ago, that I would sacrifice you in the hope of killing him. So you see, I have been trying, in distancing myself from you, to protect you, Harry. An old man's mistake ...'

He sighed deeply. Harry was letting the words wash over him. He would have been so interested to know all this a few months ago, but now it was meaningless compared to the gaping chasm inside him that was the loss of Sirius; none of it mattered ...

第37章 丢失的预言

在他情感激烈时了解他的感受——在伏地魔回归自己的肉体、卷土重来之后变得越来越明显。"

哈利连头也懒得点了。这些他都已经知道了。

"最近,"邓布利多说,"我开始担心伏地魔可能发现了你们之间的这种联系。果然,后来有一次你深入他的大脑和思想时,他感觉到了你的存在。当然啦,我说的是你目睹韦斯莱先生遭到攻击的那个夜晚。"

"是,斯内普告诉我了。"哈利低声说。

"是斯内普教授,哈利。"邓布利多轻声纠正他说,"可是你有没有想过,为什么不是我向你解释这件事?为什么我没有亲自教你大脑封闭术?为什么我几个月都几乎没有看你一眼?"

哈利抬起头来,他这才看出邓布利多显得那么悲哀而疲惫。

"是的,"哈利低声说,"是的,我想过。"

"是这样,"邓布利多继续说道,"我相信过不了多久,伏地魔就会试图强行闯入你的大脑,操纵和误导你的思想,而我并不急于刺激他这么做。我相信,如果他发现我们的关系超越了校长和学生之间的关系——或曾经如此,他就会抓住机会,利用你来监视我。我害怕他会利用你,害怕他可能试图控制你。哈利,我认为伏地魔会用那样一种方式利用你,我相信我的想法是对的。在我们难得的几次近距离接触中,我仿佛看见你的眼睛后面有他的影子在动……"

哈利想起他和邓布利多目光对视的那些时候,他体内好像有一条蛇从睡梦中醒来,准备出击。

"伏地魔控制你的目的,就像他今晚所表现出来的,并不是要消灭我,而是要消灭你。在他刚才暂时附着在你身上的时候,他希望我会为了杀死他而把你牺牲掉。所以,你明白吗,我一直跟你保持着距离,就是为了保护你,哈利。一个老人犯的错误……"

他深深地叹了一口气。哈利让这些话像耳旁风一样吹过。几个月前,他会特别感兴趣地想知道这一切,可是现在,跟失去小天狼星在他内心造成的巨大伤痛相比,这些已毫无意义,什么都无所谓了……

CHAPTER THIRTY-SEVEN   The Lost Prophecy

'Sirius told me you felt Voldemort awake inside you the very night that you had the vision of Arthur Weasley's attack. I knew at once that my worst fears were correct: Voldemort had realised he could use you. In an attempt to arm you against Voldemort's assaults on your mind, I arranged Occlumency lessons with Professor Snape.'

He paused. Harry watched the sunlight, which was sliding slowly across the polished surface of Dumbledore's desk, illuminate a silver ink pot and a handsome scarlet quill. Harry could tell that the portraits all around them were awake and listening raptly to Dumbledore's explanation; he could hear the occasional rustle of robes, the slight clearing of a throat. Phineas Nigellus had still not returned ...

'Professor Snape discovered,' Dumbledore resumed, 'that you had been dreaming about the door to the Department of Mysteries for months. Voldemort, of course, had been obsessed with the possibility of hearing the prophecy ever since he regained his body; and as he dwelled on the door, so did you, though you did not know what it meant.

'And then you saw Rookwood, who worked in the Department of Mysteries before his arrest, telling Voldemort what we had known all along – that the prophecies held in the Ministry of Magic are heavily protected. Only the people to whom they refer can lift them from the shelves without suffering madness: in this case, either Voldemort himself would have to enter the Ministry of Magic, and risk revealing himself at last – or else you would have to take it for him. It became a matter of even greater urgency that you should master Occlumency.'

'But I didn't,' muttered Harry. He said it aloud to try and ease the dead weight of guilt inside him: a confession must surely relieve some of the terrible pressure squeezing his heart. 'I didn't practise, I didn't bother, I could've stopped myself having those dreams, Hermione kept telling me to do it, if I had he'd never have been able to show me where to go, and – Sirius wouldn't – Sirius wouldn't –'

Something was erupting inside Harry's head: a need to justify himself, to explain –

'I tried to check he'd really taken Sirius, I went to Umbridge's office, I spoke to Kreacher in the fire and he said Sirius wasn't there, he said he'd gone!'

第37章 丢失的预言

"小天狼星告诉我,你在脑海里看见亚瑟·韦斯莱遭到袭击的那天夜里,感觉到伏地魔在你体内醒着。我立刻知道我最担心的事情果然应验了:伏地魔已经发现他可以利用你。为了让你武装起来抗击伏地魔对你大脑的突袭,我安排你跟斯内普教授学习大脑封闭术。"

他停住话头。哈利注视着阳光缓缓滑过邓布利多办公桌光洁的桌面,照亮了一个银色的墨水瓶和一支漂亮的红色羽毛笔。哈利感觉到周围的肖像都醒着,都在全神贯注地听着邓布利多的解释。他听见偶尔传来衣袍的沙沙声和轻轻清嗓子的声音。菲尼亚斯·奈杰勒斯还没有回来……

"斯内普教授发现,"邓布利多继续说道,"你几个月来一直梦见神秘事务司的那扇门。当然啦,伏地魔自从重新获得肉身之后,便心心念念地想要听到那个预言。他整天想着那扇门,你也是这样,虽然你不明白那是什么意思。

"后来,你看见了被捕前曾在神秘事务司工作的卢克伍德,他告诉伏地魔我们早已知道的那件事——就是存在魔法部的那些预言球都受到严密保护。只有预言涉及的人才能把它们从架子上取下来而不会精神错乱:具体来说,就是要么伏地魔自己闯进魔法部,冒着暴露自己的危险——要么让你去替他取。这样一来,你掌握大脑封闭术就显得更紧迫了。"

"可是我没有掌握。"哈利嘟哝着说。他把这些话说出来,试图减轻内心沉重的负罪感。实话实说肯定能缓解那种挤压他心脏的可怕力量,"我没有练习,我没有上心,我本来能够阻止自己做那些梦的,赫敏也总是提醒我,如果我用功一些,他就无法告诉我该去哪儿,小天狼星也就不会——小天狼星也就不会——"

一个念头在哈利脑海里突然冒出来,他需要为自己辩护,需要解释——

"我想核实一下他是否真的抓住了小天狼星,就去了乌姆里奇的办公室,在炉火里跟克利切说话,他说小天狼星不在那儿,说小天狼星走了!"

CHAPTER THIRTY-SEVEN The Lost Prophecy

'Kreacher lied,' said Dumbledore calmly. 'You are not his master, he could lie to you without even needing to punish himself. Kreacher intended you to go to the Ministry of Magic.'

'He – he sent me on purpose?'

'Oh yes. Kreacher, I am afraid, has been serving more than one master for months.'

'How?' said Harry blankly. 'He hasn't been out of Grimmauld Place for years.'

'Kreacher seized his opportunity shortly before Christmas,' said Dumbledore, 'when Sirius, apparently, shouted at him to "get out". He took Sirius at his word, and interpreted this as an order to leave the house. He went to the only Black family member for whom he had any respect left ... Black's cousin Narcissa, sister of Bellatrix and wife of Lucius Malfoy.'

'How do you know all this?' Harry said. His heart was beating very fast. He felt sick. He remembered worrying about Kreacher's odd absence over Christmas, remembered him turning up again in the attic ...

'Kreacher told me last night,' said Dumbledore. 'You see, when you gave Professor Snape that cryptic warning, he realised that you had had a vision of Sirius trapped in the bowels of the Department of Mysteries. He, like you, attempted to contact Sirius at once. I should explain that members of the Order of the Phoenix have more reliable methods of communicating than the fire in Dolores Umbridge's office. Professor Snape found that Sirius was alive and safe in Grimmauld Place.

'When, however, you did not return from your trip into the Forest with Dolores Umbridge, Professor Snape grew worried that you still believed Sirius to be a captive of Lord Voldemort's. He alerted certain Order members at once.'

Dumbledore heaved a great sigh and continued, 'Alastor Moody, Nymphadora Tonks, Kingsley Shacklebolt and Remus Lupin were at Headquarters when he made contact. All agreed to go to your aid at once. Professor Snape requested that Sirius remain behind, as he needed somebody to remain at Headquarters to tell me what had happened, for I was due there at any moment. In the meantime he, Professor Snape, intended to search the Forest for you.

'But Sirius did not wish to remain behind while the others went to search for you. He delegated to Kreacher the task of telling me what had happened. And so it was that when I arrived in Grimmauld Place shortly after they had

第37章 丢失的预言

"克利切在说谎。"邓布利多平静地说,"你不是他的主人,他可以对你撒谎而无须惩罚自己。克利切想让你去魔法部。"

"他——他是故意打发我去的?"

"是的。好几个月来,克利切恐怕一直在为不止一个主人效力。"

"怎么会呢?"哈利茫然地说,"他好几年都没有离开过格里莫广场。"

"就在圣诞节前夕,克利切抓住了机会,"邓布利多说,"当时小天狼星好像是嚷嚷着叫他'出去'。结果他以为小天狼星说的是真话,把这理解为命令他离开房子。他就去找了布莱克家族他唯一还对其保留一些尊敬的那个人……布莱克的堂姐纳西莎,也就是贝拉特里克斯的妹妹,卢修斯·马尔福的妻子。"

"你是怎么知道这些的?"哈利说。他的心跳得飞快。他觉得很不舒服。他还记得自己曾为克利切在圣诞节时莫名其妙地失踪而感到担心,并记得他后来又突然出现在了阁楼上……

"克利切昨晚告诉我的,"邓布利多说,"知道吗,当你话里有话地提醒斯内普教授之后,他便意识到你在大脑里看见了小天狼星被困在神秘事务司里。他像你一样立刻试图联系小天狼星。我应该解释一下,凤凰社成员有着比多洛雷斯·乌姆里奇办公室的炉火更可靠的联络方式。斯内普教授发现小天狼星在格里莫广场安然无恙。

"可是,你跟多洛雷斯·乌姆里奇闯进禁林后没有回来,斯内普教授就开始担心你仍然相信小天狼星还在伏地魔手里。他立刻通知了几位凤凰社成员。"

邓布利多沉重地叹了一口气,继续说道:"他联系时,阿拉斯托·穆迪、尼法朵拉·唐克斯、金斯莱·沙克尔和莱姆斯·卢平都在总部。他们都同意立刻去援助你。斯内普教授要求小天狼星留在家里,因为我随时都会赶到那里,需要有人留在总部把情况告诉我。与此同时,斯内普教授打算在禁林里搜寻你。

"可是,小天狼星不愿意在别人都去找你的时候留在总部。他委托克利切把情况告诉我。因此,当我在他们都去魔法部之后不久赶到格

CHAPTER THIRTY-SEVEN The Lost Prophecy

all left for the Ministry, it was the elf who told me – laughing fit to burst – where Sirius had gone.'

'He was laughing?' said Harry in a hollow voice.

'Oh, yes,' said Dumbledore. 'You see, Kreacher was not able to betray us totally. He is not Secret Keeper for the Order, he could not give the Malfoys our whereabouts, or tell them any of the Order's confidential plans that he had been forbidden to reveal. He was bound by the enchantments of his kind, which is to say that he could not disobey a direct order from his master, Sirius. But he gave Narcissa information of the sort that is very valuable to Voldemort, yet must have seemed much too trivial for Sirius to think of banning him from repeating it.'

'Like what?' said Harry.

'Like the fact that the person Sirius cared most about in the world was you,' said Dumbledore quietly. 'Like the fact that you were coming to regard Sirius as a mixture of father and brother. Voldemort knew already, of course, that Sirius was in the Order, and that you knew where he was – but Kreacher's information made him realise that the one person for whom you would go to any lengths to rescue was Sirius Black.'

Harry's lips were cold and numb.

'So ... when I asked Kreacher if Sirius was there last night ...'

'The Malfoys – undoubtedly on Voldemort's instructions – had told him he must find a way of keeping Sirius out of the way once you had seen the vision of Sirius being tortured. Then, if you decided to check whether Sirius was at home or not, Kreacher would be able to pretend he was not. Kreacher injured Buckbeak the Hippogriff yesterday, and, at the moment when you made your appearance in the fire, Sirius was upstairs tending to him.'

There seemed to be very little air in Harry's lungs; his breathing was quick and shallow.

'And Kreacher told you all this ... and laughed?' he croaked.

'He did not wish to tell me,' said Dumbledore. 'But I am a sufficiently accomplished Legilimens myself to know when I am being lied to and I – persuaded him – to tell me the full story, before I left for the Department of Mysteries.'

'And,' whispered Harry, his hands curled in cold fists on his knees, 'and Hermione kept telling us to be nice to him –'

'She was quite right, Harry,' said Dumbledore. 'I warned Sirius when we

第37章 丢失的预言

里莫广场时,是那个小精灵——发出一阵狂笑——告诉我小天狼星去了哪里。"

"他在笑?"哈利用空洞的声音说。

"是啊,"邓布利多说,"知道吗,克利切不能完全出卖我们。他不是凤凰社的保密人,无法告诉马尔福一家我们的地址,或告诉他们任何禁止他透露的凤凰社机密计划。他被他那个种类特有的魔法束缚着,也就是说,他不能违抗他的主人小天狼星的直接命令。但他向纳西莎提供了一些对伏地魔很有价值的情报,小天狼星一定认为那些都是鸡毛蒜皮,也就没想到要禁止他透露出去。"

"比如什么?"哈利说。

"比如小天狼星在世界上最关心的人是你,"邓布利多轻声说道,"比如你逐渐把小天狼星看成既是父亲又是兄长。当然啦,伏地魔早已清楚小天狼星在凤凰社,也清楚你知道他在哪里——但是克利切的情报使他意识到,小天狼星布莱克是你会不遗余力去搭救的人。"

哈利的嘴唇发冷、发麻。

"所以……我昨晚问克利切小天狼星在不在时……"

"马尔福一家对克利切说——他们无疑是受了伏地魔的指示——一旦你在幻觉中看见小天狼星遭受折磨,他就必须想办法把小天狼星引开。然后,如果你决定核实一下小天狼星在不在家,克利切就可以谎称他不在。克利切昨天弄伤了鹰头马身有翼兽巴克比克,你在炉火中出现时,小天狼星正在楼上照料它呢。"

哈利肺里的空气似乎变得很少,他的呼吸急切而短促。

"克利切把这些都告诉了你……并且哈哈大笑?"他嘶哑着嗓子问。

"他不想告诉我,"邓布利多说,"但我的摄神取念已相当高明,我知道对方是不是在说谎,于是我就——我就说服他——把事情的经过告诉了我,然后我就赶往了神秘事务司。"

"可是赫敏,"哈利轻声说,冰冷的双手捏成拳头放在膝盖上,"可是赫敏还总叫我们对他好一点儿——"

"她说得没错,哈利,"邓布利多说,"我们当初选择格里莫广场12

CHAPTER THIRTY-SEVEN The Lost Prophecy

adopted twelve Grimmauld Place as our Headquarters that Kreacher must be treated with kindness and respect. I also told him that Kreacher could be dangerous to us. I do not think Sirius took me very seriously, or that he ever saw Kreacher as a being with feelings as acute as a human's –'

'Don't you blame – don't you – talk – about Sirius like –' Harry's breath was constricted, he could not get the words out properly; but the rage that had subsided briefly flared in him again: he would not let Dumbledore criticise Sirius. 'Kreacher's a lying – foul – he deserved –'

'Kreacher is what he has been made by wizards, Harry,' said Dumbledore. 'Yes, he is to be pitied. His existence has been as miserable as your friend Dobby's. He was forced to do Sirius's bidding, because Sirius was the last of the family to which he was enslaved, but he felt no true loyalty to him. And whatever Kreacher's faults, it must be admitted that Sirius did nothing to make Kreacher's lot easier –'

'DON'T TALK ABOUT SIRIUS LIKE THAT!' Harry yelled.

He was on his feet again, furious, ready to fly at Dumbledore, who had plainly not understood Sirius at all, how brave he was, how much he had suffered ...

'What about Snape?' Harry spat. 'You're not talking about him, are you? When I told him Voldemort had Sirius he just sneered at me as usual –'

'Harry, you know Professor Snape had no choice but to pretend not to take you seriously in front of Dolores Umbridge,' said Dumbledore steadily, 'but as I have explained, he informed the Order as soon as possible about what you had said. It was he who deduced where you had gone when you did not return from the Forest. It was he, too, who gave Professor Umbridge fake Veritaserum when she was attempting to force you to tell her Sirius's whereabouts.'

Harry disregarded this; he felt a savage pleasure in blaming Snape, it seemed to be easing his own sense of dreadful guilt, and he wanted to hear Dumbledore agree with him.

'Snape – Snape g – goaded Sirius about staying in the house – he made out Sirius was a coward –'

'Sirius was much too old and clever to have allowed such feeble taunts to hurt him,' said Dumbledore.

'Snape stopped giving me Occlumency lessons!' Harry snarled. 'He threw

第37章 丢失的预言

号作为总部的时候,我就提醒过小天狼星必须善待和尊重克利切。我还告诉他,克利切可能会对我们构成危险。我认为小天狼星没有认真对待我的话,或者,他从来就没把克利切看成是跟人类拥有同样敏锐情感的生灵——"

"不许你责怪——不许你——这么说——小天狼星——"哈利的呼吸受到限制,没法把话说得连贯。但暂时消退的怒火又在他心头熊熊燃起:他不能让邓布利多批评小天狼星。"克利切是个谎话连篇的——可耻的——他应该受到——"

"克利切是被巫师塑造成这样的,哈利。"邓布利多说,"是的,他应该得到怜悯。他的生活跟你的朋友多比一样悲惨。他被迫听从小天狼星的吩咐,因为小天狼星是他所服侍的家族的最后一位成员,但他对小天狼星并无发自内心的忠诚。不管克利切有什么过错,我们必须承认,小天狼星并没有使克利切的生活变得轻松一些——"

"**不要这样说小天狼星!**"哈利嚷道。

他又怒气冲冲地站了起来,准备向邓布利多扑去,邓布利多显然根本就不了解小天狼星,不了解他有多么勇敢,他遭受了多少痛苦……

"那么斯内普呢?"哈利气冲冲地说,"你对他闭口不谈,是吗?我告诉他伏地魔抓住了小天狼星时,他只是像平常一样讥笑我——"

"哈利,你知道当着多洛雷斯·乌姆里奇的面,斯内普教授别无选择,只能假装不把你的话当真,"邓布利多镇定地继续往下说,"但是就像我刚才解释的,他以最快的速度把你的话通知了凤凰社。而且,是他看到你没有从禁林里回来,推断出你去了哪里;也是他在乌姆里奇教授迫使你说出小天狼星的去向时,向她提供了假的吐真剂。"

哈利对这些听而不闻。他觉得指责斯内普给他带来了一种残忍的快意,似乎能减轻他自己可怕的负疚感,而且他希望听到邓布利多赞同他的意见。

"斯内普——斯内普刺——刺激小天狼星,说他躲在家里——他把小天狼星说成是个懦夫——"

"小天狼星不是小孩和傻瓜,不会让这些软弱无力的嘲讽伤害自己

CHAPTER THIRTY-SEVEN · The Lost Prophecy

me out of his office!'

'I am aware of it,' said Dumbledore heavily. 'I have already said that it was a mistake for me not to teach you myself, though I was sure, at the time, that nothing could have been more dangerous than to open your mind even further to Voldemort while in my presence –'

'Snape made it worse, my scar always hurt worse after lessons with him –' Harry remembered Ron's thoughts on the subject and plunged on '– how do you know he wasn't trying to soften me up for Voldemort, make it easier for him to get inside my –'

'I trust Severus Snape,' said Dumbledore simply. 'But I forgot – another old man's mistake – that some wounds run too deep for the healing. I thought Professor Snape could overcome his feelings about your father – I was wrong.'

'But that's OK, is it?' yelled Harry, ignoring the scandalised faces and disapproving mutterings of the portraits on the walls. 'It's OK for Snape to hate my dad, but it's not OK for Sirius to hate Kreacher?'

'Sirius did not hate Kreacher,' said Dumbledore. 'He regarded him as a servant unworthy of much interest or notice. Indifference and neglect often do much more damage than outright dislike ... the fountain we destroyed tonight told a lie. We wizards have mistreated and abused our fellows for too long, and we are now reaping our reward.'

'SO SIRIUS DESERVED WHAT HE GOT, DID HE?' Harry yelled.

'I did not say that, nor will you ever hear me say it,' Dumbledore replied quietly. 'Sirius was not a cruel man, he was kind to house-elves in general. He had no love for Kreacher, because Kreacher was a living reminder of the home Sirius had hated.'

'Yeah, he did hate it!' said Harry, his voice cracking, turning his back on Dumbledore and walking away. The sun was bright inside the room now and the eyes of all the portraits followed him as he walked, without realising what he was doing, without seeing the office at all. 'You made him stay shut up in that house and he hated it, that's why he wanted to get out last night –'

'I was trying to keep Sirius alive,' said Dumbledore quietly.

'People don't like being locked up!' Harry said furiously, rounding on him. 'You did it to me all last summer –'

的。"邓布利多说。

"斯内普不再给我上大脑封闭术课了!"哈利咆哮道,"他把我赶出了他的办公室!"

"我意识到了,"邓布利多语气沉重地说,"我已经说过,我没有亲自教你是一个错误,不过我当时相信,没有什么比当着我的面把你的大脑进一步暴露给伏地魔更危险的了——"

"可是斯内普使事情变得更糟糕,每次我跟他上完课,伤疤都疼得更厉害——"哈利想起罗恩对这门课的看法,不顾一切地往下说道,"——你怎么知道他不是故意让我变得软弱,让伏地魔能更轻松地进入我的——"

"我相信西弗勒斯·斯内普,"邓布利多简单地说,"但我忘记了——又是老年人犯的错误——有些伤口太深,很难愈合。我以为斯内普教授可以克服他对你父亲的积怨——结果我错了。"

"但那就没事了,是吗?"哈利嚷道,不理睬墙上那些肖像愤怒的表情和不满的嘟哝,"斯内普讨厌我爸爸就没事,小天狼星讨厌克利切就不行?"

"小天狼星不是讨厌克利切,"邓布利多说,"他是把克利切看成了一个不值得关心和注意的奴仆。冷漠和忽视造成的伤害,常常比直接的反感厉害得多……我们昨晚毁坏的那座喷泉说过一个谎言。我们巫师虐待和伤害我们的伙伴太长时间了,现在遭到了报应。"

"这么说小天狼星是活该,对吗?"哈利嚷道。

"我没有这么说,而且你永远不会听到我说这样的话。"邓布利多轻声回答,"小天狼星不是一个残忍的人,他一般都很善待家养小精灵。小天狼星对克利切没有感情,是因为克利切总使他想起他所仇恨的那个家。"

"没错,他恨那个家!"哈利用发哑的声音说,转身离开了邓布利多。明亮的太阳照进了办公室,那些肖像都用目光跟随着他。他胡乱地走着,没有意识到自己在做什么,注意力也不在这间办公室里,"你把他整天关在那栋房子里,他讨厌这样,所以他昨晚才想出来——"

"我是想保住小天狼星的性命。"邓布利多轻声说。

"没人喜欢被关起来!"哈利冲着他怒吼道,"去年夏天你就是这样对待我——"

CHAPTER THIRTY-SEVEN   The Lost Prophecy

Dumbledore closed his eyes and buried his face in his long-fingered hands. Harry watched him, but this uncharacteristic sign of exhaustion, or sadness, or whatever it was from Dumbledore, did not soften him. On the contrary, he felt even angrier that Dumbledore was showing signs of weakness. He had no business being weak when Harry wanted to rage and storm at him.

Dumbledore lowered his hands and surveyed Harry through his half-moon glasses.

'It is time,' he said, 'for me to tell you what I should have told you five years ago, Harry. Please sit down. I am going to tell you everything. I ask only a little patience. You will have your chance to rage at me – to do whatever you like – when I have finished. I will not stop you.'

Harry glared at him for a moment, then flung himself back into the chair opposite Dumbledore and waited.

Dumbledore stared for a moment at the sunlit grounds outside the window, then looked back at Harry and said, 'Five years ago you arrived at Hogwarts, Harry, safe and whole, as I had planned and intended. Well – not quite whole. You had suffered. I knew you would when I left you on your aunt and uncle's doorstep. I knew I was condemning you to ten dark and difficult years.'

He paused. Harry said nothing.

'You might ask – and with good reason – why it had to be so. Why could some wizarding family not have taken you in? Many would have done so more than gladly, would have been honoured and delighted to raise you as a son.

'My answer is that my priority was to keep you alive. You were in more danger than perhaps anyone but I realised. Voldemort had been vanquished hours before, but his supporters – and many of them are almost as terrible as he – were still at large, angry, desperate and violent. And I had to make my decision, too, with regard to the years ahead. Did I believe that Voldemort was gone for ever? No. I knew not whether it would be ten, twenty or fifty years before he returned, but I was sure he would do so, and I was sure, too, knowing him as I have done, that he would not rest until he killed you.

'I knew that Voldemort's knowledge of magic is perhaps more extensive than any wizard alive. I knew that even my most complex and powerful protective spells and charms were unlikely to be invincible if he ever returned to full power.

第37章 丢失的预言

邓布利多闭上了眼睛,把脸埋在手指修长的双手里。哈利注视着他,但邓布利多难得流露出来的这种疲惫、悲哀或不管是什么,都不能使他心软。相反,他看到邓布利多居然显出软弱的样子,心里更加生气。他想冲他大发雷霆,告诉邓布利多他没有权利变得软弱。

邓布利多放下双手,透过半月形眼镜审视着哈利。

"现在,"他说,"我应该跟你说说早在五年前就该告诉你的事情了,哈利。请坐下来。我要把一切都告诉你。我只要求你耐心一点儿。等我说完,你有机会朝我发怒——做什么都行。我不会拦着你。"

哈利狠狠地盯了邓布利多一会儿,然后一屁股坐回到他对面的椅子上,等待着。

邓布利多望着窗外被阳光照亮的场地,又回过头来望着哈利,说道:"哈利,五年前你来到霍格沃茨,像我安排和计划的那样,平平安安、毫发无损。是啊——并不是真的毫发无损,你受了苦。当我把你留在你姨妈和姨父家的门口时,我就知道你会受苦。我知道我给你判了十年黑暗、难熬的日子。"

他停住话头。哈利什么也没说。

"你可能会问——你完全有理由问——为什么必须这样?为什么不能让某个巫师家庭收养你?许多家庭都巴不得把你当儿子一样抚养,并以此感到荣耀和骄傲。

"我的回答是,我首先要保证你活下来。大概只有我认识到你有多么危险。伏地魔在几个小时前被击败了,但他的支持者——其中许多人几乎跟他一样可怕——仍然逍遥法外,丧心病狂,极度凶恶。我也必须为今后的日子做出决定。难道我相信伏地魔一去不复返了?不。我不相信。我不知道他具体会在十年、二十年还是五十年之后回来,但我相信他肯定会回来,而且,凭我对他的了解我还相信,他不杀死你绝不善罢甘休。

"我知道,伏地魔的魔法知识恐怕比在世的任何巫师都要广博。我知道,如果他有朝一日卷土重来,恐怕就连我掌握的最高深、最厉害的防护咒语和魔法也都可能无济于事。

CHAPTER THIRTY-SEVEN   The Lost Prophecy

'But I knew, too, where Voldemort was weak. And so I made my decision. You would be protected by an ancient magic of which he knows, which he despises, and which he has always, therefore, underestimated – to his cost. I am speaking, of course, of the fact that your mother died to save you. She gave you a lingering protection he never expected, a protection that flows in your veins to this day. I put my trust, therefore, in your mother's blood. I delivered you to her sister, her only remaining relative.'

'She doesn't love me,' said Harry at once. 'She doesn't give a damn –'

'But she took you,' Dumbledore cut across him. 'She may have taken you grudgingly, furiously, unwillingly, bitterly, yet still she took you, and in doing so, she sealed the charm I placed upon you. Your mother's sacrifice made the bond of blood the strongest shield I could give you.'

'I still don't –'

'While you can still call home the place where your mother's blood dwells, there you cannot be touched or harmed by Voldemort. He shed her blood, but it lives on in you and her sister. Her blood became your refuge. You need return there only once a year, but as long as you can still call it home, whilst you are there he cannot hurt you. Your aunt knows this. I explained what I had done in the letter I left, with you, on her doorstep. She knows that allowing you houseroom may well have kept you alive for the past fifteen years.'

'Wait,' said Harry. 'Wait a moment.'

He sat up straighter in his chair, staring at Dumbledore.

'You sent that Howler. You told her to remember – it was your voice –'

'I thought,' said Dumbledore, inclining his head slightly, 'that she might need reminding of the pact she had sealed by taking you. I suspected the Dementor attack might have awoken her to the dangers of having you as a surrogate son.'

'It did,' said Harry quietly. 'Well – my uncle more than her. He wanted to chuck me out, but after the Howler came she – she said I had to stay.'

He stared at the floor for a moment, then said, 'But what's this got to do with –'

He could not say Sirius's name.

'Five years ago, then,' continued Dumbledore, as though he had not paused in his story, 'you arrived at Hogwarts, neither as happy nor as well-

第37章 丢失的预言

"但我同时也知道伏地魔的弱点在哪里。因此我做出了决定,应该用一种古老的魔法来保护你。这种魔法他是知道的,但他轻视它,因而一直低估了它的力量——结果付出了代价。当然啦,我说的是你母亲冒死救你那件事。伏地魔没有料到你母亲给了你一种持久的保护,这种保护至今还在你的血管里流淌。因此,我相信你母亲的血液能保护你,就把你送给了她仅存的亲人——她的姐姐。"

"她不爱我,"哈利立刻说道,"她根本就不——"

"可是她接受了你,"邓布利多打断了他,"她也许接受得很勉强,很怨恨,很不情愿,但她还是接受了你,而她这么做的时候,就使得我在你身上施的魔法开始起效了。你母亲的牺牲,使得血缘的纽带成为我所能给与你的最强大的保护屏障。"

"我还是不——"

"只要你仍然能把你母亲的血亲居住的那个地方称为家,伏地魔就不能接触或伤害你。他使你母亲流了血,而这血在你和她姐姐身上继续流淌着。她的血变成了你的庇护所。你一年只需回去一次,但只要你仍然可以称之为家,你在那里时他就不能伤害你。你姨妈知道这一点。我在那封跟你一起留在她家门口的信里讲了我做的事情。她知道收留你就会保证你在这十五年里平安无事。"

"等等,"哈利说,"等一等。"

他在椅子上坐得更直一些,盯着邓布利多。

"那封吼叫信是你寄的。你叫她别忘了——那是你的声音——"

"我当时认为,"邓布利多微微点了点头说,"或许需要提醒她记住她当初接受你时签订的那个契约。我怀疑摄魂怪的袭击会使她突然明白收养你会有多么危险。"

"是这样,"哈利轻声说,"唉——我姨父比她更害怕。他想把我赶出去,可是吼叫信来过之后,我姨妈——我姨妈说只能让我留下来。"

哈利眼睛盯着地板,过了一会儿他又说:"但是这些跟——?"

他没法儿说出小天狼星的名字。

"然后,五年前,"邓布利多继续说,似乎他的叙述并没有停顿过,"你

CHAPTER THIRTY-SEVEN   The Lost Prophecy

nourished as I would have liked, perhaps, yet alive and healthy. You were not a pampered little prince, but as normal a boy as I could have hoped under the circumstances. Thus far, my plan was working well.

'And then ... well, you will remember the events of your first year at Hogwarts quite as clearly as I do. You rose magnificently to the challenge that faced you and sooner – much sooner – than I had anticipated, you found yourself face to face with Voldemort. You survived again. You did more. You delayed his return to full power and strength. You fought a man's fight. I was ... prouder of you than I can say.

'Yet there was a flaw in this wonderful plan of mine,' said Dumbledore. 'An obvious flaw that I knew, even then, might be the undoing of it all. And yet, knowing how important it was that my plan should succeed, I told myself that I would not permit this flaw to ruin it. I alone could prevent this, so I alone must be strong. And here was my first test, as you lay in the hospital wing, weak from your struggle with Voldemort.'

'I don't understand what you're saying,' said Harry.

'Don't you remember asking me, as you lay in the hospital wing, why Voldemort had tried to kill you when you were a baby?'

Harry nodded.

'Ought I to have told you then?'

Harry stared into the blue eyes and said nothing, but his heart was racing again.

'You do not see the flaw in the plan yet? No ... perhaps not. Well, as you know, I decided not to answer you. Eleven, I told myself, was much too young to know. I had never intended to tell you when you were eleven. The knowledge would be too much at such a young age.

'I should have recognised the danger signs then. I should have asked myself why I did not feel more disturbed that you had already asked me the question to which I knew, one day, I must give a terrible answer. I should have recognised that I was too happy to think that I did not have to do it on that particular day ... you were too young, much too young.

'And so we entered your second year at Hogwarts. And once again you met challenges even grown wizards have never faced; once again you acquitted yourself beyond my wildest dreams. You did not ask me again, however, why Voldemort had left that mark on you. We discussed your scar,

第37章 丢失的预言

来到了霍格沃茨，也许不像我希望的那样快乐和壮实，但好歹是健健康康有活力的。你不是个娇生惯养的小王子，而是个普普通通的小男孩，在那种条件下我也只能希望如此了。到那时候为止，我的计划进展得很顺利。

"后来……唉，你和我一样清楚地记得你在霍格沃茨第一年里发生的事情。你出色地面对挑战，而且很快——比我预想得要快，快得多——就发现自己跟伏地魔面对面交锋了。你再次死里逃生。不仅如此，你还延缓了他恢复势力、卷土重来的时间。你像一个男子汉一样作战。我……我为你感到说不出的骄傲。

"可是我这个巧妙的计划里有一个瑕疵，"邓布利多说，"一个显而易见的瑕疵，我那时候就知道它可能会毁掉一切。然而，我知道我的计划成功实施有多么重要，就对自己说我不会允许这个瑕疵毁了全盘计划。只有我能够阻止，因而我必须强大。于是，我做了第一个试验，当时你躺在医院的病床上，因为跟伏地魔的搏斗而虚弱无力。"

"我不明白你在说什么。"哈利说。

"你记得吗，你当时躺在病床上问我，为什么伏地魔在你很小的时候就想杀死你？"

哈利点了点头。

"我是不是当时就应该告诉你？"

哈利盯着那双蓝眼睛，什么也没说，但他的心又在狂跳。

"你还没有看到这个计划里的瑕疵吗？没有……也许没有。总之，就像你所知道的，我当时决定不回答你。我对自己说，十一岁，年纪太小了，还不应该知道。我从来没有打算在你十一岁的时候告诉你。小小的年纪就知道这些，会承受不住的。

"我当时就应该看出危险的迹象。我应该问我自己，你已经提出了我知道我总有一天必须给出可怕答案的问题，但我为什么没有感到不安呢？我应该认识到我是过于乐观了，我以为那天暂时还用不着告诉你……你还年幼，太年幼了。

"然后就到了你在霍格沃茨的第二年。你再次遇到了就连成年巫师也从没有面对过的挑战；你的表现再次超出了我最大胆的梦想。但你

CHAPTER THIRTY-SEVEN The Lost Prophecy

oh yes ... we came very, very close to the subject. Why did I not tell you everything?

'Well, it seemed to me that twelve was, after all, hardly better than eleven to receive such information. I allowed you to leave my presence, bloodstained, exhausted but exhilarated, and if I felt a twinge of unease that I ought, perhaps, to have told you then, it was swiftly silenced. You were still so young, you see, and I could not find it in myself to spoil that night of triumph ...

'Do you see, Harry? Do you see the flaw in my brilliant plan now? I had fallen into the trap I had foreseen, that I had told myself I could avoid, that I must avoid.'

'I don't —'

'I cared about you too much,' said Dumbledore simply. 'I cared more for your happiness than your knowing the truth, more for your peace of mind than my plan, more for your life than the lives that might be lost if the plan failed. In other words, I acted exactly as Voldemort expects we fools who love to act.

'Is there a defence? I defy anyone who has watched you as I have — and I have watched you more closely than you can have imagined — not to want to save you more pain than you had already suffered. What did I care if numbers of nameless and faceless people and creatures were slaughtered in the vague future, if in the here and now you were alive, and well, and happy? I never dreamed that I would have such a person on my hands.

'We entered your third year. I watched from afar as you struggled to repel Dementors, as you found Sirius, learned what he was and rescued him. Was I to tell you then, at the moment when you had triumphantly snatched your godfather from the jaws of the Ministry? But now, at the age of thirteen, my excuses were running out. Young you might be, but you had proved you were exceptional. My conscience was uneasy, Harry. I knew the time must come soon ...

'But you came out of the maze last year, having watched Cedric Diggory die, having escaped death so narrowly yourself ... and I did not tell you, though I knew, now Voldemort had returned, I must do it soon. And now, tonight, I know you have long been ready for the knowledge I have kept from you for so long, because you have proved that I should have placed

第 37 章 丢失的预言

没有再问我伏地魔为什么在你身上留下了那道痕记。我们讨论了你的伤疤，哦，是的……我们当时离那个话题非常非常接近了。当时我为什么不把一切都告诉你呢？

"唉，我觉得十二岁其实跟十一岁差不了多少，还不能接受这样的事情。我让你血迹斑斑、精疲力竭，但却满心欢喜地从我的面前离开了，虽然我感到了一丝不安，觉得我或许应该告诉你一切，但这种不安很快就消失了。知道吗，你还那么年幼，我不忍心破坏那个欢庆胜利的夜晚……

"你明白吗，哈利？你现在看到我那个绝妙计划的瑕疵了吗？我跌进了我曾经预见、曾经告诉自己我能躲过也必须躲过的那个陷阱。"

"我不——"

"我太关心你了，"邓布利多直截了当地说，"我太关心你的快乐了，胜过想让你知道事情的真相；我太关心你思想的平静，胜过关心我的计划；我太关心你的生命，胜过关心那些一旦计划失败可能会失去的生命。换句话说，我的行为，完全符合伏地魔对我们这些懂得爱的傻瓜的预料。

"有什么可以辩解的吗？我认为没有人像我那样注视过你——我对你的关注超出了你可以想象的程度——你已经受了很多苦，我不愿意再把更多的痛苦留给你。只要你此时此刻还活着，健健康康，快快乐乐，我又何必去管在某个遥远的未来有大批无名无姓、普普通通的生灵遭到杀戮呢？我做梦也没想到我需要把这样一个人捧在手心里呵护。

"接着你进入了三年级。我远远地注视着你努力驱赶摄魂怪，注视着你找到小天狼星，弄清了他是谁，并且救了他。当你成功从魔法部的虎口里夺回你的教父时，我是不是就应该告诉你呢？你已经十三岁了，我的借口用完了。你虽然年幼，但已经证明自己是出类拔萃的。我的内心开始不安，哈利。我知道那个时刻很快就会到来……

"然而，去年你从迷宫里出来，目睹了塞德里克·迪戈里的死，自己从险境中死里逃生……我还是没有告诉你，尽管我知道伏地魔回来了，我必须尽快告诉你。现在，就在今晚，我知道你早已做好准备，

CHAPTER THIRTY-SEVEN   The Lost Prophecy

the burden upon you before this. My only defence is this: I have watched you struggling under more burdens than any student who has ever passed through this school and I could not bring myself to add another – the greatest one of all.'

Harry waited, but Dumbledore did not speak.

'I still don't understand.'

'Voldemort tried to kill you when you were a child because of a prophecy made shortly before your birth. He knew the prophecy had been made, though he did not know its full contents. He set out to kill you when you were still a baby, believing he was fulfilling the terms of the prophecy. He discovered, to his cost, that he was mistaken, when the curse intended to kill you backfired. And so, since his return to his body, and particularly since your extraordinary escape from him last year, he has been determined to hear that prophecy in its entirety. This is the weapon he has been seeking so assiduously since his return: the knowledge of how to destroy you.'

The sun had risen fully now: Dumbledore's office was bathed in it. The glass case in which the sword of Godric Gryffindor resided gleamed white and opaque, the fragments of the instruments Harry had thrown to the floor glistened like raindrops, and behind him, the baby Fawkes made soft chirruping noises in his nest of ashes.

'The prophecy's smashed,' Harry said blankly. 'I was pulling Neville up those benches in the – the room where the archway was, and I ripped his robes and it fell ...'

'The thing that smashed was merely the record of the prophecy kept by the Department of Mysteries. But the prophecy was made to somebody, and that person has the means of recalling it perfectly.'

'Who heard it?' asked Harry, though he thought he knew the answer already.

'I did,' said Dumbledore. 'On a cold, wet night sixteen years ago, in a room above the bar at the Hog's Head inn. I had gone there to see an applicant for the post of Divination teacher, though it was against my inclination to allow the subject of Divination to continue at all. The applicant, however, was the great-great-granddaughter of a very famous, very gifted Seer and I thought it common politeness to meet her. I was disappointed. It seemed to me that she had not a trace of the gift herself. I told her, courteously I hope, that I did not think she would be suitable for the post. I turned to leave.'

第37章 丢失的预言

接受我隐瞒了你这么长时间的事情,因为你已经证明我在这之前就应该把这副重担放在你的肩上。我唯一需要辩解的是:我注视过你在重压下的挣扎,那些负担是从这所学校毕业的任何学生都未曾承受过的,我实在不忍心再给你增加另一个负担——一个最大的负担。"

哈利等待着,但邓布利多没有说话。

"我还是不明白。"

"伏地魔在你还是个婴儿时就想杀死你,是因为在你出生前不久的一个预言。他知道有那个预言,但并不知道完整的内容。当你尚在襁褓中时,他就打算把你干掉,他相信那是在履行那个预言所陈述的事情。他付出代价后发现自己弄错了,他打算杀死你的那个咒语反弹了回去。因此,他恢复肉身后,特别是你去年很不寻常地从他手里逃脱后,他就打定主意要听听预言的全部内容。这就是他卷土重来后一直苦苦寻找的那件武器:怎样才能消灭你。"

太阳已经完全升起,邓布利多的办公室沐浴在阳光里。放着戈德里克·格兰芬多宝剑的玻璃匣子闪着乳白色的光,被哈利扔到地上的银器的碎片像雨点一样闪闪发亮。在他身后,雏鸟福克斯在铺满灰烬的窝里发出微弱的唧唧叫声。

"预言球被打碎了,"哈利茫然地说,"我当时把纳威往那些石头长凳上拖,在那个——在那个有拱门的房间里,我扯坏了他的袍子,预言球掉了出来……"

"那个被打碎的东西,只是保存在神秘事务司的一个预言记录。但预言是专门说给某个人听的,那个人有办法重新听取它的内容。"

"是谁听到的?"哈利问,其实他觉得自己已经知道了答案。

"是我,"邓布利多说,"在十六年前一个寒冷、潮湿的夜晚,在猪头酒吧楼上的一个房间里。我去那里见一个申请教占卜课的人,其实我的本意,并不打算让占卜课继续开下去。不过,那位求职者是一位非常著名、很有天赋的预言家的玄孙女,我认为出于礼貌应该见她一面。我很失望。我感觉她本人似乎没有丝毫天赋。我对她说——但愿不失礼貌——我认为她不适合这个职务。接着我就转身准备离开了。"

CHAPTER THIRTY-SEVEN   The Lost Prophecy

Dumbledore got to his feet and walked past Harry to the black cabinet that stood beside Fawkes's perch. He bent down, slid back a catch and took from inside it the shallow stone basin, carved with runes around the edges, in which Harry had seen his father tormenting Snape. Dumbledore walked back to the desk, placed the Pensieve upon it, and raised his wand to his own temple. From it, he withdrew silvery, gossamer-fine strands of thought clinging to the wand and deposited them into the basin. He sat back down behind his desk and watched his thoughts swirl and drift inside the Pensieve for a moment. Then, with a sigh, he raised his wand and prodded the silvery substance with its tip.

A figure rose out of it, draped in shawls, her eyes magnified to enormous size behind her glasses, and she revolved slowly, her feet in the basin. But when Sybill Trelawney spoke, it was not in her usual ethereal, mystic voice, but in the harsh, hoarse tones Harry had heard her use once before:

'*The one with the power to vanquish the Dark Lord approaches ... born to those who have thrice defied him, born as the seventh month dies ... and the Dark Lord will mark him as his equal, but he will have power the Dark Lord knows not ... and either must die at the hand of the other for neither can live while the other survives ... the one with the power to vanquish the Dark Lord will be born as the seventh month dies ...*'

The slowly revolving Professor Trelawney sank back into the silver mass below and vanished.

The silence within the office was absolute. Neither Dumbledore nor Harry nor any of the portraits made a sound. Even Fawkes had fallen silent.

'Professor Dumbledore?' Harry said very quietly, for Dumbledore, still staring at the Pensieve, seemed completely lost in thought. 'It ... did that mean ... what did that mean?'

'It meant,' said Dumbledore, 'that the person who has the only chance of conquering Lord Voldemort for good was born at the end of July, nearly sixteen years ago. This boy would be born to parents who had already defied Voldemort three times.'

Harry felt as though something was closing in on him. His breathing seemed difficult again.

'It means – me?'

Dumbledore took a deep breath.

'The odd thing, Harry,' he said softly, 'is that it may not have meant you

第37章 丢失的预言

邓布利多站起身,走过哈利身边,走向福克斯栖枝旁的那个黑色柜子。他弯下腰,拨开一个插销,从里面拿出那只浅浅的、边上刻着如尼文的石盆,哈利正是在这盆里看见他父亲捉弄斯内普的。邓布利多走回桌前,把冥想盆放在桌上,把魔杖举到自己的太阳穴旁。他从太阳穴里抽出一缕缕银色的、细如蛛丝的思想,再把这些沾在魔杖上的思想放进盆里。他在桌子后面重新坐下,注视着他的思想在冥想盆里旋转、飘浮。片刻之后,他叹了一口气,举起魔杖,用杖尖捅了捅那银色的物质。

一个裹着披肩的身影从盆里浮现出来,她的眼睛被镜片放大了许多倍,大得吓人;她的双脚留在盆里,身体慢慢地旋转着。当西比尔·特里劳妮说话时,用的并不是平常那种神秘而虚无缥缈的声音,而是哈利曾经听见过一次的刺耳、沙哑的声音:

"有能力战胜黑魔头的人走近了……生在曾三次抵抗过他的人家,生于七月结束的时候……黑魔头会把他标为自己的劲敌,但他将拥有黑魔头不知道的力量……他们中间必有一个死在另一个手里,因为两个人不能都活着,只有一个生存下来……有能力战胜黑魔头的那个人将在七月结束时诞生……"

特里劳妮教授缓缓地旋转着沉入下面的银色物质,消失了。

办公室里一片死寂。邓布利多和哈利,以及那些肖像都静默不语。就连福克斯也沉默了。

"邓布利多教授?"哈利说,声音很轻,因为邓布利多仍然盯着冥想盆,似乎完全陷入了沉思,"那……那意思是不是……那是什么意思呢?"

"它的意思是,"邓布利多说,"唯一有希望彻底战胜伏地魔的那个人,出生在近十六年前的七月底。这个男孩的父母曾经三次抵抗过伏地魔。"

哈利觉得似乎有什么东西向他挤压过来,呼吸好像又变得困难了。

"它指的是——我?"

邓布利多深深地吸了一口气。

"哈利,怪就怪在,"他轻声说道,"它也可能根本不是指你。西比

CHAPTER THIRTY-SEVEN   The Lost Prophecy

at all. Sybill's prophecy could have applied to two wizard boys, both born at the end of July that year, both of whom had parents in the Order of the Phoenix, both sets of parents having narrowly escaped Voldemort three times. One, of course, was you. The other was Neville Longbottom.'

'But then ... but then, why was it my name on the prophecy and not Neville's?'

'The official record was relabelled after Voldemort's attack on you as a child,' said Dumbledore. 'It seemed plain to the keeper of the Hall of Prophecy that Voldemort could only have tried to kill you because he knew you to be the one to whom Sybill was referring.'

'Then – it might not be me?' said Harry.

'I am afraid,' said Dumbledore slowly, looking as though every word cost him a great effort, 'that there is no doubt that it *is* you.'

'But you said – Neville was born at the end of July, too – and his mum and dad –'

'You are forgetting the next part of the prophecy, the final identifying feature of the boy who could vanquish Voldemort ... Voldemort himself would *mark him as his equal*. And so he did, Harry. He chose you, not Neville. He gave you the scar that has proved both blessing and curse.'

'But he might have chosen wrong!' said Harry. 'He might have marked the wrong person!'

'He chose the boy he thought most likely to be a danger to him,' said Dumbledore. 'And notice this, Harry: he chose, not the pure-blood (which, according to his creed, is the only kind of wizard worth being or knowing) but the half-blood, like himself. He saw himself in you before he had ever seen you, and in marking you with that scar, he did not kill you, as he intended, but gave you powers, and a future, which have fitted you to escape him not once, but four times so far – something that neither your parents, nor Neville's parents, ever achieved.'

'Why did he do it, then?' said Harry, who felt numb and cold. 'Why did he try and kill me as a baby? He should have waited to see whether Neville or I looked more dangerous when we were older and tried to kill whoever it was then –'

'That might, indeed, have been the more practical course,' said Dumbledore, 'except that Voldemort's information about the prophecy was incomplete. The Hog's Head inn, which Sybill chose for its cheapness,

第37章 丢失的预言

尔的预言适用于两个巫师男孩，都出生于那一年的七月底，父母都在凤凰社，两家的父母都曾经三次从伏地魔手中死里逃生。一个当然是你，另一个是纳威·隆巴顿。"

"可是……可是为什么预言上写着我的名字而不是纳威的？"

"在伏地魔对襁褓中的你下手之后，官方记录重新做了标签，"邓布利多说，"预言厅的管理人认为，伏地魔显然是因为知道你就是西比尔说的那个人，才试图杀死你的。"

"那——也可能不是我？"哈利说。

"恐怕，"邓布利多慢慢地说，似乎每说一个字都非常吃力，"就是你。"

"可是你刚才说——纳威也生在七月底——他的爸爸妈妈——"

"你忘记预言的下一部分了，那个能够战胜伏地魔的男孩，有一个最重要的身份特征……伏地魔本人会把他标为劲敌。他确实这么做了，哈利。他选择了你，而不是纳威。他给你留下了这道伤疤，后来证明这伤疤既是祝福也是诅咒。"

"但是他可能选错了！"哈利说，"他可能标错了人！"

"他选择的是他认为最有可能对他构成威胁的人，"邓布利多说，"请注意这一点，哈利，他选择的不是纯血统的（根据他的信条，只有纯血统的巫师才算得上真正的巫师），而是像他一样混血的。他还没有看见你，就在你身上看见了他自己，他给你留下那道伤疤的时候，没有像他打算的那样杀死你，反而给予了你力量和一个前途，使你能够逃脱他不止一次，而是迄今为止的四次——这是你的父母和纳威的父母都没有做到的。"

"他为什么这么做呢？"哈利说，他感到全身发冷、发僵，"我小时候他为什么想要杀死我呢？他应该等我和纳威长大一些，看看谁更危险，然后再去试着杀死那个人——"

"是啊，那样大概更加切实可行，"邓布利多说，"但是伏地魔对那个预言的了解是不完整的。西比尔图便宜挑选了猪头酒吧，那里长期以来吸引着一些比三把扫帚更加——可以这么说吧——更加有趣的常

CHAPTER THIRTY-SEVEN   The Lost Prophecy

has long attracted, shall we say, a more interesting clientele than the Three Broomsticks. As you and your friends found out to your cost, and I to mine that night, it is a place where it is never safe to assume you are not being overheard. Of course, I had not dreamed, when I set out to meet Sybill Trelawney, that I would hear anything worth overhearing. My – our – one stroke of good fortune was that the eavesdropper was detected only a short way into the prophecy and thrown from the building.'

'So he only heard –?'

'He heard only the beginning, the part foretelling the birth of a boy in July to parents who had thrice defied Voldemort. Consequently, he could not warn his master that to attack you would be to risk transferring power to you, and marking you as his equal. So Voldemort never knew that there might be danger in attacking you, that it might be wise to wait, to learn more. He did not know that you would have *power the Dark Lord knows not –*'

'But I don't!' said Harry, in a strangled voice. 'I haven't any powers he hasn't got, I couldn't fight the way he did tonight, I can't possess people or – or kill them –'

'There is a room in the Department of Mysteries,' interrupted Dumbledore, 'that is kept locked at all times. It contains a force that is at once more wonderful and more terrible than death, than human intelligence, than the forces of nature. It is also, perhaps, the most mysterious of the many subjects for study that reside there. It is the power held within that room that you possess in such quantities and which Voldemort has not at all. That power took you to save Sirius tonight. That power also saved you from possession by Voldemort, because he could not bear to reside in a body so full of the force he detests. In the end, it mattered not that you could not close your mind. It was your heart that saved you.'

Harry closed his eyes. If he had not gone to save Sirius, Sirius would not have died ... More to stave off the moment when he would have to think of Sirius again, Harry asked, without caring much about the answer, 'The end of the prophecy ... it was something about ... *neither can live ...*'

'... *while the other survives,*' said Dumbledore.

'So,' said Harry, dredging up the words from what felt like a deep well of despair inside him, 'so does that mean that ... that one of us has got to kill the other one ... in the end?'

'Yes,' said Dumbledore.

第37章 丢失的预言

客。正如你和你的朋友们付出代价才发现的那样，我那天夜里也是吃了苦头才弄清，在那个地方你永远都不能保证自己不被偷听。当然啦，当我出发去见西比尔·特里劳尼时，我做梦也没有想到会听见任何值得偷听的东西。我的——我们的运气好就好在，预言刚说到开头，那个偷听者就被发现了，然后他被扔到了屋外。"

"所以他只听到——？"

"他只听到了开头部分，就是预言一个男孩将在七月末出生，其父母曾三次抵抗过伏地魔。因此他不可能提醒他的主人，对你下手将会把力量传给你，并把你标为他的劲敌。所以伏地魔根本不知道攻击你会有危险，他应该耐心等待，多了解一些情况。他不知道你将拥有黑魔头不知道的力量——"

"可是我没有！"哈利用几近窒息的声音说道，"我并没有什么他不知道的力量，我不会像他昨天晚上那样搏斗，我不会控制别人，也不会——不会杀人——"

"神秘事务司里有一个房间，"邓布利多打断了他，"一直锁着。那里面存放着一种力量，一种比死亡、人类智慧和自然力量更奇妙、更可怕的力量。它大概也是那里的许多学科中最神秘的一门。关在那个房间里的那种力量，你拥有很多，而伏地魔根本没有。那种力量促使你昨晚去救小天狼星。那种力量也使你不受伏地魔的控制，因为在一个充满了他所憎恶的力量的身体里，他是无法栖身的。到了最后，你能不能封闭大脑已并不重要。是你的心救了你。"

哈利闭上了眼睛。如果他没有去救小天狼星，小天狼星就不会死……为了逃避再次想到小天狼星，哈利不顾会听到什么答案，脱口问道："预言的最后……好像是关于……两个人不能都活着……"

"……只有一个生存下来。"邓布利多说。

"那么，"哈利说，从内心深井般的绝望中挖掘出话语，"那么，那就意味着……到了最后……我们中间的一个必须杀死另一个？"

"是的。"邓布利多说。

CHAPTER THIRTY-SEVEN   The Lost Prophecy

For a long time, neither of them spoke. Somewhere far beyond the office walls, Harry could hear the sound of voices, students heading down to the Great Hall for an early breakfast, perhaps. It seemed impossible that there could be people in the world who still desired food, who laughed, who neither knew nor cared that Sirius Black was gone for ever. Sirius seemed a million miles away already; even now a part of Harry still believed that if he had only pulled back that veil, he would have found Sirius looking back at him, greeting him, perhaps, with his laugh like a bark ...

'I feel I owe you another explanation, Harry,' said Dumbledore hesitantly. 'You may, perhaps, have wondered why I never chose you as a prefect? I must confess ... that I rather thought ... you had enough responsibility to be going on with.'

Harry looked up at him and saw a tear trickling down Dumbledore's face into his long silver beard.

第37章 丢失的预言

两人很久都没有说话。哈利听见办公室墙壁之外的什么地方有嘈杂的人声,大概是早起的学生下楼到礼堂去吃早饭。真是令人难以相信,世界上还有人仍然渴望食物,仍然在欢笑,不知道也不关心小天狼星布莱克已经永远离去。小天狼星似乎已然远在千万里之外,尽管直到此刻哈利仍隐约相信,只要他能掀开那道帷幔,就能发现小天狼星在望着他,或许还会用狗吠般的笑声跟他打招呼……

"我觉得还有一件事需要向你解释,哈利,"邓布利多迟疑地说,"你可能想过,为什么我一直没有选你当级长?我必须承认……我考虑的是……你肩负的责任已经够多的了。"

哈利抬起目光,看见一滴眼泪顺着邓布利多的面颊流下来,落进了他长长的银色胡须里。

CHAPTER THIRTY-EIGHT

The Second War Begins

HE WHO MUST NOT BE NAMED RETURNS

In a brief statement on Friday night, Minister for Magic Cornelius Fudge confirmed that He Who Must Not Be Named has returned to this country and is once more active.

'It is with great regret that I must confirm that the wizard styling himself Lord – well, you know who I mean – is alive and among us again,' said Fudge, looking tired and flustered as he addressed reporters. 'It is with almost equal regret that we report the mass revolt of the Dementors of Azkaban, who have shown themselves averse to continuing in the Ministry's employ. We believe the Dementors are currently taking direction from Lord – Thingy.

'We urge the magical population to remain vigilant. The Ministry is currently publishing guides to elementary home and personal defence which will be delivered free to all wizarding homes within the coming month.'

The Minister's statement was met with dismay and alarm from the wizarding community, which as recently as last Wednesday was receiving Ministry assurances that there was 'no truth whatsoever in these persistent rumours that You-Know-Who is operating amongst us once more'.

Details of the events that led to the Ministry turnaround are still hazy, though it is believed that He Who Must Not Be Named and a select band of followers (known as Death Eaters) gained entry to the Ministry of Magic itself on Thursday evening.

Albus Dumbledore, newly reinstated Headmaster of Hogwarts School of Witchcraft and Wizardry, reinstated member of the

第38章

第二场战争开始了

那个连名字都不能提的人回来了

在星期五晚上的一次简要声明中,魔法部部长康奈利·福吉确认那个连名字都不能提的人已经返回这个国家并再次展开活动。

"我必须十分遗憾地证实,那个自称为魔王的巫师——唉,你们知道我指的是谁——已经获得新生,回到我们中间。"福吉说,他面对记者时显得疲惫而不安,"我们怀着几乎同样遗憾的心情报告,阿兹卡班摄魂怪发生了集体暴动,它们已经表示不愿意继续受雇于魔法部。我们相信摄魂怪目前正在为那个所谓的魔王效力。

"我们强烈呼吁魔法界人士保持警惕。魔法部正在出版家庭和个人基本防御指南,将在下个月之内免费发送到所有巫师家庭。"

部长的声明引起了魔法界的烦恼和恐慌,他们就在上个星期三还得到魔法部的保证,说"那些持续流传的神秘人又在我们中间活动的说法纯属无稽之谈"。

导致魔法部转变观念的事件细节尚不清楚,但人们相信那个连名字都不能提的人及其一伙精选的随从(名为食死徒)于星期四晚闯入了魔法部总部。

我们尚未得到阿不思·邓布利多对此事的评论。他是恢复原职的霍格沃茨魔法学校校长,恢复原职的国际巫师联合会委员和

CHAPTER THIRTY-EIGHT   The Second War Begins

International Confederation of Wizards and reinstated Chief Warlock of the Wizengamot, has so far been unavailable for comment. He has insisted over the past year that You-Know-Who is not dead, as was widely hoped and believed, but is recruiting followers once more for a fresh attempt to seize power. Meanwhile, the 'Boy Who Lived' –

'There you are, Harry, I knew they'd drag you into it somehow,' said Hermione, looking over the top of the paper at him.

They were in the hospital wing. Harry was sitting on the end of Ron's bed and they were both listening to Hermione read the front page of the *Sunday Prophet*. Ginny, whose ankle had been mended in a trice by Madam Pomfrey, was curled up at the foot of Hermione's bed; Neville, whose nose had likewise been returned to its normal size and shape, was in a chair between the two beds; and Luna, who had dropped in to visit, clutching the latest edition of *The Quibbler*, was reading the magazine upside-down and apparently not taking in a word Hermione was saying.

'He's the "Boy Who Lived" again now, though, isn't he?' said Ron darkly. 'Not such a deluded show-off any more, eh?'

He helped himself to a handful of Chocolate Frogs from the immense pile on his bedside cabinet, threw a few to Harry, Ginny and Neville and ripped off the wrapper of his own with his teeth. There were still deep welts on his forearms where the brain's tentacles had wrapped around him. According to Madam Pomfrey, thoughts could leave deeper scarring than almost anything else, though since she had started applying copious amounts of Dr Ubbly's Oblivious Unction there seemed to have been some improvement.

'Yes, they're very complimentary about you now, Harry,' said Hermione, scanning down the article. '"*A lone voice of truth ... perceived as unbalanced, yet never wavered in his story ... forced to bear ridicule and slander ...*" Hmmm,' she said, frowning, 'I notice they don't mention the fact that it was them doing all the ridiculing and slandering in the *Prophet* ...'

She winced slightly and put a hand to her ribs. The curse Dolohov had used on her, though less effective than it would have been had he been able to say the incantation aloud, had nevertheless caused, in Madam Pomfrey's words, 'quite enough damage to be going on with'. Hermione was having to take ten different types of potion every day, was improving greatly, and was already bored with the hospital wing.

第38章 第二场战争开始了

恢复原职的威森加摩首席魔法师。在过去的一年里,他坚持认为神秘人并不像人们普遍希望和相信的那样已经死去,而是又在招募随从,准备再次篡夺权势。与此同时,那个"大难不死的男孩"——

"提到你了,哈利,我就知道他们总会把你扯进去的。"赫敏从报纸上方看着哈利说。

他们是在校医院的病房里。哈利坐在罗恩的床尾,两人都在听赫敏念《星期天预言家报》的头版。金妮的脖子很快就被庞弗雷女士治愈了,此刻蜷缩在赫敏的床脚;纳威的鼻子也恢复了正常的形状和大小,他坐在两张床之间的一把椅子上;卢娜正巧过来探望,手里抓着最新一期的《唱唱反调》,正在颠倒着看,似乎根本没有听赫敏在说什么。

"不过,他又变成'大难不死的男孩'了,是吗?"罗恩不高兴地说,"不再是个受骗上当的表现狂了?"

他从床头柜上那一大堆东西里抓了一把巧克力蛙,扔了几块给哈利、金妮和纳威,然后用牙齿撕开自己那块的包装纸。他的两个前臂上仍有深深的勒痕,那是被大脑的触须缠绕时留下的。据庞弗雷女士说,思想留下的伤痕可能比其他任何东西留下的都深,不过她已经开始给罗恩大量使用乌不利博士的忘忧膏,伤情似乎有所改善。

"没错,他们现在对你赞赏有加呢,哈利。"赫敏快速浏览着那篇文章说,"一个孤独的声音说出了真相……被认为精神错乱,但始终坚持自己的说法……被迫忍受嘲笑和诽谤……唔,"赫敏皱起了眉头,"我发现他们没有提到一个事实:当时正是他们在《预言家日报》上大肆嘲笑和诽谤……"

她微微哆嗦了一下,用手按住了肋骨。多洛霍夫用在她身上的那个咒语,虽然因不能大声念出而减轻了力量,但是照庞弗雷女士的说法,仍然"非常厉害"。赫敏每天都要服用十种不同的药剂,身体恢复得很快,但她已经对病房生活感到厌烦了。

CHAPTER THIRTY-EIGHT The Second War Begins

'"*You-Know-Who's Last Attempt to Take Over,* pages two to four, *What the Ministry Should Have Told Us,* page five, *Why Nobody Listened to Albus Dumbledore,* pages six to eight, *Exclusive Interview with Harry Potter,* page nine ..."' Well,' said Hermione, folding up the newspaper and throwing it aside, 'it's certainly given them lots to write about. And that interview with Harry isn't exclusive, it's the one that was in *The Quibbler* months ago ...'

'Daddy sold it to them,' said Luna vaguely, turning a page of *The Quibbler.* 'He got a very good price for it, too, so we're going to go on an expedition to Sweden this summer to see if we can catch a Crumple-Horned Snorkack.'

Hermione seemed to struggle with herself for a moment, then said, 'That sounds lovely.'

Ginny caught Harry's eye and looked away quickly, grinning.

'So, anyway,' said Hermione, sitting up a little straighter and wincing again, 'what's going on in school?'

'Well, Flitwick's got rid of Fred and George's swamp,' said Ginny, 'he did it in about three seconds. But he left a tiny patch under the window and he's roped it off –'

'Why?' said Hermione, looking startled.

'Oh, he just says it was a really good bit of magic,' said Ginny, shrugging.

'I think he left it as a monument to Fred and George,' said Ron, through a mouthful of chocolate. 'They sent me all these, you know,' he told Harry, pointing at the small mountain of Frogs beside him. 'Must be doing all right out of that joke shop, eh?'

Hermione looked rather disapproving and asked, 'So has all the trouble stopped now Dumbledore's back?'

'Yes,' said Neville, 'everything's settled right back to normal.'

'I s'pose Filch is happy, is he?' asked Ron, propping a Chocolate Frog Card featuring Dumbledore against his water jug.

'Not at all,' said Ginny. 'He's really, really miserable, actually ...' She lowered her voice to a whisper. 'He keeps saying Umbridge was the best thing that ever happened to Hogwarts ...'

All six of them looked around. Professor Umbridge was lying in a bed opposite them, gazing up at the ceiling. Dumbledore had strode alone into the Forest to rescue her from the centaurs; how he had done it – how he had emerged from the trees supporting Professor Umbridge without so much as

第38章 第二场战争开始了

"《神秘人篡夺权势的最新尝试》，见第二版至第四版，《魔法部本来应该告诉我们什么》，见第五版，《为什么没有人听阿不思·邓布利多说话》，见第六版至第八版，《独家采访哈利·波特》，见第九版……哼，"赫敏说着，把报纸折起来扔到一边，"这肯定够他们写的了。对哈利的那次采访并不是独家的，就是几个月前登在《唱唱反调》上的那篇……"

"爸爸把它卖给他们了。"卢娜含混地说，把《唱唱反调》又翻了一页，"他卖出了一个很好的价钱，这样今年夏天我们就能到瑞典探险，看能不能抓住一头弯角鼾兽。"

赫敏似乎在内心斗争了一会儿，然后说："听起来真棒。"

金妮跟哈利对了对眼神，又笑着把目光挪开了。

"好吧。"赫敏说，把身子坐得更直一些，又痛得咧了咧嘴，"学校里怎么样？"

"还好，弗立维清除了弗雷德和乔治留下的沼泽，"金妮说，"大概三秒钟就搞定了。但他在窗户底下还留了一小片，用绳子圈了起来——"

"为什么？"赫敏惊讶地说。

"哦，他只说这是一个特别精彩的魔法。"金妮耸了耸肩膀说。

"我认为他是为了纪念弗雷德和乔治。"罗恩含着满嘴的巧克力说，"你们知道吗，这些都是他们寄给我的，"他指着身边堆得如小山一般的巧克力蛙对哈利说，"他们的笑话店肯定办得不错，是不是？"

赫敏显得不以为然，她问："那么，现在邓布利多回来了，所有的麻烦都结束了吧？"

"是啊，"纳威说，"一切都恢复了正常。"

"我猜费尔奇肯定很高兴吧？"罗恩问道，一边把一张印着邓布利多的巧克力蛙画片靠在他的水罐上。

"才不是呢，"金妮说，"实际上他特别、特别难过……"她把声音压得低低的，"他不住地说乌姆里奇是霍格沃茨有史以来最精彩的事件……"

六个人扭头望去。乌姆里奇教授正躺在他们对面的床上，两眼呆呆地凝视天花板。邓布利多独自闯进禁林，把她从马人那里救了出来。谁也不知道他是怎么做到的——怎么几乎毫发无损地把乌姆里奇带出

CHAPTER THIRTY-EIGHT   The Second War Begins

a scratch on him – nobody knew, and Umbridge was certainly not telling. Since she had returned to the castle she had not, as far as any of them knew, uttered a single word. Nobody really knew what was wrong with her, either. Her usually neat mousy hair was very untidy and there were still bits of twigs and leaves in it, but otherwise she seemed to be quite unscathed.

'Madam Pomfrey says she's just in shock,' whispered Hermione.

'Sulking, more like,' said Ginny.

'Yeah, she shows signs of life if you do this,' said Ron, and with his tongue he made soft clip-clopping noises. Umbridge sat bolt upright, looking around wildly.

'Anything wrong, Professor?' called Madam Pomfrey, poking her head around her office door.

'No … no …' said Umbridge, sinking back into her pillows. 'No, I must have been dreaming …'

Hermione and Ginny muffled their laughter in the bedclothes.

'Speaking of centaurs,' said Hermione, when she had recovered a little, 'who's Divination teacher now? Is Firenze staying?'

'He's got to,' said Harry, 'the other centaurs won't take him back, will they?'

'It looks like he and Trelawney are both going to teach,' said Ginny.

'Bet Dumbledore wishes he could've got rid of Trelawney for good,' said Ron, now munching on his fourteenth Frog. 'Mind you, the whole subject's useless if you ask me, Firenze isn't a lot better …'

'How can you say that?' Hermione demanded. 'After we've just found out that there *are* real prophecies?'

Harry's heart began to race. He had not told Ron, Hermione or anyone else what the prophecy had contained. Neville had told them it had smashed while Harry was pulling him up the steps in the Death room and Harry had not yet corrected this impression. He was not ready to see their expressions when he told them that he must be either murderer or victim, there was no other way …

'It is a pity it broke,' said Hermione quietly, shaking her head.

'Yeah, it is,' said Ron. 'Still, at least You-Know-Who never found out what was in it either – where are you going?' he added, looking both surprised and disappointed as Harry stood up.

第38章 第二场战争开始了

树丛,乌姆里奇也绝不肯说。据他们所知,自从她回到城堡之后,还没有说过一句话。而且谁也不知道她到底哪儿不对劲儿。她一贯整整齐齐的灰褐色头发十分蓬乱,里面还留着树叶和断枝,但除此之外,她似乎并没有受伤。

"庞弗雷女士说她只是受了惊吓。"赫敏低声说。

"恐怕是在生气吧。"金妮说。

"是啊,只要你发出这种声音,她就会显示出生命的迹象。"罗恩说着,用舌头发出嘚嘚的马蹄声。乌姆里奇一下子坐了起来,惊慌地东张西望。

"有什么不对吗,教授?"庞弗雷女士从她办公室的门边探头问道。

"没……没有……"乌姆里奇说着,又倒回到枕头上,"没有,我肯定是在做梦……"

赫敏和金妮用被子堵住了自己的笑声。

"说到马人,"赫敏待笑声止住一些,又说,"现在占卜课教师是谁?费伦泽会留下来吗?"

"他肯定会留下来的,"哈利说,"别的马人都不让他回去了,不是吗?"

"看来他和特里劳妮都要来教课了。"金妮说。

"我敢肯定邓布利多还希望能永远摆脱特里劳妮呢。"罗恩说,嘴里嚼着他的第十四块巧克力蛙,"告诉你们吧,要我说这门课根本就是垃圾,费伦泽也好不了多少……"

"你怎么能这么说呢?"赫敏问道,"我们不是刚刚发现确实有真正的预言吗?"

哈利的心跳加快了。他没有把预言的内容告诉罗恩、赫敏或任何人。纳威对他们说那个预言球在哈利把他拖上死刑厅的台阶时摔碎了,哈利还没有纠正大家的这种印象。如果对他们说,他必须杀人或者被杀,别无选择,他们脸上将出现什么样的表情,他还没有做好准备去面对……

"真可惜它摔碎了。"赫敏摇摇头,轻声说道。

"是啊,"罗恩说,"不过,至少神秘人也永远不会知道那里面是什么了——你要去哪儿?"他看到哈利站了起来,既吃惊又失望地问。

CHAPTER THIRTY-EIGHT   The Second War Begins

'Er – Hagrid's,' said Harry. 'You know, he just got back and I promised I'd go down and see him and tell him how you two are.'

'Oh, all right then,' said Ron grumpily, looking out of the dormitory window at the patch of bright blue sky beyond. 'Wish we could come.'

'Say hello to him for us!' called Hermione, as Harry proceeded down the ward. 'And ask him what's happening about … about his little friend!'

Harry gave a wave of his hand to show he had heard and understood as he left the dormitory.

The castle seemed very quiet even for a Sunday. Everybody was clearly out in the sunny grounds, enjoying the end of their exams and the prospect of a last few days of term unhampered by revision or homework. Harry walked slowly along the deserted corridor, peering out of windows as he went; he could see people messing around in the air over the Quidditch pitch and a couple of students swimming in the lake, accompanied by the giant squid.

He was finding it hard to decide whether he wanted to be with people or not; whenever he was in company he wanted to get away and whenever he was alone he wanted company. He thought he might really go and visit Hagrid, though, as he had not talked to him properly since he'd returned …

Harry had just descended the last marble step into the Entrance Hall when Malfoy, Crabbe and Goyle emerged from a door on the right that Harry knew led down to the Slytherin common room. Harry stopped dead; so did Malfoy and the others. The only sounds were the shouts, laughter and splashes drifting into the Hall from the grounds through the open front doors.

Malfoy glanced around – Harry knew he was checking for signs of teachers – then he looked back at Harry and said in a low voice, 'You're dead, Potter.'

Harry raised his eyebrows.

'Funny,' he said, 'you'd think I'd have stopped walking around …'

Malfoy looked angrier than Harry had ever seen him; he felt a kind of detached satisfaction at the sight of his pale, pointed face contorted with rage.

'You're going to pay,' said Malfoy, in a voice barely louder than a whisper. '*I'm* going to make you pay for what you've done to my father …'

'Well, I'm terrified now,' said Harry sarcastically. 'I s'pose Lord Voldemort's just a warm-up act compared to you three – what's the matter?'

第38章 第二场战争开始了

"呃——去海格那儿,"哈利说,"你知道的,他刚回来,我说过要下去看他,把你们俩的情况告诉他。"

"哦,那好吧。"罗恩闷闷不乐地说,望着病房窗外那一方蔚蓝色的天空,"真希望我们也能去。"

"替我们向他问好!"哈利朝门口走去时,赫敏大声说,"问问他的……他的那个小朋友怎么样了!"

哈利挥了挥手,表示听明白了,然后就走出了病房。

即使对于星期天来说,城堡也显得过于安静了。每个人都在外面阳光灿烂的场地上,享受着考试结束后的轻松,和即将到来的学期最后几天没有复习和考试困扰的日子。哈利慢慢地走在空无一人的走廊上,一边朝窗外望去。他看见人们在魁地奇球场上空悠闲地飞来飞去,还有几个学生在巨乌贼的陪伴下在湖里游泳。

他发现很难确定自己是不是愿意跟别人在一起。每当跟别人在一起时,他就想离开;而每当独自一人时,他又希望有人陪伴。不过他认为他是真的要去拜访海格,自从海格回来以后,他还没有好好跟他聊过呢……

哈利刚走下通向门厅的最后一道大理石楼梯,就看见马尔福、克拉布和高尔从右边一扇门里走了出来,哈利知道那扇门通向下面斯莱特林的公共休息室。哈利停住脚步,马尔福一伙也停住了,只听见场地上的喊声、笑声和水花泼溅的声音,从敞开的大门传进了礼堂。

马尔福扫了一眼四周——哈利知道他在察看有没有老师——然后他看着哈利,压低声音说道:"你死了,波特。"

哈利扬起眉毛。

"真滑稽,"哈利说,"那我不是应该不能到处走动了吗……"

哈利从没见过马尔福这么生气,他看到那张苍白的尖脸气得扭曲了,心头感到一种冷冷的快意。

"你要付出代价的,"马尔福用比耳语高不了多少的声音说,"我要让你为了对我父亲做的事情付出代价……"

"哎哟,我可真吓坏了。"哈利讽刺地说,"我想跟你们三个相比,对付伏地魔只是一次热身训练——怎么回事?"他又补了一句,因为

CHAPTER THIRTY-EIGHT The Second War Begins

he added, for Malfoy, Crabbe and Goyle had all looked stricken at the sound of the name. 'He's a mate of your dad, isn't he? Not scared of him, are you?'

'You think you're such a big man, Potter,' said Malfoy, advancing now, Crabbe and Goyle flanking him. 'You wait. I'll have you. You can't land my father in prison –'

'I thought I just had,' said Harry.

'The Dementors have left Azkaban,' said Malfoy quietly. 'Dad and the others'll be out in no time ...'

'Yeah, I expect they will,' said Harry. 'Still, at least everyone knows what scumbags they are now –'

Malfoy's hand flew towards his wand, but Harry was too quick for him; he had drawn his own wand before Malfoy's fingers had even entered the pocket of his robes.

'Potter!'

The voice rang across the Entrance Hall. Snape had emerged from the staircase leading down to his office and at the sight of him Harry felt a great rush of hatred beyond anything he felt towards Malfoy ... whatever Dumbledore said, he would never forgive Snape ... never ...

'What are you doing, Potter?' said Snape, as coldly as ever, as he strode over to the four of them.

'I'm trying to decide what curse to use on Malfoy, sir,' said Harry fiercely.

Snape stared at him.

'Put that wand away at once,' he said curtly. 'Ten points from Gryff–'

Snape looked towards the giant hourglasses on the walls and gave a sneering smile.

'Ah. I see there are no longer any points left in the Gryffindor hourglass to take away. In that case, Potter, we will simply have to –'

'Add some more?'

Professor McGonagall had just stumped up the stone steps into the castle; she was carrying a tartan carpetbag in one hand and leaning heavily on a walking stick with her other, but otherwise looked quite well.

'Professor McGonagall!' said Snape, striding forwards. 'Out of St Mungo's, I see!'

第38章 第二场战争开始了

马尔福、克拉布和高尔听到这个名字都像被击中了似的,"他不是你爸爸的朋友吗?你不会害怕他吧?"

"你以为你是个了不起的大人物吗,波特?"马尔福说着朝哈利逼了过来,克拉布和高尔分别在他左右两侧,"你等着吧。我会找你算账的。你休想把我父亲送进监狱——"

"我想我已经这么做了。"哈利说。

"摄魂怪离开了阿兹卡班,"马尔福轻声说,"我爸爸和其他人很快就会出来……"

"是啊,我想他们会的,"哈利说,"但至少现在大家都知道他们是什么样的卑鄙小人——"

马尔福迅速伸手去掏魔杖,但哈利出手比他还要敏捷。没等马尔福的手指伸进长袍口袋,哈利就已拔出自己的魔杖。

"波特!"

这响亮的声音从门厅那边传过来。斯内普出现在通向下面他办公室的楼梯上,哈利一看见他,内心就涌起一股强烈的仇恨,远远超过他对马尔福的憎恶……不管邓布利多怎么说,他都永远不会原谅斯内普……永远不会……

"你在做什么,波特?"斯内普一边大步朝他们四个走来,一边说道,声音和平常一样冷冰冰的。

"我正在考虑给马尔福用什么咒语,先生。"哈利情绪激烈地说。

斯内普狠狠地瞪着他。

"赶紧把魔杖收起来,"他厉声说道,"给格兰芬多扣去十分——"

斯内普朝墙上那些大沙漏望去,脸上露出了讥讽的笑容。

"啊,我发现格兰芬多的沙漏里已经没有分数可扣了。这样的话,波特,我们只好——"

"再加上一些分?"

麦格教授重重地踏上了城堡的台阶。她一只手提着一个格子呢旅行袋,另一只手拄着一根拐杖,把几乎全身的重量都倚在上面,但除此之外,她看上去状态还不错。

"麦格教授!"斯内普大步迎上前去说道,"看来,你刚从圣芒戈医院出来!"

CHAPTER THIRTY-EIGHT   The Second War Begins

'Yes, Professor Snape,' said Professor McGonagall, shrugging off her travelling cloak, 'I'm quite as good as new. You two – Crabbe – Goyle –'

She beckoned them forwards imperiously and they came, shuffling their large feet and looking awkward.

'Here,' said Professor McGonagall, thrusting her carpetbag into Crabbe's chest and her cloak into Goyle's, 'take these up to my office for me.'

They turned and stumped away up the marble staircase.

'Right then,' said Professor McGonagall, looking up at the hourglasses on the wall. 'Well, I think Potter and his friends ought to have fifty points apiece for alerting the world to the return of You-Know-Who! What say you, Professor Snape?'

'What?' snapped Snape, though Harry knew he had heard perfectly well. 'Oh – well – I suppose ...'

'So that's fifty each for Potter, the two Weasleys, Longbottom and Miss Granger,' said Professor McGonagall, and a shower of rubies fell down into the bottom bulb of Gryffindor's hourglass as she spoke. 'Oh – and fifty for Miss Lovegood, I suppose,' she added, and a number of sapphires fell into Ravenclaw's glass. 'Now, you wanted to take ten from Mr Potter, I think, Professor Snape – so there we are ...'

A few rubies retreated into the upper bulb, leaving a respectable amount below nevertheless.

'Well, Potter, Malfoy, I think you ought to be outside on a glorious day like this,' Professor McGonagall continued briskly.

Harry did not need telling twice; he thrust his wand back inside his robes and headed straight for the front doors without another glance at Snape and Malfoy.

The hot sun hit him with a blast as he walked across the lawns towards Hagrid's cabin. Students lying around on the grass sunbathing, talking, reading the *Sunday Prophet* and eating sweets, looked up at him as he passed; some called out to him, or else waved, clearly eager to show that they, like the *Prophet*, had decided he was something of a hero. Harry said nothing to any of them. He had no idea how much they knew of what had happened three days ago, but he had so far avoided being questioned and preferred to keep it that way.

He thought at first when he knocked on Hagrid's cabin door that he was out, but then Fang came charging around the corner and almost bowled him over with the enthusiasm of his welcome. Hagrid, it transpired, was picking

第38章 第二场战争开始了

"是的,斯内普教授,"麦格教授说着,抖掉身上的旅行斗篷,"我已经恢复如初了。你们俩——克拉布——高尔——"

她威严地招呼他们过去,他们的大脚在地上拖着,看上去很不安。

"给,"麦格教授说,把旅行袋塞进克拉布怀里,把斗篷塞进高尔怀里,"替我把这些拿到我办公室去。"

他们转过身,脚步沉重地走上了大理石楼梯。

"好了,"麦格教授抬头看着墙上的沙漏说,"我认为应该给波特和他的朋友每人加五十分,因为是他们提醒大家神秘人回来了!你说呢,斯内普教授?"

"什么?"斯内普厉声问道,哈利知道他其实听得清清楚楚,"哦——这个——我认为……"

"那就给波特、韦斯莱兄妹俩、隆巴顿和格兰杰小姐各加五十分。"就在麦格教授说话的当儿,一大堆红宝石像阵雨一样落进了格兰芬多沙漏的底球里。"哦——我想还应该给洛夫古德小姐加五十分。"她又说,于是一堆蓝宝石落进了拉文克劳的沙漏,"好了,斯内普教授,你好像想给波特同学扣掉十分——这样一来就是……"

几粒红宝石退回到了顶球,但留在下面的数量仍然可观。

"好了,波特,马尔福,我认为在这样一个阳光灿烂的日子,你们应该到户外去。"麦格教授语气轻快地继续说。

哈利不需要她再说第二遍。他把魔杖插回袍子里,没有再看斯内普和马尔福一眼,径直朝大门冲去。

他穿过草坪朝海格的小屋走去,炎热的太阳火辣辣地照着他。同学们躺在草地上晒日光浴,聊天,吃糖,读《星期天预言家报》。在哈利走过时他们都抬头望着他。有些人大声喊他,还有些人朝他挥手,显然在急切地表示他们像《星期天预言家报》一样,已经决定把他看成一个英雄了。哈利什么也没有对同学们说。他不知道他们对三天前发生的事情了解多少,但他这几天一直躲着被人盘问,他巴不得永远这样。

他敲敲海格小屋的门,起初以为他出去了,但是很快牙牙绕过屋角冲了过来,那股热情劲儿,差点儿把他撞翻在地。原来海格正在屋

CHAPTER THIRTY-EIGHT   The Second War Begins

runner beans in his back garden.

'All righ', Harry!' he said, beaming, when Harry approached the fence. 'Come in, come in, we'll have a cup o' dandelion juice ...'

'How's things?' Hagrid asked him, as they settled down at his wooden table with a glass apiece of iced juice. 'Yeh – er – feelin' all righ', are yeh?'

Harry knew from the look of concern on Hagrid's face that he was not referring to Harry's physical well-being.

'I'm fine,' Harry said quickly, because he could not bear to discuss the thing that he knew was in Hagrid's mind. 'So, where've you been?'

'Bin hidin' out in the mountains,' said Hagrid. 'Up in a cave, like Sirius did when he –'

Hagrid broke off, cleared his throat gruffly, looked at Harry, and took a long draught of juice.

'Anyway, back now,' he said feebly.

'You – you look better,' said Harry, who was determined to keep the conversation moving away from Sirius.

'Wha'?' said Hagrid, raising a massive hand and feeling his face. 'Oh – oh yeah. Well, Grawpy's loads better behaved now, loads. Seemed right pleased ter see me when I got back, ter tell yeh the truth. He's a good lad, really ... I've bin thinkin' abou' tryin' ter find him a lady friend, actually ...'

Harry would normally have tried to persuade Hagrid out of this idea at once; the prospect of a second giant taking up residence in the Forest, possibly even wilder and more brutal than Grawp, was positively alarming, but somehow Harry could not muster the energy necessary to argue the point. He was starting to wish he was alone again, and with the idea of hastening his departure he took several large gulps of his dandelion juice, half emptying his glass.

'Ev'ryone knows yeh've bin tellin' the truth now, Harry,' said Hagrid softly and unexpectedly. 'Tha's gotta be better, hasn' it?'

Harry shrugged.

'Look ...' Hagrid leaned towards him across the table, 'I knew Sirius longer 'n yeh did ... he died in battle, an' tha's the way he'd've wanted ter go –'

'He didn't want to go at all!' said Harry angrily.

Hagrid bowed his great shaggy head.

'Nah, I don' reckon he did,' he said quietly. 'But still, Harry ... he was

第38章 第二场战争开始了

后的园子里摘红花四季豆呢。

"好啊,哈利!"海格看到哈利走近栅栏,笑眯眯地说,"进来,进来,我们来喝一杯蒲公英汁……"

"情况怎么样?"海格问他,他们在木头桌旁坐下,每人面前放着一杯冰镇蒲公英汁,"你——呃——感觉还好吧?"

哈利从海格关切的表情知道,他指的不是哈利的身体状况。

"我挺好的。"哈利赶紧说道,因为他没心情讨论海格心里想的那件事,"那么,你去哪儿了?"

"躲在大山里,"海格说,"躲在一个山洞里,就像小天狼星当时——"

海格顿住了,粗声粗气地清清嗓子,眼睛看着哈利,喝了一大口蒲公英汁。

"反正,现在回来了。"他声音发虚地说。

"你——你气色好多了。"哈利说,他决定让话题远离小天狼星。

"什么?"海格说着,举起一只大手摸了摸脸,"哦,是啊。知道吗,格洛普现在表现好多了,真的好多了。不瞒你说,我回去的时候,他似乎很高兴见到我。他真的是个好孩子……我正考虑给他找个女朋友,真的……"

换了平常,哈利肯定要劝说海格立刻打消这个念头。想到将有第二个巨人在禁林里定居,而且很可能比格洛普还要野蛮、还要粗鲁,真是令人恐慌,但是不知怎的,哈利打不起精神来争论这个话题。他又开始希望自己一个人待着了,为了赶紧离开,他连喝了几大口蒲公英汁,把杯子喝空了一半。

"现在大家都知道你说的是对的了,哈利。"海格出人意外地轻声说,"那就好多了,是不是?"

哈利耸了耸肩。

"是这样……"海格从桌子对面朝他探过身子,"我认识小天狼星的时间比你长……他死在战斗中,他愿意这样死去——"

"他根本就不愿意死!"哈利气愤地说。

海格垂下乱蓬蓬的大脑袋。

"不,我不是说他想死,"他轻声说,"可是,哈利……他绝不

CHAPTER THIRTY-EIGHT   The Second War Begins

never one ter sit aroun' at home an' let other people do the fightin'. He couldn've lived with himself if he hadn' gone ter help –'

Harry leapt up.

'I've got to go and visit Ron and Hermione in the hospital wing,' he said mechanically.

'Oh,' said Hagrid, looking rather upset. 'Oh ... all righ' then, Harry ... take care o' yerself then, an' drop back in if yeh've got a mo ...'

'Yeah ... right ...'

Harry crossed to the door as fast as he could and pulled it open; he was out in the sunshine again before Hagrid had finished saying goodbye, and walking away across the lawn. Once again, people called out to him as he passed. He closed his eyes for a few moments, wishing they would all vanish, that he could open his eyes and find himself alone in the grounds ...

A few days ago, before his exams had finished and he had seen the vision Voldemort had planted in his mind, he would have given almost anything for the wizarding world to know he had been telling the truth, for them to believe that Voldemort was back, and to know that he was neither a liar nor mad. Now, however ...

He walked a short way around the lake, sat down on its bank, sheltered from the gaze of passers-by behind a tangle of shrubs, and stared out over the gleaming water, thinking ...

Perhaps the reason he wanted to be alone was because he had felt isolated from everybody since his talk with Dumbledore. An invisible barrier separated him from the rest of the world. He was – he had always been – a marked man. It was just that he had never really understood what that meant ...

And yet sitting here on the edge of the lake, with the terrible weight of grief dragging at him, with the loss of Sirius so raw and fresh inside, he could not muster any great sense of fear. It was sunny, and the grounds around him were full of laughing people, and even though he felt as distant from them as though he belonged to a different race, it was still very hard to believe as he sat here that his life must include, or end in, murder ...

He sat there for a long time, gazing out at the water, trying not to think about his godfather or to remember that it was directly across from here, on the opposite bank, that Sirius had once collapsed trying to fend off a hundred Dementors ...

第38章 第二场战争开始了

会坐在家里，让别人去流血牺牲。如果他不去救援，他是不会安心的——"

哈利跳了起来。

"我要到校医院去看罗恩和赫敏了。"他没有表情地说。

"噢，"海格说，神情显得十分不安，"哦……那好吧，哈利……好好照顾自己，有时间就过来……"

"行……好吧……"

哈利以最快的速度走到门口，拉开房门。海格还没有说完再见，他就又来到外面的阳光下，踏着草坪走去。他走过时又有人大声喊他。他把眼睛闭了一会儿，希望他们统统消失，这样等他睁开眼睛时，就可以发现只有他一个人待在场地上……

几天前，考试还没有结束，他还没有看见伏地魔植入他脑海的画面，他几乎愿意付出一切让巫师界明白他说的是真的，让他们相信伏地魔回来了，让他们知道他不是说谎，也没有发疯。可是现在……

他绕着湖边走了一段，然后在岸边坐了下来，躲在一大片纠结的灌木丛后面，避开路人的目光。他凝望着波光粼粼的水面，陷入了沉思……

也许，他之所以愿意一个人待着，是因为自从跟邓布利多谈话之后，他觉得自己跟大家隔离了。有一道无形的屏障，把他跟世界上的其他人隔绝开来。他是一个带有标记的人，从来都是如此。他之前只是一直没有真正明白这意味着什么……

然而，此刻他坐在湖边，内心坠着沉甸甸的悲伤，小天狼星的死带来的伤痛是这么惨烈，他没有力量去感受强烈的恐惧。这里阳光灿烂，周围的场地上都是欢笑的人们，他虽然感到离他们很遥远，似乎自己属于另一个种族，但是坐在这里，他仍然很难相信他的生命必须包括杀人或者被杀……

他在那里坐了很长时间，凝望着水面，努力不让自己去想教父，不去回忆曾经有一次，就在这里的湖对岸，小天狼星为击退一百个摄魂怪而精疲力竭地倒下……

CHAPTER THIRTY-EIGHT   The Second War Begins

The sun had set before he realised he was cold. He got up and returned to the castle, wiping his face on his sleeve as he went.

Ron and Hermione left the hospital wing completely cured three days before the end of term. Hermione kept showing signs of wanting to talk about Sirius, but Ron tended to make 'hushing' noises every time she mentioned his name. Harry was still not sure whether or not he wanted to talk about his godfather yet; his wishes varied with his mood. He knew one thing, though: unhappy as he felt at the moment, he would greatly miss Hogwarts in a few days' time when he was back at number four, Privet Drive. Even though he now understood exactly why he had to return there every summer, he did not feel any better about it. Indeed, he had never dreaded his return more.

Professor Umbridge left Hogwarts the day before the end of term. It seemed she had crept out of the hospital wing during dinnertime, evidently hoping to depart undetected, but unfortunately for her, she met Peeves on the way, who seized his last chance to do as Fred had instructed, and chased her gleefully from the premises whacking her alternately with a walking stick and a sock full of chalk. Many students ran out into the Entrance Hall to watch her running away down the path and the Heads of Houses tried only half-heartedly to restrain them. Indeed, Professor McGonagall sank back into her chair at the staff table after a few feeble remonstrances and was clearly heard to express a regret that she could not run cheering after Umbridge herself, because Peeves had borrowed her walking stick.

Their last evening at school arrived; most people had finished packing and were already heading down to the end-of-term Leaving Feast, but Harry had not even started.

'Just do it tomorrow!' said Ron, who was waiting by the door of their dormitory. 'Come on, I'm starving.'

'I won't be long ... look, you go ahead ...'

But when the dormitory door closed behind Ron, Harry made no effort to speed up his packing. The very last thing he wanted to do was to attend the Leaving Feast. He was worried that Dumbledore would make some reference to him in his speech. He was sure to mention Voldemort's return; he had talked to them about it last year, after all ...

Harry pulled some crumpled robes out of the very bottom of his trunk to make way for folded ones and, as he did so, noticed a badly wrapped package

第38章 第二场战争开始了

太阳落山之后,他才感到有些凉意。他站起来,返回城堡,一边用袖子擦去脸上的泪水。

学期结束的前三天,罗恩和赫敏离开了校医院,完全康复了。赫敏总是露出想谈论小天狼星的迹象,但是每次她一提他的名字,罗恩就发出"嘘"的声音。哈利仍然不确定自己是不是愿意谈论教父。他的想法随着情绪变化不定。但有一点他是知道的:虽然此刻他感到闷闷不乐,但是过几天回到女贞路4号之后,他会非常非常想念霍格沃茨的。他现在明白了为什么每年暑假都要回到那里去,但并没有感觉好多少。事实上,他比以前任何时候都更害怕回去。

乌姆里奇教授是在放假前一天离开霍格沃茨的。她似乎是趁吃晚饭的时候悄悄溜出了校医院,显然是希望神不知鬼不觉地离开,可是也活该她倒霉,她半路上碰到了皮皮鬼。皮皮鬼抓住这最后一次机会执行弗雷德的嘱咐,用一根拐杖和一只装满粉笔的袜子轮番打她,从场地一路开开心心地把她赶出了学校。许多学生从礼堂跑到门厅看她顺着小路跑远,几个学院的院长只是半真半假地制止他们。事实上,麦格教授有气无力地叫嚷了几声,就坐回教工餐桌的椅子上,用大家都听得很清楚的声音表示遗憾,因为皮皮鬼借走了她的拐杖,她不能亲自跑去欢送乌姆里奇。

在校的最后一晚到来了。大多数同学都收拾完行李,已经下楼去参加学期结束的晚宴了,而哈利还没开始收拾呢。

"明天再收拾吧!"等在宿舍门口的罗恩说道,"快走,我饿死了。"

"不会很久的……噢,你先走吧……"

宿舍的门在罗恩身后关上了,但哈利并没有加快收拾的速度。他最不愿意做的事情就是参加期末晚宴。他担心邓布利多在讲话中会提到他。邓布利多肯定会提到伏地魔回来了,毕竟他去年就对他们说起过这个……

哈利从箱子底部抽出几件皱巴巴的袍子,腾出地方来放叠好的衣服,就在这时,他发现箱子的角落里有一个胡乱包起的纸包。他不知

CHAPTER THIRTY-EIGHT The Second War Begins

lying in a corner of it. He could not think what it was doing there. He bent down, pulled it out from underneath his trainers and examined it.

He realised what it was within seconds. Sirius had given it to him just inside the front door of number twelve Grimmauld Place. '*Use it if you need me, all right?*'

Harry sank down on to his bed and unwrapped the package. Out fell a small, square mirror. It looked old; it was certainly dirty. Harry held it up to his face and saw his own reflection looking back at him.

He turned the mirror over. There on the reverse side was a scribbled note from Sirius.

> *This is a two-way mirror. I've got the other one of the pair. If you need to speak to me, just say my name into it; you'll appear in my mirror and I'll be able to talk in yours. James and I used to use them when we were in separate detentions.*

Harry's heart began to race. He remembered seeing his dead parents in the Mirror of Erised four years ago. He was going to be able to talk to Sirius again, right now, he knew it –

He looked around to make sure there was nobody else there; the dormitory was quite empty. He looked back at the mirror, raised it in front of his face with trembling hands and said, loudly and clearly, 'Sirius.'

His breath misted the surface of the glass. He held the mirror even closer, excitement flooding through him, but the eyes blinking back at him through the fog were definitely his own.

He wiped the mirror clear again and said, so that every syllable rang clearly through the room:

'Sirius Black!'

Nothing happened. The frustrated face looking back out of the mirror was still, definitely, his own …

Sirius didn't have his mirror on him when he went through the archway, said a small voice in Harry's head. *That's* why it's not working …

Harry remained quite still for a moment, then hurled the mirror back into the trunk where it shattered. He had been convinced, for a whole, shining minute, that he was going to see Sirius, talk to him again …

第38章 第二场战争开始了

道这里怎么会有这个东西。他弯下身,把它从运动鞋下面抽出来,仔细查看。

他几秒钟就明白了这是什么。是小天狼星在格里莫广场12号的大门里给他的。"在需要我的时候用它,好吗?"

哈利一屁股坐在床上,打开了纸包,从里面掉出一面方方的小镜子。它看上去很有年头了,脏兮兮的。哈利把它举到面前,看见里面映出的是他自己的脸。

他把镜子翻过来,背面有小天狼星写的一张潦草的纸条。

> 这是一面双面镜,共有一对,另一面在我手里。如果你需要跟我说话,就对它说出我的名字;你就会出现在我的镜子里,我也能在你的镜子里跟你说话。过去,詹姆和我分别关禁闭时经常使用它们。

哈利的心狂跳起来。他记得四年前曾在厄里斯魔镜里看见过已故的爸爸妈妈。现在,他又能跟小天狼星说话了,一定能的——

他看看周围,宿舍里空荡荡的,没有别人。他又看着镜子,用颤抖的双手把它举到面前,清清楚楚地大声说道:"小天狼星。"

他的呼吸使镜面变得模糊起来。他把镜子举得更近一些,激动的心情如潮水一般,然而,透过雾气朝他眨动的那双眼睛,毫无疑问还是他自己的。

他把镜面重新擦亮,一字一顿地说,让每个音节都在房间里回响:"小天狼星布莱克!"

什么也没有发生。镜子里那张绝望的脸庞,毫无疑问仍然是他自己的……

哈利脑袋里的一个小声音说道,小天狼星穿过拱门时没有把镜子带在身上,所以不管用了……

哈利一动不动地呆了一会儿,然后把镜子扔回箱子里,镜面摔破了。刚才整整一分钟里,他内心充满希望,相信自己肯定能见到小天狼星,能再次跟小天狼星说话……

CHAPTER THIRTY-EIGHT The Second War Begins

Disappointment was burning in his throat; he got up and began throwing his things pell-mell into the trunk on top of the broken mirror –

But then an idea struck him ... a better idea than a mirror ... a much bigger, more important idea ... how had he never thought of it before – why had he never asked?

He was sprinting out of the dormitory and down the spiral staircase, hitting the walls as he ran and barely noticing; he hurtled across the empty common room, through the portrait hole and off along the corridor, ignoring the Fat Lady, who called after him: 'The feast is about to start, you know, you're cutting it very fine!'

But Harry had no intention of going to the feast ...

How could it be that the place was full of ghosts whenever you didn't need one, yet now ...

He ran down staircases and along corridors and met nobody either alive or dead. They were all, clearly, in the Great Hall. Outside his Charms classroom he came to a halt, panting and thinking disconsolately that he would have to wait until later, until after the end of the feast ...

But just as he had given up hope, he saw it – a translucent somebody drifting across the end of the corridor.

'Hey – hey, Nick! NICK!'

The ghost stuck its head back out of the wall, revealing the extravagantly plumed hat and dangerously wobbling head of Sir Nicholas de Mimsy-Porpington.

'Good evening,' he said, withdrawing the rest of his body from the solid stone and smiling at Harry. 'I am not the only one who is late, then? Though,' he sighed, 'in a rather different sense, of course ...'

'Nick, can I ask you something?'

A most peculiar expression stole over Nearly Headless Nick's face as he inserted a finger in the stiff ruff at his neck and tugged it a little straighter, apparently to give himself thinking time. He desisted only when his partially severed neck seemed about to give way completely.

'Er – now, Harry?' said Nick, looking discomfited. 'Can't it wait until after the feast?'

'No – Nick – please,' said Harry, 'I really need to talk to you. Can we go in here?'

第38章 第二场战争开始了

他失望得嗓子眼里直冒火。他站起身,开始把东西乱七八糟地扔进箱子,扔在破碎的镜片上——

这时,他突然产生了一个念头……一个比镜子还要好的念头……一个更行之有效、更了不起的念头……他之前怎么没想到呢——他为什么从来没有问过呢?

他冲出宿舍,冲下旋转楼梯,匆忙间撞到墙上都没有注意。他跑过空无一人的公共休息室,穿过肖像洞口,顺着走廊往前跑,没有理睬胖夫人在他身后大喊:"喂,宴会就要开始了,你时间掐得真准啊!"

其实哈利根本没打算去参加宴会……

在你不需要的时候这里挤满了幽灵,现在为什么却偏偏……

他冲下楼梯,跑过一道道走廊,没有碰到一个活人和死人。显然,他们都在礼堂里呢。他在魔咒教室外停住脚步,呼呼喘着粗气,绝望地想他大概只能等待,等到宴会结束之后……

就在他放弃希望的时候,他看见了——一个半透明的人影在走廊尽头飘过。

"嘿——嘿,尼克!**尼克!**"

那幽灵又把脑袋从墙壁里伸出来,露出奢华的羽毛帽子,以及尼古拉斯·德·敏西-波平顿爵士那颗摇摇欲坠的脑袋。

"晚上好,"他说,把整个身体从坚固的石墙里退出来,笑眯眯地看着哈利,"看来迟到的不止我一个人,是吗?当然啦,"他叹息着说,"不过咱俩情况不太一样……"

"尼克,我能问你一件事吗?"

差点没头的尼克脸上浮现出一种十分古怪的表情,他把一根手指塞进脖子上的硬领里,把领子拉得更直一些,显然是为了给自己一些思考的时间。后来,他那没有完全砍断的脖子眼看就要彻底断掉了,他才停住了手。

"呃——现在吗,哈利?"尼克显得有些尴尬地说,"能不能等宴会结束了再说?"

"不——尼克——求求你了,"哈利说,"我真的需要跟你谈谈。我们能进去吗?"

CHAPTER THIRTY-EIGHT   The Second War Begins

Harry opened the door of the nearest classroom and Nearly Headless Nick sighed.

'Oh, very well,' he said, looking resigned. 'I can't pretend I haven't been expecting it.'

Harry was holding the door open for him, but he drifted through the wall instead.

'Expecting what?' Harry asked, as he closed the door.

'You to come and find me,' said Nick, now gliding over to the window and looking out at the darkening grounds. 'It happens, sometimes ... when somebody has suffered a ... loss.'

'Well,' said Harry, refusing to be deflected. 'You were right, I've – I've come to find you.'

Nick said nothing.

'It's –' said Harry, who was finding this more awkward than he had anticipated, 'it's just – you're dead. But you're still here, aren't you?'

Nick sighed and continued to gaze out at the grounds.

'That's right, isn't it?' Harry urged him. 'You died, but I'm talking to you ... you can walk around Hogwarts and everything, can't you?'

'Yes,' said Nearly Headless Nick quietly, 'I walk and talk, yes.'

'So, you came back, didn't you?' said Harry urgently. 'People can come back, right? As ghosts. They don't have to disappear completely. Well?' he added impatiently, when Nick continued to say nothing.

Nearly Headless Nick hesitated, then said, 'Not everyone can come back as a ghost.'

'What d'you mean?' said Harry quickly.

'Only ... only wizards.'

'Oh,' said Harry, and he almost laughed with relief. 'Well, that's OK then, the person I'm asking about is a wizard. So he can come back, right?'

Nick turned away from the window and looked mournfully at Harry.

'He won't come back.'

'Who?'

'Sirius Black,' said Nick.

'But you did!' said Harry angrily. 'You came back – you're dead and you didn't disappear –'

第38章　第二场战争开始了

哈利推开离他最近的一间教室的门，差点没头的尼克叹了一口气。

"哦，好吧，"他摆出一副听天由命的样子，说道，"说实在的，我早就料到会有这事。"

哈利把门打开让尼克进去，尼克却穿墙而入。

"料到什么？"哈利关上门问道。

"料到你会来找我。"尼克说，他滑到窗口，望着外面逐渐黑暗的场地，"时常会有这种事……如果有人失去了一位……亲人。"

"是啊，"哈利不愿意转移话题，"你说得对，我——我来找你就是为了这个。"

尼克什么也没说。

"因为——"哈利发现这比他料想的还要难以启齿，"因为——你是死人，但你还在这儿，不是吗？"

尼克又叹了一口气，继续望着外面的场地。

"是不是这样？"哈利追问道，"你死了，但我还能跟你说话……你还能在霍格沃茨走来走去，什么都不妨碍，是不是？"

"是的，"差点没头的尼克轻声说，"我能走路，也能说话，没错。"

"所以，你从那边回来了，是不是？"哈利急切地说，"人是可以回来的，对吗？作为幽灵回来。他们不一定完全消失。你说呢？"看到尼克还是一声不吭，他不耐烦地追问道。

差点没头的尼克迟疑了片刻，说："并不是每个人都能作为幽灵回来的。"

"什么意思？"哈利连忙问。

"只有……只有巫师才可以。"

"噢，"哈利松了一口气，差点儿笑出声来，"是的，那没问题，我要问的那个人就是巫师。所以他可以回来，对吗？"

尼克离开窗口，忧伤地望着哈利。

"他不会回来了。"

"谁？"

"小天狼星布莱克。"尼克说。

"可是你回来了！"哈利气愤地说，"你回来了——你死了，但你没有消失——"

1429

CHAPTER THIRTY-EIGHT   The Second War Begins

'Wizards can leave an imprint of themselves upon the earth, to walk palely where their living selves once trod,' said Nick miserably. 'But very few wizards choose that path.'

'Why not?' said Harry. 'Anyway – it doesn't matter – Sirius won't care if it's unusual, he'll come back, I know he will!'

And so strong was his belief, Harry actually turned his head to check the door, sure, for a split second, that he was going to see Sirius, pearly-white and transparent but beaming, walking through it towards him.

'He will not come back,' repeated Nick. 'He will have ... gone on.'

'What d'you mean, "gone on"?' said Harry quickly. 'Gone on where? Listen – what happens when you die, anyway? Where do you go? Why doesn't everyone come back? Why isn't this place full of ghosts? Why –?'

'I cannot answer,' said Nick.

'You're dead, aren't you?' said Harry exasperatedly. 'Who can answer better than you?'

'I was afraid of death,' said Nick softly. 'I chose to remain behind. I sometimes wonder whether I oughtn't to have ... well, that is neither here nor there ... in fact, *I* am neither here nor there ...' He gave a small sad chuckle. 'I know nothing of the secrets of death, Harry, for I chose my feeble imitation of life instead. I believe learned wizards study the matter in the Department of Mysteries –'

'Don't talk to me about that place!' said Harry fiercely.

'I am sorry not to have been more help,' said Nick gently. 'Well ... well, do excuse me ... the feast, you know ...'

And he left the room, leaving Harry there alone, gazing blankly at the wall through which Nick had disappeared.

Harry felt almost as though he had lost his godfather all over again in losing the hope that he might be able to see or speak to him once more. He walked slowly and miserably back up through the empty castle, wondering whether he would ever feel cheerful again.

He had turned the corner towards the Fat Lady's corridor when he saw somebody up ahead fastening a note to a board on the wall. A second glance showed him it was Luna. There were no good hiding places nearby, she was bound to have heard his footsteps, and in any case, Harry could hardly muster the energy to avoid anyone at the moment.

第38章 第二场战争开始了

"巫师可以在人间留下他们的印记,可以飘缈地走在他们生前走过的地方,"尼克难过地说,"但只有很少的巫师选择这条路。"

"为什么?"哈利说,"其实——这没有什么关系——小天狼星不会在乎这是不是反常,他会回来的,我知道他会的!"

哈利太相信这一点了,竟然真的转过脑袋看了看门,一刹那间他确实相信他会看见小天狼星,乳白色的,半透明的,面带笑容穿过房门朝他走来。

"他不会回来了,"尼克又说了一遍,"他会……继续往前走。"

"这话是什么意思,'继续往前走'?"哈利追问道,"走到哪里去?对了——你死的时候是怎么样的?你去了哪里?为什么不是每个人都能回来?为什么这个地方没有挤满幽灵?为什么——?"

"我无可奉告。"尼克说。

"你死了,是不是?"哈利激愤地说,"还能有谁比你更知道答案?"

"我当时害怕死亡,"尼克轻声说,"选择了留在后面。有时候我也会怀疑自己是不是应该……唉,非此非彼……实际上,我既不在这边也不在那边……"他悲哀地轻声笑了一下,"我对死亡的奥秘一无所知,哈利,因为我选择了似是而非地模仿生命。我相信神秘事务司里的有学之士正在研究这件事——"

"别跟我提那个地方!"哈利激烈地说。

"对不起,我爱莫能助。"尼克温和地说,"好了……好了,请原谅……宴会,你知道……"

他离开了教室,留下哈利一个人茫然地望着尼克消失的墙壁。

能再次看见教父并跟他说话的希望破灭了,哈利觉得自己几乎是又一次痛失了教父。他忧伤地慢慢穿过空荡荡的城堡,不知道自己这辈子还会不会感到快乐。

他转过那个通往胖夫人走廊的拐角,看见前面有个人正在往墙上的布告栏里钉纸条。他又看了一眼,发现是卢娜。附近没有地方可以躲藏,卢娜肯定听见了他的脚步声,而且,哈利此刻几乎打不起精神来躲避别人。

CHAPTER THIRTY-EIGHT   The Second War Begins

'Hello,' said Luna vaguely, glancing around at him as she stepped back from the notice.

'How come you're not at the feast?' Harry asked.

'Well, I've lost most of my possessions,' said Luna serenely. 'People take them and hide them, you know. But as it's the last night, I really do need them back, so I've been putting up signs.'

She gestured towards the noticeboard, upon which, sure enough, she had pinned a list of all her missing books and clothes, with a plea for their return.

An odd feeling rose in Harry; an emotion quite different from the anger and grief that had filled him since Sirius's death. It was a few moments before he realised that he was feeling sorry for Luna.

'How come people hide your stuff?' he asked her, frowning.

'Oh ... well ...' she shrugged. 'I think they think I'm a bit odd, you know. Some people call me "Loony" Lovegood, actually.'

Harry looked at her and the new feeling of pity intensified rather painfully.

'That's no reason for them to take your things,' he said flatly. 'D'you want help finding them?'

'Oh, no,' she said, smiling at him. 'They'll come back, they always do in the end. It was just that I wanted to pack tonight. Anyway ... why aren't *you* at the feast?'

Harry shrugged. 'Just didn't feel like it.'

'No,' said Luna, observing him with those oddly misty, protuberant eyes. 'I don't suppose you do. That man the Death Eaters killed was your godfather, wasn't he? Ginny told me.'

Harry nodded curtly, but found that for some reason he did not mind Luna talking about Sirius. He had just remembered that she, too, could see Thestrals.

'Have you ...' he began. 'I mean, who ... has anyone you known ever died?'

'Yes,' said Luna simply, 'my mother. She was a quite extraordinary witch, you know, but she did like to experiment and one of her spells went rather badly wrong one day. I was nine.'

'I'm sorry,' Harry mumbled.

'Yes, it was rather horrible,' said Luna conversationally. 'I still feel very sad about it sometimes. But I've still got Dad. And anyway, it's not as though I'll

第38章 第二场战争开始了

"你好。"卢娜含混地说，扭头看了他一眼，从布告栏前退后几步。

"你怎么没去参加宴会？"哈利问。

"唉，我的大部分东西都丢了，"卢娜平静地说，"你知道，是别人把它们拿走藏了起来。今天是最后一个晚上了，我确实需要把它们都要回来，所以就贴出了告示。"

她指了指布告栏，果然，那上面钉着她丢失的书本和衣服的清单，并写着请求归还的话。

哈利心头涌起一种古怪的感觉；这感觉与小天狼星死后充斥他内心的愤怒和悲哀完全不同。他过了片刻才意识到自己是在为卢娜感到难过。

"他们为什么要把你的东西藏起来呢？"他皱着眉头问卢娜。

"哦……怎么说呢……"卢娜耸了耸肩，"我猜他们觉得我有点古怪。实际上，有人管我叫'疯姑娘'洛夫古德。"

哈利看着她，这种新的怜悯感觉一下子更强烈了。

"他们没有理由拿走你的东西，"他直截了当地说，"要我帮你找到它们吗？"

"哦，不用了，"她微笑地看着他说，"它们会回来的，它们最后总是会回来的。只是今晚我想收拾东西了。对了……你为什么不去参加宴会？"

哈利耸了耸肩："不想去。"

"是啊，"卢娜说，用那双雾蒙蒙的、突出的眼睛端详着哈利，"我猜你也不想去。食死徒杀死的那个人是你的教父，对吗？金妮告诉我的。"

哈利只是点了点头，但他发现不知怎的，他并不介意卢娜谈到小天狼星。他刚刚想起卢娜也能看见夜骐。

"你有……"他开口说道，"我是说，谁……有某个你认识的人死去了吗？"

"有，"卢娜坦率地说，"我母亲。你知道吗，她是个很不一般的女巫，特别喜欢做实验，有一天，她的一个咒语出了大差错。那年我九岁。"

"对不起。"哈利轻声说。

"是啊，当时真的非常残酷，"卢娜推心置腹地说，"现在我有时候仍然会为此感到很难过。但我还有爸爸呢。而且，我又不是再也见不

CHAPTER THIRTY-EIGHT The Second War Begins

never see Mum again, is it?'

'Er – isn't it?' said Harry uncertainly.

She shook her head in disbelief.

'Oh, come on. You heard them, just behind the veil, didn't you?'

'You mean ...'

'In that room with the archway. They were just lurking out of sight, that's all. You heard them.'

They looked at each other. Luna was smiling slightly. Harry did not know what to say, or to think; Luna believed so many extraordinary things ... yet he had been sure he had heard voices behind the veil, too.

'Are you sure you don't want me to help you look for your stuff?' he said.

'Oh, no,' said Luna. 'No, I think I'll just go down and have some pudding and wait for it all to turn up ... it always does in the end ... well, have a nice holiday, Harry.'

'Yeah ... yeah, you too.'

She walked away from him and, as he watched her go, he found that the terrible weight in his stomach seemed to have lessened slightly.

The journey home on the Hogwarts Express next day was eventful in several ways. Firstly, Malfoy, Crabbe and Goyle, who had clearly been waiting all week for the opportunity to strike without teacher witnesses, attempted to ambush Harry halfway down the train as he made his way back from the toilet. The attack might have succeeded had it not been for the fact that they unwittingly chose to stage the attack right outside a compartment full of DA members, who saw what was happening through the glass and rose as one to rush to Harry's aid. By the time Ernie Macmillan, Hannah Abbott, Susan Bones, Justin Finch-Fletchley, Anthony Goldstein and Terry Boot had finished using a wide variety of the hexes and jinxes Harry had taught them, Malfoy, Crabbe and Goyle resembled nothing so much as three gigantic slugs squeezed into Hogwarts uniform as Harry, Ernie and Justin hoisted them into the luggage rack and left them there to ooze.

'I must say, I'm looking forward to seeing Malfoy's mother's face when he gets off the train,' said Ernie, with some satisfaction, as he watched Malfoy squirm above him. Ernie had never quite got over the indignity of Malfoy docking points from Hufflepuff during his brief spell as a member of the

第38章 第二场战争开始了

到妈妈了,对不对?"

"呃——不是吗?"哈利不确定地说。

她惊愕地摇摇头。

"哦,别闹了。你不也听见他们的声音了,就在那帷幔后面,是不是?"

"你是说……"

"在那个有拱门的房间里。他们只是隐藏起来了,就是这样。你听见了他们的声音。"

他们互相对视着。卢娜的脸上带着淡淡的微笑。哈利不知道该说什么,该如何去想。卢娜相信这么多奇异的事情……而他也曾相信他听见了帷幔后面有人在说话。

"你真的不需要我帮你找找东西吗?"他问。

"哦,不了,"卢娜说,"不需要,我想下楼去吃点甜点心,然后就等着它们出现……它们最后总会出现的……好了,祝你假期愉快,哈利。"

"好……好的,也祝你愉快。"

卢娜离开了他,哈利注视着她的背影,发现压在心头的沉甸甸的块垒似乎减轻了一些。

第二天,乘坐霍格沃茨特快列车回家的途中发生了好几件大事。首先,马尔福、克拉布和高尔显然一星期来都在等待机会趁老师不在时动手,他们埋伏在列车中间,想趁哈利上厕所回来时偷袭他。偷袭本来可能会成功的,结果他们鬼使神差地把地点选在了一节坐满D.A.成员的车厢外面。车厢里的人透过玻璃窗看见情况不对,立刻冲出来援救哈利。待厄尼·麦克米兰、汉娜·艾博、苏珊·博恩斯、贾斯廷·芬列里、安东尼·戈德斯坦和泰瑞·布特完成哈利教给他们的一大堆五花八门的魔法和恶咒后,马尔福、克拉布和高尔活像三只被塞进霍格沃茨校服的巨大的鼻涕虫,哈利、厄尼和贾斯廷把他们搬到行李架上,任由他们在那里渗出黏糊糊的汁液。

"我得说一句,我真盼望看到马尔福下车时他妈妈脸上的表情。"厄尼看着马尔福在他头顶上方蠕动,带着些许快意说道。厄尼一直耿

CHAPTER THIRTY-EIGHT   The Second War Begins

Inquisitorial Squad.

'Goyle's mum'll be really pleased, though,' said Ron, who had come to investigate the source of the commotion. 'He's loads better-looking now ... anyway, Harry, the food trolley's just stopped if you want anything ...'

Harry thanked the others and accompanied Ron back to their compartment, where he bought a large pile of cauldron cakes and pumpkin pasties. Hermione was reading the *Daily Prophet* again, Ginny was doing a quiz in *The Quibbler* and Neville was stroking his *Mimbulus mimbletonia*, which had grown a great deal over the year and now made odd crooning noises when touched.

Harry and Ron whiled away most of the journey playing wizard chess while Hermione read out snippets from the *Prophet*. It was now full of articles about how to repel Dementors, attempts by the Ministry to track down Death Eaters and hysterical letters claiming that the writer had seen Lord Voldemort walking past their house that very morning ...

'It hasn't really started yet,' sighed Hermione gloomily, folding up the newspaper again. 'But it won't be long now ...' 'Hey, Harry,' said Ron softly, nodding towards the glass window on to the corridor.

Harry looked around. Cho was passing, accompanied by Marietta Edgecombe, who was wearing a balaclava. His and Cho's eyes met for a moment. Cho blushed and kept walking. Harry looked back down at the chessboard just in time to see one of his pawns chased off its square by Ron's knight.

'What's – er – going on with you and her, anyway?' Ron asked quietly.

'Nothing,' said Harry truthfully.

'I – er – heard she's going out with someone else now,' said Hermione tentatively.

Harry was surprised to find that this information did not hurt at all. Wanting to impress Cho seemed to belong to a past that was no longer quite connected with him; so much of what he had wanted before Sirius's death felt that way these days ... the week that had elapsed since he had last seen Sirius seemed to have lasted much, much longer; it stretched across two universes, the one with Sirius in it, and the one without.

'You're well out of it, mate,' said Ron forcefully. 'I mean, she's quite good-looking and all that, but you want someone a bit more cheerful.'

'She's probably cheerful enough with someone else,' said Harry, shrugging.

'Who's she with now, anyway?' Ron asked Hermione, but it was Ginny who answered.

第38章 第二场战争开始了

耿于怀，因为马尔福在当调查行动组成员期间给赫奇帕奇扣了分。

"高尔的妈妈倒是会很高兴的，"跑来查看骚乱原因的罗恩说道，"高尔现在漂亮多了……喂，哈利，食物车停下来了，如果你想买东西……"

哈利谢过大家，跟罗恩一起回到他们的车厢，买了一大堆坩埚形蛋糕和南瓜馅饼。赫敏又在看《预言家日报》，金妮在做《唱唱反调》上的测试题，纳威抚摸着他的米布米宝，它在这一年里长了不少，一碰就会发出奇怪的哼哼声。

旅途中的大部分时间，哈利和罗恩都在下巫师棋，赫敏在一旁大声念着《预言家日报》的片段。现在报上的文章都是关于如何抵御摄魂怪，魔法部采取哪些措施追捕食死徒，还有一些歇斯底里的读者写信说他们那天早晨看见伏地魔从他们家门前走过……

"还没有真正开始呢，"赫敏愁闷地叹了一口气，把报纸折了起来，"但时间不会太长了……"

"喂，哈利。"罗恩轻声说，朝玻璃窗外的走廊点点头。

哈利扭头看去。秋·张从窗外走过，身旁是戴着头盔一样的帽子的玛丽埃塔·艾克莫。哈利和秋·张对视片刻。秋·张微微红了脸，继续往前走。哈利低下头来看棋盘，正好看见他的一个兵被罗恩的骑士赶出了格子。

"你们——呃——你和她到底是怎么回事？"罗恩轻声问。

"没什么。"哈利如实说道。

"我——呃——我听说她现在跟别人好了。"赫敏小心翼翼地说。

哈利惊讶地发现这消息并不令他伤心。想要征服秋·张的芳心仿佛已成往事，与他不再有任何关联。这些日子他觉得，在小天狼星死前他渴望的许多东西似乎都是这样……他最后一次看见小天狼星之后度过的这个星期，似乎格外、格外漫长，跨越了两个世界，一个世界里有小天狼星，另一个世界里没有。

"出来了也好，伙计，"罗恩坚决地说，"我是说，她长得不错，如此等等，但是你需要一个更快乐一点的人。"

"她大概跟别人在一起就快乐了。"哈利耸耸肩说。

"她现在到底跟谁好了？"罗恩问赫敏，但金妮抢着回答了。

CHAPTER THIRTY-EIGHT   The Second War Begins

'Michael Corner,' she said.

'Michael – but –' said Ron, craning around in his seat to stare at her. 'But you were going out with him!'

'Not any more,' said Ginny resolutely. 'He didn't like Gryffindor beating Ravenclaw at Quidditch, and got really sulky, so I ditched him and he ran off to comfort Cho instead.' She scratched her nose absently with the end of her quill, turned *The Quibbler* upside-down and began marking her answers. Ron looked highly delighted.

'Well, I always thought he was a bit of an idiot,' he said, prodding his queen forwards towards Harry's quivering castle. 'Good for you. Just choose someone – better – next time.'

He cast Harry an oddly furtive look as he said it.

'Well, I've chosen Dean Thomas, would you say he's better?' asked Ginny vaguely.

'WHAT?' shouted Ron, upending the chessboard: Crookshanks went plunging after the pieces and Hedwig and Pigwidgeon twittered and hooted angrily from overhead.

As the train slowed down in the approach to King's Cross, Harry thought he had never wanted to leave it less. He even wondered fleetingly what would happen if he simply refused to get off, but remained stubbornly sitting there until the first of September, when it would take him back to Hogwarts. When it finally puffed to a standstill, however, he lifted down Hedwig's cage and prepared to drag his trunk from the train as usual.

When the ticket inspector signalled to Harry, Ron and Hermione that it was safe to walk through the magical barrier between platforms nine and ten, however, he found a surprise awaiting him on the other side: a group of people standing there to greet him who he had not expected at all.

There was Mad-Eye Moody, looking quite as sinister with his bowler hat pulled low over his magical eye as he would have done without it, his gnarled hands clutching a long staff, his body wrapped in a voluminous travelling cloak. Tonks stood just behind him, her bright bubble-gum-pink hair gleaming in the sunlight filtering through the dirty glass of the station ceiling, wearing heavily patched jeans and a bright purple T-shirt bearing the legend *The Weird Sisters*. Next to Tonks was Lupin, his face pale, his hair greying, a long and threadbare overcoat covering a shabby jumper and trousers. At the

第38章 第二场战争开始了

"迈克尔·科纳。"她说。

"迈克尔——可是——"罗恩从座位上扭着脖子盯着金妮,"你不是跟他好吗?"

"现在不好了,"金妮毫不含糊地说,"他不愿意格兰芬多在魁地奇球赛上打败了拉文克劳,整天哭丧着个脸,我就把他甩了,结果他就跑去安慰秋·张了。"她漫不经心地用羽毛笔尾挠了挠鼻子,把《唱唱反调》颠倒过来,给自己的答案打分。罗恩看上去心花怒放。

"嘿,我早就觉得他有点呆头呆脑。"他说,一边把他的王后推向了哈利那个摇摇欲坠的战车,"这样很好。下次挑一个好点儿的。"

说话间,他诡谲地偷偷瞥了一眼哈利。

"没错,我挑了迪安·托马斯,你说他是不是要好一点儿?"金妮心不在焉地问。

"什么?"罗恩喊道,一把推翻了棋盘:克鲁克山扑向那些棋子,海德薇和小猪在头顶上发出愤怒的吱吱叫声。

快到国王十字车站时火车开始减速,哈利觉得自己从没像现在这样不愿下车。他甚至闪过这样的念头,如果他就是不下车,固执地留在车上,一直待到九月一号,再让列车把他带回霍格沃茨,那又会怎样呢?然而,当列车终于喷着烟雾停稳后,他还是拿下海德薇的笼子,像往常一样准备拖着箱子下车。

检票员示意哈利、罗恩和赫敏可以安全穿过第9和第10站台之间的魔法隔墙了,哈利才发现隔墙的另一边有惊喜在等待着他:一群人站在那里迎接他,而他压根儿没有料到他们会来。

这群人中有疯眼汉穆迪,他把圆顶高帽压得低低的遮住了魔眼,那模样跟他不戴帽子一样吓人,骨节粗大的双手抓着一根长长的拐杖,身上裹着一件宽大的旅行斗篷。唐克斯站在他身后,阳光透过车站顶棚上肮脏的玻璃射下来,照得她泡泡糖般粉红色的头发闪闪发亮,她穿着补丁摞补丁的牛仔裤和一件印着古怪姐妹演唱组图案的亮紫色T恤衫。在她旁边的是卢平,面无血色,头发花白,旧套头毛衣和裤子外面罩着一件长长的、磨破了的大衣。韦斯莱夫妇站在人群前面,穿着他们最好的麻瓜衣服;还有弗雷德和乔治,两人都穿着崭新的、用

CHAPTER THIRTY-EIGHT   The Second War Begins

front of the group stood Mr and Mrs Weasley, dressed in their Muggle best, and Fred and George, who were both wearing brand-new jackets in some lurid green, scaly material.

'Ron, Ginny!' called Mrs Weasley, hurrying forwards and hugging her children tightly. 'Oh, and Harry dear – how are you?'

'Fine,' lied Harry, as she pulled him into a tight embrace. Over her shoulder he saw Ron goggling at the twins' new clothes.

'What are *they* supposed to be?' he asked, pointing at the jackets.

'Finest dragonskin, little bro',' said Fred, giving his zip a little tweak. 'Business is booming and we thought we'd treat ourselves.'

'Hello, Harry,' said Lupin, as Mrs Weasley let go of Harry and turned to greet Hermione.

'Hi,' said Harry. 'I didn't expect ... what are you all doing here?'

'Well,' said Lupin with a slight smile, 'we thought we might have a little chat with your aunt and uncle before letting them take you home.'

'I dunno if that's a good idea,' said Harry at once.

'Oh, I think it is,' growled Moody, who had limped a little closer. 'That'll be them, will it, Potter?'

He pointed with his thumb over his shoulder; his magical eye was evidently peering through the back of his head and his bowler hat. Harry leaned an inch or so to the left to see where Mad-Eye was pointing and there, sure enough, were the three Dursleys, who looked positively appalled to see Harry's reception committee.

'Ah, Harry!' said Mr Weasley, turning from Hermione's parents, who he had just greeted enthusiastically, and who were now taking it in turns to hug Hermione. 'Well – shall we do it, then?'

'Yeah, I reckon so, Arthur,' said Moody.

He and Mr Weasley took the lead across the station towards the Dursleys, who were apparently rooted to the floor. Hermione disengaged herself gently from her mother to join the group.

'Good afternoon,' said Mr Weasley pleasantly to Uncle Vernon as he came to a halt right in front of him. 'You might remember me, my name's Arthur Weasley.'

As Mr Weasley had single-handedly demolished most of the Dursleys' living room two years previously, Harry would have been very surprised

第38章 第二场战争开始了

某种绿得耀眼的鳞状材料做的夹克衫。

"罗恩，金妮！"韦斯莱夫人说着，匆匆走上前紧紧拥抱她的两个孩子，"哦，还有亲爱的哈利——你好吗？"

"挺好的。"哈利被她紧搂进怀里，违心地说。他从她的肩膀上看见罗恩目不转睛地盯着两个双胞胎哥哥的新衣服。

"这是用什么东西做的？"罗恩指着那两件夹克衫问。

"最高档的火龙皮，老弟。"弗雷德说着，轻轻拉了一下拉链，"买卖兴隆，我们认为应该犒劳一下自己。"

"你好，哈利。"卢平看到韦斯莱夫人放开哈利去问候赫敏，便上前招呼道。

"你好，"哈利应道，"我真没想到……你们怎么都来了？"

"是这样，"卢平微微笑了笑说，"我们想在你的姨妈姨父带你回家之前，跟他们谈一谈。"

"我觉得这个主意不太好。"哈利立刻说道。

"哦，我认为不错。"穆迪粗声粗气地说，一瘸一拐地走近前来，"那就是他们吧，波特？"

他用大拇指往肩后一指，他的魔眼显然正透过后脑勺和圆顶高帽朝外窥视。哈利把身子往左边探过去一点儿，看着疯眼汉所指的地方。果然，德思礼一家三口就在那里，他们显然被哈利接待团的阵势吓坏了。

"啊，哈利！"韦斯莱先生说着，从他刚才热情招呼的赫敏父母那里转过身来。赫敏父母此刻正在轮流拥抱赫敏。"怎么样——现在就开始吧，好吗？"

"行，没问题，亚瑟。"穆迪说。

他和韦斯莱先生打头朝站台那边好像被钉在地上的德思礼一家走去。赫敏轻轻从母亲怀里脱出身来，也跟了过去。

"下午好，"韦斯莱先生停在弗农姨父跟前，愉快地对他说，"你大概还记得我吧，我名叫亚瑟·韦斯莱。"

两年前，韦斯莱先生仅凭一己之力就把德思礼家的客厅几乎全毁掉了，如果弗农姨父把他给忘了，哈利会感到非常吃惊的。果然，弗

CHAPTER THIRTY-EIGHT   The Second War Begins

if Uncle Vernon had forgotten him. Sure enough, Uncle Vernon turned a deeper shade of puce and glared at Mr Weasley, but chose not to say anything, partly, perhaps, because the Dursleys were outnumbered two to one. Aunt Petunia looked both frightened and embarrassed; she kept glancing around, as though terrified somebody she knew would see her in such company. Dudley, meanwhile, seemed to be trying to look small and insignificant, a feat at which he was failing extravagantly.

'We thought we'd just have a few words with you about Harry,' said Mr Weasley, still smiling.

'Yeah,' growled Moody. 'About how he's treated when he's at your place.'

Uncle Vernon's moustache seemed to bristle with indignation. Possibly because the bowler hat gave him the entirely mistaken impression that he was dealing with a kindred spirit, he addressed himself to Moody.

'I am not aware that it is any of your business what goes on in my house –'

'I expect what you're not aware of would fill several books, Dursley,' growled Moody.

'Anyway, that's not the point,' interjected Tonks, whose pink hair seemed to offend Aunt Petunia more than all the rest put together, for she closed her eyes rather than look at her. 'The point is, if we find out you've been horrible to Harry –'

'– And make no mistake, we'll hear about it,' added Lupin pleasantly.

'Yes,' said Mr Weasley, 'even if you won't let Harry use the fellytone –'

'*Telephone*,' whispered Hermione.

'– Yeah, if we get any hint that Potter's been mistreated in any way, you'll have us to answer to,' said Moody.

Uncle Vernon swelled ominously. His sense of outrage seemed to outweigh even his fear of this bunch of oddballs.

'Are you threatening me, sir?' he said, so loudly that passers-by actually turned to stare.

'Yes, I am,' said Mad-Eye, who seemed rather pleased that Uncle Vernon had grasped this fact so quickly.

'And do I look like the kind of man who can be intimidated?' barked Uncle Vernon.

'Well ...' said Moody, pushing back his bowler hat to reveal his sinisterly revolving magical eye. Uncle Vernon leapt backwards in horror and collided painfully with a luggage trolley. 'Yes, I'd have to say you do, Dursley.'

第38章 第二场战争开始了

农姨父的脸涨成了深紫色,他怒气冲冲地瞪着韦斯莱先生,却什么也没有说,这恐怕多半是因为德思礼一家的人数跟他们相比是一比二。佩妮姨妈看上去既恐惧又尴尬,不停地东张西望,似乎生怕她认识的什么人会看见她与这些人为伍。达力好像拼命把自己缩得很小,免得引起他人的注意,但他做得很不成功。

"关于哈利,我们有几句话想跟你谈谈。"韦斯莱先生仍然笑眯眯地说。

"对,"穆迪粗声粗气地说,"关于他在你家会受到什么样的待遇。"

弗农姨父的胡子似乎都气得竖了起来。大概是圆顶高帽给了他一个完全错误的印象,以为自己是在跟一个同类打交道,他对着穆迪说话了。

"我认为我家里的事情跟你们没有任何关系——"

"恐怕你不知道的事情足够写满几本书的,德思礼。"穆迪低吼道。

"问题不在这里。"唐克斯插嘴道,她的粉红色头发比他们几个加在一起更令佩妮姨妈厌恶,她闭上眼睛不去看她,"问题在于,如果我们发现你们虐待哈利——"

"——别犯糊涂,我们会了解到的。"卢平和颜悦色地加了一句。

"没错,"韦斯莱先生说,"就算你们不让哈利使用联话——"

"是电话。"赫敏小声说。

"——是啊,如果我们得到波特受虐待的任何线索,你就吃不了兜着走啦。"穆迪说。

弗农姨父的火气可怕地蹿了起来。他的愤怒似乎超过了他对这伙怪人的恐惧。

"你们在威胁我,先生?"他说,声音大极了,引得路人纷纷侧目。

"没错。"疯眼汉说,他似乎很高兴弗农姨父这么快就认清了这个事实。

"难道我的样子像个能被吓倒的人吗?"弗农姨父吼道。

"好吧……"穆迪说着,把圆顶高帽往后一推,露出那只滴溜溜旋转的凶险的魔眼。弗农姨父吓得往后一跳,重重地撞在一辆行李车上。"是的,我必须说你就是这样的人,德思礼。"

1443

CHAPTER THIRTY-EIGHT   The Second War Begins

He turned from Uncle Vernon to Harry.

'So, Potter ... give us a shout if you need us. If we don't hear from you for three days in a row, we'll send someone along ...'

Aunt Petunia whimpered piteously. It could not have been plainer that she was thinking of what the neighbours would say if they caught sight of these people marching up the garden path.

'Bye, then, Potter,' said Moody, grasping Harry's shoulder for a moment with a gnarled hand.

'Take care, Harry,' said Lupin quietly. 'Keep in touch.'

'Harry, we'll have you away from there as soon as we can,' Mrs Weasley whispered, hugging him again.

'We'll see you soon, mate,' said Ron anxiously, shaking Harry's hand.

'Really soon, Harry,' said Hermione earnestly. 'We promise.'

Harry nodded. He somehow could not find words to tell them what it meant to him, to see them all ranged there, on his side. Instead, he smiled, raised a hand in farewell, turned around and led the way out of the station towards the sunlit street, with Uncle Vernon, Aunt Petunia and Dudley hurrying along in his wake.

第38章 第二场战争开始了

他把目光从弗农姨父身上转向了哈利。

"好了,波特……需要我们喊一声。如果连着三天没有你的消息,我们就会派人过来……"

佩妮姨妈可怜巴巴地呜咽着。不用说,她是在想如果邻居看见这些人大步走在她家花园小径上会说什么。

"那就再见了,波特。"穆迪说着,用一只骨节粗大的手捏了捏哈利的肩膀。

"保重,哈利,"卢平轻声说,"保持联系。"

"哈利,我们会让你尽早离开那里的。"韦斯莱夫人轻声说,又搂了他一下。

"我们很快就会见面的,伙计。"罗恩握着哈利的手,急切地说。

"真的很快,哈利,"赫敏认真地说,"我们保证。"

哈利点点头。不知怎的,他无法用语言告诉他们,看到他们都聚集在这里支持着他,这对他有多么重要。他微微一笑,挥手告别,然后转身领头走出车站,走向阳光照耀的街道,弗农姨父、佩妮姨妈和达力匆匆跟在他后面。

WIZARDING WORLD